Maxim Jakubowski is a London-based novelist and editor. He was born in the UK and educated in France. Following a career in book publishing, he opened the world-famous Murder One bookshop in London in 1988. He compiles two acclaimed annual series for the Mammoth list: *Best New Erotica* and *Best British Crime*. He is a winner of the Anthony and the Karel Awards, a frequent TV and radio broadcaster, crime columnist for the *Guardian* newspaper and Literary Director of London's Crime Scene Festival. His latest thriller is *I Was Waiting for You*.

Recent Mammoth titles

The Mammoth Book of Time Travel Romance
The Mammoth Book of Chess
The Mammoth Book of Irish Romance
The Mammoth Book of Best New Erotica 9
The Mammoth Book of Alternate Histories
The Mammoth Book of New IQ Puzzles
The Mammoth Book of the Best of Best New Horror
The Mammoth Book of Bizarre Crimes
The Mammoth Book of Special Ops Romance
The Mammoth Book of Best British Mysteries 7
The Mammoth Book of Sex, Drugs & Rock 'n' Roll
The Mammoth Book of Travel in Dangerous Places
The Mammoth Book of Apocalyptic SF
The Mammoth Book of Casino Games
The Mammoth Book of Regency Romance
The Mammoth Book of Threesomes and Moresomes
The Mammoth Book of Drug Barons
The Mammoth Book of Paranormal Romance 2
The Mammoth Book of the World's Greatest Chess Games
The Mammoth Book of Tasteless Jokes
The Mammoth Book of New Erotic Photography
The Mammoth Book of Best New Horror 21
The Mammoth Book of Best New SF 23
The Mammoth Book of Great British Humour
The Mammoth Book of Scottish Romance
The Mammoth Book of Women's Erotic Fantasies
The Mammoth Book of Fun Brain Training
The Mammoth Book of Tough Guys
The Mammoth Book of Dracula
The Mammoth Book of Tattoo Art

THE MAMMOTH BOOK OF BEST BRITISH MYSTERIES

Volume 9

Edited by

MAXIM JAKUBOWSKI

RUNNING PRESS
PHILADELPHIA · LONDON

Constable & Robinson Ltd
55–56 Russell Square
London WC1B 4HP
www.constablerobinson.com

Published in the UK as *The Mammoth Book of Best British Crime 9*
by Robinson, an imprint of Constable & Robinson Ltd, 2012

A copy of the British Library Cataloguing in Publication
Data is available from the British Library

UK ISBN 978-1- 78033-094-5

1 3 5 7 9 10 8 6 4 2

First published in the United States in 2012 as
The Mammoth Book of Best British Mysteries 9
by Running Press Book Publishers, a Member of the Perseus Books Group

US ISBN: 978-0-7624-4431-1
US Library of Congress Control Number: 2011930508

9   8   7   6   5   4   3   2   1
Digit on the right indicates the number of this printing

Running Press Book Publishers
2300 Chestnut Street
Philadelphia, PA 19103-4371

Visit us on the web!
www.runningpress.com

Printed and bound in the UK

CONTENTS

INTRODUCTION

WELCOME TO YET another full year of British killers, investigators, femmes fatales, everymen and women in peril and the whole kitchen sink of crime and mystery fiction as practised on our hallowed shores.

These very shores where Conan Doyle gave birth to Sherlock Holmes, Colin Dexter to Inspector Morse, Raymond Chandler went to school and, less of a prestigious or nationalistic landmark, Jack the Ripper, the first universally feared serial killer, slashed his way into the hall of infamy.

Better critics than me have attempted to define where British crime and thrillers differ from their American or European counterparts. I will not attempt it. After all there are cosy US authors who work in the footsteps of Agatha Christie, as there are homegrown Brits who write as hardboiled blood-and-guts prose as Chandler and Hammett and their contemporary representatives. They have crooked and/or tormented cops; we have them too. They have long highways; we have motorways. But what they all have in common is the fact that on both continents crime and mystery writing thrives and not a year goes by without impressive new talent emerging and the genre we love is seen renewing itself constantly like waves lapping against the shore.

I've always tried to present the whole breadth of crime, mystery and thriller writing in these annual anthologies. So you won't just find gentle stories of detection, puzzling historical labyrinths full of devious characters or sharp social comment about the imperfect society we live in beneath the surface of some savage and, often, scary stories. All life is here, moods, settings, villains and goodies and all characters in between. In a nutshell, all the variety and must-read qualities of crime writers at their best. And there is little doubt in my mind that we have on our British (and Celtic) shores a wonderful assortment of outstanding talents.

We welcome back many old favourites but also big "names" like Reginald Hill, Ann Cleeves, R. J. Ellory, John Lawton and Stuart Neville for the very first time. And, as ever, it's with great joy that we have newcomers like L. C. Tyler, Chris Ewan, Ian Ayris, Col Bury, Matt Hilton and Christine Poulson on board; some are at an early stage in their careers while others have already made a mark for themselves.

Past volumes have enjoyed great critical and commercial success and we've gathered a couple of handfuls of nominations for prestigious short story awards. Phil Lovesey's story in last year's volume was shortlisted for and subsequently won the CWA Dagger, alongside John Lawton's delightful spy tale in these pages, and Christine Poulson's ingenious puzzler, also from this year's volume, was selected for an American readers' award, and I am confident more stories from this bumper edition will catch the attention in the best possible way and make crime pay, at any rate from a literary point of view.

So, close the windows tight, check the back door is locked and the front door bolts are safely in place, slip between the bedcovers and dive deep into our wonderful world of crime. When you emerge from the shimmering darkness, it will already be next year and we will have yet another menu of dark and sinister but enjoyable deeds ready for you.

Bon appétit criminel, as they say in France!

Maxim Jakubowski

MEET ME AT THE CREMATORIUM

Peter James

I WANT YOU, he texted.

I want you more! she texted back.

Trevor was fond of saying that the past was another country. Well, at this moment for Janet, it was the future that was another country. The future – and another man.

And tonight she was going to have him. Again.

A sharp erotic sensation coiled in the pit of her stomach at the thought of him. A longing. A craving.

Tonight I am going to have you. Again, and again and again!

Her past receded in the rear-view mirror with every kilometre she covered. The forest of winter-brown pines that lined the autobahn streaked by on both sides, along with road signs, turn-offs and other, slower cars. She was in a hurry to get there. Her heart beat with excitement, with danger. Her pulse revved. She had been running on adrenalin for forty-eight hours, but she wasn't tired, she was wide, wide awake. Going into the unknown. Going to meet a man who had been a total stranger until just a few weeks ago.

His photograph, which she had printed from the jpeg he had emailed her, lay on the passenger seat of her elderly grey Passat. He was naked. A tall, muscular guy, semi-erect as if teasing her to make him bigger. A tight stomach, nearly a six-pack, and she could already feel it pressing hard against her own. He had brown hairs on his chest and on his legs, thick and downy and she liked that. Trevor was white and bony, and his body was almost hairless. This man was tanned, lean, fit.

Hans.

He looked wild, like a young Jack Nicholson, his hair thinning on the top. He looked just the way he had sounded on the internet chat room when she had first been attracted to him.

Feral.

The background to the photograph was strange. An enclosed, windowless space that might be the engine room of a ship, although she had a pretty good idea what it really was. Like everything about him, it excited her. Shiny floor-to-ceiling metal casings, beige coloured, with dials, gauges, switches, levers, knobs, winking lights. It could be some kind of control room in a nuclear reactor? Or Mission Control?

She felt on a mission very much under control!

Who had taken that photograph, she wondered? A lover? A self-timer? She didn't care; she wanted him. All of him. Wanted that thing that half-dangled, half-rose, wanted to gather it deep inside her again. Wanted him so badly she was crazed with lust. Mosquitoes got crazed with blood lust. They had to land, take in the blood, even if it killed them. She had to have Hans, take him into her, into her body, into her life, even if that killed her, too.

She didn't care. For now she was free. She had been free for two whole days and that was longer than she had been free for years.

On the scratchy reception of the car's radio, struggling through the occasional interference of someone talking in German, Bob Dylan was singing "The Times They Are A-Changin'".

They were, they really were! Flecks of sleet struck the windscreen, and the wipers cleared them. It was cold outside and that was good. It was good to make love in the warmth when it was cold outside. And, besides, the cold had plenty of other advantages.

I will never let you go, Trevor had said. *Never. Ever.* He had told her that for years.

Hans explained to her precisely what he was going to do to her. Exactly how he would make love to her the first time. And he had done so just the way he had described. She liked that Germanic precision. The way he had studied every detail of her photograph. The way he already knew her body when they met. The way he told her he loved her hair, and had buried his face into it. Into all of it.

My name is Hans. I am thirty-seven, divorced, looking to start a new life with a lady of similar age. I am liking brunettes. Slim. Excuse my bad English. I like you. I don't know you, but I like you.

I like you even more!

She would be forty this year. Hans would be her toyboy, she had teased him. He had laughed and she liked that; he had a big sense of humour. A wicked sense of humour.

Everything about him was totally wicked!

She looked OK, she knew. She'd never been a beauty, but she understood how to make herself look attractive, sexy. Dressed to kill, plenty of men would look at her. She used to keep in shape with her twice-weekly aerobics classes, then, when Trevor had gone through one of his particularly nasty phases, she had turned to binge eating – and then binge drinking – for comfort. Then she enrolled in WeightWatchers, and the fat and the flab and the cellulite had come off again. Her figure was good, her stomach firm – not a distended pouch, like those of some of her friends who'd had children. And her boobs were still firm, still defying gravity. She'd like to have been a little taller, always had wished that. But you couldn't have everything.

Anyhow, Trevor, who was much taller than her, told her, the very first time they had made love, that people were all the same size in bed. That had made her smile.

Trevor used to tell her that nothing you do in life is ever wasted. He was always coming up with sayings, and there was a time when Janet had listened to them intently, adored hearing them, filed them away in her memory and loved repeating them back to him.

Loved him so damned much it hurt.

And she hadn't even minded the pain. Which was a good thing because pain was something Trevor did really, really well. The knots, the handcuffs, the nipple clamps, the leather straps, the spiked dog collar, the whips, the stinging bamboo canes. He liked to hurt her, knew how and where to inflict it, but that had been OK because she loved him. She would have done anything for him.

But that was then.

And sometime between *then* and *now* he had changed. They had both changed. His horizons had narrowed, hers had widened.

Every system can be beaten. That was one of his sayings.

He was right.

Now she was a lifetime away. So it seemed. And 1,212 kilometres away, driving through spartan December pine forest. Klick: 1,213. And in a few moments, travelling at 130 klicks an hour, with her life in the two large suitcases jammed on the rear seats, 1,214.

Hagen 3.

The turn-off was coming up. She felt a tightening of her throat, and a prick of excitement deep inside her. How many villages, small towns, big cities had she driven through or passed by in her travels, during her life, and wondered, each time, *What would it be like to stop here? What would it be like to drive into this place as a total stranger, knowing no one, then check into a hotel, or rent a small flat, and start a totally new life?*

She was about to realize her dream. *Hagen.* So far it was just images she had googled on websites. *Hagen.* The thirty-seventh largest town in Germany. She liked that. A population of two hundred thousand. On the edge of the Ruhr. A town few knew about outside of its inhabitants. A once important industrial conurbation that was now reinventing itself as a centre of the arts, the websites proclaimed. She liked that. She could see herself in a place that was the centre of the arts.

Up until now, she had not had much contact with the arts. Well, there had never been time, really. During the weekdays she was always on the road, driving from place to place, as an area sales representative for a company that made industrial brushes. Finishing brushes for the printing trade. Brushes for vacuum cleaners. Brushes for the bottom of elevator doors. For electrical contacts. She would miss her flirting and banter with her clients, the almost exclusively male buyers at the factories, the components wholesalers, the plant hire stores and the hardware stores. She was missing her comfortable new company Ford Mondeo, too, but the Passat was OK, it was fine, it was a small price to pay. Tiny.

Then at the weekends, Trevor wasn't interested in any area of the arts. He didn't want to know about theatre, or art galleries or concerts – except for Def Leppard, great music if you like that kind of thing, which she didn't – but they were not *art*, at least, not in her view. He just wanted to watch football, then either go to the pub or, more preferably, up to a particular S&M club he had discovered in London, where they had become regulars. He liked, most of all, to hurt and humiliate her in front of other people.

Ahead of her and to her left, across the railings on the elevated road, she could see the start of a town. It lay in a valley, surrounded by low, rounded, wintry hills. Everything she could see was mostly grey or brown, the colours bleached out by the gloomy, overcast sky. But to her, it was all intensely beautiful.

Hagen. A place where no one knew her, and she knew no one. Except just one man. And she *barely* knew him. A place where a stranger she was going to have sex with tonight, for just the second time, lived and worked. She tried to remember what his voice sounded like. What he smelled like. A man so crude he could send her a photo of himself naked and semi-erect, but a man so tender he could send her poetry by Aparna Chatterjee.

Lust is what I speak tonight,
Lust is what I see tonight,
Lust is what I feel tonight,
And I Lust You.
Show me your Body
Inside out …
No clothes on,
No holds barred …
Bit by bit,
Part by part,
Give me your smells.
And your sweat …

Trevor had never read a poem in his life.

The road dipped down suddenly beneath a flyover that seemed, from this angle, as if it went straight through the middle of a row of grimy, pastel-blue townhouses. She halted at a traffic light in the dark shadow beneath the flyover, checked in her mirror, for an instant – just checking – then saw a yellow road sign. There was an arrow pointing straight ahead, with the word *Zentrum*. Another arrow pointed left, and bore the word *Theater*.

She liked that. Liked the fact that the second word she saw on arriving in the town was *Theater*. This was going to be a good place; she felt it in her bones, in her heart, in her soul.

Hagen. She said the word to herself and smiled.

Behind her a car hooted. The lights were green.

She drove on past a road sign that read *Bergischer Ring,* and realized from the directions she had memorized that she was close to her hotel. But anxious as she was to see Hans, she wanted to get her bearings. She wanted to arrive slowly, absorbing it all, understanding the geography. She had all the time in the world, and she wanted to get it right, from the very beginning. It seemed too sudden that one moment she was on the autobahn, the next she was slap in the centre of the town. She wanted to feel it, explore it slowly, breathe it in, absorb it.

She turned right at the next road she came to, and drove up a steep, curving hill, lined with tall, terraced townhouses on both sides, then past a grimy church. She made a left turn at random, up an even steeper road, and then suddenly she was in scrubby, tree-lined countryside, winding up a hill, with the town below her.

She pulled over into the kerb, parked in front of a butane gas cylinder that was partially concealed by a threadbare hedge, stopped and climbed out. The central locking had packed up a long time ago, so she went around the car, making sure the doors and the boot were locked. Then she walked over to the hedge and looked down, across the valley, at her new home.

Hagen. A place that boasted, among its tourist attractions, Germany's first crematorium. Which had a certain convenient ring to it.

The town lay spread out and sprawling in the bowl beneath her.

Her eyes swept the grey, grimy urban landscape beyond the gas cylinder, below the grey, sleeting skies. She saw a cluster of industrial buildings, with a white chimney stack rising higher than the distant hills. A small nucleus of utilitarian apartment buildings. A church spire. A Ferris wheel brightly lit, although it was only three o'clock in the afternoon, reminding her that darkness would start to fall, soon. She saw a narrow river bordered by grimy, industrial buildings. Church spires. Houses, some with red roofs, some grey. She wondered who lived in them all, how many of their inhabitants she would get to meet.

It is neither fish nor meat, Hans said, telling her about Hagen. But she didn't mind what it was, or was not. It looked huge, vast, far bigger than a town of two hundred thousand. It looked like a vast city. A place where she could get lost, and hide, for ever.

She loved it more every second.

She noticed a strange, cylindrical building, all glass, lit in blue, above what looked like an old water tower, and she wondered what that was. Hans would tell her. She would explore every inch of this place with him, in between the times they lay in bed, naked, together. If they could spare any time to explore anything other than each other's bodies, that was!

She turned away from the view and walked on up the hill, hands dug into the pockets of her black suede jacket, the sleet tickling her face, her scarf tickling her neck, breathing in the scents of the trees and the grass. She followed the road up into a wooded glade, until it became a track, which after a few minutes came out into a knoll of unkempt grass, with a row of trees on the far side, and a rectangular stone monument at the highest point.

She climbed up to it, and stopped at a partially collapsed metal fence was that screening it off, for some kind of repair work. She knew it was the Bismarck monument, because she recognized it from every website – one of Hagen's landmarks. She stared at it silently, then took her little digital camera from her bag and photographed it. Her first photograph of Hagen! Then she stood still, licking the sleet off the air, feeling a moment of intense happiness, and freedom.

I'm here. I made it! I did it!!!!!

Her heart was burning for Hans, and yet strangely, she still felt in no hurry. She wanted to savour these moments of anticipation. To savour her freedom. To relish not having to hurry home to make Trevor his evening meal (always a variation on meat and potatoes, he would eat nothing else). To be able to stand for as long as she wanted beneath the statue of Otto Eduard Leopold von Bismarck, a man partly responsible for shaping the country that was about to become her adopted home, for however many days of freedom she had remaining. And she did not know how many those might be.

Better to live one day as a lion, than one thousand years as a lamb, Trevor was fond of saying, strutting around in his studded leathers and peaked cap.

Of course, he would not have approved of her being here. And particularly not of her standing like an acolyte worshipping at the statue of Bismarck. Trevor had a thing about Germany. It wasn't the War, or anything like that. He said the Germans had no humour – well, Hans had proved him wrong!

He also said the Germans were efficient, as if that was a fault!

Trevor had a *thing* about all kinds of stuff. He had a particularly big thing about crematoriums. They gave him the creeps, he said.

Whereas she found them fascinating.

Yet another thing on which they disagreed. And she always found his dislike of crematoriums particularly strange, since he worked in the funeral business.

In fact, thinking back on fifteen years of marriage, what exactly had they agreed on? Rubber underwear? Handcuffs? Masks? Inflicting modest pain on each other? Bringing each other to brutal climaxes that were snatched moments of release, escape from their mutual loathing? Escapes from the realities they did not want to face? Such as the one – fortunately, thank God now (!) – that they could not have children?

Time was, when she really had been in love with him. Deeply, truly, crazily do-anything-for-him, unconditional love. She had always been attracted by death. By people who worked close to death. Trevor was an embalmer with a firm of funeral directors. He had a framed certificate, which was hung in pride of place in the sitting room, declaring him to be "A Member Of The Independent Association of Embalmers".

She used to like his hands to touch her. Hands that had been inserting tubes into a cadaver, to pump out the blood and replace it with pink embalming fluid. Hands that had been applying make-up on a cadaver's face. Brushing a cadaver's hair.

The closer she was to death, the more alive she felt.

She liked to lie completely naked, and still, and tell Trevor to treat her as if she was a cadaver. She loved to feel his hands on her. Probing her. Slowly bringing her alive.

The best climax – absolutely the best ever, in her entire life – was one night when they had made love in the embalming room at the funeral director's. With two naked corpses lying, laid out on trolleys, beside her.

Then she had truly felt alive! The way she felt now!

And those same feelings would happen again with Hans, she knew it, she absolutely knew it! She was going to be so happy with Hans.

Love doesn't last, Trevor responded one night, when she had told him she was not happy. *Happiness is an illusion,* he had said. *Only an idiot can be happy twenty-four-seven. The wise man seeks to be content not happy.* Carpe diem.

You have to face reality, he had carped on, after she had told him she was leaving him. *You can run but you can't hide.*

She was running now.

Hit someone over the head with a big stick hard enough and for long enough and one day they will hit you back. Even harder.

She could not put a time or a date on when it had all started to go south. Not the exact moment. Could not get a fix on it the way you can pinpoint your position with a set of navigation co-ordinates. It was more of a gradual erosion.

But once you had made your decisions, there was no going back. You just had to keep running. As Trevor used to say, *It's not the fall that gets you, it's the sudden stop.*

And now of course, Hagen was that sudden stop. It scared her almost as much as it thrilled her. In truth, she had learned a lot from him.

I will never let you go, ever, he said, when she had once suggested that they might be happier apart.

Then he had punched her in the face so hard for suggesting it, she had not been able to go to work for several days, until the bruises had subsided, and the stitches had been removed. As usual she covered up for him, with a lame excuse about being knocked off her bicycle.

It was his diabetes that caused his mood swings, she had come to learn over many years. Too little sugar and he became edgy and aggressive. Too much and he became sleepy and docile as a lamb.

She retraced her steps from the Bismarck monument to her car, then threaded her way back down the network of roads, noting the pleasant houses, wondering what kind of house Hans had lived in until his marriage break-up. After a few minutes she found herself back on the Bergischer Ring, where she turned right. She drove along, past a market square where the Ferris wheel had been erected on the edge of a small fairground. She saw a row of kerb-side Christmassy tableaux, one after the other, with puppets acting out fairytale scenes. One was full of busy bearded goblins with hammers. Two small girls, clutching their mother's hands, stared at them in wonder.

Janet stared at the girls as she waited at a traffic light, and then, wistfully, at the mother. Forty was not too old. Maybe she and Hans could have children. Two little girls? And one day, she would stand here, holding their hands, a contented hausfrau of Hagen, while they looked at the hammering goblins.

Just three weeks to Christmas! She would wake up on Christmas morning, in her new country, in the arms of her new man.

As she drove on she saw, on her left, a brightly lit shop, the windows full of sausages hanging in clumps, like fruit, the name Wursthaus Konig above the door. She stopped for a moment, and checked her map. Then after a short distance she turned left into a side street, past a restaurant, then pulled over outside the front entrance of the hotel she had found on the internet.

Hans had invited her to stay with him. But after only one date – even if it had finished – or rather *climaxed* – with *the bonk at the end of the universe !!!!* – she wanted to keep her options open. And her independence. Just in case.

She tugged one bag off the rear seat of the car, and wheeled it in through the front door of the hotel. Inside was dark and gloomy, with a small reception desk to her right and a staircase in front of her. A living cadaver of a man stood behind the desk and she gave him her name. The place smelled old and worn. The kind of place travelling salespeople would stay in. The kind of dump she occasionally had found herself in during her early years on the road.

He passed her a form to fill in, and asked if she would like help with her luggage. No, she told him, emphatically. She filled in the form and handed him her passport.

And he handed her an envelope. "A message for you," he said.

Using the one word of German that she knew, she said, "*Danke.*"

Then as she went back outside to get her second suitcase, she tore it open, with eager fingers, and nails she had varnished to perfection for him. For Hans.

The note read: *Meet me at the crematorium. xx*

She smiled. *You wicked, wicked, man!*

The cadaver helped her up two flights of stairs to a room that was as tired and drab as the rest of the place. But at least she could see down into the street, and keep an eye on her car, and she was pleased about that. She popped open the lid of one case, changed her clothes, and freshened herself up, spraying perfume in all the places – except the one that she remembered Hans had liked to press his face into most of all, last time.

Twenty minutes later, in the falling dark, after getting lost twice, she finally pulled into the almost deserted crematorium car park. There was just one other car there, an elderly brown Mercedes that tilted to one side, as if it had a broken suspension.

As she climbed out, carefully locking the car, she looked around. It was one of the most beautiful car parks she had seen in her life, surrounded by all kinds of carefully tended trees, shrubs, flowers, as if she were in botanical gardens. It barely felt like December here, it felt more like spring. No doubt the intention – a perpetual spring, for mourners.

She walked up a tarmac footpath that was wide enough for a vehicle, and lined with manicured trees and tall black streetlamps. Anticipation drove her forwards, her pace quickening with every step, breathing deeper and faster. God, her nerves were jangling now! A million butterflies were going berserk in her stomach! Her boots crunched on grit; her teeth crunched, grinding from the cold, but more from nerves.

She walked through open wrought-iron gates, and continued along, passing a cloistered single-storey building, clad in ivy, its walls covered in memorial plaques.

And then, ahead of her, she saw the building.

And she stopped in her tracks.

And her heart skipped a beat.

Oh, fuck! Oh wow!

This was a crematorium?

It was one of the most beautiful buildings she had ever seen in her life. Rectangular, Art Deco in style, in stark white, with a portico of square black marble columns, with windows, high up, like portholes on a ship, inset with black rectangles. It was topped by an elegant red-tiled pitched roof.

Wow! Again.

There were steps leading up to the portico, with stone balustrading to the right, giving a view down across terraces of elegant tombstones set in what looked like glades in a forest. *When I die, this is where I would like to lie. Please God. Please, Hans.*

Please!

She climbed the steps and pushed the door, which was unlocked and opened almost silently. She stepped inside and simply stopped in her tracks. And now she could understand why the crematorium featured so prominently as one of Hagen's major attractions.

It was like stepping inside a Mondrian painting. Vertical stripes of black and white, with geometrical squares in the centre, varying in depth, width and height, at one end. At the other end was a semi-domed ceiling, with quasi-religious figures painted on a gold backdrop, above more black and white geometrics.

Beneath was a curious-looking altar, a white cross rising above what looked like a white, two-metre-long beer barrel.

As she stared at it, a noise made her jump. A sudden, terrifying sound. A mechanical grinding, roaring, vibrating bellow of heavy machinery. The barrel began to rise, the white cross with it, the floor trembling beneath her. As it rose higher, at the back, a bolt of grey silk slowly unfurled. Then a coffin rose into view. Janet stood, mesmerized. The grinding, roaring sound filled the galleried room.

Then the sound stopped as abruptly as it had started.

There was a moment of total silence.

The coffin lid began to rise.

Janet screamed.

Then she saw Hans's smiling face.

He pushed the lid aside and it fell to the floor with an echoing bang, and he began to haul himself out, grinning from ear to ear, hot and sweaty, wearing nothing but a boiler suit over his naked skin, and black work boots.

She stood and stared at him for a moment, in total wonder and joy. He looked even more amazing than she remembered. More handsome, more masculine, more raw.

He stood up, and he was taller than she remembered, too.

"My most beautiful angel in all the world!" he said. "You are here! You came! You really came!"

"Did you think I wouldn't?"

"My brave angel," he said. "My brave English angel." Then he scooped her in his strong arms, pulled her tightly to him, so tightly she could feel the contour of his body beneath the thin blue cotton, and kissed her. His breath smelled sweet, and was tinged sweetly with cigarette smoke, garlic and beer, the manly smells and taste she remembered. She kissed him back, wildly, deeply, feeling his tongue, holding it for a second, losing it, then finding it again.

Finally, breathless with excitement, their lips separated. They stood still, staring at each other, his eyes so close to hers they were just a warm blur.

"So," he said. "We have work to do, yah?"

She pushed her hands down inside the front of his trousers, and gripped him gently. "We do," she said with a smile.

He drew breath sharply and exhaled, grinning. "First we must work."

"First we make love," she replied.

"You are a very naughty little girl," he teased.

"Are you going to punish me?"

"That will depend, yes? On how naughty you have been. Have you been very naughty?"

She nodded solemnly, stood back a pace, and put her finger in her mouth like a little child. "Very," she said.

"Tell me?"

"I can show you."

He smiled. "Go and fetch the car, I will be prepared."

Five minutes later, Janet reversed the Passat up to the side entrance to the crematorium, where there was a green elevator door. As she halted the car, and climbed out, the green metal door slid open, and Hans stood there, with a coffin on a trolley. There was a strange expression on his face and he was looking at her in a way that made her, suddenly, deeply uncomfortable.

Her eyes shot to the coffin, then back to his face.

Then to the coffin.

Had she made a terrible mistake? To be alone, here, with all her bridges burned, her trail carefully covered. Had she walked into a trap?

No one at home in Eastbourne knew where she was. No one knew where she was. Only Hans. And she was alone with him at the crematorium, in the falling darkness, and he was standing, looking at her, beside an open coffin.

She felt suddenly as if her insides had turned to ice. She wanted to be home, back home, where it was safe. Dull but safe. With Trevor.

But none of that was an option any longer.

Then he smiled. His normal, big, warm Hans smile. And the ice inside her melted in an instant, as if it had flash-thawed. "In the trunk?" he questioned.

Nodding, she popped open the boot of the car, and then they both stood and stared for some moments at the black plastic sheeting, and the curved shape inside it.

"No problem?" he asked her, putting his arm around her, and nibbling her ear, so tenderly.

"He was good as gold," she said, wriggling with the excitement of his touch. "Went out like a lamb, after I swapped his insulin for sugared water. But he was heavy. I nearly didn't have the strength to get him into the boot."

Where there's a will, there's a way, Trevor was fond of saying. And of course what was particularly sweet was that Trevor had written a will, leaving everything to her, naturally, a long time ago.

"It is good he is so thin," Hans said, unwrapping him. "I have two cadavers waiting for the burners and one is very thin. I have the two certificates each from the doctors; we are all set. He will fit nicely into the coffin with him. No one will know a thing!"

Down in the basement, as they wheeled the coffin out of the elevator, Janet recognized the beige metal casings, the instruments, the dials. The word *Ruppman* was printed above them, and on other machines in the room, and on top of wiring diagrams. Opposite them, two coffins sat in front of two huge open furnaces, with gas flames licking along their lengths.

Hans smiled. A totally wicked smile.

A few minutes later, after he had pressed a number of buttons, and the mechanical doors had closed, and the roar of the burners rose to a crescendo, she felt Hans's arms around her waist. Slowly, shedding their clothes, they sank to the floor.

Smoke rose from the chimney into the night sky. They made love while the burners rose in temperature to their optimum heat, and their own body heat rose with it.

In the morning, Hans raked the remaining pieces of bone into the cremellator, then ground them to a powder that mingled with the ashes. Then they stepped through the crematorium doors, arm in arm. Outside, in the early, pre-dawn light, the world seemed an altogether brighter place. Birds were starting to sing.

Hans slipped an arm around her, then whispered into her ear, "You know, my English angel, I will never let you go."

And for an instant he sounded just like Trevor. She kissed him, then whispered back into his ear, "Don't push your luck."

"What is that meaning?" he asked.

She smiled.

WRONG 'EM BOYO

A JOE GERAGHTY STORY

Nick Quantrill

Three nights ago ...

"THERE YOU GO." He counted them out for me. "Two shirts, company tie and, of course, your cap. That's the full kit," he said.

I looked at the cap. The company badge stared back at me. Established 1974. I nodded to Tony Bagshaw, head of Bagshaw Security Limited. "You're the boss," I said to him.

He went back to the paperwork at his desk. "Any more questions?"

"No. It's fine," I said. I looked again at the cap, tried it on for size. It'd do the job. Sometimes you've got to take whatever's on offer to pay the bills.

"You're not a private investigator now," he said. "You start tomorrow."

Two nights ago ...

"You're the new guy, then?"

I nodded. I'd followed the directions Bagshaw had given me and found the control room. "I'm the new guy," I said.

"Grab a seat, then."

I put my cap on the table and sat down. "Joe," I said, holding my hand out.

He took it. "Bill."

I looked around the control room. It was dominated by a bank of CCTV screens showing the various angles and corners of the warehouse. Bill had a well-thumbed paperback and a mug on his desk. I could also see empty chocolate wrappers. "Busy night, then?" I asked him.

"Pretty much the same as any other."

"Right."

He pointed to the kettle. "Make yourself at home, lad. Tea, white, one sugar for me."

"And that's pretty much that," Bill said to me. "The grand tour."

He'd shown me around the warehouse. It was essentially a large storeroom full of toys. As we'd walked back to our office space, we passed the half-built extension to the building. Several JCBs and diggers sat still for the night.

"Company's expanding, is it?" I said.

Bill shrugged. "At least someone's doing well at the moment."

"There's always winners and losers," I said. Bill sat back down at his desk. I filled in the log to show we'd made our hourly inspection. I ticked the box to say no problems and signed my name. I put the kettle on. Again. The usual tea for Bill and coffee for me. I needed the caffeine. Even though I'd carried out countless overnight surveillance jobs in the past, it was still a shock to the system. We settled down for another spell. Bill sighed and picked up his paperback. Showed it to me, told me it was a load of rubbish. The first Stieg Larsson novel.

"The wife gave it to me," he said.

I told him I'd not read it. I had no interest, just continued to stare at the bank of CCTV images. The images were grainy, like watching a poor quality video cassette. I knew there were no other people on site. Nothing happened, nor should it. I picked up Bill's newspaper and flicked through it. All I had to look forward to was the next circuit of the warehouse in another hour's time. Time passed slowly. I tried to finish Bill's crossword for him. Failed. His mobile rang. Bill took the call, said very little, but it was obvious he didn't like what he was hearing. He ended the call.

"I thought private mobiles were banned," I said to him.

He shrugged. "What Bagshaw doesn't know isn't going to hurt him."

"Fair enough."

I waited for Bill to break the silence. "The wife," he eventually said. "She was a bit upset."

"I gathered."

"What does she expect, lad? If there isn't any overtime, what can I do? It's not my fault we're losing contracts all over the place, is it?" He pointed at the CCTV screens. "Besides, who wants to spend every waking hour looking at them?" He took a breath. "Do you get out much?"

"Not really."

"You can kiss goodbye to it, anyway. Might as well get used to the shit hours. I've been doing this since the trawler work finished." He threw the pen he'd been doing his crossword with on to the desk. "Nearly thirty years."

Now ...

We were both on edge. We didn't speak, just shared the odd grunted word, our eyes on the CCTV screens. We were supposed to patrol the site in pairs, but Bill didn't want to move. I switched my mobile on, gave him my number and set off on the hourly circuit of the warehouse. Midnight. I wasn't a jumpy sort of person, but tonight my torch was picking out shapes against the wall I knew weren't really there. I moved slowly, trying not to make a sound. I walked into the new extension area, flashed the torch around. The JCBs and diggers were neatly lined up, ready for tomorrow's work. Nothing doing. I adjusted my cap and walked back to the office. The circuit had taken me fifteen minutes. I found Bill curled up in a ball on the office floor, sobbing. I crouched down and straightened him up. His glasses were broken. I picked up the pieces and passed them back to him. I found a toilet roll and helped him wipe up the blood. I waited for his breathing to return to normal.

"What happened?" I said.

"They came."

One night ago ...

We worked until ten o'clock. There was time to make it to the pub before closing. Last chance before we started working nights. I passed him a pint of lager, sat down opposite him.

"Cheers," I said, drinking down a mouthful.

Bill said nothing. Didn't even touch his drink.

"What's up?" I asked.

He shuffled closer to me. "I've got a problem, Joe. A big fucking problem."

I wasn't sure I wanted to hear it. I put my drink down. "Go on."

Bill picked up his drink. I watched as he drained half of it in one go. "I wanted to let you know I didn't have a choice in the matter."

Now ...

"You did well, Bill," Bagshaw said. "I'm proud of you."

Bill looked at me, confused.

I nodded back.

"Thanks very much," he eventually said.

Once I'd settled Bill down, I'd made the call. Told Bagshaw what had happened.

"Did you get a look at the men?" he asked Bill.

Bill shook his head. "Balaclavas. I couldn't see their faces."

Bagshaw turned to me. "Not much to go on, then."

"Seems not," I said.

"At least they didn't get anything."

They hadn't even gone into the warehouse.

One night ago ...

"They had pictures of our Sharon in nightclubs. Pissed out of her head," Bill said to me.

"What did they say to you?"

"They didn't need to say much. They knew who she was. They knew where I worked. Told me how she could get into a lot of trouble behaving like that when she's out and about. Especially if she got separated from her mates."

I watched Bill drink the rest of his pint. He drank it down in one go. "She's only nineteen, Joe. A bairn. I can't let it happen."

Now ...

I looked at Bill. Best part of thirty years' service and it had come to this for him. Blackmailed by scrotes. I'd understood what Bagshaw had told me when he'd hired me. It wasn't the warehouse full of toys thieves were interested in. They definitely weren't worth all this effort. That was for the fly-by-night chancers with Transit vans. These people wanted the JCBs and diggers. They held their value and were easy to lose on building sites. If they were taken from here, Bagshaw Security was finished. And Bill was finished. Neither of them deserved that. Even if the insurance covered the loss, the blow to the company's reputation would be fatal. That was why Bagshaw had called me. I took my cap and tie off, handed them back to him, ignoring Bill's stare. I'd done my job. It was back to the office tomorrow and another job. "My invoice will be in the post," I said. "At the price we agreed."

Bagshaw walked over to the CCTV screens. I stood up, walked behind him and quietly took the JCB keys out of my pocket. I'd been a step ahead. Bill hadn't been able to give them what they wanted. He'd taken a kicking because the keys had been missing. But at least he still had a job. Bill's eyes widened. I winked at him. The police would catch the robbers eventually. It's always wrong to cheat the trying man. Or in this case, men. And without Bagshaw realizing what had really happened, I replaced the keys on the hook and left.

WHERE ARE ALL THE NAUGHTY PEOPLE?

Reginald Hill

A LOT OF kids are scared of graveyards.

Not me. I grew up in one.

My dad, Harry Cresswell, was verger at St Cyprian's on the north-east edge of Bradford. Once it had been a country parish but that was ages back. By the sixties it was all built up, a mix of council houses and owner-occupied semis, plus some older properties from the village days. We lived in one of them, Rose Cottage, right up against the churchyard wall. We didn't have a proper garden, just a small cobbled yard out back, and out front a two-foot strip of earth where Mam tried to grow a few stunted roses to make sense of the name. A low retaining wall separated this from a narrow pavement that tracked the busy main road where traffic never stopped day or night.

Nearest park was a mile away. But right next door to us there were four acres of open land, lots of grass and trees, no buildings, no roads, no traffic.

St Cyprian's graveyard.

The wall in our backyard had a small door in it to make it easy for Dad to get to the church to do his duties. In the graveyard the door was screened by a bit of shrubbery. My mam liked to tell anyone who cared to listen that she was a Longbottom out of Murton near York, a farming family whose kids had grown up breathing good fresh air and enjoying the sight and smell of trees and grass. She wasn't about to deprive her own child of the benefit just because of a few gravestones, so when I was a baby, she'd take me through the door in our yard and lay me on a rug to enjoy the sun while she got on with her knitting. She was a great knitter. If her hands didn't have some other essential task to occupy them, they were always occupied by her needles. I've even seen her knitting on the move! And I've never had to buy a scarf or a pullover in my life.

As I grew older and more mobile I began to explore a bit further. Mam and Dad were a bit worried at first, but Father Stamp said he'd rather see me enjoying myself there than running around the street in the traffic, and in Mam's ears, Father Stamp's voice was the voice of God.

I should say that though St Cyprian's was Church of England, it was what they called High, lots of incense and hyssop and such, and the vicar liked to be called Father. It used to confuse me a bit as a kid, what with God the Father, and Father Stamp, and Father Christmas, and my own dad, but I got used to it.

And folk got used to me using the graveyard as my playground. I think them as didn't like it were too scared of my mam to risk a confrontation. She could be really scary when she tried. For her part, she insisted I should always stay in the area between our bit of the wall and the side of the church, and not do anything naughty. *Naughty* in Mam's vocabulary covered a wide range of misbehaviour. She used to read the *News of the World* and shake her head and say disapprovingly, "There's a lot of naughty folk in this world. Well, they'll have to pay for it in the next!" I assumed she meant bank robbers and such. But in my own case, I didn't have to assume anything. I knew exactly what naughty meant – doing anything my mam told me not to do!

My designated playground area was the oldest section of the graveyard. All the headstones here dated back a hundred years or more, and no one ever came to tend the graves or lay flowers on them. There were quite a few trees here too and it was hard to get a mowing machine in, so the grass grew long and lush and on the rare occasions someone did come round this side, I could easily drop out of sight till they'd gone. Occasionally I'd see Father Stamp but I didn't hide from him because he'd always wave at me and smile, and sometimes he'd come and join me, and often he'd produce a bagful of mint humbugs and we'd sit next to each other on a tombstone, his arm round my shoulder, sucking away in companionable silence till suddenly he'd stand up, ruffle my hair and say he had to go and do something in the church.

Once I'd started at school, I soon realized the new activities I was enjoying, like playing football or cowboys and Indians, you couldn't do in a graveyard. Even Father Stamp wouldn't have cared to see a whole gang of kids rampaging round his church, cheering and yelling. So I spent less time there, but I still liked to wander round by myself sometimes, playing solitary make-believe games, or just lying in the grass looking up at the sky till Mam yelled my name and I had to go in for my tea.

Occasionally I'd have one or two of my special friends round at the house and to start with I took them through the door into my playground. I thought they'd be impressed I had all this space to roam around in, but instead they either said it was seriously weird, or they wanted to play daft games like pretending to be ghosts and jumping out on each other from behind the old gravestones. As well as being worried about the noise they were making, I found I was a bit put out that they weren't showing more respect. Father Stamp had told me that I should never forget there were dead people lying under the ground. No need to be scared of them, he said, but I should try and remember this was their place as well as mine. So after a while I stopped taking my friends there. I was still very young but already old enough to realize it mattered at school how your classmates regarded you. I didn't want to get known as daft Tommy Cresswell who likes to play with old bones in the graveyard.

I was what they called a slow learner, taking longer than a lot of the others to get into reading and writing, but when, one day when I was about seven, it finally clicked, I took to it big. I read everything I could lay my hands on, so much so that Mam and Dad went from worrying about me not reading to worrying about me reading my brain into train oil, as Granny Longbottom used to say.

I don't know exactly when it was that I realized the graveyard was full of stuff to read! I'd seen there were words carved on the headstones, of course, but I never paid them much attention. I was more interested in the variety of shapes.

Some of the headstones were rounded, some were pointed, and some were squared off. Quite a lot had crosses on top of them, some of the older ones leaned to one side like they were drunk, and a few lay flat out. The ones I liked best were the ones with statues and these I gave names to in my private games. My favourite was an angel with a shattered nose that I called Rocky after Rocky Marciano who was my dad's great hero. Never got beaten, he'd say. I think he'd have called me Rocky rather than Tommy if Mam had let him.

It was Rocky the angel that got me looking at the words. I was lying in the grass one evening staring up at him when the words carved at his feet came into focus.

Sacred to the memory of David Oscar Winstanley
taken in the 87th year of his life
loving husband   devoted father
in virtue spotless   in charity generous
and a loyal servant of the General Post Office for
forty-nine years

He was probably a pretty important GPO official, but I imagined him as an ordinary postman, trudging the streets with his sackful of letters well into his eighties, and I was really impressed that he'd been so highly regarded that they'd given him an angel to keep watch over his grave and a full-blown testimonial. This is what started me paying attention to the inscriptions on other headstones. A few were in a funny language I couldn't understand. Father Stamp told me it was Latin and sometimes he'd translate it for me. Mam was always telling me not to bother Father Stamp because he had so much to do in the parish. In the same breath she'd say I could learn a lot if I listened to him, he was such an educated man. When I wondered in my childish way how I could listen to him without bothering him, she told me not to be cheeky. Things have changed, but back then a wise kid quickly learned that in the adult world he was usually in the wrong!

I quite liked Father Stamp and I certainly liked his mint humbugs, but when it came to practical information about the graves, I turned to the men who dug them. There were two of them, Young Clem and Old Clem.

I don't know how old Old Clem was – certainly no older than my dad – but he "had a back" and seemed to spend most of his time standing by the side of a new grave, smoking his pipe, while Young Clem laboured with his spade down below. Nowadays they have machines to do the hard work in less than half an hour. Back then it took Young Clem the best part of a morning to excavate and square off a grave to his dad's satisfaction. Occasionally Old Clem would seize the spade to demonstrate what ought to be done, but after he'd moved a couple of clods, he'd shake his head, rub his back, and return to his pipe. I heard Dad complaining to Mam more than once that Old Clem ought to be pensioned off, but he got no support from the vicar. Father Stamp just shook his head and said there was no question of getting rid of Old Clem. Mam said it showed what a true Christian gentleman Father Stamp was, and I should try to be less naughty and grow up like him. When I asked if that meant that Mam was naughty because she agreed with Dad that Old Clem should be sacked and Father Stamp didn't, she clipped my ear and said she didn't know where I got it from. I saw Dad grinning when she said that.

Young Clem was my special friend. Nine or ten years older than me, he was a big lad, more than twice my size, and he always had a fag in his mouth, though that was OK in them days. Dad smoked twenty a day and even Mam had the occasional puff.

Clem had been around all my life, helping his dad out when he were still a kid, then becoming his full-time assistant when he left school at sixteen. Like me he clearly thought of the graveyard as his own personal play park. Wandering around in the dusk one spring evening I heard a noise I didn't recognize and dropped down in the long grass. After a bit, with the noise still going on, I reckoned I hadn't been spotted so I crawled forward and peered round a headstone. Young Clem was lying there in the grass with a girl. At eight, I already had some vague notion there were things older lads liked to do with girls but I'd no real idea what it was all about except that simultaneously it had something to do with courting, which was all right, and something to do with being naughty, which wasn't. We didn't have sex education in Yorkshire in them days. Whatever it was, Young Clem and his girl were clearly enjoying it. I watched till I got bored then I crawled away. I had enough sense to know that I ought to keep out of the way when my friend was doing his naughty courting so whenever I glimpsed Clem in the graveyard with a girl I made myself scarce.

But when there weren't any girls around to divert him, the years between us seemed to vanish. Young Clem just loved larking around. In his snap break, he was always up for a game of hide and seek, or tiggy-on-gravestones. Or if I had my cricket ball with me, he'd show me how to set my fingers round it so that I could bowl a googly. One day he was demonstrating how to do this up against the church wall when Father Stamp came round the corner and I thought we would be in real trouble. But Clem didn't seem bothered. He just lit a fag and blew smoke down at Father Stamp (Clem was a good six inches taller) till the vicar turned round and went back the way he'd come, like he'd forgotten something.

"He must like you too, Clem," I said, impressed.

"You could say that," said Clem. "Doesn't mean I have to like him, does it?"

That struck me as odd even then. Under Mam's influence, I'd come to think everyone in the world must like and admire Father Stamp, so it was a shock to find that my mate Clem didn't agree.

I noticed after this that Clem often seemed to show up when I was with the vicar. I recall one occasion when I was round the back of the church where there was this funny old cross, very tall and thin with the actual cross piece set in a circle and not very big at all. Another odd thing was it didn't seem to mark a grave and I couldn't see any writing on it, just a lot of weird carvings.

Father Stamp came and stood beside me and started explaining what they all meant. I didn't understand a lot of what he said but

I did take in that it had been there for hundreds of years, dating back to long before the present St Cyprian's had been built. He told me there'd always been some sort of church or chapel here right back to what he called the Dark Ages and this cross had been put up then and it was quite famous, and experts came from all over just to look at it. Then he lifted me right up on his shoulders so I could get a good look at the fancy carving on the topmost piece of the cross, and I was sitting there, clinging on to his hair, with his hands clasping the top of my legs really tight, when there was a cough behind us.

Father Stamp swung round so quick I almost fell off, and in fact I might as well have done, as when he saw it was Young Clem he dropped me to the ground so hard I was winded.

"Sorry to interrupt, vicar," said Young Clem, "but Dad were wondering if you'd a moment to talk about tomorrow's funeral."

It didn't sound to me all that important, but Father Stamp hurried away as if it was, and Young Clem said, "Giving you a ride, was he?"

"He was showing me the carvings up on the cross," I said.

"Is that right? Tell you what, Tommy. The vicar's a busy man. You want to play, you play with me. Or if you want to know about the carvings or anything, ask my dad."

Even at that age, I couldn't imagine that Old Clem would know anything the vicar didn't but I followed Young Clem round the church to where his dad was sitting on a tombstone, puffing his pipe in the sun. There was no sign of Father Lamb so they must have finished their business quickly.

Young Clem said, "Tommy here wants to know about the carvings on that old cross"

Old Clem blew some smoke into the air reflectively then pronounced, "Heathen, that's what they are. Nasty pagan stuff. Don't know what summat like that is doing in a Christian churchyard."

For all its shortness, I have to say I found this more intriguing than Father Stamp's more rambling account but when I mentioned it to Mam, she said, "You don't want to listen to Old Clem. What's he know? No, you stick close to a clever man like Father Stamp and you never know what you'll learn. But don't you go bothering him!"

Mam didn't like Old Clem much. She wouldn't use the same words as Dad, who said he was an idle old sod, but that's what she thought. And she really gave him a piece of her mind once when she found me searching through the long grass in the graveyard and I told her Old Clem had lost his rubber spade and asked me to help him find it. But she liked young Clem. She said he had a nice smile and I noticed she used to pat her hair and sound a bit different when she was talking to him. She even knitted him a scarf that he said was the best scarf he'd ever had, though I never saw him wear it.

So what with the Clems and Father Stamp, I had plenty of company in the graveyard if I wanted it. But most of the time all the company I wanted was my own and that of my friends in the ground. I had no fear of them. Why should I? They were all such good people, I could tell that by what I read on their headstones. I found it a really comfortable idea that after you were dead, folk would come and read what had been carved about you, just like I was doing, and they'd think what a great guy you must have been!

Sometimes I'd lie in the grass by Rocky, looking up at the sky and inventing things they might one day put on my own stone.

Here lies Tommy Cresswell, loving son, and the best striker ever to play for Bradford City and England.

The more I thought of it, though, the more I was forced to admit that it wasn't all that likely as Bradford were holding up the bottom division of the league back then, and anyway I was crap at football. But anyone could be a hero, I reasoned. It was just a question of opportunity. So in the end I settled for this.

Sacred to the memory of Tommy Cresswell, beloved by all who knew him, who lost his life while bravely rescuing 56 children from their burning orphanage.
"He died that they might live."

I got that last bit from the stone of some soldier who'd been wounded in the Great War and then come home to die.

The graveyard was full of such inspiring and upbeat messages. Those who reached old age had enjoyed such useful and productive lives it was no wonder they were sadly missed by their loving friends and families, while those who died young were so precociously marvellous that the angels couldn't wait for them to get old before claiming them.

But eventually, after I'd done a tour of the whole graveyard, a problem began to present itself. I went all the way round again just to be sure, and it was still there.

I thought of applying to Mam and Dad for help, but I didn't really want them to know how much time I was still spending in the graveyard.

Father Lamb would certainly be able to answer my question. After all he was in charge of everything at St Cyprian's. But he didn't seem quite so keen on talking to me as he'd once been. If we did meet and sit down for a chat, after a while he'd get restless and jump up and say he had to be off somewhere else, even if Young Clem didn't interrupt him.

Then one Monday in early October on my way home from school still pondering my problem, I spotted the Clems digging a grave and it came to me that if anyone would know the answer, they would.

It was the usual set-up, with Young Clem up to his knees in the grave, digging, and Old Clem leaning on his spade, proffering advice.

I said, "Who's this for?"

"Old George Parkin," said Old Clem. "They'll not be putting him in the hole till Wednesday, but we thought we'd get a start while this good weather holds. Poor old George. He'll be sadly missed. He were a grand lad. One of the best."

That was my cue.

I said, "Clem," – letting them decide which one I was addressing – "I know you bury the good folk in the churchyard. But where do you put all the naughty ones?"

Old Clem stopped puffing, and Young Clem stopped digging, and they both said, "Eh?"

I saw that I needed to make myself a bit clearer.

I said, "You only bury the good people in the churchyard. I can tell that from reading what it says about them on the headstones. But the naughty ones must die as well. So where are all the naughty people? What do you do with *their* bodies?"

There was a long silence while they looked at each other.

Old Clem put his pipe back into his mouth and took it out again twice.

And finally he said solemnly, "Can you keep a secret, Tommy?"

"Oh yes. Cross my heart and hope to die," I said eagerly.

"Right then," said Old Clem. "We puts them in the crypt."

Young Clem said, "Dad!" like he was protesting because his father was talking out of turn.

Old Clem said, "The lad asked and he deserves to know. The crypt, young Tommy. That's where we dump all the bad 'uns. Pack 'em in, twenty or thirty deep till their flesh rots down to mulch. Then they grind the bones to bonemeal and it all gets spread on the fields. But you're not to tell anyone else, OK? This is between you and me. Promise?"

I repeated, "Cross my heart, Clem," and went away, leaving father and son having what sounded like a fierce discussion behind me.

This explained a lot! I knew there was this sort of big cellar under the church that they called the crypt. And I knew that there'd been bones and stuff down there because a couple of years earlier there'd been some worry about the church floor sinking and I'd heard Dad talking about clearing out the crypt and setting some props to support the ceiling, which was of course the church floor. So all the naughty people's remains must have been cleared out to spread on the fields then. That thought made me feel a bit queasy, but, after all, I told myself, if you were too naughty to be buried in the graveyard, what did it matter where you ended up?

I mean, who'd want a headstone saying, **Here lies John Smith who was really naughty and nobody misses him?**

I'd never been in the crypt, of course, though I knew where the door was in a hidden corner of the church porch. There was a notice on it saying: *Danger. Steep and crumbling steps. Do not enter.* Not that there was much chance of that as it was always kept locked.

But it had to be opened some time so that more naughty people could be put in there, that was obvious. And if, as Mam said, there were a lot of naughty people in this world, it was probably getting full up again after the last big clear-out.

Suddenly I was filled with a desperate need to see inside the crypt. I wasn't a particularly morbid child, but I recall one of my teachers writing on my report, *It's never enough to tell Tommy anything; if possible he's got to see for himself.*

So now I'd got the answer to my question, all I needed was for someone to open the crypt door for me and shine a torch in so that I could glimpse all the naughty people piled up there! Then I'd be satisfied.

But I was bright enough to know that this wasn't the kind of favour adults were likely to do for a kid. I was going to have to sort this out for myself.

The answer was as obvious as asking the Clems about where the naughty people had been.

Dad could go anywhere in and around the church. Obviously he wasn't going to open the crypt door for me. But he did have a key. At least, I assumed he had a key. He certainly had a bunch of keys that opened up every other door.

And as I thought of this, I also realized that tonight being a Monday night was the perfect time to put my plan into operation. Not that I realized I had a plan till I thought of it! The thing was, Dad always went down the pub to play darts on Mondays and Mam curled up on the sofa with her knitting to watch *Sherlock Holmes*, her favourite TV series, and nothing was allowed to interrupt her.

So tonight was the night! It seemed like fate, but for a while it looked like fate had changed its mind. It turned out that Dad had been feeling a bit hot and snuffly all day and Mam was worried it was the Hong Kong flu virus that was just taking a grip around the country. But after tea, Dad said not to be stupid, it was just a sniffle that a couple of pints of John Smith's and a whisky chaser would soon sort. So off he went down the pub, and not long after I went up to bed without any of my usual arguments and lay there till I heard the swelling introductory music of Mam's programme.

It was Part Two of *The Hound of the Baskervilles,* I recall, and I was confident there was no way she'd move till it was finished. I had at least an hour.

I slipped out of bed. I didn't bother to get dressed. I was wearing track suit pyjamas and it was a warm autumn night, so warm in fact I was perspiring slightly and the thought of putting on more clothes was unpleasant. I tiptoed downstairs, carrying the torch I kept for reading under the bedclothes. The TV was going full belt, and I moved into the kitchen, plucked Dad's church keys from the hook by the back door and headed out into the night.

Our door into the churchyard was locked but I knew by touch alone which key I needed here.

As I passed through, I paused for a moment. The graveyard looked different in the dark, and the bulk of the church silhouetted against the stars seemed to have assumed cathedral-like proportions. But I switched on my torch and advanced till I spotted the comforting outline of Rocky, my broken-nosed angel keeping guard over David Oscar Winstanley, the virtuous old postman. The long grass beneath my bare feet was pleasantly cool, the balmy air caressed my skin, and I felt sure somehow that Rocky would be keeping an eye on me too.

The door to the crypt was in a corner of the church's broad entrance porch. I thought I might have to unlock the church door itself as, ever since the theft of some items of silver a couple of years earlier, the building had been firmly locked at dusk. Tonight, however, the door was open. I didn't consider the implications of this, just took it in my superhero mode as a demonstration that things were running my way.

Now all I had to do was find the right key for the crypt door.

It proved surprisingly easy. Close up, I saw it wasn't the ancient worm-eaten oak door I'd expected but a new door, stained to fit in with the rest of the porch, and instead of a large old-fashioned keyhole there was a modern mortice lock.

That made the selection of the right key very easy and the door swung open with well-oiled ease and not the slightest suspicion of a horror-film screech.

Now, however, the thin beam of my torch revealed that the bit about the steep and decaying steps hadn't been exaggerated. They plunged down almost vertically into the darkness where the naughty people lay.

Suddenly I felt less like a superhero and more like an eight-year-old boy who got scared watching *Dr Who* with his mam!

It felt a lot colder in the church porch and there seemed to be a draught of still colder air coming up from the crypt that made my sweat-soaked pyjamas feel clammy. I could smell damp earth – that was an odour I was very familiar with from hanging around the Clems while they were digging a grave. But what wasn't there, which I'd half expected, was any of that decaying meat smell I'd once got a whiff of as Young Clem's spade drove into an unexpected coffin.

Far from reassuring me, this only roused a fear that maybe the naughty people didn't decay like the ordinary good people, but somehow got preserved like the salted hams that hung in Granny Longbottom's kitchen. Maybe they even retained a bit of life!

In fact to my young mind, already well acquainted through the school playground with notions of zombies and vampires, it seemed very likely that the new door and its mortice lock hadn't been put there to keep the inquisitive public out, but to keep the still active naughty people in!

I could have shut the door and retreated and gone home to bed, and no one would ever have known of my cowardice. Except me, of course.

Daft, wasn't it? Just to prove to myself I wasn't scared, I began to descend that crumbling sandstone staircase. And all the time my teeth were chattering so hard I could hardly breathe!

What did I expect to find? Bodies hanging upside down from the ceiling? Coffins stacked six or seven deep? Heaps of bones? I don't know.

And I didn't know whether to be disappointed or relieved when all that the beam of my torch picked out was ... emptiness! Except, that is, for seven or eight pillars of steel rising from metal plates set on the packed earth floor to give them firm grounding, and with metal beams running between them at ceiling level to support the sagging church floor.

And that was it. It dawned on me that Old Clem had been having me on again, like he did with looking for the rubber spade! I should have known. Making a fool of people is what passes for a joke in Yorkshire. I felt really stupid! Also despite the chilly air down here, I felt very hot. I pulled off my pyjama top to cool down and used it to wipe off the streams of perspiration running down my face and body.

Suddenly I was desperate to be back in my bed and I turned to go.

Then I heard a noise.

And all my fears came rushing back full pelt!

It was a relief to realize the noise was coming from outside the crypt, not inside.

Someone was at the top of the stairs.

I clicked my torch off and stood in the dark.

A voice demanded harshly, "Who's down there?"

I almost answered but the thought of the trouble I'd be in at home – sneaking out after I'd gone to bed and stealing Dad's keys to get into the crypt – kept me quiet. Also, as I say, all my old fears were boiling up again. Maybe this was one of the wicked zombies returning from a stroll round the graveyard! I found myself praying to Rocky who'd never been beaten to come and help me!

Then a bigger fear erupted to push out all the others. Suppose whoever it was pulled the door shut behind him as he went away and left me locked in the crypt all night!

So I stuttered, "It's me," and began to move forward.

Then I stopped blinded as a powerful torch beam hit me right in the eyes.

I heard footsteps on the stairs and a voice I now recognized said, "Tommy! What on earth are you doing here?"

It was Father Stamp! I was so relieved I rushed forward up the steep steps and flung myself around him and hugged him close with my arms and legs. His arms went around my back and I felt his large strong hands cool against my hot skin. My track suit bottom was always a bit loose, and I think it had slipped down but I didn't care, I was just so relieved to be safe! I wanted to explain what I'd been doing but when I tried to speak, it came out as sobs, and he lifted me up and held me so close, I could hardly get my breath, and I tried to push myself free.

My memory of what happened after that is vague and confused. It was like my head was full of colours all forming weird shapes, constantly flying apart and changing into something else. And my body didn't feel as if it belonged to me, it was like a girl's rag doll that can be twisted into any shape you want, and I knew I would have fallen away or maybe even flown away if Father Stamp's strong hands hadn't been grasping my weak and nerveless flesh.

And then – I don't think I heard anything and I certainly didn't see anything – but I knew there was someone – or something – else on the steps. I just had time to think that maybe Rocky had answered my earlier call when there was an explosion of noise and violent movement, and something crashed into Father Stamp and together we went tumbling down the steep steps.

That was pretty well the end for me. I must have hit the crypt floor with such a bang that all of the breath and most of the con-sciousness was knocked out of my body. I had a sense of being embraced again but not in the strong muscular way that Father Stamp had embraced me. Maybe, I thought, this was Rocky. Then I was raised by strong arms and carried up the steps, and my lolling head gave me a view down into the crypt lit by a moving light that I think must have come from Father Stamp's torch, rolling around where he'd dropped it as we went tumbling down together.

Finally I was outside in the balmy night air and the sky was full of stars and I didn't remember anything else for sure till the moment when I opened my eyes and found myself back in my own bedroom with sunlight streaming through the window.

Four days had passed, four days that I'd spent being very sick, and sweating buckets, and tossing and turning with such violence that Mam sometimes had to hold me down. The doctor said I'd had a particularly extreme dose of Hong Kong flu, not just me but Dad too. He'd come back from the pub in almost as bad a state as me. How I got back to my bed, I don't know. I had some vague notion that Rocky had carried me there. My waking mind was awash with fantastic images of my visit to the crypt and these turned into really terrible nightmares when I sank into sleep, so no wonder I was tossing and turning so violently. I were poorly for nearly a fortnight, much worse than Dad who was up and about again after a week. And it was another two weeks after I first got out of bed before I really started getting back to something like normal.

By this time my memories and my nightmares had become so confused I found it impossible to tell the difference between them. Looming large in all of them was Father Stamp. Remembering how Mam always sang his praises as a visitor of the sick, I lived in fear of seeing him by my bedside. Finally, when Mam didn't mention him, I did.

"Father Stamp's gone," she said shortly.

"Gone where?" I said.

"How should I know? Just gone. Not a trace," she said. "Now are you going to take that medicine or do I have to pour it down you?"

I couldn't blame her for being short. Luckily for me and Dad, she'd somehow managed to remain untouched by the flu bug, but she must have been worked off her feet for the past few weeks taking care of the pair of us.

Also she'd had time to get used to Father Stamp's disappearance. When I was up and about again, I found out he'd been gone a long time. Exactly when no one was certain. It wasn't till he didn't turn up for old Mr Parkin's funeral on the Wednesday after my adventure in the crypt that folk started to get worried. He wasn't married and he lived alone in the vicarage, looked after by a local woman who came in every morning to clean the house and take care of his meals. That week she'd been down with the flu too, so there was a lot of vagueness about who'd actually seen him last and when.

Should I say something? Best not, I decided. When you're a kid, you learn it's usually a mistake to volunteer information that might get you in bother! Also once I started sharing my memory-nightmare of that night, it would be hard to stop till I got to the bit where I was carried home by a marble angel with a broken nose, and I knew that sounded really loopy!

Yet for some reason that was the bit of my memories that I clung on to hardest. Maybe, by clinging to what had to be fantasy, I was shutting out what might be reality. Anyway, soon as I felt well enough, I went back into the graveyard to say thank you to Rocky.

Young Clem spotted me and came over for a chat.

"All right, Tommy?" he said, lighting the inevitable fag.

"Yes thanks," I said.

"Me and Dad were dead worried about you," he said. "Hong Kong flu it was, right?"

I really didn't want to talk about it, but I didn't want to offend Young Clem, especially not after Mam told me he'd called round nearly every day to ask after me when I was ill.

"That's right," I said. "Hong Kong flu."

"Aye, it can be right nasty that. My Auntie Mary had it, just about sent her doolally, thought she were the Queen Mother for a bit, we have a grand laugh with her about that now she's right again. Owt like that happen to you, Tommy?"

"Just some bad dreams," I said.

"But you're all right now?"

"Yes, thank you."

"Grand!" he said, stubbing out his cigarette on Rocky's knee. "Everyone has bad dreams. Thing is not to let them bother you when you wake up. See you around, Tommy."

"Yes, Clem, see you around."

Father Stamp's disappearance was old news now. It seemed one of the papers had dug up some stuff about him having trouble with his nerves when he was a curate down south, and his bishop moving him north for his health. So most folk reckoned he'd had what they called a nervous breakdown and he'd turn up some day. But he never did.

After a while St Cyprian's got a replacement. He was nowhere near as High as Father Stamp, he wanted everyone to call him Jimmy, and he had all kinds of newfangled ideas. Dad and him didn't get on, and pretty soon there was a big falling out that ended with us leaving Rose Cottage and going to live with Granny Longbottom in Murton till Dad got taken on at Rowntree's chocolate factory and we found a place right on the edge of York.

So Mam got her wish and I was brought up breathing good fresh air, and eating a lot of chocolate, and enjoying the sight and smell of trees and grass with never a gravestone in sight. In fact, after leaving St Cyprian's, Mam seemed to lose all interest in religion, and as I grew up I don't think I saw the inside of a church again, unless you count a visit to the Minster on a school trip. I'd only been inside a few minutes when I started to feel the whole place crowding in on me and I were glad to get out into the air. After that I didn't bother.

That was forty-odd years ago. I still live with my mam. Lot of folk think that's weird. Let them think. All I know is I never felt the need to get close to anyone else. I never went courting. I did try being naughty with a girl from time to time, and it were all right, I suppose, but I could never get really interested and I don't think they liked it that much, so in the end I stopped bothering.

Maybe I should have moved out. I know Dad thought I should. I brought it up one night after he'd gone out to the pub. Mam was sitting in front of the TV, busily knitting away as she always did. That click-click-clicking of the needles is such a familiar accompaniment that it sounds strange if ever I watch a programme without it! She smiled up at me when I broached the subject of moving out and said, "This is your home, son. You'll always be welcome here."

Next year, Dad got diagnosed with cancer. After that I think he was glad I was still around to help take some of the strain off Mam. She was the best nurse he could have asked for and she kept him at home far longer than many women would have done. But three years later he was dead, and since then the thought of leaving has never crossed my mind.

As for Father Stamp and St Cyprian's, they never got mentioned at home, not even while Dad were still living. Was that good or bad? There's a lot of folk say everything should be brought out in the open. Well, each to his own. I know what worked for me. That's not to say I never wondered how different my life might have been if the events of that October night hadn't occurred. We're all what our childhood makes us, the kid is father to the man, isn't that what they say?

Though I doubt if many people looking at a picture of me back then could see much connection between little Tommy Cresswell at eight and this fifty-year-old, a bit shabby, a bit broken down, unmarried, living at home with his widowed mam.

There is, though, maybe one traceable link between that kid in the graveyard and this middle-aged man.

I'm a postman.

How much that can be tracked back to David Oscar Winstanley and Rocky, the broken-nosed angel, I don't know. I certainly don't aspire to anything like his memorial, either in form or in words. In fact I've lowered my sights considerably from the fantasies of my boyhood. **He looked after his mam, and bothered nobody** would do me. I suppose I could rate as a loyal servant to the Post Office, if loyalty means doing your job efficiently. But if it entails devoting yourself wholeheartedly to your employer, then I don't qualify. I never had any ambition to rise up the career ladder. Delivering the mail's been enough for me.

Then the other day, my first on a new round, I knocked on a door to deliver a parcel, and when the door opened I found myself looking at Old Clem.

Except of course it was Young Clem forty-odd years on.

"Bugger me," he said when I introduced myself. "Tommy Cresswell! Come on in and have a beer."

"More than my job's worth, Clem," I said. "But I'll have a cup of tea."

Sitting in his kitchen, he filled me in on his life. He'd worked most of his life for the Bradford Parks and Gardens Service (though they call it something fancier nowadays), he'd been a widower for five years, and he'd recently retired because of his health. No need for details here. Most of his sentences were punctuated with a racking cough which didn't stop him from getting through three or four fags as we talked.

"Me daughter and her two kiddies live here in York," he said. "She wanted me to move in with them but I knew that 'ud never do. But I wanted to be a bit handier so I got myself this place. How about you, Tommy? You married?"

"Who'd have me?" I said, making a joke out of it. Then I told him about Dad dying and me living with Mam. And all the time he was sort of studying me through a cloud of smoke in a way that made me feel uneasy. So in the end I looked at my watch and said I ought to be getting on before folk started wondering what had happened to their mail.

But as I started to rise from my chair, he reached over the table and grasped my wrist and said, "Afore you go, Tommy ... " – here he broke off to cough – " ... or mebbe I mean, afore I go, there's something we need to talk ... "

I should just have left. I knew what he was going to tell me, and it had been a long time since Rocky was a barrier against the truth. But I stopped and listened and let him give form and flesh to what for so long I'd been desperate to pretend was nowt but an echo of one of my Hong Kong flu nightmares.

That night as usual I cleared up after supper and washed the dishes. Mam says it's no job for a man but she's been having a lot of trouble with her knees lately. There's been some talk of a replacement but she says she can't be bothered with that. So I do all I can to make life easy for her. Most nights after we've eaten, we sit together in front of the telly and I'll maybe watch a football match while she gets on with her knitting. Like I say, doesn't matter how noisy the crowd is at the game, if that click-click-clicking of her needles stops, I look round to see what she's doing.

Tonight when I came in from the kitchen with a mug of coffee for me and cup of tea for her, she was knitting as usual but I didn't switch the set on.

I said, "Met an old friend today, Mam. Remember Young Clem? Him and his dad used to dig the graves at St Cyprian's? Well, he's living in York now. So he can be close to his daughter and grandkids."

"Young Clem?" she said. "So he has grandchildren? That's nice. Grandchildren are nice."

"Aye," I said. "Sorry I never gave you any, Mam."

"Maybe you didn't, but I never lost you, Tommy, and that's just as important," she said, her needles clicking away. "So what was the crack with Young Clem then?"

She looked at me brightly. Sometimes these days she could be a bit vague about things; others, like now, she was as bright as a button.

I sipped my coffee slowly while my mind tried to come to terms with what Young Clem had told me.

My problem had nothing to do with his powers of expression for he'd spoken in blunt Yorkshire terms.

He'd said, "I'd taken this lass into graveyard, for a bang, tha knows, and we'd just done when I saw this figure moving between the headstones. I nigh on shit meself till I made out it were your mam. She didn't spot me, but something about the look of her weren't right, so I told my lass to shove off down the pub and I'd catch up with her there. Well, she weren't best pleased but I didn't wait to argue, I went after your mam, and I caught up with her by the church door. She jumped a mile when I spoke to her, then she asked if I'd seen you. Seems she'd been watching the telly and all of a sudden something made her get up and go upstairs. When she found you weren't in bed, she went out into the yard and saw the back gate into the graveyard standing open and she went through it to look for you.

"I could tell what a state she were in – she'd nowt on her feet but a pair of fluffy slippers and she were still carrying her knitting with her – so I tried to calm her down, saying that likely you were just larking about with some of your mates. But she'd spotted that the church door were ajar, and nowt would satisfy her but that we went inside to take a look.

"Well, we didn't get past the porch. There was a noise like

someone sobbing and a bit of a light and it were coming up from the crypt. That was when I recalled what Dad had said to you when you asked where we put the naughty people. I'd told him he shouldn't joke about such things with you as you were only a lad, but I never thought you'd take it serious enough to do owt like this.

"I told your mam I'd go first as the steps were bad, and that's what I did, but she were right behind me and she saw clearly enough what I saw down below.

"That mucky bastard Stamp were all over you. He'd just about got you bollock naked. I knew straight off what were going on. I'd been there myself, except I was a couple of years older and a lot tougher and more streetwise than you. When he started his tricks on me, I belted him in the belly and I told him I were going to report him, and I would have done, only I weren't sure anyone would believe me. They'd already marked my card as a bit of a wild boy at school plus I'd been done for shoplifting by the cops. So I said nowt, but when they started talking about giving Dad the boot because of his back, I stood in front of Stamp and I let him know that the day Dad got his papers was the day he'd find himself *in* the papers. I'd been keeping an eye on him when I saw him getting interested in you, and I thought he'd got the message. But there's no changing them bastards!

"Now I were on him in a flash. He must have thought God had hit him with a thunderbolt, and that were no more than he deserved. The pair of you went tumbling down the steps. His torch went flying but it were one of them rubber ones and it didn't break. He was lying on his back, not moving. You were just about out of it. Your mam gathered you up and it was only then I reckon that it fully hit her what the bastard had been at. She put you into my arms and told me to take you up the steps.

"I said, 'What about you missus?' but she didn't answer, so I set off back up to the porch with you in my arms. Do you not remember any of this, Tommy? Nay, I see you do."

And he was right. I was remembering it now when Mam brought me back to our living room by saying impatiently. "Come on,

Tommy. Cat got your tongue? I asked what you and Young Clem found to talk about?"

"Oh, nothing much," I said. "I told him about Dad, and he told me that Old Clem had passed on too, about ten years back, heart, it was. And we chatted about the old days at Cyprian's, that's all."

"Well, I'm sorry to hear about Old Clem, though he was a bit of a devil," said Mam. "Remember that time he had you looking everywhere for his rubber spade? I gave him a piece of my mind for that!"

A pity you hadn't been around to give him a piece of your mind when he told me about the crypt, I thought. Maybe life could have been very different for me. Maybe I'd be sitting by my own fireside now with my own family around me. I thought of Young Clem, moving house so he could be handier for his grandchildren. He was clearly made of stronger stuff than me. He dealt with the crises in life by looking them straight in the face and getting on with the life not the crisis. He certainly gave no indication he blamed Old Clem and his daft lie for what happened to me in the crypt. It was just another Yorkshire joke, like sending a kid to look for a rubber spade!

Any road, the way it turned out, it wasn't strictly speaking a lie any more. Old Clem had told me that the crypt was where they put the naughty people. And the crypt of St Cyprian's was where Young Clem had buried Father Stamp's body.

It must have taken him a couple of hours or more to dig a grave in that hard-packed earth. I wonder how long the poor lass he'd sent off to the pub waited for him? Maybe she'd forgiven him, maybe she was even the one who'd become his wife. I should have asked.

But the question that bothered me was, just how naughty had Father Stamp really been? That he had problems was clear. That he'd been foolish enough to grope Young Clem I didn't doubt.

But it wasn't his fault that I'd flung myself almost naked into his arms. And it had been me who'd been desperate to cling on to him, at least to start with. For all I know his intention was simply to carry me out of the crypt and take me home. However it had looked to Young Clem and my mam, there'd been no time for him to actually *do* anything.

No, it wasn't a memory of childhood sexual abuse that had dictated the pattern of my life. It was quite another memory, one that I'd only been able to bear because I could pretend to myself that it might after all just be the product of a sick child's fevered imagination.

My half hour listening to Young Clem had removed that fragile barrier for ever.

I don't know how long Mam and me have before us living like this. Granny Longbottom lasted into her nineties so there could be a good few years yet.

There it is then. Night after night, month after month, year after year, I'm going to be sitting here in this room, still able to hear the click-click-clicking of her knitting no matter how loud the telly.

And every time I glance across at her to share a smile, I'm going to see her as I saw her from Clem's arms in the fitful light of the torch rolling around the crypt floor, I'm going to see her kneeling astride the recumbent body of Father Stamp with those same click-click clicking needles raised high, one in either hand, before she drives them down with all the strength of a mother's love, a mother's hate, into his despairing, uncomprehending and vainly pleading eyes.

A BULLET FOR BAUSER

Jay Stringer

"Is that—?"
"Yes."
"For real?"
"Yes."
"Fuuuuuck."
"Uh huh."

Bauser looked at the cold steel in his hand. Funny, he thought it would be heavier. He'd always thought holding a gun would be like holding a cannon, a real sign that you had some fucking strength in you.

He'd held an air pistol once, at his best mate Dex's house after school. He'd shot Dex in the balls and he'd walked with a limp for six months. Thing was, that air pistol was pretty much the same weight as this gun. It was a disappointment to say the least.

His little brother Marcus was staring at the gun as if it was the greatest thing he'd ever seen. Bauser had never heard Marcus swear before. He cuffed him round the ear proudly.

"Listen to you, swearing like Granny."

"I'm a man now, just like you."

Bauser laughed. Marcus was only a week past twelve years old. Which put him two weeks past the eighth anniversary of their daddy walking out. Stood there in second-hand pyjamas, a faded Power Ranger on the belly, and swearing with pride.

"Is that right? When you going to start working for a living, then?"

Marcus smiled and pulled a face. When he was younger, that had been the face he pulled if he didn't like the food he was given. Now it just made do for any time he wanted to be funny.

"Working's for looooosers." Marcus stretched it out in a high whine. "I aye never seen granny working, and she's always got money for magazines and shit."

"Shit? You're really getting the hang of these words. You been watching my DVDs?"

Marcus rolled his eyes.

"Nah. I get the words from school, man. I only watch your DVDs if I want to see boobies." He paused while his big brother gave him a high five. "But one thing? What's a clit?"

Bauser blushed and looked at the floor. Then at the wall. Then at everything else in the room other than his brother.

"I, uh, I dunno."

"Nobody ever seems to know." Marcus shook his head. Then his eyes fell to the gun again and his face lit up once more. "Why you got a gun, Eric?"

Bauser tucked the gun into the waistline of his jeans at the small of his back. He usually wore them a size up, but he needed the waistband to be tight today so he'd worn an old pair. He flinched when his brother used his first name.

"Cuz today's a big day for me." He checked himself out in the mirror to make sure the gun was concealed. "I'm getting promoted."

***

He stopped in the kitchen to kiss his mum on the cheek before going out.

She was stirring a pot while trying to stop something under the grill from turning to charcoal. From the living room Bauser's granny was shouting in a running commentary in her Caribbean lilt. Bauser and his mum shared a laugh at the old woman's rantings.

"Where you off to?"

"Doing overtime at work. They say they're gonna teach me to drive the forklift."

His mum smiled at him with a sad tilt to her mouth. She didn't call him a liar. She didn't need to.

"You'll stay for breakfast first though?"

"Nah, can't. I'll be late if I don't get off now. I'll get a pot noodle or something, don't worry about it."

"I saw Dex at the supermarket last night, he was asking about you. You don't spend any time with him any more?"

"Nah, he's with a bad lot. Gotta keep my head in the work, you know?"

Dex was working at the warehouse that Bauser was pretending to work at. He was on the straight and boring, and Bauser had new friends now.

"Mwah." His mum kissed him on the forehead and waited until he returned the sentiment on her cheek, then turned back to her cooking.

"Don't work too hard, Eric," she said.

"Mum, don't go calling me that. That's *his* name, I don't want it."

Bauser had almost made it through the living room before his granny caught him. She was settled in her usual armchair, directly in front of the telly and below a photograph of her husband. She rose out of her chair in a mass of flailing arms and legs, making a funny squealing noise at the thought of not getting a kiss. He gave her a hug and a kiss on the cheek, and then made it out the door before any more family members appeared to molest him.

***

On the tram ride into town, he could feel the lump against his back. A sweat was trickling down there, sticking between the metal and his skin. This never seemed to be a problem in the films. Not once had he seen a character pull out a concealed weapon and then have to wipe the sweat off before using it.

The conductor was someone he knew from school. Tony or Timmy, something like that. One of those faceless kids he used to steal lunch money off. Look at him now in his cheap blue blazer, tie buttoned up as if he was proud of it. Faceless Timmy saw Bauser but left him alone. The schoolyard never left some people. It would have been a free journey if some old lady hadn't taken offence at the idea and pointed Bauser out to the conductor again.

He wanted to say, *Oi, bitch, I got a gun. Shut the fuck up.* He wanted to say a lot, but words had never been his thing. And after today, he wouldn't need them. He wouldn't be riding the tram to work, he'd get picked up any time he wanted.

After today, if he needed bullets for the gun, he'd be able to get them. The Mann brothers would let him have all the ammunition he needed.

The tram station in the city centre was in front of the police station. Bauser caught a thrill. His spine tingled and his shoulders felt a hundred feet wide as he stood and looked up at the front door. For the first time, he started to feel a little bit of weight in the metal he was carrying.

* * *

Two men frisked Bauser at the door before letting him into the restaurant.

Later on it would be full of drunken football fans and students, but right now it was playing host to a board meeting. The tables in the middle of the room had been pushed to one side, clearing a space for them all to stand. The stereo was already playing the generic Indian music that would fill the room later on. Bauser suppressed a smile.

They were all there. Both Mann brothers, Gav and Channy. They had to be there to give their approval. Teek and Marvin, the guys who called the shots on the streets. Pepsi and Letisha, the two team leaders who had recommended Bauser. They all greeted him with smiles when he walked in, handshakes and backslaps, a hug from Latisha. The talking seemed to have already been done.

"So you ready to step up?" Channy Mann looked Bauser up and down as he spoke. "You think you're ready to run a team?"

"Hell yeah."

His confidence was only about fifty per cent bravado. The rest was naivety. But the Mann brothers seemed to like his answer. Channy continued.

"How long have you been with us now?"

"Four years."

"Started young."

"He aye never missed a count." Marv spoke up. "Never called in sick. Kept his mouth shut when the police pulled him."

"Yeah." Gav smiled and looked Bauser up and down as if he was sizing up a pitbull. "I think you are. You're bursting for it."

Bauser nodded, hoping he looked cool and relaxed but his heart was breaking out of his chest.

"This means, you get arrested? We'll get you bail and a good lawyer. You don't have to carry that on your own. You need to go anywhere? You get a man to drive you. You need anything? They can fetch it for you."

Bauser was liking this. It sounded like being a king.

"But, and we tell you this now, you're the man we come to. One of your boys fucks up? You carry that. You put your fingers in the till? Marv and Teek here will fuck you up."

"Totally, man. I'd never do you guys like that."

Channy nodded his head toward the door at the back of the room. Letisha tapped Bauser on the shoulder and motioned for him to follow and she and Pepsi headed over to the door. It led to the kitchen at the back of the building. It was spotless and smelled of cleaning fluids. Aside from a ratty old sofa against the wall, it was the very model of a well-run kitchen. Letisha and Pepsi slouched down into the sofa, but Bauser stayed on his feet.

"They're talking about me, right?"

"Yup."

"They like me though, right? I mean, they wouldn't have me here if they wasn't going to give me the job, right?"

Letisha shrugged and Pepsi started replying to a text message on his phone.

"What if they change their minds?"

Pepsi didn't take his eyes off the phone. "Probably kill you."

They let Bauser hang there for a moment feeling his heart stop until they started laughing. Letisha stuck out her hand and Pepsi slapped it. Bauser kicked them both in the shins.

The laughter stopped when Marv stepped into the kitchen and shut the door again after him. He was a quiet man and stillness seemed to settle in around him wherever he was.

"There's a problem." He said it in a low voice, and the room seemed to suck in around his words and drain the air away.

"Wha—?"

He pulled a gun out from the folds of his hoodie. It was Bauser's gun, the one that had been taken off him at the door.

"Did you get this from Sukhi?"

"Nah, some guy in West Brom."

"Let me tell you, it worries us. Kids come into this wanting to play gangsta? They don't last very long. What made you get a gun?"

"I thought that was how it worked. I seen Pepsi carries a gun and, you know, I thought that all you team leaders did?"

Marv stared off into space for a moment, lining things up in his mind. Then he nodded and smiled down at the gun.

"I trust you, son. That's why we're promoting you." Bauser's face lit up and he was about to speak but Marv continued. "But a gun? That's something else. This aye Birmingham. Bullets are expensive, man. You only carry if we say so, and you're not there yet."

He turned the gun over in his hand.

"Nice. Sweaty though. You nervous today, huh?"

Bauser shrugged.

"It's OK, you can admit it. We're all nervous the first time. To be honest, it's always there, just a little bit. You put it behind your back, right? Don't do that. You got a hoodie?"

Bauser nodded. He had lots of hoodies. He'd always liked them, and when the men on TV started saying hoodies were evil, he'd liked them even more.

"Cool. Wear ones with big pockets, like mine. You can carry a gun in front of you and it don't have to get wet. Or in your hood, unless there's police around. A good trick? Carry it in your sleeve a couple of times, let people see it. Then always keep your right hand covered by your sleeve and people will think you've always got it." He held up a bullet and slipped it into the cartridge. "I want you to prove yourself before you carry, and that's going to take time. But let's see if you've got what it takes."

He turned in the direction of the kitchen door and pushed through. Bauser followed. The Mann brothers had left, and in the centre of the room was a man tied to a chair. He was doing his best to shout, but the sock that they'd forced down his throat meant it was coming out as a choking sound.

He was old and tired, and his face was swollen from a beating. Through the swelling, though, Bauser could still recognize him.

He was the face from pictures on his mum's dressing table, and half-remembered trips to the cinema and McDonald's. He was a name on a birthday card every few years. His name was Eric, and he was Bauser's father. Marv handed him the gun.

"Your old man here's been running up a tab that he never intended to pay. We was going to let you talk him round, but this is a better way. All yours."

Marv went and stood by the kitchen door. Bauser felt his gut turn and try to climb its way out through his ass. His feet were made of lead. The gun in his hand felt real now, it was a serious fucking cannon. He looked down at it, at the way it shone in the dim light, and at how the outside world fell away when he stared at the metal.

His father's eyes were wide as golf balls, bloodshot and terrified. He was shaking his head and the choking sounds now sounded pleading rather than angry. As the gun came into view, he twisted and toppled the chair, and began trying to wriggle his way to the front door. It was a pathetic sight, and he didn't have the energy to move too far. Bauser just stood and watched for a moment, waiting until the old man gave up before he knelt and pressed the gun against his temple. The smell of warm piss filled the room, followed by one last whimper.

This felt fucking amazing.

Bauser's finger tightened against the trigger and he closed his eyes for a moment. When he opened them and looked back down, he noticed just how much his father resembled Marcus.

"Fuck you," he said into the old man's ear.

He got to his feet and walked over to stand with his boss.

"Why didn't you shoot him?" Marvin said.

"Like you said, bullets are expensive."

WHOLE LIFE

Liza Cody

———————————

I F EYES WERE knives she'd have cut me stone dead. Instead she gave me that look and then spat. I hate passing the bus shelter. But I have to pass it by because I can't wait for a bus there any more.

They took the shoe off of the roof of the shelter, but they still haven't mended the crazy crack where Jamie's board hit the safety plastic. It was a drenching night, that night, so when the Law arrived they say there was hardly any blood left. It gurgled away down the gutter as fast as it spilled out of Jamie's body and there's not even a stain left. Poor ginger lamb.

That's what I'd tell the woman with the eyes – poor ginger lamb. He was red-headed, plump, gay, and that night he was carrying a new skateboard. If she was even talking to me she'd tell me he was a sweet kid who never did anyone any harm. And she'd say he had "his whole life ahead of him". That's what they always say: "Whole life ahead … "

What's a whole life? Is my life without my son a whole life? Is it a whole life when I can't use the nearest bus stop? My life, minus my kid and a bus stop; my life minus respect, my reputation, two of my three jobs and all my friends, isn't a whole life, is it? It's a life full of holes.

Jamie's whole life ran red – from his eyes, mouth, ears, nose and groin. It ran away from him down a storm drain never to return. And Ben came home and said, "Can you wash my shirt, Mum? A kid had a nosebleed and it went all over me." It was his school uniform so I stuffed his clothes into the washing machine and he had a hot bath because he was shivering from the rain and cold.

I left him alone to do his homework with half a pizza in the oven and some chocolate pud in the fridge. His whole life was ahead of him. Then I went to the Saracen's Head to serve drinks to drunks.

You see, I thought I was a good mother. I washed Ben's clothes and I left a hot supper for him – I didn't just bung him a couple of quid and expect him to go back out into the rain for a takeaway.

The Law said, "Your son comes in covered in a murdered boy's blood and all you do is wash his clothes? You must've known something was up. We could charge you as an accessory."

Mary Sharp didn't wash her twins' shirts. The Law found their clothes in a soggy tangle under the bunk beds. Roseen Hardesty didn't even come home that night. Rocky Hardesty tried to wash his own uniform but the machine was bust. He ate his beans cold, straight from the can, and stayed up till five in the morning playing computer games.

There wasn't even a speck on Jamal's clothes. I think cleanness is part of Jamal's mum's religion, but I don't really know because her English won't stand up to an ordinary conversation.

Me? I was home by half past midnight. I asked Ben if he'd done his homework and he said, "Yes – why do you always go on at me?"

I told him to go to bed and I transferred his clothes from the washer to the dryer because he'd forgotten. Then I tidied the kitchen and was in bed by a quarter past one myself. I was tired and I had to be up and out at six-thirty to clean three offices by nine.

That's when I saw the police tape at the bus shelter. The one purple and white trainer was still on the roof. At that point no one knew it was Jamie's. So I still thought I had my whole life ahead of me, whereas I'd already lost it hours ago. So had Ben, although most folk round here would say he didn't lose it, he chucked it all away and got what he deserved.

"What happened here?" the bus driver asked when I got on.

"Search me," I said. "Kids?"

"Someone got knifed," a woman said. She works part time. I see her on the bus three mornings out of five.

"Not round here," I said. "They're good kids round here."

"I heard it on local radio," she said. And we all turned to look at the crazy crack on the plastic shelter as the bus pulled away.

Later, this same woman went round telling everyone that I was playing the innocent but she knew beyond the shadow of a doubt that I was lying. Do doubts have shadows? I think they must do. My whole life has been about doubts and shadows ever since.

That morning I went straight from the office block to Moby's Café where I worked during the day. I did the food preparation, waitressing and cleaning up.

Mr Moby was there when the school rang to say that Ben was with the Law. He looked daggers at me because I wasn't supposed to take personal calls while I was at work.

"It's a mistake," I kept saying. "Ben's never been in any trouble." But I had to go to the police station to find out what was wrong and Mr Moby said he'd dock my wages. He'd been on my case since that time I slapped his face in the mop cupboard.

On the other hand he spoke up for me to the Law. He said I was a hard worker and as far as he knew I was honest. But he also told them I wasn't very bright. Then he fired me because of the boycott the Friends of Jamie Cooke people organized.

The Friends made Kath and Ed Majors at the Saracen's Head fire me too. But Pauline Greenberg said I could go on cleaning offices because I wasn't working with members of the public. She said nobody cared who cleaned for them as long as they didn't have to see me. She also gave me more hours on the nightshift, so I can keep up with the rent.

I remember Pauline from school. She was a couple of years older than me but she was famous for beating up two boys and Roseen Hardesty when they called her dad a dirty Jew. She did well for herself. She employs twenty women – but never Roseen Hardesty.

She likes us to be on time so I walked quickly through the estate to Kennington Road to catch the number 3. There was no one at the bus stop but me and a gang of screaming urban seagulls. They'd torn a rubbish bag open and made a mess of the pavement. At first I thought they were fighting over a chicken carcass, but then I saw they were plucking the eyes out of a dead pigeon and stabbing their cruel beaks into its throat and breast. Seagulls have such clean white heads. Their beaks are a beautiful fresh yellow. You wouldn't think, would you, that something so clean and fresh lived on city garbage and carrion.

I just waited for my bus and minded my own business. I didn't try to shoo the gulls away because they never take a blind bit of notice, and, truth to tell, I'm a little bit scared of them. They eat, fight and shriek, and if anyone gets in their way they attack – a bit like ...

I didn't know Ben was in a gang. I just thought he had mates. He'd known the Sharp twins and Rocky since they were in Juniors together. When it all came out, he told me he'd only joined to stop the others picking on him. Jamal said the same thing too. The Law believed Jamal because Jamal's mum forced him to talk. But they didn't believe Ben. They took away his mobile phone and said they could prove that the gang members had been talking to each other non-stop all night.

But Ben is quite small; he hasn't had his growth spurt like the others. His skin is still fresh and peachy without spots and open pores. His voice hasn't broken, but he tucks his chin in and talks as low in his throat as he can. I think he was telling the truth – maybe the bigger kids would have picked on him for being not manly enough. The Law said that was probably why he wanted to prove himself and that's why he turned on Jamie.

But how can such a beautiful boy do ugly things to a poor gay ginger lamb? He can't, I know he can't. He's too innocent to be guilty.

He's sensitive. He cried when his dad forgot his thirteenth birthday and didn't even send him a card from Hull or wherever he and his new family are living now. I can't believe a boy who cried about his own father would do anything so cruel to Jamie Cooke. But the Law never saw him cry so they said he was guilty and "showed no remorse".

A white van pulled up to the bus stop and a man leant over to open the passenger door. It was Ron Tidey who lives on the estate. He drank regularly at the Saracen's Head, and he drank a lot. But he said, "I saw you waiting all by yourself. Hop in. I'll give you a ride to work."

I don't much like Ron Tidey but I got in because no one had spoken to me for weeks.

He said, "I don't care what they're all saying. It isn't your fault. It'd be even more unnatural if a mother didn't stand up for her boy."

"He didn't do it, Ron," I said, feeling suddenly so tired I could've lain down then and there and slept for a hundred years. The cab was warm and smoky.

"You aren't doing yourself any favours, Cherry. You should just shut up about it and keep your head down."

"I am doing," I said. "I'm always shut up 'cos there's no one to talk to."

"Tell you what, Cherry, why don't you and me go out for a drink later? Somewhere no one knows you. It'll take you out of yourself. You're still a young woman, more or less, and you got your whole life ... "

"Don't say it, Ron," I interrupted. But I agreed to meet him. I was that lonely.

I suppose you could say that loneliness was always my downfall. Ben's father wasn't much of a catch. But I did get Ben out of it, and I thought, if I had a baby, there'd always be someone for me to love who'd love me back. But I suppose just loving a child isn't a whole love. I wasn't living a whole life, according to Roseen Hardesty. "Get yourself a man," she said. "At least, get yourself a shag. A grown woman can't go without for long, Cherry, or she'll turn sour and grow rust on it."

"Use it or lose it," Mary Sharp agreed.

"Mary Sharp's in no danger of losing it," Roseen said later. "Her problem might be overuse."

"Meow!" I said, because I wasn't taking anything they had to say seriously. They both had new boyfriends every week as far as I could see, while their kids had holes in their shoes. Yes, I was a bit snooty back then. Now, when we meet sometimes outside the Young Offenders Unit on visiting days, we hardly exchange a word.

Tomorrow they're moving Ben to some place in darkest Wales and I don't have a car. I can still send him sweets and toothpaste but I won't hardly see him, train fares costing what they do.

"Cheer up," said Ron Tidey later that night at the Elephant and Castle. "Have another voddy and talk about something else. You're like a broken record."

So I had some more vodka and then some more after that, and at about midnight when we were in the back of Ron's van and I couldn't find my underwear Ron said, "There, you're more relaxed now, ain't ya? Don't never say Ron Tidey can't show a lonely woman a bit of sympathy." He was busy spraying himself with deodorant and chewing peppermints so's his wife wouldn't rumble him.

I felt like crying, but I didn't because Ron has a van and if he thinks I'm a miserable cow he won't want to see me again or maybe even give me a lift up to Wales.

Also, last time I did anything like this I got Ben. Maybe I'll get a whole other life out of Ron, and if I do maybe this time it'll be a girl. They say girls are better company than boys. I hope it's a girl.

A FAIR DEAL

L. C. Tyler

WHERE TO BEGIN this story? Perhaps by stating that Mr Sparrow did not defraud the old and infirm without good cause. We should always try to be fair, even to Mr Sparrow. And on this occasion he had cause to feel that he was owed something.

"Sorry," said the white-haired gentleman with an apologetic smile. "We gave the job to the other firm. They'll be clearing the house next week. I did leave a message on your mobile, saying not to come round."

"Or on somebody else's mobile," said the white-haired lady, with the knowledge of husbands that forty years of marriage bestows. "He's hopeless with technology. I'm sorry he's caused you a wasted trip."

"And everything is going?" asked Mr Sparrow, viewing as much of the Davenports' hallway as he could from his vantage point on the wrong side of the half-opened front door. It looked like good stuff – antique or first-class modern reproduction. The other firm (whoever they were) would make a bob or two on this house clearance.

"The new flat is so much smaller than this," said the gentleman regretfully. "Apart from one or two things we're taking with us, yes, it's all spoken for."

"Except his 'Canaletto'," said the lady. The word caught Mr Sparrow's attention, hidden though it was in inverted commas.

"Canaletto?"

"He wanted an extra thousand for it. They wouldn't pay."

"Sounds good value for a Canaletto, Mrs Davenport."

"Oh, it's not the real thing," said the lady.

"It certainly is," said the gentleman.

"Your father paid a fiver for it in Petticoat Lane."

"A tenner," said the gentleman. "You couldn't get a Canaletto for a fiver, even then."

"Him and his 'Canaletto'," snorted the lady, replacing the picture in its dubious quotation marks.

"Mind if I take a glance anyway, Mrs Davenport?"

The white-haired gentleman and his wife looked at each other.

"Happy to see the back of it," she said.

Left alone in front of the picture, Mr Sparrow scanned it carefully. To be fair to Mr Sparrow, and we should always try to be fair, he did know a bit about art. The picture was badly hung in an obscure corner – not properly lit even. But everything about it told him it was the genuine article. He'd expected an oil painting of the Grand Canal, with cracked glaze, gondolas and masked gallants, but this was a small chalk and brown-ink drawing of a domed church with men at work in front of it. Not the sort of thing you'd fake if you were hoping to fool the unwary. It had to be worth fifty, sixty thousand?

"It's wasted on them," he muttered under his breath.

"What do you think?" asked a voice behind him. "My old dad always used to say it was worth a few hundred, so I won't take less than a thousand."

"It's probably a fake," said Mr Sparrow. "If I had a fiver for every fake old master I've been offered, I'd be a rich man."

"My father checked it out at Christie's – that would have been forty or fifty years ago, of course. It's real. But my wife has always found it a bit dull, and it's only his oil paintings that go for big money. It's yours for a grand. Cash."

To be fair, Mr Sparrow had a conscience, though he was not always sure where he had left it. For the shortest of moments he was tempted to advise the gentleman to go straight back to Christie's. But – and this was one of Mr Sparrow's favourite maxims, quoted after work in the bar of the Feathers or at home in front of the television – he couldn't help it if other people were stupid, could

he? "We'll have the police round here one day if you're not careful," his wife would observe, whenever he chose to say it in front
of the television. "I'm always careful," he'd reply.

"My wife," said Mr Sparrow, "tells me I'm far too trusting for
this line of work. But you have an honest face, Mr Davenport."

He handed over the money in twenties.

"Do you want to count it, Mr Davenport?"

"I'm very trusting too," said the gentleman.

If Mr Sparrow had any remaining doubts, they were largely
dispelled by a painting in the hallway.

"Isn't that a Howard Hodgkin?" he asked.

"Another of dad's bargains," said the gentleman. "He had an
eye for it."

"We think we'll take that one with us," said the lady.

"Definitely," said the gentleman.

Where to end this story? Not, I think, with Mr Sparrow, driving
home with a carefully wrapped bundle on the passenger seat of
the van, wondering if he really knew as much about Canaletto as
he thought. Nor should we end with him walking confidently, a
couple of days later, up Bond Street to a well-known auctioneer to
obtain an estimate of the value of his recent purchase, though his
face fifteen minutes later ... would you mind terribly if I described
it as "a picture'? "Not a fake," said the auctioneer. "But regret-
tably, it *is* stolen. Of course, on the plus side, its real owners will
be very pleased to see it returned. I don't think there's any reward,
I'm afraid."

No, let's end the story with the Davenports, the real Davenports,
returning from holiday to discover that the lovely old couple who
had been minding their house – a couple who came with such
excellent references and to whom they had unfortunately already
issued another excellent reference – had been selling stolen goods
from their home. The couple's contact address proved to be an
ingenious work of fiction.

When their own Howard Hodgkin was stolen a few weeks later,
by a thief apparently using forged keys and with a good knowledge

of their burglar alarm, the Davenports put it down to one of those strange coincidences that occur from time to time. And, to be fair, it may have been just that.

DEATH IN THE TIME MACHINE

Barbara Nadel

M Y GRANDFATHER SAID he found the body in the back yard on the Wednesday night when he went to the outside toilet. It was by the fence in the old pen where the chickens used to live. But because my grandparents didn't have a telephone, my father didn't get to know about it until he went round with their shopping the following Saturday. My grandparents never went out.

This all happened over forty years ago, but I can still remember that day very well. We drove over in Dad's latest acquisition from his dodgy brother-in-law Brian, a 1950 Vauxhall Victor. Grandma and Granddad lived almost opposite Upton Park, West Ham United's home ground. So the streets were full of football fans all dressed in the team's colours of claret and blue. We'd picked up the shopping at the grocers near our own house in East Ham and just had to stop at a hardware shop on the Barking Road to pick up some gas mantles. Although this was 1967 my grandparents, unlike most people even in the impoverished East End of London, didn't have electricity. Year after year they hung on to the gas lamps that had been in their house on Green Street since they'd first moved in back in the 1900s. Every so often these lamps needed the mantles, the bit that contains the gas and converts it into an incandescent light, replaced. And so we stopped at the one hardware shop that still sold the things, bought the mantles and then, inevitably, my father's car broke down.

I was only six years old and short for my age but I had to drag my share of bags down the Barking Road, into Green Street and up my grandparents' garden path. My father, furious about "bloody Brian and his bleeding old wrecks", carried everything else, a limp roll-up cigarette hanging from his lips as he muttered his anger. When we got to the house, which was a battered Edwardian terrace with an overgrown front garden, Dad was further infuriated by the fact that someone had broken the door knocker. "Sodding hell!" he exploded. And then he looked up at the window that was above the door and yelled out, "Mo! Mo, you up there? Get down here and open this door for Christ's sake!"

Grandma and Granddad didn't rent the whole house. They'd always been too poor for that. They lived downstairs while upstairs was occupied by a man with a wooden leg called Mo. Unlike my grandparents, Mo did go out from time to time and it was nearly always he who answered the door. But Mo liked a drink and sometimes he would range about his flat in a drunken stupor, falling over and breaking things. When he left the building he could get into fights, he'd broken parts of the front door down in the past and the poor old knocker was always fair game. Eventually Mo, red-eyed and, as he put it, "as stiff as a board" with arthritis, came down the stairs and opened up.

My grandfather was in the hall with a shovel in his hand. The entrance to the coal cellar was underneath the stairs and he'd left what they called the parlour to go and get some coal.

"Hello," he said. "Cold out, is it?"

My father ignored him and said, "Car's buggered. Me and kiddo had to walk from the hardware shop."

Granddad began to shovel coal, when Mo, halfway up the stairs, called down, "Here George, tell them about the murder."

"The murder?"

My father's already white face blanched. My grandfather looked away.

"Some bloke. In the back yard," Mo said to my father. "Your dad found him. Dead."

Whether my grandfather would ever have told my father about the body in the yard, had Mo not said what he did, is something I still ponder on occasionally, even now. From what I remember of that day and others that proved significant afterwards, I think that he probably wouldn't.

All he said as he shovelled coal was "Your mother didn't want you bothered with it."

"*Bothered* with it!"

Dad went out of the hall, into the parlour and through to the scullery where my grandmother was washing up dishes. I followed, fascinated as I always was by the way in which the passage from the dingy hall into the darkness of the parlour plunged one into a world of browns and blacks. No outside sounds of football revelry or chatter of local shoppers entered here. Only the crackle of coal as it burnt inside the range, the hiss of the gas lamps and, sometimes, the whistle of steam as it escaped from the big metal kettle.

My father talked to a small, thin woman in a long black dress. My grandmother was in her late seventies then, the same sort of age that my own mother, who favours jeans and T-shirts, is now. I had only once seen my grandmother's hair not piled up on top of her head. One morning we turned up early and she had just got out of bed. Her hair, which was as grey as an afternoon in November, reached all the way down to her feet. But this time it was in a bun and, as usual, held up with pins made of silver and onyx and jet. She spoke to my father in low, angry tones, the long silver chains around her neck and wrists jangling as she did so.

I was looking at the many framed photographs of my ancestors that sat on the mantelpiece above the range when my grandfather came in and said, "You all right are you, my love?"

One of the photos had been laid down on its face. I said, "Granddad, one of the pictures is down."

He looked up and frowned. My grandfather was a big man. Tall and broad and completely different in build from my skinny father. A dock worker by trade, he was also a veteran of the First World War, a conflict that I knew, even then, haunted him always. He opened the door of the range and threw the coal on with the shovel. He stood up with difficulty and then looked at the mantelpiece and

said, "Your grandmother was cleaning. It must've fallen down."
He ruffled my long, mousy hair with his coaly fingers and then
stood the picture up again. I knew it well. It was a portrait of his
brother Harold. He had died long, long ago during a battle called
the Battle of Mons. Uncle Harold had been my grandfather's only
male sibling and his memory was sacred not just because of who he
had been but also because he had died so young and in service to
his country. This portrait, of a young, thin and unsmiling man who
was really little more than a boy, sat alongside others depicting
my grandfather's many sisters, his parents and my grandmother's
mother and her three brothers, David, John and Patrick. In between
all of these photographs were scattered plaster images of the Virgin
Mary, the suffering Christ and the saints. This proximity to the
divine told us all, had we not already known it, that everyone
depicted had sadly passed away.

I sat down to wait for the cup of tea and plate of bread and jam
that always accompanied any visit to the grandparents' house. My
grandfather put the kettle on the range and then, although I do
remember wanting to ask him about what Mo had said about the
dead body in the yard, I know that I didn't do so. My father and
grandmother went out into the yard, which was not what usually
happened, because neither of them had gone out there to go to the
toilet. My grandfather just smiled and I asked if I could please play
with my Box of Things. The Box of Things was in fact an old carpetbag. It contained all sorts of "treasures" that were played with by
my grandparents' many grandchildren. We all loved it. There were
wooden camels which had once belonged to my great-great-uncle
Sidney who had been in the army in Palestine, shells from a beach
somewhere in the West Country, model cats made out of Bakelite,
old bits of broken costume jewellery, a tiny New Testament, dolls
and small religious statues and two photograph albums. These two
brown, heavily stuffed books were my favourites. Full of small
black and white photographs, some dating back to the latter part
of the nineteenth century. They showed me my forebears in funny
clothes and doing things like picking hops in Kent that I had never
seen and would never do. Involved in the Box, I recall nothing

more from that day except a snatch of conversation between my parents when I got home.

My mother said to my dad, "So do the police know who he is, this man your father found?"

"No," my dad replied. "No one seems to know anything about him."

* * *

The following Saturday my father and I made our usual trip to see my grandparents in West Ham. This time we didn't go in the car because the police had apparently taken it off my father and were currently looking for my Uncle Brian. Although he had promised never, ever to sell or give my father any dodgy goods ever, Uncle Brian just hadn't been able to resist the Vauxhall Victor.

We arrived in the afternoon which, in November, meant that it was dark and as we walked into the parlour the gas lamps hissed and hummed in time to the boiling kettle. I smiled at my granddad who was in his usual position, in his chair by the side of the range. He and my grandmother were not, however, alone. Sitting on the far side of the large dining table that was wedged into the square bay window was a policeman. He looked to be about my dad's age and he was in uniform, his helmet placed before him on the table. The adults began to talk and I remember my grandmother, who was sitting next to the policeman, asked, "So he doesn't have any family then? Not come forward to claim his body?"

"No," the policeman answered. "No, nothing."

Then I said, "Is this about the man who was murdered in the back yard?"

No one spoke at first. They all looked at me and then it was the policeman who began to smile. "Well," he said as he bent down in order to speak to me across the table, "what do you know about ... "

"It was our neighbour, Mo, who said the word 'murder'," my grandmother said grumpily. "He's a cripple and a drunk and he dramatizes everything. She heard him and picked up on it."

"Oh, I know old Mo," the policeman said and then he looked at me again. "The poor man in your Gran's yard just died, sweetheart," he said. "No one killed him."

"It was his time. God took him," my grandmother added.

"Sod God," my grandfather, who had absolutely no time for religion, muttered over by the fire.

"Can I have my Box, please?" I asked then. Kids move on very quickly and I was already bored by the notion of murder, by God and by my grandfather's routine blasphemy.

My father went and got the Box and when he returned I spread all of the treasures out across the table and then began looking through the photo albums. The adults talked and I clearly remember my grandmother going on about a possible funeral or cremation. Not that that was anything unusual. Funerals and how ornate or religiously observant they were formed frequent topics of her conversation. Of course, what I didn't know then, was that all of the ceremonies she spoke about had taken place in the fifties at the very latest. My grandparents did not, after all, go out.

When I opened up my albums I was sitting beside my father with my grandmother and the policeman sitting across the table opposite. I knew that after a little while my grandmother was watching me more intently than usual, but I just smiled at her and then went back to what I was doing. I have absolutely no recollection whatsoever about what I was looking at in the album when my grandmother ripped it and the other book away from me and put them back in the old carpetbag. I do remember that I started to cry but that the look on my grandmother's face was such that I felt compelled to swallow my tears and hold my peace. She looked fierce – she could do that, like an old, old toothless cheetah.

No one asked my grandmother why some of my treasures had been suddenly denied to me. But I do remember my father looking angry and I can recall how he very obviously picked up the carpetbag and then began to flick through the album himself. Sitting next to me, he knew exactly what I had been looking at when my grandmother had ripped the album from my hands. By this time the policeman was getting up to leave and so all of us got up from the table and bade him very politely "Goodbye". Once he had gone, my grandfather, who was about as good with authority as he was with God, muttered, "Fascist!" and then promptly went to sleep in his chair.

I think I was given my albums back then. I really don't know. I do recall a feeling of discomfort afterwards, however, although at the time I didn't know why. Things were never quite right between my grandparents and my father from then on. My grandmother and my father talked frequently alone and in furious whispers.

***

My grandfather died in 1970 at the age of eighty-three and my grandmother five years later at eighty-five. The contents of the flat were distributed between my father and his two brothers with Dad inheriting most of the photographs. Until I was well into my twenties I would, from time to time, take out the old albums and the photographs that had once stood on the mantelpiece and look at them. But when I moved away to Yorkshire, in 1982, I forgot about the photographs and, to a large extent, about my grandparents too. Only when my father and his brothers got together to reminisce, if I was around at the time, did I think of them and smile.

Dad and my uncles Geoff and Eric always referred to the old house in West Ham as The Time Machine. My grandparents had chosen to stop their personal clock around about 1929 when my father had been born, or so my Uncle Eric always said.

"Even in the Blitz mother always wore long skirts and put her hair up like old Queen Mary," he said at one reunion back in the eighties. "Frightened of electricity they were, the both of them, frightened rigid."

Not that their eccentric lifestyle stopped with lack of electricity. They had no bathroom and were accustomed to washing daily in the kitchen sink. When a proper hot soak was needed they brought in the old tin bath which hung on the side of the wooden shed that was the outside toilet. God knows how many kettles they had to boil on the old range to get enough water to bathe in. They didn't have a washing machine, had no television or transistor radio, and their bedstead was made of brass which was very unfashionable back in the sixties. Now that bed, not to mention the big, black range in the parlour, would send the type of middle-class people my grandparents never met into raptures.

It was generally agreed amongst my relatives that my grandparents' strange aversion to change and modernity had a lot to do with the First World War. Granddad in particular had come from a fairly easy-going working class family who actively embraced innovations. But he'd had a bad time in the trenches. He had been gassed and wounded and had returned to London and his wife with a profoundly pessimistic take on life. Why my grandmother had seemed to follow him along this course was not known, except perhaps that women did always do what their men told them to back in those days. But both my uncles, Geoff and Eric, were born during the 1914–18 conflict, presumably conceived when granddad was at home on leave.

That said, along with Uncle Geoff, it was my belief that the death of Granddad's brother Harold possibly held the key. Blown up at the Battle of Mons, he had only been seventeen at the time. They'd been in the same battalion and Granddad always said that he'd seen Harold die. One minute he'd been by his side and the next he'd disappeared into a great ball of fire and metal and ash. There hadn't been a single trace left of him to bury, Granddad had said. Not a trace. How a person *could* get over such a thing was inconceivable to me. In the light of that it was no wonder that he had been so very weird.

Life moved on and the family photographs entered what would probably, under normal circumstances, have been their final resting place in a box in my parents' attic. I had two children by this time and my many cousins had reproduced also. It was the generation before ours that was diminishing. Both my father's brothers died in the mid-eighties and their wives followed on after them, one just before, and one just after, the year 2000. My sons were taking their

A levels when I was called by my mother to say I had to return to London immediately.

"Your dad was taken bad two days ago," she said. She didn't cry or even sound that much upset. "He's in hospital. The doctor, whoever he is, says he's got lung cancer."

I drove from Wakefield to London in four straight hours and, when I got to my parents' house, my mother was still calmly in shock. "They say he's going to die," she said. "How can that be?"

We didn't say anything at all about my father's lifetime smoking habit. We just sat in silence in my mum's living room and lit up cigarettes of our own. Suddenly, or so it seemed to me, I had blinked just once and my childhood and my youth had disappeared into a hole in the ground.

***

My father was conscious. Hooked up to machines and drips, he looked small and was yellow and the sight of him made me choke with a mixture of utter grief and total horror. Because he was on the Intensive Therapy ward I had to wear a plastic apron and gloves whenever I was near him. As I put the gloves on, I began to cry. Unfortunately Dad saw me, but he smiled anyway and said, "Got a fag, have you, kiddo?"

He hadn't called me that since I was a child. It took me back to Uncle Brian (long dead himself by then) and his stolen cars, to England winning the World Cup in 1966, to West Ham and Mum's mini-skirts and to Grandma and Granddad and the Time Machine. But then that, of course, was his intention. He and I, we had to go back there, because back there was something my father felt I needed to know.

"The doctors say I'm going to snuff it," he said as I leaned over and kissed his forehead and then sat down beside his bed.

I didn't even try to contradict him. My father had always been a pragmatic man. To tell him he was going to be fine would have insulted him.

"So now I've got to tell you something," he continued. He wasn't gasping for breath as I had imagined that he would. But then Mum had said the doctors had told her that lung cancer didn't always do that to people, at least not until the very end.

"Do you remember when your granddad found that dead body in their back yard?" Dad asked.

"Yes," I said. "Of course. In the old chicken coop. The police never identified him, did they?"

Some time after the policeman had visited the house when Dad and I had been there, another officer had turned up and told them that apparently the unknown man had been buried in a pauper's grave.

"No, they didn't," Dad said.

"I expect they would have done these days," I said. "What with DNA and everything."

"It's possible," Dad said. And then he took one of my weird purple-gloved hands in one of his equally weird yellow mitts and he smiled. "But *I* know who he was," he said.

"You?"

"Because your grandma told me," he replied. "It was a long time afterwards. Your granddad was dead. But I knew she'd known something, without knowing quite what, for years." He coughed. "Do you remember when that copper came round the house and your grandma took those old photo albums off you?"

That had always been indelibly printed on my memory, mainly because Grandma had never done that before or after that occasion. Also it was in the wake of that incident that things between Grandma and Dad appeared, to me, to cool.

"She did that," Dad said, "because as you turned the page there was a picture of the man who'd died in the yard staring up at her. An old picture admittedly, but she was frightened that that copper would recognize the corpse from it and start asking questions."

Shocked, firstly, to see my always so vital father in such a state, I was now almost beyond further reaction. I said nothing.

"I never made the exact connection at the time. Not surprising given what it was," Dad said. "But that said, I had a bad feeling about it all from then on, and one day when Grandma was in one of her moods to talk I asked her about it. She said she'd tell me provided I never told Geoff or Eric and as long as I promised never to breathe a word to the police."

"The police?"

Dad smiled again. He had such a big smile for a very thin man. "Don't worry, kiddo," he said. "You can tell them if you want to. I won't hold you to anything. Everyone's dead now anyway. I'm almost dead ... "

I began to cry then and for a while we had to break off because Mum came in and talked to Dad about how well their garden was doing and other stuff to "take his mind off it all". But then she left – she couldn't bear more than a few minutes by his side, it was all far too distressing for her to take – and Dad continued his story.

"Your granddad was a regular soldier when the First World War started," he said. "He was in his thirties and had just got married. He had, as you know, a lot of sisters and a brother who was very much younger than he was."

"Uncle Harold."

"Harold was seventeen. Sweet, he was, loved by everyone. Your granddad had a notion that the war was going to be long and vicious and bloody and he told his brother to keep as far away from recruiting officers and the like as he could. But of course he didn't listen. Thought himself patriotic like most lads then. So not only did Harold join up, he went into the self-same regiment as your granddad."

"Yes, but what ... "

"It'll all become clear," Dad said and then he coughed and coughed until his face changed colour and, although one of the nurses told him it might be better if I left for a while, he clung on to me and wouldn't let go. He had, he said, to get out what he needed to say, no matter what.

As soon as he could speak easily again, he said, "On the twenty-third of August 1914, your granddad's regiment, the Middlesex, went into battle at Mons. They fought and many of them died and your granddad was wounded in the leg and was briefly shipped back home to recover. He got a lot of sympathy because of his wound and of course because his brother Harold had been killed. Or so everyone thought."

I frowned. Uncle Harold's heroic and untimely death had always been a cornerstone of our family's mythology.

"Uncle Harold deserted," my father said simply.

I was stunned. Even though the legend of Uncle Harold was no longer at the forefront of my thoughts it was something I had been brought up with, like a half-resented, half-loved religion.

"I was just as shocked as you are," Dad said. He took my hand again.

"Did they shoot him?" I asked. Deserters were routinely shot during the First World War. Some of them were tortured too. Granddad used to mutter about "lads left tied naked in full sun to gun carriages", men slowly dehydrating and going mad.

My father shook his head. "No. Harold got away," he said. "He was a young silly kid, but your grandfather was a man and he made sure that Harold got out of there."

"How?" Fields of battle were chaotic, yes, but even so I knew enough stories about officers shooting men who ran "the wrong way" to know how hard such an endeavour would be.

"Harold was terrified," Dad said. "Sick all the time. Your grand-dad had to be behind him just to get him into the line. All he wanted to do was get out of there. The plan was simple and it could very easily have failed. In fact I think that your granddad did probably think that it had failed. Once on the field, Harold dropped to the ground as if he was shot. And there he stayed until our boys had passed him by. Your granddad behaved as if his brother had died and, when the day was over, there was indeed no sign of him."

"But if he did survive," I said, "why didn't he visit his family? Where did he go? Did Granddad not try to contact him?"

"Granddad wouldn't have contacted him," dad said with a smile. "That wasn't his job. His role, as you youngsters have it these days, was to make sure that no one ever knew the truth. You have to remember, kiddo, that deserters were regarded as scum even by their families back in the First World War. Granddad wanted to save his silly little brother's life but he couldn't tell anybody about it. That was the deal. If Harold got caught, then George, his brother, knew nothing about his desertion. If he didn't get caught then he just disappeared. He was "dead" and that was the end of it. And as the years passed, even if Granddad had wanted to tell his family, he couldn't have done so. Harold was awarded medals posthumously, he's a grave somewhere in one of the war cemeteries over on the continent. He'd become a dead man and until that night back in November 1967 he'd stayed a dead man."

Harold had come back? I began to feel chilly. I rubbed my arms with my strange purple hands and watched as Dad smiled up at me again.

"Do you remember Mo who used to live upstairs to grandma and granddad?" he said.

"Yes." Mo had been funny to a kid like me, always staggering about all the time and, occasionally, swearing.

"Mo went down the pub and left the front door open," Dad said. "Your grandma was doing the dishes in the scullery when this bloke walked into the parlour. She didn't know who he was at first, couldn't see his face. There was just a silence. Your granddad didn't speak and neither did the other man. According to her, when she did go into the parlour, they were both just standing there, looking at each other. Harold, she said, was faced away from her. But she saw the expression on your granddad's face and so she walked around so that she could see the man. She got a right shock."

"Did she?" Grandma can't have seen Harold since he was not much more than a child over fifty years before.

"Your granddad went berserk." Dad coughed. "Said that Harold had broken their pact. Told him to bugger off to where he'd come from and never come back. All Harold kept on saying, apparently, was that he was lonely, that he couldn't do it any more, that he wanted to be part of something again. Granddad hit him. He took the coal shovel in his hand and he hit his brother over the head with it. He did it just as Mo was walking through the parlour door as drunk as a sack. Harold had left it open when he walked back into your grandparents' lives."

Bile from my already grieving stomach rose up into my throat. "Granddad killed him."

"He didn't mean to. He was angry."

"And Mo saw him do it?"

Mo had used the word "murder" to describe what had happened that night. I had never known why until that point. I had never even questioned it. Mo had been a drunk. He'd eventually died in a pub brawl in 1969, a year before my granddad's death.

"Mo helped your granddad drag the body out to the yard," Dad said.

"But how did Mo never tell anyone? How … "

"He told us, inadvertently," Dad said. "But he never told the coppers. Your grandparents had the tenancy of that house. If they'd've had to go then the landlord would have chucked Mo out too. He didn't want them carted off to prison. It was really an accident."

"Granddad killed Harold!"

"He didn't mean to."

"Yes, but he did it anyway!"

"Love," my dad said, "he turned up out of the blue. It was a shock, it … The cause of the unknown man's death according to the coppers was a heart attack. He had a coronary and he hit his head on the side of the old chicken coop as he fell. That's what they said."

"Yes, but he didn't … "

"He did die of a heart attack," Dad said. "I asked and that was what I was told. The blow to the head wasn't fatal."

"So he had a weak heart anyway," I said. "Doesn't make what Granddad did right."

"No. No, it doesn't."

My father didn't know where Harold had been or what he had done in the long years that had followed the First World War. Maybe he hadn't done anything much for fear of being discovered? Or perhaps he'd had a family who had left him or died and that was why he had turned up, lonely and weary, at my grandparents' place on that ill-fated November evening? I realized then, as I realize now, that I would never, ever know.

Two days after my father told me about Harold, he slipped into a coma and died. Family and friends came from far and wide to attend his funeral and I often visit his grave up at the East London Cemetery. But about Harold I have remained silent. What good would upsetting what remains of the family about such a thing be now? Feelings still run high about the First World War even though modern opinions about desertion are more enlightened than they were at the time. I did do one thing, however. And shudder as I do when I write of it, I am glad that I did do it.

I didn't find my Uncle Harold's grave, but I did find a record of the death of the unknown man in my grandparents' yard in November 1967. It is the police doctor's estimate of Harold's age that haunts me: 17. Seventeen. Write it twice in numbers and letters, it doesn't get any better. And how can that be?

Harold, I estimated, had to have been seventy in 1967. So whoever my grandfather killed, it can't have been Harold. And yet my grandmother said that it had been. And indeed why and for what reason would my gentle grandfather have attacked and killed a perfect stranger? I've spent sleepless nights wondering whether the man who entered my grandparents' house that night was Harold's son, his grandson or just someone who happened, for whatever reason, to look like him. My grandmother was, after all, frightened enough to not want the policeman who visited them to see any of Harold's photographs, either in the albums or on the mantelpiece. But in spite of all that, was it just a case of mistaken identity? If it was, however, why did "Harold" say to Granddad that he was lonely, that he "couldn't do it any more"?

Logically the man who walked into my grandparents' house that night in November 1967 cannot have been my great-uncle Harold. It was his son, his grandson, a lookalike, someone completely different. A burglar that my grandparents, for some reason, projected Harold's image on to. Maybe there was a resemblance of some sort there. But there is something else it could have been too. Against all logic Harold did come back and he did enter that house in West Ham with the full intention of breaking the pact with his brother, maybe because his heart was weak and he knew that he was close to death. But as he entered that strange, ossified place, something happened. By magic, by the action of the place we all laughingly called the Time Machine, by some trick of biology or act of God, Harold became again the boy he had been when he disappeared. Alone and desperate, this "ghost" appealed to my grandfather for help and this time he denied him. Harold "died" again and lies in an unmarked grave somewhere in the East London Cemetery where all my family lie.

But my grandfather said that he found a body in the back yard down by the chicken coop when he went out to the toilet one cold evening in November 1967. And maybe if that didn't actually happen, then perhaps that was what was meant to happen and possibly I will just have to content myself with that. And, of course, with a load of black and white photographs that now live in boxes in my attic in Yorkshire.

SHOOTING FISH

Adrian Magson

MARAUDERS HIT MY patch again last night.

It's not much of a place for growing stuff; a thirty-by-thirty rectangle of scrubby earth behind a clutch of pine trees half a mile from where I bed down. There's a small brook where I get water just a few yards away, and a shelter, where the worst of the wind is kept back by the trees. But it's mine and all that stands between me and having to live on roots and whatever I can find, or trekking into town ten miles away.

Allotments used to be about community cohesion and getting back to the land, where a family could grow potatoes and onions and things for the table. Now, since the credit crunch went further south than anyone had predicted, and country people had moved into the towns for protection – safety in numbers, so they thought – they'd found out the harsh reality: they're about survival, pure and simple ... and defending what's yours.

I looked at the ragged holes where the potatoes used to be. Three days of hard work wasted, digging and raking until the soil was broken up and soft enough to plant. Whoever had done this – and I figured it had to be someone who knew the area – hadn't known shit about vegetables, other than maybe eating them. They'd ripped up plants wholesale only to find they'd struck too early and come up with barely enough to fill a soup bowl. Another month at least before I'd expected anything sizeable, but now it was all gone.

I picked up a smashed trellis where I'd been trying to encourage peas and beans to grow. They were gone, ripped out and thrown to one side. Trails of heavy boot prints had trekked across the neat rows, scuffing into oblivion what the visitors hadn't been bothered to bend and ease from the earth the way you're supposed to if you care about that kind of thing.

But then, marauders don't. Care, I mean. They don't have the brains, merely the greed, crawling out from under the stones they call home and living up to their name without considering the consequences.

I checked the horizon, wondering if they were still out there. There'd be at least three – they rarely travel in smaller groups, preferring to rely on numbers to intimidate rather than using intelligence or guile. And they'd be armed with whatever ordnance they'd managed to steal from abandoned farmhouses when the owners had gone: shotguns, twelve-bores, old four-tens and whatever.

I preferred to take my chances out here; at least I knew what country rats looked like. And I could read the countryside like an open book. Out here, I stood a better chance than anywhere else, even if it meant being alone.

Alone I could handle.

A couple of rooks clawed into the air from a strand of trees on the far side of a field three hundred yards away. I sank to the ground and watched. Crows are grudging, surly birds, too stupid to frighten easily. Not unless something unusual comes along. Like humans.

Something must have spooked them.

Something coming this way.

A single figure, walking solidly, stumbling occasionally over the rough ground. It had been ploughed earth once, but not for the past two years. Not since the farmer had gone. Now it was just earth, overgrown with couch-grass and weeds, a few spindly remnants of wheat and whatever else he'd planted over the years struggling to find clear air.

I waited until the figure was fifty yards away, then stood up and faced him.

Her.

The woman was pale and thin, about thirty, with long dark hair. She was dressed in a ski-jacket, combats and walking boots. The boots looked new, which meant they were looted or black-market.

She stopped twenty yards away, looking at me with wide eyes.

"Who are you?" she said. If she was scared, she didn't show it.

"My name's Dave," I replied. Well, it would have been rude not to. "You are—?"

"Angel." She looked around, beyond me, scanning the area, and I got the feeling she did this out of instinct, not training. "You got any shelter?"

"No. Not here. Where are you from?" If she said she was local, I was getting ready to fight, because she wouldn't be. I knew everyone within a fifteen-mile radius, all the other country-dwellers like me, the dispossessed and the ones who could do without company and the toxic surroundings of overcrowded towns and cities. Town dwellers I didn't know, nor did I want to.

She looked too pale to be country.

She shivered and coughed. "I came south overland. Had an argument with the people I was with and took off." She smiled, which threatened to light up her face. "Stupid, I know, but it had been brewing for ages. I had no choice, so I left." She shrugged and looked around. "Didn't expect to find anyone around here, but I'm glad I did. You got any eats?"

Then she keeled over.

She woke when I got her back to my caravan, eyes fluttering and disorientated. I'd got some tea on the brew and poured her a cup. She was skin and bone beneath the jacket and combats and weighed almost nothing.

She sat up and took a sip. Looked surprised.

"Couldn't get this in the place I was in," she said weakly, and drank it down. "Stocks ran out ages ago." She put the cup down and lay back, breathing light and fast, eyes fixed on nothing I could see.

I gave her a bowl of soup and some pitta bread, and she scoffed it down double-quick, in spite of the heat. She looked like she hadn't eaten in a long time and I wondered how close she'd come to lying down and not getting up before stumbling over my allotment.

"It's been a couple of days," she said, reading my mind. "Needed to get distance between them and me before stopping."

I didn't say anything. It wasn't my business who she was running from. Just as long as she hadn't brought them with her.

They came the following night, on the heels of a brief storm. The clouds had been heavy all day, thumping overhead like bad-tempered children spoiling for a fight. The rain had been welcome, though, I didn't mind rain. It would irrigate the allotment and keep casual travellers huddled in whatever shelter they could find. When it ended, they'd be anxious to be on their way, depressed by the way nature pushed the wind and rain through every crack and cranny, forcing water down their necks and inside their clothing.

In the drip-backed silence following the last puff of thunder, I heard a crack out in the field. I knew what it was: I'd scattered some canes out there while Angel was asleep. Still brittle even if wet, they were thin enough to give easily, thick enough to snap and give me warning of someone's approach.

I curled out of bed and went to the window. Eased back the curtain. Movement showed through the trees surrounding the caravan. A figure slipped sideways out of my field of view; another followed, going the other way. Visitors don't behave like that.

"*Angel*!" The voice came from the left, anger and command contained in just one word. "Angel, we know you're in there. Come out!"

I heard a clicking sound and my stomach flipped. It was the sound of a shotgun being racked. Deliberate, intimidating, dramatic, it carried an unmistakable message.

"Angel." Another voice, this one high-pitched like a woman, lilting, almost tuneful. But just as scary.

Behind me, Angel stumbled out of the other bunk and crept up to my shoulder. I could feel her breath on my neck, sour and hot.

"Are they your friends?" I asked.

"Not any more." She sounded almost regretful, and I wondered if I'd been set up. Find a solitary man growing food and surviving in the country, pretend to be vulnerable and afraid to gain his confidence and trust, then get your friends to come in and take him when his guard's down. Good as a Trojan Horse.

Another cracking sound, this time of undergrowth being kicked aside. It sounded about twenty feet away. Too close for comfort. If they had guns, these caravan walls would puncture like soft cheese.

I reached sideways and took hold of the shotgun I'd never used, but kept handy. It felt heavy and cold, and I desperately didn't want to use it. Guns were for other people, messy and brutal. Once used, guns couldn't be denied, an irreversible action with irreversible consequences.

A vivid flash of light and a roar of sound, and suddenly I was looking at a fist-sized hole in one corner of the caravan, and the interior was splattering with lead pellets bouncing off the walls like a hailstorm. Angel screamed in pain and ducked to the floor, and I followed.

No good being a hero if you're dead.

"You OK?"

"Yes. Stung my face, that's all." She suddenly sounded very young.

A cackle of laughter from outside, and another shot. The blast took out a window, showering us with slivers of Perspex. It came from the right, followed by the high-pitched voice again.

"Angel, sweetie!" it teased. "You got ten seconds to come out. I want my birthday pressie!"

"Who are they?" I asked, and checked the gun was loaded. If they hadn't come in already, it was because they were being cautious.

"His name's Roper," said Angel, fear making her voice tremble. "The older one. He was always after me, but his wife kept him away. The other one's Tyke." I felt her shiver with revulsion. "Roper's son. He promised me to him on his seventeenth birthday."

"When's that?"

A pause. "Today. No, tomorrow. Tomorrow."

"Nobody objected?" I scanned the darkness, waiting for the next shot. Now would have been a good idea to have a back door to slip through. Bad planning.

"Nobody dared." Her voice was a whisper. "Roper thinks he's untouchable. The last man who argued with him disappeared."

"He ran off?"

"No, They found his left hand a week later. But that was all."

Great. Psychopaths in my allotment. That's all I needed.

Suddenly another shot ripped through the walls, and a large figure flitted across my field of vision, heading for the door. He was going at a tilt that would take him through the thin wood without stopping. He'd be in among us and I knew that would be the end of it for both of us.

"First one in gets the goodies!" he roared tauntingly, as he came near, and a howl of protest came from his son, like it was some sort of contest. I realized it probably was.

I waited for the last second, then swung the door open and pulled the trigger.

He was so close the twin barrels were nearly touching his chest. The double blast lit up his face, highlighting an ugly sneer and a mouth full of rotten teeth, a consequence of insufficient flossing. It also showed a look of surprise, even shock. Then he was tossed backwards like a discarded heap of clothing.

I slammed the door shut and motioned Angel towards the back of the caravan. A window opened above the sink. With a wriggle, we might both get out before Tyke started riddling the bodywork with gunshots. I doubted he'd follow his father's example, but you can never tell. The stupid gene often just keeps on going.

A scream of anguish echoed through the trees, making the hairs on the back of my neck stand on end. It was long and high, like a screech-owl, only livid and furious in a way no animal could match. Then the shots began hitting the caravan.

I flipped open the window and pushed Angel through. She hit the ground below with a cry but was up and running instantly, testament to how scared she was of what would follow if Tyke caught us.

I dropped to the ground, ripping off half my shirt buttons on the window catch in the process, and took off after her. I still had the shotgun, although I'd just fired off the only two shells I'd had. Maybe if he came close enough I could throw it at him.

I led Angel to the allotment. It was where I felt safest; where I knew my way around. It wouldn't save us if Tyke came looking, but it might give us a better chance than trying to outrun him over level ground. Under the barrel of a gun, and with Angel being as weak as she was, we'd be easy prey.

We kipped down in the small shelter I'd built to house my tools. It wasn't meant to sleep in, being shoulder height and pitch black, with corrugated metal for a roof, but it was better than staying outside. I made Angel scurry under some old sacking at the back, then covered her over and sat down by the door with a garden fork in my hands.

Pathetic really, but running wasn't an option.

Tyke arrived just before dawn.

The crows in the trees above us gave the first warning, crabbing away to each other like old men. I heard a curse followed by the blast of a shotgun, then more cursing. It told me two things: he wasn't short of shells and didn't care if we heard him coming.

I snuck out of the shelter, motioning Angel, who'd been jolted awake, to stay where she was. Before I left, I handed her a pruning knife.

She took it, eyes wide, and sank back among the sacking.

Tyke was standing near the bean canes, staring up at the trees, his shotgun over his shoulder. He was swaying in the early light and I guessed he'd been drinking up the courage to come looking for us. I looked down at the empty shotgun and realized he was too far gone to care whether I had this or a rocker launcher.

I tossed it aside. Maybe I could fool him with guile.

I crabbed over to the compost heap near the back hedge and stuck my hands into the rotting pile along one edge, until my fingers encountered a ridge of hard metal. I dug in and lifted the sheet of corrugated roofing. Underneath was a canvas golf bag, decades old and hardened with age, like stone, but dry inside. I flipped open the lid and dragged out the magnum.

Well, it wasn't a normal magnum, but I doubt a fish would have seen the distinction.

It was made of mahogany and fired stainless steel spears with twin barbs, propelled by heavy-duty rubber bands. Hitting anything over 18 feet away was probably pushing it but I wouldn't want to stand in the way and put it to the test.

I'd found it in an abandoned barn one day, along with a load of scuba gear. I'd been attracted by the sheen of the mahogany; I'd always liked wooden things.

Tyke had spotted me by now and was walking towards me, his steps uneven, his face mottled with anger and booze. His stance told me he wanted to be up close and personal, which suited me just fine.

Then he saw the magnum and laughed. It was an ugly, yelping sound which came all the way up from his skinny belly and erupted out of his mouth, more child than adult. But I knew I wasn't facing a child.

"The hell's *that*?" he said, and laughed some more. "You think that toy's any kind of weapon against *this*?" He hefted the shotgun and fired off a blast into the trees, bringing down a shower of branches and one dead crow. He laughed at that, spit dribbling down his chin, and kicked the bird away like a spiteful kid who doesn't want to play any more.

He stopped laughing and I saw his knuckles tighten around the stock as he applied first pressure on the trigger. I felt my belly shrink at the thought of what that gun would do to me.

"Where's the bitch?" he said.

Then he looked surprised and put the gun down. Well, dropped it.

The thing about spear guns is, they're almost silent. I mean, I've never heard one go off under water, so I suppose there might be a little gurgle or two, maybe a wet *chowk* as the rubber band lets fly, followed by a line of bubbles. But out here on dry land – and right here was about as far from the sea as you could get, which was a real irony – that sound got lost in the breeze.

So Tyke never even heard the spear take off; probably didn't see it, either.

But he sure as hell felt it.

It hit him dead centre, and when he looked down to see what

it was, there was about an inch of steel shaft sticking out of his diaphragm.

Maybe he was wearing an extra heavy shirt. Slowed it down a bit.

I resisted the temptation to utter the quip from the old Bond film which I'd seen a re-run of a few years back; about the killer getting the point. Right now it seemed unseemly, somehow. Mind you, it was a struggle.

He tried to pull the shotgun's trigger once more, then realized he no longer had the weapon in his hand and fell over on his back.

I made sure Angel was OK, and showed her how to light a fire and put on some water for tea. It would be rough and ready, but it would keep away the cold and give me time to do what I had to. She didn't argue, and even looked pleased to be doing something normal.

"Will anyone else come?" I asked her. If the answer was yes, we'd have to leave here for good. I didn't want to do that, but neither did I want to die.

She shook her head, feeding sticks into the flames under the blackened water pot. "There's nobody cares enough. They all hated both of them." She looked at me. "Can I stay? I've nowhere else to go."

"We'll see," I replied. "Maybe."

She seemed happy enough at that.

While she encouraged the water to boil, I dragged Tyke's body across the allotment and buried him in the compost heap. It took a while and raised a sweat, but I made sure he was at the centre where it was nice and warm, where he'd get the most benefit. When I was sure he was bedded down, I covered him over.

Given the natural heat in there, along with the bacteria and stuff, Tyke would soon cease to exist altogether. Especially when I spread him around a bit and forked him in. Somehow I doubted he'd appreciate the irony; he might not have cared squat about the land when he was on it, but he was sure as hell going to play a part now he was in it.

THE MINISTRY OF WHISKY

Val McDermid

THERE'S TWO THINGS everybody knows about John French the minister – he likes a dram, and his wife won't have a drop in the house. That's why he spends as much time as possible out and about, making himself at home with his parishioners. Even the strictest teetotallers, the dry alcoholics and the three English families understand they have to keep whisky in the house for the minister. Newcomers to the parish who don't know the drill get their first visit seasoned with a heavy-handed version of the wedding at Cana, complete with knowing winks and exaggerated gestures. If they don't get the message, Mr French mentions in passing to one of the kirk elders that such-and-such a body doesn't seem to have much grasp of the rules of hospitality. Then the elder has a quiet word ahead of the minister's next pastoral visit. Trust me, most folks don't have to be told twice.

Don't get me wrong. Mr French is no drunk. I'm born and bred in Inverbiggin and I've never seen him the worse for drink. I know who the village drunks are and the minister isn't one of them. OK, he maybe spends his life a bit blurred round the edges, but you can hardly blame him for that. We all need something to help us deal with life's little disappointments. And God knows, the minister has that to do 24/7. Because I don't think for a minute that Inverbiggin is where he planned to end up.

I've seen folks' wedding photos with Mr French when he first came here. God, but he was handsome. You can still see it now even though he's definitely past his best. Back then, though, he looked like a cross between Robert Redford and the kind of pop star your granny would approve of. A thick mane of reddish blonde hair, square jaw, broad shoulders and a gleaming row of teeth that were a lot closer to perfection than you generally saw in the backwoods of Stirlingshire back then. The looks have faded, inevitably, though he'd still give most of the men round here a run for their money. What's more important is that he's still a brilliant preacher. At least half his congregation are agnostic – if not downright atheist – but we all still turn up on a Sunday for the pure pleasure of listening to him. It's better than anything you get on the telly, because it's rooted in our community. So imagine what a catch he was back when he started out, when he was good looking and he could preach. Obviously, his natural home would have been some showpiece congregation in Glasgow or Edinburgh. The man has ex-future Moderator of the Church of Scotland written all over him.

Something obviously went badly wrong for him to end up here. Even its best friends would have to admit that Inverbiggin is one of the last stops on the road to nowhere. I don't know what it was that he did in the dim and distant past to blot his copybook, but it can't have been trivial for him to be sent this far into exile. Mind you, back when he arrived here thirty-odd years ago, the Church of Scotland was a lot closer to the Wee Frees than it is these days. So maybe all he did was have a hurl on the kids' swings in the park on a Sunday when they should have been chained up. Whatever. One way or another, he must have really pissed somebody off.

I don't know whether his wife knows the full story behind their exile, but she sure as hell knows she's been banished. There's no way this is her natural habitat either. She should be in some posh part of Glasgow or Edinburgh, hosting wee soirées to raise money for Darfur or Gaza. One time, and one time only, she unbent enough to speak to me at the summer fête when we got stuck together on the tombola. "He's a good man," she said, her eye on Mr French as he gladhanded his way round the stalls. She gave me a look sharp as Jessie Robertson's tongue. "He deserves to be among good people." Her meaning was clear. And I couldn't find it in my heart to disagree with her.

Her obvious bitterness is neutralized by the sweetness of her husband. Mr French might have had high-flying ambitions, but having his dreams trashed hasn't left him resentful or frustrated. It's pretty amazing, really, but in exchange for the whisky, he's given us compassion and comprehension. Fuelled by a succession of drams, he seems to find a way to the heart of what we all need from him. It's not a one-way street either. The more he answers the challenge of meeting our needs, the finer the whisky that makes its way into his glass.

When he first started making his rounds, folk would pour any old rubbish. Crappy bargain blends that provoked instant indigestion, brutal supermarket own brands that ripped the tastebuds from your tongue, evil no-name rotgut provided by somebody's brother-in-law's best pal that made you think you were going blind. But gradually, his good Samaritan acts spread through the community till there was hardly a household in Inverbiggin that hadn't been touched by them. Our way of saying thank you was to provide better drink. Quality blends, single malts, single barrel vintages. You scratch my back, I'll scratch yours.

See, we all find our own ways to cope with living in Inverbiggin. The minister and his wife aren't the only ones who started out with higher hopes. Maybe it's precisely because his own dreams were dashed that he handles our failures so well. He intervenes when other people would be too scared or too discouraged to get in the middle of things. Kids that are slipping through the cracks at school – John French grabs the bull by the horns and takes on the teachers as well as the parents. Carers doing stuff for parents and disabled kids that none of us can think about without shuddering – John French goes to bat for them and scores relief and respite.

And then there was that business with Kirsty Black. Everybody knew things were far from right between her and her man. But she'd made her bed and we were all content to let her lie on it. At least if he was taking out his rage on her, William Black was leaving other folk alone.

I must have been about twelve years old when I discovered why William Black was known as BB, a man notorious for his willingness to pick a fight with anybody about anything. "He thinks it stands for Big Bill," my father told me after I'd had the misfortune to witness BB Black smash a man's face to pulp outside the chip shop. "But everybody else in Inverbiggin knows it stands for Bad Bastard." My father was no angel either, but his darkness was more devious. I got the feeling he despised BB as much for his lack of subtlety as for the violence itself.

When Kirsty lost her first baby in the fifth month of her pregnancy, we all knew by the next teatime that it had happened because BB Black had knocked her down and kicked her in the belly. We all knew because Betty McEwan, the midwife, heard it from one of the nurses at the infirmary who apparently said you could see the mark of his boot on her belly. But Kirsty was adamant that she'd fallen getting out of the bath. So that was that. No point in calling in the police or the Social Services if Kirsty couldn't manage to stick up for herself.

Wee towns like Inverbiggin are supposed to be all about community, all about looking out for each other. But we can turn a blind eye as surely as any block of flats in the big city. We all got extremely good at looking the other way when Kirsty walked by.

All except John French. He saw the bruises, he saw how Kirsty flinched when anybody spoke to her, he saw the awkward way she held herself when her ribs were bruised and cracked. He tried to persuade her to leave her man, but she was too scared. She had no place to go and by then she had two kids. The minister suggested a refuge, but Kirsty was almost as afraid of being cast adrift among strangers as she was of William Black himself. So then Mr French said he would talk to the Bad Bastard, to put him on notice that somebody was on to him. But Kirsty pleaded with the minister to stay out of it and he eventually gave in to her wishes.

I know all this because it came out at the trial. Kirsty wasn't able to give evidence herself. She was catatonic by that point. But Mr French stood in the witness box and explained to the court that Kirsty had exhibited all the signs of a woman who had been reduced to a zombie-like state by violence and terror. He told them she had been determined to protect her kids. That she'd been in fear for her own life and the lives of her children that Friday night when he'd come home roaring drunk and she'd picked up the kitchen knife and thrust it up into William Black's soft belly.

You could see the jury loved John French. They'd have taken him home and sat him on the mantelpiece just for the sheer pleasure of listening to him and looking at him. He surfed the courtroom like a man riding on the crest of a wave of righteousness rather than a wave of whisky.

The prosecution didn't stand a chance. The jury went for the "not proven" verdict on the culpable homicide charge and Kirsty walked out of the court a free woman. It took some more work from Mr French, but eventually her lawyers got the kids back from Social Services and she moved back home. Everybody rallied round. I suppose ignoring what had happened to Kirsty kind of guilt-tripped us all into lending a helping hand. Better late than never, the minister pointed out one Sunday when he gave us his particular take on the Good Samaritan story. He was adamant that we should open our hearts and put our faith in God.

But here's the thing about people like John French. Like his wife said, he does deserve to be among good people. Because being ready to think the best of folk leaves you wide open to the ones that can't wait to take advantage. And there's one or two like that in Inverbiggin.

Take me, for example. I've been out of love with my husband for years. He's a coarse, uncouth, ignorant pig. He's never dared to lift a hand to me, but he disgusts me. Worse still, he bores the living daylights out of me. When he walks in a room, he sucks the life out of it. There is one positive thing about my husband, though. His job comes with terrific death-in-service benefits. And then there's that lovely big insurance policy. Frankly, it'll be worth every penny I've spent on rare malts and exclusive single barrel vintages.

Because I've been planting the seeds for a while now. I used to do amateur dramatics years ago. I can play my part well and I can paint a bonny set of bruises on my back and my ribs. Good enough to fool a man whose vocation would never let him examine a woman's injuries too closely. I even got him to take some photos on my mobile phone. If the police examine them later, they won't be able to make out too much detail, which suits me just fine. And after all, there's precedent now. Nobody would dare to doubt John French, not after the publicity Kirsty's case earned him.

Never mind putting my faith in God. Me, I'm putting my faith in John French and the ministry of whisky.

THE ART OF NEGOTIATION

Chris Ewan

SOMETIMES WHEN I meet a new man they like to guess what I do for a living. There are certain things they always begin with, such as model or actress or air hostess. Air hostess annoys the hell out of me. Once, I asked a guy to explain his thinking and he pulled a face like he'd just snagged his ankle on a tripwire. It could have been worse. I could have told him the truth.

It's the same with my clients. My clients are all men. The ones I turn down are the types who can't handle the idea that I'm a woman. It's not a feminist crusade. Fact is, if my client can't trust me, I can't trust them. And in my line of work, trust is everything.

I had no need to ask the American in the white linen suit his business. He arranged for me to meet him in Cannes, the week of the film festival, and everything about him said he worked in the movie industry. Not just the linen suit, but the cream espadrilles and the white cotton shirt, the tan and the capped teeth and the hair plugs. He looked like money, but not the old kind. I had him pegged as a studio executive or a producer. His first words placed him a little lower down the evolutionary scale.

He said, "They didn't tell me you had ovaries."

I left my carry-on suitcase in the doorway. The apartment was empty of furniture. No curtains. Bare concrete floors. A pair of sliding glass doors led on to a balcony. Beyond the balcony was the ocean, nearer still La Croisette. Super yachts. Red carpets. Movie stars. Hangers-on.

He said, "Your fee is kinda high."

"I prefer it that way."

"They told me you'd negotiate."

"I never negotiate."

"They told me you'd consider it this time."

I returned to my suitcase, lifted it from the floor and shaped as if to leave.

"Jesus Christ." The client ran his hand through his hair. He favoured a style that had been popular during my teenage years. Centre-parting, long at the front, curling in over his eyes. "This is crazy."

I checked the time on my wristwatch. Hitched my shoulders by way of response.

"How far did you fly to get here?" he asked. "Halfway around the world, right? West Coast, I heard. And you'd walk out – just like that?"

"I never negotiate."

"All right, I get it. Jeez. Can't we at least discuss what I need?"

"Just so long as you understand that the fee is non-negotiable."

"I said I got it already."

I studied him for a moment, feeling tempted to leave anyway. But he was right, I had flown long haul. Not from the States. From Rio. But the principle was the same.

"Tell me about the job," I said, and managed to sound pleasant with it.

He licked his lip and glanced at the sliding glass doors, as if he was afraid we were under surveillance. He had no reason to be concerned. I wouldn't have been there if that was the case.

"If you're planning on wetting yourself, I'll be off," I told him.

"Just wait, OK? Lemme think a minute."

"One minute."

I tapped my toe on the floor, keeping time with his thoughts. Interrupting them, even. I didn't care. He had no need to think. He needed to act. To give me the green light.

"The gear you use is untraceable, right?" he asked.

"Completely."

"And this thing'll be contained?"

I tipped my head to one side. "Explain *contained*."

"Just his yacht. The people on it. Jesus. Can you do that?"

"If you want something clean, you should hire a sniper. If you require a statement, hire me."

The guy ran his hand through his hair again. "I guess I need a statement."

I nodded. "The blast radius will be minimal, but they tend to cram these yachts in pretty tight at this time of year. I can't control that. And you'll need to have the fee in my account by tomorrow."

"Tomorrow? That's not what I agreed."

I cocked a hip and contemplated my nails. They were an immaculate fuchsia-pink. Perhaps it was time for something different. "Things change based on my assessment of the variables. You're a variable."

"Hey, come on. Be reasonable here."

"I'm being reasonable. Your fee hasn't increased."

The American threw his hands into the air, then clutched them to his head. He ran splayed fingers down over his face. "I guess we're really doing this thing, huh?"

"Looks that way."

Two days later, I arranged for my contact to route a call to the client. The call was safe for four minutes.

"My money," I began.

"I paid half."

"That's not what we discussed."

"Hey, it's like you said, things change. Finish the job and you'll get the rest."

"I told you – this isn't a negotiation."

"Then you don't get paid."

I heard the tinkle of female laughter. The roar of a car engine. The drone of wheels on asphalt.

"Wait," I said. "Do you have me on speakerphone? Are there people with you?"

"Hey, take it easy."

"Christ's sake."

"These are my people. You can trust them."

"Hang up the phone."

"Hang up the phone? Listen lady, you're working for me now, OK, and I'll finish the call when I'm good and ready."

I pressed a button on my laptop and killed the satellite link-up. I bet myself the twerp would call back in less than a day.

The twerp surprised me and waited thirty-six hours. I could hear the shuffle of waves on a beach. No laughter. No engine noise.

"We need to talk," he said, once my contact had re-routed his call.

"Fine," I told him. "You have four minutes."

"What, you have a hair appointment?"

My burgundy nail hovered over my mouse-pad. Count to ten, I told myself. Give him an opportunity to redeem himself.

"So the truth is I don't have all the money," he said.

"Then it's a shame my organization doesn't offer refunds."

"What? No, hey, no, that's not what I'm saying. You'll get the other half. You'll have it when I do."

"You mean somebody is paying you?"

"My business partner."

This just got better. "Ask him for the money now."

"He won't pay until the fireworks are through."

"In that case, there won't *be* any fireworks."

A new window popped up on my laptop. Seemed a former colleague from Thames House was trying to private-message me. I tapped out a coded reply, my fingernails clacking across the keys.

"I'm afraid you'll have to forfeit the cash you've already paid," I told him.

"Hey, come on. Let's talk."

"*You* talk."

Four hours later, he called back.

"So I spoke to my business partner. We'll pay another twenty-five per cent of your fee."

I stayed silent.

"And I know what you're thinking. But hear me out, OK? I have a place along the coast. Antibes. It has a pool, a terrace, the works."

"Give me the address. Perhaps I'll kill you in your sleep."

He chuckled, nervously. "Here's how it works, OK? When you're done, and this whole thing is through, come visit and we'll pay the rest of your fee, plus an extra ten per cent."

"You're offering me a bonus?"

"See? That's what comes from negotiating."

I turned it over in my mind. It wasn't a bad compromise.

"You'll be watching?" I asked.

"Huh?"

"The *fireworks*."

"Oh. Sure thing. We'll both be watching – me and my business partner. You've been to our apartment, right? It has a view over the marina."

"Then take my advice. Wear earplugs."

On the given night, at the given time, I eased into the oily water in my diving suit. The suit was a snug fit, designed for flexibility, not warmth. I could live with the cold. Hell, considering the fee I was being paid, I could live with most things.

The swim didn't trouble me. Keeping fit was a requirement of the job, and I swam several hundred lengths whenever I visited my local pool. Tonight, the distance I needed to cover was less than half that far. The harbour tides were negligible, and I was wearing flippers. True, I was towing a floating bag of equipment tied off from my ankle, but it was the least of my concerns.

My primary hazard was being spotted. In most locations, approaching a super-yacht just after midnight, even a heavily guarded one, wouldn't involve a high degree of risk. Here, by virtue of the film festival, the situation was different. Floodlights bathed the geometric walls of the Palais des Festivals and the gleaming white hulls of the yachts moored beneath it, casting green halos of light into the murky waters along the quay. Partygoers were everywhere: strolling the Jetée Albert Edouard; toasting one another with chilled wine on hotel patios; gazing down from the vaulted decks and bubbling hot tubs of the yachts themselves.

The craft I was swimming towards went by the name *Lazy Jane*. She was a sleek, 100-foot Italian vessel with five cabins, eight crew and, for this week in particular, a rental cost in excess of 80,000 euros. She boasted three decks, a salon that doubled as a screening room, an aft lounge, a Jacuzzi sundeck, a shaded flying bridge and one highly recognizable target.

The target was a former action hero, from a franchise that had been big in the eighties. His accommodation sounded impressive, but the reality was that no bankable movie star would stay anywhere close. The big names were hiding out in secluded villas up in the hills, where their privacy and security could be guaranteed. Yachts were reserved for middling organizations – start-out production companies, European sales distributors, a cable porn channel. Oh, and the former star of the *Vengeance* series of espionage thrillers.

He had begun his career as a kickboxing champion with a fondness for steroid injections, a north European accent and a memorable name, and advanced until he was married to the daughter of minor Hollywood royalty, with a mansion in Beverly Hills, a three-way share in a chain of celebrity nightclubs and a shot at cementing his fame as a crossover star in a line of family comedies. It didn't work. His box office plummeted, younger stars nudged him out of the limelight, his wife divorced him and his popularity began to sag along with his pecs.

Unable to quit, he still made movies, but these days they went straight to video. Now, his star had faded so badly that he was worth more to the makers of his latest film dead than alive. Cannes was scheduled during a hiatus in shooting, but his insurance cover was ongoing. He was a cheque waiting to be cashed.

He was also standing on the aft deck of the *Lazy Jane*, bunched arms resting on the wood-and-aluminium rails, a mobile phone clasped to his ear. I was close enough by now to count the buttons on the open-neck Hawaiian shirt he was wearing, and to hear his side of the conversation. He didn't sound happy. The yacht was too noisy to sleep, he complained. There were too many tourists trying to sneak pictures of him. Some jerk from the cable porn channel hadn't let him board their ship. Didn't anyone know who he was any more?

I had a reasonable idea who he was talking to, and I could hazard a fair guess at what he was being told. The yacht was ideal. It was central. It was perfect for all the business meetings they had lined up.

And it was also vulnerable to attacks like my own.

Clutching my equipment bag to my chest, I ducked silently beneath the rippling surface and kicked for the cooler waters below the slick of diesel snaking away from the engine outlet and the wash of light from the submerged bulbs under the hull. I have the ability to hold my breath in excess of two minutes when the situation demands it, but I had no need for party tricks this time around. I came up to the side of the mini-deck at the rear of the vessel, where a pair of jet-skis were moored. Tossing my bag up before me, I gripped the smooth timber with my fingertips and heaved myself aboard in one fluid movement.

First, I dried myself with the towel I'd packed inside my waterproof bag, since I didn't want to leave a giveaway trail of water running through the inner corridors of the yacht. Then I slipped my backpack over my shoulders, removed my flippers and climbed barefoot up the metal ladder to the deck above.

It didn't take long to locate the burnished wooden door to the master cabin, and it occupied but a moment's thought for me to kneel before the flimsy lock and coax the tumblers into tumbling with my picking gun. I slipped my hand inside and flipped a light switch, then entered a sumptuous world of highly polished teak, fine cotton sheets and thick woollen carpet. I scanned the lighted interior until my eyes settled on a small drawer in the fitted cabinet beside the bed. Perfect.

I was back in my compact hire car, towel coiled around my damp hair and a pair of field binoculars raised to my eyes, when I clicked the appropriate icon on my laptop to place the call. Minutes before, I'd watched the target flick a cigarette over the side of the yacht, check his watch and disappear below deck. Once the lights in his cabin had been extinguished, I'd made the connection. The American answered on the first ring.

"Yeah?"

"Are you watching?" I asked.

"Hell, yes. What kept you? We've been waiting hours already."

"You wanted a thorough job."

"You didn't tell us it'd be this late. Christ."

I scanned the quay. "Less people means less casualties. Less witnesses, too."

"Yeah, maybe."

"You're sure you still want to go ahead?"

"Sure I'm sure. Asshole's been griping on the phone, yanking my chain about his damn issues. Thinks he's still somebody. Nothing's good enough for him. Go ahead. Toast the schmuck."

"I'll leave that to you, if I may."

"Huh?"

"Write down this number."

I delivered the sequence. He interrupted me halfway through.

"Wait. What is this?"

"Are you writing it down?"

"I don't have a pen."

"Then get one."

"OK. Jeez. Keep your panties on."

I counted to ten. Made it to twelve. I was still shaking my head when he came back on the line.

"Give it to me again," he said.

I did. Slowly. I had no desire to repeat myself.

"It's a telephone number," I explained. "For a mobile. I hid it in his cabin. You call the number and when he picks up it completes the circuit."

"Ka-boom time?"

"Indeed."

"No shit. And say, do you have some kind of master-control over all this?"

Funny. I had a feeling he might ask me that. "Not any more," I told him. "It's all down to you."

He paused. "Wait. If I use my cell, it can be traced, right?"

"It could be."

"Don't you think maybe you should have considered that?"

"Go to the kitchen in your apartment," I told him. "Open the bottom left cupboard beside the gas cooker."

"Huh?"

"Just do it."

I heard the cluck of his tongue, followed by the sound of his footsteps and the rasp of his breath. Then I heard the squeak of the cupboard hinge.

"Hey, there's a handset in here."

"It's prepaid," I told him, trying not to sound vexed. "No trace."

"Shit. You've been here?"

This time I failed to control my irritation. "You invited me in, remember?"

I waited for the cogs to mesh. It took longer than it should have done.

"Lady, you're good."

"I'm pleased that you're pleased. And I assume that I will be paid the rest of my money."

There was a moment's hesitation. "Oh, sure thing. The bonus too. Absolutely. No question. You're coming to Antibes, right?"

I let go of a weary breath and lowered the binoculars from my eyes. "There's nobody on the Jetée just now. You should make the call."

I closed the lid of my laptop, gripped hold of my steering wheel and craned my neck until my line of sight was clear. I turned the radio on low and was mid-way through a morsel of Euro-pop when I saw the bright pulse of blue-white light. The windows gave out in a flaming burst and a cloud of blackened smoke idled upwards on the faint night breeze. I muted the radio and awaited the boom.

Less than three minutes later, I was fitting my key in the ignition of my rental Citröen and getting ready to drive to the airport when

I happened to glance across to the *Lazy Jane*. Standing on deck was a man in a Hawaiian shirt. He had a mobile phone clutched uselessly in his hand and his tanned face was lifted towards the fire raging through the exclusive apartment overlooking the harbour.

My name is Rachel Delaney and there are three things you'd do well to remember about me. I never negotiate. I always do my research, so I know if a client is lying about a place in Antibes, or anything else for that matter. Oh, and I'm a huge fan of cheesy action movies, especially the ones starring Rick van Hammer.

JUNGLE BOOGIE

Kate Horsley

RAOUL STOOD ON the corner, leaning against the plaster wall of Bar El Diablo, telling himself to walk away. It was seven in the evening and the sky was a ripening bruise behind the cathedral. The August heat licked his face and a knot of girls skipped arm in arm across the zócalo. One burst into song. He told himself to go back to the museum, to lock the statue in its glass case, and if his boss asked any questions to make up some amusing story. But he'd crossed an unseen line on Barrio El Cerrillo and now he couldn't move. So he dragged on the stub of his cigarette and stared at the blonde woman on the cathedral steps.

She was wearing her new green dress with the red cherries pouting from it. It flared at the waist, making it look as if she had hips. He thought about grabbing her ass last night because he wanted something heavy to hang on to, to tether him when he came, and about how, at the crucial moment, his thumbs dug into her hip bones. She was thin and pale and tall and not his type. She wore orange cowboy boots in summer and people walking by them said that she was loco. He was addicted to fucking her maybe, or in love, or just pathetic and obsessed. He didn't know which one and he didn't care.

He dropped his cigarette and ground it out with his heel, picked up the briefcase. Walking across the zócalo towards her was like crossing the border into a better place. Her hair was gold from Fort Knox. Her teeth were silver dollars. Together they would fuck and make babies and be rich. She saw him coming and smiled a little and started walking to him, swinging her boy hips like she was doing the jungle boogie. It made him laugh. Maybe jungle boogie was the first symptom of jungle fever. Man, he had it bad.

Raoul wiped the sweat off his forehead and walked to the blonde, to the church. They met on the bottom step and kissed and he dropped the briefcase so he could hold her round the waist. She tasted of beer and cigarettes just like he did. Blue doves called from the rain trees behind the cathedral. He was half hard already. "You check out of your hotel?"

"Hours ago." Darla laughed and bit his throat. "You bring it with you?"

"You wanted it, I got it."

She pushed him away, her blue eyes narrowing. "No one suspects?"

"Not yet, but when I don't show up tomorrow—"

"Let's not get our panties in a bunch about tomorrow." She pulled a pack of Bohemios from her purse and tapped one out, pinching it in her mouth so that her lips thinned to an angry coral line.

He flicked open his Zippo and lit it for her. "Talking of panties—"

"One thing at a time. The car's nearby?" She took his zippo and tucked it into her cigarette pack, as if it had been hers all along.

"Parked on Cinco de Mayo just like we said. Don't you trust me?"

She picked up the briefcase. "Can I see?"

"In the middle of the zócalo with the whole town looking?"

"The square's empty. Not a soul."

He looked behind him. It was true. "It just doesn't seem like the place to break out something so sacred."

She laughed. "You worried about angering the Mayan gods?"

He said nothing. He'd grown up with so many stories about the ancient ruins, the jungle full of spirits and bad blood.

She dropped her cigarette and dragged her arm across her forehead. "Oh my God, you are worried. You people … "

"*You people?* You mean Mexicans?"

"No, I mean museum curators. You've got too much knowledge, not enough nerve." She pulled something out of her purse.

He thought it was the cigarettes again, but it looked too dark, too long. He didn't really see, just heard the muffled shot and felt the burst of pain. He fell on his knees. "But I love you."

"I know. That's why I asked you to do this for me." She bent down, pressed her lips on his forehead. "I'm sorry, but it's just too valuable."

He clutched his gut and watched her walk across the zócalo, briefcase in hand, boy hips doing the jungle boogie under her new green dress.

***

Sighing with relief, Darla slid into the front seat of Raoul's small red coupe. She turned the key in the ignition, heard one of the wretched local channels crackle into life, pressed down the lighter, took out a smoke. She'd pulled it off, dared to do what a lot of guys wouldn't have had the balls to. She lit up and swung out into Cinco de Mayo without looking behind her. And even though her heart chirred like a cicada, her hands were steady on the wheel.

Five miles from San Cristóbal, she thought someone was following her, a black car in her rear-view mirror, almost bumper to bumper with her. On impulse, she turned off the main road, watched him sail by behind. Now if he wanted to find her, he'd have to make a U-turn and come back. She laughed. Why was she being so paranoid? Sure, the museum police would be tailing her now, like Raoul would ever have the guts to turn her in. That's how she'd picked him out, how she knew she'd get away with it.

The coupe rolled down a dirt track with weeds sprouting in the middle and fallen branches squealing on the belly of the car, began to speed up, the crappy little path thinning as the trees on each side thickened. Who'd have thought a little road like this would go down at such a steep pitch? It was getting dark, too. She stepped on the brake. The car slowed some, but didn't screech to a halt like she thought it would.

Instead, it kept on rasping over the tall grass, headlights cutting a yellow groove into the jungle's darkness. She jammed her foot down hard. The coupe twisted sideways on a root, throwing her into the wheel. She hit her head on the top of it. The bottom dug into her ribs. The car lurched to a stop in some spiky Mexican bush or other, flinging her back against the seat, breathless and bleeding. A parrot flew up squawking through the leaves. The engine made a coughing sound, a sort of deathbed rattle before cutting out in a bleakly predictable way.

"Fuck it." She pulled the mangled cigarette out of her mouth, lighting the next from the glowing cherry. "Fuck it all to hell."

***

It was his Abuela, his tiny grandmother, muttering the rosary to herself as she stirred bread soup, who'd made him the lace handkerchief. He stuffed it into the space between his belt and the wound in his gut. As he staggered along he could feel it getting wetter and in his mind's eye he saw the silk curlicues growing brittle and black. What would Abuela say if she saw her handiwork jammed between his watch pocket and the nugget of lead? Nothing probably. She would simply take it and wash it for him, crossing herself and whispering about *la agonía en el huerto*. Then it would appear, clean and pressed, in the breast pocket of his linen jacket. He told himself that it was there now, crisply folded.

The blonde would be behind the wheel of his coupe by now, headed for Mexico City. Meanwhile, he was almost at a bar – not the Bar El Diablo, full of tourists and sugary, cold beer, panpipes blaring over the PA. No, his hand was propping up the yellow-painted wall of La Cantina del Corazon where the men sipped cane hooch in dark corners and chewed the fat. He could rest there for a little while, maybe.

He stumbled through the swinging doors, trying to hold his head high long enough to get to a table. A few people stared then turned back to their talk, probably thinking he was drunk or stoned. The bar was hot and it was hard to walk like there was no hole in his gut just next to the fake-silver belt buckle, no dark wad of silk sticking to his black cotton shirt. He slumped at an empty table and a woman with hard black eyes, long hair and a proud, straight throat came to wipe the crumbs and peanut shells into his lap. "Drinking? Eating?" She said it in English, like he was just another tourist.

"Long time since I've been in here, I guess." Speaking tore him up. He winced. It felt like that blonde had hammered nails through him, tacking his flesh into his bones. Maybe voodoo was her thing. Maybe that was why she'd wanted the statue of Xbalanque, Jaguar god of the Underworld, shadow of the shaman. Xbalanque would bring her all the darkness she could wish for if she let him.

The waitress stopped wiping. Her eyes softened. "*Una cerveza grande?*"

He nodded and smiled, relieved that she could read his mind, and watched her walk away, her ass subtly swaying under her uniform.

***

If she drove through the night, she'd be in Mexico City in time for her plane, back over the border before you could say "four hundred grand". That was the plan, and for weeks she'd stuck to it faithfully, fucking him when he asked for it, telling him she loved him when that was what he needed to hear. And truthfully, the fucking and the candlelight and all the sweet nothings hadn't been so hard. Some mornings, when she woke up in his arms and heard him breathing steady and slow behind her and the street vendors setting up their wares outside the window … Well, she didn't mind it so much. But the trouble with accomplices was goddamn guilty consciences and the trouble with splitting the money was loose ends. Darla didn't like loose ends.

Her arm ached from holding up her keychain torch and her eyes were gritty from staring down at the torn map with its stupid Mexican names. There was San Cristóbal de las Casas and there was Ciudad de Mexico, but nowhere was Stupido de Los Dirt Tracko and Automóvil Repair. She threw down the map and opened the car door, half-expecting a snake. But there was just dirt and crappy grass and her boot with some blood on it. The crushed hood belched up smoke in a pathetic plume. There was no choice but to hike back up the track and thumb for a ride on the main road.

She slammed the door and it opened right back up again, reminding her that she'd almost left something behind. She pulled out the black suitcase and hugged it to her chest like a child. "You're worth all this and more."

* * *

For the first time, he heard the guitar playing behind him, saw the old men in corners swigging out of plastic mugs and letting their ash drop on the floor. Up above, the paper lamps hung from strings tacked to the ceiling and neon signs for Bud Light and Clamato flickered on the wall. The waitress came back with his beer. He thanked her and lifted it to his lips, relishing the cool gold liquid trickling down his throat. Maybe it would run right through the hole in his belly. He almost laughed at that, but stopped when he felt another nail go through him.

The doors swung open and a little old woman in a black mantilla came in, clutching a basket under her arm. She went to a few of the tables, but people shook their heads or just ignored her. Maybe she was selling moonshine or telling fortunes. She made him think of his Abuela, so tiny, scrubbing the steps on Saturday, melting chocolate for mole, slapping his face for cursing that one time. He never swore in front of her again.

When she finally hobbled over to his table, she opened her basket wordlessly, and he saw that it was full of knitted dolls. Each one wore a balaclava and clutched a machine gun, just like the drug runners in the jungle. He felt sad then. He wanted to ask her, *When did it come down to this, the knitted dolls, the local crafts?* So far from the men in masks sacrificing blood to the Jaguar, the shaman chanting his mantra, bringing the spirits with his sacred drum.

But then, he'd drifted pretty far. He'd been about to leave this life behind for good, betray the people who'd raised him. Grimacing, he dug 60 pesos from his pocket and dropped them in her outstretched palm. In return, she handed him three dolls, stitched mouths grinning through their balaclavas, guns poised to fire woollen bullets at anyone who crossed their path.

* * *

The shapes of trees grew blacker against the lilac sky. Beyond, between, inside, night creatures chattered and rustled. Sometimes they even shrieked. A twig cracked. Darla spun around. The torch's thin beam bounced off glossy leaves that sprung back into place behind some mottled thing vanishing into the jungle's green void, slinking stealthy and feral as a jaguar. There wasn't anything as big as that in this rat hole, though, she was sure. She turned back, one hand trembling a little on the handle of the briefcase, the other clenching the torch. She stepped forward and its light faltered. She shook it hard. "Mother of shit, don't die now, battery."

When the car crashed, it had only gone a short way into the trees. She'd seen that with her own eyes, and she'd been cool and collected, tracing the tyre marks back towards the track. But the further she followed them, the denser the foliage grew. She'd been going maybe a quarter of an hour and now it was night. Her torch was failing. The place was crawling with fuck knew what tropical shit.

Back in San Cristóbal, if you mentioned the jungle, everyone was totally weird about it, even Raoul. They were superstitious, crossing themselves and talking about ancient gods, lost tribesmen, human sacrifice. It seemed to Darla there were more tangible things to worry about – the Guatemalan drug runners toting Mac-10s for one thing, the bird-eating spiders and the giant fucking snakes.

As soon as she thought the thought, something bright wriggled in the undergrowth. She shone the torch on it and it slunk away. A pinkish tinge. Probably a coral snake. She imagined it striking, all bared fangs and venom, and her going all Bear Grylls and sucking the poison out, maybe snacking on the thing when it was dead. She had to laugh at that. A loud sound interrupted her. A person laughing, an echo. But it went on too long for that, the sound stretching out into something like a howl. Underneath it a rhythmic sound boomed. Drums. The torch crapped out.

* * *

When he'd finished the first beer, the waitress brought him another, then another after that. He finished the last drop of the last beer and thought about the alcohol dribbling, spouting, gouting from the wound under his belt, except that he couldn't really feel it any more. The cantina looked softer now and the air felt cooler, clearer. A woman came out, wearing a red dress, and stood with her arms raised above her head. The guitar music stopped. A red light came on. The guitar began again, slow and rhythmic and the woman began to dance.

She wore gold hoop earrings and her gleaming hair was adorned with a white paper camellia. She danced with the heels of her shoes and her hips, holding one arm out, then the other, turning around to show the roses stitched on to her scarf. Her brows were thick and her mouth was fierce as a shaman's. A jaguar's. When she bent her arm and pressed her hand to her waist, the guitarist slapped the strings, loud and staccato, the music burning into Raoul's ears, calling the spirits forth. When she raised her arms above her head, he stroked them so gently, picking out each note like he had all the time in the world to play the song.

Raoul closed his eyes and thought of the blonde, the jungle boogie in her skinny hips, the statue hidden in her stolen suitcase. The Jaguar God was in that lump of gold and spirits always took back what was theirs. They called the dark magic. They demanded blood.

He slumped further back in the chair, listening to the dying chords of the guitar, thinking of Abuela's handkerchief folded so neat and clean in his pocket, of Darla sitting beside him in the passenger seat of the coupe, the statue in her lap, her hand on his arm, a look on her face like she was remembering the night before. When he opened his eyes, the dancer was gone and the waitress was putting another beer in front of him.

"Will she come back and dance again?"

"Will who come back?" asked the waitress. Her fingers, slipping from the sweating glass, brushed his hand. They were cool and smooth as gold. He closed his eyes again, feeling that he loved the waitress and the old woman and the dancer, and even the blonde, because the same blood ran in all their veins.

* * *

She was alone in the dark, her heart going like the Kentucky Derby, the laughter echoing around her. She put down the briefcase. "Keep it together, Darla. Don't lose your shit now, girl." Fumbling in her dress, she found her cigarettes, slid her fingers in the crumpled pack. Three left. Three cigarettes, like three wishes. She tapped Raoul's Zippo out, feeling a certain reassurance in its familiar shape. Flicking it open, she strummed the wheel. No flame, just a sad blue spark or two. Made her think of a shy cock you had to coax and coax before it was ready for use. Raoul's had been like that a couple of times towards the end, as if he knew their game was played out. Not that Darla believed in gut feelings. She turned up the gas.

On about the twentieth twang of the flint, a tall white flame leapt up, singeing her eyelashes. She sucked on her cheap Mexican cigarette, pretending she wasn't even going to look around. She didn't know what she'd been expecting to see – hundreds of shining eyes watching her, or just one pair, red-rimmed and hungry. But there was nothing.

She dragged and exhaled a plume of smoke. The Zippo was still burning away, eating up its little tank of gas. It would be dead soon, like the torch, and she would be here in the dark until the dawn broke. A wave of tiredness hit her. Her feet ached. She'd have to sit down for a while, wait for the light. Not on the ground though.

Kicking the briefcase over with her toe, she was about to sit down on it when she had an urge to know what was inside. Zippo in one hand, she flipped up the catches with the other. Inside was an old bit of lace, the kind Raoul was always mopping his forehead with. She sucked on her cigarette. "Better not be all there is."

The handkerchief was loosely wrapped around something solid and heavy. She pulled it away. Out rolled a gold figurine, smaller than she thought it would be. She picked it up, turned it in the light. From what she could tell, it was some kind of big cat, a jaguar maybe. Beneath him, back arched, legs spread, little gold mouth open and gasping, was a woman. She and the jaguar were fucking away. Not just fucking, but really staring into each other's eyes, like they loved each other.

She sat down, a strange feeling in her belly, as if all her life she'd been missing some crucial piece of the puzzle. All those long cons and short cons, boring affairs and quick, hot lays, and here was this ancient relic and just looking at it filled her with a raw desire for something. A connection. Love.

The Zippo light dipped a little, its brightness fading. All around her the jungle chirped and screeched. And there was the laughter again, the wild thump and smack of a drum. She dropped the lighter and clamped her hands over her ears. Her belly told her that she'd been a bad girl, that she'd never leave this place. But that was just stupid. Gut feelings didn't exist.

ROTTERDAM

Nicholas Royle

As SOON AS Joe arrived in Rotterdam, he made for the river. He believed that a city without a river was like a computer without memory. A camera without film.

The river was wide and grey. A slice of the North Sea.

Joe was listening to "Rotterdam", a track on the Githead album *Art Pop*. When he'd last been to Paris he'd played the Friendly Fires single of that name over and over. Earlier in the year, walking through the Neuköln district of Berlin, he'd selected Bowie's *Heroes* album and listened to one track, "Neuköln", on repeat.

He switched it off. It wasn't working. Sometimes it worked, sometimes it didn't. The chugging, wiry pop of Githead didn't fit this bleak riverscape. The breathy vocals were a distraction. Instrumentals worked better.

He didn't have long. A couple of days. The producer, Vos, wouldn't wait any longer. The American was a busy man and Joe knew he had already more than tried Vos's patience with repeated requests to have a shot at writing the screenplay, or have some input elsewhere on the movie. For now, at least, the script had John Mains's name on it and Joe knew he could count himself lucky to be scouting locations, albeit unpaid. He hoped that by showing willing and maybe coming up with some places that not only corresponded to what Vos wanted but also helped to back up his own vision of how the film could look, he might still get to gain some influence.

Joe turned back on himself and selected a cheap hotel with a river view. His room, when he got up to the fourth floor, managed to reveal very little of the Nieuwe Maas but if you craned your neck you could just make out the distinctive outline of the Erasmus Bridge. They called it the Swan; to Joe it looked more like a wishbone, picked clean. Did swans have wishbones?

The room itself was basic and while you wouldn't necessarily pick up dirt with a trailing finger, there was a suggestion of ingrained grime, a patina of grease. Joe quickly unpacked his shoulder bag, placing his tattered Panther paperback of *The Lurking Fear & Other Stories* by the side of the bed. He checked his emails and sent one to Vos to let him know he had arrived in Rotterdam and was heading straight out to make a start.

He walked towards the centre. The kind of places he was looking for were not likely to be found there, but he wanted to get a feel for the city. He'd known not to expect a replica of Amsterdam, or even Antwerp. Rotterdam had been flattened in the war and had arisen anew in the twentieth century's favourite materials of glass and steel. But really the commercial centre could have been plucked from the English Midlands or the depressed Francophone cities of Wallonia.

A figure on top of an anonymous block of chrome and smoked glass caught his eye. It was either hubris or a remarkable achievement on the artist's part that Antony Gormley's cast of his own body had, by stealth, become a sort of Everyman figure. A split second's glance was all you needed to identify the facsimile as that of the London-born sculptor.

Only absently wondering why there might be an Antony Gormley figure standing on top of an office block in Rotterdam, Joe walked on. He stopped outside a bookshop and surveyed the contents of the window as an inevitable prelude to going inside: Joe couldn't walk past bookshops. It was their unpredictability that drew him in. They might not have his book in stock, but then again they might.

This one had the recently published Dutch edition of Joe's crime novel *Amsterdam*. He stroked the cover, lost for a moment in the same reverie that always gripped him at this point. The thought that the novel was this far – *this far* – from reaching the screen.

Leaving the bookshop, Joe spotted another tall figure standing erect on the flat roof of a shiny anonymous building 200 metres down the road.

When Vos had optioned the book, Joe had thought it was only a matter of time, but delay followed delay. Vos had a director attached, but couldn't find a writer the director would work with. Joe had asked his agent to show Vos the three unsold feature-length scripts he had written on spec, but the agent had explained that Vos and his director were looking for someone with a track record. Which was why Joe made a bid to write the adaptation of Lovecraft's "The Hound", Vos's other optioned property, but the response was the same. Hence the visit to Rotterdam to look for empty spaces and spooky graveyards.

On the Westzeedijk, a boulevard heading east away from the city centre, Joe came upon the Kunsthal: a glass-and-steel construction, the art gallery had a protruding metal deck on which were scattered more Gormley figures in different positions. Lying flat, sitting down, bent double. Inside the gallery, visible through the sheet-glass walls, were more figures striking a variety of poses. Two faced each other through the plate glass, identical in all respects except height. The one inside looked taller, presumably an illusion.

Joe had missed the original Gormley exhibition in London, when cast-iron moulds of the artist's body had popped up on rooftops across the capital. Leaving the Kunsthal in his wake, he caught sight of another figure at one corner of the roof of the Erasmus Medical Centre. He realized he had started looking for them. This was Gormley's aim, he supposed, to alter the way you looked at the world. To get into your head and flick a switch. As public art, it was inescapable, insidious, invasive. Was that a good thing? Was his work really a "radical investigation of the body as a place of memory and transformation", as Joe remembered reading on the artist's own web site? Or was it all about him? All about Gormley. And if it was, did that matter? Wasn't Joe's novel all about Joe? Who's to say Lovecraft's essays were the extent of his auto-biographical work?

Joe was halfway to the top of the Euromast when his phone buzzed. The incoming text was from Vos. John Mains, the scriptwriter, was going to be in Rotterdam, arriving later that day. They should meet, compare notes, Vos advised.

Joe scowled. He reached the top landing of the structure and exited on to the viewing deck. The panorama of the city ought to have dominated, but Joe couldn't help but be aware of the ubiquitous figure perched on the railing above his head.

He tried to think of a way in which he could get out of meeting up with Mains. He'd lost his phone and not received Vos's text. Amateurish. Didn't have time. Even worse.

He checked his watch. He still had a few hours.

At the foot of the Euromast he found an empty fire station. He peered through the fogged windows. A red plastic chair sat upturned in the middle of a concrete floor. A single boot lay on its side. Joe took a couple of pictures and moved on. A kilometre or so north was Nieuwe Binnenweg. With its mix of independent music stores, designer boutiques, print centres and sex shops, this long east-west street on the west side of the city would be useful for establishing shots. At the top end he photographed a pet grooming salon, Doggy Stijl, next door to a business calling itself, less ambiguously, the Fetish Store. There were a few empty shops, more cropping up the further out of town he walked, alongside ethnic food stores and tatty establishments selling cheap luggage and rolls of brightly coloured vinyl floor coverings.

The port of Rotterdam had expanded since Lovecraft's day to become the largest in Europe. Why the late author had chosen to set his story here did not concern Joe; indeed, he had no reason to suspect Lovecraft had ever set foot on Dutch soil. The references to Holland and Rotterdam in particular were so general he could have been describing any port city. All credit to Vos, Joe conceded, that he had chosen to film here rather than in Hull or Harwich, or the eastern seaboard of the US, for that matter.

Joe's westward migration out of the city had taken him into one of the port areas. The cold hand of the North Sea poked its stubby fingers into waste ground crisscrossed by disused railway sidings. Ancient warehouses crumbled in the moist air. New buildings the size of football pitches constructed out of corrugated metal squatted amid coarse grass and hardy yellow flowering plants. Interposed between one of these nameless buildings and the end of a long narrow channel of slate-coloured water was an abandoned Meccano set of rusty machinery – hawsers, articulated arms, winches, pulleys. Elsewhere in the city this would pass as contemporary art. Out here it was merely a relic of outmoded mechanization, with a possible afterlife as a prop in a twenty-first-century horror film.

There had been a few adaptations of Lovecraft's work, successful and otherwise, and they weren't *all* by Stuart Gordon. Just most of them. Joe wasn't sure where Vos's film was destined to play, arthouse or multiplex. As he lowered the camera from his eye, he caught sight of a dark shape behind the machinery. Tasting a rush of adrenalin, he moved his head for a better view, but there was nothing – or nobody – there.

Disconcerted, he backed away. In the distance a container lorry crunched down through the gears as it negotiated a corner. A faint alarm could be heard as the driver of another vehicle reversed up to a loading bay.

Keileweg had been the centre of the dockside red-light district before the clean-up of 2005 that had driven prostitution off the streets. If he hadn't done his research, Joe wouldn't have guessed. He found Keileweg devoid of almost any signs of life. The street was lined with boxy grey warehouses and abandoned import/export businesses. A dirty scarf of sulphurous smoke trailed from a chimney at an industrial site near the main road end of Keileweg. On the opposite side, a little way down, a building clad in blue corrugated metal drew Joe's eye. Christian graffiti decorated the roadside wall: "JEZUS STIERF VOOR ONS TOEN WIJ NOG ZONDAREN WAREN". The building's main entrance was tucked away behind high gates. High but not unscalable. Approaching the dirty windows, Joe shielded his eyes to check out the interior. The usual story: upturned chairs, a table separated from its legs, a computer monitor with its screen kicked in, a venetian blind pulled down from the wall, its blue slats twisted and splayed like some kind of post-ecological vegetation.

The place had potential.

Likewise the waste ground and disused railway sidings running alongside Vier-Havens-Straat.

Slowly, Joe made his way back into town photographing likely sites, even throwing in the odd windmill in case Vos wanted to catch the heritage market.

He returned to the hotel to shower and pick up his emails, including one from Vos telling him where and when to meet John Mains. Joe studied the map. He left the hotel and walked north until he reached Nieuwe Binnenweg, where he turned left. At the junction with Gravendijkwal, where the traffic rattled beneath Nieuwe Binnenweg in an underpass, he entered the Dizzy Jazzcafé and ordered a Belgian brown beer. He drank it quickly, toying with his beermat, and ordered another. Checking his watch, he emptied his glass for the second time. As he stood up, his head spun and he had to hold on to the back of the chair. Belgian brown beers were notoriously strong, he remembered, a little too late.

Two blocks down Nieuwe Binnenweg was Heemraadssingel, a wide boulevard with a canal running up the middle of it. Joe stood on a broad grassy bank facing the canal and beyond it the bar where he was due to meet Mains. He straightened his back and breathed in deeply. He needed a moment of calm.

A soft voice in his ear: "Joe!"

He whirled around. A figure stood on the grass behind him, legs slightly apart, arms by his side. The lights of the bars and the clubs on the near side of the street turned the figure into a silhouette; the lights from the far side of the canal were too distant to provide any illumination.

Joe stood his ground, straining his eyes to see.

The figure didn't move.

And then a shape ghosted out from behind it. A man.

"Joe," said the man in a gentle Scots accent. "Didn't mean to make you jump. Well, I guess I did, but you know ... These are a laugh, aren't they?" He indicated the cast-iron mould as he moved away from it. "Easily recyclable, too. John Mains." He offered his hand.

"Joe," said Joe, still disoriented.

"I know," said Mains, smiling slyly.

He was about Joe's height with an uncertain cast to his slightly asymmetrical features that could go either way – charmingly vulnerable or deceptively untrustworthy.

"Busy day?" Mains asked, moving dark hair out of his eyes.

"Yeah."

"When did you get here?"

"This morning."

"*How* did you get here?"

"I flew."

"Shall we?" Mains gestured towards the far side of the canal.

They walked towards where the road crossed over the canal and Joe was the first to enter the bar. Rock music played loudly from speakers bracketed to the walls. They sat on stools at a high table in a little booth and a bartender brought them beers. Joe observed Mains while the scriptwriter was watching the lads in the next booth, and he wondered what anyone would think, looking at them. Would they be able to spot the difference between them? Was Mains's precious track record visible to the naked eye?

Mains looked back and it was Joe's turn to redirect his gaze.

Mains said something and Joe had to ask him to repeat it.

"I said I haven't booked into a hotel yet."

"It's not exactly high season."

"No." He took a sip of his beer. "Could you not have taken the train? Or the ferry?"

"What?"

"It's not very environmentally friendly to fly, especially such a short distance."

"It was cheaper."

"Not in the long run, Joe. You've got to take the long view."

Joe looked at the other man's dark eyes, small and round and glossy like a bird's. A half-smile.

"So what have you got for me?" Mains asked.

Joe hesitated. He wondered if it was worth making the point that he was working for Vos. He decided that since neither of them was paying him, it didn't make much difference. He was about to answer when Mains spoke again.

"Look, Joe, I know you pitched to write this script, but we do have to work together."

"I know, I know," Joe shouted into a sudden break between tracks. The boys in the next booth looked over at them. Joe returned their stare, then turned to look at Mains. "I know," he continued. "Here, have a look."

He handed Mains the camera phone on which he'd taken his pictures and Mains flicked through them using his thumbs.

"Great," he said, not particularly sounding like he meant it. "I suppose I was expecting something more atmospheric."

Joe tried to keep the irritation out of his voice – "I guess the Germans weren't thinking about that when they bombed the place to fuck" – and failed.

Another group of young men entered the bar. Joe didn't consider himself an expert on the outward signifiers of particular social groupings, particularly in foreign countries, but he wondered if Mains had brought him to a gay bar. One of the newcomers glanced at Joe, then switched his attention to Mains, his eyes lingering on the tattoos on the Scot's forearms.

"Are you hungry?" said Mains.

"I haven't eaten all day."

"Let's go get something to eat."

As they got down from their stools, Joe felt his head spinning again. He really did need something to eat, and quick.

They ate in a Thai restaurant. Joe smiled at the waitress, but it was his dining partner she couldn't take her eyes off.

"You'd better write a decent script, that's all I can say," Joe said to Mains, argumentatively, as the waitress poured them each another Singha beer. "It better not be shit."

Mains laughed.

"I'm not fucking joking. When's it set, for example? Is it contemporary?"

"It's timeless, Joe. It's a timeless story, after all. I'm sure you agree. Grave-robbing – it's never a good idea."

"Tell me you're not writing it as a fucking period piece."

"Like I say, it's timeless."

"Fuck's sake."

As they left, Mains slipped the tip directly into the waitress's hand. Joe thought he saw her fingers momentarily close over his.

Out on the street, Joe wanted nothing more than to drink several glasses of water and get his head down, but Mains wasn't done yet, insisting that they go to a club he'd read about near Centraal Station.

"I'm fucked," Joe said, pulling a face.

"Ah come on, man. It's new. I want to check it out and I can't go on my own."

Why not? Joe wanted to yell at him. *Why the fuck not?*

But instead he allowed his shoulders to slump in a gesture of acquiescence.

"Good man!" Mains clapped him on the back. "Good man! Let's go."

They walked together through the city streets, dodging bicycles. Joe knew he was making a mistake. He just didn't know how big.

They reached West-Kruiskade. The nightclub – WATT – was located between a public park and an Asian fast food restaurant. Dozens of bikes were parked outside. Bouncers looked over a steady stream of clubbers as they entered. Joe and Mains joined them.

They waited to be served at the bar.

"The glasses are made from recycled materials," Mains said.

"Right," said Joe.

A bartender cracked open two brown bottles and poured the contents into two plastic glasses.

"They have a rainwater-flush system for the loos," Mains went on.

"Brilliant," Joe said in a deliberately flat voice.

"The lighting is all LEDs. Renewable energy sources."

"This is why you wanted to come here?" A disgusted grimace had settled on Joe's face.

"The best part is over there." Mains turned and pointed towards the dance floor, accidentally brushing the shoulder of the girl next to him, who turned and stared at the two men. "It's a brand new concept," he continued, ignoring the girl, who eventually looked away. "Sustainable Dance Club. Energy from people's feet powers the lights in the dance floor."

Joe concentrated on trying to remain upright. He drank some beer from his recycled plastic glass. Something Mains had said in the restaurant came back to him.

"You know you said grave-robbing is never a good idea?" Joe looked at Mains, whose face was unreadable. "Surely what we're doing is a form of grave-robbing? Adapting the work of a dead man without his approval." Joe finished his beer. "I'm not saying I wouldn't have done the adaptation, offered the chance, but still, eh?"

Mains stared back into Joe's eyes and for a moment Joe thought he had outwitted the scriptwriter.

"I prefer to think of it," Mains said eventually, "as recycling."

Joe held his beady gaze for a second or two, then, with an air about him of someone conceding defeat but slipping a card up his sleeve at the same time, said, "I have some ideas."

"Uh-huh?"

"Mike Nelson."

"The installation artist?"

"Works a lot with abandoned buildings, something Vos told me to keep an eye out for. Plus, he's a fan of Lovecraft. He entitled one of his works *To the Memory of HP Lovecraft*. Admittedly he's quoting a dedication from a short story by Borges, but why would he do that if he wasn't a fan?"

"So what about him?" Mains asked.

"Get him on board as production designer. I suggested it to Vos. Do you know what he said? 'Production design's not art, it's craft.'"

Mains appeared to alter the direction of the conversation. "Vos optioned your novel, didn't he?"

Joe nodded.

"You realize if the Lovecraft adaptation gets made it increases the chances of yours going into development?"

Joe nodded again.

"It would make a good movie," Mains added.

"You've read it?" Joe asked before he could stop himself.

"Vos gave me a copy."

Joe felt more conflicted than ever. If Vos had given Mains a copy of his book it could mean he wanted him to adapt it, and whereas Joe would rather write any script himself, the ultimate goal was seeing a film version on the big screen, whoever got the writer's credit.

Joe saw himself buying more beers, which was madness, given how seriously drunk he was by now. He turned around to pass one to Mains, but the writer was not there. The back of his jacket could be seen threading its way between the crowds towards the dance floor.

Joe looked at the beers in his hands.

The rest of the evening was a maelstrom of pounding music, throbbing temples, flashing lights. Grabbed hands, shouted remarks, glimpsed figures. Time became elastic, sense fragmentary, perception unreliable. Joe was aware, while staggering back to the hotel, of feeling so utterly isolated from the rest of the world that he felt alternately tiny and huge in relation to his surroundings. But mainly he was unaware of anything that made any sense; there were pockets, or moments, of clarity like stills from a forgotten film. The giant white swan of the Erasmus Bridge glowing against the night sky. A heel caught between rails as the first tram of the day screeched around a bend in the track. His hotel room – leaning back against the closed door, astonished to be there at all. Looking at his reflection in the bathroom mirror and not being convinced it was his, until he reminded himself this was how a man might look after drinking as much as he had. Cupping water in his hands from the tap, again and again and again. Finally, lying in bed staring at the door and hallucinating one of Antony Gormley's cast-iron figures standing inside the room with its back to the door.

Waking was a slow process of fear and denial, the inside of his head host to a slideshow of rescued images from the night before. Tattooed flesh, strobe lights, red flashes. Someone grabbing hold of his crotch, taking a handful. A mouth full of teeth. The pulsing

LEDs in the kinetic dance floor. The Erasmus Bridge. The Gormley figure in his room. The open window admitted the sounds of traffic on river and road, the city coming to life. Knowing he would soon be spending a long period of penance in the bathroom, he looked over towards the door. The figure he had thought he had seen just before falling asleep was not there, but there was something not right about that corner of the room. He closed his eyes, but then opened them again to stop his head spinning. There was something on the wall, something that oughtn't to be there. Feeling his gorge begin to rise, he clambered out of bed, naked. To get to the bathroom he had to pass the end of the bed where there was a bit of space between it and the wall opposite. The door was beyond to the left. There was something there on the floor, some kind of dummy or lifesize doll, or a picture of one painted dark rusty red by a child. There was a lot of red paint splashed on the floor and the walls and the end of the bed, but Joe had to get to the bathroom.

He threw up in the toilet, his brain processing the images from the floor of the room, against his will. All he wanted to do was be sick and cleanse his system. As he vomited again, a small knot of pain formed towards the front of his skull, increasing in severity in a matter of seconds. He knew he had to go out of the bathroom and have another look at the floor between the wall and the end of the bed, but he didn't want to do so. He was frightened and he didn't understand. What he had seen was just a picture; hopefully it wasn't even there, it was a hallucination, like the figure as he'd lain in bed. He turned and looked out of the bathroom door. The bedspread had a busy pattern, but even among the geometric shapes, the purples and the blues, lozenges and diamonds, he could see streaks and splashes of a dirty brown. He crawled to the doorway, his heart thumping, and peered around the corner.

He spent a few seconds looking at the thing that lay on the carpet before retreating into the bathroom and being sick again.

He remembered Mains telling him, at the start of the evening, that he hadn't booked a hotel room. Had they come back together? Or had Mains followed him back and had he – Joe – let him in? Or had he broken in? Had the glimpsed figure been the writer, not one of Gormley's cast-iron facsimiles? Or had Mains already been there passed out on the floor while Joe was drifting into sleep in bed, and had the cast-iron man done this to him?

It was no more bizarre an idea than that Joe had done it. Had slashed at the writer's body until it was almost unrecognizable as that of a human being, never mind as that of Mains. There could be little blood left in the vasculature, most of it having soaked into the carpet and bedspread or adhered to the wall in patterns consistent with arterial spray.

Joe inspected his hands. They were clean. Perhaps too clean. His body was unmarked.

Very deliberately, Joe got dressed. Stepping carefully around the body, he left the room and took the lift down to the ground floor. He glanced at the desk staff as he left the hotel, but they didn't look up.

He walked towards the western end of Nieuwe Binnenweg until he found the mix of shops he needed and returned to the hotel with a rucksack containing a sturdy hacksaw, a serrated knife, some cleaning materials, skin-tight rubber gloves and a large roll of resealable freezer bags. As he stood facing the mirrored wall in the lift to go back up to the fourth floor, he pictured himself as the boys in the bar would have seen him, shouting at Mains. He recalled the waitress in the restaurant, who had been at their table precisely when Joe had been giving Mains a hard time, and then there was the girl by the bar in WATT. The latter part of the time they had spent in the club was a blank. Anything could have happened and anyone could come forward as a witness.

The lift arrived with a metallic ping and Joe got out and walked the short distance to his room. Once inside, he dumped the rucksack and stripped down to his underpants. He slipped his iPod inside the waistband and inserted the earphones into his ears. "Rotterdam" by Githead, on repeat. If it meant he would never again be able to listen to Githead, so be it. Just as he had never been able to listen to *Astral Weeks* since the traumatic break-up with Anne from Donegal, or to Cranes. He'd been to a Cranes gig in Clapham the night before his father had died and every time he tried to listen to any of their albums, it put him right back where he was the morning he got the phone call from his mother.

He moved a towel and bath mat out of the way, then dragged the body into the bathroom and lifted it into the bath, not worrying too much about the smears of blood this left on the floor and the side of the bath. He stood over the bath with the hacksaw in his hand and suddenly perceived himself as Vos might film him, looking up from the corpse's-eye view. He hesitated, then reached for the towel, which he placed over the head and upper torso.

His first job was to cut away the remaining scraps of clothes, which he dumped in the sink, and then he began working at the left wrist, just below the tattoo. The hacksaw blade skittered when it first met substantial resistance. Blood welled from the cut in the flesh and trickled down towards the hand, causing Joe's hand to slip.

In his earphones, the girl vocalist sang, "It's a nice day," over and over.

It took at least five minutes to get through the radius and another minute or so of sawing to work through the ulna. There was a certain grim satisfaction in having removed one of the hands, but the exertion had brought Joe out in a sweat and his head was throbbing. In his dehydrated state, he could little afford to lose further moisture.

He knew that he had a long job ahead of him and that it would never seem any closer to being completed while he was still thinking forward to – and dreading – the hardest part. He sat down on the bathroom floor for a moment, letting his heart rate slow down. He knew what he was about to attempt. He had decided. It was necessary if he was to survive.

It's a nice day.

Taking a breath, Joe shuffled along the floor. He turned around and leaned over the edge, pulling the hem of the towel up to reveal the neck. He placed the serrated edge of the hacksaw blade against the soft skin just below the Adam's apple. A little bit of pressure and the teeth bit into the skin causing a string of tiny red beads to appear. He leaned into the saw and extended his arm. Back and forth, back and forth. His hand pressing down on the chest and slithering and sliding.

It took a few minutes. He wasn't timing himself. It felt longer. He bagged the head by touch alone, using a plastic carrier from one of the shops on Nieuwe Binnenweg. He recycled one of Mains's shoelaces to tie it shut, then placed it in the sink.

It would be easier now. It could be anyone.

It's a nice day.

At several points over the next two hours, Joe thought he would have to give up. What he was doing was inhuman. If he carried on, he would lose his humanity. Even if he evaded capture, he would never be at peace. But each time he merely restated to himself his determination to survive. Yes, what he was doing was a crime, but it was the only crime he knew for certain he had committed.

The clean-up operation took longer.

It was some time in the afternoon when Joe presented himself at the front desk to settle his bill. The rucksack was on his back, his own bag, bulkier than on arrival, slung over one shoulder. Outside in the street he stopped and looked back. He counted the floors up and along until he spotted his open window. On an impulse, he walked back towards the hotel. There was a poorly maintained raised flower bed between the pavement and the hotel wall. Joe rested his foot on the lip of the bed as if to tie his shoelace and peered into the gaps between the shrubs. At the back, among the rubbish close to the hotel wall was a broken brown bottle. Joe reached in and his fingers closed around the neck. He placed the bottle in his shoulder bag and walked away.

On a patch of waste ground at the end of one of the docks behind Keileweg, unobserved, he started a small fire with bits of rubbish, locally sourced. When the fire was going well enough to burn a couple of pieces of wood salvaged from the dockside, Joe took Mains's torn and bloodstained clothing from his bag. He dropped the items into the flames, then added Mains's wallet, from which he had already extracted anything of use. The broken bottle, which could have originally been a beer bottle from WATT but equally might not have been, went over the side of the dock.

Satisfied that the fire had done its most important work, Joe left it burning and started walking back towards the city centre, the rucksack still heavy on his back.

At a bus stop across the street from where one of Antony Gormley's ubiquitous cast-iron moulds stood guard on the roof of another building, Joe caught a bus to Europort and boarded a ferry bound for Hull, using Mains's ticket. The writer would have approved, he thought. When the ticket control had turned out also to involve a simultaneous passport check, a detail he had somehow not anticipated, Joe's heart rate had shot up and a line of sweat had crept from his hair line, but the check had been cursory at best and Joe had been waved on to the boat. He sat out on the rear deck, glad to relieve his shoulders of the weight of the rucksack. With an hour to go before the ferry was due to sail, he watched the sky darken and the various colours of the port lights take on depth, intensity, richness. Huge wind turbines turning slowly in the light breeze, like fans cooling the desert-warmed air of some alien city of the future. Giant cranes squatting over docksides, mutant insects towering over tiny human figures passing from one suspended cone of orange light to the next. Tall, slender flare-stacks, votive offerings to some unknown god. The lights of the edge of the city in the distance, apartment blocks, life going on.

Soon the ferry would slip her mooring and glide past fantastical wharves and gantries, enormous silos and floating jetties. She would navigate slowly away from this dream of the lowlands and enter the cold dark reality of the North Sea, where no one would hear the odd splash over the side in the lonely hours of the night.

SMALL PRINT

Ian Ayris

"DRINNGG, DRINNGG. DRINNGG, drinngg."

That's me phone. Always let it ring three times before I pick it up. It's like not steppin on the cracks in the pavement or walkin under ladders. Black cats and all that shit.

"Drinngg, drinngg."

There we go. And then I count to three. Don't say nothing. Gives me the upper hand, see, if it's a punter. Gets 'em right on edge from the start. If it's me mum, just pisses her off and she gives me a right ear-bashin, but more often than not, it's a punter.

"Er … Mr Splinters? Charlie Splinters?"

One. Two. Three. It's a geezer's voice. And he sounds just like when you're up in front of the school gettin caned by the headmaster or when you're doin a ton down the motorway. Or when you've just beat a man to death with your bare hands. Fear and panic all runnin round inside but all you wanna do is laugh your fuckin head off.

"Yes," I says.

Geezer breathes hard, like he's blowin all the fear back out.

"Mr Splinters. I need a favour."

Cos that's the business I'm in. "Favours". I do anyone a good turn, me. For the right price. And me rates is pretty reasonable. Ain't got much in the way of letters and education, but I got a head for business, you might say. Undercut every other fucker on the manor, do the job clean and quick, take the money, and see you later. Everyone's a winner. Other than the poor sod in question, of course, but that's sort of the point of it, really.

"Come round to the office," I says.

"You've got an office?" he says, sort of surprised, which I've got a bit of the arse about straight off to tell you the truth, him thinkin I wouldn't have a place of business, and all that.

"Yes, I've got an office," I says to him, a bit fuckin narked. I can tell by how his breathing's gone he knows he's done a wrong 'un. Won't be no more of that I can fuckin tell you.

"The Three Rabbits, half eight, in the snug," I says.

All right, it ain't strictly an office as such, but like I says, it's me place of business and it does very nicely thank you.

Geezer says he'll be there, and puts the phone down.

One. Two. Three.

Time for business.

* * *

The Rabbits is a shit-hole. I'll give you that. But that's part of the beauty of the place. Always quiet. Never no disturbances, or nothing. And in the snug, there's normally just me and No-Arms Maurice, if his old girl's let him out. Lost both his arms in a run-in with Harry the Hatchet. Harry's sister done a bit of waitin tables in a Greasy Spoon on the Old Kent Road, and Maurice took a bit of a fancy to her. Used to slap her arse as she went by his table. No harm meant. Just Harry never see it like that. Called Maurice over to his butchers one night. It was a Friday. I think. Took both his arms off at the shoulder with a fire axe.

Seemed a bit harsh at the time.

But Maurice ain't here tonight. It's just me. And this weedy lookin geezer at the bar what's looked round soon as I've come in.

"Mr Splinters?" he says, desperate look on his face.

I mean, I pretty much look the part, but I suppose he's gotta be sure.

I stare him down. One. Two. Three.

"Yes," I says. And I say, "Take a seat, Mr … "

"Briscoe. Tommy Briscoe." And he holds out his sweaty palm for me to shake. Which I do. Business is business, as they say.

We sit in the corner, opposite the door. Standard procedure. And I go through the particulars with him.

Turns out it's his boss needs doin. Some row about money, or something. Same old shit. I get one of me contracts out me pocket, flatten it out a bit, and hand it over to him. He's a bit confused, at first. Asks me what it is. I says it's a contract, you know, between me and him. So things is done proper. He nods, and feels in his pocket for a pen. Pulls out a pencil. See, that's no good, a pencil. Gotta be black ink, for legal purposes and all that. My mate Terry told me. He went to college and everything. Woodwork, I think, but he knows his stuff with fillin forms and stuff.

I go up to the bar and call round for Eddie.

"Eddie?" I says. "You gotta pen?"

I can see through the other bar Eddie's servin a punter.

"Be a minute, Charlie," he shouts back.

"All right, Eddie," I says. "No problem, mate."

When Eddie's sorted me out with a pen, I goes back and gets down to the matter at hand. His name's Mr Hammond. Not the geezer in front of me, he's Briscoe, like I said. The geezer what needs sortin, that's Hammond. Won't say his first name, just says him as Mr Hammond.

Computers or something, something to do with the buildin trade, that's what he says he works in, this Briscoe geezer. Says this Hammond's been stitchin him up with overtime money and stuff. There's other things, but I start losin the will to fuckin live when punters start goin into their personal shit and that, their reasons, you know. Long and short of it, they want a job done. That's all it comes down to at the end of the day.

"So what do you want me to do?" I says to the geezer.

"What do you mean?" he says.

"Well, you know, it's all about degrees, ain't it, mate."

He nods, like he understands what I'm getting at.

"I got a price list here, if you wanna gander."

I get me "menu", as I like to call it, out me other pocket. It's a bit screwed up and the writing's a bit smudged where I've had me hand in me pocket, but it'll do.

I hand it over to him. It's me basic list, but I can get as creative as they want, for the right money, if you know what I mean.

He puts down the contract what he's been holdin and has a close look at me list. Up and down. Got a face on him like a kid in a sweet shop.

"What's this?" he says, showin me the list, his face all screwed up. "Andycappin?"

"Andycappin. You know, break their legs, feet, toes, whatever you want. Andycappin."

"Oh," he says. "Handicapping."

"That's right," I says. "Andycappin," I take me list off him and start reading it out. "Andycappin, neecappin, kidnappin."

I tell him the kidnappin thing ain't their kids and that. I don't do none of that shit. I got me morals. I'm dead serious when I say that to him. I ain't no perv or nothing.

"They're me Level Ones," I says. "Then it's up a level to your basic shootin and your stabbin."

I look dead in his eyes. Hold him there.

"So, what'll it be?" I says.

He's gone all quiet. He's thinkin hard on whether he really wants what he thinks he wants. They all go like this when I show em the list. I ain't got no truck with timewasters, see, so I lay it on pretty thick at this stage.

But, to his credit, he comes up smilin.

"I want him gone, Mr Splinters. Taken out. I'm prepared to pay whatever it takes."

That's what I like to hear.

I nudge the contract across the table towards him.

"Have a read of that, and sign at the bottom, please, mate."

He gives it a quick once-over and asks me for the pen.

"Don't you wanna read the small print, you know, acquaint yourself with all the particulars?" I says.

And he don't. He takes the pen and he signs and he shakes me hand and he's off.

Never even read the small print.

***

Briscoe tipped me off this Hammond geezer worked late at the office on a Thursday. In the industrial park on the outside of town. So here I am. Behind a stack of pallets. Waitin. All blacked up, I am. Not like Al Jolson or nothing, I mean, just me clothes. The only light's from the office, so when that goes out it'll be dark as fuck out here.

I got me shooter down the front of me trousers. Don't even know what it is, you know, the make or nothing. Never been interested. Got it second-hand off Twinkles MacKenzie from the bookies. I never give him nothing for it, but I slice him off a wedge whenever it comes into play, like. Got a silencer and everything. Never let me down yet, it hasn't.

The light in the office goes out. Pitch black. Door opens. Door shuts. Locks up. Here he comes. I wait till he's just passed before I make me move. Then I jump him. Before he knows it, he's got his face in the dust and me knee in his back. I pull the shooter out the front of me trousers. Touch it to where the back of his head meets his neck, pointin up a bit.

Phht. Phht. Job done.

I'm just gettin up when I see something move from behind another load of pallets to me left. A shadow in the dark. Comes straight for me, holdin out his hand. That Briscoe bloke. The fuckin idiot. Wanted to see his boss go down in a right load of bullets like off the Westerns. Right made up, he is.

"Mr Splinters, this is the happiest day of my life. You've no idea how—"

He's stopped. Cos I'm pointin the gun in his face. He's proper shittin it. To be expected, I suppose. Given his situation.

One. Two. Three.

"Did you not read the small print, Mr Briscoe?" I says, knowin he knows I know he never.

He shakes his head. Slow and scared. I move the shooter to the middle of his forehead.

I know this one off by heart. Thought it up meself when I was talkin the whole deal over with Ronnie one night in The Rabbits.

"In the event of the punter – that's you – turnin up to have a gander at the contracted party – that's me – doin the business, the contracted party – that's me again – is beholden unto himself to do the punter in by any means necessary. That's you again, I'm afraid, Mr Briscoe."

I stuck this one in the small print as a safeguard, if you like. Happens more often than you think. Matrimonial cases, normally. Want to see their cheatin other half get what's comin to em. But I can't have no witnesses, see. Gotta look after meself. No other cunt's goin to.

That's the thing with the small print. The thing this Briscoe bloke ain't counted on. All them words at the bottom that are too little to see, if you don't keep your eyes peeled, it's them little words what's gonna fuck you up. Cos they're too easy to overlook. That's what it is. We don't pay enough attention. We just wanna go on our merry little way, thinkin everything's gonna be all right. But it ain't.

It's like when you're born. You come bouncin out, eyes full of wonder. You've chose your mum and you've chose your dad. You've read the contract: go to school – get a job – get married – two kids, one boy, one girl. And you live happily ever after.

Piece of piss.

But you never bothered to read the small print. The dad that beat the crap out of you if you ever dared open your fuckin mouth. Small print. Gettin beat to shit every day at school for bein a fuckin moron and watchin your old man beatin the shit out of your mum and you not bein able to do a fuckin thing about it. Small print. The sound of her cryin and screamin through your bedroom wall breakin your heart as you lay awake at night. Small print.

Your nan, your dear old nan, the only person you loved in the whole world, peggin it on your thirteenth birthday. Small print. The tears you shed that day. Small print. The gettin laid off at the factory and never gettin a proper job ever again. Small print. The wife that left you for the plumber downstairs. Small print. The kids. The kids you never had. Fuckin small print.

One. Two. Three. Deep breath.

Phht. Phht.

Briscoe crumbles to the ground, blood spillin out a hole between his eyes.

Small print.

EAST OF SUEZ, WEST OF CHARING CROSS ROAD

John Lawton

UNHAPPINESS DOES NOT fall on a man from the sky like a branch struck by lightning, it is more like rising damp. It creeps up day by day, unfelt or ignored until it is too late. And if it's true that each unhappy family is unhappy in its own way, then the whole must be greater than the sum of the parts in Tolstoy's equation, because George Horsfield was unhappy in a way that could only be described as commonplace. He had married young and he had not married well. In 1948 he had answered the call to arms. At the age of eighteen he hadn't much choice. National Service – the Draft – the only occasion in its thousand-year history that England had had peacetime conscription. It was considered a necessary precaution in a world in which, to quote the US Secretary of State, England had lost an empire and not yet found a role. Not that England knew this – England's attitude was that we had crushed old Adolf and we'd be buggered if we'd now lose an empire – it would take more than little brown men in loincloths ... OK, so we lost India ... or Johnny Arab with a couple of petrol bombs or those Bolshy Jews in their damn kibbutzes – OK, so we'd cut and run in Palestine, but dammit man, one has to draw the line somewhere. And the line was east of Suez, somewhere east of Suez, anywhere east of Suez – a sort of moveable feast really.

George had expected to do his two years square-bashing or polishing coal. Instead, to both his surprise and pleasure, he was considered officer material by the War Office Selection Board. Not too short in the leg, no dropped aitches, a passing knowledge of the proper use of a knife and fork and no pretensions to be an intellectual. He was offered a short-service commission, rapidly trained at Eaton Hall in Cheshire – a beggarman's Sandhurst – and put back on the parade ground not as a private but as 2nd Lt H. G. Horsfield RAOC.

Why RAOC? Because the light of ambition had flickered in George's poorly exercised mind – he meant to turn this short-service commission into a career – and he had worked out that promotion was faster in the technical corps than in the infantry regiments and he had chosen the Royal Army Ordnance Corps, the "suppliers", whose most dangerous activity was that they supplied some of the chaps who took apart unexploded bombs, but, that allowed for, an outfit in which one was unlikely to get blown up, shot at or otherwise injured in anything resembling combat.

***

George's efforts notwithstanding, England did lose an empire, and the bits it didn't lose England gave away with bad grace. By the end of the next decade a British Prime Minister could stand up in front of an audience of white South Africans, until that moment regarded as our "kith and kin", and inform them that "a wind of change is blowing through the continent". He meant "the black man will take charge", but as ever with Mr Macmillan, it was too subtle a remark to be effective. Like his "you've never had it so good" it was much quoted and little understood.

George did not have it so good. In fact the fifties were little else but a disappointment to him. He seemed to be festering in the backwaters of England – Nottingham, Bicester – postings only relieved, if at all, by interludes in the backwater of Europe known as Belgium. The second pip on his shoulder grew so slowly it was tempting to force it under a bucket like rhubarb. It was 1953 before the pip bore fruit. Just in time for the coronation.

They gave him a few years to get used to his promotion – he boxed the compass of obscure English bases – then Lt Horsfield was delighted with the prospect of a posting to Libya, at least until he got there. He had thought of it in terms of the campaigns of the Second World War that he'd followed with newspaper clippings, a large cork board and drawing pins when he was a boy – Monty, the eccentric, lisping Englishman, versus Rommel, the old Desert Fox, the romantic, halfway-decent German. Benghazi, Tobruk, El Alamein – the first land victory of the war. The first real action since the Battle of Britain.

There was plenty of evidence of the war around Fort Kasala (known to the British as 595 Ordnance Depot, but built by the Italians during their brief, barmy empire in Africa). Mostly it was scrap metal. Bits of tanks and artillery half-buried in the sand. A sort of modern version of the legs of Ozymandias. And the fort itself looked as though it had taken a bit of a bashing in its time. But the action had long since settled down to the slow-motion favoured by camels and even more so by donkeys. It took less than a week for it to dawn on George that he had once more drawn the short straw. There was only one word for the Kingdom of Libya – boring. A realm of sand and camel shit.

He found he could get through a day's paperwork by about eleven in the morning. He found that his clerk-corporal could get through it by ten, and since it was received wisdom in Her Majesty's Forces that the devil made work for idle hands, he enquired politely of Corporal Ollerenshaw, "What do you do with the rest of the day?"

Ollerenshaw, not having bothered either to stand or salute on the arrival of an officer, was still behind his desk. He held up the book he had been reading – *Teach Yourself Italian*.

"*Come sta?*"

"Sorry, Corporal, I don't quite … "

"It means, 'How are you?' sir. In Italian. I'm studying for my O level exam in Italian."

"Really?"

"Yes, sir. I do a couple of exams a year. Helps to pass the time. I've got Maths, English, History, Physics, Biology, French, German and Russian – this year I'll take Italian and Art History."

"Good Lord, how long have you been here?"

"Four years sir. I think it was a curse from the bad fairy at my christening. I would either sleep for a century until kissed by a prince or get four years in fuckin' Libya. Scuse my French, sir."

Ollerenshaw rooted around in his desk drawer and took out two books – *Teach Yourself Russian* and a Russian-English, English-Russian Dictionary.

"Why don't you give it a whirl, sir, it's better than goin' bonkers or shaggin' camels."

George took the books and for a week or more they sat unopened on his desk.

It was hearing Ollerenshaw through the partition – "*Una bottiglia di vino rosso, per favore*" – "*Mia moglie vorrebbe gli spaghetti alle vongole*" – that finally prompted him to open them. The alphabet was a surprise, so odd it might as well have been Greek, and as he read on he realized it was Greek and he learnt the story of how two Orthodox priests from Greece had created the world's first artificial alphabet for a previously illiterate culture by adapting their own to the needs of the Russian language. And from that moment George was hooked.

Two years later, and the end of George's tour of duty in sight, he had passed his O level and A level Russian and was passing fluent – passing only in that he had just Ollerenshaw to converse with in Russian and might, should he meet a real Russki for a bit of a chat, be found to be unequivocally fluent.

Most afternoons the two of them would sit in George's office in sanctioned idleness talking Russian, addressing each other as "comrade" and drinking strong black tea to get into the spirit of things Russian.

"Tell me, *tovarich*," Ollerenshaw said. "Why have you just stuck with Russian? While you've been teaching yourself Russian I've passed Italian, Art History, Swedish and Technical Drawing."

George had a ready answer for this.

"Libya suits you. You're happy doing nothing at the bumhole of nowhere. Nobody to pester you but me – a weekly wage and all found – petrol you can flog to the wogs – you're in lazy buggers' heaven. You've got skiving down to a fine art. And I wish you well of it. But I want more. I don't want to be a lieutenant all my life and I certainly don't want to be pushing around dockets for pith helmets, army boots and jerry cans for much longer. Russian is what will get me out of it."

"How d'you reckon that?"

"I've applied for a transfer to Military Intelligence."

"Fuck me! You mean MI5 and all them spooks an' that?"

"They need Russian speakers. Russian is my ticket."

***

MI5 did not want George. His next home posting, still a lowly First Lieutenant at the age of twenty-nine, was to Command Ordnance Depot Upton Bassett on the coast of Lincolnshire – flat, sandy, cold and miserable. The only possible connection with things Russian was that the wind which blew bitterly off the North Sea all year round probably started off somewhere in the Urals.

He hated it.

The saving grace was that a decent-but-dull old bloke – Major Denis Cockburn, a veteran of the Second World War, with a good track record in bomb disposal – took him up.

"We can always use a fourth at bridge."

George came from a family that thought three card brag was the height of sophistication but readily turned his hand to the pseudo-intellectual pastime of the upper classes.

He partnered the Major's wife, Sylvia – the Major usually partnered Sylvia's unmarried sister, Grace.

George, far from being the most perceptive of men, at least deduced that a slow process of match-making had been begun. He didn't want this. Grace was at least ten years older than him and far and away the less attractive of the two sisters. The Major had got the pick of the bunch, but that wasn't saying much.

George pretended to be blind to hints and deaf to suggestions. Evenings with the Cockburns were just about the only damn thing that stopped him from leaving all his clothes on a beach and disappearing into the North Sea for ever. He'd hang on to them. He'd ignore anything that changed the status quo.

Alas, he could not ignore death.

When the Major died of a sudden and unexpected heart attack in September 1959, seemingly devoid of any family but Sylvia and Grace, it fell to George to have the grieving widow on his arm at the funeral.

"You were his best friend," Sylvia told him.

No, thought George, I was his only friend and that's not the same thing at all.

A string of unwilling subalterns were dragooned into replacing Denis at the bridge table. George continued to do his bit. After all it was scarcely any hardship, he was fond of Sylvia in his way, and it could not be long before red tape broke up bridge nights for ever when the Army asked for the house back and shuffled her off somewhere with a pension.

But the break-up came in the most unanticipated way. He'd seen off Grace with a practised display of indifference, but it had not occurred to him that he might need to see off Sylvia too.

On 29 February 1960, she sat him down on the flowery sofa in the boxy sitting room of her standard army house, told him how grateful she had been for his care and company since the death of her husband, and George, not seeing where this was leading, said that he had grown fond of her and was happy to do anything for her.

It was then that she proposed to him.

She was, he thought, about forty-five or -six, although she looked older, and whilst a bit broad in the beam was not unattractive.

This had little to do with his acceptance. It was not her body that tipped the balance, it was her character. Sylvia could be a bit of a dragon when she wanted, and George was simply too scared to say no. He could have said something about haste or mourning or with real wit have quoted Hamlet, saying that the "funeral baked meats did coldly furnish forth the marriage table". But he didn't.

"I'm not a young thing any more," she said. "It need not be a marriage of passion. There's much to be said for companionship."

George was not well acquainted with passion. There'd been the odd dusky prostitute out in Libya, a one-night fling with a NAAFI woman in Aldershot ... but little else. He had not given up on passion because he did not consider that he had yet begun with it.

They were married as soon as the banns had been read, and he walked out of church under a tunnel of swords in his blue dress uniform, the Madame Bovary of Upton Bassett, down a path that led to twin beds, Ovaltine and hairnets worn overnight. He had not given up on passion, but it was beginning to look as though passion had given up on him.

* * *

Six weeks later, desperation led him to act irrationally. Against all better judgement he asked once more to be transferred to Intelligence and was gobsmacked to find himself summoned to an interview at the War Office in London. London ... Whitehall ... the hub of the universe.

Simply stepping out of a cab so close to the Cenotaph – England's memorial to her dead, at least her own, white dead, of countless Imperial ventures – gave him a thrill. It was all he could do not to salute.

Down all the corridors and in the right door to face a Lt Colonel, then he saluted. But, he could not fail to notice, he was saluting not some secret agent in civilian dress, not Bulldog Drummond or James Bond, but another Ordnance officer just like himself.

"You've been hiding your light under a bushel, haven't you?" Lt Colonel Breen said when they'd zipped through the introductions.

"I have?"

Breen flourished a sheet of smudgy-carbonned typed paper.

"Your old CO in Tripoli tells me you did a first-class job running the mess. And I think you're just the chap we need here."

Silence being the better part of discretion and discretion being the better part of an old cliché, George said nothing and let Breen amble to his point.

"A good man is hard to find."

Well – he knew that, he just wasn't wholly certain he'd ever qualified as a "good man". It went with "first-class mind" (said of eggheads) or "very able" (said of politicians) and was the vocabulary of a world he moved in without ever touching.

"And we need a good man right here."

Oh Christ – they weren't making him mess officer? Not again!

"Er ... actually sir, I was under the impression that I was being interviewed for a post in Intelligence."

"Eh? What?"

"I have fluent Russian sir, and I ... "

"Well, you won't be needing it here ... ha ... ha ... ha!"

"Mess Officer?"

Breen seemed momentarily baffled.

"Mess Officer? Mess Officer? Oh, I get it. Yes, I suppose you will be in a way, it's just that the mess you'll be supplying will be the entire British Army 'East of Suez'. And you'll get your third pip. Congratulations, Captain."

Intelligence was not mentioned again except as an abstract quality that went along with "good man" and "first-class mind".

＊

Sylvia would not hear of living in Hendon or Finchley. The army had houses in north London, but she would not even look. So they moved to West Byfleet in Surrey, on to an hermetically sealed army estate of identical houses, and as far as George could see, identical wives, attending identical coffee mornings.

"Even the bloody furniture's identical!"

"It's what one knows," she said. "And it's a fair and decent world without envy. After all the thing about the forces is that everyone knows what everyone else earns. Goes with the rank, you can look it up in an almanac if you want. It takes the bitterness out of life."

George thought of all those endless pink gins he and Ollerenshaw had knocked back out in Libya, and how what had made them palatable was the bitters.

George hung up his uniform, went into plain clothes, War Office Staff Captain (Ord) General Stores, let his hair grow a little longer and became a commuter – the 7.57 a.m. to Waterloo, and the 5.27 p.m. back again. It was far from Russia.

Many of his colleagues played poker on the train, many more did crosswords and a few read. George read; he got through most of Dostoevsky in the original, the books disguised with the dust jacket from a Harold Robbins or an Irwin Shaw, and when he wasn't reading stared out of the window at the suburbs of South London – Streatham, Tooting, Wimbledon – and posh "villages" of Surrey – Surbiton, Esher, Weybridge – and imagined them all blown to buggery.

The only break in the routine was getting rat-arsed at the office party a few days before Christmas 1962, falling asleep on the train and being woken by a cleaner to find himself in a railway siding in Guildford at dawn the next morning.

It didn't feel foolish – it felt raffish, almost daring, a touch of Errol Flynn debauchery, but as 1963 dawned England was becoming a much more raffish and daring place – and Errol Flynn would soon come to seem like the role model for an entire nation.

***

It was all down to one person really – a nineteen-year-old named Christine Keeler. Miss Keeler had had an affair with George's boss, the top man, the Minister of War, the Rt Hon. John (Umpteenth Baron) Profumo (of Italy) MP (Stratford-on-Avon, Con.), OBE. Miss Keeler had simultaneously had an affair with Yevgeni Ivanov, an "attaché of the Soviet Embassy" (newspeak for spy) – and the ensuing scandal had rocked Britain, come close to toppling the government, led to a trumped-up prosecution (for pimping) of a society doctor, his subsequent suicide and the resignation of the aforementioned John Profumo.

At the War Office, there were two notable reactions. Alarm that the class divide had been dropped long enough to allow a toff like Profumo to take up with a girl of neither breeding nor education, whose parents lived in a converted wooden railway carriage, that a great party (Conservative) could be brought down by a woman of easy virtue (Keeler) – and paranoia that the Russians could get that close.

For a while Christine Keeler was regarded as the most dangerous woman in England. George adored her. If he thought he'd get away with it he'd have pinned her picture to his office wall.

It was possible that his lust for a pin-up girl he had never met was what led him into folly.

* * *

The dust had scarcely settled on the Profumo Affair. Lord Denning had published his report entitled unambiguously "Lord Denning's Report" and found himself an unwitting bestseller when it sold 4,000 copies in the first hour and the queues outside Her Majesty's Stationery Office in Kingsway stretched around the block and into Drury Lane, and the country had a new Prime Minister in the cadaverous shape of Sir Alec Douglas-Home, who had resigned an earldom for the chance to live at No. 10.

George coveted a copy of the Denning Report but it was understood to be very bad form for a serving officer, let alone one at the Ministry that had been if not at the heart of the scandal then most certainly close to the liver and kidneys, to be seen in the queue.

His friend Ted – Captain Edward Ffyffe-Robertson RAOC – got him a copy and George refrained from asking how. It was better than any novel – a marvellous tale of pot-smoking West Indians, masked men, naked orgies, beautiful, available women and high society. He read it and reread it and, since he and Sylvia had now taken not only separate beds but also separate rooms, slept with it under his pillow.

About six months later Ted was propping up the wall in George's office, having nothing better to do than jingle the coins in his pocket or play pocket billiards whilst making the smallest of small talk.

Elsie the tea lady parked her trolley by the open door.

"You're early," Ted said.

"Ain't even started on teas yet. They got me 'anding out the post while old Albert's orf sick. What a diabolical bleedin' liberty. Ain't they never 'eard of demarcation? Lucky I don't have the union on 'em."

Then she slung a single large brown envelope on to George's desk.

"I see you got yer promotion then, Mr 'Orsefiddle. All right for some."

She pushed her trolley on. George looked at the envelope.

"Lt Colonel H. G. Horsfield."

"It's got to be a mistake, surely?"

Ted peered over.

"It is, old man. Hugh Horsfield. Half-colonel in Artillery. He's on the fourth floor. Daft old Elsie's given you his post."

"There's another Horsfield?"

"Yep. Been here about six weeks. Surprised you haven't met him. He's certainly made his presence felt."

With hindsight George ought to have asked what Ted's last remark meant.

Instead, later the same day, he went in search of Lt Col. Horsfield, out of nothing more than curiosity and a sense of fellow-feeling.

He tapped on the open door. A big bloke with salt-and-pepper hair and a spiky little moustache looked up from his desk.

George beamed at him.

"Lt Col. H. G. Horsfield? I'm Captain H. G. Horsfield."

His alter ego got up and walked across to the door and with a single utterance of "Fascinating" swung it to in George's face.

Later, Ted said. "I did try to warn you, old man. He's got a fierce reputation."

"As what?"

"He's the sort of bloke who gets described as not suffering fools gladly."

"Are you saying I'm a fool?"

"Oh, the things only your best friend will tell. Like using the right brand of bath soap. No, I'm not saying that."

"Then what are you saying?"

"I'm saying that to a high flyer like Hugh Horsfield, blokes like us who keep our boys in pots and pans and socks and blankets are merely the also-rans of the British Army. He deals with the big stuff. He's artillery after all."

"Big stuff? What big stuff?"

"Well, we're none of us supposed to say, are we. But here's a hint. Think back to August 1945 and those mushroom-shaped clouds over Japan."

"Oh. I see. Bloody hell!"

"Bloody hell indeed."

"Anything else?"

"I do hear that he's more than a bit of a ladies' man. In the first month alone he's supposed to have shagged half the women on the fourth floor. And you know that blonde in the typing pool we all nicknamed the Jayne Mansfield of Muswell Hill?"

"Not her too? I thought she didn't look at anything below a full colonel?"

"Well, if the grapevine has it aright she dropped her knickers to half-mast for this half-colonel."

What a bastard.

George hated his namesake.

George envied his namesake.

* * *

It was someone's birthday. Some bloke on the floor below, whom he didn't know particularly well but Ted did. A whole crowd of them, serving soldiers in civvies, literally and metaphorically letting their hair down, followed up cake and coffee in the office with a mob-handed invasion of a nightclub in Greek Street, Soho. Soho – a ten-minute walk from the War Office, the nearest thing London had to a red-light district, occupying a maze of narrow little streets east of the elegant Regent Street, south of the increasingly vulgar Oxford Street, north of the bright lights of Shaftesbury Avenue and west of the bookshops of the Charing Cross Road. It was home to the Marquee music club, the Flamingo, also a music club, the private boozing club known as the Colony Room, the scurrilous magazine *Private Eye*, the Gay Hussar restaurant, the Coach and

Horses pub (and too many other pubs ever to mention), a host of odd little shops where a nod and a wink might get you into the back room for purchase of a faintly pornographic film, a plethora of strip clubs and the occasional and more-than-occasional prostitute.

He'd be late home. So what? They'd all be late home.

They moved rapidly on to Frith Street and street by street and club by club worked their way across towards Wardour Street. The intention, George was sure, was to end up in a strip joint. He hoped to slip away before they reached The Silver Tit or The Golden Arse and the embarrassing farce of watching a woman wearing only a G-string and pasties jiggle all that would jiggle in front of a bunch of pissed and paunchy middle-aged men who confused titillation with satisfaction.

He'd been aware of Lt Col. Horsfield's presence from the first – the upper-class bray of a bar-room bore could cut through any amount of noise. He knew H. G.'s type. Minor public school, too idle for university, but snapped up by Sandhurst because he cut a decent figure on the parade ground. Indeed, he rather thought the only reason the Army had picked him for Eaton Hall was that he too looked the officer type at a handsome five foot eleven inches.

As they reached Dean Street George stepped off the pavement meaning to head south and catch a bus to Waterloo, but Ted had him by one arm.

"Not so fast, old son. The night is yet young."

"If it's all the same to you, Ted, I'd just as soon go home. I can't abide strippers, and H. G. is really beginning to get on my tits if not on theirs."

"Nonsense, you're one of us. And we won't be going to a titty bar for at least an hour. Come and have a drink with your mates and ignore H. G. He'll be off as soon as the first prozzie flashes a bit of cleavage at him."

"He doesn't?"

"He does. Sooner or later everybody does. Haven't you?"

"Well ... yes ... out in Benghazi ... before I was married ... but not ... "

"It's OK, old son. Not compulsory. I'll just be having a couple of jars myself then I'll be home to Mill Hill and the missis."

It was a miserable half-hour. He retreated to a booth on his own, nursing a pink gin he didn't much want. He'd no idea how long she'd been sitting there. He just looked up from pink reflections and there she was. Petite, dark, twenty-ish and looking uncannily like the dangerous woman of his dreams; the almost pencil-thin eyebrows, the swept-back chestnut hair, the almond eyes, the pout of slightly prominent front teeth and the cheekbones from heaven or Hollywood.

"Buy a girl a drink?"

This was what hostesses did. Plonked themselves down, got you to buy them a drink and then ordered house "champagne" at a price that dwarfed the national debt. George wasn't falling for that.

"Have mine," he said, pushing the pink gin across the table. "I haven't touched it."

"Thanks, love."

He realized at once that she wasn't a hostess. No hostess would have taken the drink.

"You're not working here, are you?"

"Nah. But ... "

"But what?"

"But I am ... working."

The penny dropped, clunking down inside him, rattling around in the rusty pinball machine of the soul.

"And you think I ... "

"You look as though you could do with something. I could ... make you happy ... just for a while I could make you happy."

George heard a voice very like his own say, "How much?"

"Not up front, love. That's just vulgar."

"I haven't got a lot of cash on me."

"'S OK. I take cheques."

* * *

She had a room three flights up in Bridle Lane. Clothed she was gorgeous, naked she was irresistible. If George died on the train home he would die happy.

She had one hand on his balls and was kissing him in one ear – he was priapic as Punch. He was on the edge, seconds away from entry, sheathed in a frenchie, when the door burst open, his head turned sharply and a flash bulb went off in his eyes.

When the stars cleared he found himself facing a big bloke in a dark suit, clutching a Polaroid camera and smiling smugly at him.

"Get dressed, Mr Horsfield. Meet me in the Stork Café in Berwick Street. You're not there in fifteen minutes this goes to your wife."

The square cardboard plate shot from the base of the camera and took form before his eyes.

He fell back on the pillow and groaned. He'd know a Russian accent anywhere. He'd been set up – trussed up like a turkey.

"Oh … shit."

"Sorry, love. But, y'know. It's a job. Gotta make a livin' somehow."

George's wits were gathering slowly cohering into a fuzzy knot of meaning.

"You mean they pay you to … frame blokes like me?"

"'Fraid so. Prozzyin' ain't what it used to be."

The knot pulled tight.

"You take money for this?"

"O' course. I'm no Commie. It's a job. I get paid. Up front."

He had a memory somewhere of her telling him that was vulgar, but he sidestepped it.

"Paid to get you out of yer trousers, into bed, do what I do till Boris gets here."

"What you do?"

"You know, love … the other."

"You mean sex?"

"If it gets that far. He was a bit early tonight."

A light shone in George's mind. The knot slackened off and the life began to crawl back into his startled groin.

"You've been paid to … fuck me?"

"Language, love. But yeah."

"Would you mind awfully if we ... er ... finished the job?"

She thought for a moment.

"Why not? Least I can do. Besides, I like you. And old Boris is hardly going to bugger off after fifteen minutes. He needs you. He'll wait till dawn if he has to."

* * *

Walking to Berwick Street, along the Whore's Paradise of Meard Street, apprehension mingled with bliss. It was like that moment in Tobruk when Johnny Arab had stuck a pipe of super-strength hashish in front of him and he had looked askance at it but inhaled all the same. The headiness never quite offset and overwhelmed the sheer oddness of the situation.

In the caff a few late night "beatniks" (scruffbags, Sylvia would have called them) spun out cups of frothy coffee as long as they could and put the world to rights – while Boris, if that really was his name, sat alone at a table next to the lavatory door.

George was at least half an hour late. Boris glanced at his watch but said nothing about it. Silently he slid the finished Polaroid – congealed as George thought of it – across the table, his finger never quite letting go of it.

"This type of camera only takes these shots. No negative. Hard to copy and I won't even try unless you make me. Do what we ask, Mr Horsfield, and you will not find us unreasonable people. Give us what we want and when we have it, you can have this. Frame it, burn it, I don't care – but if we get what we want you can be assured this will be the only copy and your wife need never know."

George didn't even look at the photo. It might ruin a precious memory.

"What is it you want?"

Boris all but whispered, "Everything you're sending East of Suez."

"I see," said George, utterly baffled by this.

"Be here one week tonight. Nine o' clock. You bring evidence of something you've shipped out – show willing as you people say

– and we'll brief you on what to look for next. In fact we'll give you a shopping list."

Boris stood up. A bigger bugger in a black suit came over and stood next to him. George hadn't even noticed this one was in the room.

"Well?" he said in Russian.

"A pushover," Boris replied.

The other man picked up the photo, glimmed it and said, "When did he shave off the moustache?"

"Who cares?" Boris replied.

Then he switched to English, said, "Next week" to George and they left.

George sat there. He'd learnt two things. They didn't know he spoke Russian, and they had the wrong Horsfield. George felt like laughing. It really was very funny – but it didn't let him off the hook ... whatever they called him, Henry George Horsfield RAOC or Hugh George Horsfield RA ... they had still had a photograph of him in bed with a whore. It might end up in the hands of the right wife or the wrong wife, but he had no doubts it would all end up on a desk at the War Office if he screwed up now.

***

He got bugger all work done the next day. He had sneaked home very late, left a note for Sylvia saying he would be out early, caught the 7.01 train and got into the office very early. He could not face her across the breakfast table. He couldn't face anyone. He closed his office door, but after ten minutes decided that that was a dead giveaway and opened it again. He hoped Ted did not want to chat. He hoped Daft Elsie had no gossip as she brought round the tea.

At 5.30 in the evening he took his briefcase and sought out a caff in Soho. He sat in Old Compton Street staring into his deflating frothy coffee much as he had stared into his pink gin the night before. Oddly, most oddly, the same thing happened. He looked up from his cup and there she was. Right opposite him. A vision of beauty and betrayal.

"I was just passin'. Honest. And I saw you sittin' in the window."

"You're wasting your time. I haven't got the money and after last night ... "

"I'm not on the pull. It's six o' clock and broad bleedin' daylight. I ... I ... I thought you looked lonely."

"I'm always lonely," he replied, surprised at his own honesty. "But what you see now is misery of your own making."

"You'll be fine. Just give old Boris what he wants."

"Has it occurred to you that that might be treason?"

"Nah ... it's not as if you're John Profumo or I'm Christine Keeler. We're small fry, we are."

Oh God, if only she knew.

"I can't give him what he wants. He wants secrets."

"Don't you know any?"

"Of course I do ... everything's a sodding secret. But ... but ... I'm RAOC. Do you know what that stands for?"

"Nah. Rags And Old Clothes?"

"Close. Our nickname is The Rag And Oil Company. Royal Army Ordnance Corps. I keep the British Army in saucepans and socks!"

"Ah."

"You begin to see? Boris will want secrets about weapons."

"O' course he will. How long have you got?"

"I really ought to be on a train by nine."

"Well ... you come home with me. We'll have a bit of a think."

"I'm not sure I could face that room again."

"You silly bugger. I don't work from home, do I? Nah. I got a place in Henrietta Street. Let's nip along and put the kettle on. It's cosy. Really it is. Ever so."

How Sylvia would have despised the "ever so". It would be "common".

Over tea and ginger biscuits she heard him out – the confusion of two Horsfields and how he really had nothing that Boris would ever want.

She said, "You gotta laugh, ain't yer?"

And they did.

She thought while they fucked – he could see in her eyes that she wasn't quite with him, but he didn't much mind.

Afterwards, she said, "You gotta do what I have to do."

"What's that?"

"Fake it."

George took this on board with a certain solemnity and doubt. She shook him by the arm vigorously.

"Leave it out, Captain. I'd never fake one with you."

***

The best part of a week passed. He was due to meet Boris that evening and sat at his desk in the day trying to do what the nameless whore had suggested. Fake it.

He had in front of him a "Shipping Docket" for frying pans.

"FP1 Titanium Range 12 inch. Maximum heat dispersal. 116 units."

It was typical army-speak that the docket didn't actually say they were frying pans. The docket was an FP1 and that was only used for frying pans, so the bloke on the receiving end in Singapore would just look at the code and know what was in the crate. There was a certain logic to it. Fewer things got stolen this way. He'd once shipped thirty-two kettles to Cyprus and somehow the word "kettle" had ended up on the docket and only ten ever arrived at their destination.

He could see possibilities in this. All he needed was a jar of that new-fangled American stuff, "Liquid Paper", which he bought out of his own money from an import shop in the Charing Cross Road, a bit of jiggery pokery and access to the equally new-fangled, equally American, Xerox machine. Uncle Sam had finally given the world something useful. It almost made up for popcorn and Rock'n' Roll.

Caution stepped in. He practised first on an inter-office memo. Just as well, he made a hash of it. "Staff Canteen Menu, Changes to : Sub-section Potato, Mashed : WD414" would never be the same again. No matter, if one of these yards of bumf dropped on to his desk in the course of a day, then so did a dozen more. He'd even seen one headed "War Office Gravy, Lumps in."

He found the best technique was to thin the Liquid Paper as far as it would go, and then treat it like ink. Fortunately, the empire had only just died – or committed hara-kiri – and he had in his desk drawer two or three dip pens, with nibs, and a dry, clean, cut-glass inkwell that might have graced the desk of the Ass't Commissioner Eastern Nigeria in 1910.

And – practice does make perfect. And a copy of a copy of a copy – three passes on the Xerox – makes the perfect into a pleasing blur.

Titanium was fairly easily altered to Plutonium.

A full stop was added before Range.

12 inch became 120 miles.

He stared, willing something to come to him about maximum heat dispersal and when nothing did concluded it was fine as it was. And 116 units sounded spot on. A good healthy number, divisible by nothing.

He looked over his handywork. It would do. It would ... pass muster, that was the phrase. And it was pleasingly ambiguous.

"FP1 Plutonium. Range 120 miles. Maximum heat dispersal. 116 units."

But what if Boris asked what they were?

* * *

Boris did, but by then George was ready for him.

"FP means Field Personnel. And I'm sure you know what Plutonium is."

"You cheeky bugger. You think I'm just some dumb Russki? The point is to what aspect of Field Personnel does this document refer?"

George looked him in the eye, said, "Just put it all together. Add up the parts and get to the sum."

Boris looked down at the paper and then up at George.

Whatever penny dropped George would roll with it.

"My God. I don't believe it. You bastards are upping the ante on us. You're putting tactical nuclear weapons into Singapore!"

"Well," George replied in all honesty. "You said it, I didn't."

"And they shipped in January. My God, they're already there!"

George was emboldened.

"And why not – things are hotting up in Viet Nam. Or did you think that after Cuba we'd just roll over and die?"

And then he kicked himself. Was Viet Nam, either bit of it, within 120 miles of Singapore? He hadn't a clue.

Mouth, big, shut.

But Boris didn't seem to know either.

He pushed the Polaroid across the table to him. This time he took his hand off it.

"You will understand. We keep our word."

George doubted this.

And then Boris reached into his pocket, pulled out a white envelope and pushed that to George.

"And I am to give you this."

"What is it?"

"Five hundred pounds. I believe you call it a monkey."

Good God – here he was betraying his country's canteen secrets and the bastards were actually going to pay him for it.

He took it round to Henrietta Street.

He didn't mention it until after they'd made love.

And she said, "Bloody hell. That's more'n I make in a month," and George said, "It's more than I make in three months."

They agreed. They'd stash it in the bottom of her wardrobe and think what they might do with it some other time.

As he was leaving for Waterloo, George said, "Do you realize, I don't know your name?"

"You din ask. And it's Donna."

"Is that your real name?"

"Nah. 'S my workin' name. Goes with my surname. Needham. It's like a joke. Donna Needham. Gettit?"

"Yes. I get it. You're referring to men."

"Yeah, but you can call me Janet if you like. That's me real name."

"I think I prefer Donna."

***

It became part of the summer. Part of the summer's new routine.

He would ring home about once a week and tell Sylvia he would be working late.

"The DDT to the DFC's in town. The brass want me in a meeting. Sorry, old thing."

Considering that she had been married to a serving army officer for twenty years before she met George, Sylvia had never bothered to learn any army jargon. She expected men to talk bollocks and she paid it no mind. She accepted it and dismissed it simultaneously.

George would then keep an appointment with Boris in the Berwick Street caff, sell his country up the Swanee, and then go round to the flat in Henrietta Street.

Even as his conscience atrophied, or quite possibly because it atrophied, love blossomed. He was absolutely potty about Donna and told her so every time he saw her.

Boris didn't use the Berwick Street caff every time, and it suited both to meet at Kempton Park racecourse on the occasional Saturday, particularly if Sylvia had gone to a whist drive or taken herself off shopping in Kingston-upon-Thames. Five bob each way on the favourite was George's limit. Boris played long shots and made more than he lost. It was, George thought, a fair reflection on both their characters and their trades.

As the weeks passed, George doctored more dockets, pocketed more cash – although he never again collected £500 in one go (Boris explained that this had been merely to get his attention), every meeting resulted in his treachery being rewarded with £100 or £200.

Some deceptions required a bit of thought.

For example he found himself staring at a docket for saucepans he had shipped to Hong Kong from the makers in Lancashire.

SP3 PRESTIGE Copper-topped 6 inch. 250 units.

Prestige was probably the best-known maker of saucepans in the country. He couldn't leave the word intact – it was just possible that even old Boris had heard of them.

But once contemplated, his liar's muse came to his rescue and it was easily altered to read ...

FP3 P F T Cobalt-tipped 6 inch. 250 units.

He'd no idea what this might mean, but, once in the caff with two cups of frothy coffee in front of them, as ever, Boris filled in most of the blanks.

Yes. FP meant what it had always meant. He struggled a little with P F T, and George waited patiently as Boris steered himself in the direction of Personal Field Tactical, and as he put that together with cobalt-tipped his great Russian self-righteousness surfaced with a bang.

"You really are a bunch of bastards aren't you? You're fitting hand-held rocket launchers with missiles coated with spent uranium!"

Oh, was that it? George knew cobalt had something to do with radioactivity, but quite what was beyond him.

"Armour-piercing cobalt-tipped shells? You bastards. You utter fockin' bastards. Queensberry Rules, my Bolshevik arse!"

Ah … armour-piercing, that was what they were for. George hadn't a clue and would have guessed blindly had Boris asked.

"Bastards!"

After which outburst Boris slipped him a hundred quid and called it a long un.

Midsummer, George got lucky. He was running out of ideas, and somebody mentioned that the Army had American-built ground-to-air missiles deployed with NATO forces in Europe. A truck-mounted launcher that went by the code-name of *Honest John*. It wasn't exactly a secret and there was every chance Boris knew what *Honest John* was.

It rang a bell in the great canteen of the mind. A while back, he was almost certain, he had shipped fifty large stewpots out to Aden, bought from a firm in Waterford called *Honett Iron*. It was the shortest alteration he ever made, and lit the shortest fuse in Boris.

"Bastards!" he said yet again.

And then he paused and in thinking came close to unravelling George's skein of lies. George had thought to impress Boris with a fake docket for a missile that really existed, and it was about to blow up in his face.

"Just a minute. I know this thing, it only has a range of fifteen miles. Who can you nuke from Aden? It doesn't make sense. Every other country is more than fifteen miles away. There's nothing but fockin dyesert within fifteen miles of Aden."

George was stuck. To say anything would be wrong, but this was one gap Boris's fertile imagination didn't seem willing to plug.

"Er ... that depends," said George.

"On what?"

"Er ... on ... on what you think is going on in the er ... 'fockin dyesert'."

Boris stared at him.

A silence screaming to be filled.

And Boris wasn't going to fill it.

George risked all.

"After all, I mean ... you either have spyplanes or you don't."

It was enigmatic.

George had no idea whether the Russians had spyplanes. The Americans did. One had been shot down over the Soviet Union in 1960, resulting in egg-on-face as the Russians paraded the unfortunate pilot alive before the world's press. So much for the cyanide capsule.

It was enigmatic. Enigmatic to the point of meaninglessness but it did the trick. It turned Boris's enquiries inward. Meanwhile George had scared himself shitless. He'd got cocky and he'd nearly paid the price.

* * *

He lobbed another envelope of money into the bottom of Donna's wardrobe. He hadn't counted it and neither of them had spent any of it, but he reckoned they must have about £2,000 in there.

"I have to stop," he said. "Boris damn near caught me tonight."

* * *

Two days later, George opened his copy of the *Daily Telegraph* on the train to work and page one chilled him to the briefcase.

"Russian Spy Plane Shot Down Over Aden"

He had reached Waterloo and was crossing the Hungerford footbridge to the Victoria Embankment before he managed to reassure himself with the notion that because it had been shot down, the USSR still didn't know what was (not) going on in the "fockin dyesert".

He told Donna, the next time they met, the next time they made love. He lay back in the afterglow and felt anxiety awaken from its erotically induced slumber.

"You see," he said. "I had to tell Boris something. There's nothing going on in the 'fockin dyesert'. But the Russians launched a spyplane to find out. On Boris's say-so. On my say-so. I mean, for all I know the Viet Cong are deploying more troops along the DMZ, the Chinese might be massing their millions at the border with Hong Kong ... this is all getting ... out of hand."

Donna ran her fingers through his hair, brought her lips close to his ear, with that touch of moist breath that drove him wild.

"Y'know Georgie, you been luckier than you know."

"How so?"

"Supposin' there really had been something going on out in the 'fockin dyesert'?"

"Oh Christ."

"Don't bear thinkin' about, do it? But you're right. This is all gettin' outa hand. We need to do something."

"Such as?"

"Dunno. But let me think. I'm better at it than you are."

"Could you think quickly? Before I start World War III."

"Sssh, Georgie. Donna's thinkin'."

* * *

"It's like this," she said. "You want out, but the Russkis have enough on you to fit you up for treason, and then there's the Polaroid of you an' me in bed an' your wife to think about."

"I got the Polaroid back months ago."

"You did? Good. Now ... thing is, as I see it, they got you for selling them our secrets 'bout rockets an' 'at out East. Only you gave 'em saucepans and tea urns. So, what have they really got?"

"Me. They've got me, because saucepans and tea urns are just as secret as nukes. I'm still a traitor. I'll be the Klaus Fuchs of kitchenware."

"No. You're not. The other Horsfield is, 'cos that's who they think they're dealing with."

George could not see where this was headed.

"We gotta do two things, see off old Boris and put the other Horsfield in the frame. Give 'em the Horsfield they wanted in the first place."

"Oh God."

"No ... listen ... Boris thinks he's been dealing with Lt Col. Horsfield. What we gotta do is make the Colonel think he's dealing with Boris ... swap him for you and then blow the whistle."

"Or let the whistle blow," said George.

"How do you mean?"

"If I understand that cunning little mind of yours aright you mean to try and frame Horsfield."

"'S right."

"I know H. G. He's a total bastard, but he can't be scared or intimidated. We make any move against him, he catches even a whiff of Russian involvement, he'll blow the whistle himself."

"Y'know, that's even more than I hoped for. Let me try for the full house then. Is he what you might call a ladies' man?"

"How do you mean?"

"Well, no offence, Georgie, but you was easy to pull. If I was to try and pull H. G., what would he do?"

"Oh, I see. Well if office gossip is to be believed he'd paint his arse blue and shag you under a lamp-post in Soho Square."

"Bingo," said Donna. "Bingo bloody bingo!"

***

They dipped into the wardrobe money for the first time.

"I can't do this myself, and I can't use the room in Bridle Lane. I'll pay a mate to do H. G., and I know a house in Marshall Street that's going under the wrecking ball any day now. It'll be perfect. I get a room kitted out so it looks like a regular pad and then we just abandon it. The grey area is knowing when we might get to H. G."

"It's Ted's birthday next week. Bound to be a pub and club crawl. I could even predict that at some point we'll all be in the same club you found me in."

"What would be H. G.'s type?"

"Now you mention it ... not you. He goes for blondes, blondes with big ... "

"Tits?"

"Quite."

"OK, that narrows it down. I'll have to ask Judy. She'll want a ton for the job and another for the risk, but she'll do it."

* * *

Ted's birthday bash coincided with George's Boris night at the Berwick Street caff. Something was going right. God knows, they might even get away with this. "This" – he wasn't at all sure what "this" was. He knew his own part in this, but the initiative had now passed to Donna. She had planned the night's activity like a film script.

He slipped away early from Ted's party. Ted was three sheets to the wind anyway. H. G. was in full flight with a string of smutty stories and the only risk was that he might get off with some woman before Judy pulled him. As he was leaving, a tall, busty blonde, another Jayne Mansfield or Diana Dors, cantilevered by state-of-the-art bra mechanics into a pink lambswool sweater that showed plenty of cleavage and looked as solid as Everest, came into the club. She winked at George, and carried on down the stairs without a word.

George went round to Bridle Lane.

It was a tale of two wigs.

Donna had a wig ready for him.

"You and Boris are about the same size. It's just a matter of hair colour. Besides, it's not as if H. G. will get a good look at you."

And a wig ready for herself. She was transformed into a pocket Marilyn Monroe.

He hated the waiting. They stood at the corner of Foubert's Place, looking down the length of Marshall Street. It was past nine when a staggering, three-quarters pissed H. G. appeared on the arm of a very steady Judy. They stopped under a lamp-post. He didn't paint his arse blue, but he groped her in public, his hand on her backside, his face half-buried in her cleavage.

George watched Judy gently reposition his hand at her waist and heard her say, "Not so fast, soldier, we're almost there."

"We are? Bloody good show."

George hated H. G.

George hated H. G. for being so predictable.

Donna whispered.

"Ten minutes at the most. Judy'll pull a curtain to, when he's got his kit off. Now, are you sure you know how to work it?"

"It's just a camera like any other, Donna."

"Georgie – we only got one chance."

"Yes. I know how to work it."

When the curtain moved, George tiptoed up the stairs, imagining Boris doing the same thing all those months ago as he prepared to spring the honeytrap.

At the bedroom door he could hear the baritone rumble of H. G.'s drunken sweet nothings.

"'S wonderful. 'S bloody amazing. Tits. Marvellous things. If I had tits ... bloody hell ... I'd play with them all day."

Then, kick, flash, bang, wallop ... and H. G. was sprawled where he had been and he was uttering Boris's lines in the best Russian accent he could muster.

"You have ten minutes, Colonel Horsfield. You fail to meet me in the Penguin Café in Kingly Street, this goes to your wife."

He was impressed by his own timing. The Polaroid shot out of the bottom of the camera just as he said "wife".

H. G. was staring at him glassy-eyed. Judy grabbed her clothes and ran past him hell-for-leather. Still, H. G. stared. Perhaps he was too drunk to understand what was happening.

"You have ten minutes, Colonel. Penguin Café, Kingly Street. *Das Vidanye.*"

He'd no idea why he'd thrown in the *"das vidanye"* – perhaps a desperate urge to sound more Russian than he had.

H. G. said, "I'll be there ... you Commie fucking bastard. I'll be there."

Much to George's alarm he got up from the bed, seemingly less drunk, bollock-naked, stiff cock swaying in its frenchie, and came towards him.

George fled. It was what Donna had told him to do.

Down in the street, George arrived just in time to see Judy pulling on her stilettoes and heading off towards Beak Street. Donna took the Polaroid from him, waved it in the air and looked for the image.

"Gottim," she said.

George looked at his watch. Didn't dare to raise his voice much above a whisper.

"I must hurry. I have to meet Boris."

"No. No, you don't. You leave Boris to me."

This wasn't part of the plan. This had never been mentioned.

"What?"

"Go back to the party."

"I don't ... "

"Find your mates. They must be in a club somewhere near. You know the pattern, booze, booze, strippers. Find 'em. Ditch the wig. Ditch the camera. Go back and make yourself seen."

She kissed him.

"And don't go down Berwick Street."

* * *

Donna stood awhile on the next corner, watched as H. G. emerged and saw him rumble off in the direction of Kingly Street. Then she went the other way, towards Berwick Street, and stood behind one of the market stalls that were scattered along the right-hand side.

She could see Boris. He was reading a newspaper, letting his coffee go cold and occasionally glancing at his watch. He was almost taking George's arrival for granted, but not quite.

She was reassured when he finally gave up and stood a moment on the pavement outside the caff, looking up at the stars and muttering something Russian. Really, he wasn't any taller than George, just a bit bigger in the chest and shoulders. What with the wig and flashbulb going off, all H. G. was likely to say was "some big bugger, sort of darkish, in a dark suit, didn't really get a good look, I'm afraid."

That was old Boris, a big, dark bugger in a dark suit.

Her only worry was that if Boris flagged a cab and there wasn't one close behind, she'd lose him. But it was a warm summer evening, and Boris had decided to walk. He set off westward, in the direction of the Soviet Embassy. Perhaps he needed to think? Was he going to shop George for one no-show or was he going to roll with it, string it and George out in the hope of keeping the stream of information flowing?

Boris crossed Regent Street into Mayfair, and headed south towards Piccadilly. He seemed to be in no hurry and paid no attention to cabs or buses. Indeed, he seemed to pay no attention to anything, as though he was deep in thought.

She matched her pace to his, trying to stay in shadow, but Boris never looked back. In Shepherd Market he turned into one of those tiny alleys that dot the northern side of Piccadilly and she quickened her step to get to the corner.

The light vanished. A hand grabbed her by the jacket and pulled her into the alley. The other hand pulled off her wig, and Boris's voice said, "Don't take me for a fockin fool. Horsfield doesn't show and then you appear in a silly wig, trailing after me like a third-rate gumshoe. What the fock are you playing at?"

It was better than she'd dared hope for. She'd been foxed all along to work out how to get him alone, this close, in a dark alley. And now he'd done it for her.

She pressed her gun to his heart and shot him dead.

Then she leant down, tucked the Polaroid into his inside pocket, put her wig back on, walked down to Piccadilly and caught a number 38 bus home.

* * *

The first George heard was from Daft Elsie, pushing her trolley round just after eleven the next morning.

"Can't get on the fourth floor. Buggers won't let me. Some sort of argy-bargy going on. I ask yer. Spooks and spies. Gotta be a load of old bollocks, ain't it?"

"Two sugars, please," said George.

"And I got these 'ere jam donuts special for that Colonel 'Orsepiddle. 'Ere love, you have one."

"So." He tried to sound casual. "It all revolves around the good colonel, does it?"

"Let's put it this way, love. 'E's doin' a lot of shoutin'. An' it's not as if he whispers at the best of times."

So – H. G. wasn't so much blowing the whistle as shouting the odds.

After lunch Ted dropped in, dropped the latest, not-yet-late-final-but-almost edition of the *London Evening Standard* on to his desk.

George pulled it towards him.

"Soviet Embassy Attaché Shot Dead in Mayfair."

George said nothing.

Ted said, "Could be an interesting few weeks. Russkis play hell. Possibly bump off one of ours. A few expulsions, followed by retaliatory expulsions ... God, I'd hate to be in Moscow right now."

"What makes you think we did it? I mean, do we shoot foreign agents in the street?"

"Not as a rule. But boldness was our friend. I gather from a mate at Scotland Yard that they're clueless. No one saw or heard a damn thing. Anyway ... change the subject ... what was up with you last night? Throwing up in the bogs for an hour. Not like you, old son."

"Change it back – does this have anything to do with the hooha going on on the fourth floor?"

"Well. Let me put it this way. Be a striking bloody coincidence if it didn't."

***

It became received wisdom in the office that the Russians had tried to set up H. G. and that he would have none of it. Less received, but much bandied, was the theory that rather than keep the meeting with the man attempting blackmail, H. G. had simply rang MI5 who had bumped off the unfortunate Russki on his way across Mayfair. That one Boris Alexandrovich Bulganov was found dead within a few yards of MI5 HQ in Curzon Street added to veracity, as did a rumour that he'd had a photograph of H. G. in bed with a prozzie in his pocket. Some wag pinned a notice to the canteen message board offering £10 for a copy but found no takers.

Ted was profound upon the matter, "Always knew he'd end up in trouble if he let his dick do the thinking for him."

It became, almost at once, a diplomatic incident. Nothing on the scale of Profumo or the U2 spyplane, but the Russians accused the British of assassinating Boris, whom they described as a "cultural attaché". The British accused the Russians of attempting to blackmail H. G. Horsfield, whose name never graced the newspapers – merely "unnamed high-ranking British officer" – and George could only conclude that neither one had put the dates together and worked out that they had been blackmailing *an* H. G. Horsfield for some time, but not *the* H. G. Horsfield. If they'd swapped information, George would have been sunk. But, of course, they'd never do that.

H. G.'s "reward" was to be made a full colonel and posted to the Bahamas. Anywhere out of the way. Why the Bahamas might need a tactical nuclear weapons expert was neither here nor there nor anywhere.

George never heard from the Russians again. He expected to. Every day for six months he expected to. But he didn't.

* * *

Six months on, Boris's death was eclipsed.

George arrived home in West Byfleet to find an ambulance and a crowd of neighbours outside his house.

Mrs Wallace, wife of Jack Wallace, lieutenant in REME – George thought her name might be Betty – came up oozing an alarming mixture of tears and sympathy.

"Oh, Captain Horsfield ... I don't know what to ... "

George pushed past her to the ambulancemen. A covered stretcher was already in the back of the ambulance and he knew the worst at once.

"How?" he asked simply.

"She took a tumble, sir. Top o' the stairs to the bottom. Broken neck. Never knew what hit her."

George spent an evening alone with a bottle of Scotch, ignoring the ringing phone. He hadn't loved Sylvia. He had never loved Sylvia. He had been fond of her. She was too young, a rotten age to go ... and then he realized he didn't actually know how old Sylvia was. He might find out only when they chipped it on her tombstone.

Grief was nothing, guilt was everything.

Decorum ruled.

He did not go to Henrietta Street for the best part of a month.

He wrote to Donna, much as he wrote to many of his friends, knowing that the done thing was the notice in *The Times*, but that few of his friends read *The Times* and that the *Daily Mail* didn't bother with a Deaths column.

When he did go to Henrietta Street, he cut through Covent Garden, fifty yards to the north and bought a bouquet of flowers.

"You never brought me flowers before."

"I've never asked you to marry me before."

"Wot? Marriage? Me an' you?"

"I can't think that 'marry me' would imply anything else."

And having read the odd bit of Shakespeare in the interim, George quoted an approximation of Hamlet on the matter of baked meats, funerals and wedding feasts.

"Sometimes, Georgie, I can't understand a word you say."

She was hesitant. The last thing he had wanted, though he had troubled himself to imagine it. She said she'd "just put the kettle on" and, when she had, seemed to perch on the edge of the sofa without a muscle in her body relaxing.

"What's the matter?"

"If ... if we was to get married ... what would we do? I mean we carried on ... once we got shot of the Russians, we just carried on ... as normal. Only there weren't no normal."

George knew exactly what she meant, but said nothing.

"I mean ... oh ... bloody Nora ... I don't know what I mean."

"You mean that serving army officers don't marry prostitutes."

"Yeah ... something like that."

"I have thought of leaving the Army. There are opportunities in supply management, and the Army is one of the best references a chap could have."

The kettle whistled. She turned it off but made no move towards making tea.

"Where would we live?"

"Anywhere. Where are you from?"

"Colchester."

Colchester was the biggest military prison in the country – the glasshouse, England's Leavenworth. Considered the worst posting a man could get. He'd never shake off the feel of the Army in Colchester.

"OK. Well ... perhaps not Colchester ... "

"I always wanted to live up north."

"What? Manchester? Leeds?"

"Nah ... 'Ampstead. I'd never want to leave London ... specially now it's started to ... wotchercallit? . . swing."

"Hampstead won't be cheap."

"I saved over three thousand quid from the game."

"I have about a thousand in savings, and I inherited more from Sylvia. In fact about seven and a half thousand pounds. Not inconsiderable."

Not inconsiderable – a lifetime of saving roughly equivalent to a couple of years on "the game".

"And of course, I'll get a pension. I've done sixteen years and a bit. I'll get part of a pension now, more if I leave it, and at thirty-five I'm young enough to put twenty or more years into another career."

"And there's the money in the bottom of the wardrobe."

"I hadn't forgotten."

"I counted it. Just the other day I counted it. We got seventeen hundred and thirty-two pounds. O' course there been expenses."

Donna was skirting the edge of a taboo subject. George was in two minds as to whether to let her plunge in. Who knows? It might clear the air.

"I give Judy two hundred. And there was money for the room ... an 'at."

George bit, appropriately, on the bullet.

"And how much did the gun cost you?"

There was a very long pause.

"Did you always know?"

"Yes."

"It didn't come cheap. Fifty quid."

In for a penny, in for a pound.

Marry without secrets.

George cleared his throat.

"And of course, there's the cost of your return ticket to West Byfleet last month, isn't there?"

He could see her go rigid, a ramrod to her spine, a crab-claw grip to her fingers on the arm of the sofa.

He hoped she'd speak first, but after an age it seemed to him she might never speak again.

"I don't care," he said softly. "Really I don't."

She would not look at him.

"Donna. Please say yes. Please tell me you'll marry me."

Donna said nothing.

George got up and made tea, hoping he would be making tea for two for the rest of their lives.

SISTERHOOD

Nigel Bird

"VEIL AND EVIL." This was the part Brandon enjoyed the most. "Same four letters. Ever noticed?"

The three women tied to the chairs that used to sit round his grandfather's table offered no response. Just stared.

Ever since Grandad had gone into the home, Brandon had been using the house as a base. Seemed fair enough – he spent his week teaching brats who didn't want to learn to pay for the old goat to stay there.

"The Chamber", he called it. He liked to hear himself say it out loud.

Brandon and his mates loved weekends. A couple of pints at the meeting followed by a trawl round town to do their bit to clean the streets.

Seemed like their lucky night when they saw three of them together.

When they bundled them into the van they made no attempt to struggle. Wasn't so much fun without having to beat them into submission, but there was still time to get their kicks.

Billy was all for chucking them into the Ribble, leaving their fate to the undertow, but Brandon ordered them to head for the usual place.

Number 36 was in the middle of a red-brick terrace.

Newspapers taped to the windows stopped neighbours taking a nose.

The Chamber was upstairs at the back. Soundproofed and blacked-out, it was perfect.

"See, in Britain, we like to see people's faces." Billy had stripped down to his boxers. Sweat dripped from his armpits to his waist as he coiled a studded belt around his hand. He always undressed in front of their prey. Like it was part of a ceremony or something.

Brandon gave Ian a nod.

Ian pulled scissors from the bag, wandered over and cut the hijabs to the knees.

Brandon's skull tingled at the sight of their skin. He itched to take them there and then. Waiting for their tears, for the begging and the squirms, merely heightened the pleasure.

They never came.

"Maybe we're not getting our point across." Brandon picked up a blowtorch and turned the valve.

Billy reached over and gave it a light. The flame hissed orange and blue.

"I'll take off the niqabs then our mouths are going to get intimate." He flicked his tongue up and down. Shook his shoulders with delight. "And Billy's lips wouldn't mind a friend tonight, eh?"

Billy licked the studs at his knuckles and smiled.

"Don't co-operate and you'll need those masks to hide the scars."

Brandon stepped over to the first girl, noted the smell of spices. Decided to go for a curry afterwards.

He reached for the veil. Tore it from her face.

"Watch yourself with that bloody razor." As Yusuf pulled his leg away from Arash he kicked over his mug of tea.

"Dickhead. Mum'll be furious." Arash took off his T-shirt and rubbed the carpet clean. "We're supposed to be slick. Fuck would Naz say?"

"Sorry, mate," Yusuf said, "but you cut me."

"Can't take a nick from a razor, how the hell are you going to sort out these fascists?"

Yusuf, Zeeko and Ahmed sat in a line on the sofa watching the North End with the sound down. All three had their legs stretched out covered in shaving foam.

"We'll take what they give," Zeeko said. "They won't be coming for any more of our women after tonight."

Arash set about his work again, stripped away the leg-hair and sent them off to get showered and dressed.

"Jesus." Brandon pulled his hand away as if he were about to be bitten. "It's the bearded fucking woman."

Billy ripped off the veils from the others. Two more beards. "Shit."

"It's a bloody trap," Ian said, backing away.

"Cool it, man," Billy said. "They're the ones in the snares."

Brandon felt anything but cool. He'd been lusting after men. It didn't feel right. Nobody should play tricks like that. He put his feet on the chest of the biggest and pushed him over. Grabbing the scissors from Ian, he stabbed them into the man's thigh.

"Crazy bastard," the man shouted, writhing in his upturned chair in spite of the bindings. It was the first sound he'd made since they'd taken him from the street.

There wasn't much blood until Billy pulled the scissors out. After that the trickle was steady.

"You girls need a facial, know what I mean?" If they hadn't, it didn't take long for them to find out.

Brandon took the blowtorch. Went straight for the face. The smell of singeing hair, accompanied by Brandon's laughter and the victim's screams, filled the room.

Arash pulled up a couple of doors down. Reversed into the space outside number 42. Caught the front wing on a scaffolding pole sticking out from the back of the flatbed he was trying to avoid.

"I'm a dickhead. A total knob." Arash jumped out of the car to inspect the damage. "Mum's going to kill me." He licked his fingers and gave the scratches a rub. They didn't go away.

In the passenger seat Naz wound down the window and took the headphones from his ears. "Park the bloody car and let's get to work." He looked behind him to his brothers, their necks bent, heads pushing dents up into the roof.

Arash slapped the truck. Pulled back his hand and got ready to punch it. Decided he'd be better off saving himself for later. Got back behind the wheel, edged forward and started again.

The car ended up two feet from the kerb. It would do.

The boys in the back contorted themselves to get out when Naz pulled up the front seat then uncurled to their full height once on the pavement. They looked down at the car and nodded.

"I'll get better after my lessons," Arash told them.

"When you're old enough," Naz said. He unzipped his holdall, checked the contents and closed it up again. "Now move."

It was the first time Brandon had actually used the torch. They usually folded at the sight of it. Gave in to whatever they wanted.

What they wanted was always the same. Sex and the promise that they'd show their faces when in public from then on. That or stay indoors.

It had been working. The head of the Preston Chapter had been pleased with their work. Fewer Muslims in traditional dress. Fewer Muslim women on the street full stop.

Brandon and Billy were in line for a promotion. Ian, well, he might make it if he held tight to their tailcoats, but Brandon didn't really care what happened to him. He was soft. Took all of the pleasures but had to be carried.

"I'm definitely not screwing them now," Billy laughed. "Shame they wasted all that eye make-up."

"Don't know if these guys'll get laid ever again," Brandon said. He looked down on the three men lying on the floor, still trussed to their chairs. The screaming had stopped. Instead all three of them cried softly. Maybe the tears were nature's way of cooling the burns, Brandon thought. "In fact we're going to have to make sure of it."

"What do you mean?" Ian asked.

"Sometimes you're slower than a bloody tractor," Billy said.

"Aye. They came to sort us out, I reckon. We have to send a message."

"Can't you just write it down?"

"Gotta get rid of them for good." Brandon turned down the flame and put the torch over on the mantelpiece.

"Needs to be done," Billy said.

"Hear that, boys? Your Krishna's not going to be any good to you now."

"Paper, scissors, stone?" Billy asked.

The three men formed a circle and clenched their fists.

Naz went up to the door followed by his younger brothers Zulfi and Ali.

The three of them were destined for greatness, Arash was sure of it. They were the kind of people that nothing ever touched. It was rare for them to get involved in battles these days. Most of their time was spent studying or down at one of their gyms. If they didn't make it at boxing it would be basketball. Had their sights on a scholarship in the States. Anything had to be better than a life on the Broadgate.

Arash came from the side, his head turning from left to right, checking for witnesses. He knew it was pointless. A street like that, full of curtain-twitchers and old folk, and they might as well have been posting photos of themselves through every letterbox.

Replacing his headphones and switching on his tunes, Naz opened up the bag and passed out the goodies. The Amir boys should be able to scare the shit out of anybody without needing weapons, but having a few to hand wasn't going to do them any harm.

The scimitar, curved and polished, caught the light even though the sun was already setting. Zulfi took that. Ran his thumb across the blade. Felt the weight of it in his hand.

Arash was given a ball and chain. It was a token gesture and Arash knew it. He could swing it and look intimidating, but the brothers wouldn't let him get close enough to do any damage. They just needed his mother's car and his brains.

Ali had a bow and a handful of arrows. Placed one of them into the string ready for action. His head nodded up and down to the dubstep that was probably ruining his hearing.

It was going to be the first medieval battle since the Middle Ages,

Arash thought. Made him feel better to have that picture in his mind.

Naz took the crossbow for himself. "Ready?"

Without being asked, Ali leant his shoulder into the door. Stood back to give it a good bash.

Putting his fingers on the handle, Naz pushed down gently. The door opened without making a noise.

Ali turned, rubbed the arm of his shell-suit as if removing dirt and turned down his tunes.

Everyone nodded and they followed Naz inside.

Ian was first out, just like always. No matter how random the game should have been, he never guessed right.

On the count of three, the finalists threw down their hands. Billy's was open, Brandon's clenched.

"Paper wraps stone," Billy said and punched the air. "Yes."

Brandon was pissed off. Maybe he was losing his touch. Not that it mattered. He'd still get his turn.

"Eeny, meeny, miny, mo," Billy pointed at the three men in turn. Mouthed the rest of the rhyme to himself. Settled on the one in the middle.

"Come on, Billy," Ian said. "They're not going to say anything. Look at the one you chose. He's pissed himself already."

The man in the middle lay in a puddle, his body shaking like he was freezing to death.

It was the last time they were going to work with Ian, Brandon decided. He was worse than fucking useless. Didn't have the stomach for this anymore.

"Today," Billy said, "I shall be using the belt, followed by whatever knives I can find in the kitchen." He stood over his intended victim and pulled back his arm.

Brandon heard a creak on the stairs, then another. Turned his head towards the door as it was kicked open. Found himself looking straight at a crossbow.

Arash stayed at the bottom of the stairs. It was like his body gave up on him. He looked at the spikes on his weapon then gave the chain a swing. Let the ball take out a chunk of plaster from the wall. No way he could do that to someone's head.

The others took the stairs three at a time. Strolled up like they were about to throw a few practice hoops.

Ali went to take the door. This time Naz let him. He kicked it in with the heel of his trainers and they were out of sight before Arash could let out his breath.

He heard the ping of the bow-string and the jolt of the crossbow, then nothing.

"Where the fuck have you been?" someone was yelling. Sounded like Zeeko. "Where the fuck have you been?"

There was a strange sound, like a gas leak.

"No way man. Please. No way." Someone was begging. One of the white kids. Should be saving his breath.

Next he knew a human fireball was tearing down the stairs. Looked like he was wearing a suit and tie, but Arash couldn't be sure. He resisted the urge to lift up his leg and trip him over – the way the flames were swirling round the body and those arms were gyrating, it would have been a mean trick.

Arash watched the ball of fire run out of the door, cross the road and jump clear over the wall into the river. By the time he got there to investigate there were only a couple of ducks to be seen.

From the house spilled the tinny sound of a hip-hop track, hitting the beat in perfect time with Arash's pulse.

"He just reversed into it like it wasn't even there, Mum."

"Did you get the plate number?"

Arash hadn't worked through the whole story. He'd been too busy getting his mates to the hospital. "Nah, Mum. He was too quick."

He didn't see it coming but he felt his cheek sting as the slap landed.

It was the kind of slap he liked. Reminded him of who he was. Where he came from. "Thanks, Mum.'

He gave her a kiss on the forehead and ran up to his room without needing to be told, a great big grin spread right across his face.

RULES OF ENGAGEMENT

Zoë Sharp

A LONG TIME ago, when Angel was just starting out in the busi-ness, an old pro she met lurking in a doorway opposite the Russian embassy in Paris laid down the Rules of Engagement. "Get in. Take the shot. Get out," he'd said, with the careful solemnity of a man not quite sober at ten o'clock in the morning.

To this advice Angel had since added a bitter rider of her own. *Always get the money.*

The fees for Angel's particular line of work were elastic, only sometimes connected to the difficulty of the shot. In this case, the money was nowhere near enough to justify attempting to evade capture across 200 acres of jealously guarded parkland in Buckinghamshire. Not for an off-chance glimpse of her targets at the limit of her operational range.

There was only so much she could do for a decent covert photo – even with a 1000mm mirror lens.

"So, what exactly," she'd demanded of George, when she'd but-tonholed him in his office on the thirtieth floor and wheedled the assignment out of him, "are you expecting from this?"

"Pictures of the happy couple holding hands, bit of snogging maybe," said the rumpled little man who was her occasional employer, scratching his chin. "Wouldn't hope for much else. The groom-to-be isn't so love-struck that he hasn't twisted a deal with Blackley's for piccies of the nuptials themselves. They'll have that chapel sewn up tighter than a fish's armpit."

"How much?" Angel perched on the edge of George's desk, reaching for one of her Turkish cigarettes.

George, a forty-year nicotine addict, yelped "Don't!" jerking his eyes upwards. "They've turned up the sensitivity on the sprinkler system again – bastards." He nipped the unlit cigarette out of Angel's fingers and threw it into the filing cabinet behind him. He'd known her long enough to know she'd light up anyway, just to watch the indoor rain.

"How much is Blackley paying, George?" she asked now, voice husky.

George shivered. That voice went straight through him, plugged into his cerebral cortex and set his nerve endings quivering. She knew exactly what effect it had – even on men a whole lot younger and less susceptible. He was determined it wouldn't get to him – not this time.

"A mil," he blurted, to his own dismay. "Look, what's this to you, Angel? This is no bent judge or perverted politician. Just some pop star and some actress. I thought you hated celebrity fluff? You of all people."

Angel raised an eyebrow, jiggling the little silver hoop through the corner, and snagged the job sheet off the pile.

"You remember when *those* pictures came out?" she said eventually, seemingly fascinated by the view behind the desk, out over Canary Wharf. "Of me—"

"I remember," George cut in softly.

"Blackley syndicated them," she said, flat. She turned her gaze back on to him. Her eyes were startling violet today, with the slightest shimmer. "That's what put him on the map. Anything I can do to wipe him off it again will be worth it."

She slid off the desk and headed for the door with that long catwalk stride she'd never lost.

"Angel! Hey, kiddo, I—"

At the doorway she stopped, turned back with a wicked, dazzling smile.

"Trust me, George. Get a deal, and I'll get you pictures," she promised. "Besides, Johnny Franz is not just *some pop star*. He has a certain ... reputation. Maybe I just want to see for myself, up close and personal, if he deserves it."

***

Now, lying under a rhododendron bush only 400 metres from the great west wing of the house, Angel began to question her breezy confidence.

The tabloids had whipped themselves to a frenzy for months over the "Wedding of the Year". Johnny Franz was a playboy rock star whose ego matched his prodigious talent with a Fender Stratocaster. Born on a council estate in Sheffield, he'd shrugged off his working-class beginnings further with every platinum disk.

Johnny's chosen bride was Caro Urquart, an English beauty whose tiny, perfect figure was made for crinoline and corsets, and she had the genuine cut-glass accent to match. Her diminutive stature – ensuring all her leading men seemed giants by comparison – was just one reason behind her international stardom.

They'd met at a Hollywood party and, oblivious to the eyes of the gossip press, struck instant sparks. By midnight they'd flown down to his villa in Mexico by private jet, ostensibly to watch the sunrise. Nobody had seen either of them for a solid week.

And now they were tying the knot at the bride's family estate, with all the pomp their fame and wealth could supply. Johnny's PR guru had issued a statement declaring he'd found his true love, was finally ready to settle down. Caro's studio press release claimed she'd never been happier and didn't care who knew it.

Blackley's picture agency paid seven figures for exclusive rights to the wedding photos, and hired an army of security to make sure nobody else got a look-in.

But that didn't mean Angel couldn't try.

Getting into the grounds hadn't been hard. Guile and flattery, for the most part, learned during the time Angel had spent taking her clothes off for a living. Even now, something of that former life exuded through her pores like raw sex.

The dogs hadn't caused her undue problems, either. She'd found the kennels the first night and bribed the motley collection of hounds. When they picked up her scent on their rounds they reacted as to a canine friend rather than an intruder. The handlers tugged the animals away, whining, from any proximity to her hiding place.

But Angel was bored. And boredom brought a restless reckless-ness that made those who knew her check nervously for the nearest emergency exit. She'd been here three nights without a sniff. Now, the sun had risen on the big day and she'd failed to snap a single frame. She was, she recognized, probably on the verge of doing something stupid.

And then somebody else did it for her.

She heard laughter. A girlie giggle, coquettish, pretending shock but hiding an edge of triumph. Angel recognized the giggle of a woman who's leading a man by the balls and both of them know it, and neither of them care.

She felt the slight tremble of footsteps through the earth beneath her. A pair of shapely female legs, clad in pale stockings, came within a metre of Angel's nose, picking carefully through the dewed grass, careful of telltale stains on the dainty satin shoes. The man's legs were in official pinstripe morning dress.

They passed close enough for her to smell their excitement.

The bride's mother was known as an uptight aristocrat who would never countenance the happy couple sharing a suite in antici-pation. Maybe that was why they'd evaded their own babysitters for this last, unfettered quickie.

Angel kept her head down until the legs had gone by, squirmed round in time to see the couple weaving away across the billiard-table lawn. There was no mistaking the trademark wild black hair of Johnny Franz.

As soon as they were too far to hear the whirr, Angel brought the camera up to her eye and kept the shutter pressed.

The Canon digital she was using was capable of ten frames a second and buffered just as fast. She took a long sequence of the couple's back view, their hands all over each other.

The gardens had been laid out in the mid-1800s, a vast testa-ment to formal good taste, manicured within an inch of its life. At the end of the impossibly vibrant lawn, invisible from the main residence, was a wooden summer-house, built on a distant whim and rarely used. Angel knew entire families in Brixton who could have moved in and luxuriated in the extra space.

The couple headed for the summer-house with clear intent, oblivious, almost grappling in their urgency. Johnny Franz had his hands up his intended's skirts and Angel wondered if they would even wait until they got inside.

George is going to want to have my children for this.

And then, just as he grabbed for the door, Johnny swung the girl around so that Angel's telephoto lens got a clear shot of her face for the first time, and she realized that wasn't all her boss was going to have. *A heart attack, most likely.*

Because the still-giggling girl Johnny pushed into the summer-house was not who she was supposed to be. The long blonde hair was a similar shade and length, but the face was not the one that stared down from billboards and buses all over London. Angel checked the playback just to be sure, but there was no doubt.

So, Johnny Franz was cheating on his beautiful, famous bride on the morning of their wedding with, unless Angel was very much mistaken, one of the bridesmaids.

Even as the door closed behind them, Angel levered up, grabbing the padded backpack that held a second camera body, attached to a mid-length zoom lens. For this, she intended getting as close as she dared.

She sprinted across the grass. If the way Johnny had been tugging at the bridesmaid's dress was anything to go by, he wasn't planning a slow seduction.

The summer-house had two windows and Angel edged closer to one where the light would fall without the need for flash, not if she bumped up the ISO speed just a touch. For what she was about to give him, George could put up with a little noise in the pictures. Too perfect and they looked fake.

There was nothing fake going on inside the summer-house. By the time Angel silently set down her bag, raising the viewfinder to her eye, Johnny had the bridesmaid thrust face down over a stack of lounger cushions, her skirts thrown over her back.

With his trousers halfway down his skinny thighs, Angel could just make out yet another tattoo added to Johnny's collection since *Vanity Fair* shot him coyly naked for their best-selling summer issue. The name "Caro" in gothic script across his left hip. Angel shot a decent close-up, just in case there were any later accusations of Photoshop.

Johnny reached forwards and wrapped his hand in the girl's hair like taking up the reins of a horse. He dragged her head back, his teeth bared in what might have been a snarl.

This isn't about the sex, Angel thought. *This has never been about the sex.*

She lowered the camera and stumbled back, knowing she'd got more than enough, seen more than enough. Knowing, too, that she wouldn't clear the foul taste from her mouth, even if she gargled with Stolichnaya for a fortnight.

She scooped up her pack and ran for the trees. By the time the couple re-emerged, less urgent but more furtive, adjusting their clothing, Angel had the memory card bluetoothed to her Blackberry and uploading to her secure home server. Even if they caught her now, trashed her gear – as they had before – it would be too late.

She shifted back to the telephoto and took a series of them walking away. From this she surmised the bridesmaid had not altogether enjoyed the experience. Not enough to overcome an instant blossom of guilt. She hurried, flushed, awkward, not waiting when Johnny paused infuriatingly to dip his head and light a cigarette as if he'd all the time in the world.

Through the pin-sharp magnification of the lens, crosshaired by the focusing array, Angel watched him track the bridesmaid's hasty retreat as he blew out the first wreath of smoke. He didn't raise his head, but something about the predatory watchfulness of those legendary ice-blue eyes made her skin shimmy. Then he flicked the spent match into a nearby ornamental fountain, and he smiled.

That was what did it.

***

In her spacious bedroom suite at the top of the east wing, Caro Urquart fussed with her hair. When she and Johnny first met, the length and the colour and the weight of it had captivated him.

She'd been preparing for another wretched period drama – Africa this time. Growing her own hair was less cumbersome, less hot, than using one of her selection of wigs.

Normally, the first thing she would have done after the final wrap party would have been to visit her stylist in New York for a total makeover. Her screen agent warned her keeping static wasn't good for her career. "You mustn't risk typecasting, darling," he'd fretted at Cannes. "You have to keep reinventing yourself."

But when Johnny played her the hastily mixed demo for the new album, featuring "The Girl with the Sun in Her Hair" as title track and debut single, how could she have it cut or dyed? The song had debuted at number one, the album following suit, and Johnny had given her the platinum disc as a keepsake.

Besides, once they were married she'd be cherry-picking roles anyway. On Jay Leno, Johnny declared he liked the idea of a working wife, but she knew that was just image talking. That secretly he'd be delighted to have her on the road with him, touring with the band – for part of the year, at least. Besides, she'd heard the rumours about those groupies ...

Caro teased her fringe into artfully casual disarray. Nobody realized how much effort it took, looking this damned natural all the time. She twisted her head sideways. And maybe it was time for the little nip-and-tuck her beauty therapist suggested. She *was* nearly twenty-seven, after all.

A small stone flipped against the window pane behind her, making her start. Her rooms were right at the top of the house, five storeys up. Who ... ?

Then a smile lit her face. *Johnny*!

The window led out on to a small balcony, level with the many-turreted rooftop. The suite had once been servants' quarters, but Caro loved the view and had long since claimed it as her own.

She flung open the window and stepped out.

In the far corner of the balcony lounged a tall figure, just in the process of lighting a cigarette. She had the high slanted cheekbones of a model, black and white spiked hair, and she wore urban-cam

cargoes and a skinny sleeveless T-shirt that revealed a strange inter-
woven Celtic symbol tattooed on her shoulder.

Definitely not Johnny.

For a moment Caro froze. Then her eyes flicked to the bag at the
girl's feet. To the very pro-looking camera balanced on the top of it.

"Get out!" she thundered, voice quivering with anger. "How
dare you!"

The girl exhaled, giving Caro a narrow-eyed stare through a
lungful of smoke. "I'm here to give, not take," she said mildly.
"Call it an early wedding present, if you like. And it took some *dare*
to climb that ivy, I can tell you." For the first time Caro noticed
that the girl's hands were shaking, her skin unnaturally pale and
sheened with sweat.

"Are you *so* desperate to snatch some grubby shot of me in my
wedding gown, you'd risk your neck for it?" Caro demanded,
incredulous.

"I've got all the shots I want, and not of you," the girl said. "I
was never here for that – not really."

Cold fear trickled down the back of Caro's spine. She shivered in
her elaborate dress, despite the balmy air.

"I know you," she said, uncertain. "You were that model. That
one who—"

"Became a *paparazza*, yes," the girl said flatly. "I take pictures
people don't want taken, of them doing things they don't want
publicized." She took a last long drag on her cigarette and looked
up suddenly into Caro's face. The girl's eyes were a remarkable
shade of amber, golden like a cat. *Coloured contacts?* "And I've got
something you really need to see."

Caro recoiled instinctively. "I don't want—"

"Didn't say you'd *want* to, babe," the girl said, almost gently.
"But I've already cut a deal on these pictures. By tomorrow, you're
not going to be able to avoid them. And then it'll be too late. Then
you'll have married the slimeball."

Caro swallowed. Common sense urged her to yell for help and
have this insolent stranger thrown out. To watch as she was marched
down the drive with Caro's largest minder twisting her arm up her

back, and kicking the bag of expensive cameras alongside him as he went. But the image of those groupies still clung.

She stepped sideways, to the edge of the parapet, and glanced downwards. The creeper-clad stone walls stretched away towards the gravel below.

"You really climbed all the way up here," she murmured, "just to show me some pictures?"

"Yes," the girl agreed gravely. "And I don't fancy going back the same way. So, if you're going to have me chucked out, at least do it through the tradesman's entrance, would you?"

She picked up the camera. Caro stiffened, but the girl merely held it out to her. Cautiously, Caro took it from her. The action brought her near to the parapet again and her gaze returned to the seemingly impossible climb.

It was more years than she could count since someone offered a favour and expected nothing in return, and Caro had grown cynical. She held the camera out over the long drop. It was surprisingly heavy.

"What's to stop me simply letting go?"

The girl grinned. It transformed her face into that of a street urchin. "Absolutely nothing," she said cheerfully. "But those Canons have a magnesium shell and are tough as old boots, so the lens would be knackered, but the memory card would survive. And that's the bit you should worry about."

Caro considered for a moment, then slowly brought the camera back inside the parapet. "You've already made copies, haven't you?" she realized bitterly.

"Hell, yes," the girl agreed, fervent. "Made copies and sold the rights, worldwide."

"So, what do you want from me?" Caro asked with brittle dignity. "Money?"

The girl laughed outright. "Didn't I already say I wasn't selling? Johnny Franz deserves what's coming to him." She put her head on one side. "The only question is ... do you?"

"He loves me." But even an actress of Caro's skill heard the underlying uncertainty.

"Hm. I'm sure that's what all those starstruck teenagers thought, before he damn-near raped them," the girl said deliberately. "You know how many he's paid off?" When Caro didn't respond, she shrugged. "Well, can't say I didn't warn you."

She took the camera out of Caro's momentarily nerveless fingers, squatted to repack it into its padded bag, adding in conversational tones, "Personally, I don't see what all the fuss is about with that boy. From what I saw, I'd rate him maybe a four out of ten – for energy if not for style. And that's only because sometimes I can go a little rough." She rose easily, flashed Caro a doubtful smile from beneath that Cruella de Vil-style hair. "Good luck, babe – you're going to need it."

* * *

When Caro Urquart began her walk down the aisle, gasps from the assembled congregation greeted her appearance. The dress with its mile-long silk train carried by a single bridesmaid, that distinctive golden hair under the diaphanous veil, the perfect bunch of white orchids in her hands.

It took them a moment to wonder why she wasn't on the arm of her father, and another to realize she seemed in something of a hurry to meet the handsome rock star in his trademark swaggered pose alongside the waiting priest.

Caro reached the altar faster than rehearsals had predicted, paused while the organist tried to catch up and eventually floundered into silence. Her cheeks were faintly flushed, lips slightly parted, the bridesmaid fussing with her train.

Johnny Franz failed to notice any of this lapse in timing. He stepped forwards with that famous killer smile and gently lifted the veil away from his fiancée's face.

"You are the love of my life," he murmured, just loud enough to carry to the guy ghost-writing his autobiography, seated two rows back.

"Really?" Caro said blandly, her own voice the one she'd perfected on the West End stage to be clearly audible in the Gods. "So, who was the little bitch-in-heat you were shagging in the summer-house this morning, then?"

Johnny's guilty eyes flew to the bridesmaid, only then realizing that she was taller than he remembered. She hadn't been wearing a blonde wig then, either, and he was pretty sure there'd been no tattoos.

And she definitely hadn't had a camera hidden somewhere that she was now using to fire off frame after frame of unflattering close-ups.

Bewildered by his own rush of guilt, his gaze jerked back to Caro.

"'The Girl with the Sun in Her Hair'?" she thundered, temper finally breaking loose. "How about 'The Girl with Her Fist in Your Face', you cheating bastard!"

Johnny never saw the first punch coming.

***

The tabloid banner headlines quoted her verbatim the following day, above one of Angel's exclusive photographs from the church. It showed Caro's delicate clenched fist frozen at the very moment of contact, square on the side of Johnny Franz's jaw. A perfect shot, with his chin tucked back and his eyes shut and his cheeks bloated in shocked surprise, just a fleck of spittle spraying outwards to show the force of the blow.

Caro's own face had blazed with righteous fury, proving that she was one of the few women who truly *was* more beautiful when she was angry.

Immediately afterwards, Caro's agent started fielding calls from the major studios, offering her leading roles in big-budget action adventures. She chose that of an ice-cool assassin in a sci-fi epic, playing it with golden contacts, spiked black and white hair, and a number of curious tattoos.

She refused to be drawn by David Letterman on her source of inspiration. The movie became the blockbuster hit of the summer.

After Angel's pictures from the summer-house hit the Internet, three girls came forward to lodge formal complaints about Johnny's often vicious sexual style in the back of the tour bus after gigs. One of them was only fifteen.

The resultant police investigation meant the second single from *The Girl with the Sun in Her Hair* barely made it into the Top Twenty on release, and dropped rapidly down the charts. His next album tanked.

Blackley's agency attempted to recover their outlay, but since the pictures Angel took were, strictly speaking, not of the wedding, Johnny's lawyers were stalling. He had other things to worry about.

Caro sent Angel an open-ended offer to be her bridesmaid for real – as and when the actress made another trip down the aisle. Angel's texted refusal was more regretful than it sounded. She had no desire to become her own prey.

George, who perhaps knew her best of anyone, sent her a case of Stolichnaya.

With her commission, Angel went to Oklahoma for the start of the tornado season, capturing shots of an F4 touching down just outside Tulsa, which she sold to *National Geographic.*

"Stunning," George said, thoughtful, when she brought him a copy of the magazine. He peered at the invented by-line. "Bloody shame you couldn't use your real name on this, kiddo."

Angel was lounging by the cracked-open office window, blowing experimental smoke-rings out over Canary Wharf. Today, her hair was pink and her eyes were a vivid aquamarine. She shrugged. She hadn't forgotten the guy in the doorway opposite the embassy.

Always get the money.

"As long as they get my name right on the cheque," she said, with a smile that didn't quite reach her eyes, "what do I care?"

LOVELY REQUIEM, MR MOZART

Robert Barnard

THE COMMISSION CAME into my life accompanied by Mr Lewis Cazalet. The arrival of that gentleman was announced by Jeannie, my unusually bright and alert maid of all duties.

"There's a wee mannikin to see you. Says he has a proposal, something to your advantage."

I did not jump up with the alacrity I would once have shown. My position as piano teacher to the Princess Victoria brought me, as well as great pleasure, none of it musical, a great number of prestigious pupils. I stirred reluctantly in my chair, only to have Jeannie say: "Don't hurry. Let the body wait."

I nodded, and went to the piano and played a showy piece by my friend Clementi, sufficiently *forte* to penetrate walls. Jeannie came in as I was finishing.

"He's walking up and down. He's a mite ... unappetizing."

I raised my eyebrows, but I relied on Jeannie's judgement, and told her to show him in.

The gentleman whom she ushered in was not short, but there was a sort of insubstantiality about him: he was thin to the point of meagreness, his gestures were fluttery, and his face was the colour of putty.

"Mr Mozart?" he said, taking my hand limply. "A great honour. I recognized one of your sonatas, did I not? Your fame is gone out to all lands."

I was not well disposed towards anyone who could confuse a piece by Clementi with one of my sonatas.

"Mr ... er?"

"Cazalet, Lewis Cazalet."

"Ah – a French name," I said unenthusiastically. That nation had virtually cut the continent of Europe off for twenty years, the very years of my prime, when I could have earned a fortune.

"We are a Huguenot family," he murmured, as if that was a guarantee of virtue and probity.

"Well, let's get down to business. I believe you have a proposition for me." We sat down and I looked enquiringly at him.

"Perhaps as a preliminary—" No, please! Spare me the preliminaries! "I should say that I am a man of letters, but not one favoured by fame and fortune like yourself." Did my sitting room look as if I was favoured by fortune? "As a consequence I have been for the last five years librarian and secretary to Mr Isaac Pickles. You know the name?"

I prevaricated.

"I believe I have heard the name mentioned by my son in Wakefield."

"You would have. A great name in the North. Immensely wealthy. Mr Pickles – his father was Pighills, but no matter – is one of the foremost mill-owners in the Bradford district. He is, in newspaper parlance, a Prince of Industry."

"I see," I said. And I did. A loud vulgarian with pots of money and a power lust.

"A most considerate employer, and generous to boot on occasion. I have no complaints whatsoever."

"That's good to hear. In sending you to see me this, er, Pickles has some end in view, I take it?"

Mr Cazalet hummed and hawed. Then he suddenly blurted out: "A Requiem. He wishes you to write a Requiem."

"Ah. I take it you mean a requiem mass. Is Mr Pickles a Catholic?"

"He is not. His religion is taken from many and is his own alone."

"And the person for whom this requiem is to be written?"

"Is immaterial."

"I assure you it is not. If it is for His late Majesty King George

IV it would be very different to what I would write if it was for the Archbishop of Canterbury, for example."

"I would imagine so!" He hummed again, let out something like a whimper, then said: "It is a requiem for his wife."

"I see. Mr Pickles was a devoted husband, I take it?"

"Mr Pickles is the complete family man – affectionate, but wise ... I must insist, however, that the information I have just given you remain completely confidential. Com-plete-ly."

"It will. But there must surely be a reason for this request?"

He looked at me piteously but I held his gaze.

"The lady in question is still alive."

I sat back in my chair and simply said "Phew."

In the next few minutes he confided in me the facts of the case. The wife in question was sick, sicker than she herself recognized; the doctor was certain her illness was terminal, but would not commit himself to a likely date. All the uncertainties of the commission would be reflected in the fee, and there was one further condition that Mr Pickles absolutely insisted upon.

"That is that you tell no one of this commission, tell no one that you are writing a Requiem, tell no one when it is performed that you wrote it, and give total and absolute rights in the work to Mr Pickles, along with all manuscript writings."

"I see," I said. "And the fee he suggests that he pay me?"

"The fee he is willing to pay you is fifteen hundred pounds."

Fifteen hundred! Riches! Good dinners, fine silk clothes, rich presents for my children and grandchildren. O wondrous Pickles!

"Say two thousand," I said, "and I am Mr Pickles's to command."

* * *

I was not deceived by the conditions. Mr Pickles was an amateur musician who wanted to pass my work off as his own. When his wife died he wanted to impose on the world by pretending that the superb Requiem that was performed for her was written by his good self, divinely inspired (rather as that arch imposter Samuel Taylor Coleridge tries to pretend that his poems were in fact written by the

Almighty, with himself acting merely as amanuensis). And it would all be in vain: every society person with any musical knowledge would know it was not by him, and anyone of real discernment would guess it was by Wolfgang Gottlieb Mozart.

The only fly in the ointment was spelled out for me by the Princess Victoria at her next weekly piano lesson, where she murdered the works of lesser men than I (I had learned the lesson of not encouraging her to her painful operations on works of my own). When she had screwed out of me the reasons for my lightness of heart (unusual, even with her delightful presence) she said:

"He seems a very dishonest man, Mr Mozart."

"Distinctly devious, my dear."

"Devious! What a lovely word. If he can rob you of credit for the music, he can hardly be trusted to pay you for it."

It was something I resolved to bear in mind.

From the start Mr Pickles showed he had learned lessons from the negotiations of Mr Cazalet.

"The fee I'm offering," he said to me in his Hyde Park mansion, "is two thousand pounds. Subject, naturally to some safeguards."

Two thousand pounds, as asked for! I wouldn't like to say how long it would take me to earn that amount by more legitimate pursuits. Kensington Palace paid me thirteen and sixpence an hour for my lessons with the Princess. We were sitting on a superb sofa, which must have been in Mr Pickles's family since the time he started to make a fortune from his niche in the cotton industry, which was warm underwear. I could have done with a pair of his long combinations now: this luxurious sofa was about half a mile from the nearest of two fires in the high-ceilinged drawing room of his mansion. I got up and strolled over to his fine grand piano, much nearer the fire. I played a few notes.

"This will need tuning," I said. Mr Pickles was outraged.

"I assure you it is just as it came from the makers."

"That is the problem. Pianos go out of tune."

"But the finest singers and pianists have used it," he neighed, like a child wailing. "My musical soirées are famous."

"Mr Pickles, I played for King George III when he was a young man. I know when a piano needs tuning."

He backed away at once.

"Yes, yes, of course. But we haven't gone over the cond– the safeguards."

"For a fee of two thousand pounds I accept those without question. If I understand Mr Cazalet they are that you will own the piece absolutely, my name will not be attached to it, nor will I verbally lay claim to it. I suggest you might like to call it the Pickles Requiem, and state on the title page that it is 'by a gentleman'."

Mr Pickles almost purred.

"Yes, yes. They have a ring to them. 'The Pickles Requiem'. In memory of my late wife, of course."

"Of course. I didn't realize that your wife had died since I talked to Mr Cazalet."

"She has not. I refer to her proper designation when the great work comes to be performed."

"I see." (But I didn't.)

"I want the piece to be sung within a week of her death, as a direct statement of my grief and sense of loss."

"Of course, I quite understand … You might find it advisable to let the orchestra and choir rehearse as much as possible in advance."

"Ah yes, I see. Well spoken, Mr Mozart. It must be done in the most tactful way possible."

"Totally secret, I would suggest. The public prints take any opportunity for ridicule … Now I think our business is over?"

"You accept my conditions? And will compose the work entirely in this house, and leave the manuscript and any notes here always?"

"I do accept, and will write the piece as you stipulate."

We shook hands on it. I had not thought it necessary to mention that nothing in the "safeguards" prevented me from writing out a second copy at home when I was satisfied with a movement.

On the following evening a message arrived from Pickles Palace (as I called it in my mind) with the news that the Danish couple I had recommended, Hr Bang and Dr Olufsen, had been and tuned the piano. No expense spared, obviously. I felt quite sure Mr Pickles noticed no difference.

I began work next day. An anteroom next to the drawing room was assigned entirely to me – the lowly room being chosen not to downgrade my position and purpose in the household but to give easy access to the piano. I say "began work" but I had begun work on it in my heart before Mr Cazalet had closed the front door. It was to be a work not full of grandeur, still less grandiloquence, with no trace of suffering or hellfire. It was to be gentle, gracious, kind on the ear – a feminine Requiem, you might say, for the wife of a wealthy industrialist who must surely be his superior in manners, knowledge of the genteel world, and kindness.

On my third day of working in Pickles Palace, when I was just completing the Sanctus, which I had decided to write first, I had the honour of a visit. I was sitting in the great drawing room, with welcome spring sunshine coming through the high windows, and trying things over on the piano, which was now a superb instrument and sounding like one. I was conscious after a time that I was not alone. I looked round in the direction of the door towards the hall, and saw a figure standing near the fire.

"Very beautiful, Mr Mozart. Very lovely."

The voice came as if from a great distance. It was genteel – no, aristocratic – and it proceeded from a slim, graceful yet commanding woman of perhaps thirty-five or forty, elegantly dressed in a loose-fitting day gown. What a contrast she made to the mighty Pighills himself!

"I am honoured by your approval. Do I have the pleasure of—?"

"Mercy Pickles," she said, distaste creeping into her tones. "I hope you will create one of the great ecclesiastical musical works. It should have a life beyond the immediate one marking the death of my husband's mother."

"Mo—?" I pulled myself up. "I suppose all composers would like to think their works will last."

"He is very fond of his mother," she said, in the same distant tones she had used hitherto. "She used to make the mill-children's gruel and beat them when they went to sleep. Naturally he's devoted to her, but I found her less than charming."

"A wife seldom gets on with her husband's mother," I said.

"When my father sold me, at the age of sixteen, to a man more than twice my age, his mother made it her business to make my life an endless swamp of misery. When she suffered the onset of senility I made it my business to return her treatment in kind. It palled after a time. There was little joy in mistreating someone so far removed from the world that she could not appreciate the fact that she was being mistreated. Now all I wish is that she would hurry up dying." She stopped, possibly feeling she had said too much. "And then we can all hear your wonderful Requiem." She thought for a second, then said: "Take care, Mr Mozart."

She glided from the room. "Take care" is a popular form of farewell that sat ill with her aristocratic air. But perhaps she meant it to be taken not as a courtesy but a warning.

My first encounter with the Pickles sons was no less confusing, but even more thought-provoking. I was playing over a first sketch for the Libera Me section – a grand, sweeping theme with a hint of yearning – when the doors of the drawing room opened and two young men began a progress across the great expanse of the drawing room, talking loudly. I went on playing. The voices rose to a crescendo. I was intrigued and stopped playing to listen. The voices immediately ceased. I was impressed: they knew enough about music to notice when it stopped. They turned round and saw me.

"You must be Mr Thingummy."

I waited. I am not a Mr Thingummy.

"Mozart."

It was the taller of the two. He pronounced it Mo-zart instead of Moat-zart, a deplorable English habit. However I bowed – a reward for a good try. They began over towards me.

"You're the johnny who's teaching my father composition."

"Well, not—"

"You've got a hard job on your hands. You're starting from scratch."

"Typical of my father," came from the shorter boy. "Wasting

our inheritance on futile projects. Who will believe that he wrote it?"

"And who would believe," chimed in the older boy, "that he'd lavish all that money and time on a damned librarian?"

"A damned what?" I couldn't stop myself saying.

"Faithful servant and all that. But a piece of *music*? Choirs and solo singers, orchestral johnnies, the whole caboodle. For a book-duster? It should be a case of, when he dies, slipping a ten-pound note to his widow."

"He's not married, Jimmy," said the other. "Not at all, if you get me."

"Well, in that case you're ten pounds to the good." The pair turned and resumed their marathon.

It was around this point in the execution of the contract that Mr Pickles began to take a more active interest in the progress of my composition. I found one afternoon when I went to play over the day's inspirations that cups and jugs of chocolate had been set out on a small table, and I had no sooner begun playing than a footman came in with napkins and biscuits (biscuits are my weakness but the servants so far had not remembered to offer me any), followed a second or two later by Mr Pickles, who sat himself down and – to be fair to him – listened. At the first pause in the playing he called me over.

"Mr Mozart, you must be in need of refreshment."

I bowed my head briefly, and made my way over. He had poured into my cup some of the fragrant refresher, while pouring himself a cup from the other jug. Made with the finest Brazilian coffee beans, he explained. It was a country with which his mills had strong financial links. The drink was slightly bitter-tasting but acceptable.

"So how is it going, then? Are you well on the way?"

I had the reputation for extreme facility in the writing of my scores. It was a reputation fully justified when it concerned my pieces written to order for members of the aristocracy or the theatre. Still, four weeks for a full-scale Requiem was ridiculous.

"I have five movements well advanced, either on paper or in my head," I said. "I have fragments of ideas for the other nine sections. Time will tell which are usable."

"Ah yes. This question of time—"

I was so daring as to interrupt him.

"Great work is not done in days. Remember, sir, I have strong connections with Kensington Palace. If the princess on whom all our hopes turn hears this is a workaday piece that anyone could have written she will not attend. But if it is a work worthy of Wolfgang Gottlieb Mozart then she will come if I persuade her, and I will not need to say anything about my participation in the piece."

"Oh my!" said my patron, as if he could barely comprehend the joyful possibility. "A magnificent prospect! A wonderful culmination to our mutual collaboration."

What a mutual collaboration was I could not guess. All we had was a willingness to pay money on one side and an eagerness to accept it on the other, a purely commercial transaction.

So things went on. Now and then Mrs Pickles came in, usually listened for a time, then went out possibly with a banal compliment, sometimes with a barbed remark about her husband or his family, depending on her mood. The boys (James and Seymour were their names, the second being his mother's family name) came either singly or together, greeted me with "Hi" or "Good morning", and sometimes added a sarcastic comment, such as "Earning your daily crust, eh, Mr Mozart?" I didn't like them. Their father was at least fond of music, even if he knew nothing about it. The boys were simply vessels, without learning or achievement. I heard from the servants that they were both very deep in gambling debts.

The course of my time with the Pickleses changed one afternoon at the beginning of May. I had been forced, on my way out of Pickles Palace, to make a quick visit to the privy, the nature of which I won't go into. I was just washing my hands in the bowl of lukewarm water renewed every hour by a lower footman, when I heard two voices passing along the corridor outside. One was Mr Cazalet, whose work in the library prevented my having much to do with him while I was in the house, and the other was his, and temporarily my, employer, Isaac Pickles.

"The uncertainty is playing on your mind, I fear, sir."

"Oh, I'm perfectly all right. Masterpieces are not made in days, or even months, as Mr Mozart says. But I worry a little about him. He is not a young man. He looks increasingly ill every time I see him."

"I see him very little," said Mr Cazalet neutrally.

"Just so long as he lasts long enough to complete the great work," came Mr Pickles's voice fading down the long corridor. Then I heard him laugh – a silly, childish laugh. I stayed in the privy, frozen to the spot, looking at my reflection in the glass.

I was not looking ill, not "increasingly ill" every time I came to the Pickleses. If I was, the Princess would have noticed and been concerned. She is very conscious of the great gap between my great age and her little one. She has so few congenial souls around her that she is desperate not to lose one of them. No, I was not looking more and more sickly.

On the other hand, there was the bowel trouble that had taken me to the privy in the first place.

There was another thing that troubled me. the foolish laugh as the pair disappeared from earshot. It sounded not just silly, but less than sane. Senile. And I thought of the fearsome mother now apparently sunk into imbecility for many years. Was senility heritable? Did that explain the multitude of reasons given for the Requiem's composition? To me it was for his wife; to his wife it was for his mother; to his thoughtless and senseless sons he gave the least likely explanation of all – that it was for his librarian. It all sounded like a foolish jape. It suggested softening of the brain.

I told all this to the Princess Victoria at the beginning of her next lesson. Her performances that day were more than usually inaccurate and insensitive, and I drew her attention to this several times. Finally, as the lesson ended, she pulled down the piano lid and said: "I'm sorry to play so badly, Mr Mozart. The truth is, I am worried."

"Oh dear. Your mother and Sir John again?"

"Not at all. Well, yes, they *are* at it, but it's you I am worried about, and what you told me about Mr Pickles. Has it occurred to you that, if he is so concerned to hide the authorship of this Requiem, the most convenient death for him would be your own?"

I fear I was so surprised that I could make no adequate response. I took my leave, made for the door, and turned to bow my farewells. The Princess had not finished with me.

"What was the nature of this little room from which you overheard this interesting conversation, Mr Mozart?"

My mouth opened and shut and I scurried out to make my escape.

Arsenic. That's what it was. I wondered at the Princess's knowledge of the ways of the criminal world, but then I remembered she had grown up surrounded by plots and conspiracies. Threats on her life (usually involving the Duke of Cumberland, the next in line to the throne) had been the staple of society and newspaper gossip. Arsenic, the poison that is best administered first in small doses, leading up to a fatal dose. Illness of an internal kind is first established, than accepted as the cause of death. Simple.

And who, after all, questions the cause of death of a seventy-nine-year-old man? I was a sitting duck. And my murderer, insultingly enough, was a brain-softened vulgarian from the North of England!

On the next occasion, later that same week, that Mr Pickles came to hear my latest inspirations I put into action a cunning but simple plan. Standing by the small table, with the chocolate already poured out, I remarked to Mr Pickles that the magnificent proportions of the room were remarkably similar to those of St Margaret on the Square, one of the churches we had considered for the first performance of the Requiem. I suggested he go to the far end of the room to hear how my latest extracts, from the Benedictus, would sound. He was childishly delighted with my proposal. As he walked the length of the room I changed our cups around. The biter bit! I played some of the Benedictus and Mr Pickles expressed his delight: the music penetrated to the far end of the room and was wonderful. We resumed our discussion over chocolate and I looked closely to see if a grimace came over the Pickles face when he tasted it, but I could see nothing.

My next conversation with a member of the Pickles family came two days later. I was sketching a crucial moment in the Rex

Tremendae when the door to my little anteroom opened and the younger son, Seymour, put his head in.

"I say, Mr Mo-zart."

"Yes?"

"This Requiem you're writing and pretending my Dad did it all – who is it supposed to be *for*? I mean, who is it commemorating, if that's the right word? Eh? Who is dead?"

"I believe it is to commemorate your mother."

"Well, she's alive and blooming and if she's ill she's quite unaware of it. And *we'd* – that's Jimmy and me – heard it was for Cazalet the book johnnie. Damned unlikely, what? And now I've heard it is for Gran, who *is* alive but not so you'd notice and there won't be much difference when she finally goes over the finishing line."

"I couldn't comment. Maybe your father is confused. Many people who have lived exceptionally active lives do get ... brain-tired earlier than most of us. Or perhaps he has just been joking."

"Pater doesn't joke. And a Requiem's a pretty funny thing to joke about. But you think senility, maybe? I think I ought to talk to a lawyer. He could be declared *non compos*. Stop him throwing his money around."

"I doubt it. I have seen no signs of it except for the stories about the Requiem. His condition would have to be much further advanced before you could start trying to jump into his shoes."

"I say, you make it sound unpleasant. I mean, I'm deuced concerned—"

I got up and shut the door on him.

A crisis in an affair such as this should not be too long delayed. In a comedy it would come in the third act, with the outcome in the last. Two days after my conversation with Seymour, Isaac Pickles and I had one of our afternoon meetings. We talked first, I explained my aims in the Tuba Mirum, he got up of his own accord and by the time he reached the end of the room the jugs had been shifted round and I was at the piano ready to play and add a sketchy vocal performance as well.

"Enthralling, Mr Mozart," he said, when he returned to the table. "You have excelled yourself – as I always say because you always do." He took up his little jug of chocolate, poured it into his cup, added sugar, stirred, and then took a great, almost a theatrical gulp at it.

It was as if his eyes were trying to pop out of his face with astonishment – he let out a great, flabbergasted yell, then cried out in fear and outrage. As he weakened he bellowed something – a command, a query, a protestation of innocence. I could only assume he had put a hefty dose of arsenic in my chocolate jug, and was now really getting the taste of it for the first time. I ran to the door, but before I got there Seymour had appeared through the door at the room's other end, and before I could shout servants were running into the room from all quarters. When I got back to the table the butler was trying to induce vomiting, others were banging him on the shoulders or trying to put their fingers down his throat. Soon two footmen came with a stretcher and said the doctor had been sent for. He was taken, crying out and retching, to his bedroom. The family physician arrived twenty minutes later. By six o'clock in the evening he was dead. The doctor, though he had not been consulted recently, heard from servants and family Isaac Pickles's complaints about an upset stomach. The lower footman who serviced the privies gave more specific evidence. The doctor signed the certificate. I was left to ponder what in fact had happened.

On the long walk back to my house in Covent Garden I subjected my assumption to detailed scrutiny. Would a man who had just popped a hefty dose of arsenic into my chocolate jug take a first taste of his own chocolate in the form of a massive gulp? I would have thought that, however confident he was of having got the right cup, some primitive form of self-protection would ensure he took a modest sip.

Then again, why would he try to poison me *now*? The Requiem was barely half complete in rough form. If he had waited a few months it could have been in the sort of shape that would mean it could be completed by one of my pupils – the dutiful but uninspired Frank Sussman sprang to mind. Certainly Isaac Pickles couldn't complete it himself. By poisoning me at this point he was spoiling all his own plans, mad as they were, by killing the goose that was laying the golden egg. If senility was setting in – and I rather thought it was – it was strongly affecting his judgement and his logic and causing him to act in his own worst interests.

Was there an alternative explanation? The chocolate, on days when Mr Pickles intended honouring me with his company, was put outside the drawing room on an occasional table, the jugs protected by their padded cosies. When Pickles arrived the chocolate was brought in by the footman if one was around, or by the Great Man himself if one was not. Either outside the drawing room or once he'd got in Mr Pickles added a small amount of arsenic to my jug or my cup. His plan was a very small increase in amount so that my death could be timed to coincide with the completion (or the as-near-as-makes-no-difference completion) of the Requiem. He was already anxiously scrutinizing my appearance and convincing himself I was looking ill, as in the early stages of the operation I must have been.

Someone knew I was switching the jugs or the cups. Someone knew that, after a certain time, the arsenic was going not to me but to the master of the house instead.

Two days after Pickles's death I received a note from Mr Cazalet "written at the request of Mrs Pickles" expressing the hope that I would continue with the Requiem "so that it may be ready in the course of time to commemorate the melancholy passing of her husband." The note did not say that the old conditions no longer applied and I could compose the remaining movements in the comfort of my own house, so I was entitled to assume that the conditions were still in force. I hoped by returning to Pickles Palace I could be in a position to solve the mysteries of its master's death.

The *éclaircissement* was not slow coming. After three hours spent in composing (initial uneasiness being settled by the glorious business of creation) I went to the drawing room to play through the near-complete section of the Kyrie – with occasional contributions from my own fallible voice. As I drew to a close, the far door was opened and the figure of Mrs Pickles wafted towards me.

"Ah, Mr Mozart. Still gloriously in full flood, I'm glad to hear."

I bowed.

"You do me too much honour."

"The tenor solo you sang yourself reminded me of the soprano solo in the Benedictus. I suppose that is intentional?"

She looked at me as she spoke. I held her gaze.

"Intentional of course ... So you have heard some of my compositions for the Requiem already – perhaps from the far door?"

"Retreating when my husband came down to test the acoustics – yes."

"And perhaps at other times taking peeps through the keyhole?"

"Yes. It's rather a large one, conveniently. I could not see you at the piano but I had a good view of the little table and chairs. And of course of the tray, with the jugs under the cosies."

"I see," I said, unusually stuck for words.

"As soon as I saw your little manoeuvres with the jugs or the cups I knew that my warning had at last got through to you. My husband was in the grip of vast senile fantasies in which he was recognized as a great composer. I feared the logical outcome of these delusions, and of all the silly games he played in the household over the person to whom it was to be a memorial, would have to be your death ... But arsenic is a slow-working poison in small doses, and when my husband became your intended victim – because I knew that is what he would have become – I decided to hurry the process up, for reasons I will not go into."

She looked at me.

"It has worked very well," I said. "For both of us."

"For both of us indeed," she said. "I will leave you to your great work. Please remember that if any of this gets out, the first victim of the authorities' suspicions will be yourself. Farewell, Mr Mozart. We shall doubtless meet when the Requiem is performed. You will – what do they call this new trick? – *conduct*, will you not? I shall play the afflicted widow to the best of my abilities."

And that was how my involvement with the Pickleses ended. When, four months later, the Requiem was performed at St Margaret's (a church whose vicar went in for the newfangled business of Catholic ritual and costuming), the glorious work was attributed to me, as all would have known in any case, and

Mr Pickles's only look-in was as the "commissioner and dedicatee of the Requiem who tragically only lived to hear the first-written movements of the score". The Princess Victoria was present with her adulterous mother, and though she said she was "quite prepared to be bored" she had insisted on a place from where she could see the Pickles family, those whom I described in my introduction to the performance as "his grieving widow and his inconsolable sons" (one of whom had a racing journal hidden inside his word sheet). I also saw the family, both when I spoke at the beginning and at the end of the performance, acknowledging the silent (idiotic English habit in a church) expression of enthusiasm. I saw in one of the walled-off family pews a footman put around Mrs Pickles's shoulders a capacious black shawl, preparatory to attending her out to her carriage. There was on his thick-necked, rather brutal face something close to a leer.

Eight months after her husband's death Mrs Pickles was delivered of what was universally accepted to be a daughter of the late Isaac. The London house had been closed up and sold, and Mrs Pickles – in charge of all family affairs until her sons (uncontrollably angry) reached the age of thirty – had moved up North. A year after my last sight of her she had married one of her one-time footmen, now her steward. I hope this time she married for love, though my brief sight of him with her did not suggest it was a wise one.

"He reminds me of Sir John," said the Princess with a shiver. She was on the whole a forgiving little thing, but she never was able to reconcile herself to her mother's lover. I wondered whether, when she came to be our queen, her reign was going to be a lot less fun than most people were expecting.

BEASTLY PLEASURES

Ann Cleeves

WHEN I FAILED my A levels my parents weren't sure what to do with me. But then they've never been quite sure what to do with me. I emerged into the world yelling, fighting to make my presence felt, an alien creature to them, and so I've remained. They are gentle souls, considerate and unworldly, and they consider me a monster. I tell myself that it isn't entirely my fault: my parents were older than most when I was conceived and I am an only child, carrying the weight of their expectations. In a different family, in a freer, less ordered household, I might have been respected, even admired. As it is they regard me with dismay and anxiety. How could someone so unconventional, so physically lovely, belong to them? I am the dark-eyed, shapely cuckoo in their nest.

Of course I set out to fail the exams. It was a challenge: to complete the paper and still achieve so few marks that I'd fail. Almost impossible these days. And harder, I might say, than getting the four As for which the dears had been hoping. All my life I've been bored. I have only survived by playing games. I don't intend to hurt people.

But of course I had hurt *them*. We sat in the garden discussing my future. They looked grey and disappointed and for a very brief moment I wished I'd passed the bloody things so that for once they'd have something to celebrate in me. It was very hot. There was a smell of cut grass and melted tar. In the distance the sound of a hosepipe running and a wood pigeon calling.

"You do realize," I said, "that I could have passed them if I'd wanted."

"Of course." My father looked at me over his glasses. He was a senior social worker and thought he should understand me.

"You've always been a bright girl." My mother wore floral print dresses, which might have been fashionable when she was a student in the seventies. She illustrated children's books – cats were her speciality, though I'd never been allowed pets because she was allergic to their fur.

"We've decided," she said, "that you should go and work for Uncle George."

George wasn't a real uncle, but a distant cousin of my father's. I'd only met him once at my grandmother's funeral and remember him as a rather glamorous figure, with the look of a thirties movie star. During the service he shot several admiring glances in my direction, but even then I was used to men staring at my body and I took no notice. Vanessa, his wife, was pale, draped in purple chiffon. My parents spoke of the couple occasionally but in no detail. George was a businessman and of course they disapproved of that; I had been brought up to believe that money was grubby and something to be ignored. George and Vanessa lived in London and that alone gave me a frisson of excitement. In the big city there would surely be scope for new adventures and I'd find a way to keep boredom at bay.

It seemed anyway that I would have no say in the matter. With an uncharacteristic decisiveness my parents told me that everything had been arranged. I would leave by train the following morning. I would become Uncle George's assistant and return at the end of the year to re-sit my A levels. Working for a living might give me a sense of responsibility. The next day they took me to the station. They stood on the platform waving me off, looking at once sad, guilty and very relieved.

Uncle George had a house in Camden, between King's Cross and Regent's Canal. He was waiting for me at Paddington and in the cab he talked, not expecting any reply.

"Our neck of the woods has certainly gone up in the world. One time you'd only find whores and bag ladies here. Now we live next door to the *Guardian* and a major publishing house."

I said nothing. I was aware of him sitting beside me. He smelled of sandalwood and something else I couldn't recognize: a chemical,

almost medical scent. It occurred to me that for the first time in my
life I was nervous. We stopped in a street that seemed industrial
rather than domestic in character. George took my hand to help me
out and held it for a little longer than necessary. I recognized him
as a kindred spirit then, someone for whom the normal boundaries,
the conventional rules of everyday life had no meaning.

He pushed open arched double doors in a high brick wall and
I followed him into a cobbled courtyard. The rest of the neighbourhood might have been gentrified but this felt like stepping
into a scene from Dickens. There was an L-shaped warehouse or
workshop, with grimy barred windows. On the nearest door a
sign said "Show Room" though from outside there was nothing to
indicate what was being shown. I was suddenly curious about what
George's "business" might be. My parents had never discussed it,
even when they told me I was to be his assistant.

To our left was a tall, narrow house, Victorian Gothic, with
stone steps leading to another arched door. George took a brass
key from his pocket and unlocked it. It was late afternoon, gloomy
for midsummer, with the threat of thunder. I could see nothing of
the room inside and paused for a moment on the threshold. George
switched on a light and suddenly we were in a different continent.
Or even in a different dimension of being. Organic rather than
concrete. It was as if we'd been swallowed by a whale or sucked
into the belly of a huge beast.

It was an entrance hall with a grand staircase leading away from
the centre. But there were no hard edges. The walls were covered
with animal skins – zebra and different kinds of deer. On the floor
were fur rugs, the fur deep brown in colour, dense and very soft.
So many that there were only glimpses of polished wood. I stood
in astonishment then couldn't help reaching out to stroke the nearest wall. The skin was smooth and surprisingly cool to my touch.
George nodded approvingly.

"You obviously have a feel for the work," he said. He set my
rucksack next to an umbrella stand made from an elephant's foot
and led me on to meet Aunt Vanessa.

He explained more about the business over dinner. We ate steak, very rare as I like it, and drank strong red wine. My parents are practically vegetarians, so the meal alone made me feel I'd moved into quite a different world.

"My great-grandfather founded the company," George said. "He was a big-game hunter and saw the opportunity. All the expat British wanted trophies, a record of the things that they'd shot. And it reminded them of Africa when they came home. A memory of the glories of Empire." He gave a little sigh.

"But surely that sort of thing is outlawed now. Do people shoot game any more? I thought all animals were protected." My parents were members of the Green Party.

"The business is certainly different." He sighed again. "Taxidermy isn't what it was. We have to work with museums now. But I still have private clients, at home and abroad. Of course discretion is essential." He gave a sudden wolfish grin. "Occasionally we operate on the very edge of the law." And I saw that was how he liked to operate. He was a game-player too. A risk-taker.

Throughout this conversation Vanessa was almost silent. Her skin was the colour of a white butterfly's wing. How could she eat red meat and drink red wine and stay so pale?

Over the next few weeks I learned more about the business. Only two other people worked in the echoing workshop. All the rooms in the attic were unused, though once there'd been several dozen employees. A serious young man called Harry prepared skins for museums. These were all birds and animals that had died of natural causes or had been killed accidentally. When I first met him he was stuffing a pine marten that had been knocked down on a road in the Highlands. He'd constructed a wire frame and wrapped it with wood wool, before stretching the skin of the animal over it. The marten was a rare and beautiful creature, he said, and most people would never have the opportunity to see it living. He was evangelical about his craft and explained that his exhibits had brought an understanding of natural history to visitors to the museums.

The other employee was Arthur, an elderly man, who'd been in the place since George's father's day. He worked with vats of chemicals and very sharp knives in his own room in the basement.

He dealt with the specimens imported from overseas. Only George was made welcome there. Arthur regarded me with suspicion and seldom spoke. Vanessa looked after the show room but few customers turned up by chance. Most of George's personal clients slipped into his office unannounced. I never saw the victims of their slaughter arrive but the completed objects – polished ivory tusks on brass plaques or mounted wildebeest heads – were returned to them in an anonymous transit van. I had no moral problem about these transactions. The extinction of a great African mammal would have no real impact on me, and I'd always considered that laws were for breaking. Besides, it was clear that most of George's income came from these illegal commissions. Harry of course would have been horrified, but Harry was engrossed in preparing his museum exhibits and never quite understood what was going on.

As I got to grips with the process of preserving skins, de-scaling tusks and preparing heads for mounting, my relationship with George developed in an unexpected and tantalizing way. I had assumed that he would want sex with me. All men did. Harry certainly blushed every time I came within yards of him and even the elderly Arthur watched my legs through narrowed eyes as I walked away from him and breathed more heavily when I approached. George, however, seemed impervious to my charms. There would have been no sport in seducing Harry, but George became a challenge. I wore more provocative clothes, allowed my breast to brush against his bare arm when we worked together. Still there was no response. The more that he ignored me, and the longer he made me wait, the more I wanted him. He became an obsession. I dreamed about him at night and woke up thinking about him. He was a married middle-aged man who smelled of sandalwood and borax, but still I wanted him more than I had wanted anything in my life.

It happened quite suddenly when I was least expecting it. By now it was October, damp and misty, with sodden leaves on the canal path and in the Bloomsbury squares where occasionally I wandered when I felt the need to spend some time away from the business. There were no wild London adventures. I spent my evenings with

George and Vanessa or alone in my room. I had begun to study for my exams. I wanted to cause a sensation, to jump from the lowest A level marks the school had ever known to the highest, and realized that even for me that would take some effort.

Harry and Arthur had just gone home and Vanessa had closed the showroom and walked over the courtyard into the house to prepare dinner. George put his hand on my shoulder, startling me. Since that first day in the taxi he hadn't touched me.

"We've had a new acquisition," he said. "Would you like to see it?"

Of course I said I would. I'd have agreed to anything he asked at that time. He took my hand and led me upstairs to the empty rooms at the top of the building. There was no corridor – one cavernous space led directly into another. Each was lit by a bare bulb. In the shadows were piles of sacking, the occasional moth-eaten skin, odd tools the function of which I could only guess. As we moved further into the attic, I felt my heart rate increase. I was almost faint. At last we arrived at the furthest door. George asked me to close my eyes. I did as he asked immediately. He stood behind me with his hands on my shoulders and walked forwards with me. I felt his body against my spine and my buttocks. With my eyes tight shut I lost all sense of balance and would have stumbled if he hadn't been holding me.

"Now! Open them!'His voice was unsteady with excitement.

It was a tiger. The animal had been skinned where it had been killed in India and the soft tissue of the head, the eyes and the brain removed. That was standard procedure. George had unrolled it and laid it out on the dusty floor for my inspection. In the small, dimly lit room the colours glowed like fire.

"Well?" he demanded.

I thought he'd set this up for me. He'd acquired the tiger just for this moment. It was a token of his admiration. Then he added: "Do you know how much money this will make me? The risk I'm taking by having it here?" And I saw I wasn't the object of his excitement at all.

"It's magnificent." But I couldn't take my eyes from the holes where once the eyes had been. I imagined the skin covering muscle and bone.

"So are you," he said. "You're magnificent too." And now all his attention was focused on me and I pushed away my doubts. He made me wait a little longer while he looked at me at arm's length. He ran his fingers over my head and across my shoulders then lightly over my breasts, exploring me as I had touched the skins on his wall on my arrival at the house. He undressed me and laid me on the tiger skin and that was where we made love.

He must have realized that we might be interrupted. Perhaps for him that added to the thrill of the encounter. If I'd thought about it I'd probably have been excited by the possibility of discovery too. George had turned no locks. In fact Vanessa must have seen us as soon as she arrived at the top of the stairs, through the string of open doors across the empty rooms to the small chamber where George had laid out the tiger.

We weren't aware of her until it was all over. She could have been watching for some time because she was in the next room when we saw her, motionless and silent. I still don't know if she'd guessed what would take place or if she'd come looking for us with an innocent message about dinner or a phone call. Her face was still white except for two perfectly round red patches on her cheeks. In her hand was a knife she must have snatched from the pile of tools on her way through the attic. George pulled on his trousers and stood up, his hands upturned in supplication.

"Vanessa. I'm sorry."

I saw that he had a small paunch, like a young mother's bulge in the early months of pregnancy. It hung slightly over his belt.

Her face became suffused with red and she lunged at him with the knife, hit him at the top of the paunch and pushed it home. I heard the sound of shattering bone and soft flesh. Then the knife was in the air, spattering blood over the tiger skin. She stabbed him again and again until she was sure he was dead. I slid away from her, holding my clothes to my body.

At last she stood still. "I don't blame you," she said, looking down at me, her face still flushed. She looked more human than I'd ever known her; it was as if someone had blown life back into a ghost. "You're not the first of his playthings."

"What will you do now?" I struggled into my clothes.

"I suppose I should phone the police."

"No!" I was horrified at the thought. Perhaps I was more conventional than I'd believed. The idea of this story becoming public knowledge, of my parents reading about it in the Sunday newspapers, was more than I could bear. And it was clear that I'd meant very little to George. Rather than acquiring the tiger as a gift for me, he'd used me to make his experience of the beast more intense.

"What then?" Vanessa turned to me now as if I were a coconspirator, as if we'd planned this murder between us.

"In this place there must be a way to dispose of a human body."

"Oh, I don't really know. I've never been involved in that part of the business." We caught each other's eyes and began to laugh. There was something deliciously ludicrous about the whole conversation.

"I know," I said. "I know what to do."

We rolled George's body in the tiger skin and carried him down to Arthur's basement. I've always been a quick learner. The skinning was less complex than I'd expected – I'd watched Harry working often enough and it wasn't as if we needed a perfect specimen for the purposes of taxidermy. We weren't planning to preserve Uncle George. That would have been macabre. The bones and pieces of attached flesh went into the bin with the other biological waste for disposal by Camden Council and the skin dissolved very quickly in one of Arthur's buckets. The tiger skin, spattered with blood, was a trickier problem. It had already been rubbed with borax and was partly preserved. In the end we cleaned it as best we could and hung it on the wall in a small room at the back of the house. The stains hardly showed in the dim light and there were other skins of endangered species there. If challenged, Vanessa would say that it was ancient. The man who had shot it could hardly go to the police to make a complaint.

I left London by the last train home, having told my parents that I felt uncomfortable in the presence of Uncle George, implying that he'd made unwelcome advances. They weren't surprised; he must have had that sort of reputation and they seemed almost pleased that I'd decided to return to them. Vanessa drove me to Paddington and we made plans on the way. She was quite a different woman now, full-blooded and decisive. She said she'd tell the staff that George and I had run away together. And then she'd sell the house and the workshop. Even in this climate, the area had changed so dramatically that there'd be a market for all that land, so close to St Pancras and the Eurostar terminal.

A few weeks later I re-sat my exams and achieved marks that brought tears of joy to my parents' eyes. "We always knew you were a *good* girl," my mother said. I had decided to read politics at university. I thought I had all the necessary qualities to be an effective politician.

I moved into my little room in Oxford almost a year after Vanessa had stabbed her husband. From my suitcase I took a small wooden box. Inside was a perfectly preserved part of George's anatomy. A memento of those months in London, as potent for me as the tiger had been for him. The exhibit was surprisingly small. In the end, that day, I hadn't resisted the temptation to practise my skills at taxidermy. In more than one sense I had stuffed Uncle George.

THE WALLS

Mark Billingham

IT WAS PROBABLY not the nicest hotel in Huntsville, but I had a good idea that it wasn't the worst either, so I didn't have a lot to complain about. Truth was, I'd booked the Palms over the Internet, so I didn't know too much about anything until I checked in. Besides which, I'd stayed in places that made this one seem like the damn Ritz or whatever, so I was happy enough with a bed I could sleep in and food that didn't come back to haunt me.

That was when I first saw her, in the restaurant at the Huntsville Palms Hotel.

It was seven o'clock or somewhere around there and the place was pretty packed and she was sitting at a big table just across from my small one. She and everyone else at the table with her were talking in hushed voices, which made a nice change from the loudmouth pair behind me who talked about the cost of bedroom furniture for an hour or more, like they were saving the planet or some shit. I turned around to stare at one point. I was hoping they'd see that they were putting me right off my chicken-fried steak, but it didn't do any good. I really don't know how either of them had the time to eat anything with all that jabbering, but they clearly did because they both looked like Mack trucks with heads.

I'd seen a lot of people that size since I'd arrived in Texas.

From where I was sitting I didn't have a great view of her, but what I could see looked pretty good, so I kept glancing over and eventually she turned to try and catch the eye of the waitress. There wasn't really a *moment* between us, nothing like that. But there *was* maybe a half-smile or something before she got the waitress's attention and turned away. I just kept on eating and flicking through the local paper, happy enough to make up the rest of it in my head, the way men do sometimes.

She presses something into my hand when I run into her on the way out of the men's room. Her room number scrawled on a napkin.

She says, "Let's not bother with names," when we get together later on, while she's looking me straight in the eye and taking off her shirt. "Let's just enjoy each other," she whispers. "Get out of our heads and go crazy for one night ... "

There was plenty of strong drink on her table, bottles of beer and red wine. It looked like some sort of family party, even though nobody looked too excited to be there or smiled a whole lot. Looking back, it's not hard to understand why, but at the time I didn't think a great deal of it. There weren't a whole lot of parties in what passes for my family, so it's not like I'm any great expert or anything. They were putting it away, is all I'm saying, her as much as anyone, reaching for those bottles to fill in the silences. That time she tried to find a waitress? That was so she could order another couple of beers.

"You like what you see?" she says, when she's finally naked, and I think it's pretty obvious that I do, because I'm naked too by then. She finishes the beer she's drinking and puts the empty bottle down. I say something that makes her laugh and she reaches out for me, pulls me down on to the bed then moans as she rolls on top.

I had the two older women at the table marked down as the mother and maybe an aunt and I figured that the young guy with the shaved head was her brother. He had the same eyes and the features were pretty similar. He was probably a couple of years younger than me, while she was around the same age I was. I couldn't be sure, because I hadn't got a good look at her close up.

The bedroom-furniture couple had squeezed out from behind their table and gone, which made hanging around easier.

I ordered pecan pie with whipped cream.

I watched the cars pulling in and out of the lot outside.

I spent a few minutes looking at the crossword then gave up.

I wasn't drinking, myself. It's been a good few years since I did

any of that, so I sat there with coffee once I'd done eating, trying
to make the newspaper last. There was plenty of stuff about what
would be going down at the Walls the following day, but I skipped
all that and lingered instead over the local news and the crazy clas-
sifieds. I've always loved that stuff.

The shit that people try to sell, the lonely hearts, the adult
services.

For a small town with only one major industry and a good per-
centage of its population behind bars, there were plenty of massage
parlours and the like. Escort agencies and strip joints and saunas.
I knew the women in the pictures were not the ones anyone was
likely to get if they showed up, but I'm not a monk or anything and
they were nice enough to look at for a while. I turned the paper
over when the waitress came to the table with a refill, then sat and
drank sweet black coffee for another ten minutes, while the day
dimmed outside and the restaurant started to empty.

Just sipping coffee and watching the girl across the top of the
mug. Staring through the steam at the chain around her ankle and
the hand she laid on one of the old women's arms. At the back of
her neck, where the fine blonde hairs ran down beneath the collar
of her blouse.

I'd been thinking about trying to catch a movie or something,
but in the end I just drove around for a while, trying to find a
station that wasn't playing cowboy music. I took the car on to
I-45, south-west into Walker County, and after a while I picked
up signs to Huntsville State Park. I parked in the picnic area next
to a gathering of RVs and camper vans and got talking to a guy
who was cooking sausages and pork chops on one of those cheap
barbecue sets you can pick up at gas stations. He seemed decent
and we chatted about nothing in particular for ten minutes or so,
then I walked down to the lake. The moon was like a dinner plate.
You could see clear across the water to where the pines were thick
and black on the other side, but after a while it started to get cold
and I only had a thin jacket on, so I walked back through the trees
to the car and drove back to the hotel.

I swear I was thinking about nothing but television, but when I walked towards the stairs, I caught sight of her sitting at the small bar in a room just off the reception area. She had her back to me, but I knew it was her. She was on her own, dipping nachos into a bowl of salsa and talking to the woman who ran the place, and I decided there probably wouldn't be anything much worth watching on TV anyway.

I sat a couple of seats away and ordered a Coke and, when I'd got it, I asked if she wouldn't mind sliding the nachos along. I know it sounds like a line, but the truth was, those chops and sausages had made me hungry again. She passed the bowl and moved into the chair next to mine, said she was glad someone was taking the damn nachos away, because otherwise she might have eaten every single one.

"I love these things," I said, grabbing a handful and thinking that she hadn't got any need to worry about a few extra pounds.

"I'd ask if you wanted to have a drink with me." She nodded towards my glass. "But that's not the sort of drink I had in mind."

"Sorry."

"I'm sorry too."

She had that great accent, you know? All those long, flat vowels, but not syrupy and stupid like some. Musical more than anything, and definitely sounding good on her.

"Can't you just pretend it's got rum in it?" I asked.

"I like rum and Coke," she said. "I might have one myself when this is finished." She raised her beer bottle and I leaned over and touched my glass to it.

"Happy to keep you company though," I said.

She was probably a couple of years older than me, but the light wasn't too good in the place and I wasn't bothered either way. Her hair was dirty-blonde, a bob growing out, and though her eyes were already starting to glaze over just a little, they were big and green enough. She wore a dark blouse and skirt and when she leaned towards the bar I could just see a thin, white bra-strap and the gap between flesh and material a little lower down.

"How long are you in town for?" she asked.

"I'm heading home tomorrow."

"Where's home?"

"It keeps changing," I said.

"Originally, then."

"Wisconsin."

She smiled and emptied her bottle. "Bit warmer down here," she said.

I said, "Right," and laughed and took her hand when she offered it to me.

"I'm Ellen," she said.

"Chris ... "

"So why are you in Huntsville, Chris?"

"I'm supervising some construction out at the mall," I said.

"You like it?"

"It's all right."

She ordered more drinks. Another beer for her and an "invisible rum" and Coke for me. When she'd served us, the owner wandered down to the end of the bar and began cleaning glasses. She was a lousy eavesdropper.

"I don't normally drink very much," she said. She put a third of her bottle away in one, and wiped her mouth. "And I know you're thinking that lots of people who drink like fish say that, right?"

"It's not my business," I said.

She laughed, dry and empty. "It's kind of a special occasion."

"That why you're here with your family?"

She nodded, took another drink. "You might not think 'special' is the right word," she said. "Not ... appropriate or whatever. If I tell you why it is we're here."

"You don't have to tell me anything."

"You want to go outside for a cigarette?" She reached down for the handbag at her feet. "God, I *need* a cigarette."

"I don't smoke," I said. "But I'll come with you if you like."

She waved the idea away, then turned on her chair and stared at me. She said that she might just as well talk to a complete stranger about what was happening because she and her family weren't talking about it a whole lot. She cleared her throat and finished her beer. Put down the bottle, then turned back to me.

"I'm here, because tomorrow at six o'clock they're executing the man who killed my sister."

I could not think of a single thing to say.

"Heavy, I know." She reached across me for the nachos. "I bet you're wishing you'd drunk your soda and walked away, right?"

"Maybe."

"You've still got time."

I shrugged. "Sounds like you could do with someone to talk to."

She nodded, pleased, and put a hand on my leg for just a second or two. "My head's buzzing with it, you know? My mom and her sister and my psycho brother have just gone to bed like it's no big deal, or that's what they're telling themselves at any rate, but Jesus, I can't just sit up there in that shitty room and take my make-up off and say goodnight like we're all on some shopping trip or something." She shook her head. "I mean, we've known it's been coming for a while, but still, I can't just pretend this is ... normal, you know?"

"You're right," I said. "It's not normal."

She smiled and let out a long sigh, like she was relieved that I hadn't freaked out or something. She could see that I had barely touched my drink but she said she was going to have another one anyway and waved the woman across from the end of the bar. She ordered another beer and a rum and Coke, and watched me while the drinks were being prepared. After a minute or so she said, "Aren't you going to ask me what he did?"

"Sure."

"What that animal did to her?"

"Look, it's up to you—"

"He beat her so bad they needed dental records to identify her." She leaned close, but made no effort to lower her voice. "He beat her and raped her then he cut her throat like she was no better than a pig and when he'd finished, he sat down and made himself something to eat. He sat there with a sandwich while my nineteen-year-old sister bled out in her bedroom."

"Jesus ... "

"So, you know, tomorrow doesn't make it anywhere near even. Not for what he did, right? Not for *that*."

I grunted something and glanced up at the woman who was laying the drinks down in front of us. She caught my eye and raised a painted eyebrow before walking back to the other end of the bar.

"So, what do you think?"

It was not the easiest question I'd ever been asked. "I think I can understand why you're angry."

"I doubt it," she said.

"Fair point," I said. "She wasn't my sister."

"No, she wasn't."

"It can't be easy holding on to that though. Not for so long." I reached for my drink, moved the ice around in the glass. "I mean, these guys are on death row for years, right?"

"Anthony Solomon Johnson has been on death row for a little over four years and seven months," she said. There was no emotion in her voice. "That's how long we've been waiting for this."

I nodded slow, like I was impressed or something. "For revenge."

"I don't care what you call it," she said. "I've met folks who say that a killer should be put to death the same way he did his killing, but I don't hold with that eye for an eye stuff." She stared down, straightened her skirt. "I don't really give a damn if it hurts, mind you. It *should* hurt." She took a drink. "You agree with me, right, Chris?"

I thought about it. She asked me again.

"They don't know if the needle hurts or not, though, do they?" I pulled the nachos across the bar but the bowl was empty. "I mean, it's not like anyone's around long enough to tell anybody."

She shrugged. Said, "I hope I can see it in his eyes ... "

The rum was going down every bit as easy as the beer and she was starting to slur her words a little. She said something after that, but I didn't catch it and when I leaned closer all I could smell was the booze.

"We're going to have to call it a night, folks."

I looked up and the woman behind the bar was pulling the

empties towards her. I opened my mouth to speak, but she shook her head and even now I'm not quite sure what she meant by it. I glanced at the bill and put thirty dollars on the bar and when the woman had taken the cash away, Ellen began talking again. It was not much above a whisper, but this time I caught it easily enough.

"I can't be alone," she said.

"You've got your family," I said. "Your mother's upstairs."

"You know I don't mean that." Her eyes were wide suddenly, and wet. "You want me to beg?"

"No, I don't want that," I said.

She and her mother were sharing a room, so we went to mine. There was not a great deal of choice in the mini-bar, but she didn't seem too picky, so I told her to help herself. She took a beer and a bag of chips and we sat together on the bed with our feet on the quilt and our backs against the headboard.

The window was open a few inches and the traffic from I-45 was just a hum, like an insect coming close to the glass every so often and retreating again.

"I don't know how I'm going to feel," she said.

"Afterwards?"

She nodded.

I remembered her face when she'd been talking in the bar. The way she'd talked about wanting it to hurt. "Pretty good, by the sound of it," I said.

"Yeah, I'll feel good … and *relieved*. I mean how I'm going to feel when I'm watching it happen, though. It's not something everyone gets to see, is it?"

"No, it isn't."

"Probably something you never forget, right?"

She made it sound like she was going whale-watching. She slid down the bed a little and she kept on closing her eyes for a few seconds at a time.

"You think you might feel guilty after?" I asked.

Her eyes stayed closed as she shook her head. "Not a chance."

"I hope you're right."

"Why the hell should I feel guilty when he never did?"

"You know that for sure?"

She opened her eyes. "Well, it wasn't like I was visiting him every week or nothing, but I don't think a man like that has any normal human feelings." She took a swig of beer, ignored the dribble that ran down her neck. "He wrote us a letter a month or so back and he said he was sorry, all that shit, but it's easy to come out with that stuff when you know the needle's just around the corner, right? Probably told to do it by his lawyer. So they've got something to show when they're pushing for a stay, you know?" She tried to brush away the remains of the chips from her shirt. "Said he'd found God as well."

"I think that happens a lot."

"Yeah, well, tomorrow he'll get a lot closer to Him, right?"

"You religious?"

"Sure," she said.

"So this isn't a problem for you?"

"Why should it be?"

"What happened to 'thou shalt not kill'?"

"Shame *he* never thought about that."

"He obviously didn't believe in anything back then," I said.

She shook her head again and screwed her face up like she was getting irritated. "Look, it isn't me that's going to be doing the killing, is it?" She raised the bottle, then thought of something. "OK, smart-ass, what about 'as you reap, you shall sow'? It's something like that, right?"

I nodded. "Something like that, yeah."

"Right." She turned on to her side suddenly and leaned up on one elbow. She slid a leg across the bed and lifted it over mine. "Anyway, what the hell are we talking about this stuff for?"

"You were the one started talking about God," I said.

"Yeah, well, there's other things I'd rather be talking about." She blinked slowly, which she probably thought was sexy, but which made her seem even drunker, you know? "Other things I'd rather be *doing*."

"I'm not sure that's a good idea."

"Come on," she said. "I know that's what you want. I saw you looking in the restaurant."

"Yeah, I was looking."

"So?"

"You've had too much to drink."

"I've had just enough."

I smiled. "You won't feel good about yourself tomorrow."

"I've got more important things to worry about tomorrow," she said. She put a hand between my legs. "Now are you going to get about your business, or what?"

I did what she was asking. It didn't take long and it was pretty clear that she needed it a damn sight more than I did. She cried a little afterwards, but I just let her and I'm not sure which of us got to sleep first.

I left early without making any noise, and when I turned at the door to look at her wrapped up in the thin hotel sheet, I was thinking that, aside from the fact that I *am* crazy about nachos and salsa, almost everything I'd told her about myself had been a lie.

God only knows why they call it "The Walls". They're thick enough and tall enough for sure, but the men behind them have got a damn sight more to worry about than what's keeping them inside.

The Huntsville Unit in particular.

One of the deputy wardens led me across the compound from the Visitors' Waiting Area and in through a grey metal door. They try to keep the families separate until the last possible moment, which is understandable, I suppose, and even though there was only me and some crazy woman who'd been writing to Anthony for the last few years, we had our own escort. The prison chaplain would be a "witness" too, of course, but I guessed he had no choice but to be kind of neutral about what was happening, so he didn't really count.

The deputy warden's highly polished shoes squeaked on the lino-leum floor as we walked towards the room next to the execution chamber. Then he opened the door and politely stood aside as I walked in.

The place was pretty crowded.

I knew there would be a few State officials as well as representatives from the media, but I hadn't figured on there being that many people and it took me a few seconds before I spotted her. She was sitting on the front row of plastic chairs, her mother on one side of her, the other older woman and her psycho brother on the other side. Like everyone else, she'd turned to look when the door opened and I saw the colour drain from her face when I nodded to her. Her mother leaned close to whisper something, but she just shook her head and turned round again.

I walked towards the front of the room and took a seat on the end of the second row. We sat in silence for a couple of minutes, save for some coughing and the scrape of metal as chairs got shifted, then one of the officers ran through the procedure and raised the blind at the window.

Tony was already strapped to the gurney.

There were three men inside the chamber with him and one of them, who I figured was the Warden, asked Tony if he wanted to say anything. Tony nodded and one of the other men lowered a microphone in front of his face.

Tony turned his head as far as he was able and said how sorry he was. For what he'd done, and for all the shit he'd laid at his own family's door down the years. He finished up by saying that he wasn't afraid and that everyone on the other side of the glass should take a good look at his life and try to learn something. I'm not quite sure what he meant by that and, things being how they were, it wasn't like I had the chance to ask him.

He closed his eyes, then the Warden gave the signal and everything went quiet.

Three drugs, one after the other: the sedative, the paralytic and the poison.

It took five minutes or so and Tony didn't really react a great deal. I saw his lips start to go blue and from then until it was finished, I paid as much attention to *her* face as his. She knew I was watching her, I could tell that. That I was thinking about all the things she'd said, and the things she'd asked me to do to her the night before at the Huntsville Palms Hotel.

Wanting to see just how good she felt about herself the next day.

I left the room before she did, but I waited around just long enough to get one last look at her. Her face was the colour of oatmeal and I couldn't tell if her mother was holding on to her or if it was the other way around. I guessed she was right about one thing; that it would not be something she would forget.

I had to shield my eyes against the glare when I stepped back out into the courtyard and walked towards my car. I drove out through the gates and past a small group of protesters with placards and candles. A few of them were singing some hymn I couldn't place and others were holding up Tony's picture. Later on, I would be coming back to collect my brother's body and make the arrangements, but until I did, he wasn't going anywhere.

Right then, all I wanted was to get away from "The Walls" and drive south-west on I-45.

To get another look at that big beautiful lake in the daylight.

MOON LANDING

Paul Johnston

I⟨T WAS THE⟩ morning after the longest day that Moon made his decision. It didn't help that his head was splitting after James's party, his throat parched and his fingers quivering. The night before had been a disaster, but the truth was he'd been wearing donkey's ears for weeks. He'd tried to be understanding, he'd tried to be a good neighbour, but he'd been wasting his time. Some people just didn't care. The noise had got worse, the dogs barking all night and the baby screaming as if it was possessed by the most anti-social fiend in the underworld. As for the music ... either the daughter was tone-deaf or she'd been paid by some caterwauling boy band to play their songs 24/7. He wasn't going to take it any more.

Things had looked good when he'd moved into the fourth-floor flat in the converted warehouse behind the City Chambers. Moon – tall, dark and what he thought was handsome – was a business lawyer in a big firm. He'd used contacts to secure the luxury three-bedroom for a price less steep than an ordinary mortal would pay. He'd taken every reasonable precaution, running checks on the building's other occupants. His next-door neighbour was a stock-broker who spent a lot of time travelling, while the people below were softly spoken bankers whose idea of a raucous evening was to worship at the shrine of Jeremy Paxman. Angela, the middle-aged woman who rented the penthouse, had seemed to be no problem. She was a freelance writer who worked on her own and had few visitors.

All that suited Moon – he was Kevin to his mother, but anyone who wanted to be his friend soon learned to use his surname; he spent at least four evenings a week with his laptop in the room he'd equipped as a study. His days were filled by power breakfasts, high-level meetings, alcohol-free business lunches and visits to clients, so he had to do the research and reports in his own time. That didn't bother him. His friends, most of them lawyers about to be offered partnerships, did the same.

For three months Moon had done that without breaking much of a sweat. The flat was great, even though the best view was across the lane to another renovated Victorian block, full of men and women who came home wearing tailored suits and changed into designer casual wear. That was no hassle. The only view he wanted was of his new silver Audi parked below in the designated resident's space. He worked, he chilled, he listened to his music – Waits, fado, Calexico – at a respectable volume. At least, no one complained. He'd been invited round by all his neighbours, including Angela in the penthouse. She was in her late forties, he reckoned, her bobbed hair dyed auburn and her figure interesting enough beneath the loose clothes she wore. Moon had even thought about trying his luck with her.

Then the daughter, the grand-daughter and the dogs materialized.

Moon didn't see the new arrivals, but he smelled and heard them as soon as he came in the street door. There was a stain on the carpet and the frantic howling from above made it clear that a four-legged specimen had cocked a leg or squatted. The lift was full of the sweet-and-sour reek of infant puke and, as he got out on his floor, Moon heard high-pitched screams join the canine racket from the penthouse. They were followed by the yell of an irate woman. Letting himself into his flat, he realized the sounds were even louder there. They were loudest of all in his study.

Moon stood with his fists clenched and told himself not to panic. He went into the kitchen and poured himself a glass of organic orange juice, no bits. So Angela had visitors. Pretty noisy, dirty visitors for such a pleasant woman, but they'd soon be gone. They'd better be. He had a report to write.

But they stayed. And they got noisier. It was nearly a month now. Moon had waited a few days before calling Angela. His report had been markedly less well received than his efforts normally were, and his sleep not so much disrupted as destroyed – earplugs were no help at all. His neighbour was apologetic. Her daughter Sharon had broken up with her husband and had nowhere else to go. Her grand-daughter Mimi was teething, but she'd soon be over it. Yes, she knew the dogs were a problem, she wasn't getting much sleep herself. "Don't worry," she said. "Sharon will find her own place in a week or two."

But she hadn't. And Mimi was still squealing. She must have had a full set of fangs coming through. Maybe the dogs – one a mongrel with a face that looked like it had been stoved in by a frying-pan, the other a scrawny terrier – were howling in terror. Moon had tried everything to get his work done. He stayed late at the office, though the cleaning team made a racket that was only marginally less distracting. In the flat, he put on his top-of-the-range headphones and cranked up the decibels, but concentration then became impossible. He even swallowed his pride and bought a supermarket CD of "relaxing sounds", but the attack dogs and the demon child cut through that like a knife through crème caramel.

Moon realized he was being too soft and decided to hit back. The whole of Led Zeppelin Two at the top end of the dial obscured the sounds from the penthouse, but brought a pained rebuke from the bankers below – and made Mimi screech even louder. Next morning, Sharon came down the stairs from the penthouse in a rush when he was leaving for work.

"I suppose you thought that was funny, pal." Her voice was much less refined than her mother's. "Well, I didn't and neither did my baby." Above, the dogs were barking, their claws rattling on the door.

Moon looked into bloodshot eyes. Sharon was thin and wan, her face marked with fading bruises. The skin round one of her eyes was blackened. He felt his antipathy well up and then suddenly drain away. He turned away with his head down, but the injustice soon got to him. What right did she have to complain when he countered her noise with his?

Come on, man, you're a lawyer, Moon told himself later. He called the company that owned the penthouse and got them to write Angela a letter about the noise and presence of animals. As for the baby, the tenant was entitled to have her grand-daughter to stay – the woman on the phone made him sound like the unreasonable one. He contacted the council's noise pollution unit. They were polite, but made it clear that they had greater priorities than a self-proclaimed luxury apartment block. He even spoke to the police, who brusquely declined to get involved. The other neighbours were useless. They didn't get the full force of the din and, anyway, they were about as confrontational as a fish supper.

His workmates suggested official letters and court action. Before he started down that line, he was called in by the senior partner and informed that the firm could do without one of the people it had invested so much in being distracted by a personal case at such a sensitive phase of his career. The quality of his work had become uneven. Did Mr Moon get the message?

He did and he was devastated. Without work he was nothing. Going to the nearest pub, he knocked back a couple of whiskies and got his breathing under control. Not only had the witches and their familiars ruined his private life, they were fatally damaging his career. But his nerves were so shot, his brain so churned, that he couldn't come up with a coherent plan. At least his mate James was having one of his famously over-the-top parties at the weekend. He'd think about how to close down the penthouse zoo after that.

The party started well. James, a hyper-flash advocate who specialized in keeping murderers out of jail, had hired a nightclub. The catering was by one of the city's top operators. After several glasses of Krug and a platter of oysters, Moon found himself in a clinch with Vivienne, a statuesque blonde who worked with James. He was surprised, considering the dark rings around his eyes and the twitch that sleep deprivation had given him, that she was interested. And even more surprised when she suggested they go back to his place – apparently the woman she shared with was having her parents to stay. Maybe his luck was finally changing, he thought, as he tapped in the code of the street-door. When they emerged from the lift, he heard no sound from above.

Not for long. As soon as they got into Moon's place, the music started, even though it was after midnight. "Shake it, baby, shake it, yeah, yeah, yeah," sang the pimply boys against a pounding beat.

"Yeah, baby," Vivienne said, frowning.

Then the dogs started, arhythmically. Moon could hear Mimi screaming in the background too.

Vivienne looked around the flat, giving no sign of being impressed. "Is it always such a madhouse here?" she asked, with a mocking smile. "Why don't you do something about it?"

"Watch me," Moon said, the weeks of inadequacy making his cheeks blaze. He ran up to the penthouse. As he hammered on the door, he looked down and saw Vivienne on the landing below.

The door opened and, before he could move, the dogs were on him. The pig-ugly mongrel went for his groin, while the terrier nipped away at his ankles. In a desperate attempt to save his man-hood, Moon went to ground, giving the Jack Russell even more targets. The bites hurt, as did the slap that Sharon gave him. She was screaming about her baby being terrified of him and that music was the only way she calmed down. Her mother was a witness to the way he was hassling them, he was nothing but a stuck-up twat.

Worst of all for Moon was the look on Vivienne's face as she helped him back into his flat. She left him to get to the hospital on his own for a tetanus jab.

On his way home in the early morning, the birds in full voice, Moon finally saw the light. He'd tried not to allow himself to be dragged down to Sharon's level, but there was no point. It was time to play hard ball and Wee Stevie was the answer.

Before Moon had joined the firm, he'd worked for a small Legal Aid partnership. Back then he had some crazy idea about saving society's unfortunates from the vicissitudes of life. A lot of the work was petty crime and he soon got bored with the fecklessness of his clients. Then he met Wee Stevie and realized immediately that the guy was a serious piece of work. Smart, a half-smile perpetually on his lips, brought down only by his cretinous pals, Stevie had nerves of steel. He was also, despite his wiry body and pretty-boy looks, the most violent individual Moon had ever come across. After

Moon got him off an assault charge by digging the dirt on the sole witness, Wee Stevie told him he was for ever in his debt.

"You ever need any business doing, I'm your man," he said, winking conspiratorially. "The sky's the limit, Mr Moon."

All it needed was a phone call. Moon was going to be out with James and his friends the next Saturday night. He'd make sure he wasn't back before 3 a.m. Wee Stevie would be long gone by then, leaving behind a pair of dead dogs and couple of traumatized women. Moon had told him not to lay a hand on Angela or Sharon, and especially not on the baby. But it was to be made clear that they were all to be gone the next morning and the lease terminated forthwith. And if they wanted the kid to make it to primary school, they'd better keep their mouths shut.

Saturday came and Moon managed to enjoy himself, despite Vivienne's ironic smiles. He told her he'd solved the problem, though he wasn't going to invite her back, not tonight anyway. At half-past two, having consumed a heavy load of cocktails, he left the club and headed home. He'd sobered up considerably by the time he got to the lane. For once he didn't cast more than a glance at his precious Audi. This was going to be very interesting.

Punching in the code he'd given Wee Stevie, Moon opened the street door and made no less noise than he normally would coming back late. There was no sound from above, even when he came out of the lift on the fourth floor. This was looking good, but his heart was pounding. Wee Stevie was an animal. What if he'd lost it and laid into the women? What if he'd done something to Mimi?

Moon moved towards his door. He had to keep his cool. If he went up to the penthouse, he'd potentially link himself to whatever the lunatic had done. But he couldn't hold himself back. Now the noise had finally stopped, his mind was clear again, despite the booze. The need to know was overwhelming.

Leaving his shoes behind, he went up the stairs. The door was ajar. Had Stevie dealt with the dogs as planned? What about the women? Could they have left already?

After listening at the gap, Moon took a deep breath and slowly pushed the door further open. The penthouse had a large open living space to the left. There was no sign of anyone in it. To the right, the doors of the bedrooms and bathroom were all wide open. The place was still, as silent as an ancient tomb. Moon tried to swallow, his throat suddenly drier than the Sahara. Where were they? Where were the dogs? He wasn't necessarily in the clear yet. They were occasionally quiet, so Sharon must have been able to shut them up somehow.

Tiptoeing across the stripped-pine floor, he reached the master bedroom and gasped. Angela was on her back, motionless, her arms outspread. Before he could move towards her, he heard a sound that made the hairs spring up on the back of his neck. It was a soft and sibilant laugh.

"Mr … Moon," said Wee Stevie from the floor by the door to the en suite bathroom. Then he coughed and dark blood slopped out over his lips. His head rolled to the side and his eyes glazed.

Moon went to him, then stopped when he saw the figure that appeared in the doorway.

"You did this," Sharon said hoarsely, Mimi clamped to her chest. "You told him I was here."

Moon took in her wide-eyed stare and then glanced back at Stevie. He was clutching a short length of piping in his right hand. There was a patch of blood on his abdomen, the handle of a kitchen knife protruding from it. "I … " Moon looked at her. "You know him?"

"He's my husband," Sharon said, her face hardening as she moved forwards. "And you told him where to find me."

Moon took a step back when he saw the other knife in her hand. "I … no, I've never seen him … " The lie was feeble. "What … what happened to your mother?"

"He hit her. I think she'll be all right." Sharon was getting closer. "Which is more than can be said for you, shithead. You're a lawyer. Self-defence should cover me, don't you think?"

Moon panicked and made a dash for the door, Sharon shielding Mimi from him. He felt his socks skid on the wooden floor. "What about the dogs?" he said, looking around.

Sharon gave him an empty smile. "And there was me thinking

you didn't like them." She jerked open the door of the broom cupboard. "Get him, girls!"

Moon started to run as the mongrel and terrier came for him. He went towards the sofa to put it between him and them, but his feet went from under him and he found himself flying towards the window. Arms extended, body stretched in a loose dive, he braced himself for impact.

Unfortunately for him, the window-lock had been disengaged. As he hit the glass, it swung open and he was through in a flash.

All this for a bit of peace and quiet, he thought.

Moon carved a graceful arc through the lightening sky, the barking of the dogs and the baby's cries filling his head as he landed on the roof of his Audi and died.

PARSON PENNYWICK IN ARCADIA

Amy Myers

"MY DEAR JACOB, it is death who addresses us, not a gentleman who has indulged in the idyllic pastoral life of Arcadia. You are most certainly wrong in your interpretation of the phrase. Et in Arcadia *ego*, remember. Death is present even in Arcadia." This was a familiar conundrum for us both, all the more enjoyable as there is no answer to it. Two elderly parsons may be allowed a little fun, especially as I feared that our visit to the Palladian mansion of Fern House might not prove to be as delightful as it sounded.

Jacob adjusted his wig before giving me his earnest attention, always a sign that my friend is about to stand firm – usually on marshy ground, alas. "Self, Caleb. The *et* qualifies the *ego*, not the Arcadia. My source is Schidoni. *Et ego in Arcadia vixi.* Translated, that is: And I too have lived in Arcadia."

Death must have the last word. I was about to reply somewhat heatedly that Schidoni was irrelevant, owing to his inclusion of the word *vixi*, which altered the construction and thus the meaning of the phrase. At that moment, however, our host appeared to greet us. Many guests were already present, judging by the numbers of carriages in the forecourt.

The Honourable Horatio Simple was an eccentric gentleman, devoted more to his continental travels and collection of antiquities than to his fellow human beings, whom he approached with distrust. Alas, this applied even to his betrothed. I had a great fondness for Eleanor Herrick, and my heart was sad that she was being forced by impoverished parents into marriage with Horatio rather than bestowing her hand on his younger brother. Mr John Simple was a straightforward and honest young man, who smarted with pain for her loss.

Horatio was a far different kettle of fish – which reminded me, in the way that my mind can nowadays all too frequently jump, of Mortimer Kettle, who was perhaps the most famous collector of relics of classical times. In public they maintained their rivalry was purely good-natured, but knowing Horatio I found that hard to believe. I wondered whether Mr Kettle would be here today for the much awaited opening of Fern House's newly designed gardens.

I had always had a great admiration for these gardens, around which I frequently strolled when Horatio's and John's father, Percival Simple, was alive. Their formal design and colour, surrounded and enhanced by famous yew hedges, gave the eye much pleasure, but times and fashions change, alas, and even gardens can no longer rest in peace. When Percival died three years ago, he can hardly have dreamt of the havoc to fall upon his beloved estate at the hands of his heir Horatio.

"Parson Pennywick, Parson Trent," Horatio greeted us affably. "Pray do not fail to visit my tomb."

Such oddity did not disturb me, as I knew Horatio better than did Jacob, and I replied politely, "We should be delighted."

"Renaissance, of course, carved for one of the Medicis and newly brought from Florence," our host explained. "One far-off day it shall have the honour of enclosing myself."

I saw Jacob blench, but perhaps that was more at our host's chosen costume than at the proposed visit to the tomb. Horatio was dressed as an Arcadian shepherd. Tight-fitting breeches adorned his lower body, perhaps because the weather was chilly for an Arcadian May, but the upper half was clad in Grecian shepherd style – or at least in accordance with the various painted impressions of it provided to us by artists over the centuries.

"But you are not dressed for Arcadia," Horatio continued querulously.

Our invitations, splendidly embossed with flower and small

animal designs, had been for "An Afternoon in Arcadia", and we had been encouraged to dress appropriately for the occasion.

"…… dressed for Arcadia," Horatio's companion, young Nathaniel Drake, echoed indignantly in support of his master. He had a habit of repeating Horatio's words as if by this method he could ensure his continued employment. He was clad as a much humbler shepherd, I noticed, and no breeches had been permitted for him, merely a smock. I had not realized that even Arcadia had its hierarchical distinctions.

"I serve the Good Shepherd," I replied amiably to Horatio. "As His loyal sheep, I prefer not to compete with His authority."

Horatio did not seem amused, and Nat looked anxious. I felt sorry for Nat, now a young man approaching thirty and dependent on Horatio for his livelihood. He was a bright lad, and though he accompanied Horatio everywhere his aspirations for independence had come to nothing. Nevertheless he did his best to support his employer at every turn.

"Behold," Horatio said proudly, after we had entrusted our horses to the groom and been escorted through the house to the terrace. I had been amazed at the countless antiquities that had sprung up within it since my last visit during his father's lifetime, and even more at the addition of an orangery. "Pray feast your eyes on Arcadia itself."

"I shall indeed. It is a spectacle of great wonder," I managed to reply honestly. "Capability Brown's work, no doubt?"

There was a disapproving silence, which I did not at first understand. Nor Jacob either, I imagine. We were too overwhelmed at the vista before us. Gone were the formal gardens I had loved. Instead, a pastoral scene greeted us. The eye was swept into the far distance where water shimmered – a lake perhaps? Hills, trees, follies and pools greeted the eye wherever it fell. Carefully created wildness replaced order and varying hues of green the bright colours of the flowers I had loved so well. Even from this terrace, I could see antique statues sprouting between the bushes and in every nook and cranny, peeping out as though surprised to find themselves in Arcadian England.

I disliked this new landscaped garden, and mourned the loss of Percival's emphasis on grace and tradition. I was aware, however, of Horatio's shrewd eye on me, and kept an admiring expression, while murmuring that elderly people move more slowly with the times.

In the midst of this pastoral bliss, I could see a maypole, targets set out for archery and various arbours where guests might dine and drink. None of these connected with any vision of Arcadia that I could recollect, and I sensed Jacob stiffening with disapproval at my side. Little wonder. Arcadian costume – or an eighteenth-century interpretation of it – was to be seen everywhere. The lady shepherdesses looked more delightful than the gentlemen, needless to say, although their huge flowery hats and wide skirts would surely have been an inconvenience in tending Arcadian flocks. As for the gentlemen shepherds, those who had nobly forgone breeches might well have repented of the decision, I thought, as I saw the amount of naked leg displayed between boot and smock or sheepskin.

There was an air of uncertainty about the guests, perhaps due to the sheep who wandered cautiously amongst them. Sheep in society Kent were usually safely divided from the viewer by a ha-ha ditch, and their introduction at these closer quarters might not be receiving universal acclamation. I did not dare glance at Jacob, who is my very dear friend but more accustomed to greeting Arcadia in the pages of his library than in person.

Then I realized the reason for the disapproving silence of our host, as Horatio replied heatedly, "This paradise is my masterpiece. I am its designer."

" ... my masterpiece," repeated Nathaniel anxiously. "I am its designer."

He was ignored by his master. "The perfect home for my Aphrodite."

" ... home for my Aphrodite."

"And the Renaissance sarcophagus?" I enquired.

Horatio giggled mysteriously. "Perfection, the crowning jewel, Parson. It will reveal its secrets at four o'clock, and your presence is required. Meanwhile, dear friends, pray disport yourselves merrily in Arcadia."

Jacob and I duly endeavoured to disport ourselves, but our merriment was feigned. There was a curious atmosphere in this Arcadia, as though each shepherd and shepherdess glanced warily at his or her neighbour to see what degree of smile would be most fitting to display. Perhaps I imagined this in my regret for the destruction of a garden I had loved.

Nevertheless, Horatio's garden was not without its merits. In the hours that passed Jacob and I came upon a pool so exquisite, so covered with lilies, and a small rustic bridge so silent among the rocks surrounding it that nature herself seemed to hold her breath, overcome with what art could achieve. For it was undoubtedly art to have positioned the lilies so cleverly, to plant varied trees and bushes both to entice the curious onlooker and to create mystery as to what they might be shielding from his sight. Many other gardens boast such features, but this pool and the cunningly designed grotto that formed an arc around it showed that art could complement, not battle with, nature. The water sparkled as it trickled down rocks to a series of tiny pools until it reached the one at which we stood so admiringly. The only obvious sign of man's intrusion was a small antique statue of a woman gazing into the pool as if, so I remarked to Jacob, she would woo her own reflection, like Narcissus in the old legend.

"She is fine, is she not?"

The harsh voice at my side startled me, for it was certainly not Jacob's. I turned to see a gentleman I recognized as Mr Mortimer Kettle at my side. His round, portly figure and bright ginger unbewigged hair were unmistakable.

"She is *my* Aphrodite," he continued, full of angry passion. "Do you realize, Parson, how *rare* it is to find a statue of the goddess of love? I would know mine anywhere, and this is it, stolen from me by our noble host."

Unfortunately the loyal Nathaniel, who was standing by a sundial nearby, had overheard, and at once defended his master. "Aphrodite is rightfully here, sir. As is the Medici sarcophagus—"

"He has that too?" Kettle struggled for composure. There were tears on his face but whether of anger or loss was not clear.

"Horatio bade me to come to this place at four o'clock. Is he to apologize for his perfidiousness? I shall not leave here today without my Aphrodite."

Nathaniel skilfully placed himself between the statue and her would-be abductor. "There are others joining us, sir. We must all go together." He looked nervous now, and no wonder. Montague Kettle was not the only person to have strong emotions where Horatio was concerned. Whatever our host had planned for this ceremony – if that is what it was – he would need to take care. *Caveat canem*, I thought; there might be dogs a-plenty snapping at his heels.

Squire Carstairs, hardly to my surprise, as he is lord of the manor of this parish of Farnley, now joined us, together with dear Eleanor, and John Simple, who both looked as though they would fain be elsewhere. When Horatio commanded, however, they had little choice, and I was glad of the Squire's presence, as he is our local justice. Nothing, I told myself, could therefore be amiss. Even Horatio would plan no mischief if the Squire was to be present.

Our small group followed Nathaniel as he led the way up a stone path cunningly concealed by the side of the grotto. At a last twist this led to a high rocky outcrop looking down over the gardens and on to the pool beneath. On its far side a hillside seemed to lead down to wild woodland, and the outcrop itself was framed by bushes forming a delightful arc around it and providing for a small arbour with a seat for two. The outcrop was an impressive sight, dominated by the large open stone sarcophagus with splendid carvings that suggested it had indeed been created for a powerful and rich occupant.

Horatio was not yet present, but in the bushes I was sure I could see old Tom Hawkins, Percival's knowledgeable gardener of many decades, who shared my own deep love of his master's gardens, and had none for Percival's heir. What, I wondered, was he doing here? I saw Montague Kettle edge forward to inspect the side of the sarcophagus, I saw Eleanor and John hold back, I saw Nathaniel walk over to the tomb.

His cry of horror pierced us all, and I rushed to his side.

Death had indeed come to Arcadia. Horatio's bloodied body lay in the bottom of the sarcophagus. Across his chest lay an arrow, as if, having done its foul work, it had been disdainfully flung in after him.

In times of shock, the eye can be a keen observer, because such a moment as we had experienced remains frozen in time and memory, every detail as crystal clear as the trickling water cascading down the rocks below us. I remember the look on John's face, as he realized that the brother who had barred his way all these years was dead, but I could not then interpret it. I remember the blankness of Eleanor's expression and Mr Kettle's mingled shock and triumph as he looked on his rival's body. I remember Nathaniel's pale face, as he collapsed on to the arbour seat. I remember the hatred in old Tom's face, as he came forward from the bushes, belatedly doffing his cap in respect. I shuddered for us all, but mostly for Horatio, who had met such a dreadful end as a result, surely, of his own actions.

"Squire?" I asked tentatively.

The Squire looked a gentleman more inclined to the bottle after luncheon than such a task as he must now face. I suspected he had no more liking for Horatio than I, but he had a duty to perform. He was the local magistrate and this was surely a task beyond the parish constable's handling. It was the Squire who must call for the coroner.

It was clearly an unwelcome task, but he took charge immediately. "Stay, if you please," he snapped at John, who was about to escort Eleanor down the steps, his arm tenderly about her waist.

John looked as if he were about to protest, but wisely did not. Nor did Mr Kettle who had already begun to run down to the gardens below us. He meekly returned to join us. The Squire next turned to Jacob and myself. "A doctor should be summoned and the innkeeper."

As I was not from this parish, the latter surprised me, until I realized that the innkeeper might be the coroner here. Having some experience in cases of sudden death, I reluctantly decided that I should remain here, but Jacob very willingly departed on his errand.

"A prayer for the soul of Horatio Simple," I said quietly.

The Squire reddened at his previous emphasis on the secular demands of the situation, as I recalled our small group to the fact that there was a dead man here, no matter what their liking or otherwise might have been for him.

I drew the Squire to one side after my simple plea to our Lord was concluded, so that we might speak privately. "My services are at your disposal, Squire."

He looked surprised. "Why, I need none," he told me gruffly. "The affair is shocking but simply solved. The gardener was present when we arrived and there is but one entrance to this place. He is our man."

I was aware that Tom had retreated to the far side of the outcrop, too scared to venture forth, and I knew then that not only were my services going to be necessary but diplomacy also. Tom would not have been an invited guest to this place, so why was he here?

"That may be so," I agreed. "Tell me, Squire, what do you make of the arrow?"

"Make of it?" He looked bewildered.

I explained. "The arrow has been pulled out of the wound by the murderer, leading to the amount of blood we can see on the body. However, if Mr Simple were killed on the ground here, and his body thrown into the sarcophagus after, then his blood would be scattered on the ground around us, but I see none. Why should the gardener trouble to conceal his crime in such a way?"

The Squire paled, and hastened to check my words. Then he straightened up. "Are you telling me the poor fellow was forced to climb into his own tomb and was then shot from above?"

"So it would appear." And yet my answer did not satisfy me.

"Then a woman is indicated." The Squire did not name Eleanor or turn to look at her, but his meaning was clear, even if he was reluctant to put it into words. I could see that her face was still a mask under the large hat which partially shielded it. What her real emotions might be were known only to her. "To put a body in this tomb would take more strength than a woman possesses," the Squire continued, "but a woman would have to persuade a man to lie there of his own accord." He was about to stride over to interrogate her further, when I stopped him.

"Nathaniel guarded the only apparent passage up here," I pointed out.

"Quite. So Tom's our man," the Squire agreed in the belief that we were at one.

"Ask Nathaniel what he knows," I said gently. "He was alone while he guarded the steps."

"Bless me if you're not right, Parson."

Squire Carstairs walked over to the apprehensive Nat, without suggesting that I join him, but I hastened to follow as he planted himself in front of the poor fellow. "What do you know about this affair, Nathaniel?" he roared.

To Nat the Squire must have looked a fearsome sight, but he answered bravely enough. "Mr Horatio said no one was to come up to the tomb until the sundial showed four o'clock, and then only yourself, Parson Pennywick and his companion, and those others he had asked to attend."

"Those others who perhaps had reason to hate him most," I murmured. "Strange." The Squire brushed my comment aside, however, and continued to fire questions at Nat.

"When did you begin these guardian duties of yours?"

"Two o'clock, sir."

"Was Mr Simple already here?"

"No, sir, he came about three o'clock."

"You must have come up here when you arrived. Was anyone else here?"

"No, sir."

"And who came after that?"

"Save for Mr Simple himself, no one, sir, until we all came up an hour later."

Nathaniel seemed to have answered honestly, but it served him ill. "That looks bad for you." The Squire frowned.

I knew Nat was generally well liked and, eager though the Squire was to find the perpetrator of this terrible deed, he would not wish it to be Nat.

Nat went white with fear. "Why should I wish to kill Mr Simple, sir? He was my employer. I owe everything to him."

"If no one else could come up here without your noticing, it must have been you who killed him." The Squire looked glum, but seemed satisfied with his reasoning.

I was not. "But Tom must surely have arrived later than Nat?"

The Squire looked at me sharply, and turned to the assembled company. "Is there another entrance to this place?"

"I know of none," Eleanor faltered.

"Nor I," John immediately confirmed.

"I am a stranger here." Mr Kettle looked highly relieved that this was so.

"Then if there is no other entrance, you or Tom must be guilty, Nat," the Squire said sadly. "Or both."

"Not so," I said firmly. "Even Arcadia needs work upon it to keep it idyllic – provided of course the workmen are not seen by those enjoying its perfection. Tom," I called to him, and he approached fearfully, "is it not true that weeds, leaves and pruned branches must be removed from this outcrop by some other path than the steps leading to the main gardens?"

I was about to go on to ask him the reason he had come here, but at that moment, Jacob returned to assure us a doctor was on his way and the coroner been sent for. He was so overcome by the rush and importance of his mission that he had to be calmed lest he collapse. Once this was accomplished, we turned back to Tom, but there was no sign of him.

"Where's the old man gone?" the Squire cried out in fury. "How did he get away?"

"By the same way he came." I speedily investigated the bushes and found a most interesting hedge which had been so trained as to completely hide another narrow set of steps leading down the hillside at the rear.

"Tom," I called out sternly, as the rustling of the branches made me sure he was still nearby. "Come hither to face your Lord."

Whether I referred to his secular or religious lord was immaterial. Tom was frightened enough to creep back to join us.

"Thomas," I addressed him formally, "you were here when we arrived. For what reason?"

I thought at first he would not reply, but finally he growled, "I wanted to speak to Mr Simple. I saw him come up here. He turned me away yesterday. All for saying I liked his father's garden better than his."

I sympathized, but could not show it. "Did you kill him, Tom?"

He glared at me. "No. He was lying there just like he is now. Dead. Then I heard you all coming. With that old cock-brain out of the way, I thought I might stand a chance. He'd told me I'd to be out of my cottage, me and my family, by the end of the week."

John exclaimed in distress. "You shall not leave, Tom. You are safe now that I am the master here. My brother's death puts an end to his cruelty to Miss Eleanor and to you."

Mr Kettle then decided to join the attack. "He was a shark up to every dodge," he maintained. "I discovered Aphrodite in the ruins of Pompeii, and this sarcophagus was mine too. Nathaniel will tell you so, won't you?"

I thought at first Nat would not agree through loyalty to his dead master, but at last he spoke, albeit unwillingly. "Mr Kettle is correct. Mr Simple did steal them and Arcadia—"

Then there was uproar, as everyone, including the Squire, burst out with his own tales of Horatio's cheating ways.

"Stop!" I cried out in horror. "This is not seemly."

But my words had little effect. Even when Mr Kettle rushed away down the stairs, saying he would take his Aphrodite *now*, only Nathaniel made any attempt to stop him. In vain, however. Mr Kettle had gone.

We were all so engaged in our varying capacities with this bitter discussion that none of us paid any attention to what else might be going on around us, until a familiar voice remarked:

"What a jolly hoax, eh?"

It was Horatio. We turned in disbelief to see him standing upright in the tomb, merrily laughing at us.

As we gaped at that dreadful sight, wondering whether this were a sudden recovery from death's cold grasp or the work of the devil,

Horatio, seeing he had our full attention, kindly explained that he had merely, in the common parlance, been gaming us.

"I always thought I'd like to be present at my own death," he chortled. "That was more than you could offer me, Parson. You'd have me packed off to hellfire like the rest of them here. Splendid to know what everyone thinks of me, all for the price of an arrow and some red paint. Pity about the ruined sheepskin but worth it to see your faces. Look at you all. No one glad to see me returned from the dead, eh?"

Still none of us spoke.

No matter, Horatio was eager to do that for us. "Eleanor, my faithless betrothed," he grinned. "John, my envious brother, Montague Kettle, my avaricious rival, wherever he is. And dear old Tom, our reluctant gardener, packing me off to the devil before my time, and of course Nat, my faithful Grecian echo." His gaze swept over the anguished Nat, then switched back sharply to Mr Kettle who had returned to join us. "Kettle," Horatio screamed out, "you can put that statue back where you found it. It's mine."

Kettle stood there, eyes popping, with Aphrodite clasped to his bosom, looking as though he had just seen Jupiter descending from the clouds aiming a thunderbolt right at him. Eleanor had swooned into John's arms and John looked as if he would stab Horatio with the very arrow he had mocked us with. And I? I stood there, torn between outrage that I had been deceived into playing a role in this tawdry jest and misery on behalf of those whom Horatio would now proceed to punish.

"You'll be out of that cottage tomorrow, Tom," Horatio continued gleefully. "You too, Nat. I need no more of you around. Nor you, loving brother John. I'll only keep one of you for myself." He paused. "My sweet Eleanor."

Jacob and I sat in that so-called Arcadian paradise for another two hours. The doctor and coroner had duly arrived, Jacob had broken the news to them that their services were not required and they had returned to their homes unimpressed with the jests of Horatio

Simple. Jacob is not accustomed to having hoaxes played upon him, and required much soothing as we waited. Waited for what? I did not know, but something would surely draw this dreadful day to a close.

We had watched as the guests began to leave. First a few crept away singly, then, as more gained courage, they left in small groups, then in a flood, but at last the sound of hooves and carriages rattling over the gravel was dying away. The Squire had long since departed, I had seen nothing of Mr Kettle, nor of Eleanor, nor of John, nor of Nathaniel. Only old Tom refused to leave the garden and wandered about, reluctant to return to tell his family of what must happen on the morrow. I had seen nothing of Horatio either, and I was grateful for that.

My heart was heavy and even Jacob had lost his taste for classical argument, now that the notorious Hellfire Club seemed to have re-established itself in Kent. I had heard of the devilish capers that went on in those caves, but I had not thought that such outrages could take place here. It seemed to mock God Himself, and God will not be mocked.

At last as the sun set over Arcadia, Jacob and I stretched our weary souls and legs, and strolled back to Fern House to make our way home. It was only then, as we passed through the orangery, that we saw Horatio Simple again, lying amidst the exotic leaves and fruit in what had been another of his extravagant innovations.

He was dead. No arrow had been used this time, and there had been no hoax. He had been brutally and savagely strangled.

"What is amiss?" Eleanor cried, as I entered the drawing room. She must have seen from my face that something was very wrong. "What worse news can there be?"

John looked as if he were drained of the will to live. "There can be none, Parson. Eleanor is condemned to a life with a monster and I to a loveless future." He might have added, "a penniless one, too," since his only income depended on his brother. "We have been discussing what we might do, but there is nothing. Either we condemn Eleanor's parents to starvation, or Eleanor and I must part for ever. We have decided upon the latter and I shall sail for the Indies shortly."

"Do not," I said gently, "for all has changed. Your brother is dead, John."

He did not seem to take the words in, just looked hopelessly at me.

"Another jest, Parson?" Eleanor said wearily. "I would not have believed that of you."

"This time it is certain," I assured her.

"He has taken his own life?" John asked.

"Another took it."

I should have condemned the look of hope and joy that crossed their faces, but I prayed for forgiveness because I could not do so. Surely their reaction could not be feigned? Horatio's fate had been unknown to them.

"Come with me, John," I bade him. "There is much to be done."

The Squire was once more sent for, but he was from home. With John's permission, therefore, I bade the servants carry the body to a more seemly resting place until the Squire should join us.

Death's grinning skull was before my eyes as I looked my last on this would-be Arcadia. I was contemplating who had finally brought death to Horatio Simple. I thought back to Jacob's and my conversation earlier, and then I knew beyond a doubt who it had been. I sought the guilty one out, with a heavy heart. It was not difficult. He was sitting on the terrace looking out upon his handiwork, admiring it.

"Why did you do it, Nathaniel?" I asked.

Why had I not noticed the strangeness of his eyes before? They looked right through me as though they saw nothing but himself, like the mythical Narcissus who was oblivious to all others, even the lovely nymph Echo. Echo had been condemned only to repeat the last words of others, and Nathaniel too. Or so I had believed, but Nat saw only his own reflection in the pool.

"He took it away from me," he explained at last. "He took everything I discovered. I found Aphrodite, I found the sarcophagus, but it was Arcadia whose loss I minded, when he claimed it as his own. My heart is here, for I designed it, not he."

Nathaniel had not always been echoing Horatio's words, he had been telling us pathetically the truth that he was the designer.

"But because of what I said at the tomb," Nat continued, "when I believed him dead, Mr Simple was going to turn me from the house, from my own creation. He came to me and said that he would ensure I would never design or travel again."

"You put Arcadia before God's commandments to man."

Nat bowed his head, and had no reply for me.

I sighed. "Then it is not Arcadia you dream of, Nathaniel," I told him bluntly, as I heard a carriage approaching. "It is yourself. Arcadia is merely your reflection."

The Squire had come at last together with the doctor, coroner and parish constable, and I could do no more. I was sad indeed as Nathaniel was taken away, and I gave one last look at what had been one man's vision of Arcadia. The sheep had gone, the garden looked dreary. What had been delightful wildness now looked merely untidy and ordinary, and I longed for my home.

Jacob rode back to his vicarage at Tunbridge Wells, and I to Cuckoo Lees where my beloved parsonage and my loving housekeeper Dorcas awaited me.

She was standing at the door as I rode up. "Where have you been, Caleb?" she cried, tears of relief running down her face, as I had been expected much earlier.

"In one man's bubble of a dream," I told her sadly.

She looked at me in bewilderment, and then smiled. "I have a wheatear pie and fine tansy pudding for supper, Caleb."

I took her hand, and said I would stable my horse and be with her. My heart grew warm again, for I was about to enter my home. I too live in Arcadia.

THE LONG DROP

Tony Black

SOMETIMES IT WAS the thing to do.

There was no keeping the needle under seventy; eighty was a trial but the lights went out when the grille clipped the dumpster. These dark country roads called for careful driving; stick in the dirt from the slips and the wet – and the fact that this was the night luck ran out on us – we were always going to go to shit.

The Toyota came to rest on its roof; Craven watched the wheels spinning and shook his head. He tried to crack his backbone into place. "The car's fucking finished. We're finished."

"Oh, y'think?" said Lois. She had a deep cut above her left eye; it looked like jello when she dabbed it with her shirtsleeve. As her flannel rode up I saw the SIG Sauer was still tucked in her waistband. That was something.

"You need to get rid of that," said Craven, "We're finished!"

She turned to me, gave a slight sigh, then looked back to her shirtsleeve. "Oh, I'm good for now."

Her tone was enough for Craven to fire up, "Someone's been killed. We're fucked."

He strode forward and flagged his arms like he'd lost control again.

Lois didn't like that. The way her lip twitched, the way she narrowed her eyes … I could almost smell her anger.

She removed the pistol.

I knew to look away.

For a second, the spinning wheels of the car were lit by the muzzle flash.

* * *

I'd met Craven at NA. It was three weeks after my split with Pam, two weeks before Lois crossed the dark divide into the long drop that was my life.

Craven was an old hand at kicking; he was wrapped far too tight for the real world and meth was his crutch. I liked to think I had the edge on him in that regard. When I used, it was because I was bored. Or working a job.

"So, how'd you end up here?" Craven collared me at the coffee counter. He twitched and oozed sweat from his heavy brows. His hairline was receding and some freckles on his crown looked like they were ready to slide down his face.

"Do I know you?"

He shot up his hands. "Whoa, easy, cowboy!"

"Don't call me that, please."

"You object to being called cowboy? Or you're just not real friendly?" The tone was queer, but I didn't have him down as a homosexual. Either way, it had taken less than two minutes for me to tire of him. "I don't like people messing with me."

"Well, fuck you!"

He made a dramatic flourish with his coffee cup and some grey liquid spilled on the floor. A few heads turned.

I moved off, found a vantage point by the doorway – it seemed a good place to assess the crowd. I soon had them sussed. The room was full of trembling, bug-eyed losers. All except the one. I watched over the cold decaf as Craven made a bee-line for her.

I wished I had his courage – Pam had taken that.

* * *

The lot held only two vehicles, three if you included the trail bike a group of kids were using to burn donuts on the asphalt. I watched them from below a to-let sign hung over the door of a long-vacated Ho-Joes. The neighbourhood had lost its sparkle. Brownstones were being boarded-up left and right; cops kept clear.

"This'll do," said Craven.

"You sure?" I said.

"Oh, yeah ... these Toyotas, can't kill 'em with an axe."

I took his word. Watched him approach with his steel rule out-stretched; it didn't take him long to make the ignition kick, then the engine purred to life.

I ran to the passenger's door. Craven gunned the gas.

As we drove he lit a Montecristo; said it was "his thing" on a job. I didn't question it – I had met a lot of guys with strange rituals and superstitions. This wasn't any take-down, though. We'd moved up a league. The thought made me edgy.

"Hey buddy boy ... you keeping it together there?" said Craven.

I turned to face him, "Me?"

"You think I'm talking to Mr Magic Tree? Fucking-A I mean you."

"Don't worry about me."

His voice dropped, took on a mocking tone, "Oh, but I do, buddy boy ... I do."

"Cut the shit, Craven ... just spit it out, where you going with this?"

He started to laugh. He laughed me up. "I ain't going any-where ... and neither are you! Ain't that what your little woman used to say?"

I felt a rush of adrenalin enter my veins; I grabbed the SIG and pushed it in his throat. "Pull this fucking piece of shit over now!"

His face changed colour, dropped several shades. His mouth turned down towards his chest. As he grabbed for breath his words came falteringly. "Jesus ... I'm, I'm ... only messing with you, man."

I moved the gun from his throat to the middle of his temple.

"How many times I got to tell you? I don't like people messing with me ... Pull the fuck over!"

*　*　*

The job was bloody, I never meant for it to be that way. I knew Lois wouldn't approve; she had insisted on one thing only – no body bags. We'd cleared the city, made the highway in good time but

Craven wasn't in any kind of condition. I took the wheel from him but I wasn't in much better shape. She was only a girl.

"Man, this is wrong, dead wrong," Craven whined.

"Shut the fuck up!"

"Why was she in the middle of the road?"

"I said, shut the fucking hell up, Craven." He rocked to and fro in the passenger seat. Tears streamed down the sides of his face as he tugged at the few tight red curls that sat above his neck. I could see the streaks of blood where he'd cradled her head on the front of his jeans; it had already dried dark on the pale-blue denim.

"What was she, man ... six?"

I couldn't listen any more. It was his fault; he rolled out way too fast after we cut Pam loose. Craven had fucked up twice now – tested our luck – and that was fucking fatal. If I had to produce the gun again I'd fire it in his face; make that two body bags.

"Craven, listen ... now listen. Are you listening?" I needed him to chill out; for all our sakes.

He sobbed louder, brought his knees up under his chin.

"We have to collect Lois from the drop ... if she has the money, we can still make this work. Do you hear me? We can still clear out ... go our ways like we planned. Only richer, a hell of a lot richer."

Craven didn't answer. As the wind and rain picked up, and the sky darkened I started to think of Lois. It had all been her idea – the kidnapping. I had never had a thought to it; not even when Pam had turned me out without a dime, not even then. There was something about that line of business that brought nothing but bad luck; that's what the old boys said. But Lois was certain we could pull it off ... "You don't need to be part of the gig ... just feed us what we need to know," she had said.

I never believed her. I knew better, but Pam had taken something from me and I wanted to take something from her. Christ Almighty, my mind was ablaze. I was full of thoughts of the past, the present meant nothing to me, and Lois had this way of making me believe anything was possible. Anything at all.

***

Craven pulled the Toyota into the side of the street. The SIG started to feel heavy in my hand; my palm was sweating. If he had made contact with the mark then we were finished before we'd even started. We were skating close to the edge on this job as it was; it would take one look from Pam, one hint that I was back in her ambit, and her father would have her back under security. Billionaires are funny that way about only daughters.

"What the fuck do you know about what Pam used to say to me?"

Craven knew he'd fucked up. He had set about riling me, taking me for a ride ... but he hadn't thought it through properly. He didn't see where his joking would end.

"I ... I ... didn't do anything."

He looked pathetic, his eyes looping in wide circles, searching for some answer that was never going to come.

"*I didn't do anything* ... Is this fucking kindergarten? ... Am I playing with you, here?"

"No. No ... I ... "

I smacked him with the gun. His cheekbone opened up, a little blood spilled out. "Tell me now ... when did you speak to her about me?"

He lowered his eyes to his lap, looked at his palms. "In the diner."

I hit him again; the force of it sprained my wrist. "What did you say to her?"

"She didn't know me ... she didn't know who I was ... I just sat next to her at the counter and she asked me to pass the mayo ... we started talking and she said something about an ex she had. I just put two and two together ... that was it. I promise. She had no idea who I was ... she'd never know me again. I promise. I promise you ... "

I took the SIG in my other hand; I was ready to blow his fucking dumb head through the window.

"Craven, you stupid motherfucker. You stupid son of a bitch ... you never heard of tempting fate."

* * *

If I had been anything like the man I once was I would have pulled the trigger myself, but he was gone. Pam had turned me around, made me believe I could change ... and I did. I had changed so much that I wasn't capable of living the life any more. I'd grown soft; that's what the meth was about. It was recreation to begin with, a break from carrying shopping bags in Beverly Hills, some kind of reminder of the old days, the old kicks. I knew I'd taken it too far. Pam knew that too ... or maybe she was right when she said I was never going anywhere.

"What the fuck happened?" Lois yelled. Her blonde hair was tied back tight from her face. It made her look harder than usual. Her features seemed severe as she squinted through the falling rain.

"Get in!" I shouted.

"What the fuck's going on?" She looked at the dent on the fender, where Craven had hit the girl ... throwing her little body in the air.

"What happened?"

I let her get inside the Toyota. She looked at Craven rocking to and fro and yelled at me again, "Tell me what the fuck is going on ... "

"Take this, keep it on him." She took the SIG Sauer from me.

"What is this?"

"Never mind ... Did you get the money?"

Lois wrestled the rucksack off her back, stayed calm. "Every dime ... let's hope we hold on to it."

I gripped the wheel tighter; I was already upping the revs as we sped into the rain.

Lois spoke, "What the fuck happened back there?"

Craven was stirring. "We're finished ... the girl. That poor fucking girl."

"What's he on about?"

I tried to keep the needle below eighty, but I was desperate to put some distance between us and the scene.

I felt a cold gun on my ear. "I'm not going to ask again," said Lois.

"We killed a fucking little girl ... she was in the fucking road!"

Lois turned back to Craven. He was still cradling his head in his hands as I yelled, "You fucking killed her ... you dumb bastard! You killed that girl when you spoke to Pam in the diner."

"No. No. No!" Craven mumbled and sobbed.

"You burned our luck ... You fucking burned us!"

Lois couldn't take it any more. She exploded, "You spoke to her? You fucking spoke to the bitch!" She levelled the gun at him; I turned, saw her eyes widen, her breathing stilled. I tried to grab the gun – her shot broke the windscreen. I went to right the wheels but the car was on the verge already. I pumped the brakes but it only made matters worse. We fell into an uncontrollable skid.

The second the car turned over on its roof, I thought we were all dead. As we rolled to a stop I wished I had died ... Outside I tried to find the courage to go and take the SIG from Lois, but I knew Pam had been right about me all along, I was going nowhere.

A little girl had died, but I did nothing.

Sometimes it was the thing to do.

TERATOMA

Keith McCarthy

J OHN BARCLAY, THE buffoon, greets me the next morning.

"Got a cracker for you, Doc." He guffaws at this – not "laughs", not "chuckles", not "titters", but actually, really *guffaws*: the phone line can barely contain this amount of merriment. He is a Coroner's Officer and I have known many of these people. Most of them have been very good at a very difficult job; they have to deal with the bereaved, perhaps having to ask them difficult questions, perhaps having to tell them things they do not want to hear. John Barclay, though, wings it; he does not just cut corners, he rips them apart; he lies by omission, by commission and by inference; he does not pass the buck so much as make sure that it never even knows he is in the room; he is, as Carter, the mortuary technician, says, a right "see you next Tuesday", only Carter says it in a rich Gloucestershire accent that I cannot hope, and would not dare, to essay.

"Have you?" I say. I am wary.

"A right loony."

As I have just said, most Coroner's Officers I have had the pleasure of working with have been exemplary; one used to be regularly on the verge of tears after speaking with next of kin, because of the empathy he could not help but feel. John Barclay does not consider empathy to be part of the job description; he looks on death as a source of amusement, as a substrate for his chortling.

"Really?" I am in my office. It is Monday morning and it is October and I don't want to be here. I could have taken compassionate leave, which is the type of leave you never want to have to take and the type you certainly don't want to talk about when you do; I have decided not to, because it is better to work through these things.

This time it is definitely more of a chuckle as he explains, "She topped herself because she heard voices coming from her stomach."

And the phone line again has to bear the strain of his inane hilarity.

My secretary comes in. Joanna has the curse of being older than her name; a Joanna should be between forty and fifty, yet this one is sixty-three, cursed to have had avant-garde parents. She is not particularly efficient and irritatingly maudlin; work, to this Joanna, is an extension of her social life. I can see from her lax eyes and developing jowls that she is filled to the quivering brim with concern for me, and this is nothing more than an emetic to me.

How does she know, I wonder. Clearly she does, though. I dare not let her guide the course of the conversation, so I say at once, "Morning, Joanna. John Barclay was just telling me about this morning's PM."

Thankfully, I succeed in this misdirection. Her opening mouth closes again and, holding the paperwork out, she says, "There's only the one. I expect you won't be sorry to hear that."

As I take it, I say, "No, I'm not."

She does not leave; I can see her looking at me with that soppy look that I know so well; Joanna has never moved on from mother-hood and never will. She trails maternal instincts like snail slime. I see she is going again to say something commiserating and so once more I pre-empt her. "I'd better go to the mortuary and identify the body so that Carter can start."

Her opening mouth closes again. I am aware that I am being brusque, but her sympathy is a weapon that I can use against her. I stand and she nods and smiles weakly – she does everything weakly, though – and she precedes me out of the office.

Miss Valerie Templeman

DOB: 14.4.1965

Age: 45

DOD: 14.4.2010

Address: Flat 3, Millikan Road, Cheltenham, Gloucestershire GL51 9QQ

Circumstance: Miss Templeman was found hanging in her bedroom by her boyfriend, Steven Damon, who had become concerned when she failed to attend a dinner date and had not been answering her phone. She had improvised a noose from an old brown leather belt. Mr Damon says that she had been acting very oddly for the past few weeks, claiming that there was a spirit inside her stomach that was talking to her.

From the GP: Miss Templeman was lately a frequent attender at the surgery with gynaecological problems including subfertility and irregular menses. She was due to attend at the gynaecology outpatients department at Cheltenham General Hospital next month. She had recently become very depressed about her inability to conceive a baby. She had been having aural hallucinations of a spirit living within her for which she had been prescribed citalopram.

Hangings are for men, usually, although that is far from exclusive; woman prefer tablets, something a little more sedate. The bloody, extroverted deaths are almost always men, or occasionally the severely psychotic woman. It's the way of the world.

Carter has the body out on the dissection table, although he hasn't taken it out of the body bag. As I walk past his office he comes out and follows me into the dissection room. I put on some disposable gloves while he unzips the white bag and pulls the sides down away from the body. Tied around her left wrist and to her right big toe are labels; I compare the details on these – name, date of birth and address – with those on the post mortem request that has been faxed through from the Coroner's office. Satisfied that we have the right body, I say, "OK, you can start."

Carter is in his mid-fifties with a bushy, greying moustache and long silvered hair. We get on well, and he knows me better than to ask how I am. He says, "You got anything to do upstairs first?" He is referring to the other tasks of a consultant cellular pathologist, such as dissecting or reporting surgical specimens. I want to hide down in the mortuary, though, and say, "Nothing that can't wait for a while."

I retreat into the changing room where I send a surreptitious text to Anna - *How are you? xxx* – before changing. At the same time, as Ken Bruce earns his crust by providing brainless entertainment over the radio waves, Carter strips the clothes from Miss Valerie Templeman; he does this roughly, without thought for either dignity or decorum. By the time I am in my scrubs, she is naked. She is slightly overweight but otherwise nondescript; all corpses are nondescript, though. The belt has been cut from the neck and is in the body bag with her. Around her neck is a faint, broad mark that has reddened but barely indented the skin. I take the belt and compare it with the mark; it fits, more or less. The mark is deepest – but at that, only a millimetre or so – just beneath the angle of the jaw on the left-hand side, fading on the exactly opposite side. This pattern is what one expects when the body has been hung and not strangled, which I have to consider; the blood has pooled in the lower half of the body – "post mortem lividity is caudal in distribution", in the jargon – which is another reassuring sign (at least, if you are a pathologist). There are no other significant signs to detect; no ligature marks around the wrists or ankles, no signs to suggest that she was not alone when she died.

Happy that I am not going to make a prat of myself and blunder into a murder, I give the nod to Carter and he eviscerates her.

e-viss-er-ate.

One hell of a word for one hell of a thing to do, yet Carter does it once, twice, even three or four times a day, and he always does it quickly and efficiently, and without any deep thoughts. And I watch him do it, as I have done many times before, again without any serious consideration of what is happening. From the carcase – because now it is really only that – he lifts the "pluck".

Pluck.

One hell of another word, only in a different sense. Anglo-Saxon rather than Latin, I fancy. How many people appreciate that all the organs bar the brain hang together from the tongue? How many people *want* to appreciate that?

Valerie Templeman's pluck, though, is different, for there is spherical grey mass at its base. Carter lifts it effortlessly – it is quite heavy, you know – from the body cavity, transferring it to a stainless steel bowl, then taking this to the dissection board where I am to do my bit. Carter says, "She's got a tumour."

Ken Bruce prattles on, unaware of what he is talking over.

I already know what the tumour is and so, when Carter asks, I say confidently, "It's a teratoma."

Teratoma.

Pathology is chock-a-block with interesting words, you see.

This one is derived from *Teros*, which is Greek for "monster". A teratoma is a tumour that is derived from the egg and, because eggs develop into all the tissues of the body, so the teratoma can grow *anything*. Most often, they grow skin and so you get a cyst which is filled with grease and hair, and makes the strongest of pathologists want to puke. When you look under the microscope, you will usually see small amounts of other things like bone and gristle; often there will be a bit of brain, muscle, fat, gut lining; rarely there will be retina, liver or thyroid. Disgusting rather than monstrous. It is benign and of passing interest only, because it did not kill her; death is so much more interesting than all else, you see.

It is my job to determine why Valerie Templeman died; she *appears* to have hanged herself, but until all other possible causes are excluded, until I can be sure that she didn't die of brain haemorrhage just before the noose tightened, that she didn't swallow kettle descaler as well as gobble down some potassium cyanide, no assumptions can be made. Accordingly, although it seems obvious that she died from hanging, there is no cause for her death until I have completed all my investigations.

I examine all the major organs, including her brain, which Carter has extracted from its osseous nook. I ask him to get blood and urine for toxicological analysis. This done, he labels the containers, then says, "How's things, Doc?" He says it casually, so that it is bearable. I say, "Fine, thanks, Carter," which is the end of that, because he nods and gets on with his job. Again, I wonder how people know.

At the end, it is all as I have hoped: non-specific changes consistent with hanging, and nothing natural of significance. All the main stuff is done now. I examine the gut without opening it, slice into the bladder, slice into the uterus, then turn to the teratoma. The knife goes in and, as I suspected, sebum and black, coarse hair billow out. "Yuk," says Carter. The grease is terrible, clings to everything with a stale, rancid odour; even through thick disposable gloves, the feel of slime is all too apparent. I hold it under the tap to clean it out, which is when I see that I was wrong, that this is no ordinary benign teratoma.

As the grease releases its cloying grip on the inside wall of the cyst, there comes to light a small baby.

"Anna?" I say as soon as the ringing in my ear stops, but her mobile just goes to answerphone. I hate it when it goes to answerphone, but I have to try to communicate with her. Impatiently I wait for the recorded voice to take me through its automatic inanities, then, "Anna? Are you all right? I'm getting worried. Can you ring me?"

I put the phone down and wonder why it is suddenly important to talk to her.

Because you're worried about her. Because she is severely depressed. Because she has just lost her baby. And that brings me back to the thing on my desk.

Carter swears. He is good at swearing, has a rich vein of obscenity and vulgarity to mine, and does so enthusiastically at times. This time, it is with awe that he digs deep into profanity. I am too stunned to do or say anything; my brain is numbed; for a moment I cannot even reassemble the components of what my vision is telling me into a coherent whole. I am temporarily autistic, only slowly beginning to function properly once again.

It is about eight centimetres only. It is shaped as a baby should be, with two arms and two legs, all of approximately appropriate length, a torso and a head. It lies at the base of the cyst, fused to a small, solid, partly calcified area at the small of the back. It is the head that is really ... really ... *disturbing*.

It is slightly too large, and not quite right. The eyes are open, and that is not right either. The mouth is open, although thank the Lord there are no teeth; it looks as if it has been caught in the midst of a scream ...

I become aware of Carter talking to me.

" ... What is it, Doc?"

Homunculus.

That is the name, and they have been reported before, although they make hen's teeth seem tediously commonplace in comparison. An entire being, somehow constructed by the random forces of neoplasia. An oddity, nothing more ...

I explain to Carter, who whistles. "Spooky, or what?" he says, then asks, "Is it male or female?" He is peering shamelessly at it as he asks.

My voice is soft and far away as I reply, "Insofar as it's anything at all, it's female. It has to be. No sperm has ever been anywhere near it."

He straightens up. He does not seem to have noticed that I am having trouble; trouble breathing, trouble thinking, trouble in not screaming. "What are you going to do?"

What, indeed? This rarest of rare phenomena is nothing to do with her death, and I am forbidden by the oh-so-sainted Human Tissue Act to do anything that is unconnected with satisfying the Coroner and the law of this free and liberal democracy, at least without written, informed consent from the next of kin, which is never really possible. And it's horrible, too. It gives me the creeps, if truth be told (which it so rarely is). It should be returned to the body cavity – "reunited" is the correct term – and thereafter disposed of, in a "fitting manner".

Yet …

And Anna's name comes into mind. Her name and her pain and …

In my mind I go back to the Coroner's information. " … Aural hallucinations about a spirit living inside her' …

No. No, no, no, no …

Why won't Anna answer? I am afraid … I look again at the "homunculus" – a nasty word, shot through with nasty connotations – and try to be objective. It is just a freak of nature; it has never been alive, never will be, never could be. It is also just a coincidence that it should come into my life now.

It has to be.

Carter says, "Shame we're not allowed to keep things like that any more. It would make a fantastic exhibit if we could put it in formalin."

I know Carter. Sooner or later it would occur to him to "disappear" the exhibit, perhaps make a nice little profit on it. I smile, therefore, and point out that it is no longer legal to do such things, not since the Human Tissue Act promised miscreants the possibility of a £5,000 fine and three years in chokey. He sighs, the very model of an honest academic thwarted by unnecessary bureaucracy.

But, having said that …

I say, "I'd like to photograph it, though, Carter. Put it in a jar of saline. I'll ring the Coroner's office to get them to contact the next of kin for consent." Now, we cannot even take photographs without somebody's say-so, you see.

He obliges me.

Joanna comes into my office; my face freezes into a smile of rigid insincerity. She says, "It's the monthly management meeting in an hour. Are you going to go?"

It is a reasonable question for a secretary to ask, yet I hear subtexts in it, and react accordingly. "Of course I am," I reply too brusquely, and have to rely yet again on her sympathy to protect me from her reproach. And I don't even want to go.

She sees the homunculus on my desk and her face betrays all those emotions at which I know she is so good – shock, surprise, disgust ... the list goes on. I say at once, "Interesting, isn't it?"

She says nervously (why nervously, I wonder?), "Yes ... I suppose so."

"I'm going to ask permission to keep it." I see something on her face that tells me she does not think that this is right. "As a pathological exhibit," I hasten to explain. She nods, but it is born of enthusiasm, that nod. She leaves and I am alone with the prospect of the monthly management meeting, a sorry affair and one that no one normal can enjoy. Desultory conversation about the problems of staffing, the problems of decrepit equipment, the problems of the backlog, the problems of the problems. I am not even head of department any more, so could make a more or less plausible excuse for my absence, but it is important to me not to appear the invalid, the one who is marked by tragedy, the one who has problems.

Babies have caused me a lot of misery and, over the years, they have given me much reason to hate them. They scream at an intolerable pitch and frequency until we are close to insanity, even as they soil their nappies in idiotic glee, even as they keep us awake for hour after ever longer hour during hot nights. They paralyze us with terror when they become febrile, or puke, or green snot runs from their noses and they labour to breathe. They drive us to distraction as they minutely examine electrical sockets, flames, carelessly discarded tablets, knives and kettle flexes. They refuse to eat their food, they love to eat their faeces, they become sticky and messy, and they knock things over. They demand so much and yet give us love without knowing what that is; they rely on us, yet manipulate us; we are puppets who are deluded into thinking that we are masters.

Yes, I hate them.

Because Anna and I cannot have them.

"John? It's David Fairclough."

"Hello, Doc. What can I do for you?" John Barclay is forever hearty, some sort of expression of merriment only a breath away, be it chuckle, guffaw, titter or bellow.

"I was wondering if you could do me a favour."

"If I can, Doc. If I can. You know that."

John Barclay is like that, at least with me; he will do anything, short of murder (and maybe not even short of that). With those he can bully, things are slightly different, though.

"Today's post mortem ... "

"That poor loony? Yes, how could I forget?" And there it is, the release of humour energy, emitted this time with a chuckle, polluting the radio waves and thence the air with its awkwardness.

"I found something rather interesting. I'd like to keep it for teaching purposes."

"Really? What is it?"

But for some reason I do not want to say precisely. "It's a rare type of tumour of the ovary."

"But nothing to do with her death? She definitely died from hanging?"

"Definitely nothing to do with her death." But I am wondering whether that is the truth or a lie, or both. She died from hanging herself, but did she hang herself because of that strange little thing inside her? Could it somehow have spoken to her? Was she driven to suicide by its tiny whisperings?

"And this ovarian thing, what are you going to do with it?"

"Keep it in formalin in the department. It will be useful for teaching medical students and nurses. It's a type of teratoma."

"Sounds disgusting," he opines. This time he treats me to a guffaw. Before I can argue, he says, "Only joking, Doc. Let me have it in writing and I'll see what I can do. I'm sure there won't be a problem."

I am forty-two, Anna is forty-four. We married eleven years ago, after a three-year engagement. Love at first sight? That counts for nothing, I think. Love at millionth sight is the only thing worth having. And we managed that, although a pall was gathering, imperceptibly, as the clocks ticked and the calendars told of days passing. At first, we did not want children, wanted just to enjoy each other; after all, I had a new job as a consultant cellular pathologist, she as medical PA to one of my colleagues, a consultant surgeon. But it was not only the sidereal clock that was ticking, for Anna began to change, perhaps psychologically, perhaps biologically, perhaps both; I cannot say when it began, but I do know that I became aware that she looked at the world and, more importantly, our relationship differently. Whereas until then she had considered, and whereas I still considered at that time, two was the optimal number, at the time she donned a different perspective, wore glasses of a different type, a stronger prescription. The pairing had run its course; she wanted to move on, as she saw it. I saw it as change, as boat-rocking, as dissection and reassembly, and not necessarily for the better.

But you know women. I at first refused to see that there was a problem, then I refused to believe that it was a major one, then I refused to talk about it, then I refused to argue about it. Then I capitulated.

I rationalized that things had changed anyway; Anna was no longer satisfied to waltz down the corridors of time with only me, and the rosy tint of retrospection was all I had remaining of the first part of my marriage. Anyway, a baby might not be too bad. Slowly, then, I began to foster paternal feelings and, such was my success, that they grew strong, but nowhere near as strong as Anna's. Nowhere near.

She became obsessed, I belatedly realized. This was more than a desire and little less than an obsession; it became the achievement by which she was to be measured. Nothing less than success was permissible. She even had names; she asked me for my opinion on these, but this was too strange and strong for my blood, and I declined. So, without my input, our baby-to-be became either Samuel or Samantha, and she talked in her restless sleep to her little "Sam".

Trouble was, something was wrong. Just as it took me a while (because I am dim, you see) to spot that Anna yearned for an end to our exclusive relationship, so it was a year or more before it dawned on me that really by then something should have happened. The contraceptive pills had been consigned to the sewers for fourteen months by the time I realized that Anna's eyes were haunted by the fear of infertility. She didn't say anything, but it was there; perhaps she feared to speak its name and thereby conjure the beast.

The management meeting is as I feared. We sit in an airless, windowless, spiritless room and we are all imbued with a sense of hopelessness at our failures. Beset by worries of finance, we who run the department are doomed to run around the same, worn arguments of how best to combat the failures, fight the failures, battle against a rising tide of entropy; it is easy to see how dire the situation is, because we revert to the code that is management speak, so that we talk glibly (and meaninglessly) of "rapid improvement events", "doing a piece of work" on such and such, of auditing this, that and the other, of the rising number of "code red adverse clinical incidents". No one looks me in the eye, even when they greet me as I sit down. It is, I am sure, my imagination, that the conversation died as I entered the room.

We were tested, by which I mean, I suppose, "humiliated". No doctor wants to be a patient, to experience the role of supplicant; you go into medicine to be above other people, giving it out, rather than below them and dependent on them. It was worse for Anna, of course – questions after questions, blood tests, urine tests, swabs, smears and pipelles, even a laparotomy – but I had my fair share. I had the questions, I had the blood tests and urine tests and, of course, I had the small cubicle (sound-proofed, I fervently hoped), the sterile pot, the adolescent thoughts of dirty women, and the wrist action.

After all of which, it transpired, I was the one at fault. Of course, that was not the language used – the patois was strictly non-blame, neutral and sympathetic – but the implication remained the same, no matter what linguistic cosmetic was used. I was the commander of a less than optimally trained army; my little lads were few and far between; many of those who did turn out on parade were a bit weak if not seriously crippled; barely one in a thousand was going to manage that long swim through treacle that is the lot of the spermatozoa. They hastened to assure us that we should keep trying, that it was not impossible that we might conceive, but I could see that Anna, like me, did not credit their no doubt well-meant platitudes. Her disappointment distorted her face, even as she tried not to show it. When she looked at me, I wondered if I saw reproach, but it was only fleeting; even if it had been there, what would have been the point in protest, in pointing out that it was not my fault? Of course it was my fault. If not mine, then whose? And we live in a society that, despite the rhetoric, must always find someone to blame.

"Dr Fairclough speaking."

A pause, then a slight gulp. "Sorry to bother you."

"What can I do for you?" The automated telephonist at the hospital has a wicked sense of humour; I frequently field calls for what in PC-speak is the GUM clinic but what most right-minded people refer to as the clap clinic.

"You did the ... the examination on my fiancée. On Valerie."

And the tenor of the conversation, of my mood, of the whole wide world and all its hidden places, changes. "Oh." It is my turn to hesitate. "Yes, I did." It is an admission of guilt, of course, as much as confessing to murder or theft or rape. Or perhaps all three. I do what I do without a thought of what I am doing, until someone rings me up and accuses me of it, and then I am forced to confront my crimes.

"The Coroner's Officer – John Barclay – rang me up. Said you wanted to keep something from it."

My eyes do not flick to the jar on my desk because they have been there since I came to appreciate who was talking to me. Has it changed expression? Is the mouth now a little more closed, are the legs a little less flexed? Rubbish.

"You're the next of kin?"

"There's no one else," he assures me. "What is it that you want to keep?"

My mouth is not dry, but it is filled with viscid saliva that soon becomes mixed with sophistry. "Just a small thing. She had a small growth in her ovary; it's quite interesting, for a pathologist. It could be used to teach nurses and doctors, and suchlike."

"A growth? You mean like a cancer?"

"Oh, no. Not like that ... "

"She said that she couldn't sleep at night. She said that she heard a voice. Not 'voices', just one voice."

His is a voice I don't want to hear, I think. All I can find to reply with is "Did she?"

"She said it was like a child's voice."

Oh, Jesus, no ...

"It didn't say anything that made sense, she said. But then it wouldn't, I suppose, would it? Not if it was a child."

He is just talking, I realize, because he needs to talk. He is grieving. I look again at the homunculus. No, I am sure, it hasn't moved. *This is all just coincidence.*

To him, I say, "It must have been very distressing."

"She didn't leave a note, either." He sounds half puzzled, half angry at this lapse in etiquette. "I'll never know why she did it. Not really. But I wonder if it was the voice that made her."

"Maybe," is my weak offering.

There is another long pause before he says, "Well, if it'll help with training and suchlike, I don't see any harm."

"Thank you," I say, although it is little more than a croak and a little less than a whisper.

We continued to try for a baby, "for Sam" as Anna put it, either unknowing or uncaring of my shudder each time she said this. The months turned, as they will, into years, but without the success of a pregnancy. We had success aplenty in other things – in our careers, in our friends, in the trappings of modern, western, secular life – but not the one thing that she most needed. No, in the *only thing* that she needed. And because of her unhappiness, I fulfilled my side of the marriage contract, and I became unhappy too. No marriage can survive two unhappy people; one, and it might just make it, but not two. The bonds perished, became little more than cracked dust. We would have divorced within the year.

And then the miracle occurred. Anna fell pregnant, and everything was all right again.

I am seriously worried. She really should have answered by now. I do not recall that she said anything about visiting her parents, or going shopping, but I tell myself that I really should not be worried. Anna has always been independent. The loss of the baby hit her hard – how could it not – but only for a short while; she is still fragile, but I know she will survive. She does not need to be wrapped in swaddling clothes, I know.

I try to report – cases of inflammatory bowel disease, gastritis, colonic polyp – but cannot. It has been many years since the delights of the pigments of histology looked like high art to me; now, at a superficial level, they merely resemble cartoons and, at a deeper one, everything in my life that I abhor. The thing in the jar does not look at me – it cannot for so many reasons – although I cannot but feel that we are aware of each other. Yet what is it thinking? Part of me knows that it is not thinking at all, part of me is completely certain that it is, although I cannot say what. What would such a thing think? What could it think? I am a scientist, a rationalist, and I know that all it has ever experienced is darkness, grease and hair; without experience, there can be no sentience.

So why do I *know* that it is thinking, even if I do not know what it is thinking?

It turned out that it wasn't all right, though; and it turned out, too, that I was being dim again. She was happy – of that there was no doubt – but it wasn't total happiness; I had expected ecstasy and I merely got satisfaction. More than that, I now see, it was satisfaction undercut with trepidation. As for me, I told myself that I was relieved, and that I was excited, and that having a child was going to be fantastic. True, I do not think that I could work out the particulars of that fantasy, but I persuaded myself of a vague, generic concept of wonderfulness. I expected the pregnancy to progress – from first to second trimester – and for things to change, the tension behind Anna's eyes (no doubt there because of her fear that she would miscarry) to fade, and for my own misgivings to become excited expectations.

Except that it did not. If anything, the tensions increased.

I leave early, at half past four, my concern for Anna synergizing with my boredom and distaste for my work and thus prompting me to skive. The traffic is quite light, except for the roadworks along the Tewkesbury Road – soon due to get even worse when they close the carriageway completely for a month. I am home in forty-five minutes though. It is a nice house, with five bedrooms, set back from a quiet road, with a paddock at the back, although we do not have a pony. Her car is on the drive, so my heart lifts. And yet, having opened the front door, when the first thing I do is to call out Anna's name, there is no reply, not even an echo; the sound is deadened, swallowed by an empty house. Where can she be? I look at my phone for the hundredth time, but there are still no messages.

I go into the study, sit down, try to think, but it is only an image of the homunculus that comes to my mind. Why cannot I think of anything else? Perhaps a drink …

Anna was defiant at the same time as she was ashamed and sorry. There were tears in her eyes that refused to stay put and had soaked the make-up of her cheeks, and were now making her sniffle defiantly. I was stunned, just for a moment, but what it lacked in length, it made up for in depth. Reality and realization were not long in returning. Her qualified pleasure, the haunted look, the very fact of the pregnancy itself.

I had been so stupid.

It is dark when the doorbell rings. I am very drunk. I have been dreaming, I think, of the homunculus, although I am confused, and I could be wrong. I make my way to the front door, slowly and, before I reach it, the bell sounds again, this time longer and somehow with greater insistency. I open the door to two men; one in front who is tall, curly-haired, almost boyish-looking; behind him is a squatter, older man who looks unpleasant. The tall one holds something out; the hall light is dim but I make out a shield of some sort. He says, "Inspector Sauerwine. This is Sergeant Beech. May we come in?"

I am confused, addled I suppose with drink and doziness. I ask, "What's all this about?" I let them walk in past me, then I realize. "Is it Anna? Is something wrong?" They are both looking around in that inquisitive, detached air that police seem to have. I say, "Come into the study."

I lead them to the back of the house, proffer seats. The one called Sauerwine sees the whisky bottle and remarks, "Have you been drinking, Sir?"

"Yes. Is that a crime?" I have reacted badly and realize it immediately; wonder immediately, too, why. He does not answer. I ask again, "Is it about Anna? She's not here. I don't know where she is."

"We've had a phone call from her mother."

"Is that where she is?"

I might as well have not spoken, for he does not respond to my question. He says, "She is very concerned about her daughter's welfare. It appears you had some sort of row last night."

I frown. Did we? I don't recall that. I say, "No, that's not true. She's been sick. She lost her baby, you see … "

He is remorseless, refusing to allow me the satisfaction of having my side of things heard. "Anna's parents have been away. They returned to find a message on their answerphone this evening."

His words make no sense. The homunculus comes into my mind; it is now no longer screaming, but almost smiling, it seems to me. Can I hear a child's voice somewhere? Sauerwine, meanwhile has turned to the other one – I have forgotten his name – and nodded, at which he leaves the room. I watch him go while Sauerwine reaches into his pocket and pulls out a small portable recorder. He presses the play button. It is not good quality, but it is Anna's voice, yet not as I have ever heard it before. It is hysterical, sob-ridden, almost unintelligible.

... *Oh, my God* ...

... *Help, please, help* ...

... *Mummy, please answer* ... *please* ...

... *He's trying to kill me* ...

And then there is nothing. No scream, just a sudden, absolute silence.

I look up at Sauerwine who is looking at me, his eyes full of interest, yet dead, as if he has cut himself off from me. I do not know what is going on. This is complete madness. What can she be talking about? I say, "I don't understand. She miscarried last night. It was quite sudden. She refused to go to hospital, though. I tried to persuade, but she would have none of it ... "

The door opens and the other man comes back in. I see him look at Sauerwine and I see Sauerwine return that look. There is a lot of meaning in the exchange, all of it beyond me. Sauerwine says to me, "Would you come with me, Sir?" His voice has not changed; it is not loud and it has a questioning tone, but I do not think it wise or even possible to argue. We move, Sauerwine behind me, his companion leading. It is a short journey, for we go into the front room of the house. It is Anna's favourite room, where she likes to go and watch interminable episodes of *Lost*. I have never seen the appeal, myself.

She is in there now, I see. We see her head above the back of the armchair. For a moment I wonder why I did not realize it, but then remember that I have not been in here since I got home. She must be asleep ...

I am led to the front of the chair and my puzzlement increases.

Why is the carving knife on the carpet in front of her? And what is that mess of tissue beside it? And why is there so much blood over her belly?

So much blood.

I hear a small child's voice whisper to me in my darkness. I fear that I will hear it for ever more.

CLUTTER

Martin Edwards

"YOU WILL BE aware that your grandfather died in, ah, rather unusual circumstances?"

I bowed my head. "We can only hope his last thoughts were pleasurable."

Beazell raised bushy eyebrows. "At least his, um, companion, did her best by calling an ambulance. And she tried to administer the kiss of life herself. To no avail, sadly."

"I gather there was no suspicion of ... foul play?"

"Goodness me, no. The doctor was emphatic, and of course a second opinion is required for a sudden death. There is no doubt the poor fellow died of a heart attack, brought on by excessive exertion. Your grandfather was seventy and unfit, he'd led a sedentary life, and frankly, cavorting with a nineteen-year-old foreign woman was the height of folly. I recall advising him ... " Beazell cleared his throat. "Well, that wasn't why I asked you here this afternoon. The important question concerns his last will and testament."

Beazell was a lawyer with a shiny suit and a glass eye with an in-built accusatory stare, as if it suspected me of concealing a dark secret. His offices occupied a single floor above a kebab house in a back street in Manchester, and the posters in the waiting room spoke of legal aid, visas for migrant workers and compensation for accidents. I was unsure why Rafe (as my grandfather liked me to call him) had entrusted his legal affairs to such a firm. Beazell's services must come cheap, but Rafe was by no means short of money. Certainly, though, the two men had one thing in common. Beazell's floor was stacked high with buff folders bulging with official documents, and fat briefs to counsel tied up in pink string.

He'd needed to clear a pile of invoices from my chair before I could sit down. Rafe too gloried in detritus; perhaps he regarded Beazell as a kindred spirit.

"I don't suppose wills are ever read out nowadays?" I said. "And presumably there's nobody apart from me to read it to?"

"My understanding is that you were his only close relative."

I nodded. My grandparents divorced a couple of years after my grandmother gave birth to their only child, my father. She had a stroke a month before my parents married, and they, in turn, succumbed to cancer and coronary disease respectively shortly after I left school and took a job as a snapper for a local newspaper. My mother was an only child, and her parents had died young. I was alone in the world – except for Hong Li.

"I saw very little of him, I'm afraid, even before I moved overseas. But we got on well enough. He had artistic inclinations, as you must know, and he encouraged my interest in photography."

Beazell exhaled; his breath reeked of garlic. "Artistic? Candidly, I never thought much of his sculpture. However, he told me that, in his opinion, you were a man after his own heart."

"That was kind of him," I said, although Beazell had not made it sound like a compliment.

"The will is straightforward." The lawyer could not keep a note of professional disapproval out of his voice. "He left you the whole of his estate."

My eyes widened: I had not known what to expect. "Very generous."

"There is, however, one condition."

"Which is?"

"The will stipulates that you must live in Brook House for a period of five years after his death, and undertake not to dispose of any items of his property whatsoever during that time. You are, of course, at liberty to enjoy full use of your own possessions, upon the proviso that you retain all of your grandfather's."

The glass eye glared. Presumably Beazell thought my own possessions wouldn't amount to much, and he was right. Since coming back to England six months earlier, I'd rented a one-bedroom flat in

Stoke-on-Trent and, although I was by nature a voracious hoarder, I'd had little opportunity to accumulate belongings on my travels. Even so, the flat resembled a bomb site. My chronic reluctance to throw anything away was the one thing which provoked Hong Li to outbursts of temper.

"But I would lose the whole caboodle if I didn't agree to live there and keep his things?"

"In the event that the condition of the bequest fails to be satisfied," Beazell said, refusing to recognize *caboodle* as a legal term, "the estate passes to charities supporting the homeless."

I'd never thought of Rafe as a charitable donor. He must have expected me to toe the line. "Is that legal? To force someone to live somewhere, I mean?"

"There is no compulsion, the choice is yours." Beazell swivelled in his chair. "I may not specialize in the drafting of wills, but I can assure you that challenging your grandfather's testamentary provisions would be a costly exercise, and litigation is always fraught with uncertainty."

"What field do you specialize in, may I ask?"

"Criminal law." As if to remind me that his time was money, Beazell consulted his watch. A fake Rolex, I suspected, possibly supplied by one of his clients. "Indeed, I am due to appear at the magistrates' court in half an hour. Perhaps you would advise me by the end of the week whether or not you will undertake to accept the condition of the bequest?"

"No need to wait," I said. "My grandmother was right. I once heard her say that whatever Rafe wanted, he got. I'll take the house, and all his clutter."

* * *

"This is an adventure," Hong Li said, as we turned off the motorway.

"I hope you'll like the place … "

She fiddled with the silver bracelet I'd given her after our first night together. "I'm sure I shall love it. Life in the English countryside! I can't believe this is happening to me. Six weeks ago, I was working shifts in a chip shop in Stafford for half the minimum wage, now … my only worry is, how will the people in the village take to me?"

"Rafe never worried about other people, and you shouldn't, either. Besides, the village is little more than a shabby pub and half a dozen cottages a mile's walk from Brook House."

"Sounds idyllic." Her voice became dreamy. "So tell me more about Rafe."

"My grandmother never had a good word to say about him. According to her, he didn't really want a wife, but a servant at his beck and call. He and I didn't even meet until after my parents died. What I'd heard about him made me curious."

"He sounds rather sexist."

"I prefer to think he was just a product of his time. Neither Grandma nor my father talked much about him. They blamed him for the marriage breakdown, though I never found out precisely what caused it. It was as if they wanted to air-brush him out of our lives. I could understand their bitterness. Even so, the degree of their hostility seemed unfair."

"You like to see the good in people."

"Why not? I wanted to find out what he was really like."

"And did you?"

"Sort of. He was a small man, bald with dark gleaming eyes, rather charismatic. Yet I found him almost … scary. When we talked, he always seemed to be enjoying a private joke. He inherited the farm from a bachelor uncle when he was in his twenties, but he had no interest in farming. He sold off the bulk of the land and lived on the proceeds for the rest of his life."

"After your grandmother left him, he never married again?"

"No, but he cohabited with various women he called housekeepers. He had a rather old-fashioned attitude towards what he liked to call the fair sex."

Hong Li raised her eyebrows. "Actually, you're not exactly a new man yourself."

I chose to ignore this. "The first time I visited him, someone called Ramona was looking after him. Paraguayan and voluptuous, with a low-cut top and a spangly brooch on her bosom."

"So he didn't recruit her simply for her housekeeping skills?"

"Even he described her as sluttish, though he made it sound like high praise. The house was such a mess that it would send anyone who was remotely house-proud into a tailspin. He never believed in putting things away – he used to say he liked to have everything handy. Every cupboard and every drawer overflowed. Shelves buckled under the weight of books, ornaments and knick-knacks. The floors were covered with his things. I suppose it's no real wonder that his marriage fell apart."

Hong Li frowned. She'd come from Canton to England three years ago, and she wasn't supposed to have stayed here so long. The immigration laws are draconian; they don't give such people a hope of staying if they play by the rules. So they lurk in the twilight, taking work where they can to make ends meet. We met when I called in her shop for a bag of chips, and was smitten at first sight. Hong was not only a perfect model for any photographer, she also spoke better English than most people born and bred here. I felt a yearning for a passionate woman, and my only complaint was that her passion extended to tidiness. She was worse than my grand-mother, whose mantra was *a place for everything, and everything in its place*. Hong enthused about *feng shui*, and tried to persuade me there was more to it than an aesthetic approach to interior design. Given half a chance, she would chatter for hours about discovering correlations between human life and the universe, and energizing your life through positive *qi*. For her, clutter was a metaphor for negative life circumstances. She wouldn't have suited Rafe, that was for sure.

"When did you last visit Brook House?"

"Four years ago, before I left for France. Ramona had moved on, and he'd installed a Thai girl he'd met through the internet. She wore thick spectacles and seemed very earnest, but he hinted that when she let her hair down ... "

"I really don't think I would have liked Rafe," Hong said.

"But he was generous to a fault. He paid to bring these women to England on extended holidays, and looked after them well. He was just … idiosyncratic, that's all."

"It did him no good in the long run," she said. "What about the girl he was with when he died?"

"From Turkey by way of Berlin, according to Beazell. Poor kid, she called the emergency services when Rafe keeled over, and her reward was to be put on the first plane out of Britain."

Hong murmured, "You won't tell anyone about my situation, will you? I know I must get things sorted. I want to have the right to live in England, but it takes time to tick all the boxes."

"No need to worry," I said in a soothing tone, hoping she wasn't about to drop another hint about marriage. I might have promised to live in Brook House, but there's a limit to how many commitments a man can take on. Hong Li was the most accommodating model I'd worked with in ages, and I understood why, after the long and difficult journey from Canton, she felt a need to create order out of the chaos of a life in the shadows. But sometimes chaos is impossible to avoid. "There's no way the authorities will come looking for you here."

***

"This is such a weird place," she said that evening, as we lay together on the sofa, in front of a roaring fire.

"I was afraid you'd loathe it," I murmured.

"Because of all the rubbish?"

There was no escaping Rafe's clutter. Since my last visit, he had spent another four years accumulating stuff. You could barely move in any of the downstairs rooms for junk. It wasn't only the discarded lumps of stone, the incomplete bits of sculpture that he'd abandoned whenever he chiselled off one chunk too many. He collected indiscriminately. Stacked next to the sofa was an early run of copies of *Playboy* from the fifties, side-by-side with a pile of P. G. Wodehouse paperbacks and a dozen bulging postcard albums. He'd indulged in philately for years, but seemed to have become bored with the hobby in recent years, since countless unopened packets of gaudily coloured stamps from all four corners of the world were stashed away in cupboards and in between the elderly encyclopaedias crammed on groaning shelves.

"I know you can't bear mess."

"Come on, sweetheart. Mess is too mild a word, you must admit. There's so much negative energy here. We really have to start clearing up tomorrow."

"It won't be easy. It's a big house, but there isn't much room left to put all this stuff away."

"We drove past a waste disposal site on the way here."

"You can't be serious," I protested. "Remember the terms of his will?"

Hong shifted on the sofa, edging away from me. "You don't have to take everything so literally."

"It's a legal requirement. You wouldn't want me to lose my inheritance, would you?"

"Nobody would notice if you carried out a bit of ... what's the right word? Rationalization?"

"Don't you believe it. Councils hide cameras on wheelie-bins these days, they spy on folk who put electrical goods in containers meant for cardboard, it's scandalous."

"Out here in the middle of nowhere? You're making feeble excuses."

"Not in the least. It's a nightmare to dispose of anything. So easy to infringe some by-law or environmental regulation."

"That evening we first met, when I told you my story, you said laws were made to be broken."

"It was a figure of speech."

"Look!" She ran her finger along the arm of the sofa, showing me the dust. "Dirt interrupts the flow of natural energies. And the springs in the sofa have gone, it's so uncomfortable, we really must replace it."

"But it's flammable. Even if I wasn't bound to comply with Rafe's will, it would be impossible to chuck it out without a fistful of licences and bureaucratic permissions."

She sighed. "This house needs some positive *chi*."

I put my arms around her, not bothering to argue. Better prove that I had all the positive *chi* she needed.

* * *

Brook House stood on a winding lane in a quiet corner of Lancashire, surrounded by tumbledown sheds packed with misshapen sculptures and rusting cars that Rafe had driven into the ground and then abandoned. A preliminary reconnaissance indicated that he'd never got rid of a single thing. There wasn't another house in sight, which suited Rafe, who was not gregarious by nature. It suited me, too. The land that once belonged to the farm was now occupied by a business that hired out plant and machinery. A row of huge skips lined the horizon, but, as I'd made clear to Hong, it would be unthinkable to use them as a dumping ground for Rafe's possessions. It wasn't simply about complying with legal niceties; to flout his wishes would be a betrayal.

I've never cared for an excess of noise and chatter, but it was bound to take Hong longer to adjust to a new life. She came from a large family, and loved to socialize. Unlike me. During my years in Europe, I'd had a number of relationships, but none of them worked out. At least I'd got the wanderlust out of my system. When I admitted I was an old-fashioned chap at heart, and felt it was time to settle down, Hong took it as a precursor to tying the knot. Which was not what I meant at all.

"Lucky that girl was with him when he had his heart attack," she hissed, glaring at a tower of boxes full of Rafe's correspondence from the past thirty years. "If he'd died alone, it might have been weeks before his body was discovered. Imagine being buried under a load of magazines, broken toasters and old shirts. Do you have any idea how many ancient sinks are outside the kitchen? Not one, but two!"

"Let's recycle them," I suggested, in a spirit of compromise. "They make ideal planters."

"And this whole house smells," she complained, throwing open the windows in the living room. "Musty books, old pairs of underpants. It's unhealthy."

"Hey, we'll freeze if you're not careful," I said. "Let me build up the fire."

"With some of those old yellow newspapers in the scullery?"

"No way. They go back twenty years. Some of them might be valuable."

"You must be joking. And what about this?" With a flourish, Hong produced a tin box and fiddled with a small key to open it.

"You found the key!" Extraordinary. Two whole drawers in the sideboard were packed with keys of all shapes and sizes, none bearing any tag to indicate to which lock they belonged.

"It took an hour and a half of trial and error, and now I've broken in ... well, see for yourself."

She lifted the lid of the box to reveal half a dozen locks of hair. Red, fair, and black, wavy and straight.

"Who do you think they belonged to?"

"Old girlfriends, some of the housekeepers, who knows? Rafe must have had a sentimental streak, hence not wanting me to dispose of his clutter. I guess he kept snippets of their hair long after they'd moved on."

"They spook me." She pulled a face. "For pity's sake, be reasonable, sweetheart. We have to clear this crap out, it makes me ill just to look at it all."

I picked up one of the dark strands of hair. "I bet this was cut from Ramona's head. It's precisely her shade."

Hong shivered. "Creepy."

"You don't understand. They are keepsakes. It's touching that they meant so much to him."

As I spoke the words, I knew instinctively how Rafe had felt about his souvenirs. Our possessions define us. Throw them out, and you throw away your history, your personality, the very life that you have lived. When we are gone, our possessions remain; they give our loved ones something to remember us by.

"You're right," she muttered, "I don't understand."

* * *

The next day I continued to sift through the endless clutter. Hong set out for a long walk, much to my relief. I'd been afraid that she might embark on a clear-out when I wasn't looking. I dropped in on the pub for a snack lunch, and found myself chatting to the Russian barmaid. Anya was a pretty student, on a gap year. Something prompted me to ask for her phone number, and she wrote it down for me with a coquettish smile.

When Hong returned late in the afternoon, she was sneezing and out of humour. I pointed out that opening windows on a damp winter's day had been unwise, and she stomped off to bed with a glass of whisky and a paperback of *Zuleika Dobson* that she'd found under a pile of coffee filters in a kitchen cupboard. She was a voracious reader of English fiction, one of the reasons why she had mastered the language, and I said she ought to be thrilled to live in a house containing as many novels as a public library. She sniffed and headed upstairs without another word.

As the bedroom door slammed, I picked up the phone, and dialled Beazell's office.

"How did you come to meet my grandfather?"

The solicitor hesitated. "Why do you ask?"

"You're a criminal lawyer. Did Rafe do something wrong?"

"Certainly not." Beazell sounded as if I'd impugned his integrity. "Innocent until proven guilty, that's the law of the land."

"But he was accused of something?"

"He was a man of certain … tastes, shall we say? His lifestyle was by no means risk-free, his untimely demise is evidence for that."

"What happened?"

Beazell sighed. "He is dead now, so I am not breaching a confidence. A young Filipina accused him of whipping her black and blue; she claimed he was a sadist. He insisted that the, um, acts in question were consensual."

"Was he prosecuted?"

"A summons was issued, but the complainant dropped the charges and refused to testify. The case collapsed."

"A change of mind? Or did he buy the girl off?"

"I will not dignify that question with an answer." I pictured Beazell puffing out his sallow cheeks. "Suffice to say that I gave my client certain advice as to his future conduct. He went to his grave without a stain on his character."

I put the phone down and stared at the contents of the casket I'd discovered under Rafe's bed after returning from the pub. It wasn't covered in as much dust as the rest of his possessions, and I suspected that he regularly inspected its contents. When I grew frustrated after trying a couple of dozen keys in the lock, I took a hammer he'd kept in the dining room and smashed open the lid. Inside the casket were photographs, some of which I recognized. A portrait of Ramona was among them, another showed the girl from Thailand in the nude.

But it wasn't the photographs that made me catch my breath, but the spangly brooch that once adorned Ramona's prominent chest, the little round spectacles worn by the Thai girl, the heart-shaped locket containing a picture of a Slavic woman. Hooped ear-rings which I recognized from another woman who posed for one of Rafe's photographs. And a whip streaked with dark blotches.

In my head, I heard my grandfather's silky tones. A conversation I'd forgotten until this very moment.

"You may consider it strange that I surround myself with so much ephemera, but the most precious of my possessions make me feel more *real*. Tangible reminders of the life I've lived, and those with whom I've shared it. Memories of the highs and the lows, the ups and downs. These are things to be cherished, not tossed away as if they never mattered."

"I think I understand," I'd said, although, until now, I had not.

He'd smiled and said, "Well, well, my boy. I believe you do."

* * *

When Hong came downstairs, she was in a mood to conciliate. The whisky had brightened her eyes, and made her voice rather loud.

"We don't need to clear out much," she announced. "Just the bare minimum. Enough to enable us to turn this place into a decent home."

"You know," I said, almost to myself, "I think I've finally found somewhere I can be myself."

As she squeezed my hand, her bracelet brushed my wrist. "We don't need to clear out everything."

"Tell you the truth," I said. "I really don't want to clear out anything at all."

Her pleasant face hardened. The smile vanished, and for an instant I saw her face as it might look in forty years' time.

"We have a perfectly good incinerator outside the back door," she hissed. "Why not use it?"

I gave a long, low sigh, as I surrendered to the inevitable. Rafe was right, I was a man after his own heart. I patted the mobile in my pocket. Anya's number was safely stored.

"All right." I ran my fingertips along her silver bracelet. I must no longer think of it as a present, but as a souvenir. "Tomorrow, I will."

COLT

Ken Bruen

DAMN COLT 45.
    Jammed.

Doggone it all to hell.

Darn thing is supposed to work every time and I clean it like I do my tin cup, plate, every evening.

I'd landed up in a one-horse town named Watersprings, and I ain't joshing you, one horse is what they had and that was mine. Well, OK, I'm joshin you a bit here but my ride was the best, apart from the sheriff's and the owner of the saloon, who had three Palominos.

Sweet, sweet horse.

I've had my Sorrel since the Injun trouble and that baby ain't never quit, nohow.

I had me a thirst, been riding hard, real hard to get way the hell outa Arizona. They wanted me real bad in that godforsaken place.

The why is a whole other yarn and I ain't gonna bother you none with that hokum now.

Doggone, no.

This here is about a gal.

Ain't it always?

I tethered my horse outside the rail at the saloon. Couple a neer-do-wells given me that slack-eyes jaw look. I touched the brim of me beat-up Stetson, said, "How de?"

Not too friendly, didn't want em getting no damn fool notions but enough to show I meant no injury, leastways I was pushed.

I took my Winchester outa its pouch, and I could see they knew it'd been well worn. Make em think twice about foolin around some.

They done muttered some answer. I didn't detect nuttin there to reach for my Colt so I carried on up to the saloon.

Real bird place, darn right.

Couple guys moseying at card playing but not more'n a buck on the table. Big stakes, huh, but I noticed they was all carrying iron, watching me over them cards.

I seen em.

The bartender, big, burly, like a grizzly I seen one time up near Canada, too damn cold up there, and I had my Winchester, that bear in my sights and I swear, the beast turned, looked at me, like he was thinking, "I hurt you?"

I lowered the rifle, and never had a day's regret, not a one. He was kinda, I dunno the word ... noble. He sure a shotting was a big mother.

The grizzly behind the counter gives me a slow eye, asks, "What's it gonna be, partner?"

Could have said, "I ain't your partner, mistah." But no point touching trouble, one way or the damn other, the stuff done find me anyways.

I jacked my boot up on that brass foot-rail, laid my Winchester lightly against the bar, said, "Whiskey."

Didn't put no please or nuttin on there. My daddy used to say, "Son, I ain't got a whole lot to teach you cept how to shoot, shoe a horse and this, don't start nuttin you ain't aiming to finish."

I ain't gonna lie to you none, I haven't always followed my daddy's saying, the reason I got me a bullet hole in my leg, drags a bit but I ain't a moanin, the other guy, he's not doing no walking, not nohow 's I see it.

Grizzly sets the bottle on the counter, shot glass, and it weren't durty but it weren't clean neither. I figured the whiskey will wash it most ways.

I knock back two fast ones and damn, tasted real fine, like the Tucson sun after six months' hitch in the State Pen.

He's lookin at my holster, goes, "That there a Colt?"

The hell else it be?

Real slow, I reach, take it out, let him see it. Don't let no man touch it, not unless he's got the draw on me, and even then, well, he better be prepared to do more than mouth.

He lets out a slow whistle, said, "You rode with the Cavalry?"

The guy was whole lot smarter than he looked. The Colt was Army issue, and the notches on the butt, an old horse soldier tradition. Mine was riddled.

I nodded, not a story I wanted to share with some damn barkeep.

He reached out his massive hand, about to touch it, and felt, rather than saw me stiffen, pulled back, asked, "You ever run into Custer?"

That Yallah. And I ain't even talking bout his hair.

I downed another shot, let it warm me belly, then real easy said, "Man never passed a mirror he didn't love."

Let it out there, see where he stood on that whole darn mess.

He poured himself a shot, downed it in one, grimaced, the whiskey of Custer?

He said, "He sure ran into one mountain of shinola that day."
OK.

Then he done told me about those fine horses he had and I gave him the face that asks, "*Say I was in the market for a horse?*"

I put a few bits on the counter and he asked, "You fixing to stay a few days?"

And when I didn't answer, it's real foolhardy to be asking a stranger his business these wild days, he added real fast, "Reason I ask is, we got us a hanging, folks coming for miles round, ain't often you gets to see a woman dangle."

I seen most stuff, lynchings, burnings, scalpings, and I don't got me no taste for it, especially not the legal ones. But I was interested, who wouldn't be, and I repeated, "A woman?"

"Yeah, done shot her husband and now they gonna stretch her pretty little neck, see if they don't."

I dunno, I still can't get me a fix on it, I was aiming to get some chow, get my horse seen to and then hit out next day. I had business over in Shiloh and I was antsy to git movin but I asked, "She local?"

He was shaking his head, wiping down the counter with a greasy rag, said, "Hell no, outa Virginia, name of Molly Blair."

The whiskey stuck in me gullet and I'd to fight real hard to keep me face tight. I tipped my Stetson, said I might stick around for the rope party and he shouted as I reached the swing door, "Real purty little thing, shame to let all that fine woman go a begging."

My hand went to my Colt, pure instinct, I would have drilled that sum of a gun for two cents.

Outside, I had to grab me some deep breaths.

Molly, damn her to tarnation, the only gal I done ever loved.

I hawked me a big chunk of spittle and let it out on the board-walk ... looked round and could see the sheriff's office down a ways.

Cussin nine ways to Sunday, I hitched my gun belt, headed on over, thinking, "The hell I had to go running off me fool mouth."

I glanced at my horse, tired as he was, tired as I was my own self, we could have bin outa there in two seconds flat, left her to rot, like she did me but ...

Darn story of my life, I just can never mosey on the other way.

I put a chaw of bacca in me cheek, began to walk towards the jail, me fool heart thundering like the Injuns reining down on Custer.

Stepping up to the porch outside the sheriff's office, I heard loud hammering and looked to my left, damnation ... how in all that's shottin did I miss seeing it?

The scaffold, ugly looking thing but then, I guess, they ain't building em for purtyness.

Damn thing was near done too, they was even trying out a sack of taters, body weight I guess, though Molly, a cup of sugar would have been about right with her.

Petite sweet thing I'd thought way back in Tennessee when I done first run into her.

Sweet? ... Like a coyote on heat.

They let the bag fall, and it startled me, I had to shake me own self, get it tight.

I opened the door and a man was sitting behind a desk, cup of gruel going, cheroot dangling in his mouth, boots up on the desk and I thought, "Uh oh."

Frontier lawmen, a real mean breed of buzzard, they get that tin on them, they're as dangerous as a herd of buffalo in a Cheyenne autumn. He had him a belly there, a man who liked his vittles and his drinking if his flushed cheeks were any story. Round thirty, I'd hazard, and all them years, mean as can be.

He had him a smirk too, like he knew I wasn't bringing him no good news.

He got that right.

He drawled, "Help yah?"

Sounding like that was a darn fool notion.

I kept my hands loose, no threat showing, least not yet, said, "I'm kin to Molly."

He mulled that over then spat to his side, said, "That so."

Not a question.

I kept with it, tried, "Yessir, on my Momma's side, we ain't been real close or nuttin but I figured I'd better come, pay my respects."

He had a metal cup on the table and lazy as can be, he reached over, his cobra eyes never leaving my face, took his own time in a long swallow, making noises like a hog, said, "Funny, ain't it?"

What?

I went, "What?"

Then stuck on, "Sir?"

Let the beat in.

He blew a cloud of smoke at me, said, "The murdering gal ain't mentioned no kin?"

I gave a real slow grin, the *gee shucks* I keep for killing vermin, said, "Like I said, sheriff, we ain't been real close."

He stood up, real sudden and I kept very still. He grabbed a bunch of keys, asked, "Well, whatcha waiting on son, you're real keen to visit with yer kin, am I right?"

Sumofapistol ... *son* ... I had a good ten years on him. I nodded and he led me back.

She looked even more damn beautiful than I remembered and before the sheriff could try his game, I said, damn near hollered, "Coz, Momma done told me to come visit, see you be needing anything?"

He gave me the look then and his eyes showed most of what he was, a piece of trash with a Smith and Wesson, nothing no mo in that.

Molly, sharp as always, smiled, and I swear, even squeezed a tear out, shouts, "Cousin Lucas, I was believin my family washed their hands offa me."

I turned to the sheriff, asked, "Mind if I have me a moment with my kin?"

He minded, heck, he minded a lot. He spat right next to my boots, said, "You got five minutes and I'll be right outside."

I done already said about me and my running off mouth and even now, I had to go, "That'll be a comfort, sir."

His eyes sparked and he moved right in my face, drawled, real slow, "You sassing me, boy?"

Like I was nigrah.

I shot men for less.

I heard Molly say, "Now sheriff, he's just a country type, don't know a whole lot how to behave round decent folk."

He thought about it, said, "I'll be talking some more to you, boy."

He was closing a nickel to a dollar on that.

Course, a lard ass like him, he ain't going to let it go easy, said, "I'll be needing that there Colt."

I gave it up, real slow, seeing another notch on the butt already and this time, it would be a whole lot of funning.

He made lots of grunting on his way back to his coffee. I hoped it would choke him ... slow.

She gave that radiant smile, that damn melt yer heart and yer senses, all in one, done make a fool outa a man everytime.

She reached out her hand, touched my arm, said, "You lookin real fine, darling."

Cold to her heart.

I'd made me some gold offa a claim that was already staked out and I was looking to spend it, met Molly in a saloon and she not only took off with my stash but my dumbass heart as well.

Broke, hungover, I had me some real trouble to git on outa there with my skin.

I asked, "Why'd you throw me over, wasn't I good to you?"

She lowered her eyes, said, "I was real young, real reckless, what do you know at seventeen?"

I whistled, went, "Boy howdy."

She was caressing my arm and I got riled, said, "You didn't know enough that leaving me without cash could have got me killed. Them fellahs in that saloon didn't take kindly to some greenhorn saying he couldn't pay the freight, they done give me a horse whipping, took my boots and ran my ass outa town."

She let her eyes melt in the honey way she had, said, "Lucas, I'm so damn sorry, can you forgive me?"

Dammit.

Then she said, "You gotta get me on outa here."

I laughed, not with any merriment or anything, asked, "And how you fixing on me doing that, that fat ass took my Colt."

Now her real smile showed, the smile of a woman who is one hundred years old and means to live another, said, "You telling me, darling, you ain't still got that derringer in your boot."

I always had that spooked feeling she knew things she never should have known and like a lovesick pup, I reached in my boot, took out the tiny pistol, two shots.

She said, "Give it here, hon."

The gun felt tiny in my hand, small as the focus of my thinking. I asked, "You're fixing to do what?"

A cloud passed briefly over them lovely features, then was gone and she asked, "You want to see them hang me, see me spoil me bloomers as the rope bites in, you want that, lover?"

I handed it over and she hollered, "Sheriff, git on in here."

He did and she shot him in the face.

Now her voice was hard as the Rockies in that big snow we had a time back, she said, "Get the keys."

I did and took my Colt back, turned to see her level the derringer at me. She said, "I'm sorry, coz, but you'd only slow me down."

I pulled the trigger of the Colt and it jammed ... you believe it, she gave me that almost sad look and pulled the trigger on the second load. Took me right in the gut. She stepped over me, reached in my vest, took what money I had.

The Colt was lying a few feet from me. She glanced at it then stepped away, said, "They'll be coming, make sure it doesn't jam again."

And she was gone, I swear, leaving a trail of perfume that was warm as that first time I ever set my eyes on her.

The dead sheriff's dead eyes are staring at me and his cheroot is lying real close. If I could stop the blood for a moment, I might get a smoke before they come.

The Colt is a little outa reach and the damn thing let me down, you think I'm gonna trust it again.

Another inch, I might grab me that cheroot.

OPEN AND SHUT CASE

Marilyn Todd

OFFICIAL PAPERWORK OR not, sir, I am the Great Rivorsky, and that is how I wish my name to be recorded. That's R-i-v – but I see you're already familiar with the spelling from the posters. How rewarding. Though perhaps you'd be kind enough to cross out the words *no fixed abode* in the address line. The phrase smacks of gypsies, tramps and circus performers, whereas my show is a reputable spectacular that just happens to tour Europe on a continual basis. An extravaganza of mystery, magic and illusion that has performed in all the major cities, and in front of royalty on more occasions than I care to count.

Indeed, our last such performance was before Archduke Ferdinand and his charming wife, Sophie, last year in Vienna, and take it from me, Inspector, His Grace's proposals to grant ethnic minorities independence will guarantee him a long and glittering future. Unlike your own King Edward. How is his Majesty's health, by the way? Still shaky? We played for him in Biarritz not long after his mother died, and he was chesty even then. Indeed, half the audience thought the smoke from his cigars was part of the act, and it certainly made Pepé disappear. Sick as a dog behind the stage door he was, but then Pepé is a dwarf. Working the wires from the ceiling, he was subjected to the full force of the royal smoke as it rose. And though there is only half as much of him as the rest of us, he seems to be doubly absorbent when it comes to toxic pollution.

So you see, *no fixed abode* gives quite the wrong impression, and while we're about it, I wish to make clear that it is not customary for us to sleep in caravans and operate out of a marquee. Dear me, no. The Great Rivorsky? Working out of a *tent*? But after that unfortunate incident during rehearsals in Amsterdam – you did not hear?

It all came about when the fire-eater coughed at an inopportune moment, causing the curtains of the backdrop to catch light. The props immediately fell victim to flames, and of course our boxes are wood and we can't have our contortionist squeezing herself into unseasoned timber, can we? To cut a long story short, Inspector, the theatre became an inferno before you could blink, and what else could an impresario do? With a troupe to pay and suddenly no income to cover the disbursement, my only option was to hop across the Channel and stage a series of impromptu shows.

What? Sack the fire-eater? Certainly not. It was hardly his fault Zorba the Freak chose that moment to drop his trousers and show Mimi his enormous— Which is why I'm not worried about the insurance claim. The company have agreed to settle, but these things take time, though Mimi has not been the same since. Such a sensitive soul. Not at all the type of girl to whom a man should expose his enormous— Oh, I was as shocked as you, sir. Absolutely. So when Mimi shrieked, it was quite understandable that the fire-eater jumped, causing him to cough on the kerosene. Terrible. A perfectly good spring season ruined, all thanks to one fist-sized navel.

Ooh. Tea. How very kind. But if I may be so bold as to correct your report while you stir in the sugar?

When I mentioned the contortionist a moment ago – that's right, Jeannette Ridoux, though you've missed off the "x" at the end of her name. Not that she'd take offence. In fact, she'd bend over backwards to accommodate anyone, but my point is, you've written *love affair* in the margin and I feel I must take issue with that. Affair, certainly, but love? Perish the thought, though when you meet her – and I see from your notes that you haven't yet – you will understand the attraction. Not to put too fine a point on it, Inspector, the combination of raven-black hair, blue eyes and the ability to wrap her left ankle around her neck is quite powerful, though your observation was correct. All the ladies in the troupe are stunning, but then that is a requisite of the magician's trade.

Their beauty is necessary to distract the eye, where even the slightest movement will suffice. She moves her hands in a natural gesture, and see? The ten of diamonds *was* the card you picked out earlier, was it not? Yes, yes, put it back anywhere you like, and oops, there it is again. Ten of diamonds. No, sir, not in the deck. Underneath your notes. Which, unfortunately, bring us back to my dalliance with the lovely Jeannette Ridoux, and the dispute it caused with Madame Rivorsky.

You say you have twenty-three witnesses who heard Carla screaming at me two days ago, and the only surprise is that the number is that low, Carla being theatrically trained. Then again, what virtuous woman wouldn't raise her voice when she walks in to find her husband playing "Find the Lady" with his contortionist in her own marital bed?

Very well, if you wish to split hairs, my arrangement with Carla did not actually constitute a *legal* contract of marriage. But I am a gentleman, sir, and honour bound to protect a lady's reputation, even though, technically speaking, I am still married to the first Madame Rivorsky. And perhaps a couple of others, I can't be sure, though that ceremony in Rome was declared unlawful a year afterwards, and I still have my doubts about Lisbon.

But dear me, you have not brought me all the way to your police station to charge me with bigamy.

You have arrested me for Carla's murder.

* * *

Carla Bonetti had it all. Blonde hair, flawless skin, perfect memory, sleight of hand. Everything, in fact, that made her a first-rate mind-reading act.

The first time I saw her was in Prague. Our schedule took us there two years ago, during that particularly vicious hot August. I had wandered into St Nicholas' church to cool down, passing a pleasant hour or two imagining the magnificent baroque paintings that used to adorn the interior, until the late Emperor Josef ordered them to be removed. Silly fool. Anyway, walking back into the square was like stepping into a furnace, in which the entire population seemed to be melting. Except one.

She'd set up a table in the shade of the Town Hall, well aware that each day, hundreds of people flock to see the famous astronomical clock. If you haven't seen this gigantic masterpiece of engineering and entertainment, allow me to enlighten you. Every hour, on the hour, larger-than-life-size figures of Christ and the apostles march past the upper window, turning to look out over the square as they pass, while the skeleton of death tolls the bell. It is a spectacle admired by princes and peasants alike and the crowds are ferociously large. But what attracted me to Carla, Inspector, wasn't that while her audience were mopping their foreheads and fanning themselves she remained cool as the proverbial cucumber, in her virgin white dress and blonde hair swept up, as she slid *koruna* after *koruna* into her tin. It was that she'd chosen to work the *Mystical Card* trick right under the great circle of the zodiac that is mounted directly beneath the clock.

Let me clarify. You see these? They are the very pieces she was using that day, and as you can see they are leather. They could just as easily have been parchment or wood, the material's irrelevant, but you see how she's painted mystical symbols round the edge of each of these five little sheets? Then inscribed four numbers across and four down in a square in the middle? Once the ink was dry, she'd have scrubbed the leather to make the pieces appear ancient, reinforcing her claim that these little treasures came from a pharaoh's tomb, an Indian mystic, an Aztec princess, whatever.

I shall dispense with the hocus-pocus for now. The power of the symbols … The channelling of energy … The transference of your thoughts to mine … I shall simply point out what you will have already noticed, namely that the numbers range from one to thirty-one, and now ask you to tap each of the pages on which your birthday appears. Aha. 28 April. A most pleasant time of the year to be celebrating, though I see even you, an experienced police officer, are surprised. Of course, you are right. The numbers are not written randomly at all, and I confess, the date is not mind-reading, but basic arithmetic. Guessing the month, though? Sadly, I am not at liberty to disclose how that's done. The Magic Circle would have my head in a noose—

Hm. A rather unfortunate expression, given the circumstances, so I shall quickly skip on.

From the moment I saw how Carla had not only positioned her pitch to catch those who flocked to the clock, but also primed their minds with the zodiac signs, I realized that here was a highly polished performer, who deserved a wider, and more lucrative, audience.

She jumped at the chance to tour with us, and from the moment I watched her opening act, in which she invited spectators to draw a picture on the blackboard, then opened a pre-sealed envelope to reveal that same drawing, I knew my instincts were right. Without resorting to stooges or trickery, she would manipulate the audience with her "psychic" abilities, and have them eating out of her hand. With her dazzling white dress and soft-spoken voice, who would suspect such a fragile creature of being an actress? Even Archduke Ferdinand was enchanted by Carla Bonetti. When she called for volunteers during our tour in Vienna, I clearly remember him jumping up and shouting, "I'll give it a shot!"

Inspector, you should have seen the look on his face, when she gave all three members of the Royal party a bundle of baggage labels bearing the name of a different city, asked them to memorize any one that took their fancy, then lifted the sheet on a black board on which she'd already written the names of the cities they'd chosen.

I was spellbound. Full of admiration for making fragility part of her act when, in fact, that soft-spoken voice carried to the back of the theatre. But at the same time, sir, Cupid never strays far from a theatrical troupe. In no time, I had lost my heart to this beautiful, talented but above all professional lady, and within three months of that meeting beneath the clock tower, Carla Bonetti was my wife.

That is to say, we went through the motions of a civil ceremony, for I know false papers when I see them. And whatever other characteristics the Italians might have, fair skin and blonde hair is rarely among them. Especially when accompanied by a Scandinavian accent.

Who cared? None of us is perfect, sir, none. The point is, her fame increased, her popularity grew, and within six months she was almost as famous as The Great Rivorsky himself, and I begrudged her none of the limelight. Quite the contrary, in fact. We were a team. We were in love. We had such a brilliant future ahead of us! She talked of expansion. Of America. New York, San Francisco, Boston, Chicago, dear me, she almost had the itinerary booked! But what I had forgotten – the quickness of the hand deceiving the eye and all that – is that, at heart, Carla Bonetti was a con-artist.

Fate may have brought us together that hot August day, but from that moment on, she had been feeding me the way she fed her audience. Were I not so besotted, I would have realized. Good Lord, I'd even remarked on the speed with which she'd pocketed those *korunas*, attributing this to a fear of thieves and pickpockets in Prague's crowded main square. With hindsight, though, it was obvious. Carla, Inspector, was motivated by one thing, and one thing only. Money.

She had no friends, no relatives (at least none with whom she kept in touch) and no desire to mix with the rest of the company. She led me to believe she was a lonely, damaged individual, and maybe that part was true. But in her eyes, I was nothing more than a stepping stone to bettering herself, and she threw herself into honing her act.

When I proposed marriage, she saw an even faster route to financial success. Half my takings, half my savings, possibly even more, had I coughed up for that ill-fated American Dream, for I feel sure she had no intention of remaining with me. I hand her the money for the transatlantic crossing, bearing in mind the number of berths this troupe needs – and pff! Carla Bonetti disappears in the night, while Madame d'Orcale turns up in New York, an angelic psychic to whom you'd entrust your life.

And the silly thing is, she'd have got away with it, had greed not got the better of her.

Pardon me leaning closer, but what I am about to tell you is a delicate matter, and I would beg you to think carefully before you commit such confidences to paper. You see ... how can I put this? What with one city after another, the packing, the unpacking, the rehearsals, the hiring, the firing, that lawsuit with the Siamese twins (and despite what they claim, I am *certain* Pepé was not the father of the dark-haired one's baby; Zorba is not known as The Freak for nothing) ... But my point is, these activities take time and, ahem ... energy. For several months, the Rivorsky marital bed saw little activity other than sleeping, and when I finally had vigour enough to rekindle the spark, Carla made it clear she was no longer interested.

I worship you as a husband, a leader, a father-figure to myself and the group, she told me, and dear me, there were even tears in her eyes. *The pedestal I have put you on is so high, that I need time to adjust and put a proper perspective on our marriage.* She kissed my cheek. *I will be a wife to you again, darling, I promise. Just give me time.*

The brush-off didn't bother me, Inspector. I already had the measure of Carla by then, and it was around this point that Jeannette joined our company. You have seen my "Slicing the Lady in Three" trick? Oh, you should, sir, you should. Bring your wife, she'll be amazed. Far superior to "Sawing the Lady in Half", which has become somewhat overworked of late, and also requires two female assistants to be successful, whereas this relies on just the one. Let me explain how it works.

We start with a tall, upright box whose door has a large oval hole at the top for her head, two small round ones for her hands, and two more at the bottom to accommodate her feet. My beautiful assistant steps into the box. I close the door. She places her head, hands and feet through the openings, and I invite the audience to pass her any small object of their own for her to hold. Sometimes it is a comb, sometimes a pocket watch, sometimes an embroidered hankie or necklace, but whatever they choose, it is important that the items belong to members of the public and they can see there is no sleight of hand.

I now bring out my blades, and show people that these are not trick pieces that collapse or disappear into the handle, and that by heaven, the edges are sharp. Fashioned from the finest steel, these are truly the deadliest of weapons, which is why we always keep them under lock and key. And also why my assistant and I need to practise, practise, practise, sir. One false move could be fatal.

But of course it was not Jeannette Ridoux who was murdered.

Nor one of those blades that killed the lovely Carla ...

To continue. Having locked Jeannette in the box, where she is merrily waving the audience's personal effects, I brandish the first blade then proceed to push it across the full width of the box at roughly the level of her armpits. She twists her lip a bit, and frowns, but eventually it goes right the way in. I then repeat the process at a point about mid-thigh – which, incidentally, is a very shapely one – and, as you would expect of a knife sawing off your legs, she winces even harder. But my assistant is no cry-baby, sir. She continues to wave the pocket watch, hankie or whatever, her smile broader than ever.

Now for the moment of truth! I push on the side of the box. Heave, heave, heave, and hey presto! To a rumble of drums, the middle section, the part between the two blades, slides to the left, leaving Jeannette – ta, da! – in three separate pieces.

The top part is still in its original and upright position. You can see her smiling, and waving whatever the audience gave her to hold in her left hand. The bottom part hasn't moved either. You can still see her wriggling her pretty little toes through the cut-outs. But with the middle section pushed completely to one side, there is nothing now but a gaping hole where Jeannette's torso used to be, and yet, look! Her right hand, now stuck out way to the side, is still waggling the object she'd been given!

To prove there are no mirrors involved, I plunge my arm through the gap, then throw a ball through the space, backwards and for-wards, backwards and forwards, to prove there is nothing there except air. I walk behind it, bending down, making faces, pushing my hand through, then invite the owners of the items to come forward and verify that these are indeed their possessions. The middle section is then slid back into place, out come the blades, click, click, and when I open the door again, out steps Jeannette, all in one piece!

The applause is rapturous, as you can imagine. But because the trick is new and, I repeat, extremely dangerous, timing is everything. My new assistant and I spent many hours together, perfecting the act, and I suppose it was inevitable that contortion and illusion would eventually join in collusion.

Which is why I wanted to make clear just now that it was purely a physical attraction, one in which love played no part. Jeannette is supple and sultry, and whilst one could argue that one good turn deserves another – especially in her case – Cupid had already hit me with one misguided dart. I was in no hurry to lose my heart again, and besides. I needed to dislodge that first mischievous arrow, and here was a conundrum, if ever there was one. Do I fire Carla and lose the best mind-reading act I'd ever had? Or put up with the situation, no matter how difficult, and try to make the most of it?

A tricky predicament, as you'll agree. One that unfortunately pales in comparison to the one I find myself in now, though I do see the logic behind the arrest.

You find me covered in blood ... beside the body of my bigamous wife ... in the marital bed ... with a bread knife sticking out of her heart ... and the caravan locked from the inside.

Might I have another cup of tea, do you suppose?

* * *

Motive, means and opportunity. The Great Rivorsky has all three, and in terms of a police investigation, I fully understand why you see this as an open and shut case. So do I. Carla was looking to bleed me dry, and money is a magnificent incentive to murder. Knives are commonplace in a theatrical troupe, especially with Chief Red Sky's knife-throwing act, though how many Cherokee Indians you see in Glasgow is dubious. Or red skies, come to that. And finally, of course, who else had the opportunity to kill Carla, since all the bolts on the caravan doors were in place when you broke in, and with a wound like that, it was clearly not suicide.

It doesn't look good for me, does it?

On the other hand, you have to take into account that I am an illusionist, sir. A master of deception, disguise and dexterity, who makes his living from things that are not what they seem.

For instance, look how you found me. Dressed in my stage suit, with its hidden pockets, false buttons, even this lovely white rabbit. Incidentally, you wouldn't have a lettuce leaf on the premises, would you? It's well past this little chap's breakfast. Thank you, thank you. Most kind.

Anyway, Inspector, as I was saying. Did you not think it odd that the police broke in this morning, to find me fast asleep and still in the clothes in which I had been performing? The prosecution could argue that I had fallen into a drunken stupor, and there's no denying I enjoy a port and brandy or two after the show. But if I had been so hammered as to fall asleep fully clothed, would I have had the presence of mind to lock the caravan doors – four bolts, don't forget – and then drive a knife into a sleeping Carla?

Or hadn't you noticed that she was killed as she slept?

No rumpled bedsheets. No arcing spurts of blood. No tangled nightdress or hair that had been messed up in a struggle.

And I know you will already have established from witnesses that she was alive when I entered the caravan, and this, I feel sure, is the reason you've charged me. Half the company would have seen us through the open doors, possibly overheard us dissecting the night's performance and debating how it could be improved on. For if there was one thing to be said in favour of that disastrous relationship, it was a sense of professionalism.

I was still drinking port and brandies when the church bell tolled midnight, and shortly afterwards I locked up. I remember waving to Pepé and blowing a kiss on my fingers to Mimi, or at least that's what I had intended to do, it just came out the wrong way round. No matter. The important thing is that Carla took herself off to her side of the bed, I bolted all four sections of the small stable doors, and that's the last thing I remember until your flat-footed sergeant hauled me off the bed and into a pair of handcuffs. I gave them back to him several times, but he insisted on replacing them.

I have them in my pocket, by the way, if you'd like me to return them.

**

The caravan is delightful. Round, like a barrel, with sailmaker's canvas stretched over the frame, the oak from which it is made is intricately carved and even more exquisitely painted. The cold is banished by a cast-iron "Queenie" stove, and the interior is so sumptuous, it rivals the most opulent hotel. Lavishly painted and comfortably furnished, it boasts a small bow window with lattice panes at the back, under which the bed frame has been built. Meaning one is not then obliged to draw the rich velvet curtains that hang over the window, but is at liberty to lie in bed and gaze up at the stars. With its mahogany panelling and gold leaf on the mouldings, the caravan provides luxury and comfort, and combined with the gentle rock of the horse drawing it along, offers a lifestyle which has much to recommend it.

Except, it appears, when it comes to privacy.

You tell me the police were called after Colonel Tom Thumb peered through the latticework, saw carnage on the bed and promptly raised the alarm. My first comment here is that you should go gently when interviewing him. Far from the Peeping Tom you take him to be, he is, in fact, a normal, lively six-year-old boy who just happens to have an unnaturally deep voice and has been coached to walk, talk and behave as a man, even to smoking cigars, drinking whisky and yes, I admit it, even cussing. The latter being a family trait – dear me, the mouth on his mother!

On the other hand, there's no need to tread softly when interviewing the bearded lady. She is none other than Samson O'Reilly, blessed, as luck would have it, with delicate, sculpted features not usually found in a family of dockers, and a minuscule Adam's apple that is easily disguised by a sparkling ruby necklace. As always with illusion, sir, it is a question of distracting the eye. Rather like our "Southseas Mermaid", I suppose. A testimony to the skill of the taxidermist, the creature is half-fish, half-monkey to which blonde human hair has been glued, but all this is beside the point.

Namely, was the discovery of Carla's body down to a young boy's natural curiosity, or a bit of prompting from a third party?

A question that hadn't occurred to you, I can see, but ask yourself this. What circumstances would make a man drive a bread knife into his sleeping wife's heart, knowing he'd get blood all over his precious stage suit, then fall into so heavy a stupor that he doesn't wake up even when the alarm has been raised, and is still sleeping when the police break down the door?

Wait, wait, wait. That was a rhetorical question, not a challenge, Inspector, though I do see your dilemma.

If I didn't kill Carla, then who did? Professional to the core as she was, and exceedingly pleasant on the eye, she wasn't popular with the troupe. Not at all. And I doubt you will find anyone who'll admit to liking her, not even Pepé, and usually he looks up to everyone. Which makes it a doubly difficult situation for me, given that a woman who makes no friends makes no enemies, either. Indeed, I defy you to find anyone who hated her for that matter, and a lukewarm dislike is hardly a motive for murder!

So then. We've ruled out love, hate, jealousy, greed, and even revenge can be crossed off the list, since she was not a person who aroused high emotions in others, having no passion herself—

Oh, no, that screaming match when she caught me *in flagrante* was pure theatrics, I assure you. Granted, Inspector, it was ungentlemanly conduct on my part to seduce my assistant in the marital bed. But Jeannette dropped by unexpectedly to discuss the act, and somehow it just happened. One moment I was minding my own business, waxing my moustache in front of the mirror. The next I had a contortionist coiled round me like an anaconda, dislocating her joints in every direction.

Carla did not usually return before noon, and hand on my heart, I never intended to hurt or humiliate her. I was in the wrong, I admitted it, and took great pains to apologize for my behaviour. On the other hand, the manner of her outburst was completely unjustified, a cheap theatrical ploy designed to publicize my shabby conduct, thus adding to the list of reasons why I should not assault her icy virtue. I am not ashamed to say that, once Jeannette left, I threw the whole lot back at her, albeit in the form of a tired, old joke.

About how I'd picked this up poor, bedraggled waif, who told me she hadn't eaten for three days.

"In my compassion, Carla, I brought her home and warmed up the shepherd's pie I cooked for you last night, the meal you wouldn't eat because it was too fattening."

Not the first dinner I had prepared for her that had been passed to the dogs.

"And since the orphan's clothes were so ragged, I gave her that blue dress I bought you on our honeymoon, which you never wore because you said it's too tight. Along with the straw bonnet I bought as an anniversary present, but which has never come out of the box, because you feel the flowers on the brim aren't dignified enough."

Again, all true.

I pressed on. "I donated the velvet choker Mimi gave you for Christmas that you don't use simply to annoy her, along with those expensive button boots you never wear because Chief Red Sky's wife has an identical pair, as well as the jade brooch you've never put on, because you say I have no taste."

Carla was taken aback by my bitterness, Inspector, but I wasn't done.

"In fact, the waif was so grateful for my sympathy and support," I continued, "that as I walked her to the door, the poor girl turned to me with tears in her eyes and said, *"Please, sir. Do you have anything else your wife doesn't use?"*

The joke was intended to soften the effect, though too late I remembered Carla had no sense of humour. But if motive is a sticking point in her murder, so, too, is opportunity. Knowing as we do that all four parts of the twin stable doors were bolted from the inside, how could anyone get in? And it has already been established that the lattice window is too small for even my contortionist to squeeze through, which means, and apologies if I appear to be doing your job, the solution lies in the character.

Take you, for example, Inspector. From what I've seen, you obviously pride yourself on being objective, and do not readily accept theories without proof. Neither do you suffer fools gladly. But what of the qualities that are not quite as apparent? Let me see …

Yes, I'm starting to sense that much of the time you are unruffled and in control, yet when you are alone with your thoughts, there are times when you are prone to worry. About your family, at a guess. Your wife and your children, and also over your finances. Feelings are also coming to me that you are self-critical, constantly strive to do well and earn the respect that you deserve, especially from your superior officers, and that you also read books to broaden your mind. In addition, I'd say you thrive on a certain amount of challenge and change – not too much, though – but become deeply frustrated when your efforts are hampered by pettiness, bureaucracy and shortage of time. I will even go out on a limb and suggest there have been times in your life, Inspector, and more than one, when you have had serious doubts about whether you've made the right decision. Am I right? Of course I am, but my skills are nothing compared to Carla's.

Now I don't wish to disillusion you, sir. Not at all. But that character reading applies to one hundred per cent of the population in one way or another, being so vague and ambiguous that the assessment cannot help but fit. A few frown lines indicate a tendency to worry, your frayed cuffs point to money problems, and the library card on your desk is well used. Carla, though, was far better at manipulating her public, relying on them reading a lot more into her words than there was substance. After all, sceptics don't pay to visit psychics and mind-readers. Only those who already believe.

What, to the "psychic", is a vague but nonetheless suggestive assertion is simply bait for the sitter to take. If there is no response, or the assessment falls wide of the mark, the "psychic" will quickly change tack and fish for alternative clues, constantly reading the sitter's response and taking their lead from that. Like illusionists, they bank on people seeing what they want to see. Never underestimate the human desire to make sense out of the most incongruous rubbish!

So there we are, Inspector. Now we know how Carla was killed, and by whom. It will soon lead us to why.

Ooh, more tea. How lovely. When it comes to hospitality, you English just cannot be beaten.

* * *

If no one got in and no one got out, *ipso facto* the killer must be in the caravan. Yet your men found only Carla and me, which brings us, Inspector, to the open and shut case.

Earlier I mentioned my "Slicing the Lady in Three" trick. Providing you give me your oath not to tell anyone else, I shall enlighten you as to how it is done. The knives are real, so are the hands, the feet and the face that smiles through dismemberment. Yet there is a gaping hole in the middle where my assistant's torso should be, and a compartment at the side where it actually is.

Or where it appears to be, I should say.

Once my assistant steps into the box, she puts her face through the window, and also her hands, and her feet through the holes at the bottom. She wiggles them all to prove it is real, and the audience pass her their personal items to hold. But once they have returned to their seats, she kicks off her left shoe and twists her body flat to the side of the box. Using her right foot, she manoeuvres the shoe to make it look like it's moving, alternating with the foot that is actually poking through the hole. Her hands remain in position.

The dangerous part comes when I push in the blades. If you look closely, you will see that the blades are not quite as wide as the box, the operative words there being "not quite". The contortionist has to really flatten herself against the wall, while still keeping her face pointing forward. This, sir, is no mean feat. The trick will not work without the most accomplished contortionist.

And of course the other thing is, such is the optical illusion of the wavy lines painted on the woodwork, that the box appears to be the same thickness on both sides. In reality, the left side is a good few inches wider, which, when coupled with the slightly narrower blades, allows just enough space for my assistant's body turned sideways. After that, it is simply a question of her stretching her arm in the part I slide sideways, and hey presto, the illusion is complete.

There is nothing in the middle except air!

And unfortunately it is air that lies at the heart of this mystery. While I drink my tea and read your excellent *Times* newspaper, I suggest you return to the caravan, Inspector, and examine the suitcase on top of the wardrobe. I'm betting it has holes bored in the back. Curled up inside, you see, Mademoiselle Ridoux would have needed to breathe.

I suspect you will also find traces of blood on the inside. Carla's blood, obviously, for one cannot drive knives into people without certain consequences. And at the same time, I suggest you have men search Jeannette's caravan, where you will surely find the blood-stained leotard that she hasn't yet had time to wash. Why not? Oh, for the same reason you haven't interviewed her. She was still coiled inside the suitcase when the police broke in this morning, and with your men tramping in and out, undertakers and so on, she'd have been obliged to remain there until the coast was clear.

Let me tell you what I believe happened last night.

After Carla finished her mind-reading act, she returned to the wagon, where she stowed her dazzling white gown in the suit-case, as she did after every performance, to protect it. Clad in an ordinary frock, she then attended the regular post-performance party – a short celebration, but an important one. The troupe need to know they are appreciated, even those who work behind the scenes. Jeannette would have used the diversion to slip in to the Rivorsky wagon, remove Carla's gown and at the same time tak-ing the opportunity to drug the port or the brandy with bromide, possibly both.

When you search her quarters, I daresay you will also find the white sequinned dress, and I suggest you ignore any assertion that Carla asked her to look after it for her, because, dear me, this of all items? The gown she wore every night on the stage? Carla Bonetti would never entrust such a precious gown to anyone, much less the woman she'd found in her own bed with her husband!

Yes, as to that unfortunate incident – as a man of the world, Inspector, I am well aware when a woman has no deep emotional feelings for me. But a lonely heart will take comfort where it is offered, though once again, I failed to see that the affair was set up. A smoke-screen to cover Jeannette's plan to kill Carla, then frame me for the murder.

What I suspect happened is this.

Jeannette asked Carla for a reading, little realizing it was nothing more than a cheap display of manipulation, suggestion and flattery. Like illusion, where people see what they are expecting to see, when it comes to mind-reading, fortune-telling and psychics, sittters are also predisposed to hear what they expect to hear, and invariably remember the successes over the failures.

I don't know what secret Jeannette was hiding, but for a sceptic to resort to consulting someone like Carla, she must have been very afraid. She'll probably tell you she was running away from a violent husband, and was terrified he'd track her down. I suggest a more likely scenario involves the police, and since Carla's murder was so meticulously planned, I doubt it was beginner's luck.

Naturally, I don't know what Carla told Jeannette, either. Indeed, I doubt she'd even remembered herself. To her, this would have been just another routine exercise, picking up clues then feeling her way as she went along. Whatever she'd told her, it would have been exceedingly nebulous, yet that scam, sir, cost Carla her life.

Jeannette would have seen things from a different angle entirely. In her eyes, Carla knew her every dark secret and, for that reason, had to be silenced. So she seduces the Great Rivorsky in his own bed, no doubt planting something of Carla's in the caravan knowing my poor wife would be needing it during rehearsals. The steaming row would have been the icing on the cake.

I'll bet the bitch even sharpened my own bread knife while she was at it.

* * *

Ah, there you are, Inspector. And me not halfway through this excellent paper. You found the holes in the empty suitcase? Blood on the inside? Carla's stage dress under Jeannette's bunk. Good. Well, not good. For all her faults, poor Carla is dead, and this is not how I would have wished the marriage to end.

And you have also unmasked Jeannette Ridoux? Amazing detective work, sir, I compliment you. Janet Reed from Basingstoke, eh? Wanted for poisoning three elderly gentlemen for their life savings, and no doubt planning to spend it, once she was free of your English borders. Probably why she chose this particular troupe. In a matter of days, we'll be gone again, won't we? Budapest, my home town, as it happens.

I must say, I feel partly responsible for Carla's death. If I hadn't succumbed to Jeannette's entwining charms, she could not have put her plan into action.

Or yes. Maybe, Inspector, you have hit the nail on the head. Maybe she would have found someone else to frame for the murder. A man who would not have been able to prove his innocence, and been hanged for a crime he didn't commit ...

But I, of course, am the Great Rivorsky. I can get out of any tight spot.

Contortionists, on the other hand, twist their joints and their bodies, just as in Jeannette's case they twist the truth.

Though I fear that, this time, the hangman's noose is one thing Janet Reed won't wriggle out of.

QUEEN OF THE HILL

Stuart Neville

CAM THE HUN set off from his flat on Victoria Street with fear in his heart and heat in his loins. He pulled his coat tight around him. There'd be no snow for Christmas, but it might manage a frost.

Not that he cared much about Christmas this year. If he did this awful thing, if he could actually go through with it, he intended on drinking every last drop of alcohol in the flat. He'd drink until he passed out, and drink some more when he woke up. With any luck he'd stay under right through to Boxing Day.

Davy Pollock told Cam the Hun he could come back to Orangefield. The banishment would be lifted, he could return and see his mother, so long as he did as Davy asked. But Cam the Hun knew he wouldn't be able to face her if he did the job, not on Christmas, no matter how badly he wanted to spend the day at her bedside. He'd been put out of the estate seven years ago for "running with the taigs", as Davy put it. Still and all, Davy didn't mind coming to Cam the Hun when he needed supplies from the other side. When Es and blow were thin on the ground in Armagh, just like any other town, the unbridgeable divide between Loyalist and Republican narrowed pretty quickly. Cam the Hun had his uses. He had that much to be grateful for.

He crossed towards Barrack Street, the Mall on his right, the old prison on his left. Christmas lights sprawled across the front of the gaol, ridiculous baubles on such a grim, desperate building. The Church of Ireland cathedral loomed up ahead, glowing at the top of the hill, lit up like a stage set. He couldn't see the Queen's house from here, but it stood just beneath the cathedral. It was an old

Georgian place, three storeys, and would've cost a fortune before the property crash.

She didn't pay a penny for it. The Queen of the Hill won her palace in a game of cards.

Anne Mahon and her then boyfriend had rented a flat on the top floor from Paddy Dolan, a lawyer who laundered cash for the IRA through property investment. She was pregnant, ready to pop at any moment, when Dolan and the boyfriend started a drunken game of poker. When the boyfriend was down to his last ten-pound note, he boasted of Anne's skill, said she could beat any man in the country. Dolan challenged her to a game. She refused, but Dolan wouldn't let it be. He said if she didn't play him, he'd put her and her fuckwit boyfriend out on the street that very night, pregnant or not.

Her water broke just as she laid out the hand that won the house, and Paddy Dolan's shoes were ruined. Not that it mattered in the end. The cops found him at the bottom of Newry Canal, tied to the driver's seat of his 5-Series BMW, nine days after he handed over the deeds. The boyfriend lasted a week longer. A bullet in the gut did for him, but the 'Ra let Anne keep the house. They said they wouldn't evict a young woman with newborn twins. The talk around town was a Sinn Féin councillor was sweet on her and smoothed things over with the balaclava boys.

Anne Mahon knew how to use men in that way. That's what made her Queen of the Hill. Once she got her claws into you, that was that. You were clean fucked.

Like Cam the Hun.

He kept his head down as he passed the shaven-headed men smoking outside the pub on Barrack Street. They knew who he was, knew he ran with the other sort, and glared as he walked by. One of them wore a Santa hat with a Red Hand of Ulster badge pinned to the brim.

As Cam the Hun began the climb up Scotch Street, the warmth in his groin grew with the terror in his stomach. The two sensations butted against each other somewhere beneath his navel. It was almost a year since he'd last seen her. That long night had left him drained and walking like John Wayne. She'd made him earn it, though. Two likely lads had been dealing right on her doorstep, and he'd sorted them out for her.

Back then he'd have done anything for a taste of the Queen, but as she took the last of him, his fingers tangled in her dyed crimson hair, he noticed the blood congealing on his swollen knuckles. The image of the two boys' broken faces swamped his mind, and he swore right then he'd never touch her again. She was poison. Like the goods she distributed from her fortress on the hill, too much would kill you, but there was no such thing as enough.

He walked to the far side of the library on Market Street. Metal fencing portioned off a path up the steep slope. The council was wasting more money renovating the town centre, leaving the area between the library and the closed-down cinema covered in rubble. Christmas Eve revellers puffed on cigarettes outside the theatre, girls draped with tinsel, young men shivering in their shirtsleeves. The sight of them caused dark thoughts to pass behind Cam the Hun's eyes. He seized on the resentment, brought it close to his heart. He'd need all the anger and hate he could muster.

He'd phoned the Queen that afternoon and told her it had been too long. He needed her.

"Tonight," she'd said. "Christmas party at my place."

The house came into view as Cam the Hun climbed the slope past the library. Last house on the terrace to his left, facing the theatre across the square, the cathedral towering over it all. Her palace, her fortress. The fear slammed into his belly, and he stopped dead.

Could he do it? He'd done worse things in his life. She was a cancer in Armagh, feeding off the misery she sowed with her powders and potions. The world would be no poorer without her. She'd offloaded her twin sons on their grandmother and rarely saw them. No one depended on her but the dealers she owned, and they'd have Davy Pollock to turn to when she was gone. No, the air in this town could only be sweeter for her passing. The logic of it was insurmountable. Cam the Hun could and would do this thing.

But he loved her.

The sudden weight of it forced the air from his lungs. He knew it was a foolish notion, a symptom of his weakness and her power over him. But the knowledge went no further than his head. His heart and loins knew different.

One or two of the smokers outside the theatre noticed him, this slight figure with his coat wrapped tight around him. If he stood rooted to the spot much longer, they would remember him. When they heard the news the next day, they would recall his face. Cam the Hun thought of the ten grand the job would pay and started walking.

For a moment he considered veering right, into the theatre bar, shouldering his way through the crowd, and ordering a pint of Stella and a shot of Black Bush. Instead, he thought of his debts. And there'd be some left over to pay for a home help for his mother, even if it was only for a month or two. He headed left, towards the Queen's house.

His chest strained as he neared the top of the hill, his breath misting around him. He gripped the railing by her door and willed his heart to slow. Jesus, he needed to get more exercise. That would be his New Year's resolution. Get healthy. He rang the doorbell.

The muffled rumble of Black Sabbath's "Supernaut" came from inside. Cam the Hun listened for movement in the hall. When none came, he hit the doorbell twice more. He watched, through the glass above the front door, a shadow move against the ceiling. Something obscured the point of light at the peephole. He heard a bar move aside and three locks snap open. Warm air ferried the sweet tang of cannabis and perfume out into the night.

"Campbell Hunter," she said. "It's been a while."

She still wore her hair dyed crimson red with a black streak at her left temple. A black corset top revealed a trail from her deep cleavage, along her flat stomach, to the smooth skin above her low-cut jeans. Part of the raven tattoo was just visible above the button fly. He remembered the silken feel against his lips, the scent of her, the firmness of her body. She could afford the best work; the surgeons left little sign of her childbearing, save for the scar that cut the raven in two.

"A year," Cam the Hun said. "Too long."

She stepped back, and he crossed her threshold knowing it would be the last time. She locked the steel-backed door and lowered the bar into place. Neither bullet nor battering ram could break through. He followed her to the living room. Ozzy Osbourne wailed over Tony Iommi's guitar. A black artificial Christmas tree stood in the corner, small skulls, crows and inverted crosses as ornaments among the red tinsel. Men and women lay about on cushions and blankets, their lids drooping over distant eyes. Spoons and foil wraps, needles and rolled-up money, papers and tobaccos, crumbs of resins and wafts of powder.

"Good party," Cam the Hun said, his voice raised above the music.

"You know me," she said as she took a bottle of Gordon's gin and two glasses from the sideboard. "I'm the hostess with the mostest. Come on."

As she brushed past him, sparks leaping between their bodies, Cam the Hun caught her perfume through the room's mingled aromas. A white-hot bolt crackled from his brain down to his groin. She headed to the stairs in the hall, stopped, turned on her heel, showed him the maddening undulations of her figure. "Well?" she asked. "What are you waiting for?"

Cam the Hun forced one foot in front of the other and followed her up the stairs. The rhythm of her hips held him spellbound, and he tripped. She looked back over her naked shoulder and smiled down at him. He returned the smile as he thanked God the knife in his coat pocket had a folding blade. He found his feet and stayed behind her as she climbed the second flight to her bedroom on the top floor.

The décor hadn't changed in a year, blacks and reds, silks and satins. Suspended sheets of shimmering fabric formed a canopy over the wrought-iron bedstead. A huge mound of pillows in all shapes and sizes lay at one end. He wondered if she still had the cuffs, or the—

Cam the Hun stamped on that thought. He had to keep his mind behind his eyes and between his ears, not let it creep down to where it could do him no good.

"Take your coat off," she said. She set the glasses on the dressing table and poured three fingers of neat gin into each.

He hung his coat on her bedpost, careful not to let the knife clang against the iron. She handed him a glass. He sat on the edge of the bed and took a sip. He tried not to cough at the stinging juniper taste. He failed.

Somewhere beneath the gin's cloying odour, and the soft sweetness of her perfume, he caught the hint of another smell. Something lower, meaner, like ripe meat. The alcohol reached his belly. He swallowed again to keep it there.

The Queen of the Hill smiled her crooked smile and sat in the chair facing him. She hooked one leg over its arm, her jeans hinting at secrets he already knew. She took a mouthful of gin, washed it around her teeth, and hissed as it went down.

"I'm glad you called," she said.

"Are you?"

"Of course," she said. She winked and let a finger trace the shape of her left breast. "And not just for that."

Cam the Hun tried to quell the stirring in his trousers by studying the black painted floorboards. "Oh?" he said.

"There's trouble coming," she said. "I'll need your help."

He allowed himself a glance at her. "What kind of trouble?"

"The Davy Pollock kind."

His stomach lurched. He took a deeper swig of gin, forced it down. His eyes burned.

"He's been spreading talk about me," she said. "Says he wants me out of the way. Says he wants my business. Says he'll pay good money to anyone who'll do it for him."

"Is that right?" Cam the Hun said.

"That's right." She let her leg drop from the arm of the chair, her heel like a gunshot on the floor, and sat forward. "But he's got no takers. No one on that side of town wants the fight. They know I've too many friends."

He managed a laugh. "Who'd be that stupid?"

"Exactly," she said.

He drained the glass and coughed. His eyes streamed, and when he sniffed back the scorching tears, he got that ripe meat smell again. His stomach wanted to expel the gin, but he willed it to be quiet.

"So, what do you want me to do?" he asked.

She swallowed the last of her gin and said, "Him."

He dropped his glass. It didn't shatter, but rolled across the floor to stop at her feet. "What?"

"I want you to do him," she said.

He could only blink and open his mouth.

"It'll be all right," she said. "I've cleared it with everyone that matters. His own side have wanted shot of him for years. Davy Pollock is a piece of shit. He steals from his own neighbours, threatens old ladies and children, talks like he's the big man when everyone knows he's an arsewipe. You'd be doing this town a favour."

Cam the Hun shook his head. "I can't," he said.

"Course you can." She smiled at him. "Besides, there's fifteen grand in it for you. And you can go back to Orangefield to see your mother. Picture it. You could have Christmas dinner with your ma tomorrow."

"But I'd have to—"

"Tonight," she said. "That's right."

"But how?"

"How? Sure, everyone knows Cam the Hun's handy with a knife." She drew a line across her throat with her finger. "Just like that. You won't even have to go looking for him. I know where he's resting his pretty wee head right this minute."

"No," he said.

She placed her glass on the floor next to his and rose to her feet, her hands gliding over her thighs, along her body, and up to her hair. Her heels click-clacked on the floorboards as she crossed to him. "Consider it my Christmas present," she said.

He went to stand, but she put a hand on his shoulder.

"But first I'm going to give you yours," she purred. "Do you want it?"

"God," he said.

The Queen of the Hill unlaced her corset top and let it fall away.

"Jesus," he said.

She pulled him to her breasts, let him take in her warmth. He kissed her there while she toyed with his hair. A minute stretched out to eternity before she pushed him back with a gentle hand on his chest. His right mind shrieked in protest as she straddled him, grinding against his body as she got into position, a knee either side of his waist. She leaned forward.

"Close your eyes," she said.

"No," he said, the word dying in his throat before it found his vocal cords.

"Shush," she said. She wiped her hand across his eyelids, sealed out the dim light. Her weight shifted and pillows tumbled around him. Her breasts pressed against his chest, her breath warmed his cheek. Lips met his, an open mouth cold and dry, coarse stubble, a tongue like ripe meat.

Cam the Hun opened one eye and saw a milky white globe an inch from his own, a thick, dark brow above it, pale skin blotched with red.

He screamed.

The Queen of the Hill laughed and pushed Davy Pollock's severed head down, rubbing the dead flesh and stubble against Cam the Hun's face.

Cam the Hun screamed again and threw his arms upward. The heel of his hand connected with her jaw. She tumbled backwards and spilled onto the floor. The head bounced twice and rolled to a halt at her side. She hooted and cackled as she sprawled there, her legs kicking.

He squealed until his voice broke. He wiped his mouth and cheeks with his hands and sleeves until the chill of dead flesh was replaced by raw burning. He rolled on his side and vomited, the gin and foulness soaking her black satin sheets. He retched until his stomach felt like it had turned itself inside-out.

All the time, her laughter tore at him, ripping his sanity away shred by shred.

"Shut up," he wanted to shout, but it came out a thin whine.

"Shut up." He managed a weak croak this time. He reached for his coat, fumbled for the pocket, found the knife. He tried to stand, couldn't, tried again. He grabbed the iron bedpost with his left hand for balance. The blade snapped open in his right.

Her laughter stopped, leaving only the rushing in his ears. She looked up at him, grinning, a trickle of blood running to her chin.

"What are you?" he asked.

She giggled.

"What are you?" A tear rolled down his cheek, leaving a hot trail behind it.

"I'm the Queen of the Hill." Her tongue flicked out, smeared the blood across her lips. "I'm the goddess. I'm the death of you and any man who crosses me."

"No," he said, "not me." He raised the knife and stepped towards her.

She reached for Davy Pollock's head, grabbed it by the hair.

Cam the Hun took another step and opened his mouth to roar. He held the knife high, ready to bring it down on her exposed heart.

He saw it coming, but it was too late. Davy Pollock's cranium shattered Cam the Hun's nose, and he fell into feathery darkness.

He awoke choking on his own blood and bile. He coughed and spat. A deep, searing pain radiated from beneath his eyes to encompass the entire world. The Queen of the Hill cradled his head in her lap. He went to speak, but could only gargle and sputter.

"Shush, now," she said.

He tried to raise himself up, pushing with the last of his strength. She clucked and gathered him to her bosom. He stained her breasts red.

"We could've been good together, you and me," she said.

His mouth opened and closed, but the words couldn't force their way past the coppery warm liquid. He wanted to weep, but the pain blocked his tears.

"You could've been my king," she said. She rocked him and kissed his forehead. "This could've been our palace on the hill. But that's all gone. Now there's only this."

She brought the knife into his vision, the blade so bright and pretty. "Close your eyes," she said.

He did as he was told. Her fingers were warm and soft as she loosened his collar and pulled the fabric away from his throat.

The cathedral bells rang out. He counted the chimes, just like he'd done as a child, listening to his mother's old clock as he waited for Santa Claus. Twelve and it would be Christmas.

It didn't hurt for long.

GHOSTED

Peter Lovesey

THIS HAPPENED THE year I won the Gold Heart for *Passionata*, my romantic novel of the blighted love between an Austrian composer and a troubled English girl getting psychotherapy in Vienna. I have never had any difficulty thinking up plots even though my own life has been rather short of romantic experiences. You will understand that the award and the attention it brought me were a high point, because up to then I had written forty-five books in various genres that received no praise at all except a few letters from readers. I hadn't even attended one of the romance writers' lunches at which the awards were presented. I was a little light-headed by the end. I still believe it wasn't the champagne that got to me and it wasn't the prize or the cheque or shaking the hand of one of the royal family. It was the envy in the eyes of all the other writers. Utterly intoxicating.

Whatever the reason, I can't deny that my brain was in such a whirl when I left the Café Royal that I couldn't think which way to turn for Waterloo Station. I believe I broke the rule of a lifetime and took a taxi. Anyway, it was a relief finally to find myself on the train to Guildford, an ordinary middle-aged lady once again – ordinary except for the drop-dead Armani gown under my padded overcoat. That little number cost me more than the value of the prize cheque. Just to be sure my triumph had really happened I took out the presentation box containing the replica Gold Heart, closed my eyes and remembered the moment when everyone had stood and applauded.

"Is that it?" a voice interrupted my reverie.

I opened my eyes. The seat next to me had been taken by a man with cropped silver hair. He was in a pinstripe suit cut rather too sharply for my taste, but smart. He had a black shirt with a silver tie and he wore dark glasses that he probably called shades.

"I beg your pardon," I said.

"I said is that it – one day as a star and you shove off home with your gong and are never heard of again?"

I tried not to catch his eye, but I'd seen the glint of gold teeth when he spoke. I've never liked ostentation. Whoever he was, this person had caught me off guard. Quite how he knew so much I had no idea. I didn't care for his forwardness or the presumption behind his question. Besides, it was the coveted Gold Heart, not a gong. I decided to let him know his interest wasn't welcome. "If you don't mind me saying so, it's none of your business."

"Don't be like that, Dolly," he said, giving me even more reason to object to him. My pen-name is Dolores and I insist that my friends call me that and nothing less. The man was bending his head towards me as if he didn't want the other passengers to overhear. It's unnerving at the best of times to be seated next to someone in a train who wants a conversation, but when they almost touch heads with you and call you Dolly, it's enough to make a lady reach for the emergency handle. He must have sensed what I was thinking because he tried to appease me. "I was being friendly. You're right. It's none of my business."

I gave a curt nod and looked away, out of the window.

Then he added, "But it could be yours."

I ignored him.

"Business I could put your way."

"I don't wish to buy anything. Please leave me alone," I said.

"I'm not selling anything. The business I mean is a runaway best-seller. Think about it. What's this book called – *Passion* something?"

"*Passionata.*"

"It will sell a few hundred extra copies on the strength of this award. A thousand, if you're lucky, and how much does the author take? Chickenfeed. I'm talking worldwide sales running into millions."

"Oh, yes?" I said with an ironic curl of the lip.

"You want to know more? Step into the limo that will be waiting at the end of your street at nine tomorrow morning. It's safe, I promise you, and it will change your life."

I was about to ask how he knew where I lived, but he stood up, took a black fedora off the rack, held it in a kind of salute, winked, placed it on his head and moved away up the train.

I didn't enjoy the rest of my journey home. My thoughts were in ferment. *Worldwide sales running into millions?* Success on a scale such as that was undreamed of, even for the writer of the best romantic novel of the year. The man was obviously talking nonsense.

Who could he possibly have been? A literary agent? A publisher? A film tycoon? I couldn't imagine he was any of these.

I decided to forget about him and his limousine.

I think it was the anticlimax of returning to my cold suburban semi that made me reconsider. Some more of the paint on the front door had peeled off. There was a rate demand on the doormat along with the usual flyers advertising takeaways. Next door's TV was too loud again. At least it masked the maddening drip-drip of the leaky kitchen tap. I deserved better after writing all those books.

Perhaps the award had really changed my luck.

After a troubled night, I woke early, wondering if the man in the train had been a figment of my imagination. If the car materialized, I'd know he had been real. Generally I wear jeans and an old sweater around the house. Today I put on my grey suit and white blouse, just in case. I looked out of the window more than once. All I could see at the end of the street was the greengrocer's dirty white van.

At five to nine, I looked again and saw a gleaming black Daimler. My heart pounded. I put on my shiny black shoes with the heels, tossed my red pashmina around my shoulders, and hurried in as dignified a fashion as possible to the end of the street. The chauffeur was a grey-haired man in a grey uniform. He saluted me in a friendly fashion and opened the car door.

"Where are we going?" I asked.

"I believe it's meant to be a surprise, ma'am."

"You're not telling, then?"

"That would spoil it. Make yourself comfortable. If you don't want the TV, just press the power switch. There's a selection of magazines and papers."

"Will it take long?"

"About an hour."

London, I thought, and this was confirmed when we headed along the A3. I was too interested in where we were going to look at the in-car TV or the magazines. But once we had left the main road I lost track. Before the hour was up, we were into parts of West London I didn't know at all. Finally we stopped in front of a gate that was raised electronically, the entrance to a private estate called The Cedars with some wonderful old trees to justify the name. Even inside the estate there was a ten-minute drive past some huge redbrick mansions. I was beginning to feel intimidated.

Our destination proved to be a mock-Tudor mansion with a tiled forecourt big enough to take the Trooping of the Colour.

"Will you be driving me home after this?" I asked the chauffeur.

"It's all arranged, ma'am," he said, touching his cap.

The front door opened before I started up the steps. A strikingly beautiful young woman greeted me by name, my pen-name, in full. She had a mass of red-gold hair in loose curls that looked almost natural. She was wearing a dark green top, low-cut, and white designer jeans. Her face seemed familiar, but I couldn't recall meeting her. She was younger than any of the women I'd met at the awards lunch.

"I'm so chuffed you decided to come," she said. "Ash was dead sure he'd reeled you in, but he thinks he's God's gift and not everyone sees it."

"Ash?" I said, not liking the idea that anyone had "reeled me in".

"My old man. The sweet-talking guy in the train."

"He made it sound like a business proposition," I said.

"Oh, it is, and we need you on board."

She showed me through a red-carpeted hallway into a sitting room with several huge white leather sofas. A real log fire was blazing under a copper hood in the centre. A large dog with silky white hair was lying asleep nearby.

"Coffee, Dolores?"

"That would be nice," I said to her. "But you have the advantage of me."

Her pretty face creased in mystification. "Come again."

"I don't know your name."

She laughed. "Most people do. I'm Raven. Excuse me." She spoke into a mobile phone. "It's coffee for three, and hot croissants."

Even I, with my tendency to ignore the popular press, had heard of Raven. Model, singer, actress, TV celebrity, she made headlines in whatever she'd tried. "I should have known," I said, feeling my cheeks grow hot. "I wasn't prepared. I was expecting someone from the publishing industry."

"No problem," she said. "It's nice not to be recognized. People react to me in the dumbest ways. Did you tell anyone you were making this mystery trip?"

"No. I kept it to myself."

"Great. You live alone – is that right?"

"Yes."

"And you've written all those amazing romances?"

I glowed inwardly and responded with a modest "Some people seem to like them."

"I've read every one, from *Love Unspoken* to *Passionata*," Raven said with genuine admiration in her voice.

This came as a surprise. Her own life was high romance. She didn't need the sort of escapism my books offered. "I'm flattered."

"You're a star, a wonderful writer. You deserved that award. You ought to be a best seller by now."

I secretly agreed with her, but I'm not used to receiving praise and I found it difficult to take. "I don't think I could handle fame. I'm rather a coward, actually. I sometimes get asked to give talks and I always turn them down."

"Who looks after your PR?"

"No one."

"You must have an agent."

"I wouldn't want one. They take a slice of your income and I can't afford that."

"So you do all the business stuff yourself?"

I nodded.

Raven seemed to approve. "You're smart. If I could get shot of all my hangers-on, I would."

At this moment a woman arrived with the coffee on a trolley.

"I wasn't talking about you, Annie," Raven said. "You're a treasure. We'll pour it ourselves."

The woman gave a faint smile and left.

"How do you like your coffee, Dolores?"

"Black, please."

"Same as me. Same as Ash. He's Ashley really, like that footballer."

I don't follow football and I must have looked bemused, because Raven added, "Or that guy in *Gone With The Wind*, but no one calls him that. He'll be with us any sec. His timing is always spot-on. Ash is smart, or he wouldn't own a pad like this."

Raven poured three coffees. The croissants were kept warm by a kind of cosy on the lower shelf of the trolley. Mine almost slipped off my plate at the sudden sound of husband Ashley's voice behind me.

"Sensible girl."

I'm not used to being called a girl, but I was junior to him by at least ten years, so I suppose it was excusable. I got a better look at him than I had when he was seated beside me in the train. He was seventy if he was a day, as wrinkled as a Medjool date. Today he was in a combat jacket and trousers and expensive trainers.

He held out his hand and I felt his coarse skin against mine. The grip was strong. My hand felt numb after he'd squeezed it.

"Can't say I've read any of your stuff," he said. "I've never been much of a reader. She tells me you're the best at what you do."

"She's too generous," I said.

"How much do you make in an average year?"

This wasn't the kind of question I was used to answering. "Enough to live on," I said.

"Yeah, but how much?"

"A writer's income fluctuates," I said, determined not to give a figure. "I've earned a living at it for fifteen years."

"What sort of living?" he asked. "Don't get me wrong, Dolly, but a semi on the wrong side of Guildford ain't what I call living."

Raven clicked her tongue. "Ash, that isn't kind."

He ignored her. His brown eyes fixed on me. "You put in the hours. You do good work. You deserve better. I made my first million before I was twenty-three. It was dirty work nobody wanted, so I did it. Collecting scrap from house to house. Waste management. Landfill. I've covered every angle. Now I have the biggest fleet of refuse lorries in the country. Ash the Trash, they call me. Doesn't bother me. I'm proud of it. I've got houses in London, Bilbao, New York and San Francisco. I did skiing every year until my knees went. And I'm married to the bird half the men in the world are lusting over."

"That's crude," Raven said.

"It's a fact." Now his eyes shifted to his young wife. "And you're more than just a pretty face and a boob job. I rate you, sweetheart. You've got ideas in your head. Tell Dolly your story." He turned to me again. "This'll get you going." He sat next to her on the sofa opposite mine. "Come on, my lovely. Spill it out."

"Well," she said, "I don't know what Dolores will think of it. She's a proper author."

"She has to get ideas," Ash said, "and that's where you come in."

"He never lets up," Raven said, fluttering her false lashes at me. "It needs a bit of work, but it goes like this. There's this little girl living in East Sheen."

"We'll change that," Ash said. "Make it Richmond."

"All right. Richmond. And when she gets to thirteen, she's already got a figure and her mum puts her in for a beauty contest and she wins, but then one of the other girls points out that she's underage. You had to be at least sixteen under the rules, so I was disqualified."

"She," Ash corrected her. "She was disqualified."

"She."

"We're calling her Falcon," Ash said.

"I was coming to that," Raven said.

Ash turned to me. "What do you think, Dolly? Is Falcon a good name?"

"Fine," I said, not wishing to fuel the obvious tension between husband and wife.

"OK," Raven said. "So this girl – Falcon – has to wait until she's older, but she learns all she can about beauty and make-up and fashion and then she enters for another contest even though she's still only fifteen."

"And she won a modelling contract," Ash said.

"You're spoiling it," Raven said.

"That's what happened."

"Yes, but I'm telling it. I was building up to the modelling. You don't come straight out with the best bit of the story, do you, Dolores?"

"Suspense is a useful device, yes," I said.

"See?" she said to Ash. "Now shut it."

"Before you go on," I said to Raven. "I'm not entirely sure why you're telling me all this." In truth, I had a strong suspicion. "If it's your life story and you want to get it published, surely you should write it."

"It's not supposed to be about me. Well, it is really, but it's a romance. I'm leaving out the stuff I don't want people to know."

"And beefing up the good bits," Ash said.

"In that case it's autobiography dressed up as fiction. I still think you should write it yourself."

"She can't write," Ash said.

"He means I'm not a writer," Raven said. "I can spell and stuff."

"Which is where you come in," Ash said to me.

"We want you to do the writing," Raven said, "give it a make-over, if you know what I mean."

"We're not daft," Ash said. "Her fans will know it's her life story and buy a million copies."

"But if it isn't in Raven's own style, no one will believe she wrote it."

"So you rough it up a bit," Ash said to me. "Knock out the long words. Give it plenty of passion. You're good at that, I was told. All the celebs hire someone to do the writing. It's called ghosting."

"I know what it's called," I said. "I'm sorry to disappoint you, but I'm not a ghost writer. I write original fiction. I've never attempted anything like this. I wouldn't know how to start."

"It's all on tape," Ash said. "You write it down, juice it up a bit and with her name on the cover we've got a bestseller."

"I'm sorry," I said. "I can't do it."

"Hold on. You haven't heard the deal," Ash said. "You walk out of here today with ten grand in fifty-pound notes. Another ninety grand on delivery, all in cash. No tax. How does that strike you?"

The figure was huge, far more than I earned usually. But what would a ghosted book do to the reputation I'd built with my forty-six novels?

Ash gave me instant reassurance. "You won't take any flak for writing it. We're keeping you out of it. As far as Joe Public is concerned, Raven wrote every word herself. That's why it will be a bestseller. She's got fans all over the world and she'll get more when the book hits the shelves. They want the inside story of the nude modelling, the catwalks, the reality shows, the pop concerts, all the stars she's met—"

"And how I met you," Raven said to him. "They want to know what I see in a man forty-two years older than me."

"True love, innit?" Ash said in all seriousness. "I'm nuts about you. That's why I'm funding this bloody book."

She kissed his cheek and ruffled his silver hair. "My hero."

All this was bizarre. I was actually thinking what I could do with a hundred thousand pounds. The task of writing Raven's life story might not be creatively fulfilling, but it was within my capability, especially if she had recorded it in her own words. "Just now you said it's on tape."

"God knows how many cassettes," Ash said. "Hours and hours. She's left nothing out."

This disposed of one concern. Any writer prefers condensing a script to padding it.

"You take them home today, all of them," Ash said.

"I'm not saying I'll do it."

"What's the problem, Dolly? You've got the job."

"But we haven't even talked about a contract."

"There isn't one," Ash said. "There's only one thing you have to promise, apart from doing the book, and that's to keep your mouth shut. Like I said, we're passing this off as Raven's book. If anyone asks, there wasn't no ghost. She done the whole thing herself. I wasn't born yesterday and neither was you. We're paying well over the odds and buying your silence."

"How soon do you expect this book to be written?"

"How long do you need? Six months?"

This seemed reasonable if it was all on tape already. I wouldn't wish to spend more than six months away from my real writing. Heaven help me, I was almost persuaded. "And if I needed to meet Raven again to clarify anything, is that allowed for?"

"Sorry. Can't be done," Raven said. "I'm doing reality TV in Australia for the next few months and no one can reach me, not even Ash."

"So you want the book written just from these tapes, without any more consultation?"

"It's the best way," Ash said. "Raven is so big that it's sure to leak out if you keep on meeting her. You won't be short of material. There's loads of stuff on the internet."

"What happens if you aren't happy with my script?"

Raven answered that one. "It won't happen. That's why I chose you." She fixed her big blue eyes on me. Her confidence in me was total.

I warmed to her.

"But I'm sure to get some details wrong. Anyone would, working like this."

"She'll straighten it out when it comes in," Ash said. "Let's agree a date."

* * *

I must be honest. I'd been persuaded by the money. At home over the next six months I set about my task. The tapes were my source material. Raven had dictated more than enough for a substantial book, but she had a tendency to repeat herself. With skilful editing I could give it some shape. Such incidents as there were had little of the drama I put into my own books. I would have to rely on the reader identifying with "Falcon" and her steady rise to fame and fortune.

The first objective was to find a narrative voice closer to Raven's than my own. I rewrote Chapter One several times. The process was far more demanding than Ash had predicted. "Knock out the long words," he'd said, as if nothing else needed to be done. Eventually, through tuning my ear to Raven's speech rhythms, I found a way of telling it that satisfied me.

The absence of a strong plot was harder to get over. Her story was depressingly predictable. A romantic novel needs conflict, some trials and setbacks, before love triumphs. I had to make the most of every vestige of disappointment, and the disqualification from the beauty contest was about all she had provided. In the end I invented a car crash, a stalker and a death in the family just to "beef it up", as Ash had suggested.

The biggest problem of all lay waiting like a storm cloud on the horizon while I worked through the early chapters: what to do about Ash. How could I make a romantic ending out of a relationship with an elderly scrap dealer, however rich he was? If I took thirty years off his age he'd probably be insulted. If I changed his job and made him a brain surgeon or a racing driver, he'd want to know why. He was justly proud of becoming a legend in refuse collection, but it wasn't the stuff of romantic fiction.

And I have to admit that he frightened me.

Deliberately I put off writing about him until the last possible opportunity. By then I had shaped and polished the rest of the book into a form I thought acceptable, though far from brilliant. Ash was the last big challenge.

In desperation I researched him on the internet. Being so successful, he was sure to have been interviewed by the press. Perhaps I would find some helpful insights into his personality.

I was in for a shock.

In 1992 Ash had been put on trial for murder and acquitted. His first wife, a young actress, had gone missing after having an affair with the director of a play she was in. Her family suspected Ash had killed her, but her body had never been found. The word "landfill" was bandied about among her anxious friends. Before she disappeared, she had written letters to her lover telling of mental and physical cruelty. A prosecution had been brought. Ash had walked free thanks to a brilliant defence team.

All of this would have greatly assisted the plot of the book. Of course, I dared not use it. I felt sure Ash didn't want his dirty washing aired in Raven's romantic novel. Nor was I certain how much Raven knew about it.

After reading several interviews online, I concluded that Ash was a dangerous man. He had defended his empire of landfill and dust-carts against a number of well-known barons of the underworld who had threatened to take over. "You don't mess with Ash," was one memorable quote.

For the book, I called him Aspen, made him a grieving widower of forty-nine, called his business recycling, gave him green credentials and charitable instincts. He fell in love with Falcon after meeting her at a fund-raising concert and they emigrated to East Africa and started an orphanage there. The book was finished with a week to spare. I was satisfied that it would pass as Raven's unaided work and please her readers.

At nine on the agreed day in March, I walked to the end of my street with a large bag containing the manuscript and Raven's tapes and stepped into the Daimler. Even after so many years of getting published I always feel nervous about submitting a script and this was magnified at least tenfold by the circumstances of this submission.

As before, the front door of the mansion was opened by Raven herself, and she looked tanned and gorgeous after her television show in Australia. "Is that it?" she asked, pointing to my bag, echoing the words Ash had used when we first met in the train.

I handed over the manuscript.

"I can't tell you how much I've been waiting to read this," she said, eyes shining.

I warned her that I'd made a number of changes to give it dramatic tension.

"Don't worry, Dolores," she said. "You're the professional here. I'm sure whatever you've done is right for the book. Coffee is on its way and so is Ash. I'm going to make sure he reads the book, too. I don't think he's read a novel in the whole of his life."

"I wouldn't insist, if I were you," I said quickly. "It's not written for male readers."

"But it's my life story and he's the hero."

"I took some liberties," I said. "He may not recognize himself."

"What's that?" Ash had come into the room behind me, pushing the coffee trolley. "You talking about me?"

"Good morning," I said, frantically trying to think how to put this. "I was explaining that for the sake of the book I had you two meeting at an earlier point in life."

"So?"

"So you're a younger man in the story," Raven put it more plainly than I had dared.

He frowned. "Are you saying I'm too old?"

"No way," she said. "I've always told you I like a man who's been around a bit."

"So long as he's got something in the bank. Speaking of which," he said, turning to me, "we owe you ninety grand."

"That was what we agreed," I was bold enough to say.

His eyes slid sideways and then downwards. "Will tomorrow do? The bloody bank wanted an extra day's notice. They're not used to large cash withdrawals."

"But you promised to pay me when I delivered the manuscript," I said.

He poured the coffee. "I'll make sure it's delivered to you."

"A cheque would be simpler."

He shook his head. "Cheques can be traced back. Like I told you before, this has to be a secret deal."

I have to say I was suspicious. It had been in my mind that Ash could easily welsh on the agreement. True, I'd been paid ten thousand pounds already, but I wanted my full entitlement.

As if he was reading my mind, Ash said to Raven, "Is the message from the bank still on the answerphone? I'd like Dolly to hear it, just to show good faith."

"What message?" she said.

He got up and crossed the room to the phone by the window. "The message from the bank saying they wouldn't supply the cash today." He pressed the playback button.

Nothing was played back.

He swore. "Must have deleted it myself. Well," he said, turning back, "you'll have to trust me, won't you?"

"But I don't even have the address of this house, or a phone number, or anything."

"Better you don't."

"But you know where I live."

"Right, and so does my driver. He'll deliver the money tomorrow afternoon."

At that moment I acted like a feeble female outgunned by an alpha male. I left soon after, without any confidence that I would ever receive the rest of the payment.

* * *

Three days later I read in the paper that Ashley Parker, the landfill tycoon and husband of Raven, was dead. He had apparently overdosed on sleeping pills and lapsed into a coma from which he never emerged. He was aged seventy-two.

Raven inherited his forty-million-pound estate, and went on record as saying that she would gladly pay twice that amount to get her husband back.

The inquest into Ash's death made interesting reading. There was some gossip in the papers that Raven had overplayed the grieving widow to allay suspicion that she had somehow administered the overdose. This was never raised at the inquest. There, she melted the hearts of the coroner and the jury. She said Ashley had always been a poor sleeper and relied on a cocktail of medication that "would have knocked out most men". He had been happy to the last, a man with a clear conscience.

A clear conscience indeed. I never did receive the second payment for my work on the book. In fact, I have never heard from Raven since. However, she had enough sense not to publish. I believe she worked out the truth of what happened that morning I visited the house.

You see, when Ash told me I wouldn't get paid that day, I became suspicious. I'd delivered the book and they had no further use for me, but I remained a risk to Ash's scheme. While I was alive I could pop up any time and earn a fat fee from the papers by revealing that I had ghosted the masterpiece supposedly written by Raven. I had become disposable, ready for the landfill. Easier still, I might succumb to an overdose and no one would ever know how it happened, or connect me with Raven and Ash. I'd heard of doctored drinks known as Mickey Finns, and I could believe that some slow-acting drug might sedate me until I got home and finally kill me. And that was why after the coffee was poured I took the sensible precaution of switching my cup with Ash's. The opportunity came when he acted out his little charade with the answerphone.

What neither of them knew is that as well as romantic novels I write whodunits.

TEXAS IN THE FALL

R. J. Ellory

"GENTLEMEN, GENTLEMEN, PLEASE, we're off-track again. This isn't a specific thing ... this is a multitude of things. It's no longer a question of political allegiance, it's a matter of national allegiance. It is simply a matter of taking responsibility for the consequences of our decisions ... "

"Which is easy for you to say. You're not the one who'll have to clean up the mess afterwards."

"We're all going to have to deal with that, believe me."

"No, not all of us ... when did you last have your dinner guests stay to wash dishes?"

"What happens afterwards is what happens, gentlemen ... we cross those bridges as they come. Certain agreements have been made, and those agreements have been compromised. It has happened before, it will happen again."

"OK, back to the point here. The first questions to answer are how and when—"

"I think the most important question is who, wouldn't you say?"

"That question we have answered already, you'll be pleased to know. We have someone. We have the who for this project."

***

Later, considering the details, I realized I had felt nothing at all.

You would think that such a thing would hurt ... but for some considerable time I felt nothing at all.

Perhaps some small comfort – not for myself, but for others. I was without pain. I was without fear.

And then, ultimately, I was without myself.

* * *

We had to go down there. No choice really. We'd taken Texas by
a little more than forty-six thousand votes; knew we had to secure
it or we wouldn't stand a chance in the fall, and we had those
two troublemakers – Connally and Yarborough – at each other's
throats.

No one writes off twenty-five electoral votes, even if it means
flying a thousand miles into redneck country to patch things up.
Didn't want to go, but hell, I didn't have a choice.

I had a premonition that day. We came in at Fort Worth a little after midnight as I recall, went straight to the Hotel Texas.
During those hours, it seemed – at least to me – that things were
fine between us. For sure, they had been a little awkward for a
few weeks prior, but they seemed to have straightened out OK.
I wasn't worried about her ... tell you the truth, I never really
worried about her.

Thinking back I reckon that was half the problem right there:
that I didn't worry about her enough. She was being what the world
expected her to be, being what she imagined I wanted her to be.
But always there were questions. There must have been. If she was
perfect, then how come I saw so much imperfection? How come
the world that we had created was not the world within which I
wished to reside?

I know better now. Now it is too late.

Hindsight, as always, is the cruellest and most astute advisor.

* * *

"So tell us ... who is this guy?"

"He's ex-military, Communist affiliations ... all the right
credentials."

"Sounds like a candidate for the Senate."

"Very funny ... very funny indeed."

"He has a history?"

"It's enough. Been into Russia. Got involved with all that pro-Cuba noise down south—"

"But enough of a history to make this thing stick?"

"Christ, are you serious? Machinery we have in place could make anything stick to anyone."

"No one's questioning your belief in this thing, George ... but we have the whole world out there. The whole world has to believe whatever we tell them. History has demonstrated that in such circumstances people just grasp whatever is given them. They need something, anything ... we deliver it, and they will accept it."

"I agree. Remember Hitler ... bigger the lie the more easily it will be believed."

"But you're *sure* we can present it in such a way as it will be accepted?"

"Acceptance is not what we're looking for. When did we ever look for acceptance? We obscure everything. We give them one thing, and if they start to question it then we simply give them fifteen or twenty other possibilities, and no one will know what to believe."

"Point taken."

"Good. So we have our man. Now it's a question of when."

***

We came out the following morning just before ten, and I remember speaking to Connally in the parking lot before we went back to the suite. I spoke to John Nance Garner as well, just for a little while. He was a good man. I always liked him. One time he told me that his job was something like a pitcher of warm spit.

A little while later Lyndon came up and introduced us to his sister, and then at eleven-thirty or so we flew down to Love Field. We left in the motorcade about five minutes before noon. The sun was high and bright. The air was fresh. The people would have already gathered to see me, and – perhaps, if I was honest – I wanted to see them. Every once in a while it was good to be reminded of why.

Jackie didn't like the heat. Didn't like it in Mexico, didn't like it in Texas. She ran with the program, but she got lost amongst the Communications Agency people with their codenames and unintelligible language. I remember seeing Clint Hill on the running board, back and forth, back and forth, sweating like a pig on barbecue day. His name was Dazzle, and then there was Deacon and Daylight and Domino, and they had these handheld radios, all this talk going back and forth about Volunteer in Varsity with Velvet and Venus ...

The circus started then. I remember waving, coming out of Main and Poydras and waving like a maniac. I was saying "Thank you, thank you ... ", and then I glanced at Governor Connally's wife, Nellie, and the expression on her face was like I was crazy, like she was thinking, *What the hell's he doing? Doesn't he understand these people can't hear him?* It was just force of habit. I didn't think about it. Perhaps it was nothing more than the way I'd been raised. I kept on waving. I kept on thanking people. We went down Lamar and Austin, and then we hit Main and Market, and hell if the place didn't look like crap. Bail-bond shops, a line of bars and gyms, and then there was the courthouse and the Records Building, and it was then that I felt the unnerving sense of premonition.

I looked up at the sky. Just for a second. A single heartbeat. It was blue, almost perfect, almost cloudless, and I believed it was possible for a hole to open right up and snatch me from the earth.

I felt insignificant.

I felt like nothing.

I felt no more important than a breath of air.

***

"We'll look at when in a moment."

"But we have to decide on the when. Until we make a decision on when we won't have a location. Without a location—"

"He's right. We need a location."

"There's two bills coming through the House in the summer. I can't risk having any difficulty—"

"There are no favorites here. We have to look at *when* it's going to work, gentlemen, not whether it suits some individual agenda."

"The overall agenda is the thing here, no question about it."

"I think it should be near to Christmas. Once the worst of the panic is over it'll be the holiday season. Something to take people's minds off of it."

"I agree. Not before the end of the summer, not too close to Christmas."

"Which gives us October or November."

"So let's take a look at what we have in October and November. You have the schedule there?"

"I think I have a copy in my case."

* * *

I didn't figure I was paying that much attention to it, but looking back it comes right at me. We went into Elm Street, and then we hit Houston and the motorcade was cut up into a three-part zig-zag - SS 100 X up front, Halfback and Varsity behind us, and then lastly there was the VIP bus and the signals car. I remember seeing Kinney then, right there on the bumper, and I remember how hot the sun felt. The underpass was right ahead of us and I thought how nice it would be to drive beneath it and feel the shade it would afford. I heard Nellie say to Jackie, "We're almost through. It's just beyond that." She pointed to the tunnel, and I saw her turn and look in that direction.

And the premonition arrived.

It was quiet and slow and insidious.

I saw images. Images of Lawson, Greer, Roy Kellerman. I saw Nellie's horrified face. The impression of a dark-haired woman at a switchboard as all the lights came on simultaneously, and then throwing her hands up in despair as the exchange overloaded and shut down. And though these images lasted no more than a heartbeat it must have registered on my face, because I remember Jackie leaning towards me and asking if I was OK. "Sure," I said, "just a little hot," and I recall running my finger around the inside of my shirt collar and being aware of how much I was sweating.

I thought of John Junior and the way he complained about the heat when we took him to Hyannisport.

I thought of all the children, especially the one we had lost.

Jackie had changed after. That was the time she needed me the most, and that was the time I was the furthest away.

***

"So we're agreed on the South?"

"The South it is."

"They're going to take a beating. People're gonna say it couldn't have happened in the North ... "

"Hell. The South always takes a beating, but you know what they say."

"The South will rise again."

"I'm not sure about Texas."

"Not so sure about what? The place itself or the people?"

"The people ... how they will react."

"You can't predict people. Doesn't matter who they are."

"Texas is the best place. He's in Texas in the third week of November."

"A month before Christmas."

"A month is good. Not too close, not too far away."

"Country'll be through the worst of it within a month."

"I still don't like Texas—"

"Who the hell *does* like Texas?"

"I'm from Texas ... my whole goddamned family's from Texas."

"See what I mean?"

"This is a democracy here. We'll take a vote on it."

***

James Rowley – Secret Service Chief, Jerry Behn – Head of the White House Detail; both of these guys were ultimately responsible for anything that might happen, either to me, my family, or those in Halfback and Varsity.

Later, amongst the details, I would consider how their lives would be from that point forward. How do you live with such a failure? You accept a responsibility. You assume the burden of duty. And then you fail. And no small failure, but a failure the world would never forget.

How do you live with such a thing?

When you wake – perhaps chilled, in the cool half-light of nascent dawn; as you stand at the window looking into darkness and feel the memory of all of this crawling back inside you like a ghost – what do you tell yourself?

What words can you say that will assuage what you feel?

Do such words exist?

Even I can see the moment now, the moment we approached the overpass, and then there was the sound, and it could have been anything, a cherry bomb, a car backfiring, and the guys weren't used to hearing a sound like that in such an open space. The Secret Service undertook two courses a year in outdoor shooting at the National Arboretum, a wide-open space with its own particular acoustical anomalies. They didn't know what gunfire sounded like when it reverberated between buildings, but that's what it was, and they had no idea, and all I felt was this sudden tension in my neck, and I remember reaching up my hands and trying to determine why there was an awkward tension around my throat, and I recalled how I had looked up at the cloudless blue sky, and how I had imagined a hole opening right up and how I could be snatched from the earth by some invisible hand …

And in that moment I thought of her. I thought of *her*. Of how I'd felt when I'd heard she was dead. I thought of Marilyn. Of how she was gone. Gone for good. Of how I'd known it would happen, but I had not known when, or by what means, or the month or week or day or hour. But I had known. There was no way she would come back. And maybe, just maybe, I felt that I had created my own justice for letting that happen.

An eye for an eye.

The bullet went through the back of my neck.

It skidded across my right lung, it ripped my windpipe, exited through my throat. It kept on going. A hole had been punched through the sky and inevitability came tearing through.

Everyone was looking everywhere.

Everyone was looking at everyone else waiting for someone to tell them what had happened. No one knew, no one could be sure, and I just sat there for a moment wondering why I felt the way I did. I figured it was the heat, that I was dehydrated, and that maybe I was going to faint. Jackie turned and looked at me, and then there was another shot, and that's when the pigeons took off – band-tailed pigeons, first in twos and threes and fours, and then a vast wave of them, like a cloud, and I remember sensing them overhead, and I could hear them, a sound like helicopters, and I remember thinking, *Helicopters? I don't remember anyone saying anything about helicopters ...* , and then there was a tugging sensation at the back of my head, and I remember reaching up my hand to ease the sensation, and when my hand reached the back of my skull I realized it wasn't there.

The hole in the sky was in the back of my head.

I half-smiled.

I think I half-smiled.

Strange how the mind plays tricks.

* * *

"So everyone knows what they have to do."

"Who's dealing with Lyndon and Walter Jenkins?"

"I am ... that's my baby."

"And Bobby ... what's the deal with him?"

"We have the Hickory Hill birthday party on the twentieth ... he'll stay back. He'll not go down to Dallas there with them."

"Who else do we have?"

"Clifton, Kilduff, Godfrey—"

"Get me a list together. You can do that?"

"Sure I can."

"So get me a list together ... I'll work out who speaks to who, who'll need to know what on the day."

"No problem."
"Anything else for now?"
"No, I don't think so."
"So we'll meet again in a week."

* * *

My perspective changed.

Suddenly, irreversibly.

I had never believed in out-of-body phenomena, but I had the unmistakable sensation of rising upwards, and then it was as if I was floating above the car, and my body was down there, and though the confusion centered around my body, for some strange reason I felt that none of it had anything to do with me.

Strange how the mind plays tricks.

Everything went in slow-motion, and it was quiet but for the sound of the wind and the birds. I saw Hickey waving the barrel of his AR-15 aimlessly around. He didn't know what to do but wanted to look like he was doing something. I saw a man throw his son to the ground and lie over him like a shield. Ken O'Donnell and Dave Powers were in the jump seats. O'Donnell crossed himself, and I could hear Powers whispering, "Jesus, Mary, mother of God ... ", and I knew no one else could hear him, and it made me think of my father, and because of my father I thought of Roosevelt, and the *Eleanor hates war. James hates war* ... Presidential Address he gave in August of 1936, and how my father used to tell me what he thought of FDR, how he had finally capitulated and led us into the Second World War.

And then Sam Kinney stamped on the siren button to alert Kellerman and Greer. That siren started up like a tornado, right there on Halfback's bumper.

SS 100 X slowed down.

I could see Jackie spattered with blood, and I remembered thinking, *Blood? Whose blood? Where the hell has all this blood come from?*

And then Jackie was screaming, and even now I can recall

exactly the words that came from her mouth: "My God, what are they doing? My God, they've killed Jack, they've killed my husband ... Jack, Jack!"

I could see her sprawled across the back of the car, and for some reason I had the idea she was trying to gather my head together, gather it all together and put it back where it came from ... and I could feel myself smiling, and the feeling I had was one of peace, peace and quiet, because somehow I knew I would never have to sit up late into the night worrying about what was happening with the world, and what the Russians might be doing in Cuba, and whether Connally and Yarborough would bury the hatchet so we could take Texas with something more than an eyelash margin in the fall ... all these things ...

Police Chief Curry's Ford couldn't keep up with SS 100 X and Halfback. I could see him shouting at a motorcyclist.

"Anybody hurt?" he asked, and the motorcyclist shouted, "Yes", and then Curry radioed his HQ dispatcher and told them to call Parkland Hospital and have them stand by. The dispatcher's microphone button was stuck, and it was three minutes before Parkland was notified. Three minutes before they got the message "601 coming in on Code 3, stand by". Then the motorcade arrived at 12.36, and they weren't ready. The Chief Surgeon was in Houston, the Senior Nurse at a conference fifteen miles away ...

I was dead by the time we got there. Jackie was holding on to my body, and though Dr Burkley was there, there was nothing he or anyone else could have done. Six minutes it had taken to get to Parkland, and I had been dead for all of those six. Clint was there, Ralph Yarborough and Dave Powers. They had to get John Connally out in order to reach me, and – once they had him – Clint tried to tell Jackie to let me go, but she wouldn't. She held on to me for dear life, and when he asked again she said, "I'm not going to let him go, Mr Hill," and then Clint said "We've got to take him in, Mrs Kennedy", and she said, "No, Mr Hill. You know he's dead. Let me alone." Clint took his coat off then, and he handed it to Jackie, and she wrapped it around my head. She didn't want the world to see me like that. And then they took my body out and laid it on the stretcher, and Jackie was moving alongside it and holding the coat together so the world wouldn't see what had become of me.

I remember the corridor inside, the tan-coloured tiling, and red-brown linoleum on the floor, and we were travelling down this corridor past O. B., Triage, Gynaecology, X-Ray, Admittance. Someone said that Connally was in Trauma Two, and I figured maybe he was dead too, and the first thought that came to mind was how this really was the end of the feud between him and Ralph Yarborough. Yarborough was the first one the reporters got to, and he said something which I will never forget. He said, "Gentlemen, this has been a deed of horror. Excalibur has sunk beneath the waves ... "

24740, Gunshot Wounds. That's who I was at Parkland, and then at 2 p.m. I was pronounced dead by Kemp Clark, and apparently there were already seventy-five million Americans aware of what had happened, but not until five minutes later did Bobby find out, and it wasn't until 2.14 that Lyndon knew. He left Parkland twelve minutes later, and half an hour after that he called three Dallas lawyers in an attempt to locate a copy of the Oath of Office. He knew the thing had been done. He knew he was President, and it scared the living Jesus out of him.

McNamara summoned a meeting of the Joint Chiefs of Staff, Washington's phone system broke down, and then at 3.20 Katzenbach dictated the Oath of Office to the crew aboard AF1. Eighteen minutes later Lyndon was sworn in as the thirty-sixth President of the United States of America. They took off for Andrews Field, and then at eight in the evening they started my autopsy.

The country kind of fell to pieces for a while, you know? November twenty-third they questioned this Oswald guy for less than three hours, and then on Sunday Jack Ruby shot him on NBC, and by the time Sunday evening rolled around there were 200,000 people around the Capitol. The following day, Monday, was the funeral. Jackie lit the Eternal Flame. Broken Taps were played.

But you know, the hardest thing of all, the thing that cuts me up even now, is that Monday was John Junior's birthday party. You imagine that? Three days after his dad is killed little John Junior has his birthday party, his third birthday party. Jackie did that. Jackie went ahead and did that, despite everything. And it was in that moment I realized how much I loved that woman, how much I cherished everything she did, everything she'd done to help me get where I was, and it was then, maybe for the first time, that I understood how much I had hurt her with the other women …

And now you're gonna ask me whether I know who it was who killed me.

I'm sorry, I cannot put you out of your misery on that one. We know, we *all* know, that it could never have been this Oswald character. Impossible feat – two shots, perhaps even three, from the sixth-floor window of the Texas School Book Depository? I understand that the FBI and the Army have tried this numerous times with a succession of brilliant marksmen, and none have accomplished it. They won't ever accomplish it, because it can't be done. The Warren Report was what it was: a whitewash. No one will ever really know, because the people who know are very likely dead themselves, and anyone who might be left will take it to their graves. But hell, they won't get an Eternal Flame like I did.

Always has to be a fall guy … always has to be someone who takes the rap for these things, and more often than not they're no more guilty than Oswald.

* * *

"We do this, it'll set a precedent."

"There's a pun there somewhere."

"There's always a pun with you."

"So once we have this one taken care of we'll talk about Bobby."

"We'll talk about Bobby if he campaigns."

"He will, believe me. I know the kid as well as anyone."

"Then we'll nominate you for that project."

"Well, this'll shut him up for a little while, that's for sure."

"This will shut everyone up for a little while."

"It'll change everything—"

"That's what it's supposed to do."

* * *

And you know something? Perhaps it would have been so much worse had it not been for Bobby. Bobby was always there, always back and to the left of me. I knew he was right behind me, knew he would just pick up the torch and keep carrying it.

He would make it.

I knew that in my heart.

That's what Dad would have wanted.

That one of us – just one of us – would make it all the way.

* * *

"So we're done then."

"Seems that way. It'll roll forward just the way we've discussed. We'll have that bastard Jack Kennedy out of the White House, the whole world blindsided by some bullshit Communist plot, and the country back in safe hands."

"Couldn't agree more. Here's to Texas in the fall."

"Sure as damn it, my friend ... Texas in the fall."

THE FEATHER

Kate Ellis

THE PIANO IN the corner of the parlour hadn't been used for over three years ... not since Jack first left for France. Nobody had had the heart to lift the lid since we received the dreadful news because the very sight of those black and white keys brought back memories of how he used to sit there and play.

Jack had known all the latest tunes and I can see him now, turning his head round and telling us to join in. "Come on," he'd say. "I'm not singing a solo." And when he sang, unlike me, he'd always be in perfect tune. Our Aunty Vi used to say he should be on the stage.

I stood in the parlour doorway and stared into the room with its big dark fireplace and its heavy oak furniture. It looked as it always had done, polished and spotless. The best room that we only used on Sundays. Sometimes I wondered what was the use of having a room you only used one day a week, but that was the way things were done in all the houses round here. Except when Jack had played the piano and sent a ray of sunshine into the solemn, polish-scented gloom.

"Ivy, what are you doing?"

My mother's voice made me jump and I swung round, feeling guilty. I'd been daydreaming again and in our house daydreaming was regarded as a major sin.

"I was just on my way to the washhouse."

"Well, go on then. Don't leave your sister to do all the work while you stand around thinking of higher things."

I knew from the way she snapped the words that she wasn't having a good day. Perhaps Mondays were the worst. We'd had the telegram from the War Office on a Monday when our hands were wet and red from the washing.

"I'm going next door to take Mrs Bevan some soup," she said, nodding towards the jug she was holding; our best jug covered with a clean white cloth.

She'd been taking soup to Mrs Bevan for the past week, even though our neighbour had a daughter to nurse her in her time of sickness. In my opinion Mrs Bevan didn't deserve our kindness but Mother was like that to anyone who was ill or had fallen on hard times. When Dad was alive he'd called her a saint.

As she adjusted the cloth, I caught the salty aroma of the soup and I suddenly felt hungry. But it was washday and there was work to be done.

I spent the rest of the morning helping Rose in the washhouse and when Mother didn't appear to supervise our efforts like she usually did, I began to worry. My sister, however, didn't seem at all concerned and I guessed she was relieved that Mother wasn't there to scold her for her clumsiness. But when an hour passed and Mother still hadn't returned, even Rose began to feel uneasy.

"Perhaps Mrs Bevan's taken a turn for the worse," Rose said. "Betty Bevan wouldn't be much help in the sickroom. She's never liked getting her hands dirty."

I shared Rose's opinion of our neighbour's daughter, who had obtained employment as a lady typist and considered herself above the menial work necessary to run a household if one could not afford servants. Betty Bevan had always been an impractical girl with ideas above her station and I knew she wouldn't be able to cope on her own if Mrs Bevan was really poorly. But the thought of Mother pandering to her whims made my blood boil with anger.

As I put a sheet through the mangle, I noticed a feather on the cobbled floor, wet and curled. A white feather, probably from a pillow or eiderdown. I stared at it for a few moments then I kicked at it and the dirt from my boot stained it the same dirty grey as the stone floor. I was about to pick it up when Mother appeared in the doorway. She was wiping her hands on her apron and, from the look of distress on her face I knew something had happened.

Rose and I waited for her to speak.

"She's dead," she said after a few moments, speaking in a whisper as though she didn't want to be overheard. "Mrs Bevan's dead."

I bowed my head. Another death. Our world was full of death.

* * *

Mother laid Mrs Bevan out. Betty hadn't known what to do and, besides, she hadn't stopped bursting into tears since it happened, twisting her silly scrap of a lace handkerchief in her soft, well-manicured fingers.

I gathered that Betty was planning a rather grand funeral, Mrs Bevan having paid into an insurance policy to ensure that she had a good send off, and she told Mother proudly that the hearse was to be the undertaker's best, pulled by four black horses with black glossy plumes. Normally Mother would have relished the prospect of seeing such a spectacle outside our terraced house, but when she returned home she seemed quiet and preoccupied. I knew for certain that it wasn't grief that had subdued her spirits, for she had never regarded Mrs Bevan as a close friend. Something else was preying on her mind and I longed to know what it was.

I was to find out later that day when a police constable arrived along with the doctor. Mother had summoned them and they were making enquiries into the cause of Mrs Bevan's unexpected death.

* * *

Rose told me in a whisper that Mrs Bevan's body had been taken to the mortuary to be cut up. The intrusion seemed to me obscene and I shuddered in horror at the very thought. Even Jack hadn't had to suffer that indignity. He had been trundled off on a cart and buried near the battlefield. A soldier known unto God. It was said that poppies grew where he fell, taking their scarlet colour from his innocent blood. Perhaps one day I would see those grim flowers for myself.

Mother would not tell my sister why she had alerted the police. She set her lips in a stubborn line and resisted all Rose's attempts to wheedle the truth out of her. But when she had first returned from the Bevan house she had asked my advice so I knew exactly why she had acted as she did.

I recalled her words, spoken in a whisper so that Rose would not hear.

"There's something amiss, Ivy," she said. "And that Betty was acting as if she didn't give a cuss until she saw me watching her then the waterworks started."

"What do you mean, amiss?" I asked.

"That was no chill on the stomach. She couldn't keep my good soup down and she was retching and soiling herself as though ... as though she'd been poisoned."

I remember gasping with disbelief. "You think Betty poisoned her mother?"

"She always was a nasty spoiled child. And she's turned into a nasty spoiled woman. That's what I'll tell the police."

"But you can't just accuse ... "

"That woman was poisoned. I'm as sure of that as I am of my own name."

Once Mother set her mind to something she could never be dissuaded. Therefore, when Mrs Bevan was lying in the big front bedroom next door, washed and laid out neatly in her best night-gown, it came as no surprise when Mother walked down to the police station and told the desk sergeant that she wished to report a murder.

***

The police searched the house next door, of course, and I heard later that they'd found a quantity of arsenic hidden in the wash-house. At first Betty swore that she had no idea how it came to be there. Then later she changed her story and said that her mother was probably keeping it there to kill mice.

The story didn't convince Mother or myself. And it certainly didn't convince the police because a few days later two constables called next door to arrest Betty Bevan.

Rose and I watched from the window as the younger constable led her away, holding her arm gently like a bridegroom leading his bride from the altar. Betty's head was bowed and I knew she was crying. But I could feel no pity for her.

* * *

It was three days after Betty's arrest and even the most inquisitive of our neighbours had failed to discover what was happening. Mother talked little about the tragedy next door; Rose, however, chattered on about it with unseemly enthusiasm and I had to do my best to curtail her curiosity. Terrible murder is one of those things that should not be treated as entertainment for wagging tongues but I confess that I too wished to know what had become of Betty Bevan.

At number sixteen we tried our best to carry on as normal but on Thursday afternoon something occurred that made this impossible, for me at least.

I was peeling vegetables for the evening meal in our tiny scullery when I heard a scraping noise coming from next door. Our scullery was attached to the Bevans' and the walls were thin so we could often hear their voices, sometimes raised in dispute. However, I knew the Bevans' house was supposed to be empty so I stopped what I was doing and listened.

I could hear things being moved around next door; a furtive sound as though somebody was shifting the contents of the scullery shelves to conduct a clandestine search. I put down my knife and wiped my rough hands on my apron, telling myself that it was probably the police – but then the police have no need for secrecy. I had been no friend of the Bevans but if robbers were violating their empty house, I felt it was my duty as a neighbour to raise the alarm.

I crept out of the back door into our yard. The wall between the back yards was too high for me to see into next door so I let myself out into the back alley and pushed the Bevans' wooden gate open, trying not to make a sound. Once inside their yard, I crept past the privy and caught a whiff of something unpleasant. It had not been cleaned and scrubbed like our privy next door, but then I could hardly imagine Betty Bevan, or her mother for that matter, getting down on her hands and knees to wipe away the worst kind of filth.

When I reached the back door, I tried the latch and, to my surprise, it yielded and the door swung open. I do not know who was more surprised, myself or the young man standing there with a tea caddy in his hand. He was dressed in a dark, ill-fitting suit and his ginger hair was short and slicked back. With his sharp nose and small moustache, he reminded me a little of a rodent ... a rat perhaps. As soon as he saw me his lips tilted upwards in an ingratiating smile and I saw that one of his front teeth was missing.

"You didn't half give me a shock," he said with forced jocularity. His accent was local but I didn't think I had ever seen him before.

"Who are you?"

"Friend of Betty's. The name's Winslow ... Albert Winslow. Here's my card."

He produced a card from his pocket and handed it to me with a flourish. I studied it and learned that Albert Winslow was an insurance man. The local accent I'd detected in his unguarded greeting had vanished and now he spoke as if he was a person of the better sort, like the officers I'd overheard talking when Jack's regiment had marched through town. I had no doubt he wished to impress me and I felt myself blush.

I handed the card back to him. "You haven't said what you're doing here?"

"Neither have you, Miss." There was impertinence in his statement but I knew he had a point.

"I live next door. I heard a noise and I knew the house was empty so ... "

"You thought I was a burglar. I'm sorry to disappoint you. I've just come to retrieve something I left here on my last visit so you've nothing to worry your head over. And what a pretty head it is, if I may say so."

I felt myself blushing again but I tried my best to ignore the remark. "I take it you know that Betty's ... "

He nodded, suddenly solemn. "It's a bad business. She's innocent, of course. Devoted to her mama, she was."

"Are you and Betty courting?"

He hesitated for a moment before nodding. "We were hoping to get engaged this summer."

"When did you meet?" I was curious for most young men – those who had survived – had recently returned from the war.

"I first met Betty when I called here regarding a life assurance policy." He edged closer to me and I could smell some kind of cloying scent, his hair oil perhaps. It made me feel a little sick. "They'll let Betty out soon, won't they? I mean she couldn't have done what they say."

"I couldn't possibly say, Mr Winslow. The police think she is the only one who had the opportunity to poison her mama."

Winslow looked worried as he shut the tea caddy he was holding and replaced it on the shelf.

"If they find her guilty she will hang."

His body tensed and for the first time I felt I was witnessing true emotion. "She can't. She's innocent."

"How can you be so sure, Mr Winslow?"

When he didn't answer I experienced a sudden feeling of dread. I was alone with this man and I only had his word that the story of his association with Betty Bevan was true.

I decided to enquire further. "You served in the war, Mr Winslow?"

"Naturally. I was at Wipers and Passchendaele. Why? You didn't think I was a conshy, did you? I wouldn't have got far with Betty if I had been. She could never stand cowards."

"You were fortunate, then."

"How do you mean?"

"To have got back alive. My brother, Jack, died in the last days of the war. He was, er ... wounded in 1916 and he came home. But after a year he said he felt a little better and he insisted on going back. He didn't have to because he still wasn't right but ... He felt … he felt obliged." I could feel my hands shaking and my eyes were stinging with unshed tears. I knew that I had been foolish to bare my soul to this man. But feelings long suppressed can bubble to the surface when one least expects it.

I saw Winslow shuffle his feet as though my raw outburst had embarrassed him. "I'm sorry," he said quietly. "I understand, I really do. I saw things over in France that … " His face clouded. Then he straightened his shoulders and gave a cheerless smile. "But you have to keep your spirits up, don't you … think of the future. Pack up your troubles in your old kit bag and smile and all that."

I took a deep breath. Some things were best dealt with by stoicism and a cheerful attitude. Other ways might lead to madness. And there was a question I had to ask.

"The life assurance policy you mentioned … was it for Mrs Bevan?"

His pale-blue eyes widened in alarm for a second then he composed his features. "That information's confidential, I'm afraid, Miss."

"You might have to tell the police. If Betty stands to gain from her mother's death … "

"I know what you're hinting at and it's nonsense," he said, taking another step towards me.

"Why did you really come here, Mr Winslow?" I felt I had to know the truth.

"If you must know I came to find something to prove Betty's innocent."

"And have you found it?"

He paused and I knew he was making a decision. After a few moments he spoke. "I might as well tell you. If she's charged it'll all come out anyway. Three weeks ago she insured her mother's life for a hundred pounds and I fear that she might have … "

"Poisoned her own mother?"

He nodded and, unexpectedly, I found myself feeling sorry for him.

***

It was a week after my encounter with Albert Winslow that we received the news that Betty Bevan was to stand trial for murder at the Assizes. Little was said of the matter in our house. It was done and it was over and soon she'd be dead ... just as my brother Jack was dead. I had never had any liking for her or her murdered mother and it would have been hypocritical in the extreme to start feigning grief now. I saved my tears for those who deserved them.

The following Monday Mother, Rose and I began our normal washday routine, setting the copper boiling in the washhouse ready to receive our soiled linen. When I heard a loud knocking on our front door I wondered who would come calling on a Monday morning, a time when we never expected to receive visitors. I answered the door in my apron with my hair pinned untidily off my face and I was surprised to see Albert Winslow standing on the freshly scrubbed doorstep.

As he raised his hat I suddenly felt uncomfortable. I looked like a washer woman, hardly the sort an insurance clerk would take into his confidence, but he seemed not to notice the state of my apparel. In his right hand he held a small tin box as though it was something fragile and precious and his well-polished shoe hovered on the threshold.

"May I come in?" he said. The arrogance I had detected at our first meeting had vanished and he reminded me now not so much of a rat, but of a puzzled child.

I stood aside to admit him then I led him into the parlour, for I knew that this was a matter between ourselves. I had no wish for our conversation to be interrupted by my mother or my sister.

I invited him to sit and he placed the box on the small table beside the armchair. Suddenly self-conscious I took off my apron and sat up straight on the hard dining chair, my rough, reddened hands resting in my lap.

I waited for him to begin for I felt it was up to him to explain the purpose of his visit. Eventually he cleared his throat and spoke.

"When we parted the other day, I made a further search of the house next door."

I tilted my head politely. "And did you find anything of interest?"

"I'm not sure."

"You told the police about the insurance policy?"

"Not yet. I wanted to see Betty before I ... "

"Haven't you seen her?"

He shook his head. "They won't let me speak to her but I feel I must. I need to ask her what it means."

"What what means?"

He picked up the box as though it was hot to the touch. "I found this."

He handed the box to me and I opened it. Inside were five white feathers and a piece of paper.

"It's a list," he said quietly. "Your surname is Burton, is it not?"

I nodded, fearing what was coming next.

"The list includes the name Jack Burton. You mentioned your brother Jack died in the last days of the war." He paused. "This is a list of men Betty or her mother describe as cowards."

"My brother was no coward," I snapped. "He fought for his King and country and he lost his life. My brother was a hero."

"Yes, of course. But his name is on the list in this box."

"Mrs Bevan and Betty were always too ready to judge others. Perhaps they put Jack's name on their nasty little list before he signed up for the army, and omitted to remove it."

A look of relief appeared on Albert Winslow's face. "Of course."

I looked him in the eye. "There might be another reason. At one time Betty was rather sweet on Jack but another girl caught his eye. I think Betty was displeased with him and she might have included his name on her list out of spite."

"You think that Betty is a spiteful girl?" He sounded as if his disappointment was deep and bitter. His goddess had feet of rough and dirty clay.

"She was spiteful and sinful and if I were you I'd forget all about her, Mr Winslow. It is likely she will hang, especially if you tell the police what you know about the insurance. I think you should go along to the police station and tell them now. Justice must be done."

Albert Winslow nodded slowly and stood up. "We must do our duty ... do the right thing."

I touched his hand. It was softer than mine. "Chin up, Albert. Think how you'd feel if you said nothing and she went and did it again. Because they say when you've killed once it's easier next time."

He knew I was right. I watched him disappear down the road, slowly with his head bowed like an old man.

***

Betty Bevan was hanged at the end of May. It was a beautiful day, cloudless and warm.

That morning I walked in the park and listened to the sound of the birds, glad it was over.

As I rested on the bench, enjoying the sun on my face, I held a conversation with Jack in my head. I often talked to him, told him things. If he'd been alive, I'm not sure how he would have taken the news but I felt I couldn't keep it from him. I was his loving sister after all. And everything I'd done had been for him. I'm sure sin isn't really sin when it's in a good cause.

Sitting there in the warmth of the May sun, I spotted something on the ground and my heart skipped a beat. It was a feather, shed by some passing bird. A white feather. I bent to pick it up then I held it for a while, turning it in my fingers before throwing it back onto the ground and grinding it into the grass with my heel. Such small things can have such catastrophic consequences.

Jack had been sent home from France, unfit to fight. Every loud sound had made his body shake and he had woken each night, crying out at the unseen horrors that tormented his brain. He'd wander, half crazed, from room to room, staring with frightened, unseeing eyes until one of us would guide him gently back to his own bed. How Mother cried in that year to see her only son, a boy who had always been so cheerful and good-natured, with his mind blasted into insanity by war. Sometimes I wished he could have been maimed some other way; even losing an arm or a leg wouldn't have been as bad as the way he suffered. But his body had been intact ... then.

It was when Jack had been home almost a year that Betty Bevan and her stupid mother began their campaign. All men not at the front, they said in their loud, braying voices, were cowards. They collected white feathers and distributed them to the men they accused, haranguing them with insults as they did so. Their tongues were spiteful and wicked. How I wished I could have had them sent to the front to see how they liked crawling through mud and corpses to certain death.

Jack had always been a proud man and the accusation of cowardice caused him such shame. Mother, Rose and I tried to tell him that he was sick but he didn't understand. He saw only his strong body and his intact limbs and he swore that he was fit to return to France to fight. Nothing we said would dissuade him from contacting his regiment to say that he was recovered and ready. But his regiment had not heard his screams of terror as he dodged those phantom shells and bullets each night and they hadn't seen the empty fear and bewilderment in his eyes.

The Bevans must have known how he was. His cries through those thin walls must have kept them awake as they did us. But those two women ignored my mother's pleas and explanations and a month after Jack left for France, we received the telegram to tell us that he had died a hero.

The Bevans showed our family no mercy. And I showed them no mercy in return. It was a simple matter to soak fly papers and add the arsenic they produced to the soup Mother took to Mrs Bevan each day. It had suited my purpose well for Betty to get the blame when the police found the powder I had placed in their scullery. And now the law had punished her – albeit for the wrong crime for she killed my dearest brother as surely as if she had rammed a knife into his heart.

I suppose the death of Betty Bevan had been my second murder and it had been so easy, just as second murders are reputed to be. A third, I suppose, would be easier still. All sins, I imagine, improve with practice.

I examined the little watch pinned to the front of my dress. It was nearly time for my appointment with Albert Winslow. He said that on our marriage, he will insure his life for a large sum of money so that, should the worst happen, I would be very well provided for.

How I look forward to our wedding day.

THE DECEIVERS

Christopher Fowler

THIS IS A police statement, but they said I could tell it in my own way. So I'm not writing it down, I'm dictating it into the desk sergeant's laptop, like he even knows how to operate it. He sticks Post-It notes on the lid, the keys are filthy and there's software on it from before I was born.

I'm not worried. I'm going to get out of here because there's someone coming who can prove what really happened.

They want me to put everything down, so first I have to explain about the hill.

The boundary line between Devon and Cornwall is dotted with small villages that pretend they're towns, but they're not. For a start, everyone who lives in them is either really old, over forty at least, and has lived there all their lives, or they're from London and only come down at the weekends. The locals all hate them, although my Dad says we should smile as we charge them double, like the French do. There's no one of my age to hang out with here, and nowhere to go if you do find someone. If you travel to one of the bigger towns with your mates, there's a good chance you'll get beaten up just because you're from somewhere else.

My folks are obsessed with getting fresh air. "Let's go for a walk and get some fresh air", like there's ever anything else to do. "Let's go up to the hill." We live in a village called Trethorton Hill. It consists of a short high street, about a hundred and twenty houses, two pubs and a hill. That's it. There's nothing even remotely interesting about the hill, it's just a huge pimple of grass and scrub with a single white rock set in the top, not even a proper standing stone, and when they get up there hikers say things like "You can see all the way to Dartmoor from here", as if that's a good thing. I hate hikers, with their billycans and red knees and woollen hats, and their rulebooks and guidebooks and hard little eyes. But that's what everyone around here does every Sunday. On Saturdays they go to Liskeard for their shopping, and on Sundays they go up the hill. I used to think that was boring until I realized that people actually come here from other towns to go up the hill, and what does that make their villages, if it's more interesting here than staying where they are?

The locals think they're cool and that they've been around, but they haven't. I heard some old guy in the supermarket telling the cashier that he'd just been up North, and she was reacting in amazement, like he'd just told her he'd been to Alpha Centauri. Then he added, "Yes, I went all the way to Tintagel", and I realized he meant North Cornwall. Jesus.

I have an older sister, and she got out while she could. I say "got out", what she did was get pregnant by some docker who'd gone to work on container ships out of Liverpool, so now she's stuck in Swansea with two bulldog-faced kids, in a hell of her own making.

Not for me. Once I get a job offer you won't see me for dust. I'm smart, I'm awake, I've got a mind. But it doesn't pay to be too clever in a village. People get suspicious of you. Best to keep your mouth shut and stay indoors mucking about on the internet, talking to smart people on the other side of the world. Someone asked me if we had Wi-Fi, and I had to explain we don't even get decent mobile phone reception here. The internet stops you from getting too lonely, because there are people in places with exotic sounding names, and they're just as bored as you are, so it makes you feel better.

I made one friend but he's not my friend any more, a kid called Daniel who came from the next village. I met him at IT club, and then at the Trethorton Charity Climb – we weren't taking part, we were just hanging around – and I thought, "We're alike. He's awake too." Daniel lives in a damp shadowy dell called Crayshaw. It's a village which loses its sunlight before lunchtime even at the height of summer. Daniel's parents are rich – his old man had invented rubberized flooring for factories and had sold it all around the world. So Daniel got an amazing allowance but had no one to share it with, because he had a gimp leg which meant he couldn't play football, and the flybrains at school treated him like dirt because he was from the wrong village and couldn't do sports. He never told them he had money, but he told me after I stuck up for him in a fight.

Daniel got excused from double games on Fridays (he only did the midweek swimming) and I didn't go because I hated it. I once forged a doctor's letter to Mr Phelps the gym teacher saying I had a defective heart valve and couldn't do contact sports, and the moron never even bothered to check it out with my folks. So every Friday afternoon we kicked around Trethorton Hill looking for ways to annoy the hikers. Once we tied fishing wire over the grass and filmed them, all falling over, on our phones.

Although Daniel had money he couldn't really spend it. He was only allowed to catch the bus as far as Liskeard because of his leg, so it wasn't like we were going to whip off to Ibiza for the weekend, but we bought stuff online, and for a while we had a lot of fun hanging out together.

My old man says when things go wrong there's always a woman involved, and in this case it was a girl called Tara Mellor. She was in our year and had been suspended twice for wearing incorrect school uniform. She was tall and thin with cropped blonde hair, and I was nuts about her, but for some incredible reason she seemed to prefer Daniel. But at the start the three of us hung out together a lot.

The lardy desk sergeant just came by, saw what I was writing and said could I get to the point. I wanted to say, "Could you get to the gym?" but he'd already waddled off.

I think the problem was that Daniel and I kept trying to impress Tara. To his credit, he never flashed his cash at her – he was too cool for that – and besides, she wasn't interested in money. She wasn't like the other girls we knew from school, who spent all their spare time planning shopping trips to town on Saturdays. She read a lot, and was interested in ancient history. The trouble started on the day she dragged us to Liskeard's "Man, Myth & Magic" Museum. The locals wanted to get rid of the word "man" because they said it was sexist, and rename it "The Liskeard Early Civilization Centre". We wrote in to the *Liskeard Gazette* with a suggestion of our own, but I guess they worked out that the acronym we suggested would be pronounced "Dogs' Cocks" and they didn't run our letter.

We were in the museum and there was a section on local legends, the usual guff about ghosts, human sacrifices, phantom hounds and highwaymen, and Tara said there was no proof that any of the stories were true, they were just made up by drunk old publicans, and she pointed out that Trethorton Hill didn't even have any decent legends attached to it, that's how lame the place was, and that's when we decided to make one up.

We decided it had to be a believable legend, something with evidence to back it up. It also had to be something that could scare the hikers off the hill. So Daniel said how about aliens, and I said no because crop circles had been discredited years ago, all you needed was a couple of dopeheads armed with a piece of rope and a plank. We needed something more sophisticated. I thought we should create a plausible unsolved mystery, so we decided on a desperate sailor who had come ashore after murdering his violent captain in a mutiny, and who for some unknown reason dragged a local girl up the hill and cut her throat. Then we added a supernatural element that would provide proof of the legend, a ghostly wailing you could hear on certain nights when the air was still.

PC Porky just came by again and asked me if I was writing a novel, and I told him if I was I'd let him know so he could hire someone to read it to him.

Daniel knew quite a lot about sound technology, and figured we could rig outdoor speakers around the hill, running from two synced-up MP3 players. We decided to record the ghost crying and phase the sound so that it appeared to circle the hill, and preset the time so that we wouldn't have to be there when it happened. I didn't involve Tara in this because I wanted to surprise her, to show I was interested in myths and stuff. We ordered the components we needed on Daniel's Paypal account, and when they arrived we tested everything in the fields beyond Trethorton, down near the river.

Next, we needed to record the sound of the crying woman, and

Daniel said he had a bit of software that could replicate the human voice but also distort it. We aimed for something between a child in pain and a fox at night. It had to be haunting and other-worldly, and after a weekend of experimentation we had mixed it to perfection. The effect was so spooky it made the hairs on my arms stand up.

Then it was time for the trial run.

Late one night we loaded the equipment into our backpacks and set off for the hill. It took over three hours to set up the sound parameters because we hadn't allowed for the wind noise up there, but we eventually got it so that the crying echoed from one speaker to the next. The effect was subtle, so that you weren't aware you were being directed between the speakers. And Daniel had recorded it a dozen times, switching the equalizer settings so that you never heard the same sound arrangement twice. He was also able to vary the start times, so we set the switch-on at different hours between 11 p.m. and 2 a.m. We figured the battery charge on the MP3 players would hold for a long time because they were only being used for a few minutes at a time. Then we sealed the players in plastic bags and buried them. The four speakers were more of a problem because we needed them to be above ground. We put one deep inside a hawthorn bush and another in a wet ditch, after first making sure that the connections were all covered. The other two we hid in clumps of grass, hoping that no one would stumble across them.

Then we went home to write the letters. We targeted both of the local papers, the *Gazette* and the *Chronicle*, and used false names. We assumed different identities, becoming hikers and pensioners, fathers and kids, and varied the content of the letters. One said he'd heard a sound like a trapped animal on the hill, another said it sounded like a woman being tortured, and so on. Daniel thought there was a risk the paper might check the senders' addresses, but I said why would they? Two weeks after the first letter appeared, we hooked our first outsider – some old guy had been walking his dog and heard the sound for himself, and wrote in to the *Gazette*.

After another two weeks had passed and a handful of letters had been published, describing the eerie sounds on the hill, we hit them with Phase Two – the legend. This letter appeared to have been sent from a retired schoolmistress, now living in Wales (I got my sister to post it, but I didn't let her read the contents). The schoolmistress explained the source of the strange sounds on Trethorton Hill. She repeated the bare bones of our legend about the sailor and the girl, and the *Chronicle* published it as their star letter of the week.

I know what you're thinking. How bored did we have to be to do this? Pretty damn bored, I guess, but it was fun winding up the locals. Soon, the hiking club members were taking turns to check out the ghost of Trethorton Hill, and created a chart detailing exactly when and where the ghost could be heard, according to which direction the wind was coming from. They put it up in the village hall and asked others to add to it with different coloured marker pens. Hikers like stuff like that.

The main thing, from our point of view, was to get everyone in the village to believe in it before we exposed the whole thing as a hoax. It was our revenge on everyone for being so boring and sheep-like. With each passing week, the letter pages became more polarized between huffing walkers who refused to believe the legend, and others who said they'd heard it for themselves.

Daniel and I went up the hill at the weekends and found whole groups of drunk Emos hanging around waiting to hear the cry of the murdered woman. We thought they'd start poking about, trying to find out where the sound was coming from, so Daniel periodically turned off the system from his remote, because we were worried they might start digging up the ground and tearing the bushes apart, but most of them seemed content to lie around on the grass drinking and making out. I think they really wanted to believe.

The week after this, Tara suddenly became much more friendly with me, and was cooler around Daniel, to the point where it seemed like she didn't want to see him. They'd obviously had some kind of falling out, but neither of them was prepared to talk about it. Maybe he'd tried it on with her and she wasn't having it. Daniel acted like he wasn't bothered and it didn't affect our friendship, and then I realized that Tara and I were kind of going out, so everything was OK.

Hang on, the sergeant is waving his stubby sausage fingers at me. It turns out he just wanted to offer me a cup of tea. Bless.

So. Then one Friday – this was about six weeks after the whole thing had started – I opened the *Chronicle* to find a letter from a genuine schoolteacher – some retired guy in Portsmouth, citing precedence for the legend.

> *Dear Sir,*
>
> *I have been following the discussions about Trethorton's Sobbing Woman with great interest. When I was a child, I well remember my late father taking me to the top of the hill to hear the cries of this poor tortured soul. He told me that she was a local Liskeard girl who had been murdered by her swain some time in the 1800s. Whenever I think of my holidays there, the memories of our trips to the "Black Hill" send shivers down my spine.*
>
> *Yours sincerely,*
>
> *Arthur Parkyn*
>
> *Schoolteacher (retired)*

Black Hill? It was never called the Black Hill. What was he on about? Not to be outdone, a builder from Liskeard wrote in and put a lot more meat on the bones. I still have the cutting here.

> *Dear Chronicle Letters,*
>
> *Concerning the legend of Trethorton's Sobbing Woman, the name of the victim was Ennor Maddern. From the age of eight she worked at what was then called the Anchor Inn (demolished in 1893), where she eventually met and fell in love with a sailor named Carne Greenway. Carne was a sailor on board the HMS Sans Pareil. He served under a cruel, violent captain named either Sambourne or Sanborn, and led the mutiny against his captain in*

*March of 1827. The captain was killed and thrown over-
board to general approval of the long-suffering crew, but
as Greenway was the leader of the mutineers, he was
hunted by the local sheriffs as soon as he set foot on land.*

*The horrors of the mutiny affected this young man
dreadfully. He was hounded from one county to the next
and became a smuggler in order to survive. When he
was finally able to make his way back to see his beloved
Ennor, he discovered that she was about to marry the
corrupt town magistrate. Carne came calling at her
window one wild night, and she pretended to be thrilled
to see him, and arranged to meet him later at Trethorton
Hill. But when he arrived there Carne found that Ennor
had betrayed him, and had rallied a gang of ruffians to
join with her from Portlooe, where HMS Sans Pareil was
docked. These men sought revenge for the death of their
captain. In the ensuing fight, Carne took the girl as a
hostage, and as the men came at him he took a knife to
her throat as punishment for this act of betrayal.*

*The ghostly cry that can be heard on the Black Hill is not
the sound of Ennor's death, but her sobbing in contrition
for her own foolishness in ever doubting her beloved. It
resonates from the standing stone which appeared after
her death, placed there by villagers in commemoration,
although there are those who believe her spirit resides
within it. I hope this clears up the mystery surrounding
this phenomenon.*

Yours,

James Talbot

Liskeard

Needless to say, Daniel and I were pissing ourselves. The following
week brought another letter, this one from a vicar who added a new
detail to the story. He said "When a local magistrate identified the

disguised sailor, Greenway kidnapped his daughter and brought her to the Black Hill, demanding that the magistrate deliver money and a horse, but the magistrate betrayed him, and in desperation Greenway killed the woman he loved".

It was inevitable that this point of view should be quickly revised. A woman called Dr Megan Stander, an academic from University College London, wrote in. I didn't keep a copy of her letter, but it said something like: "Typically, Mr Parkyn twists an important piece of local history to a patriarchal viewpoint in which Ennor Maddern takes the hag-role of the traditional Cornish witch or siren, luring an innocent sailor to his doom, and Carne Greenway is whitewashed to become the dominant male-hero of the story."

Another letter agreed with her, pointing out that Parkyn had reversed the legend, as the cruel sailor had in fact kidnapped Ennor and raped her on the hill, cutting her throat in a state of frenzied blood-lust. Meanwhile, the myth was taken up by a local reporter in the *Gazette* who reckoned he'd uncovered the truth about the "Sobbing Virgin of Trethorton Hill". According to records she had indeed been "cruelly violat'd upon the Tor" and had cut her own throat with a straight razor out of shame. He suggested the town should erect a statue to her on top of the hill.

It was all too good to be true. Daniel and I could see that everyone was just getting in on the act, each challenging the next to come up with a new addition to the story, but I wondered: was there a possibility that they actually believed what they were saying?

The *Gazette*'s reporter was the worst; he kept adding all kinds of details to the myth, citing unspecified "local records". But even he never explained what this girl was doing on top of a hill at midnight with a straight razor in her pocket, or why she'd become known as the Sobbing Virgin if she'd been violated. It was the most exciting thing to happen in our village in years. Even Tara became fascinated by the legend; it gave us something in common to talk about. I was dying to tell her the truth, but I decided to wait until the time was right.

The next time Daniel and I went up to Trethorton Hill, we realized that the time had come, because the entire hill was covered with people. The white stone had been roped off by the council, and there was an incredible party atmosphere; kids were selling beer from cold-bags and there was even a guy serving overpriced hot dogs. So, early the next morning, before anyone was around, we went there again and dug up the speakers. We had to go in daylight because my mobile didn't have a flash. I took shots of every step, the unearthing of the wires, the MP3 player being removed from the plastic bag, then we wrote a long letter to both the *Gazette* and the *Chronicle* about how we'd done it, and how we'd wanted to prove that people were gullible enough to believe anything. We included pictures of us removing the equipment.

The only thing I forgot to do was tell Tara about the hoax.

That was when things started to get weird. I don't think either of us had realized the effect of what we'd done. The first sign of trouble was an editorial in the *Chronicle*, which was now engaged in a circulation war with the *Gazette*, thanks to each side's determination to get to the truth of the legend. The piece was entitled; "Local Youths Deny Historic Past", and pointed the finger of blame at me and Daniel. I remember one section vividly. It said; "The story of Ennor Maddern and Carne Greenway has touched the hearts of everyone in the South West. Their tragic romance stands as a symbol of an extraordinary time in our history. It has proven to be both inspirational and instructive. For some, it is a tale of honour and oppression, a classic example of machismo and the subjugation of women, for others it is a dire warning about the way in which class and status corrupts innocent lives. And yet in these celebrity-obsessed times, it seems that whenever new light is thrown on our past, someone tries to push into the spotlight by refusing to believe that it ever happened." The article named us and printed our pictures, saying that we were using the legend to try and claim some fame for ourselves.

It didn't stop there. So many people swore they'd heard the sound of the sobbing woman – and, of course, they had – that the story was picked up on the national news, and even more visitors arrived to see what the fuss was about. The next Saturday night, Daniel and I went back up on to Trethorton Hill and found dozens of people still up there, waiting to hear the climax of the legend being played out. And even though the speakers were no longer hidden around the stone, several of them swore they'd heard her crying. The legend was out of our hands now. It was bigger than us, and all we could do was sit back helplessly and watch it grow.

The next morning I answered the front door and was punched in the face by some mad hiker who swore at me for "trying to ruin the reputations of the Trethorton Three". I'd read somewhere that this was what they were now calling the legend, as it was suggested that there had been a love triangle between the captain of the HMS *Sans Pareil*, the sailor and the woman who loved them both. One school of thought was that Ennor Maddern had killed herself for the love of the captain Carne Greenway had killed. The legend was open to so many different interpretations that you could fall in with a group standing for any one of them.

Overnight we became outcasts in our own village. My parents had their car defaced. Someone spray-painted the word LIARS over our garden wall. Daniel's father stopped his allowance after some people accused him of conspiring with his son at a PTA meeting. But worst of all, Tara came around one evening to tell me that she didn't want to see me anymore.

"I identified with Ennor Maddern," she told me. "As soon as I heard her story, it was like something inside me became more complete, like I'd discovered a sister. I could feel her pain."

"I don't know how you can say that, because she doesn't exist," I told her angrily. "We made her up. There's no such person."

Tara shook her head, close to tears. "Why would you lie like this?" she asked. "I know Ennor was real. I researched her life, I even saw her picture."

"Where?"

"There are websites dedicated to her story," she told me.

"Yeah, and they've all been put together by the kind of stoners who lie on the hill at night thinking that passing satellites are space ships. Believing in something doesn't make it come true. They're just trying to make their lives more interesting."

"That's not fair," she said. "You can't disrespect us by calling us

stupid. I don't know why you would want to hurt us all like this."
And she walked away from the front door without once looking
back.

I had to prove I wasn't going mad. I searched the websites
and found a number of them using a coloured lithograph of a
baby-faced girl in a linen smock, labelled "Ennor Maddern, aged
seventeen years, just before her tragic demise." It took me a couple
of evenings to trace the picture back to an old painting of a French
peasant girl which hadn't even been produced in the right country
or the right century, but that didn't seem to matter to anyone. A bit
of proper research should have cleared the whole matter up, but no
one wanted to do it. I thought about pointing this out in another
letter to the press, but decided against it. I knew that anything I
said now would just make people angry.

Then Daniel got beaten up by a couple of kids in masks who
stopped him on the way home from school. He came out of Liskeard
Infirmary with nine stitches in his face, and said he'd had enough.
We decided to make one last-ditch attempt to clear our names by
sending the CD with the recording of the sobbing woman to the
press. We posted it to the *Chronicle* and the *Gazette*, and sat back
to see the result. I think we believed that in the worst case they'd
just say we were making it up again, trying to get our names in the
papers. But I had this pathetic fantasy that some smart young journalist might show enough initiative to get a few witnesses together
who'd agree that this was what they'd heard, and then discredit the
recording by having it broken down into component parts.

I think, on the whole, I over-estimated the intelligence of the
press.

What happened instead was something entirely unforeseen. The
journalists were happy enough to believe that the transcription was
genuine, and had us both taken into custody. According to them
the sound is real, and it's a series of callous real-time recordings of
a girl being raped.

Both my parents and Daniel's have admitted that to their knowledge the only girl we ever hung around with was Tara Mellor,
so now it's down to her to clear our names. I'm sitting here in

Liskeard police station with this shitty computer and my father outside smoking himself to death, waiting for Tara to come and provide a witness report.

OK. The sergeant says I have a chance to amend my statement now, in the light of what I've just heard.

All I can tell you is that I don't know why Tara would say this – that Daniel raped her. She says that the week after we saw the Emos on the hill, we took her up there and Daniel pinned her down on the stone, and begged her to have sex with him, and when she turned him down he held her by the throat and raped her. She says she thinks I must have been there as well to record the sound, which makes me an accessory. She says I covered up for Daniel because he was my best friend.

Part of me knows she's lying because I wasn't there, and because Daniel has a gimp leg and she's tall and strong enough to look after herself. Besides, he just wouldn't do something like that, even though he can be strange and difficult sometimes. Also her timing is out, because why would I be recording the sound if we were already playing it to visitors by that time? She says I was trying to replace the recording with a more realistic version, like that makes any sense.

But part of me also remembers how she changed toward Daniel around that time, and started to shudder whenever he came near her, like she was scared of him. And I can't get rid of the feeling that perhaps he did do something bad to her.

The worst part was in the last section of her statement. She says that ever since then, she's been going up on Trethorton Hill at night and she hears the sound of the crying woman, and the sobbing is real, and she can't tell if it's the anguished cries of Ennor Maddern, or if it's her, and it was her all along.

I don't know if Tara was raped or not. I don't know who are the deceivers any more. But there's an easy way to sort it out. Take me up to the hill at night and I'll show you where the speakers were planted, and you'll hear there's nothing there now except the wind. Going up the Black Hill is the only real way to prove my innocence. Even though part of me is terrified that I'll hear the sound of crying.

LOVE AND DEATH

Michael Z. Lewin

SPURRED BY BOREDOM, Salvatore Lunghi rolled the chair from behind the office desk to a place by the office window. He watched the traffic on Bath's Walcot Street below.

The cars were hardly moving. People on the pavement couldn't be seen beneath their umbrellas which were black, black and – whoops, there was a blue one. It all seemed like a painting of what was inside his head. Nothing in there was moving. He had no woman he was interested in. His life had little colour.

It was all also typical of this *awful* – cold, wet, dark – summer. Where was global warming when you needed it? Salvatore sighed. How had his life brought him to this place when he was the son and brother who had carved his *own* path? He had resisted relentless pressures to join the family detective business, becoming a painter instead. Yet here he was, in the agency office, minding the silent phone, painting nothing. What had *happened*?

He rolled the chair back to the desk, not even detouring to visit the kettle. He wouldn't have minded a cup of coffee but not the instant rubbish that was available. His family was Italian, for crying out loud. Couldn't they lay on an espresso machine? But no. If he wanted *real* coffee he had to go down the street to Harriett's Café.

Or settle for tea. Gina – his brother's wife – preferred tea, so the makings of a decent cuppa were always available in the office. And fair enough, the office side was mostly Gina's terrain. And Gina worked hard.

Not just in the business. For a start she had her in-laws upstairs and nobody could call Mama or the Old Man *easy*. Then there was

Angelo and their two kids. And with her sister-in-law living in the same house too, Gina was a saint.

Salvatore sighed again. Gina and Angelo were at the Crown Court in Bristol for the rest of the week, key witnesses in a fraud case that had occupied them for the last six months. Which is how Salvatore came to be recruited to mind the office.

Although if he *really* got cabin fever he could recruit his father to fill in for a bit. But calling for the Old Man was an option of last resort. It would take longer to set up than it was worth. "You think I don't know how? Huh!" his father would say about all the things he didn't know how to do these days, what with the new technologies.

And Salvatore *was* being paid for his time. Which meant he'd make the rent. Last month's rent, to be accurate. It's just that sometimes the cost of money felt too great.

Life was a bitch at the moment. Not happy and carefree like it used to be. Even the women he met in the local pubs and clubs weren't as light-hearted as they used to be. Take the blonde from last night. *Lovely*, sure. And funny and clever. But with two kids and two exes? Talk about baggage ... Where were the blank-canvas twenty-year-olds of yesteryear?

Hanging around with blank-canvas twenty-year-old boys. Or thirty-year-old boys. Because face it, Salvatore told himself, *you're* not as young as you used to be either. Or without baggage, despite having no ex-wives or children.

He wasn't going to have to grow up and settle down at last, was he?

He rolled the chair back to the window. And just as he was in position to watch the street again something unexpected happened.

The office doorbell rang.

* * *

The Lunghi Detective Agency got very few clients who hadn't made appointments first. Walk-ins happened, but they were rare. And walk-ins who looked like this one ... Well!

Hel-*lo*, Salvatore said to himself as he followed her up the stairs.

He held the door open for her. As she entered the office he said, "Would you like a cup of tea?"

She turned and smiled – a *gorgeous* smile. "That would be great."

Following into the office Salvatore was struck by how gloomy it was. Books on shelves, filing cabinets ... No fish tank. No *paintings*. That was a terrible oversight. What better introduction to a client could he have than for her to admire a painting and for him to be able to say, "Well, actually ... "

Instead he said, "A cup of tea is the least we can offer after those stairs." The Lunghis' home and business premises were spread across the upper floors of a number of interconnected buildings. The ground-level shops provided stable rental income when agency business was slow and icing on the family cake when it wasn't. "Do sit." He gestured to the chairs facing the desk.

The woman was about thirty, tall but not skinny. She wore her rich black hair down to her shoulders. Her plain, quiet suit set off her natural colouring beautifully. Both clothes and demeanour said that she was something professional.

Then, as he watched, Salvatore suddenly saw – *saw* – a painting. A woman – this woman – leaning over a desk, one hand extended. Was it so she could balance herself, or was she heading for one of the desk's drawers? Was the desk hers, or someone else's? The painting would be titled *Opportunity*.

He *almost* asked if she had ever modelled. But as the woman sat Salvatore realized he was breathing heavily. Get a grip, he told himself. To the woman he said, "How do you take your tea?"

She looked up at him – an oval, symmetrical face and huge blue eyes. "Milk, no sugar," she said. "Skimmed if you have it."

"Just semi, I'm afraid."

"That will do fine."

And she wasn't at all out of breath from the climb. Fit in more ways than one.

"I'm Salvatore Lunghi."

"Polly Mainwaring."

"Pleased to meet you, Polly." He turned toward the heating

kettle, took a few biscuits from a tin and arranged them on a plate. He put the plate on the desk before her. "Full service detectives," he said as he went back to the teapot. The kettle boiled. He poured the water and carried pot, milk and mugs to the desk on a tray. He sat behind the desk while the tea steeped. "Give it a moment. Then I'll be mother."

She smiled.

Then, leaning forward just a little and speaking quietly, Salvatore said, "People who come to a detective agency are often uncertain whether it's the right thing to do. I want to stress that anything you say here is in complete confidence."

"OK, thank you."

"And if you would prefer to talk to a woman, my sister is working nearby and I can ask her to come in. Either way, our first job is to decide if what we do here can help you. No charge for that, of course." He gave it a moment and then unleashed one of his famous and devastating smiles.

But Polly Mainwaring didn't seem to need gentle unpicking of a knot of uncertainty. Nor did she seem to react to the smile. She just said, "It's my fiancé."

A *fiancé*. Salvatore caught sight of the ring. With its big rock.

Ah well.

"What about your fiancé?"

"Something weird happened and I can't get a straight answer from him. I think he's lying to me, and that's no way to begin a new life together." And suddenly the controlled, businesslike face of Polly Mainwaring puckered into wrinkles of distress.

Salvatore wanted to take her in his arms. He wanted to say, I'll help you ditch this lying scumbag. He *wanted* to ask her to model for him. However, what he did say was "Tell me about it."

"Jack and I met at the hospital. I was visiting my Aunt Elaine. She had kidney cancer, though she's OK now."

Salvatore hadn't expected the history of the relationship but Polly seemed to want to tell it. He nodded sympathetically. And he did enjoy looking into her eyes.

"Jack's a nurse, and a really good one. Everyone on Auntie's ward loved him. She'd told me about him even before I met him. But when I did, when we did, it was, like, boom. You know? Love. The real thing. Wonderful."

"How long ago was that?"

"Months now. Seven."

"And you decided to get married?"

"Six weeks ago. But neither of us wanted a bells and whistles wedding."

"No?"

"The money's better used to start us off in our new life together. Jack has plenty, but I don't have much left over each month and my family's just, you know, comfortable."

"Uh huh."

"So six days ago we went to the Register Office to make arrangements." Polly's face began to contort again. "And the registrar ... She greeted Jack by name. By *name*. 'Hello, Jack,' she said when we walked in."

Salvatore waited but there was no more. "I don't understand."

"Neither did I. I mean, how does a registrar know somebody's name when he walks into her office? But it was more than that. Her tone ... It was like she was meeting an old friend." Polly gave a little nod of punctuation.

"Is there some reason they shouldn't be friends?"

"She's, like, fifty and talks posh. Anyway, he *says* they're not."

"Or mightn't she have been a patient or visitor to the hospital and got to know him as a nurse?"

"He *says* no to that too."

"So how *did* he explain her greeting?"

"He just laughed and said it was nothing. He said that she knew his name because he'd rung her to make our appointment to go in. He said that using people's first names must be the way she puts people at their ease."

"And you didn't think that was a reasonable explanation?"

"She didn't know *my* name. She didn't put *me* at my ease. With me she was more a stuck-up cow."

OK ... "And ... ?"

"I'm a legal secretary, Mr Lunghi. I've done the job for seven years and we get cases that you wouldn't believe. And I have a good sense of when things are right and when they're not. And this is not right. That 'Hello Jack' was the 'Hello, Jack' of someone who *knew* him. There's nothing wrong with that but then he *denied* it, and now he won't even talk about it. And it's hanging over me like a Sword of Damocles, if you know what I mean. There's *something* going on, Mr Lunghi. I just know there is."

"You mean between Jack and the registrar?"

"Not an affair. But they were conspiratorial. That's the word. Conspiratorial. Even after the 'Hello, Jack' I saw little looks between them. I'm not a genius or anything – I've never had to be. But my instinct says that something's *wrong*. And the last thing I want to do is marry a man, have children with a man, who is the *wrong* man."

"Of course not."

"Maybe the very fact he's being evasive should be enough for me to break it off," she said. "But I love him. I *love* him." And then the dam burst. Polly started to cry.

* * *

"I *bet* she's a babe," Rosetta said at the kitchen table that evening.

"Don't be silly," Salvatore said to his sister. But he felt his face flush. Good thing the kitchen was hot from cooking.

"It's the vacant look on your face when you talk about her," Rosetta said. "I've seen it before. Do you see it, Angelo? Gina?"

Angelo said nothing. Gina said, "See what?"

"That Sally's smitten with this Polly woman." Rosetta turned back to her elder brother. "But calling a marriage off because the registrar greeted her fiancé by name? How flaky is that?"

Unmarried – not even engaged recently – Rosetta was eager, even desperate, to find Mr Right. To put a wedding in doubt because of a greeting was an alien concept.

"Polly's instincts tell her something's wrong," Salvatore said. "Pass the gnocchi, please."

Rosetta and Mama had pitched in to prepare food for everyone but because teenagers Marie and David were out, the meal was adults-only. The special circumstance was the return of star witnesses Angelo and Gina from Crown Court in Bristol.

However, neither witness felt celebratory. "We're shattered," Angelo declared as they arrived at the table.

"Shattered?" the Old Man said. "*Shattered?*"

"Like panes of glass, Papa," Gina said. "We're in bits."

The Old Man picked up a piece of bread. "*Shattered?* It sounds ... excremental. Shattered. Doubly excremental. Huh! There's more butter?"

"But still you testified?" Mama refilled Gina's wine glass and ignored her husband's request for his own good.

"We began our testimonies," Angelo said. "It's complicated, this fraud. We're testifying bit by bit rather than giving all our testimony at once."

"But you two will make it clear as glass for them." Mama refilled her younger son's wine glass. "Until you shatter, of course."

"*Shat-tered,*" the Old Man said quietly. He held his glass out too.

"So this Polly," Rosetta said, "she thinks her fiancé is carrying on with the registrar?"

"Only that they were conspiratorial. But it's destroying her that she doesn't know what they're conspiring about," Salvatore said.

"You took the case?"

"Of course. They hire us, we do the job."

"She pays, this Polly?" the Old Man asked.

"She paid a retainer, Papa. She works for lawyers, so she knows how it all goes."

"Which lawyers?"

"Baum and Carteret."

"Ah." An established firm the Lunghis had often been employed by. "It explains how she knows to come to us."

Salvatore turned to Gina. "The new case does mean that I'll be mostly out of the office tomorrow."

"I can cover it," Rosetta said quickly. She and Gina glanced rapidly at the Old Man who was drinking.

He saw the glances but didn't understand them. "What?"

Mama did. She said, "Where did you say Marie and David are tonight?" intentionally changing the subject. Everyone knew that putting the Old Man at the end of the agency telephone for a day was like rolling dice. You couldn't be sure what he'd do.

"They're at the films," Gina said.

"Oh, isn't that nice," Mama said.

"Not together, Mama. Not the same film. That would be far too easy."

"On a school night?" Rosetta asked.

"They swore they've done their homework. Marie has lines to learn for the play she's in, but that's really her business." Gina shrugged. Both children were responsible students, although with very different interests and talents. Marie was dramatic and arty. David was scientific and mathematical. But their parents cut them both some slack. So many teenaged children were much worse.

Rosetta said, "Where will you start with Polly's Jack, Sal?"

"A registrar does more than marriages," the Old Man said.

"True," Salvatore said.

"Deaths and births as well. Maybe this Jack comes in with all his babies."

"Maybe, Papa," Salvatore said, "but I'm going to start by checking out where he works and where he lives."

"What's his job?"

"He's a nurse."

"A nurse?"

"Although he went to university and read Spanish," Salvatore said. "Polly says he didn't know what to do after university so he got a care job and one thing led to another."

"A nurse, he is?" the Old Man said. "Helpful to people, if he isn't using it to kill them instead." The table went quiet. "What?" He looked around. "You think I'm foolish now? Nurses, doctors, they know things."

"No one thinks you're foolish, Papa," Gina said.

"Then why don't they ask me to cover their telephone while our Salvatore goes out to hunt for this fiancé's conspiracy?" The Old Man sipped from his wine. "Huh!"

* * *

Years of working cases in Bath had provided the family with many friendly contacts in the Royal United Hospital. Unfortunately the same years had seen most of those contacts move on or retire.

When he began work in the morning Salvatore could not call on a single hospital nurse for information. However an administrative secretary was on the family's unofficial list of informants and Salvatore's call intrigued Dorothy Simbals sufficiently for her to agree to a coffee break in the large café area by the main entrance.

There was one small problem. Salvatore had never met her. "But you wear a name tag, right?"

"And you're happy to walk around a large room looking at every woman's chest?"

"Happy to have an excuse," Salvatore said.

"Even so ... Why don't *you* carry ... a magnifying glass. I'll recognize you as a detective by that."

"I could wear a geranium in my buttonhole."

"Humour me, Mr Lunghi. My job here is *very* boring."

So a magnifying glass it was. With Rosetta's help he eventually found one in Marie's room – part of a school kit that had never been used.

And, as things turned out, Dorothy Simbals' chest was entirely worthy of attention. She was not a young woman, but she was in very good shape. *Shape* ... Salvatore was pleased to meet her.

"Can I get you a coffee? Or something else?" he asked.

"A coffee, please," she said. "You'll get it cheaper from the machine over there." She pointed. "But better if you queue at the counter." The opposite direction.

"Nothing but the best for you."

"Is the right answer."

Salvatore brought back two lattes and a *pain au chocolat*. He suggested they split the pastry when he sat. "Don't want you to waste away."

"I think I'll start wearing my name tag on my shoulder."

He laughed and then offered to clink coffee cups with her. "*Salute*."

"Cheers."

They clinked and sipped.

Then she said, "Jack Appleby. Or Jonathan Aloysius Appleby, to be more exact."

"Lordy," Salvatore said.

"Not a name you see every day. What do you know about him?"

"I was told that he gravitated to nursing after graduating from uni."

"Got his degree from Cardiff thirteen years ago."

"Making him ... ?"

"Thirty-six."

"What does one intend to use a degree in Spanish for?" Salvatore wondered aloud. "Teaching?"

"Jonathan Aloysius's CV says that he travelled for a year and then did volunteer work in a hospice."

"Where?"

"Weston." An area in the northeast of Bath. "His grandmother was there and instead of just visiting he decided to try to help out. He stayed ... " – she consulted a thin file she'd brought with her – "for about a year. His next stop was to train as a care assistant. You do that on-the-job and he trained in the oncology unit here. They rated him highly and he spent a year or so here. Then he moved to another hospice, and after that to a nursing home." She turned to a new page. "Another hospice, and then another."

"Is bouncing from one place to another like that the way it usually works for care assistants?"

"I'm not an expert but probably not. Yet it happens. If you get to care – I mean personally – for people in hospices you can be affected when they ... go."

Salvatore nodded. "And perhaps he has a special affinity with people in acute distress."

"All his references praise his work. Then a few years ago he did proper nurses' training. That was in Bristol, where he was again rated highly. Then he came back here. He's been at the RUH nearly two years and his performance evaluations have been outstanding. Care to guess what ward he works on here now?"

"Oncology?"

"He began there, but then six months ago he switched to maternity."

Salvatore laughed. "So, a new speciality."

"So it seems."

"What else is in the file?"

"You expect a lot for a coffee," Dorothy Simbals said.

"Is there anything else I can do to encourage you to feel helpful?" Salvatore flashed the big smile.

"You can understand that I'm only here because your father helped my mother when she was being badly treated by the printing company she worked for. It was years ago and your dad sorted it all out. She still mentions his name sometimes."

"He's one of the good guys."

She returned to her papers. "Do you have Jonathan Aloysius's home address?"

"Yes. But I'd be grateful for anything else you have in there."

"References, health reports, evaluations. Nothing unusual, apart from the unanimity of people's appreciation of him. Usually *somebody* finds something to complain about. Otherwise ... He's got a parking permit for his ... oh, it's a BMW."

"Nice ... "

"Not new. The registration number makes it ... five years old."

"Nevertheless ... " Salvatore raised his eyebrows.

"Posh for a nurse?"

"Maybe his grandmother left him some money."

"Sorry. Our records don't include copies of the wills from near relatives."

"Anything else?"

"Nothing unusual. Except ... "

"What?"

"Well, he's unlucky to be as young as he is and be a widower."

"He was *married*?"

"You didn't know about that?"

"No. Do you have any information about who his wife was, when they were married, what she died of?"

She shook her head.

OK. "And do you have a personal impression of Jonathan Aloysius?"

"Never met him. But you could make up a story and go to Maternity and have a look for yourself."

"Or you could take me there on the pretext of showing me around. After your shift, say?" Salvatore said.

"After my shift I'll be heading home with my husband," Dorothy said with a smile. "But it's been very nice to meet you." She stood up.

Salvatore stood too. "You have my number."

"Oh, I think I do."

Salvatore watched her until she was out of sight. He liked her, for all the good it did him. If it wasn't baggage in the form of children then it was the baggage in the form of husbands. Ah well.

* * *

"Rose can feed herself," the Old Man said.

"But if she's in the office, she won't eat good," Mama said. "She'll just eat easy."

"So let her eat easy."

"When I can make her wholesome?"

"Stop fussing."

"You don't mind my fuss when I feed *you* just because the clock says you're hungry and not your stomach."

"To feed me you have five steps into our very own kitchen. Or six. Or seven. Maybe you don't stride out like you used to."

"Why don't *you* make lunch for us? Save me all those steps."

"I could do that." What could he make if he had to? An egg? Boiled? Two eggs, in water? How hard could it be? "Huh!"

"Or would you prefer me to make it?"

There was no escaping this. "You."

"Well, I'll make lunch for us, the two."

"Good."

"It will be served downstairs. In their kitchen, or in the office if Rosetta insists. It will be ready in twenty-five minutes."

* * *

Salvatore decided against visiting the RUH's maternity department. As things stood, Jonathan Aloysius Appleby didn't know him. If something came up that required surveillance, there was no point making it easy for Jack to think, I've seen that guy somewhere.

Better to follow up the widower thing. But before he went home he took a detour, to the staff parking lot.

Jack's BMW was red. A convertible. *Nice* car ...

* * *

Rosetta's feet were on the desk. A cup of tea with feet up was her reward for bringing the agency's invoices up to date. One reward, but she planned another. She had decided to join an online dating agency.

It was time to be proactive. If she didn't want to spend the rest of her life in her parents' house, she was going to do something about it.

Lots of couples met online these days. Not always for ever but she was coming around to thinking of "for ever" as an outdated ideal in the modern world.

It was fine for old people, like her parents. And for old-fashioned couples, like Angelo and Gina. But it needn't be the template for a *modern* relationship. And a modern relationship would do her nicely now, ta very much. And where better than the internet to find one?

Or even two.

With that saucy thought Rosetta smiled to herself.

And then the telephone rang.

She gave some care to her tone of voice. "Lunghi Detective Agency. Rosetta Lunghi speaking."

"You sound about as businesslike as a massage parlour, Sis. No offence." It was Salvatore.

"Offence taken," Rosetta said. "Did you ring for anything more than to give me a hard time?"

"Is it easy to get marital records online? It turns out that my client's fiancé was married before, but his wife died. Before I speak to Polly I'd like to find out something about the dead wife."

"What's the wife's name?"

"Beyond Mrs Appleby I don't know."

"Birth date? Date of the marriage? Date of the death? Location of any of the above?"

"The only thing I do have is the full name of the husband. Jonathan Aloysius Appleby."

"Aloysius ... A slim thread. You care to spell that?"

He did. "Once I've driven past Jonathan Aloysius' house, I'll come back home. Maybe fifteen minutes?" He hung up.

Oh well, Rosetta thought. The dating website would wait. The important thing was her decision to do it.

***

Mama carried a tray to the office. She was surprised to find Salvatore there as well as Rose. "Why are *you* here?"

"Hello to you too, Mama."

"You know I don't mean it like that," Mama said. "But you were out, working your case."

"And now I'm in, working my case."

Mama put the tray down on the desk.

Rosetta said, "I can't eat all that, Mama."

"It's not so much."

"It's enough for six people."

"Your brother should eat too, if he's case-working."

"None for me, thanks," Salvatore said.

Rosetta said, "Sally's learned something about his client's fiancé. We were just talking about the cost of searching for more information. There's no easy way to get it online for free."

"Ah, my little girl and her computer." Mama knew how proud Rose was to be the family's IT expert. Even more than David. "Well, computers have to eat too."

"I'm not really hungry," Rosetta said.

"Your father gets hungry with the clock," Mama said. "But this will wait for your stomach. Except the hot soup – that you should have now. And I'll go get something else for Salvatore since what I already made isn't good enough for him."

"Nothing for me," Salvatore said.

"*Nothing*?" Mama looked at her first-born. "You are not so fat you need to diet. A man *should* have substance. With substance you can find a nice girl to make children."

"Mama ... " Salvatore began.

"I know, I know. Shut up. Make food that nobody eats. I know my place."

"I'm going *out* to lunch."

This news transformed Salvatore's mother. "A date you have? Who with? A young lady? She's single?"

"A fat, ugly, married man. I'm getting too old to be choosy."

All three heard noises from the kitchen. "Your father, he too mocks me." Mama left the office.

Salvatore turned to his sister. "*Am* I getting fat?"

***

It wasn't a long walk from Walcot Street to the Circus. The eighteenth-century circular street was rimmed by tall, elegant buildings but these days the Georgian homes had been converted into flats and offices, including Baum and Carteret's.

Polly Mainwaring was already putting on her jacket as Salvatore entered. "You're on time. Thank you. I don't have long."

"I do my best."

"And you have something to report?"

"As well as questions to ask."

"Good. I can't tell you how upsetting all this uncertainty is."

You *can* tell me, Salvatore thought, but he just followed as Polly led the way to the nearby Assembly Rooms, site of countless social gatherings in Bath's Georgian heyday and countless dance scenes in films about Georgian Bath's heyday. The building had a large café and tearoom.

Polly picked a table well away from other customers. She sat and put her bag on the floor. "Do you know what you want?"

Only in one sense, Salvatore thought. But he skimmed the menu rapidly and nodded.

The waitress arrived. "Something to drink?"

"We're ready to order," Polly said. "I'll have smoked salmon on multi-grain, no butter but with lettuce and tomato. Water with ice. Tap, not bottled."

The waitress's eyes were not made up and slightly swollen, making her look sleepy, as if lunchtime was her sunrise. "Sir?"

"The chef's salad and a latte."

When they were alone Salvatore said, "Did you know that Jack has been married before?"

To his surprise, Polly gave a quick nod. "Her name was Belinda. She died. She was older than he was."

"You didn't mention it yesterday."

"It didn't occur to me."

"But mightn't that explain how Jack knows the registrar? She might have registered Belinda's death."

"I didn't think of that." But Polly wrinkled her nose, and gave her head a little shake. "The registrar's tone didn't sound like 'I have met you in sad circumstances before.' It was more 'Hi, Jack, nice to see you again, my friend.'"

"Isn't that quite a lot to conclude from a brief encounter?"

"It was also ... her body language, the way she looked at him while we were talking. No, I'm sure I'm right."

Polly *was* the client ... So Salvatore moved on. "Yesterday you told me that Jack owns his flat. I drove past it today. It's very nice."

"Yes."

"As is his car – the Beemer convertible."

"Oh, I *love* that car. Especially on warm days. Not that we've had many this year."

"Polly, how does Jack afford it all?" Property in Bath was notoriously expensive. Beemers were expensive everywhere.

"It's not like he owns the flat outright. He has a mortgage."

Nevertheless … "Does he have money beyond his nursing salary?"

"His wife left him an income."

"An income rather than capital?"

"That's what he said. We talked about it when all the credit crunch stuff hit the news."

"It must be quite a large income."

"I'd never ask him a thing like that."

"Even though you're about to get married?"

"He said he doesn't owe anybody anything, apart from the mortgage, and I believe him."

I take it Jack's body language said, "Trust me", Salvatore thought.

"But you're right," Polly said. "He must be reasonably well off. His flat is furnished *very* nicely."

Salvatore leaned forward and looked serious. "Polly, if I'm to unravel Jack's connection to the registrar, it would really help me to look at his personal papers. Things like his bank and credit card statements. His photographs."

"Oh!"

It was clear that Polly didn't like the sound of where this might be going.

However … "When people come to a detective, they have questions. But they don't always realize what it will cost to get answers. The cost beyond the money. That can include doing things that are distasteful, things that you would never consider in normal circumstances. You wouldn't poke into Jack's personal effects but that really is what you've hired me to do."

Polly's lips tightened. For a moment Salvatore thought she was about to become an ex-client. But then she gathered her bag from the floor, fished in it and put a set of keys on the table. "To Jack's flat. Copy them and drop the originals back to me at the office this afternoon."

Salvatore nodded solemnly.

"His shift today ends at five. He won't be home before twenty past."

* * *

The Old Man was dozing in front of a jigsaw puzzle when there was a knock at the door. He wasn't sure he'd heard it at first. But then the knock was repeated.

"The door!" he called to Mama.

He had just remembered that Mama went out shopping when Rosetta called back, "It's me, Papa," and entered.

"Hello, my darling girl," the Old Man said. "You come to visit? I make you some coffee. Wait, is it tea you prefer?" He readied himself to get up.

"Nothing to drink, thanks, Papa. I want to ask you a favour."

"A favour." He considered. "You want money to start a computing business?"

"I need to go out – to make a visit on Salvatore's case. Would you cover the office for an hour?"

"You want I should cover the office?"

"But if you have something else to do … "

"I have so much to do." He glanced at the puzzle. "Huh! I will be down the stairs in a minute. Or two. Best I go to the bathroom first, like before a trip. Who knows how long you must be out on Salvatore's visit."

"An hour and a half at most, Papa. I'll see you downstairs."

* * *

Jonathan Aloysius Appleby's flat was on the first floor in a well-maintained building overlooking a park. It wasn't huge – two bedrooms, a living room and a kitchen – but it was immaculate.

Even the light-switches looked new. Jonathan Aloysius clearly liked his things just so.

It was in the smaller of the bedrooms that Salvatore found the cache of documents he was looking for – bank and credit card statements, employment and personal correspondence, even Jack's will. They were in file folders in the drawers of a lush mahogany desk. Because Salvatore was on a timetable he took photographs of everything he could find rather than studying the documents one by one.

Just past four, when he was about to open the last drawer, his phone vibrated. It was Rosetta. "Hi, Sis. How'd you do?"

"I managed to get fifteen minutes." After leaving Polly at lunchtime, Salvatore had asked Rosetta to try to interview the registrar. "She was very professional."

"Did she acknowledge knowing Jonathan Aloysius?"

"She agreed that they know each other."

"Personally?"

"She laughed when I asked. Then made a cross with her index fingers."

"What? Like to keep vampires away?"

"Exactly."

"Jack is a vampire?"

"I'm sure she just meant that she would never get personal with him. Very jolly and bright, but beyond what I've already said she wouldn't say anything. And she does wear a wedding ring and is in her fifties, which would reduce the odds. How are you doing there?"

"Taking lots of snaps but nothing has jumped out at me so far."

"We can download the pictures and have a look when you get back. Will you be long?"

"I don't want to get caught *in flagrante*. I don't think I've got much more to do."

"See you soon then." Rosetta rang off.

Salvatore opened the last drawer in Appleby's desk. It held only one folder but it was pretty thick. Opening it, he found that the top document was a Death Certificate.

***

David Lunghi returned from school at about five-fifteen – later than usual because of football practice. Being wiry and quick rather than muscular and tall meant the ground-level game suited him. He wasn't interested in it the way a lot of his classmates were but David enjoyed the strategic side of the game. He was a passer rather than a shooter and because of that his goal-scoring contemporaries liked playing with him. His passes made them look good.

In turn, David enjoyed the respect from schoolmates that arose from physical qualities rather than his brainpower. It was a gratifying development in his school life. He was even being noticed more by girls.

But when he dropped his school bag in the kitchen and headed for the office, it wasn't to recount his latest footballing successes. He wanted an update on the agency's current investigations. Because if he liked football and enjoyed physics, it was the family business that he loved.

In the office David found his grandfather, who was looking out the window. "Hi, Grandpa."

The Old Man turned with a smile. "My David. Welcome to the hub, the heartbeat of the agency."

"Has it been busy?"

"Only in my head. So … You are back from school."

"Has Uncle Sal learned anything for his new case?"

"Your uncle thinks he has located important documents. He and Rose wanted to study these documents here." The Old Man patted the monitor on the desk. "And send me back to my pasture, to my stable. But I told them, Go look at your pictures on Rosetta's better computer. I can finish the day here, no extra charge."

"So they're in Auntie Rose's room?"

"With their important pictures. You want to look?"

"I think I do."

"So look. And when you've looked, come back. If the telephone should ring, you can answer."

David enjoyed saying, "Lunghi Detective Agency, David Lunghi speaking." With a nod and a smile, he left for Rosetta's room. There he found his aunt and uncle peering at Rose's screen. "Amazing," Salvatore said.

David could see only that the screen was split between two images.

"She can't possibly know," Rose said. "Can she?"

"She would have said."

"Will you warn her tonight?"

There was a pause while Salvatore thought. In the gap David said, "Hi."

Neither of the adults looked up or answered.

Finally Salvatore said, "I shouldn't think it's necessary."

Rosetta waved a hand in David's direction. "Hi, David."

Salvatore said, "Best to get it all together first, chapter and verse."

Rosetta said, "I agree." Then her telephone rang.

The adults ignored it, continuing to concentrate on the screen. After four rings David picked up the receiver and said, "Lunghi Detective Agency. David Lunghi speaking."

"David?" It was his grandmother. "That's David?"

"Yes, Grandma."

"Your aunt's not in her room? Because she's not in the kitchen."

"She's here, Grandma."

"Good. Good. Give her to me, OK?"

David tapped Rosetta on the shoulder and then passed the telephone over. Rose took it without looking away from the screen.

* * *

Thursday was one of the three times a week that the family routinely ate together. Usually Rosetta made a curry. But when Marie arrived about six, exhausted – ex-*hausted*, dahling – from rehearsing *Hedda Gabler* at school, there was neither the smell of a curry nor anybody working at the cooker when she entered the kitchen. *What* was going on?

Marie tossed her hair. How was a star – a *stahr*, dahling – supposed to cope with neglect and famishment? The hair-toss and the attitude were not really appropriate for Hedda, her first starring role, but Marie was not a method actor. She was able to leave Hedda at school and be herself at home.

"Hey," she called. "*Hey!*"

But there was no answer.

She thought for a moment. Her parents were in court and apparently not back yet. Uncle Sal was supposed to be out working today. So Auntie Rose would be in the agency office. Which must be why she wasn't cooking. But it was a bit much – a *bit* much, dahling – when not only was it close to dinnertime, it was a *family* dinnertime. Did nobody respect tradition any more?

But just as Marie was about to look for David – whose bag she saw lying awkwardly by the door – she heard noises from above. Her grandparents were on the move, on their way down. Them, at least, she could count on. Mama would cook. All would be well.

Marie dropped on to a chair and let her hair hang back. A tableau of fatigue. Mama and the Old Man would appreciate quality in a weary grandchild, even if nobody did.

But when the descending footsteps arrived outside the kitchen door, they didn't stop to turn into the flat. They continued down the stairs that led to the street. Mama and the Old Man were going *out.*

What on earth was happening? Was she doomed – *doomed*, dahling – to expire here? Drained. Unreplenished. Ignored.

* * *

Gina and Angelo arrived home even later than the day before, but their spirits were high. Everyone could see it as soon as they stepped into the kitchen. "Honeys, we're home," Angelo said.

"And home to stay," Gina said. "The case is over. The bad guys changed their pleas. All of them. They're guilty, guilty, guilty."

There was a murmur of congratulation from around the table.

"What's this?" Angelo said, looking at an array of plastic containers. "Not Rose's curry?"

"We did Suko tonight, Dad," David said, referring to the Thai restaurant down the street.

"Celebrating or just busy?" Gina asked.

"Auntie Rose and Uncle Sal made progress on a case, but they haven't reported yet. They wanted to wait for you."

"Which case?" Angelo asked.

"The fiancé, from yesterday," Salvatore said. "We made a breakthrough. It may even be *murder*." He opened his eyes theatrically wide and looked from David to Marie and back again.

"Wash your hands," Mama said.

Gina said, "We won't be a minute."

"Murder he talks about, this Salvatore," the Old Man said. "Do you hear that? *Murder*." Only the Old Man had ever solved a murder case for the agency. "What I could tell you about a murder."

A moan rose from around the table.

"What?" He looked around.

"Not now," Mama said. "Here, have more king prawns with cashews."

The Old Man liked his cashews. And his king prawns. After a moment he moved his plate closer so she could serve. Sharing his wisdom could wait for later.

*   *   *

Gina and Angelo were not away long.

"It's not that we want to hear about any more *cases*," Angelo said as he sat. "I just don't want Papa eating all the prawns."

Faces turned to the Old Man to see what response he'd make to this nudge. But he just said, "What? You think I can't take a joke? Huh! Also I can take a *hint*." He pushed a plastic tray closer to Angelo.

"So, c'mon, Sally, tell us," Gina said.

As the food made the rounds, Salvatore said, "Well, to recap, my new client objected to the familiarity with which the registrar greeted her husband-to-be when they went in to arrange their wedding. Well, it turns out that the registrar *does* know Jonathan Aloysius Appleby. Quite well." Salvatore spread his hands. Everyone recognized this as an invitation to speculate about the case.

"Personally?" Gina asked.

"Strictly business," Rosetta said.

"Interesting. Because a registrar's business is births, deaths, and marriages. Is there anything else they do?" Gina turned to her husband.

Angelo shrugged.

"If there is," Salvatore said, "you needn't look for it."

"Births, deaths and marriages?" David said. "So did Jonathan thingy have a lot of children?"

"By different mothers?" Marie said. "Or maybe with this registrar herself?"

"Or he just registered them all with this registrar?" Angelo asked.

"No," Salvatore said. "Nothing to do with children."

"That only leaves marriages and deaths," David said.

"Correct," Rosetta said.

"Which?"

"Both."

"There's marriage and death in *Hedda Gabler*," Marie said. "If anybody cares." She tossed her hair.

***

The family agreed that, really, Salvatore *should* ring Polly Mainwaring after dinner.

Oh *well*, Salvatore thought. If I *must* ring the most gorgeous woman I've met in ages and tell her news that ought to end her engagement ...

He contemplated how he would feel about being a rebound boyfriend.

He decided he'd feel just fine.

However, when he rang, Polly's phone was switched off. "I have new information for you, Ms Mainwaring," he said in his message. "It's quite important, so I would like to see you either later tonight or tomorrow morning. Ring me. Anytime."

He hoped that he'd managed to balance urgency and not frightening her. However, when Polly called at 9.50 she *was* frightened.

"Mr. Lunghi? What is this *about*? You've found out things that I should know?"

"Yes, but there are documents you really need to see, so I'd prefer to meet you so you can see them for yourself. If you'd like me to come over now ... "

* * *

Polly's flat was much more modest than her fiancé's and not in the city centre. It took Salvatore twenty minutes to get there and it would have been longer without the satnav because her building was at the end of a cul-de-sac that was missing its street sign.

Polly opened the downstairs door immediately when he pulled up outside. She must have been watching from upstairs and guessed his would be the only car arriving at that time of night.

Once in her flat she turned to face him. "What have you found out? Because Jack is acting like everything is completely normal."

"Please," Salvatore said, "let's sit somewhere."

She pointed to a couch. She picked a matching armchair.

"As you know, Jack has been married before," Salvatore began after he'd put a black folder on the table in front of them.

"To Belinda. I told you that this afternoon."

"Belinda Rogers." Salvatore removed prints of two documents. "Marriage and death certificates."

Polly's face showed her puzzlement. She did not reach for the papers.

Then Salvatore pulled out two more pieces of paper. "Harriet Martinson." Then two more. "Rosalind Perry." Two more. "Gladys Anne Horowitz." Two more. "Felicity Jarbaum." Two more. "Arabella Marlow."

"What are these?"

"Marriage and death certificates."

Polly's eyes widened.

Quietly Salvatore said, "Jack has been married six times. At least six times. These are copies of documents he keeps in a folder in his desk."

"*Married* six times?"

"And, in each case his wife died within a few months of the wedding."

The large eyes got larger still. "*Died*?"

"Yes."

"You're ... you're saying that he *murdered* them?"

Salvatore shook his head. "I can't say anything of the kind. In each case the death certificate gives a natural cause of death, a cancer as either the primary or a secondary cause."

"But ... you can't kill someone by giving them cancer."

"I don't know enough about medicine to know what is or isn't possible." He paused and watched her fill in a blank: possible for someone with *medical* training. "I can look into that if you want me to. However you should also know that in each case – all six times – the wedding was conducted by Beverley Norbury."

"But that's—"

"Ms Norbury is, indeed, the registrar Jack took you to the other day. She's been a registrar here in Bath for nearly fifteen years. Jack's first wedding was twelve years ago."

"Twelve," Polly said quietly.

"And," Salvatore said, "you should know that Beverley Norbury also registered all six deaths."

Polly Mainwaring sat holding the documents.

"So it's no wonder that Ms Norbury knows Jack. She's met him on at least a dozen previous occasions. She says—"

"You *talked* with her?"

"My sister did. Ms Norbury acknowledged knowing Jack but she denied that the relationship is personal."

"But if she's in *league* with him ... If she helps him marry women and then kill them ... "

"I haven't said or suggested any such thing. All we know are the dates and details of these twelve events. They do explain why Ms Norbury might call him Jack. However, they don't explain why she greeted him in that personal and friendly way."

"Yes," Polly said. "Yes, she did."

"There may be a good reason," Salvatore said, "and I'm making no accusations. But I hope you see why I thought you ought to have this information sooner rather than later."

"Yes," Polly said. Quietly.

Salvatore could see that his client was upset. "Look, can I get you a cup of tea? Or something stronger?"

* * *

As the evening went on, the Old Man became restless. The television was on but he wasn't watching it with his usual critical attention.

"Why do you twitch?" Mama said.

He thought about it. Then he realized. "The certificates. Salvatore's marriage and death. I don't like them."

After a moment Mama said, "They don't have to be a murder."

"I don't care about *that*." They always thought his murder was so precious to him. "Huh!"

"No?"

"Let the boy solve a dozen murders. Or half-a-dozen, if that's how many. Maybe the boy will be proud and work full-time and give up painting that doesn't pay."

"He values his independence too much."

"That we all value. Doesn't mean he shouldn't work here. Let him paint in spare time. We could even make him a room." He didn't know which room but there was bound to be one. The Old Man rocked forward.

"You go somewhere?"

"Downstairs. To talk."

"About the independence or because you don't like the certificates?"

"Yes."

"Why not? Give them your benefit. But don't be out all night."

* * *

Gina and Angelo sat in the living room. They were finally beginning to relax after the case that had occupied them for months.

And made them a *lot* of money. "Cheers." Angelo offered his glass.

"Cheers." They clinked wine glasses, not the first time in the evening.

Rosetta came in. "Join us." Angelo held up the wine bottle.

"No Sally?"

"Not yet. You have something? Tell us."

Rosetta sat and Angelo poured.

"What do you think of computer dating?" Rosetta asked.

He looked at her as if she'd asked his opinion of holidays on the moon. But Gina said, "It seems like a good thing, if you're reasonably cautious."

"Thank you," Rosetta said with a nod.

"*That's* what you've been doing since dinner?" Angelo asked. The idea of putting personal things on a computer made him shiver.

"No. I've been going through the documents from the Jonathan Aloysius flat."

Gina said, "And you've found something?"

"Jonathan Aloysius has an income. Or, more accurately, incomes. Every month seven deposits go into his account and only one is the salary from his job."

The room's door opened. David's head peeped around it. "Is he back yet?"

"Go to *bed*," Gina said.

David bowed with mock respect. "Yes, oh ancient one." He left.

"Cheeky," she said with a fond smile. "Go on, Rose."

"*And* eleven payments leave his account every month."

"Payments?" Angelo said. "For what?"

"Named people. No indication of what they're for."

"For how much?"

"About half the value of the non-salary deposits."

"Usually, regular payments ... " Angelo frowned. "They'd be mortgages or credit cards."

"There's a mortgage payment," Rosetta said. "And he uses a credit card but he pays that off each month."

"Hmmm."

"*And* he has five-figure savings. I can't tell where most of that money came from, though. During the period I have records for only a little has been added to savings."

"Low five figures? Not life-changing but ... " Angelo lifted his glass. "Enough to celebrate, from time to time. Here's to savings."

"Savings?" the Old Man said as he came through the door. "Savings I happily celebrate."

* * *

When Salvatore returned at 10.30 he found Rose, Gina, Angelo and his father waiting for him. "Wow. A welcoming committee."

Gina said, "David wanted to be here too. But I beat him with a stick and sent him to bed."

"What? No Marie?"

"I think she fell asleep learning lines."

"I bet David's listening outside the door," Angelo said.

"He'd better not be," Gina said. Then louder, "He'd better not be!"

"So," the Old Man said, "you told this Polly that her Aloysius Jack plans to kill her?"

"No, Papa. I just showed her the marriage and death certificates."

"And did she know about the other weddings?" Rosetta asked.

"The five additional wives were news to her."

"And their deaths," the Old Man said. "Don't forget their deaths."

"And, of course, she didn't know about them either," Salvatore said. "Jack told her he was a widower. Polly couldn't swear he ever *said* he'd only been married once. But even if he cloaked the words to avoid telling a literal untruth, she certainly feels that he has lied to her about all this."

"And misled her," Rosetta said.

"She must feel terribly betrayed," Gina said.

"So how did she react when you told her?" Angelo asked.

"She went quiet."

"A lot to take in."

"I offered to make her a cuppa or pour something stronger but she didn't want anything."

"Did you offer to stay and comfort her?" Rosetta asked, with raised eyebrows.

In fact Salvatore *had* offered to stay. But to his sister he said, "No, no." He wasn't proud of his willingness to take advantage of Polly's vulnerability.

"Tell me something else," the Old Man said.

"What, Papa?"

"All of these married dead women, they share a registrar ... "

"Beverley Norbury."

"But did they have the same death *doctor*?"

"Doctor?"

"To sign for the natural cause of these married deaths."

"I haven't had a chance to study the certificates for that." Salvatore looked at Rose.

"I didn't either," she said. "I concentrated on the bank records."

"Because," the Old Man said, "this certifying is well and good for history and for weddings that aren't white, but if Aloysius Jack was murdering them, he had to murder them past a doctor."

The others looked at each other.

"To murder them all past one doctor is one thing, but past six different doctors? That's hard, unless his method is perfect."

"Where are our copies of the certificates?" Salvatore asked Rosetta.

"In my room. I'll get them. But it also makes me wonder if any of the payments Jonathan Aloysius makes each month are to doctors."

"Payments?"

"Money he pays every month to different named people. We can compare the names with those on the certificates."

Angelo said, "Polly won't confront Jonathan Aloysius tonight, will she, Sal?"

"I don't think so. When I left she was going to take a sleeping pill. I asked her to ring me in the morning. It's not like she's in immediate danger. Unless he shows up at her door at midnight and drags her off to Gretna Green."

"Gretna Green wouldn't work anyway," Gina said. "He only gets married with his favourite registrar."

"Six wives, all dead?" the Old Man said. "Even the famous Henry VIII couldn't match Aloysius Jack for that."

***

Salvatore slept over in case Polly Mainwaring rang the office line in the morning. Although he *had* given her his mobile number and told her to ring at any time.

Before he went to bed, he and Rosetta went through the names on Appleby's bank records. None matched that of a doctor on a death certificate. And to answer his father's question, five doctors had shared the six causes of death, one having two. Salvatore couldn't think of anything unreasonable about that.

Less reasonable was Rosetta's asking what he thought of online dating sites. "Refuges of the desperate," he said immediately. "Does *anybody* post an up-to-date picture?"

"Really? That's what you think?"

But as Salvatore lay in bed in the morning he wondered if he had been too hasty. Only a bad brother would discourage a single sister from trying to find someone. A good brother would introduce her to his friends. If he had any friends who were male.

Salvatore shook his head and got up, although 7.30 was early for him. But Polly's call didn't come as the time reached business hours. Nor did it come as the day progressed.

All morning he sat sketching versions of Polly leaning over a desk while Gina and Angelo took turns being the agency person on duty. They also talked with Rosetta about whether they should buy a new range of micro cameras.

Just before noon Salvatore rang Polly's mobile. His call went straight to voicemail. So he rang Baum and Carteret and was told that she hadn't come to work.

"Is she ill?"

"I don't know," a young man said. "I know she rang in but that's all."

So, she was sufficiently alive this morning to make a call to work. But why not a call to me? Where was she and what was she doing?

Salvatore rang the Royal United Hospital and asked for the maternity ward.

"Putting you through to neonatal," the operator said.

Salvatore asked for Jack Appleby.

"I don't think he's in," a woman there said. Salvatore heard her ask someone nearby. "No, Jack's not in today. Can someone else help you?"

"Wasn't he scheduled to be in today?"

"Yes, but he called in sick."

Nothing too trivial, I hope, Salvatore thought. "OK. I'll maybe try him at home."

Which was an option. Salvatore still had keys to Jonathan Aloysius's flat. But should he just wait for Polly, or should he try to *do* something?

In all likelihood Polly and Jack were together, each having taken the day off work. And they *did* have things to discuss. Whether they would live happily ever after, or whether he was planning to murder her ...

But was Polly safe?

Probably. But ... suppose Jonathan Aloysius *was* a serial murderer, and suppose Polly had told him that she knew his secret. How would he react? And how would Salvatore feel if something happened while he was waiting for Polly to call?

He went to the kitchen. Angelo was heating something in the microwave. "A word, bro."

* * *

Jonathan Aloysius's flat was closer than Polly's so they went there first. After a perfunctory ring on the bell Salvatore used the keys and he and Angelo went inside.

Things appeared to be just as they were the day before. There was certainly nobody home.

So they headed for Polly's. But as they got out, Salvatore said, "I don't think they're here. At least he's not here. I don't see his car."

Even so they tried the bell. Nothing perfunctory this time. They rang several times without response. They tried the other flats' doorbells, hoping to be let in to try Polly's own door. But without response. Short of finding a ladder and looking through her windows there was nothing more to do.

"And now?" Angelo asked. "Someone where she works might know details of her family if she's gone to stay with them."

They might even track down Polly's family through the phonebook. How many Mainwarings could there be? But something else occurred to Salvatore. "Come on," he said.

He drove them to the registrar's office. Jack Appleby's red BMW convertible was in the parking lot.

With the waiting room unlocked, they went in. A sign asked visitors to take a seat but they heard voices in the registrar's office. A glance from Angelo asked if Salvatore recognized Polly's.

Salvatore nodded. He knocked on the door but opened it immediately and went in. Polly sat beside the registrar's desk, eyes puffy and hair every which way. Facing her was a man in his thirties – presumably Jonathan Aloysius Appleby.

From behind the desk a handsome older woman said, "*Please*, wait outside until you are called." Her tone was firm. Beverley Norbury.

"Polly," Salvatore said, "are you all right?"

Polly blinked a couple of times. Then she rose and rushed into Salvatore's arms. "No," she wailed. "I'm *not* all right."

* * *

"So where is Sally now?" Gina asked as Angelo told his wife and sister about his afternoon.

"Last I saw, he was leading Polly to the registrar's car park. But who knows where they are now."

"He fancied that one from the moment he met her," Rosetta said.

"He just left you there with Jonathan Aloysius and the registrar?" Gina said.

Angelo nodded.

"What did you do? Call the police?"

"As it happened, there was no need."

***

Once Polly was in the car Salvatore had suggested that they go to her flat. Her snuffling noises didn't sound like disagreement so that's where they went. When they arrived, she had her key out.

"Shall I come in, make you a cuppa?" Salvatore asked.

More snuffling. She left the door open for him.

"Sit yourself down," he said.

Polly sat on the couch that Salvatore had occupied alone the previous night.

"Tea?"

"Mmm." The sound was nearly a word.

In her kitchen Salvatore found the kettle and a canister with the word "tea". He managed to find the fridge even though it wasn't labelled. There was an open container of skimmed milk inside.

Remembering her order in the Assembly Rooms, he said, "You take milk, but do you want sugar today?"

"No."

An actual word. "Won't be long."

"I hate him," Polly said.

"What?"

"I hate him. I *hate* him."

***

Angelo said, "Let's invite Papa and Mama down to eat tonight."

"Will Sally be back by dinner time?" Gina asked.

Angelo shrugged.

Rosetta said, "Maybe he'll get lucky." When they're on the rebound, and someone like Salvatore is at hand, it could be days before he gets back. She didn't aspire to having whatever it was Salvatore had, but ten per cent would be nice. She shook her head.

"He won't be coming back, Rose?" Gina said.

"Dunno. Sorry." Then, "Do you want me to cook?"

"There are plenty of leftovers."

"Papa will want to hear how about the certificates," Angelo said. "He'll want to know if his murder is still the only one. He's probably going on to Mama about it right now."

Gina and Rosetta smiled. They could imagine.

***

Salvatore put two mugs of tea on coasters on the table in front of Polly's couch. "You're very kind," she said.

"Not at all."

"No, I mean it. *Very* kind."

She was more beautiful than ever. For a moment it took his breath away. He sat on the couch but kept to the other end. That said, the couch wasn't a big one.

***

"So," the Old Man said, "*no* murders?" He turned to Mama. "More chutney. I feel like chutney." The improvised meal offered more food than most of the family's specially prepared dinners.

"No murders, Papa," Angelo said. "Not even a little one."

"But all those dead wives," David said. "What killed them?"

"Cancer."

"*All* of them? But isn't *that* suspicious? What are the odds?"

Angelo turned to the table and spread his hands in invitation.

"Oncology," the Old Man said.

"Give the man his chutney."

"Oncology?" David asked.

"Jack Appleby worked in places where the patients had cancer. Having cancer's nothing like it used to be, but a lot of people still don't survive it, though they may not die quickly."

"So all the women he married had cancer already?" Rosetta said.

"Correct," Angelo said with a smile.

"He has a thing for dying women?" She scratched her head. "But Polly's healthy, isn't she?"

"Cancer was not the only thing his wives had in common." When nobody offered a speculation Angelo continued, "Each was relatively young – forties and fifties. And single – obviously. Each had one or more children. And each had a career with a good pension plan, one she'd paid a lot of money into."

He looked around the table, but they were all waiting for him.

"In every case, if the woman was single when she died, her pension would die with her. All the money she'd paid in would be lost. However, in each case the terms stipulated that if the woman was married, her pension would continue to be payable to her husband."

"He married them for their pensions?" Marie asked. "Cool."

"So," Rosetta said, "the six regular payments to Jack's bank are from the dead wives' pensions?"

"Exactly," Angelo said. "Pension payments that would have been lost if the women had died unmarried."

Gina said, "I see what was in it for Jonathan Aloysius but why did those poor women marry him?"

"Because Jack agreed with each of them to pay half the pension money to their children."

"Ah," Rosetta said, "the payments going out of his account."

"So there are eleven children currently getting money that would otherwise have been lost to them."

"So he didn't love his wives?" Marie said.

"No. It was entirely a pragmatic arrangement."

"Cool."

"And where does Beverley Norbury fit in all this?" Gina asked.

"She conducted the ceremony for the first wedding. When Jack went in to register Belinda Rogers' death and Ms Norbury sympathized, Jack explained why he wasn't grieving in the usual way. Then, when it was time for the second wedding, he went back to Ms Norbury because she already understood the kind of marriage it would be. Ms Norbury says she's certain nobody was taking advantage of anybody else. It was win-win."

"And so she became his personal registrar?" Rosetta said.

"In a way."

"But where does Polly fit in all this?" Gina asked.

"Jack met her when she came to the RUH to visit an aunt – an aunt who eventually recovered. And she and Jack fell in love. When that happened he transferred out of oncology."

"He didn't think to tell Polly about his marital history?"

"How do you tell a new woman that you've been married six times, always to women you didn't love who then died? It's not a chat-up line that's going to get you a phone number."

"But why didn't he tell her later?"

"He *said* it just never seemed the right time. And then he thought that if Beverley Norbury performed the ceremony, he might not have to tell Polly at all."

"But Beverley Norbury didn't *act* her part well enough," Marie said. "Acting is a special talent. So few people have it." She tossed her hair.

"Or Polly is unusually intuitive about people," Angelo said.

"Or," Mama said, "this registrar was really happy for this marrying young man who found love at last. Did you think of that?" She glared at Angelo.

"But," Rosetta said, "despite the innocence of it, despite the good that he did, Polly wasn't happy with the explanation?"

"He lied to her, at least by omission," Angelo said. "No, she was *not* happy."

* * *

When the meal was finished, everyone but Marie repaired to the living room to wait for Salvatore. Marie's mind was on other things.

"Would you like me to help you with your lines?" Gina asked her.

"No need. You carry on with your weddings and funerals."

But once in her bedroom she called a boy at school named Sam.

"Ullo," Sam said.

"Hi. It's Marie."

"Yeah, hi."

"I'm in the most awful fix. I hate to bother you but ... Oh, I don't know. Maybe I shouldn't ask."

After a moment, Sam said, "What fix?"

"It's my lines. Everyone at my house is, like, *totally* preoccupied with something else. I can't get anyone to test me, and to read opposite me. I know it's the most awful cheek to ask, but are you doing anything now? It's just, what with your living fairly close and all ... "

"You want me ... to come over?"

"Or I could come there. It's just that with your being in the lighting crew you *know* how awful the whole thing will be if I don't know my lines. And Ms Noodles-For-Brains will go mental if we don't rehearse without scripts by next Monday."

Sam chuckled and said, "Ms Noodles-For-Brains. That's good." And Marie knew she had him.

* * *

Salvatore's mood was bittersweet as he returned to the family home and headed up the stairs. Polly was in her flat, tucked in bed with a telephone, water and a banana on the bedside table. She was calmer, comforted by his attentions. Or the passage of time. Hard to be sure which.

Salvatore entered the kitchen as quietly as he could. His intention was to gather the overnight things he'd brought the day before and then go back to his own flat.

From the living room he heard laughter and speech. He listened, checking the voices. All the grown-ups except Mama. Well, he didn't really feel like going through it all, making what almost felt like a confession.

So he glided silently into the hallway that led to the bedrooms. There wasn't much to pick up. He got his things together and tiptoed back into the hall.

"Uncle Sal?"

It was David. "Nephew Dave."

"What happened with Polly?"

"She's fine."

"They were talking about it at dinner. Is she your girlfriend now?"

"My *what?*"

"That's what Aunty Rose thought. That you like Polly and now that she's not engaged any more you'd be making your move." David smiled. He even winked.

"Polly isn't my girlfriend and she won't be."

"Don't you want her to be?"

That was a painful question. "I think she'll get back with Jack."

"She will?" Wide eyes.

"It's not like he committed any crime, David." Except a crime against romance. That was not a small thing, but it was something one could be pardoned for.

"But he tried to hide all those dead wives."

"What he did helped him, but he also helped those women by making sure their children would be better off."

"Yeah, but he didn't *tell* Polly."

"And that was very wrong." Yes, Salvatore thought, a grown-up really does need to take responsibility for what he does and what he is. "And it was cowardly. But, as I told Polly, if you care *deeply* for someone ... If you think that person really *gets* you, and understands who you are underneath appearances ... That's very very rare, David. It's something your parents have, and it's something we all should aspire to. And it's not something to throw away lightly."

David didn't quite understand.

But Polly had. Salvatore had said, "Did you *really* feel that you connected with Jack before all of this? That he connected with you?"

Her response was instant. "Yes."

"That is not a trivial thing."

"But he lied to me."

"But he didn't *betray* you."

"No."

"And as soon as he fell in love with you, he switched wards."

"Yes."

"He stopped looking for another woman to marry because he'd found the woman he wanted for a *wife*. Someone he wanted to be a *real* husband to."

"Yes."

"You should at least talk to him, Polly. You should at least *try* to get past this."

"Yes," she'd said. Faintly. But then, with more resolve, "Yes, I will try. But I will *never* live on those poor women's money. Their children should have it all."

Polly would get back together with her Jack.

"So," David said, "aren't you going to tell everyone what happened? Because they want to know."

What Salvatore *wanted* to do was to go to his own place and space. He *wanted* to find a way to ignore the fact that Polly and Jack, Gina and Angelo, Mama and the Old Man all had something valuable. Something that he wanted. Something that he didn't have.

But to go home wouldn't be taking grown-up responsibility. "Yes, I'll tell them." Salvatore patted David on the head.

And when he caught a moment with Rosetta maybe he'd suggest they go speed dating together. It wasn't the same as an internet site but it was still a positive action. And at least with speed dating nobody could use a faked photograph.

BLOOD ISLAND

Barry Maitland

I WAKE WITH a jolt, a roaring in my ears. It takes me a moment to realize that it's the howl of jet engines. Dark cloud is rushing past the window by my shoulder, and then abruptly clears and I am looking down on a sea dotted with dozens – no, hundreds – of islands scattered like green confetti across the slate-grey surface. Now a landmass comes rolling into view, fractured and creased by inlets and rivers and more islands. The plane is dropping rapidly, and I can make out the roofs of buildings, farms perhaps or isolated houses, among the trees. But where is this? And then it comes back to me, my brain soggy with fatigue and jerlag. Sweden. Stockholm. And as if in response, the plane banks to reveal the red and brown roofs of a city spread out ahead.

I'm filled with a sense of unreality. Just how long ago? I check my watch, still on Australian time. Just four hours ago I flew into Heathrow, expecting my older sister Abbie to meet me at the airport. The plan was that I would stay with her for a few weeks while I looked for a job and got myself organized for a year in London now that I'd finished uni. She has been living there for five years already, doing well working for an art dealer with a posh Bond Street address. Only she wasn't at the airport. Instead there was a bloke holding a plastic carrier bag in one hand and a piece of cardboard with my name written on it in the other.

"Matt!" the stranger said, "Good to meet you. How was the flight? I'm Rich. Close friend of Abbie's. She sent me to meet you. Let's get a cup of coffee."

He led me to a café table and ordered two coffees. He was a Londoner by his accent, around thirty, but I couldn't remember Abbie mentioning a close friend called Rich.

"There's been a change of plan, mate," Rich said, stretching out his long legs. He had a smooth, confident air about him as if nothing would ruffle him. "Abbie had to go over to Stockholm on business, and thought it would be great for you to go and spend the weekend with her. You ever been there?"

I shook my head, feeling dazed after the long flight, trying to grapple with this new development. "No. First time out of Australia," I mumbled.

"Really? Oh, you'll love it, beautiful city, Stockholm."

"This weekend?" I tried to remember what day it was.

"Yeah. Your flight leaves in two hours. Not from this terminal though. Drink up and I'll take you over there."

"But ... " I rubbed my face in confusion. What I really wanted was a long hot shower and a change of clothes. "Right now? Another flight?"

"Just a short hop."

"Blimey." I looked at my suitcases, all the stuff Mum had insisted on me bringing, summer clothes, winter clothes, presents for Abbie.

"You can leave most of that with me if you like," Rich said, as if reading my mind. "Just put enough for a couple of days in your backpack. I'll take the rest back to Abbie's."

So he had a key to her flat. "Yes ... s'pose so."

I set about repacking my bags.

"Got a thick jacket?" Matt said. "Bit cooler up there."

It was the start of October, a warm spring back home, but autumn here.

When I was finished, Rich lifted up the plastic bag he'd been carrying. "And Abbie asked if you could take this to her." He handed it over carefully. It was surprisingly heavy, a solid slab of something, wrapped in brown paper.

"What is it, a bomb? Drugs?"

Rich gave a laugh, as if I'd just said something highly amusing. "No, no, just a book. An art book. Abbie needs it for reference.

Expensive, though, so whatever you do, don't leave it behind in the overhead locker, eh?"

For a brief moment I saw an anxious intensity in the other man's eyes, then he relaxed and grinned.

"No worries."

Later, going through the security checkpoint, an official asked me if I'd wrapped the sealed package myself, and I lied, just to keep things simple, and said that I had. It didn't seem to set off any alarms on the scanner.

And so here I am, looking down on a city spread out across a landscape of rivers and wooded islands, dropping towards Arlanda airport. I try to think what I know about Sweden: Abba, Volvo, IKEA, but mainly Stieg Larsson. The funny thing is that I've brought the third of his books, *The Girl Who Kicked the Hornet's Nest*, with me, and one of the movies they were showing on the plane from Australia was *The Girl with the Dragon Tattoo*. It almost seems as if this visit to Stockholm was pre-ordained. Kind of eerie really. I open my wallet and count the Swedish krona banknotes that Rich gave me in London, and read again the typed instructions for me to get to the hotel where Abbie will meet me. There is something definitely odd about all this, but perhaps it's just the jet lag that's making me feel disoriented.

When the plane lands I get my backpack and the package for Abbie from the overhead locker, remembering Rich's insistent instructions not to forget it, and make my way to the station for the high-speed train connection into Stockholm. While I'm waiting I ask at a kiosk for a map of the city, and of course they have a Millennium Map, showing all the locations that are featured in Larsson's three thrillers. Excellent. The train glides in and twenty minutes later I'm emerging from the vault of Central Station and walking out on to a broad avenue, giving a shiver as a gust of cold wind catches me. I open the map and try to work out the direction I should take when an elderly man stops and asks if he can be of assistance. He examines the note and says, "Ah yes. You want Gamla Stan, down there, across the bridge."

"Thanks a million!" I say.

He looks at me oddly. "Emilion? No, my name is Stieg."

I laugh. "Yes! Of course it is!"

He looks very puzzled as he walks away.

Gamla Stan is the oldest part of Stockholm, where the city began, on an island that looks on the map like a plug in the waterway that runs through the centre of Stockholm, connecting the Baltic Sea on one side to the freshwater Lake Mälaren on the other. As I walk across the bridge towards it my spirits lift. From all those Scandinavian crime series I'd watched on TV I expected the whole country to be shrouded in a gloomy twilight, but instead I see white ships bobbing on sparkling water, and golden-hued old buildings glowing in the sun beneath spires reaching into an azure sky, and I think how elegant and clean and beautiful it all is. My hotel is just beyond the Royal Palace, right on the cobbled stone quay. I run up the front steps expecting to see my big sister waiting in the lobby, but it's empty except for a blond hairy Viking sitting behind the reception desk.

"Good afternoon," I say. "Do you speak English, please?"

"Of course," he says, as if the question is insulting. "My name is Mikael."

Mikael Blomkvist? I almost ask, but stop myself in time. Perhaps he's not a Larsson fan. I tell him who I am and he nods as if he knows already. As I fill in a registration form I tell him that I'm expecting to meet my sister, but he knows nothing about that. Instead he pokes about behind his counter and comes up with a padded envelope with my name on it. He doesn't know how it got there. He hands me the keys and I take the lift up two floors to my room. As I'd hoped it faces out on to the quay, and I throw open the window and look out across the water to an impressive three-masted schooner tied up on the far side in front of an elegant white eighteenth-century mansion in a lush green park. I sit down on the bed and rip open the envelope and a mobile phone with recharging cable drops out. I switch it on and a text message appears on the screen: *dearest matt so sorry not here to greet u tied up on business 24 hours see u 2morrow noon in outer courtyard royal palace luv sis.*

I try to phone the sender number, but it appears to be switched off. Instead I text: *ok sis no worries luv matt.* The truth is that I am disconcerted, but there's nothing I can do. I decide to go for a walk up through the narrow winding streets of Gamla Stan, taking in the ancient buildings, the intriguing little shops – colourful children's clothes and Viking toys, antiquarian books, tourist souvenirs. I stop at a café for a burger and a beer and then wander back to the hotel, where I have a hot shower and collapse into a deep sleep.

I wake late the next morning and go downstairs for a smorgasbord breakfast in the hotel restaurant. When I return to my room I try to contact my sister again, but still her phone is turned off and there are no messages. Finally I decide to take a look at the mystery package I've brought over for her. I carefully undo the wrapping and find that, just as her friend Rich told me, it is a thick art book, of the drawings of Leonardo da Vinci. It looks expensive, with bright red leather covers and gold lettering. I rewrap it, put it into my backpack and set off to meet Abbie.

According to Mikael at the front desk, the "Inner Courtyard" is the parade ground behind the Royal Palace, where there is a changing of the guard every day at noon. He gives me directions, and I set off up the now familiar narrow streets of Gamla Stan. After a while I notice a girl riding towards me on a bicycle and as she gets closer I'm struck by her fierce expression and jet-black hair. To my startled eyes she looks exactly like Lisbeth Salander, the Girl with the Dragon Tattoo – or rather, like Noomi Rapace, the Swedish actress who plays her part in the movie. Struck by the resemblance I stand motionless for a moment, before being suddenly grabbed from behind and flung hard against the brick wall at my shoulder. I feel hands wrenching at my backpack, but the straps are tight and they are having difficulty. My arm feels as if it's being torn out of its socket and I give a yell. There are two men, shaved heads, black leather jackets, one pushing me to the ground, the other pulling at the backpack. I look up and see the girl on the bike swerving towards us and then crashing into us. One of the men screams, the other curses and the hands release me. Instinctively I scramble to my feet and take off, pelting up the street, around a corner, down a narrow laneway, and find myself suddenly in a crowd of tourists.

I'm gasping for breath, hurting all over, limping in one leg, but I still have the backpack. The crowd surges towards an opening and we find ourselves in a large semi-circular courtyard, surrounded by classical buildings. Ranks of soldiers occupy the centre of the space, the crowd packed around the edge, watching them, taking pictures. The soldiers are both men and women, in dark uniforms with white belts, gloves and spats, blue berets and long rifles. Orders are being shouted, and they march and do arms drill and exchange flags. They come to a halt and there is silence, and all the while I am frantically scanning the crowd, looking for Abbie. Where is she?

A bell chimes midday, and from the streets outside the square comes the sound of a military band approaching. Soon it turns into the parade ground, bandsmen in blue uniforms and silver helmets as brightly polished as their instruments, and as they stride across the granite sets I catch sight of a black leather jacket and a red-faced shaven head approaching through the crowd to my left. I turn to the right, and see the other one. They've followed me here! Surely they won't attack me in the middle of all these people? But then the crowd cranes forward and I get a clearer glimpse of the man on my right. He looks angry and there is the glitter of a blade in his right hand.

I stare at the knife in the man's hand as he closes in on me, imagining it rammed into my back, me falling and them running off with my bag before anyone realizes that something is wrong. There is a solid wall behind us and the parade ground in front. I really have no alternative. I take a deep breath and push my way through the crowd, jump over the perimeter rope and begin running across the open square. In front of me the band wheels around and heads straight for me. There are shouts, a roar of surprise and some laughter from the crowd as I find myself dodging through the instruments, knocking the big bass drum, and the bandsmen struggle to maintain their tune. Now I'm on the other side. There is a gap in the buildings ahead and I make for it as several soldiers run forward to cut me off. Looking back over my shoulder I see no sign of the two men trying to follow me. I charge on and just make the opening ahead of the soldiers and find myself in a narrow lane heading away from the palace and into the maze of streets beyond.

When I finally slow down I realize that this is not a random mugging and that I have probably only delayed the men who will still be after me. Where can I hide? Then it occurs to me that it isn't me they want, it's my backpack, and Abbie's book inside it, though why they should I can't imagine. Where can I hide it? Somewhere behind me I hear a shout and panic grips me. And then I see the antiquarian bookshop ahead of me. What better place to hide a book than in a bookshop? I rush in, the doorbell tinkling. There appears to be no one around, although it's hard to tell among all the bookshelves. Opening my bag I rip the paper off the book and shove it on to a high shelf in a dark corner. I grab another heavy book and ram it into my bag and run out into the street again, just as the two men appear at a corner, not fifty metres away. They give chase as I dash off, heading downhill. My leg is in agony now and they're gaining on me. Ahead I see the quay; I must turn left or right. I choose left, towards the city centre across the bridge. They are gaining on me. I dodge across the street, behind a car – a Volvo, naturally – with a ski rack on its roof, and as it passes I lob my bag onto the rack.

We come to a gasping stop, the three of us, them on that side of the road and me on this. Then they shout to each other and turn and chase after the Volvo. I watch it disappearing over the bridge, the two of them in hot pursuit.

I jog painfully back to my hotel and Mikael at the desk tells me that I've had two visitors, men in black leather jackets. My heart gives a jolt – they've been here, they knew where I was staying! I ask Mikael not to tell them I am here if they come back, and I limp up to my room and collapse on the bed. I try Abbie's number again without success and text her: *where the hell r u ive been attacked*. After several minutes a reply comes back: *where r u*.

I hesitate. Why doesn't she speak to me? How do I know this is Abbie? It could be anybody texting. I send another message: *prove u r abbie*. The answer comes back: *dodger 4 ur 10 bday*.

For my tenth birthday our parents bought me a Labrador puppy called Dodger. I breathe a sigh of relief and text back: *hotel*, and get the reply, *rich will come*. Rich, I think, why Rich? Why not you, Abbie? I'm almost tempted to go to the police, but I don't know if that would make things difficult for her. And anyway, they'd probably arrest me for disrupting the changing of the royal guard.

It's evening when Mikael rings up from reception. Someone called Rich wants to see me. I tell him to send him up. Rich is all concern for my troubles and makes soothing noises, but I'm not in a mood to be mollified. However, he's brought a bottle of Swedish akvavit, which is pretty powerful stuff, and after a couple of glasses I'm feeling a bit more relaxed and my leg hardly hurts at all. While we sip the firewater I tell him some of what's been happening to me. He shakes his head, looking worried.

"This is bad, Matt," he says, but seems hesitant to explain it to me.

"It's about that book you gave me, isn't it?" I prompt.

He nods reluctantly. "Yes." He looks around the room. "Is it safe?"

I haven't explained about the bookshop and the Volvo. "It is, but it isn't here."

"Where is it?"

"I'll tell Abbie when I see her, face to face."

"It's difficult, Matt. She can't get away right now. I'm here for her."

"Sorry. You'll have to do better than that."

So eventually he relents and tells me the story.

"In the last couple of years," he begins, "Abbie's role at the art dealer's where she works has been to go around the UK to auctions, regional dealers and house clearances, looking for bargains."

"Like *Antiques Roadshow*," I suggest.

"Yes. She's got a pretty good eye for it and she's been quite successful, though her boss, a pompous old git, hasn't recognized it in her pay. Anyway, a couple of months ago she came across an elderly lady who wanted her to look at a small sketch she owned, of the head of a bearded man. She'd inherited it from her mother, who'd been in service to an eccentric lord up in Scotland, and he'd given it to her when she retired. She assumed it was a portrait of one of his ancestors, and hoped it might fetch a hundred pounds or two. But Abbie had seen a very similar sketch once before, in Turin in Italy, a self-portrait by Leonardo da Vinci."

"Leonardo? You're joking!"

"No, I'm not. It looked very like the real thing and Abbie told the owner that it could be worth much more, possibly several thousands, but she would have to take it away to authenticate it. The old lady was delighted and agreed. When she got to London Abbie used all the expertise at her disposal and discovered a fingerprint embedded in the red chalk material of the drawing. She compared it to a fingerprint that had been found in da Vinci's painting of St Jerome in the Vatican, and got a match."

"Wow. What would it be worth?"

"Thirty, maybe forty million dollars."

I'm stunned. "Her boss must have been delighted. Will she get a good commission?"

"No, he doesn't give her commission, just her basic salary, maybe a modest Christmas bonus. And he wasn't delighted, because she didn't tell him."

"Oh?"

"Matt, this is a once in a lifetime discovery, a moment of truth. If she tells them, the old lady will get more money than she knows what to do with and will die next year and leave it all to the dogs' home, and Abbie's boss will stuff himself with even more big lunches and French champagne than he does already and have his coronary a little earlier than otherwise."

I'm not sure I like this story. It doesn't sound like Abbie at all. Has London changed her? "So what did she do?"

"She came to me for advice."

"And who are you, exactly?"

"I work for Scotland Yard, Fraud Squad. Abbie and I met during a forgery investigation last year, and got on well. When she told me the story I advised her to keep the Leonardo, give the old lady five thousand and buy a few extra paintings for her boss, and both would be delighted."

"Only five thousand?"

"Abbie wanted to give her more, but the old woman would have told everyone and word would have got back. Really, she was over the moon with that."

"You advised Abbie not to tell the owner that she had a multi-million-dollar masterpiece on her hands?"

Rich looks uncomfortable. "It was only Abbie's knowledge and expertise that made it that, Matt. I thought she deserved the profit, not the owner or her boss. Then I told her she had to find a special kind of buyer, a collector who wouldn't care about where it came from as long as the scientific tests proved authenticity, which the fingerprint certainly did. And I thought I knew of the perfect customer, a Swedish billionaire recluse by the name of Martin Gräven, who is reputed to have bought stolen artworks in the past. He lives on his private island east of Stockholm, on the edge of the Baltic Sea. It's called Blod Ö, which means Blood Island – apparently it was the site of a massacre during the Thirty Years War back in the 1600s."

I sit back, trying to digest all this. "So you're a cop with Scotland Yard, and you're helping Abbie to break the law?"

"It's only a technical breach, Matt, and like I said, this is a once in a lifetime chance for Abbie. She'll walk away with half the true value of the sketch and set up her own gallery and show the lazy bastard she works for."

"And what do you get out of it, Rich?"

"I'll be her business partner, mate, maybe more than that if things work out – I'm very fond of Abbie as it happens. And who knows, we'll probably need a bright lad like you to open an office for us down under." He gives me a friendly pat on the shoulder.

"But something's gone wrong, hasn't it?"

He frowns. "Yeah. I knew that Gräven had a reputation for being ruthless, but I hadn't counted on him being quite such a bastard. The problem in this situation is making a deal without anyone getting ripped off – I mean, you can hardly complain to the cops afterwards. So we decided that one of us would come to Sweden to negotiate with him while the other waited for the all clear. Abbie had to be the one to come over, because only she could convince him of the technical verification, but Gräven's made her a virtual prisoner on his island, and he seems to be very well informed about us, including our plan to have you smuggle the drawing into the country."

"You mean ... he's forced it out of Abbie? Tortured her?"

He hesitates. "I don't know. But I'm going to have to go to his island to get her out of there, and I can't take the drawing with me or he'll just take it and kick us out, or worse."

I'm appalled. "He'd go as far as murder?"

"For something like a Leonardo original self-portrait as good as this one, I reckon he'd do pretty much anything."

"Then give it to him!"

"First we have to get Abbie out, and the Leonardo is the only lever we've got. It's hidden behind the inside lining of the back cover of the book. You're sure you have it safe?"

"Yes. I had to hide it when those two thugs came after me, but I can get to it anytime."

"Then we've got to keep you out of trouble. You'll have to find another hotel."

"Right, and I can still keep in touch with the mobile phone Abbie left for me."

"Let me see that." He examines it. "You've had it on all the time?"

"Of course."

"That's probably how they've been able to keep tabs on you." He switches it off. "Come on, pack your things."

We go down to the lobby and pay Mikael, asking him to call a taxi for us. It pulls up at the door and we slip into the back and head into the commercial district across the river. The cab drops us outside a Vodafone shop where Rich buys me another mobile, and then we walk through the shopping streets until we find a small commercial hotel where I check in. We shake hands.

"Good luck," I say. "Give Abbie my love when you find her."

"Sure. Don't worry. You just wait for my call," and he strides away, leaving me feeling worried sick.

I don't hear from Rich again that day and the following morning I decide to go back to Gamla Stan to check on Abbie's book in its hiding place on the shelf of the antiquarian bookshop. On the way I call in at a department store in the centre of the city and buy a parka and a cap in the hope that the skinheads won't recognize me if they are still out there. It's another cold crisp day with dark clouds threatening the blue sky as I walk back across the bridge and up the cobbled streets of the old town. I turn a corner and there is the bookshop in front of me. A small crowd is gathered outside around a man wearing a fluorescent yellow jacket with the word POLISEN printed on the back. As I approach I see that the shop door is barred by a striped plastic tape. At the edge of the crowd I ask a woman what is happening, and she tells me that the old man who owned the shop has been found murdered, the place ransacked. I work my way to the window and peer in. The lights are on and I see two people in white nylon overalls inside. The word printed on their backs is FÖRMIDDAG, which I guess means *forensic*. Behind them the bookshelves seem undisturbed, and I can see the place where I hid Abbie's volume. But there is no red spine visible there now.

I feel suddenly sick, heart pounding. Without that book Abbie's life is forfeit. Should I speak to the policeman? Then I'm aware of a woman sobbing by my side, and when I look at her she says something in Swedish.

"I'm sorry?" I say.

"Oh, you're English? I said, poor Mr Palmgren." She wipes her eyes.

"You knew him?"

"I work here. It happened last evening, after I left. Mr Palmgren was alone in the shop. The bastards must have been after the cash box, but they didn't have to kill him, did they?"

"I am sorry. I came here yesterday and I saw a book I wanted to get. It was on the top shelf, a book of Leonardo's drawings, but I can't see it now. Maybe they took it."

"Oh, I remember the one. You're out of luck. I sold it yesterday afternoon."

"Really?" I feel a tiny glimmer of hope. "I don't suppose you remember who to?"

"It was to one of our regulars. She buys a lot of our books. Her name is Vera, Vera Kulla."

"Oh. I did want that book very much. Maybe she would sell it to me."

"Well, I suppose you could try. I may have her address ... "

I hold my breath as she rummages through her bag and eventually produces a well-thumbed address book. "Yes, here we are – she has an apartment in Fiskargatan. That's a street on Södermalm."

I take a note of the address and thank her and tell her again how sorry I am about Mr Palmgren. Then I hurry away to study my Millennium map of Stockholm for the address. The map pinpoints all the places mentioned in the Stieg Larsson trilogy, and I discover that many of them are located on Södermalm, a much larger island that lies just to the south of Gamla Stan. I head that way, crossing on the bridge that links the two islands and climbing up into the busy district of mixed commercial and residential buildings. Here my map takes me past Mikael Blomkvist's fictional apartment, and then along Götgatan to the offices of his *Millennium* magazine, where I turn off into quieter residential streets towards Fiskargatan, which my map tells me was where Lisbeth Salander bought herself an apartment in the second book, *The Girl Who Played with Fire.*

When I reach the block I press the entry phone button marked *V. Kulla* at the front door. After a moment a woman's voice says, "Ja?" and I give her my name and say I'd like to talk to her about the book she bought from Mr Palmgren. There's no reply, but the security door clicks open and I step inside.

I climb the stairs to Vera Kulla's front door. When it opens I'm astonished to see the girl on the bicycle who crashed into my assailants yesterday, the girl who looks so much like Lisbeth Salander in *The Girl with the Dragon Tattoo* movie.

I just stare at her, open-mouthed, and she steps back and waves me inside. I look around at the IKEA furniture, just like in Stieg Larsson's description of Salander's apartment.

She folds her arms. "Well?"

I say I want her to sell the book to me, and she raises a sceptical eyebrow. "Why should I?"

"It's a matter of life and death," I say. "Please!"

She stares at me for a moment, then tells me to sit down at the table. She brings two mugs of coffee and sits opposite me, lighting a cigarette and holding it up the way Lisbeth Salander would have done. She eyes me coolly. "Tell me."

I feel I'm going crazy and I blurt out, "Are you one of them? Are you working for Gräven too?" although as I say this I realize it doesn't make much sense.

I take a deep breath and try again. "Look, yesterday you rescued me by crashing your bike into two thugs who were trying to rob me. Did you follow me after that? Or were you in the bookshop when I ran in and hid the book on the shelves?"

She takes a draw on the cigarette and says nothing.

Getting angry now, I say, "So now I come here and meet you again, looking like Lisbeth Salander and living in her flat. Well, I'll tell you this – I wish you were Lisbeth Salander, because I could really do with her help right now."

She leans forward and says, "Tell me about Gräven."

So I do, I tell her everything, including about the Leonardo drawing. It's no doubt an impulsive and stupid thing to do, but I desperately need help and I feel I can trust her, although that is probably just the illusion of her fictional character.

When I finish she gets up and brings the Leonardo book to the table and we examine the lining of the inside of the back cover. Sure enough, it does look as if it may have something hidden beneath.

Vera closes the book. "Your sister is very foolish."

I start to protest, but she goes on, "Martin Gräven is an extremely dangerous man. People are afraid of him. It is whispered that he was behind the murder of our Prime Minister, Olof Palme, back in 1986, because Palme tried to put a stop to his crooked business dealings. No one has dared challenge Gräven since then. There are other rumours too, of people who go to his island and do not return."

She picks up a pen and doodles his name, MARTIN GRÄVEN, on a notepad, and as I watch her another unnerving thought comes into my head. "Martin *Vanger* was the name of the serial killer in *The Girl with the Dragon Tattoo*, wasn't it? It's an anagram – Vanger, Gräven."

"Very good," she says. "You think it's a coincidence? Stieg Larsson was a crusading journalist, very like his fictional character Mikael Blomkvist. Sometimes fiction and reality are hard to disentangle."

I shake my head in confusion and reach for the book. "Look, Vera, you understand now why I must have this. It's my sister's passport to freedom. I'll give you back whatever you paid for it, plus something for your trouble."

"But the problem is, how do you use that passport?" she says. "They will find you again, and when they do they will take the book and you will have no passport left. Better that you leave it here with me. Don't worry, I won't run off with it."

That does seem to make sense – I have no idea where else in Stockholm I can safely hide it, but can I really trust her?

"I saved it once before," she reminds me, and so I reluctantly agree to leave the book with her.

I leave and wander through Södermalm, always looking over my shoulder to see if I'm being followed. I come to the Kvarnen Bar, which my map tells me is where Lisbeth Salander met the girls in the rock band Evil Fingers, and where Mikael Blomkvist and his colleagues at *Millennium* magazine came for a drink. They seem like real friends now, and I go inside. The pub used to be an old high-ceilinged beer hall, now done up as a trendy café-bar with a dance floor and resident DJ, and is busy. I order a cup of coffee and find a quiet corner to check my phone. There are no messages and I text both Abbie and Rich but get no reply, and have a sick feeling as I remember what Vera said about people disappearing when they went to Blood Island.

When I return to my hotel I have barely stepped into my room when the phone beside the bed begins to ring. I pick it up and a man's voice says, "Hello, is that Matt?"

The voice sounds cultured, a Swede with a good command of English, a middle-aged man, I guess, quite relaxed and friendly.

"Yes, who's this?"

"My name is Dirch. I am Mr Gräven's personal assistant."

I stop breathing. "Oh?"

"We have some business to discuss, I think."

"Is my sister all right?" I blurt out.

"She is perfectly well, as is Rich."

"Let me speak to them."

"One moment ... "

There is silence on the line for a long while, and then, finally, I hear my sister Abbie's voice. "Hello, Matt. How are you?"

"I'm fine!" I cry with relief. "But what about you?"

"We're ... all right." She doesn't sound all right to me, but she goes on, "I want you to do what Dirch asks. Then we can go home."

"You're quite sure?"

"Just do what he says, please, Matt."

Dirch comes on the line. "Now Matt, I will pick you up this afternoon at five o'clock at the Museikajen quay beside the National Museum. It's just ten minutes from where you are now."

"How will I recognize you?"

"Don't worry, I will know you. And of course, you will bring the Leonardo book with you, yes? Five o'clock. Don't be late."

When we ring off I call Vera and tell her what's happened. She tells me I shouldn't go to the island, and definitely shouldn't take the book, but I tell her I have no choice, and finally she agrees to meet me at her flat in an hour for me to pick up the book.

At five o'clock I am standing outside the front steps of the National Museum. It is almost dusk, and the streetlights have come on above heavily wrapped pedestrians scurrying against gusts of a bitter east wind. The last tourist boats are returning to their berths in front of the Grand Hotel and a Baltic cruise liner is moving slowly out across the darkening water. I feel lonely and far from help.

"Matt? Hello, I am Dirch." I turn to see a very tall man with a severe, bony face surmounted by a crop of pale blonde hair. He peels off a black leather glove and offers his hand, which I shake cautiously. His face splits in a wide smile. "You see, we are friends. And you have the book?" He nods at my backpack.

"Yes."

"Good, follow me."

He leads the way to one of the piers jutting out into the water, and I see a powerful motor launch waiting there with a man in a skipper's cap at the wheel. We climb aboard and roar away across the bay. Gradually the spaces between the islands become wider and the lights of the suburbs more distant, until, as night closes in, they become isolated points in the dark. The water becomes rougher, the wind sharper as we bounce out of sheltered waters into the Baltic. I bow my head against the freezing spray and cling to the rail of the boat and try not to think the worst.

After half an hour the boat swings suddenly to port and throttles down, and I see the flash of a navigation buoy ahead. The captain speaks into a radio, and lights appear in the darkness, illuminating a jetty. The two men help me up onto the timber decking, and Dirch and I walk towards the land, a dark mass of foliage and rock.

"Welcome to Blod Ö," he says softly. I smell the brine of the sea mixed with the decay of autumn foliage.

A black 4WD is waiting for us, and I recognize the driver as one of the two skinheads who attacked me in Gamla Stan. He gives me an ugly smile as we get in. It's hard to make out much more than tree trunks and rocks in the headlights as we climb up a steep hillside. Then the view opens out to a large mansion with a portico of classical columns framing a front door at which we pull to a halt. Inside a uniformed manservant takes my coat and cap, but I hang on to my bag.

Dirch leads me to a sitting room, where a log fire is blazing in a hearth. He offers me something to warm me up, coffee or something stronger, but I decline, saying I just want to see my sister. He nods gravely and says he will arrange it and leaves. I wait by the fire, trying to thaw the chill in my bones, and then the door opens and Abbie comes in and we rush to each other and hug with relief.

I think how haggard and disoriented she looks, and I wonder if they have been giving her drugs. We sit in front of the fire and clutch each other's hands and I ask her if they've hurt her.

"I'm all right, Matt, really."

"You don't look well, sis."

"It's nothing, just lack of sleep. They won't let me sleep, you see. It's their way of making me come to terms. It's amazing how obliging you become after a few days without sleep. But I'll be all right now. You've brought the book?"

"Yes, but how do we know they'll let us go after we give it to them?"

"They don't want to keep us here. We have agreed a price, and once they have the drawing they will pay me and we can leave."

"How much?"

"Fifty thousand."

"But it's worth millions!"

"It's enough, Matt. I just want this to be over."

"What about Rich? Is he here?"

"Yes, we spoke when he first arrived." Abbie frowns. "He became angry and said I shouldn't agree to their terms, and they took him away and I haven't seen him since. But they've promised to let him leave with us."

I don't like the sound of this, but there's not much I can do, and as if he's been listening to our conversation, which he no doubt has, Dirch opens the door and says, "Well now, we will conclude our business and let you go home to your nice warm beds."

"Will we meet Mr Gräven?" I ask.

"Of course. He is most anxious to be present at the final transaction. Follow me."

I don't much like the sound of *final transaction*, but we do as he says, me taking Abbie's arm when she seems unsteady on her feet, bumping into the doorway.

He leads us along a corridor and down a staircase into the basement, very different in character from the upper floor, with clinical white walls and fluorescent light fittings, like a laboratory or a morgue. Dirch opens a door for us into a large room lined with workbenches on which a variety of high-tech equipment is set out – computers, special lamps, and an elaborate microscope. A man in a white coat looks up from a keyboard and comes towards us.

"What is this place?" I ask.

"This is Mr Gräven's art conservation laboratory," Dirch says. "We shall be able to examine your drawing under perfect conditions here. Ah … "

We turn to see Rich being pushed roughly into the room by the two skinheads. He looks terrible, his face swollen and bruised, one eye completely closed, his hands cuffed in front of him. He gives me a wry grin and a wink with his good eye.

A pair of double doors on the far side of the conservation room open and the manservant comes in pushing a wheelchair in which sits the hunched figure of an old man with a tartan rug spread across his knees. The pair come to a stop and the seated man peers up at me intently. It is an unsettling experience, as if he is trying to look inside my head. The two sides of his face don't quite match, and I guess he has had a stroke.

Dirch goes to the seated man and bows to hear him murmur something in a hoarse whisper. Dirch nods and turns to us. "Mr Gräven is impatient to view your merchandise. Shall we proceed?"

The man in the laboratory coat draws on a pair of white gloves and comes towards us. I open my backpack and give the book to Abbie, who lays it on the bench in front of us and opens it at the back cover.

"The drawing is inside a protective envelope beneath the lining of the cover."

She indicates to the technician, who runs his fingers across the surface, feeling for the extra thickness beneath. He nods and fetches a scalpel and tweezers, and begins delicately peeling back the lining. We are all focused on his work, holding our breath as the white envelope is revealed. When it is free he picks it up carefully and carries it reverently across to Martin Gräven, whose divided face has taken on a greedy, predatory look, and pulls a trolley out from beneath a bench and positions it in front of Gräven, then places the envelope on the surface, opens its flap with the tweezers, and slowly slides out the contents. For a moment no one speaks, then everyone starts talking at once. With a shock I recognize the thing lying there on the trolley, and it isn't a Leonardo self-portrait. It is the cover of a paperback book, *The Girl with the Dragon Tattoo*.

As the cries of consternation and anger die away, everyone turns to stare at me. I'm speechless.

Then Gräven spits a stream of Swedish at Dirch. Gräven has

gone pale, trembling with anger. He gives us one last furious glare and the manservant wheels him around and propels him out of the room. Dirch is speaking to someone behind us, and we turn to see the two skinhead thugs standing there. They grab hold of Rich and me and drag us out into the corridor, followed by Dirch and Abbie. Abbie is calling to me, a desperate cry, "Matt, what have you done?" We are bundled into another room, where Rich and Abbie are pushed on to steel chairs against the wall. A third chair is dragged out into the middle of the room and I am shoved down hard on to it. One of the skinheads stands with Rich and Abbie while Dirch and the other confront me.

"Now," Dirch says, "you will kindly explain."

I watch the thug at his side pull a set of brass knuckle-dusters out of his pocket and fit them to his large right fist, and I quickly begin talking.

"After I got away from these two at the changing of the guard, I ran into an antiquarian bookshop and hid the book on a shelf there."

"Yes," Dirch nods, "we worked that out."

"You killed the owner, didn't you?"

He waves his hand impatiently. "Get on with it."

"The next day I returned to retrieve the book and found the police there. I spoke to one of the shop assistants, who told me she had sold the book to a regular customer, and gave me her address. I went to see her, and told her the whole story, about the Leonardo drawing and everything."

"What?" Abbie cries in disbelief.

"I thought she seemed trustworthy, and I had no one else I could turn to for help," I continue desperately. "She warned me that Martin Gräven was a very dangerous man, and I agreed to leave the book with her until I knew what was happening. She must have opened the lining and taken the drawing."

I hear Rich give a groan, and Abbie sobs, "Matt, how could you be so stupid!"

"Be silent!" Dirch snaps.

I can see from the dark scowl on his face that Dirch is having difficulty believing my story.

"It's true, I swear."

"So, who is this woman, what does she look like?"

"She looks ... exactly like the face on the front of that book cover – Lisbeth Salander. Her name is Vera Kulla, and she lives in an apartment on Fiskargatan, on Södermalm."

Dirch draws back, his face stony, and when he speaks his voice is ominously quiet. "You must think we are very stupid. In the second book of the Millennium Trilogy, *The Girl Who Played with Fire*, Lisbeth Salander bought an apartment in Fiskargatan ... "

"Yes," I stammer, "I know, but ... "

He cuts me off. "She bought it using an assumed name – V. Kulla."

I'm stunned. "I ... I didn't remember that ... "

He shakes his head sadly. "You are determined to make things difficult for yourself, Matt. Do you think you are a tough guy, eh? Did you think you would impress your sister? Why don't you tell him, Abbie, tell your idiotic young brother to stop playing these games."

"Yes," Abbie sobs. "Matt, please, this is madness. Tell him where the Leonardo is!"

"She must have it," I whisper, "Vera Kulla ... "

Dirch gives a grunt of disgust and turns to the skinhead with the brass knuckles and gives him a nod. The man draws back his fist and I close my eyes.

There is a sudden commotion, a crash, I open my eyes again and see Rich on his feet, gripping his steel chair like a club and swinging it at the men who are stumbling away from him. "Run!" he cries, "Run!" and I realize he's talking to me. I leap to my feet and shove past the startled Dirch and dive for the door, out into the corridor, turn right, run, then skid to a halt as the manservant appears at the corner ahead of me. I turn back but Brass Knuckles is out now and coming for me. Then a door in front of me opens and the technician peers out, wondering what the commotion is. I shove him back inside and follow, locking the door behind me, and stand there gasping, looking around me.

This is a different room, dark walls, ceiling and floor, subdued pools of light focused on a series of images hanging on the walls.

It is an art gallery, I realize, Martin Gräven's private collection, and one of the paintings catches my eye. I have seen it before, in an art book, a portrait of a young man with extraordinarily long arms and a red waistcoat, rendered in the broken brushstrokes of Cézanne. Looking around the room I see other paintings which, although I don't recognize them, are in the style of famous artists – a Rembrandt over there, a Picasso surely, and doesn't that look like a Vermeer?

My attention is interrupted by banging on the door, the handle being rattled. I look around, my eyes becoming used to the dim light, and I realize that there is no other exit.

The technician has backed away, staring at me with wide nervous eyes. Then a voice sounds over some kind of intercom. I recognize Dirch.

"Matt, you are being very stupid. Open this door at once."

"No," I call back loudly. "I don't think so."

"That room is equipped with a fire suppression system that sucks out all the oxygen and floods the space with carbon dioxide. If you do not open the door I will activate it and you will be suffocated."

The technician looks alarmed and calls out, "No, no! Nej! Behaga!"

I notice that he still has his instruments in the top pocket of his coat, and I leap at him and snatch the scalpel. I call out to the invisible speaker, "Please don't do that, Dirch. Your conservator here would be very upset, and so would I. And I have his scalpel, and before I die I'll slice the Cezanne to ribbons, and as many of the others as I can, too."

There is a lengthy silence during which I try to work out what my options are. It feels as if I'm playing chess with just one pawn left and my opponent with all his pieces intact. Finally I walk across the room to the Cézanne and say to the technician, "All right, open the door."

He does it, and Dirch is standing there flanked by his two heavies. I raise the blade of the technician's scalpel to the surface of the painting and tell Dirch to get Abbie and Rich. He makes a move forward, into the room, and I jab the tip of the blade into the canvas. He gives a horrified gasp and hesitates.

"Do as I say, Dirch."

He turns abruptly and whispers to the skinheads, who disappear. In a moment they return with the other two. One of the men hands Dirch something and he grabs hold of Abbie's hair and pulls her into the room.

"Well now, Matt," Dirch says. He is trying to remain calm, but he is breathing very heavily. "Here is Abbie, and here ... " – he lifts up his hand – " ... is *my* scalpel." He presses it to Abbie's throat. "Now let us examine the logic of this situation. If you do not sur-render I will cut your sister's throat. What good will it do you then to damage that painting? Which is more valuable, the painting or your sister? Now be a sensible fellow."

He nods one of the skinheads forward, and there is nothing I can do. I hand him the knife and he takes it carefully and then slams his fist hard into my stomach. I double up in agony and through the pain I hear Dirch say, "We could have so easily done a deal. But now, thanks to your stupidity, that is impossible." Then the skinhead hits me again, and again. I pass out to the sound of Abbie screaming.

I come round to find that we are slumped together on the floor of a small room, like a prison cell. They have obviously roughed Rich up some more and he looks as bad as I feel.

"Are you all right, Matt?" Abbie whispers.

I mumble a yes. Trying to clear my brain, I remember the last words I heard. "What did he mean, that it's impossible now to do a deal?"

"Because we saw the paintings," Abbie says. She sounds exhausted and resigned.

"What do you mean?"

"The Cézanne *Boy in a Red Vest* was stolen from a gallery in Switzerland in 2008. The Rembrandt seascape, the only one that he ever painted, was taken from a Boston museum in 1990, along with the Vermeer, which is reckoned to be the most valuable painting that has ever been stolen. And it's the same for all the others – they're all masterpieces that have been taken during the past twenty years and never been traced. He can't let us go now that we've seen them here."

I groan. "What do you think they'll do with us?"

By way of reply, the door opens and Dirch comes in. "There is a 200-metre deep trench in the floor of the Baltic Sea some fifty kilometres south of here," he says. "Many unwanted things end up down there. Come, it is time to go."

We are hauled roughly to our feet and marched up a flight of stairs and out into the cold night air, hands manacled. They lead us across a gravel yard and we pass a truck being loaded with heavy concrete weights, each with a chain attached. We reach a path that descends steeply through woods towards the muffled roar of the sea breaking on a rocky shore. When we reach the foot we see their boat tied up against the jetty. The skinheads prod us forward, and we obey, shuffling like sheep to the slaughter. Then something comes out of the darkness from the trees to our right. I catch only a glimpse of it before the first skinhead drops to his knees with a strangled cry and falls flat on his face. The second whirls around and there is a sudden crackling noise and he too gives a scream and falls, and I see Vera Kulla standing behind him with a Taser gun in her hands.

"Come on," she says urgently, and begins running across the rocks into the trees. Behind us on the path, Dirch, who was bringing up the rear, has retreated and is shouting back up the hill for help. We rush after Vera with our bound hands and come to the small dinghy she has pulled in among the rocks. In silent panic we slip and stumble across the wet boulders and fall into the boat and she starts the outboard and we set off.

It is a tiny boat, and with four of us in it the choppy waves spill over the side and drench us. For several minutes we are alone in the darkness, sawing at our ropes with a knife Vera gives us, but then we see a beam of light to our stern, searching for us. Being so low in the water saves us for a while, and the light veers away to starboard, then swings around, sweeping, probing, until finally it catches us. We look back like dazzled rabbits as it fixes on us and grows brighter as their more powerful boat narrows the distance; all except Vera, I notice, who is staring fixedly ahead. I turn to see what she is staring at, and make out a great shoal of rocks and reefs jutting out of the water ahead, picked out by the spotlight. I remember seeing all this from the air as I flew into Stockholm, the sea scattered with thousands of tiny islands and outcrops of rock.

Vera heads straight for it without slowing down and I grip the side of the boat tight with numb fingers, certain that we will crash at any moment. Now we're into the shoals, swinging wildly from side to side as jagged rocks jump out of the darkness ahead of us. Again and again the aluminium hull scrapes and thumps against outcrops, the engine howling. After ten heart-stopping minutes of this, Vera abruptly throttles back. I realize that the light from the pursuing boat is less bright, and keeps losing track of us. "They're not coming into the rocks?" I ask Vera, and she nods grimly. She weaves the boat more slowly, further and further into the shoal, the visibility almost nil as the light behind us fades. For perhaps an hour we move cautiously through the maze, until finally the stretches of water become more open, and I notice a glow of light in the sky up ahead – Stockholm! It is another hour before Vera reaches the city and tucks the boat into a mooring between dozens of others and, shaking with cold and cramp, we climb ashore. We are at the western end of Södermalm Island, she tells us, about three kilometres from the city centre to the north, and the same distance to the apartment in the eastern part of Södermalm where I visited her.

"I have a friend here who will shelter you for tonight. It isn't safe for you in Stockholm. Gräven's people will be searching for you. What's wrong?"

She says this to Abbie, who is staring at her, seeing her in the light for the first time. "You *do* look like Lisbeth Salander," Abbie says.

Vera shakes her head impatiently. "Tomorrow you must leave."

"Yes," Abbie agrees. "We'll catch a flight to London."

"Not from Stockholm, they'll be watching for you at the airport and the Central Station. First thing tomorrow my friend will drive you down to Helsingborg, where you can cross over to Denmark, and catch a plane or a train back to England from Copenhagen."

She has brought us to the door of a small house, where there are three doorbells. She rings one of them and an Asian girl answers. "This is my friend Miriam," Vera says, and says something to her friend in Swedish. Miriam gives us a big smile and we stagger thankfully into a small apartment, blissfully warm and welcoming.

One by one we have hot showers, and Miriam dresses our wounds and gives us hot soup. Abbie is so exhausted after having had only brief snatches of sleep for a week now that she immediately falls into a deep slumber in an armchair. Rich and I talk to Vera for a while until we too are overcome with exhaustion. Rich asks her if she will inform the police about Gräven and his collection of stolen paintings, but she shakes her head. "There's no point," she says. "Even if the police agree to get a warrant they will find nothing. One day Martin Gräven will face his punishment, but not over this." There seems something personal in the way she says this, but she refuses to elaborate. Rich nods and closes his eyes and soon he too falls asleep.

Then I say, "I have to thank you for saving our lives, Vera. But you put us in danger in the first place, by removing the Leonardo drawing."

"No, Matt. You did that by insisting on taking the book to Blood Island. Gräven was never going to let any of you go free, it was too risky for him. All I could do was follow you out there and wait for my chance."

I feel very naive and tell her so, thanking her again.

"Actually it's your sister and Rich who were naive," she says. "Very naive to think they could negotiate with Gräven. They should have known – Rich especially – that such a man doesn't negotiate with people like us, he just gobbles us up."

"So, the Leonardo?" I say.

"Ah yes, the Leonardo … "

***

It is strange that not once on our return journey to London do either Abbie or Rich mention the Leonardo drawing, and I put it down to their sobering realization of how utterly, dangerously naive their get-rich scheme has been. And maybe a sense of shame too, for Abbie at least, that she could have contemplated such a fraud.

It's not until we are safely inside her flat that Abbie finally says, "Well, Matt, I hope your extraordinary friend has more luck with Leonardo's drawing than we did." And that's when I open the backpack Vera gave me and take out the Scandinavia road atlas inside, and open it to the Stockholm page to which a white envelope is taped. I hand it to Abbie and say, "This time, sis, do it right."

The next day Abbie takes the drawing in to the gallery where she works and shows it to her boss, together with her report authenticating it as a genuine lost Leonardo da Vinci self-portrait. He is, naturally, astonished and overjoyed. So is the elderly lady who owns the drawing, when it realizes thirty-two million dollars at auction three months later. So also are the numerous friends, charities and dogs' homes to which the lady promptly gives almost all of the money. And so too is Abbie when her boss, on the strength of her coup, makes her a partner in the firm.

I'm pretty happy to get a job as a barista in a coffee bar in Covent Garden, and I'm happy too that we see less and less of Rich, who seems to be losing interest in Abbie. He was never right for her, and I say so in my emails home to Mum and Dad, though of course I don't breathe a word about Sweden and Blood Island, which increasingly seems like a distant and unreal nightmare. I do think about Vera Kulla quite often, and wonder who she really was.

A week after the auction, Abbie receives a postcard at her gallery with a Swiss stamp on it, postmarked Zurich, from the Foundation E. G. Bührle in that city. It shows a famous painting, *The Boy in the Red Vest*, by Paul Cézanne, and on the reverse a text explains that on 10 February 2008, four paintings worth $162.5 million were stolen from the Bührle collection. Eight days later two of the paintings were found in a car in a nearby hospital car park, but the remaining two, the Cézanne and a Degas, have never been recovered.

Beneath this text is a hand printed message.

To Abbie and Matt, Take care now.

FEST FATALE

Alison Bruce

GETTING DRESSED WAS my first mistake. I chose high heels, an angora sweater and a black pencil skirt. I imagined the event would be glamorous and I wanted to stand out amongst the authors whose books I'd so avidly read. I should have known better: the area behind the bookstall was cramped with no ventilation and nowhere to sit. Every time there was a rush of customers I found myself raking around in the stock boxes beside the sales counter. It was another tiny space and I found it impossible to be down there without my skirt riding up and my knees scraping on the carpet ... not that I'm averse to a bit of *that* in a flash hotel, it's just not the position I usually end up taking in front of so *many* strangers.

No one took any notice of me in any case, it was like being a spectator at a huge love-in; authors, fans and books with only eyes for each other. Even Dan and Chloe from the bookshop were ignoring me.

I tried a bit of lame conversation. "It's hot in here."

"Mmm," Chloe managed.

Dan grinned with the kind of sickly enthusiasm that I've only seen from religious nuts and new mothers. "It's creative energy."

He turned back to dear old Chloe like those three words were inspiration enough. Wow.

I caught a muffled round of applause and knew that the doors leading from the main seminar door were due to open. I grabbed a copy of the nearest novel and the festival programme then dropped to the floor and crawled behind the banqueting cloth skirting the nearest table.

Dan's answer was right, but he'd missed the whole point of my irritation. I'd volunteered to work at this event so I could meet these people, learn more about the writers behind the words and get tips on how I could fulfil my own authorly ambitions. I'd worked with Dan and Chloe for three years and doubted they knew my last name, never mind guessed that I had created a trilogy featuring my tattooed axe-wielding detective, Vance Thorn. There would be agents and publishers here. I was damned if I was going to spend the whole time standing behind a shop counter.

So for the next two and a half hours I hid under it instead.

The book I'd grabbed was Joli Brown's latest. I'd chosen it for the cover; her protagonist, Jack, had a tattoo of a rose and a skull on his right bicep. I was about forty pages in when I noticed the toe of a man's brogue poking under the table cloth. I stopped reading. He was talking. There was tension in his voice.

"How are people supposed to buy it if they're not even aware that it's been released?"

"Everyone's in the same boat." It was a woman who answered. She was gravel-voiced with that old-fashioned forty-a-day grittiness to her tone.

"No, they're not; I see adverts for books on tube posters, magazines, bus stops even … "

"That's different, top-selling authors command a bigger advertising budget."

"So the rich get richer? Great, it's the same old story."

"Trevor."

"No. No. I'm not listening to any more of your attempts to make me settle for less than *Scalped* deserves. It's a great book and if the sales don't reflect that, it will be your fault for failing to give it a fighting chance."

R. V. Bold was the author of *Scalped* and I didn't remember selling a single copy.

I put my book away then and quietly opened the event programme. It was R. V. Bold's debut novel, "following the exploits of a Victorian barber turned sleuth through the poverty-stricken East End of London". Nope, not my cup of tea either …

I stayed under the table simply because the toe of R.V.'s brogue was still pointing in my direction and I didn't fancy getting exposed as an eavesdropping skiver. Then he started talking again and I just couldn't resist listening.

"Richard!" He sounded like he was calling to someone at the other end of the room but the answering voice came from close by.

"Trevor. I'm glad I've caught you."

"Oh good."

I could feel R. V. grinning. It seemed like the same sort of inane grin as Dan's.

"No, it's not, actually," the other man replied and I could tell he wasn't grinning at all. "Why in Hell's name have you published under the name R. V.? I'm R. V., I have been R. V. for ten books. In fact I've been R. V. since birth. Richard Victor, and you're Trevor. Trevor what?"

"Just Trevor."

"Then use J. T., not bloody R. V. when R. V.'s mine. And you didn't stop there, did you? Did you come up with the surname Bold so you'd sit next to me on the shelf? R. V. Bold, R. V. Bolton, it's like a sick merger."

"It's a compliment. We thought you'd be flattered."

"Getting your shitty reviews posted against my name's no compliment. And who is 'we'?"

"Monica and I ... "

"Monica? Our editor? It's bad enough that we're with the same bloody publisher without her handing my identity over to some deranged stalker."

R.V. 1, that's Trevor R. V., took a step closer to the table. I could see both of his shoes now and the tablecloth swayed as he backed up. "Sorry," he muttered.

"Sorry? You'll both be sorry. Between the two of you you've murdered my reputation. She planned this; why else would she have published your pitiful excuse for a novel?"

I had a pen in my skirt pocket. I took it out and began scribbling notes on the back of the programme.

I knew of Monica Daws, of course – everyone who's anyone did. Even I hadn't managed to escape her sharp words. Monica was the dynamic and charismatic crime editor from Page Force Publishers. I should have guessed it was her when I heard her husky voice. She was forty-something, a ripe-busted brunette with long legs and a ruthless streak. She sounded like Honor Blackman and in her day had probably looked like a Bond girl too.

One of her most celebrated rejects was Tom Monroe, author of *Cut and Shut*. After finding success with a rival publisher Tom Monroe had commented, "A face-to-face rejection from Monica was like being whipped by a beautiful woman; painful but not totally unpleasant."

She had countered with "I'm delighted that Tom has had some success *at last*, he will be able to pay for the kind of attention that he hoped to receive from me."

And so the public spat continued until Tom's book hit number 1 in the bestseller list and Page Force's books filled the rest of the top five. As they say, no such thing as bad publicity ...

With a crick in my neck and numbness creeping up my legs I was just about to abandon my position when I heard Monica's voice again. "Neil, Scarlet ... "

Neil Wilson and Scarlet Barton.

I ignored the numbness and prepared to take more notes.

I wrote more in those two and a half hours than in any other writing day I've had. If I'm honest a full writing day for me includes making sure my desk and chair are ergonomically efficient, eating a nutritious and unrushed breakfast, choosing "mood" clothing for inspiration, dealing with any pressing emails, post and phone calls and having a mid-morning drink and snack to keep me going until lunch.

I couldn't wait to get back to the bookstall the next morning – this was a perfect working environment; I'd be tucked away, making notes and being paid by the bookshop *at the same time*.

It was heading towards elevenses before Chloe and Dan stopped fiddling with the displays on the top of the desk. I had a fresh pad ready and two new Biros; perhaps they sensed I was up to something.

Dan went to the gents and Chloe finally spoke to me. She scowled and said, "What's up with you this morning?"

"Nothing."

"You keep fidgeting."

"I do not," I argued but realized I was shifting my weight from one foot to the other.

"Suit yourself," Chloe muttered. She sneered, shrugged and turned away in one deft move.

I lifted the hem of the table cloth, bobbed under then pulled the pad and pens in after me. For one moment I thought the move had been too slow and clumsy, that Chloe would drag me straight back out again. In the next moment I didn't care.

I wasn't alone under there. Monica Daws sat at the other end of the crawlspace. Her wrists were tied to each table leg and she was gagged with a scarf. She was leaning against a couple of boxes of books, wide-eyed and staring straight at me.

Her lips were purple and a polished ballpoint pen protruded from her heart. I'm no medical expert but she didn't look well.

I scuttled back out, dragging on the table cloth and knocking a pile of first editions on to the carpet. Shit, things were getting bad.

Dan was back and Chloe just stared at me. Customers stared at me too. I felt strangely calm, oddly aware that all hell was about to break loose the second I spoke. I looked at the table then back at the faces staring at me and in that moment I was lost for words. And really inappropriately I thought *I've got writers' block*.

So I screamed then screamed some more.

Chapter 44

I'd first seen DCI Wilde about an hour after I'd found Monica's body; I think he may have spoken to me but I don't remember. We'd all been kept at the hotel and now two days later he'd gathered everyone together in the main conference room. I looked around; there were authors, their agents, publishers, hotel staff and me, Dan and Chloe.

DCI Wilde started with an introduction for those that hadn't met him. The fact that he looked like Brad Pitt c. 1995 helped everyone pay attention.

"Obviously I seem very senior to be involved in every mundane facet of this investigation, however I have delegated all the boring elements in the knowledge that whatever I look into will ultimately be relevant to the conclusion. It's a talent I have." He surveyed the audience. He was about six four with a rich voice and an American accent. He seemed to read my mind. "Sure I sound like a native New Yorker but my parents were English and I only followed them back to the UK after I'd served three years in the Bronx. It gives me this kinda Transatlantic perspective, my boss calls it my unique selling point."

By this time the assembled authors were riveted.

"My intention today is to bring you up to date with the investigation and to unmask the culprit. But firstly, and only because you are crime writers and I'm a fan, I'm going to reveal the suspects. At the risk of using a cliché, 'The killer of Monica Daws is in this room.'"

He paused, as if waiting for an audible intake of breath, but let's face it, we'd all heard *that* one before.

He cleared his throat to fill the silence.

"Some of the most warped and devious minds belong to crime writers and there are a few here who have particular reasons for wanting Monica Daws dead."

He turned suddenly, pointing to a frosty-looking blonde in the front row. "Scarlet Barton, witnesses have heard you complaining that Monica failed to provide publicity for your book and you felt humiliated when there were none of your readers at this event." That drew a sharp intake of breath but Wilde barely paused, switching his attention to the man next to her. "Neil Wilson, your advance was so small that you begged Monica for more money, saying you couldn't afford to eat properly."

I saw several other authors nod in agreement.

"And" he continued "you, R. V. Bolton, feel that Monica Daws encouraged R. V. Bold to change his name, stealing your identity.

You've lost your race to stand out from the crowd now, haven't you? But then let's look at the other R. V., R. V. Bold aka Trevor Stout. You've battled for years to see your first book in print only to discover that no one's ever going to hear of it, or you. You're as anonymous as ever and you lay the blame for that at Monica's door, don't you?"

A few people looked at one another in shock, but most of us knew how tough it was to get into print.

"And finally, bestseller Tom Monroe. Why would you want to see Monica harmed? Your public sparring has helped you both, you have given each other great commercial success and yet ... " DCI Wilde paused and everyone held their breath. Here was Tom Monroe, bestselling author, the man we all wanted to be. Why would he want to jeopardize it all to kill Monica? "You have writer's block," Wilde announced. "You complained that you'd run out of ideas and Monica ridiculed you, laughed in your face, didn't she?"

As one we looked at Tom Monroe. He nodded.

The atmosphere was taut with shock and I knew that everyone's thoughts were with Monica.

What kind of evil person doesn't sympathize with writers's block, for God's sake?

With a flourish of notes Wilde went for his closing speech. "Monica Daws is dead, and at least one of you can identify the killer. This person is wicked, a twisted individual who deserves to have their civilized façade taken down in the full glare of the media, who will stand in court and be found guilty of murder, the worst of all crimes. Then it will be life in prison.

"Prison."

DCI Wilde took a step backwards and ran his gaze around the room. "Not the prison in your books but real prison, full of real criminals, all the first-hand research you can dream of, and an abundance of time in which to write it. You'll lose your independence, your social life, you'll have a routine of eating and sleeping and earning a fiver a day with nothing to spend it on but the next ream of paper. And anything you publish will cause outrage, every newspaper in the country will eat you for breakfast. Do not protect this person, they deserve the full weight of the law and … "

He never completed the sentence. There was a flurry in the front row as Scarlet Barton tried to stand. Neil Wilson was grabbing her arm, trying to pull her back into her seat. She was shrieking something I couldn't make out at first, then from the other side of the room Tom Monroe yelled, "I did it, it was me."

Scarlet and Neil replied as one, "No, I did it."

But they were outdone by the two R. V.s. R. V. Bolton shouted "I'm sorry, I'm sorry" and held out his hands to be cuffed while R. V. Trevor went for the more theatrical sobbing of "I never meant to do it. It was an accident."

Research, publicity, the excitement of publishers and paid time to write: DCI Wilde had painted a very rosy picture. I was tempted to confess myself, but as I really *had* done it I just slipped away through the back door. I had a book to finish.

THE GIFT

Phil Lovesey

EVERYONE ALWAYS TOLD Mary she had "the gift"; family, friends, even astonished strangers. And in the face of such relentless, overwhelming pressure, who was she to doubt it? Right from the start, in those first few moments when she'd picked up crayons and pencils and began scribbling on just about any surface that would take an infantile image, the shocked praise and quiet admiration had begun. But only "infantile" in terms of Mary's age – the pictures themselves, whether rendered on paper, walls, old envelopes, even white household appliances, were really quite something; special, accomplished, far in advance of her tender years.

Mary's parents, quick to recognize such an early blossoming talent, encouraged their daughter as best they could, making frequent trips to the local art shop to buy paint sets, felt-tip pens, pads and boards for the youngster to use. As an only child, they could afford to spend a little extra on her, and besides, as Mary's father often said, the art materials were an investment. Who knew how famous she might be in the future? Paintings sold for thousands of pounds. If Mary continued to excel artistically, she could keep all of them very nicely indeed. Already they were saving a fortune on Christmas and birthday cards, Mary's handmade efforts easily better than the shop-bought options.

Plus, word was getting round. One or two neighbours already had framed Mary Collins pictures in their houses, and her art teacher was quick to recognize and encourage Mary's talent in secondary school, resulting in a series of first prizes in local and regional art competitions.

Art college followed, together – unfortunately – with Mary's first rejection. The Slade and the RCA didn't want to know. This was the mid-nineties, and pop stars, East End barrow boys and drunks from seaside towns were being propped up and supported by the media as the blossoming new face of Brit Art. Mary Collins just didn't fit the bill, didn't have the necessary depressing childhood, the wild and experimental adolescence deemed necessary at the time. Mary Collins, it was decided, although a talented artist in herself, was just too boring, dull and suburban for a world increasingly peopled by the bizarre, ridiculous and outrageous.

At twenty, Mary met Steve, a decorator from Slough, and a little over a year later, the two of them moved into a small starter-home they could just about afford, with his decorating work and her job as a sales assistant in the local art shop. She still painted, but as Steve was sometimes a little too quick to point out, he made far more rolling vinyl-silk on to walls than she ever did painting "poxy little flowers" on canvas.

As the credit-card debts grew, Steve helpfully suggested Mary get another part-time job. He'd seen an ad in one of the local newspapers, something about "them wanting arty people to help prisoners".

That word "arty". Mary shuddered at it, with the connotations of all things vapid and sensational that she'd come to despise about her talent.

However, a few days later, intrigued and more than a little bored with simply selling watercolour sets to pensioners, Mary sought out the ad and began thinking that maybe this really was one area in which she could use her skill and earn some extra money, too. The following day, she applied for the post, was accepted, underwent six months' paid training and became – as her lapel badge now proudly declared – "*Mary Collins – Visiting Art Therapist*" at the nearby prison.

Even though HMP Berryfield was a women's open prison, housing mainly low-risk, category C prisoners at the end of their sentences, for Mary this was a dangerous yet strangely fascinating new world. Often teased by Steve for her "wide-eyed, bloody naiveté", Mary felt the new job was as much of an education for her as it was to provide therapeutic help for the inmates. Indeed, Mary's only previous encounter with anything remotely unlawful had been when she'd shoplifted a sable brush as a shamefaced teenager. The shopkeeper at the time, confronted with the crying girl, had let Mary off with a stern warning, making her promise never to break the law again, or the police and her parents would be informed. It was enough for Mary, and ever since she'd led the perfect law-abiding existence.

But now, approaching her mid-twenties, with little sign of Steve ever going to pop the question, marry her, have kids and settle down, Mary Collins was getting increasingly restless, as her suppressed adolescence pushed its way through the constraining veneer of respectability that had held her prisoner for so long. Now was the time to experiment a little, live a bit, pull the blinkers away, search and use new experiences and – who knows? – maybe even kick-start her art again after so many years.

Those first few sessions at HMP Berryfield couldn't be counted as an instant success, by any means. Mary had more yawning prison wardens in her class than inmates, as she struggled to combine the elements of comfortable conversation with artistic expression.

"The point," her training instructor told her, "isn't to create some kind of exhibition of the prisoners' work. No, it's to gently lead them to explore their own feelings, emotions and fears through a combination of experimental therapies and artistic interpretation."

"But what if," Mary had countered, "they simply want to paint?"

"I'm sorry?"

"I mean," she'd continued, feeling slightly stupid, "suppose they're really good artists, and they simply want to paint again? Just for the joy of it?"

The instructor had given Mary the same look Steve so often did, usually as she asked him to explain a particularly disturbing news item to her. "My dear," she was slowly informed, "it's vital that you always remember that these people broke the law. They're inside to pay a debt to society, not to be indulged with whatever creative whims they have."

The next session, however, proved more fruitful. Whether word had simply got round the female prisoners that doing art on a Wednesday afternoon was a good doss away from the otherwise mundane prison routines that merged one dull day into the next – or that Annie Morgan was going to attend – is up for debate. The result, however, wasn't. When Mary arrived in the brightly lit recreation room that particular afternoon, there were eleven new classmates smiling expectantly. Most sat in pairs behind the uninspiring tabletops, either with friends or wardens; all except Annie Morgan herself, a solitary, glowering, imposing figure who sat by herself in the far corner of the room.

Imposing mostly because of the sheer physical size and condition of the woman. Close on twenty stone, Mary reckoned, lank grey hair hanging like a pair of musty plastic shower curtains on either side of her face. A formidable pair of cold blue "stay well away from me" eyes seemed to stare right through Mary as she introduced herself and the aims of the classes to the others. For the rest of the afternoon, however, as Mary got to know the other inmates, gently guiding them through the rudiments of pencil sketching a tabletop still-life of some seashells, Annie Morgan simply busied herself with her own painting, using her own paints in the far corner of the room. Whenever Mary approached, those steely eyes warned her well away.

"Well," the chief warden asked her as she helped put tables and chairs away after the session had finished, "what did you make of our Annie, then?"

Mary paused, then said, "She's quite scary, isn't she?"

The warden smiled. "What, our Annie? Harmless, she is. Keeps herself to herself, mostly. Won't talk to the others. Just stays in her cell. Paints most of the time. Guess that was what made it so special this afternoon, having her here with the others. Quite a big step for our Annie, was that."

Mary recalled the woman, the scowling glare, and wondered just how "harmless" she was. "What's she … ?"

"In for?" the warden replied. "Double murder."

Mary almost dropped the chair she was carrying. "Murder?"

"A double. Two of them. Her old man and her sister."

"Her sister?"

The warden nodded. "Annie came back from work and caught the two of them at it in bed. Her bed. Caved their heads in, then covered them in petrol and burnt the bodies right there. House went up in flames."

"My god."

"Then she went straight to the police and confessed. Famous case at the time. Early seventies, it was."

"Before my time," Mary apologized, feeling slightly nauseous. The room felt too hot now, the thought of that monster woman sitting in the corner, just silently painting, the revelation of what she'd done … just dreadful.

"Got two life sentences, she did," the warden continued. "Served the first fifteen years in a maximum-security psychiatric unit. Then another ten years as Category A in Hull, before finally, they sent her down here to us. Didn't think she was a risk any more. They wanted to let her serve out the last of her time in a more productive environment."

"What do you mean, not a risk any more?" Mary asked.

"The shrinks in Hull assessed her, took her previous conduct into account – she's been the model prisoner, has Annie. Never caused any trouble, just likes to paint, that's all." The warden walked to the door, then stopped, turned, paused. "Only weird thing about Annie," she said, "is that bloody picture of hers."

"What about it? She wouldn't let me get close enough to even see it."

"She needs to trust you," the warden explained. "She's nearly seventy, spent the last twenty-five years inside. She's not going to suddenly let you see her closest possession. They reckon she's had that painting with her ever since she was on remand awaiting trial. Part of Annie, it is now. But give it time, Miss Collins, and who knows, maybe one day she'll let you see it."

Steve was watching the match on Sky when Mary got home. She cooked, and over supper told him about Annie Morgan. To her surprise, he didn't go and watch the finish of the game afterwards, instead booting up the computer and spending up to an hour on the Internet, as Mary dutifully tidied the small house.

"Gotcha!" he finally exclaimed, as she set down a cup of tea beside the keyboard. "Annie Morgan."

Mary looked at the screen, saw the news article from the archive website, a younger, slimmer Annie Morgan being led in handcuffs from the Old Bailey into a waiting police car after sentencing. A crowd of photographers and jeering passersby filled the background of the grainy news photo. "That's her, yeah?" Steve asked. "Your murdering pyromaniac?"

"I think so," Mary replied. "I mean, she's much younger. But, sure, I think that's her."

Steve was scrolling down, busy reading the text. He gave a low whistle, then turned to Mary. "Oh my love," he said, smiling. "We could have really hit gold here. Big-time."

Mary pulled up a chair, sat beside him.

"Says here," he went on enthusiastically, "that Annie Morgan was one of the coldest-hearted killers the judge had ever met. Says that in all the people he tried, he'd never come across a defendant who was so calculating or vicious." Steve pointed to a paragraph. "Seems that she had this job cleaning up at this big country house in Derbyshire somewhere. Been doing it for years. Well thought of, she was. The owner of the place couldn't praise her highly enough."

"Only when she was up there ... "

Steve sniggered. "Her husband was doing a bit of French polishing of his own."

"With her own sister," Mary quietly added.

He turned to her, gave her the "look" again. "What, you feel sorry for this woman? God's sake, Mary, thousands, millions of folk have affairs. Point is, most people don't murder them and burn the bloody house down, do they? Woman's a nutcase. Says here she bludgeoned them both to death with a hammer, then set fire to the place. Psycho, she is."

"Not any more. She just paints," Mary replied, lost as to why she felt it even remotely necessary to defend the woman. After all, Annie Morgan had hardly been the perfect student with her hostile attitude, and no one could deny that she'd done the most heinous thing. Maybe Mary did it simply to annoy Steve, his cocksure bloody know-it-all attitude, the way he was practically salivating over the monitor screen. She'd seen him like this before, most often when he had another one of his "schemes" in mind.

She watched as he scrolled down further.

"But here's the kicker, Mary," he said. "Seems her old man was a right mean type. Known for it in the area. And guess where he kept all his money?"

"Under the bed?"

"You got it, love. In an old suitcase, apparently. Like a bloody cliché, isn't it? But yeah, he stashed his cash under the bloody bed. Thousands of it. Your demented friend Annie Morgan even admitted as much in court." He read on. "Now according to her confession, she comes back from the cleaning job early, catches her old man and her sister in the bedroom, does the deed, then calmly walks away from the blaze and goes back to the big old country house to confess to some copper that was always hanging around up there." He turned to her. "'Sweird, isn't it?"

"Maybe she knew she'd get caught," Mary suggested, trying to picture the bizarre scene. "Perhaps she wanted to make a clean break of it. Couldn't bear to go on the run."

"But guess what the forensics people discovered when they went through the ruins of the fire?"

Mary shrugged.

"Underneath the burnt-out bed, they found the charred remains of the suitcase. And inside and surrounding it? Newspaper. Little bits of neatly cut and bundled newspaper. The same size as the old ten-pound notes."

"I don't follow you."

Steve rubbed his forehead, exasperated. "God's sake Mary, how dense are you? Think about it. Annie Morgan comes home early, kills her husband and sister in an insane jealous rage – then gets the cash from under the bed and replaces it with cut-up newspaper, hoping it would be destroyed in the blaze. But the fire brigade put the fire out too early, so the suitcase and some of the newspaper still remained." He turned to her, looked her intently in the eyes. "She nicked the money. Don't you see? Killed them, then up and offed to the manor house to hide it somewhere before turning herself in to this copper that used to hang round there. It's flamin' obvious, isn't it?"

Mary tried to think. "But in her trial – they must have mentioned the missing money? I mean you said she told everyone about it. She confessed to killing them, setting the fire. How did she explain the money turning to newspaper?"

Steve scrolled back up, reread the relevant section. "She told them that her husband must have found a new hiding place for it, worried someone would find it. She told the court he must have been giving a fair whack of it to her sister during their affair."

"That's possible, isn't it?"

Steve gave up, "God, Mary, you're just so ... bloody naive, woman! Think about it! Why bother setting fire to the bodies if she was going to confess to killing them anyway? The reason she torched the place was to try and burn the suitcase, make it look like the cash had gone up in flames, too." He took a large, loud slug of tea. "I reckon she thought she'd only get ten years max by confessing, playing the spurned wife. Then when she's released, she nips back to the manor house and retrieves the loot. Simple as that."

Mary turned, walked away from the computer, muttering, "Maybe it's not me that's the naive one round here."

He was up from the seat and on her in an instant, whirling her round to face him. "Listen, love. Do you see how big this is? Just say I'm right, and she stashed all that cash – what a story, eh? All you have to do is find out."

She was aghast. "What?"

"You know, get the old girl's confidence through that arty stuff you do. Get her to tell you where she hid it."

"*If* she hid it in the first place."

"It's the only explanation that makes sense," Steve insisted. "Why go back to the manor house after setting the fire? I reckon she buried it in the grounds or something. Then she goes looking for this copper to turn herself in, thinking the evidence back at her house is destroyed. But the fire brigade get there quicker than she expected, so she makes up this cock-and-bull story about her husband giving money to her sister." His grip tightened on her forearms. "But if he's really done that, why bother putting bits of cut-up newspaper in the suitcase? From the sound of it, he was a right git – he wouldn't have given a stuff if his own wife had discovered there was money missing. See what I'm saying – it had to be Annie Morgan who switched the money."

"And you want me to find out?"

"Makes sense, doesn't it? You're the woman's therapist, for God's sake."

Mary's head began to swim. The whole thing was bloody ridiculous! "Steve," she insisted, "I've only met the woman once. And I really didn't think she took that much of a shine to me. Besides, it's all wrong. Morally and professionally wrong. Can't you see that? God's sake, I can't use my job to discover inmates' secrets. It's unethical. I'd be fired."

He nodded. "Perhaps. But say she tells you where she stashed it. I mean, we're made, aren't we?"

Mary laughed at this. "Oh, I see. Annie Morgan tells me she buried the lot underneath the bloody croquet lawn, and we pop round later that night and dig it all up? Christ's sake Steve, this is really lame, even for you. That money's got to be nearly twenty-five years old. Even if it was there, the notes have all changed. How the hell do you think we'd spend it?'

He released his grip, smiled. "We're not going to spend *her* money, love. Oh no. We're going to spend the money we get from selling the story to the papers. Just imagine, they'll pay thousands for the exclusive. TV cameras will be there to film it being dug up. Christ's sake, it could even be a bloody movie – *Morgan's Missing Millions*." He gave her a short hug. "Like I say, love, I reckon we've hit paydirt here. You simply need to dig around a little bit, then we unearth the big one."

Regardless of her own distaste and scepticism, Mary couldn't deny that Wednesday afternoons took on a curious new significance from that point on. Annie Morgan continued to attend, always sitting solo at the same corner table, always painting the same picture.

"All her sentence she's been working on it," the warden quietly informed Mary. "Paints the thing, then whites it out and starts all over. She's never used another canvas as far as I know. I think it goes back to her time in the psychiatric unit, the staff only permitting her the one canvas that she had to reuse. Sad. I guess. Just a sort of habitual behaviour, now, endlessly repetitive. Like one of those big old bears you see in a zoo, always pacing over the same sorry circuit."

Gradually, however, as weeks progressed, Mary found herself able to get a few steps closer to Annie before being halted by the familiar icy glare, as if the distance was being controlled by the older woman, as if Mary's progress into her territory was a result of Annie's tolerance, rather than any of the "therapy" Mary offered other inmates.

"She's learning to trust you," the warden observed one afternoon. "Very few of us have got as close as you have without Annie kicking off. You've obviously got the gift, Miss Collins."

It's true that Mary felt empowered by these words, and also honoured to be allowed within six feet of the woman. For, repulsed as she was by the crime, Mary was also drawn to Annie Morgan – the conundrum of her existence, the many unanswered questions that surrounded this huge, unkempt, yet meticulously painting woman. For she did paint continuously, regardless of the noise and commotion in the room. And by the look of it, had indeed been doing so for years, on the small canvas now layered nearly an inch thick with built-up paint. Picture after picture, Mary supposed, laboriously slaved over, then, the moment she considered a piece finished, out would come the chalk-white oil paint, and Annie Morgan would obliterate the work, allow it to dry and begin again on the fresh surface.

Steve, of course, had his own theories about the painting. To him, the case of Annie Morgan had become something of an obsession, so convinced was he that a fortune lay buried somewhere deep within it.

"Just think," he said one night as they lay in bed together. "All those pictures painted on the same bloody canvas by some nut-job. I mean, it's got to be some sort of confession. Like, maybe, clues as to where to find the money. That's all she does, is it, just paint?"

"Yeah," Mary answered, sick and tired of his speculation. "Because she enjoys it."

"But over and over – on the same bloody canvas? That has to be significant, doesn't it?" He rolled over, thought for a while, then said, "I want you to get it, bring it home."

"What?"

"Tell her you need it for a course or something. She's nuts, she won't know the difference. Get it, bring it back here. Then get the mad old crone a new one. Say the old one got spoilt or something. Just get the thing here. I'm willing to bet everything we have that there's some kind of clue in it."

"No way!" Mary protested. "And besides, she takes it everywhere, even back to her cell."

"Exactly – which just proves she's obviously got something to hide, eh? Just be a good girl, Mary, and get that bastard painting. We can sell it to the papers. They've got these infrared cameras that can see through paint layers. It'll make us a fortune."

"No. It's hers. It's private."

"Yeah, and it's our chance of a ticket to a better life, Mary. Just you remember that."

The breakthrough came after eleven weeks. Glorious Wednesday, Mary would later come to call it, the day Annie Morgan finally spoke to her.

"You enjoy your work, Miss Collins?" were those first six, unexpected words.

Mary reeled in shock, partly to even be addressed by the woman, but more so at the soft, educated voice.

"Yes," she cautiously replied. "I think I do."

"And you paint yourself?"

"When I have the time."

Annie Morgan smiled at this. "Time. Well, I've had plenty of that, Miss Collins." And with that, she carefully packed up her paints, brushes and precious, thickly laden canvas and took herself back to her cell.

Gradually, over the following few weeks, to both inmates' and prison staff's amazement, an uneasy friendship grew between the two artists, with Mary even allowed the hallowed privilege of having a cup of tea with Annie in her cell after the Wednesday session had finished. It was, Mary realized, very one-sided, the older woman ceaselessly asking questions about Mary's childhood, her home life, her relationship with Steve. And although the cell door remained open, and a warden never too far away, it was, Mary felt, an intensely private experience.

One Wednesday the prison governor told her why she permitted these "visits". "Annie has no one," she explained. "No friends, no family. And although she's technically up for parole later this year, there's severe doubts about her health."

"Oh?" Mary said.

"She had two massive heart attacks last year. Refuses to lose the weight, take care of herself. Really, Miss Collins, it's just a matter of time for our Annie. And whilst your visits might be a little unorthodox, I think Annie's earned the right to have tea with a friend every week, don't you?'

The news came as a shock. "Thank you," was all Mary could say.

Mary broke up with Steve just a few weeks later. His continual insistence, insane schemes and emotional bullying finally became too much, even for previously mild-mannered Mary. After a huge row, he left, vowing to "stay over with a proper girl I sometimes knock about with from time to time". The revelation didn't come as much of a blow to Mary, more of a relief that he'd be out of her life. Mostly, she pitied the "proper girl".

She thanked Annie when she next saw her, telling the old inmate that she'd never have had the courage to cause the row in the first place if Annie hadn't advised her to do so.

Annie smiled, nodded, yet seemed older, slower. "Well, he sounded like a right rum lot to me, dear. You're well shot of that sort, believe me."

And then, without prompting, Mary told Annie of her ex's madcap ideas, the research into the crime he'd done, the obsession with the missing money, the almost daily insistence that she steal Annie's precious canvas.

Annie gently laughed, looked over at the picture, its pride of place on her small table. "Well, he was one idiot who added two and two and made fifty-five, Miss Collins.'

"Five hundred and fifty-five," Mary added.

"He really thought I'd buried my husband's money up at the manor house? Preposterous!"

Mary nodded. "He wasn't the brightest colour on the palette." She paused, not knowing whether to ask the next question.

Annie sensed the hesitation. "And now you have something to ask me?"

"Is it OK?"

"Fire away, Miss Collins."

"Why did you go back there, to the house, after you ... ?"

"Killed them?"

Mary nodded.

Annie smiled, seemed to drift back through time to a better place. "To see the constable, Miss Collins. The one who was always hanging around. I needed to confess, after all." She looked over at the ageing canvas, heaped with years of paint, then back to Mary. "Promise me this one thing. If you have the chance, then you'll paint again, Miss Collins."

"I'd love to, but ... "

She put a finger to her lips. "No buts, Miss Collins. Too many of those. I've lived a life of them. I did a truly terrible thing, and have paid the price ever since. Now, I simply want to hear if there's no 'buts' from you."

Mary took a breath. "*If* I had the chance," she slowly replied, "then there's nothing more that I'd like to do than paint."

The old woman nodded, her eyes suddenly tired and heavy, yet also seeming to glimmer and shine with something that Mary hadn't seen in Annie Morgan before – contentment.

Annie Morgan passed away three days later – another prison

suicide. At the end, she had decided to take final matters into her own hands and used a bed-sheet and gravity to take her from this world into the next. On her bedside table was a sealed, handwritten envelope addressed to "Miss Collins", together with Annie Morgan's old canvas, both of which were given to Mary by the governor after the funeral.

"Sad," the governor observed, handing her both items. "All there is to show for a life is a load of paint on an old canvas. Still, it's yours. She wanted to leave it to you as a gift. Not quite sure what you'll do with it, though."

Mary took the treasured canvas in her hands. The last picture Annie Morgan had painted before her death was a crude likeness of Mary herself, painting in a vast studio, sunlight streaming through wide, imaginary windows. At the bottom, the title – *The Gift; for Mary, from Annie.*

Back home, Mary placed the picture gently on the mantelpiece and opened the letter:

Dear Miss Collins,

Well, dear, here's the picture your repulsive ex-boyfriend wanted so much – together with a few answers he'd have craved even more.

Strange though it is to admit, however, he did get a few things right. After disposing of my husband and sister, I did indeed take the money from underneath the bed and replace it with torn-up newspaper before setting the fire, then returning to the manor house.

Why did I go there? Not to bury it, but instead to give it to the owner, a sweet and caring old woman who needed it far more than I. One of those classic cases, Miss Collins, a large house doesn't necessarily mean a massive income. She loved the place, couldn't bear to sell it, but was being forced to sell the antiques and old paintings simply to meet the upkeep. I gladly gave her the money after telling her what I'd just done. Shocked though she was, she reluctantly took it – our secret. Remember, at that time, I was convinced everything would be destroyed in the fire. I had no idea those damned burnt newspaper fragments would be found.

On remand, whilst I was awaiting trial, she came to visit me and gave me this small, white, unframed canvas, which I instantly recognized by its dimensions. It had hung in the main hall, largely unnoticed, but was a favourite of mine ever since I'd begun work in the house. She'd taken it down, removed it from its frame, carefully painted over it in white, then passed it on to me as a gift, together with some paints. Seen as harmless by the authorities, I was allowed to keep it, and began a series of paintings from that very day, each one layered over the next, until you see the final bizarre monstrosity that I leave you now.

I assume she thought I'd be shown mercy from the courts and receive a much lighter sentence, and could therefore use the painting in the future. However, that was not to be. I got two life sentences, and she died long ago, but always knew I treasured her gift, took it wherever I went, never let it leave my sight.

And now, Mary – it's yours. My "time" is done. Some will say I took the cowardly option, and maybe they're right, but in our hearts don't we all have choices? Mine is to end my life as and when I see fit. We've talked about yours, Miss Collins. Given the choice, you'd rather paint. Now you have that choice. Do with this gift what you will. However, it might be rather rash to take your ex-boyfriend's advice and sell my story and this picture to the papers. Trust me, there are no maps, there is no money to find. Any money was spent many years ago.

Although, it might interest you to know more about "the policeman that hung around the manor house" that I was so eager to see on the day of the murders. Like I said, he was a constable. A John Constable – the picture in the hallway, the one you now have, my gift to you.

Interesting, isn't it, what happens when we peel away the layers and reveal what's underneath? I suggest a very mild turpentine solution to start with. Good luck, Mary, and please: for me, my former employer and even Constable himself, enjoy your painting.

In appreciation,

Annie Morgan

THE SKIN WE'RE IN

Matt Hilton

COUSIN BILLY WASN'T happy, and he told me.

"I'm no happy, Alec."

His voice was nasal Glaswegian, the same accent I'd tried for years to lose. Brought me too much trouble this side of Hadrian's Wall.

"Everything will be OK. Trust me."

He gave me the look, eyebrows steepled, tip of the tongue just peeking from beneath his protruding front teeth. "Trust you, Alec? It's because I listened to you that I'm in this shite in the first place. You told me to stand up to him and all that got me was a death sentence."

"Don't worry." I showed him the Browning pistol. "This time things'll be different."

"That's what I'm no happy aboot."

"I'm not gonna use it. I'm only gonna show them it so they know we mean business."

"And what then? What if they dunnae listen to you? Are you gonnae use it then?"

I didn't have an answer for him. "Just quit worrying, will ya? You're making me nervous now."

"So let's just get the fuck oota here and forget all about them."

"Here" was in my beat-up Volkswagen Golf, just across the street from the hangout of the man Billy was so terrified of.

"Can't, Billy. We do that, we'll never be able to walk these streets again."

"Won't be walking anywhere if Gardy kills us."

I laid the bullshit on thick. "So go to your grave with your honour intact. I'd rather be a dead hero than a living coward."

"I'm no a coward."

"Didn't say you were. Just making a point."

"I'd rather be a *live* hero, but."

"Exactly my point. That's why I brought my gun."

Before he could say anything else, I slipped out of the Golf, jamming the Browning into my belt at the back. I hid it under the tail of my sweatshirt, pulled up my hood. Billy didn't follow. Good lad. He wasn't there to back me up, just save me if things went tits-up and a quick getaway was in order. Billy scooted over into the driving position, and turned on the ignition. He drove the Golf away and into a parking space next to a Spar shop on the corner. I watched him nose the car round and then reverse into the shadows. The lights went off, but I could still hear the low thrum of the idling engine. Out of sight, but not out of mind. I left Billy there and walked across the street to the pool hall.

Couple of kids in the doorway gave me the thousand-yard stare, eyes like jaundice pouring from manhole covers. High. I pressed between them and they grunted, didn't want to move, but they'd no option. One of them pressed his forearm to my lower back but that was the extent of his defiance. I gave him the dead eye: the old silent promise. Maybe he'd felt the weight of the gun in my belt 'cause he quickly moved away, towing his drug buddy along with him. I let them go; they meant nothing to me.

First thing I noticed was the smell of pot, heavy in the air like a dampener. Next was the stench of sweat. Something else. Wank juice. Smelled like teenagers. There was a short vestibule, which doubled as an occasional toilet judging by the stains on the walls. Then there was a narrow flight of stairs leading up into darkness. From up there in the rafters came the clack of cues on balls. There was the low rumble of conversation, punctuated by harsher curses and raucous cheers. I felt like my arsehole was doing a Betty Boop pout, but I went up the stairs. Like I told Billy, rather be a dead hero ...

If someone came down, maybe that's as far as I'd get. I went up the last few steps with my hand tucked under my sweatshirt, thumb on the gun's grip, ready to tug it out and start blasting. But no one came down. Thought, *thank fuck for that*, and kept going.

Another corridor.

This one was graced with strip-lights. One of them flickered. A bluebottle bounced along the plasterboard ceiling, doing a crazy waltz. I tried to ignore the loud buzz, but it was much the same as the sound inside my head. They blended and grew exponentially, juxtaposing one on top of the other. My mouth felt dry, like Ghandi's flip-flop. Like Billy's credit score.

There was some hip-hop shit playing through a speaker. Couldn't stand the stuff. All these young lads in the pool hall playing at being gangstas. Would've made me laugh if they weren't so serious. Now I wasn't happy. Maybe Billy had a point. Wasn't too late to walk away.

Of course it was. I'd made it all the way into the pool hall and it was like in those old westerns my dad used to watch on a Saturday afternoon. If there was a pianist, he'd have stopped playing. The hip-hop jagged on, and that was the only thing that spoiled the effect.

There were kids in the big room, slouching round green baize tables with cues held like torches to ward off the dimness. They were all in the obligatory hoody and baggy trousers. Chains hung from a couple of pockets, beanie caps pulled low like it was winter outside. I ignored them. They were just tag-alongs. I walked across the room, down the centre of the dozen pool tables. I was watched all the way. Mouths hung open. No one spoke, they didn't have to. Their faces said, *What the fuck is he doing here?*

I told them.

"This has got fuck all to do with any of ya. I'm here to see Gardy."

"Dead man walking," someone said, like prison rap.

Maybe he was right. I was taking a big chance throwing myself into the lion's open mouth, but hey, sometimes you've gotta live dangerously just to get by.

The pool hall was spread over two floors. The boys, they had to hang out down here in the shitty quarters; the men, they all went upstairs into the loft. It was like they were saying that they were above the others, and I'm not talking literally.

This time I didn't get a free walk up the steps.

I was stopped by two guys. One of them was a hard bastard I knew as Toad. No one called him that to his face, 'cause it was nothing he'd go by. The other I didn't know. In my head I called him Skank, 'cause that's the way he smelled, like a whore bitch.

Toad was an ugly man. No one would deny it, not his mother even. He'd a round head, warty texture, flat nose, and wide lips. Get the picture?

"The fuck you doin' walking in here?" he said with a hand flat on my chest.

"No other way in."

"Who says you're goin' in?"

"Me," I said, "and Gardy. He's expecting me."

"Whatcha carrying?"

I showed him my empty hands.

He snorted at the other man, who began wiping me down.

"You like how that feels?" I asked the skank. "Rubbing yoursel' all over another man?"

"The fuck's this?" he asked touching the bulge in the back of my pants.

"I shit mesel on the way in when I knew you'd be here to stop me," I told him

He withdrew his hand, looked at Toad for what to do. Toad knew I was packing, but asked anyway.

"You packin', Alec?"

"'Course I am."

"Gonna have to have it."

"Touch it," I said smiling, "and you'll *get it* all right."

Toad rocked back on his heels. His tongue went from one side of his lips to the other. I half expected his eyes to roll back as he blinked, but they didn't.

I could hear the silence behind me, as contradictory as that seems. It was as if the hush was a tangible weight pressing down on my shoulders. The gangsta music had faded so even it was indistinguishable from the buzzing in my skull. My peripheral vision retracted, like I was a horse in blinkers. I zoned down on the hand pressing on my chest.

"Take your hand off me, Toad, or I'll break it."

"Fuckin" Toad?"

"You heard."

Toad removed his hand.

But only to coil it into a fist.

He should have hit me then. But he didn't. He was hard when he got going, but he was a pussy beforehand. No real bottle. He flicked his gaze to the skank standing at my shoulder and I guessed that's who would kick off first. I smashed the prick in the throat before he got the chance. Point of my elbow bone right in his voice box; fucker couldn't even scream.

Toad flinched, but not far enough.

My forehead cracked him on the bridge of his nose.

He went back, hands cupping the blood spewing into his palms. I hoofed him in the bollocks.

I said the bastard was hard. He didn't go down, but that was only a minor setback. I grabbed him by his skull and battered my knee into his chest, then used his head like a bowling ball, fingers inserted in his nostrils to swing him down and round and across the floor.

Don't know if that was him out of the fight or not, 'cause I immediately went up the stairs and into the room they called the Gods. I'd filled my hand on the way up, the Browning feeling like a clumsy and unfamiliar weight. Shouldn't have, I used to carry one all the time, but it had been a few years. It was a single action pistol, with thirteen 9mm rounds in the magazine, and I had the hammer cocked back, the safety catch on, ready to go.

There were five of them up there. Four punks and the biggest arsehole of them all. The one in the middle was Raymond Gardner. Or Gardy to friends and foes alike. I showed him the barrel of the Browning so he could see the black hole that was gonna suck him into oblivion.

"Heard you were expecting me, Gardy?"

He had to take a spliff out of his mouth to speak.

"Alec Duncan, me ol' pal," he grinned. "How long's it been? Fuck me, must be three years."

The Browning never wavered from his skull. Give him his due, he didn't look bothered. As if having a gun pointed at him was a daily occurrence. Maybe it was these days.

His pals didn't look as confident, they were antsy, trying to move away without making it obvious. I read Gardy's face; wasn't difficult, being the proverbial open book.

"Pity me an' you can't be friends again. You see the wankers I have round me nowadays? Not like it was back in the Regiment."

The Regiment was a whole lifetime away for both of us now. His if I didn't get my way.

"Things were different back then," I told him.

"Dunno about that. I've still got the same enemies. Micks and ragheads."

And at least two Scots, I wanted to add. Me and Billy Reid.

"I'm here about my cousin Billy."

Gardy came round a pool table, putting his head even closer to the barrel of my gun. He sat on the edge of the table, folded his arms like he was fuckin' Simon Cowell offering scathing criticism. He put on a passable Glaswegian accent. "It's the difference between Bing Crosby and Walt Disney. Bing sings but Walt disnae."

"The fuck you on about?" Not that I hadn't heard that old joke about a million times.

"I'm speaking in metaphors," Gardy said.

"You're talking shite," I corrected.

He smiled, thumbed the spliff back between his teeth. I wanted to remind him that the *no smoking* ban also applied to toking on a joint, but that would have just made me look like an idiot. Holding an illegal handgun on someone wasn't viewed favourably by the law either. I let it go.

Gardy was a wiry fucker, always was. In the last three years since I last saw him he'd put on the beef, but it was all round his neck and shoulders. He still looked like an ex-squaddie. Right down to the short hair, the rubber-soled boots. He was still dangerous. The difference was I was clean, but he was wired. The gange wasn't the only thing he'd taken judging by the twitching round his eyes. I glanced, saw white residue from a couple lines on the pool table rim. Coked up. Speed maybe. I'm not that up on the different substances people snort up their noses these days. Didn't care for them or the people that peddled them. I had to hang with Billy only because he was blood.

"Billy says he owes you money," I said.

"Like I said, Bing sings—"

I got it this time. Billy had reneged on paying his supplier.

"You can't get blood from a stone," I reminded him.

"It's all about the ways and means, Alec, me ol' pal."

"You wanted him to steal money from our grandmother, you bastard."

"She's eighty-two, ain't she? What does she need with a heap of cash?"

I flicked off the safety. Almost shot the prick there and then.

His friends had made themselves scarce, backing off into the corners, still trying to look like hard-cases, but failing. I wondered if any of them were carrying; if they were they weren't making a move yet. I kept the gun on Gardy. Like stink on shit as they say.

Gardy studied the end of his spliff. Looked like it had gone out. Told me he was blowing instead of sucking. Bad sign; meant he wasn't afraid of me or the gun. That's what comes of coke, makes you feel indestructible, I heard.

"Billy owes you no nothin'. That's it, Gardy. Leave it at that an' we stay good ol' pals."

Gardy shook his head.

"Can't be done, me ol' china." The fuck had he switched to a cockney accent for? That was Gardy, though. He used to be good fun, would have us all grinning at his Sean Connery or Billy Connolly, his Tommy Cooper or Prince Charles. I used to laugh with him, now I was laughing at him. I saw now that he used the accents and mimicry cause he just wasn't happy with the skin he was in. Was why he'd reinvented himself from a Special Forces soldier to a drug-peddling smackhead, I supposed. Pathetic bastard.

Then there was me. I was also once an SAS bad-arse. Now look at me. Running around like a common criminal, defending someone who I should've smacked round the head a few times for even thinking of burgling my granny's bungalow. Give Billy his due, he'd come to me before he did it. Made me wonder what would have happened if I hadn't been in town, though. I was there protecting one deadbeat from another.

Gardy jutted out his chin, lips tight on his teeth as he looked me up and down.

"You're lookin' fit, Alec. What are ya doin' these days?"

"Hod carrying," I said. "Building site over Yorkshire way."

"Fuckin' labouring?"

"Carrying bricks beats carrying shit."

"Depends on your perspective. See, the shit pays better. Come to work for me, Alec. I'll let Billy's debt go."

"Kiss my arse."

"Not my style. I've kicked plenty in my time." He laughed. "Kicked yours once, as I recall."

He had too. Gave me a right leathering. But that was then.

I lowered the Browning.

"Got a deal for you," I said.

"Shoot," he said.

Maybe I should have, but I'd a point to prove.

"Ooh, bad choice of word, eh?" he grinned. "What I meant was —"

"I know what you meant. Me an' you, we get it on. I win, Billy's debt is clear."

"What do I get outa the deal?"

I lifted the gun. "You get to stay on living."

Gardy stuck the spliff back between his lips like it was a cheroot. Said, in his best Clint Eastwood, "You gonna use that gun or whistle Dixie?" He laughed. "Where? When?"

"Right here right now, if you want?"

He shook his head. "Where's the money in that? I'm a fuckin' businessman these days, Alec. Don't fight for nothin', you know."

He glanced round his four pals. "Which one of you pricks thinks Alec can take me?"

They all grumbled out uneasy laughter. Like, what the fuck were they gonna say?

"Put a ton on me, lads," he said. "I win, I take the pot. Four hundred should do it. It'll cover Billy's debt." He squinted up at me. "You want to put up a wedge, Alec?"

"I carry bricks, not cash."

Somehow I got the impression that Gardy's pals weren't too happy about putting up the stake, not when it looked like a sure winner for their leader. But it was an out for them, a way of getting back into his good graces. They counted bills on to the corner of a pool table.

Gardy picked up the stack of twenties and tens. Riffled them under his nose. "I love the smell of cash in the morning." He mangled the *Apocalypse Now* quote, but his pals laughed with him. I shook my head. Wondered where we were doing it, so I asked him.

"Where we doing it?"

"Out the back," he said. "We'll pick up the others on the way down, get a real purse going."

I led the way down. Trusting Gardy was like I said earlier, like putting your head in a lion's mouth, but I got the impression the money and the accolades meant more to him than if he cold-cocked me from behind like a bitch. Toad and the perfumed skank were nowhere to be seen and maybe that was a good thing. Blood spatters on the floor showed which way they'd gone. Into the pisser to clean up. Fuck 'em; I didn't need any more enemies clamouring round me 'cause Gardy was dangerous enough for any man to contend with.

We went out through the back of the pool hall and down a flight of metal steps. The young gangstas followed us out, brave now that their vaunted leader was among them. They were all talking excitedly, dissing me behind my back. Telling Gardy to *fuck me over real good*, like they'd been raised in South Central LA instead of here in northern England.

There was a cobbled yard, dustbins, a shell of a car. Recognized it as an old Ford Escort like one my dad had back in the early eighties. Could've been the same one for all I knew 'cause someone boosted it from outside our house and we never saw it again. Couldn't fathom how the car got here because the yard was fully enclosed by a high wall; maybe the car was here before the wall and they just built around it like it was a museum piece in need of protection. Right.

Gardy took off his shirt. Threw a couple of lightning-fast punches, danced like Ali for the crowd. They were all cheering him, money passing back and forward.

I put the Browning down on one of the bins. Took off my sweatshirt and piled it on top. Stood there in my vest like Bruce Willis. Some of the crowd shut the fuck up, 'cause I was a wiry bastard mesel. I shook the kinks out of my hands as I walked forward.

Gardy bounced on the balls of his feet.

I said, "Remember, I win, that's it."

"My hand on it," he said, like I was going to fall for that old trick.

"Your word will do."

"OK, we've a deal." He turned to the crowd. "No one steps in. No one does nothin', got it?" He got sounds of assent from them. "If Alec beats me, then that's everythin' over with. No one touches Billy Reid."

I nodded at him. For old time's sake.

"Rules?" he asked.

"You've seen *Butch Cassidy and the Sundance Kid*?"

He nodded. "I have."

"Good," I said and front-kicked him under the chin. As he picked himself up off his arse, hand massaging his jaw, I said, "You should've seen that one coming, Gardy."

He smiled at me, blood trickling from between his lips like he was a vampire fresh from a virgin's throat.

"Sneaky bastard," he laughed. "That's the way I got you the last time."

"We're square now," I told him. "We start from scratch."

"OK." He came at me quick.

He punched me in my chest, then hooked at my head with a left. His knuckles scraped my skull but I was ducking. I sunk a dig into his guts. It was like punching a drum. I folded my arm, slammed him with my elbow, and that had more effect. He arched his back, got a hold on my face with both hands. Dug his thumbs into my eyes.

Could have tried to fight his hands off me, but while I was doing that he'd have demolished me. I rammed forward, hit my forehead against his. Kneed him in the bollocks. I've heard about guys on steroids; abuse makes their testicles shrivel. Maybe that was the case with Gardy 'cause he didn't flinch, just came back at me with a knee of his own. Got me in the solar plexus and nearly knocked the wind clean out of me. But at least his thumbs were out of my eyes.

We rattled round the yard, grunting and swearing, trading punches and kicks, none of them landing too cleanly. The crowd moved with us, baying for blood. All of it mine, of course. One of them spat on me; would've broken his nose given the chance but Gardy wasn't giving me a second. I grappled him and we both rolled across the floor, digging and clawing. We spilled apart. Someone *accidentally on purpose* stepped on my hand. I swung a kick at him from the floor, caught him on his shins and the prick jumped back. Then it was back to Gardy. We had a hold on each other, his fists twisted in my vest, mine in his mouth and on his belt. We used that prop to struggle back to our feet.

Gardy tried to bite my fingers and I jerked my hand free. We backed away a step. But that was all. Then we were back into it.

I looped a right over the top of him, hit him in the back of the neck. Tried for his mastoid with the edge of my hand, missed but nearly tore his ear off. He backed away, touching his lug-hole like it was a prized possession. "Fuck me," he said.

I intended to.

I threw a punch at his windpipe.

Gardy stepped quickly to the side and caught my arm. Hand on wrist, hand on elbow. He rolled my arm, locked me tight, then pushed down on the joint. I felt a tendon rupture. Fuck me but it hurt. Gardy kept pressing, trying to give my arm a two-way hinge. I kicked my heel into his shins, and threw myself away. Nearly tore my arm out of its socket, but at least it wasn't broken.

Gardy didn't stop to think how I'd got away, just monopolized, coming after me while I was still off balance. He kicked me in the arse with the toe of his boot. Dunno if you've ever been kicked there for real, but it's not the playful admonishment that most people think of. A blast of pain went right up my spine to the crown of my head. Then it went all the way back down again.

Could hardly stand.

Couple of Gardy's pals were in my way and I grabbed at them to steady mesel. They shrugged me off, swung me round and Gardy planted his fist in my left eye socket.

Jesus! White light, a taste of metal in my mouth, pain like a son of a bitch.

They didn't know it, but Gardy's pals had helped me. Put me back on my feet and ready to give back everything I got. I jabbed Gardy in the mouth. Stuck a one in his gut, another in his ribs. He winced with every shot and I followed him. Palm under his chin, heel hooked round his knee in a judo trip.

Gardy wouldn't be caught so easily; he hooked me under an armpit, swung round, got his hips under me and threw me with a judo hip-toss of his own.

Flat on my back there was no escape from the heel he stamped on my chest.

It was like having the stuffing forced out of every orifice in my body. I must have yelled in agony, 'cause Gardy looked like he was pleased with himself and tried again. This time I was ready for him and I swept his leg over me with both arms. He straddled me, looking down at me with the red-rimmed eyes of a mad bull. I punched him in the balls.

Maybe he wasn't on steroids after all, or my knee hadn't been on target last time, because the result here was the absolute opposite. He collapsed down on me, knees folding, and he spewed on the floor over my left shoulder. I got a hot and sticky wash all down my neck, and that kind of galvanized me to get the fucker off me. I grabbed his precious ears, twisting his head with them as if they were handlebars and Gardy went over on to his back. I rolled with him, let go with one hand so I could punch his face to mush. I landed one, two, going for the third when someone grabbed my bicep. Couldn't help the natural reaction, I glanced up at who it was and got a smack in the teeth for my trouble.

Toad was back.

Bad Toad, bad.

I was going to swarm up, give him some, when I was surprised to hear Gardy shouting, "The fuck you doin'? Didn't you hear what I said?"

He wasn't shouting at me.

To be fair Toad hadn't been there when Gardy set the rules. But he got the message. Cowed, Toad let go of me and I swung back to Gardy, my fist cocked.

He laughed through his split lips. "Fuckin' hell, Alec, you've learned a thing or two since we last fought."

"Yeah," I agreed. "How's about this?"

Forgot about the punch and dropped my elbow instead. Smashed his head into the floor. Three times I got him just like that, and I could see his eyes rolling in his head. Wasn't finished though, so I bunched my fist, hit him again, seen his lips split under my knuckles. Rearing back again, I got ready, fist angled at his windpipe. Killer blow now that his throat was an open target.

Gardy's arms were by his sides. Not fighting now.

I pressed the fist on his chest. Not to hold him down but to help mesel up.

Standing over him, I looked around the crowd. They were like rabid things, all panting, their fingers twitching: the pack mentality about to let loose its fury. I coiled my hands, ready to give them as much as they brought.

"Alec won."

I blinked down at Gardy. While I was distracted he could've got me in the bollocks or stamped my knee out of joint. He was just lying there, breathing heavily, wearing a whimsical look on his face as if he'd just had the best shag of his life.

I held out my palm for him, and he took it. I hauled him to his feet. He wouldn't release my hand and for a second I tensed, waiting for him to try and pull me on to a head-butt.

"Take it easy, me ol' mucker," he said, his voice kind of John Lennon mixed with the Gallagher brothers. Don't know what he was going for this time. "You beat me, fair and square."

He shook hands with me, then let me go. He patted me on the shoulders for all to see. Friends again.

"We were good once," he said, touching his swollen ear. "Let's get back to the old days, huh?"

"Can't, Gardy. Not when you're into this shite."

"All I've done is traded one pile of shit for another, Alec."

"You're right there." I stood back, massaging my elbow. I looked at my old sergeant. He'd taught me well, made me the bad-arse I'd turned out. He was the one who'd given me the physical tools to defend my family. Couldn't help but feel he hadn't been trying his hardest to break my arm. Once over he'd have done it in a second. He winked at me.

"You won, Alec. A deal's a deal in my book. Billy's back in the black."

I stared at him, mindless of the crowd round us all looking on in dumbfounded silence.

Gardy turned to his mates. "He won. Got it? Now give him the purse."

"Don't want the money. Just knowing that Billy's safe is enough."

He winked again, leaned in close to my ear. "Take the purse and you can give it to your ol' pal Gardy when we meet for a drink later."

Couldn't help but grin at the sneaky twat. Made himself a heap of cash, paid off Billy's debt and got himself a whole lot more. And he'd done it in a way that bought me some respect and didn't dent any of his. I winked back at him. "You're on. The local, yeah?"

"Got it."

Maybe I misjudged him. Maybe he wasn't as far gone to the dark side as I'd assumed.

Nah, he was still a bastard.

I pulled my sweatshirt on. Tucked the Browning into my belt. Picked up the large stack of notes someone had put on the next bin along.

When I looked back, Gardy and the others had all filed back up the stairs. Probably there'd be a celebratory spliff passed around in the Gods when he got back up there. I felt like it would be good to have a pint with my old friend, without the baggage of all the bullshit that life had served us lately.

I didn't go back through the pool hall. Didn't want another run-in with Toad or the perfumed skank; I was hurting too much. I climbed up on the bonnet of the Ford Escort, boosted mesel over the high wall and into a narrow alley running alongside the hall. Walked out, across the street towards the Spar shop.

Billy's Golf was still in the shadows. *Some get-away driver*, I thought, *has he fallen asleep?*

The engine was purring, but that was it. Couldn't hear any snoring.

"Billy? Billy." I shot forward, yanking open the driver's door. "Oh, shit, Billy!"

He was dead.

Didn't need to be a doctor to tell. His head was arched back over the headrest. Mouth open, full to the brim of spew. His left arm was splayed out across the gear stick, sleeve rolled up. Rubber tube hanging loosely round his bicep, bloody smear on his arm, among all the other scabby wounds where he'd jabbed needles. There was a hypodermic syringe lying in the foot-well, a burnt spoon and lighter, all the paraphernalia. To think I'd just fought the battle of my life for things to end this way. What good had I done?

I stood there. My little cousin, Billy Reid. Seventeen years old, a junkie for the last four. Dead.

"Billy, you stupid dumb fuck."

I massaged my elbow. Shook my head. Looked down at the forlorn waste of a young life. Why'd he do that? Obviously he didn't trust me to make things right. Or he didn't trust himself. Maybe Gardy wasn't the only one unhappy with the skin he was in.

Me neither if the truth was told.

Only one consolation I could think of: my granny's house wouldn't be burgled by Billy now.

The day was saved.

Who dares wins?

Yeah, right.

Some fucking hero me.

LITTLE RUSSIA

Andrew Taylor

"Little Russia?" Jill said. "Where?"

Amy Gwyn-Thomas looked up from her shorthand pad. "It's on the other side of the river. You can see it from the road to the Forest."

"That can't be its real name."

"It's what everyone calls it. It's a little valley that doesn't get much sun even in summer. It's always cold. Anyway, it's where Stalin lives."

"What *are* you talking about?"

"His real name's Mr Joseph, but people call him Stalin or Uncle Joe. He's a widower – and a frightful stick-in-the-mud. He's always writing to us about how awful everything is. You know the sort."

Jill did. "What's this about a crash?"

"It's the children I feel sorry for," Amy continued, turning the pages of her notebook. "The girl's a sweet little thing. I hear she's in the accounts department at Broadbent's. At least the boy's got away from home – there's something to be said for National Service."

"But this crash?" Jill said.

"I made a note here." Amy tapped the tip of her pencil on the page. "They think the driver took the bend too fast – it's a hairpin – and the car went over the edge. It's a steep drop."

Jill glanced at her watch. "When did it happen?"

"Yesterday evening."

"I think I'll go to the press briefing." Jill avoided Amy's eyes and opened a drawer of her desk. "The police must know more by now, and it would do as the lead. It's not as if we've got much else."

"But Miss Francis – we haven't done the post yet, and I know Mr Marr wanted to see you about the advertising figures."

"Later." Jill found her notebook, slammed the drawer shut and stood up. "Everyone else is out. You might as well type those letters now."

Amy departed, tight-lipped with suppressed irritation. Jill put on her coat and adjusted her hat in front of the mirror. It was only a few hundred yards from the *Gazette* office to police headquarters. She walked quickly down the High Street. She had spent the last few days in London and by comparison Lydmouth looked grubby and undersized, like a slum child who has never had much of a chance in life.

At the police station the desk sergeant gave her a nod of recognition and waved her into the conference room. The press briefing had already started. Jill's arrival caused heads to twitch around the big mahogany table; after several years in London she had only recently returned to Lydmouth to edit the *Gazette*. She took a seat near the door, unbuttoned her coat and let it fall behind her on the chair. A fog of smoke blurred the outlines of the uniformed officer at the head of the table, who was talking in a soft Welsh accent.

Sergeant Lumb was chairing the briefing. Not Richard Thornhill, Jill thought; not important enough for him or the Deputy Chief Constable. Lumb was talking about a spate of shoplifting. She began to make notes. Not Richard. Her vision blurred. Her eyes were watering. The smoke was irritating them.

There was a sound behind her, and a sudden draught of cool air on her neck. Once again, the heads twitched around the table. She did not look round.

"And then there's last night's fatality," Lumb said, and paused with a sense of occasion to relight his pipe. "Nasty business." The match went out and there was another pause. "Car went off the Forest road about 11 p.m. Misty night, as you know. He took the Little Russia bend too fast by the look of it. Nasty drop there. Poor chap was dead when we got there."

"Who was he?" Fuggle of the *Post* asked. He glanced at Jill as he spoke – no, not at her, but past her.

"Timothy Wynoll – young chap," Lumb replied, glancing down

at his notes. "He was at university in London. Parents are abroad. Singapore. They've been notified by now. His aunt lives up near Ashbridge. It was her car, as a matter of fact."

"Isn't it term-time?" Jill asked, wondering if there was someone behind her, and if so, who. "What was he doing in Lydmouth?"

"The aunt's away – on a cruise, lucky for some, eh? – and he promised he'd come down and check the pipes hadn't frozen after that cold snap. There was a letter from her in his pocket."

"These students. All paid for with our taxes. Marvellous." Fuggle rearranged the phlegm in his throat, making a sound like shingle shifting beneath a retreating wave on the seashore. "Been drinking, had he?"

"I'm afraid I can't say, Mr Fuggle." Lumb sat back in his chair. "No doubt the details will come out at the inquest."

Jill raised her hand. "Anyone else involved? Another car?"

"Not that we know of, Miss Francis."

She glanced over her shoulder. Richard Thornhill was in the doorway. He gave her a hint of a smile and retreated. The door closed behind him.

"Chicken," she murmured to herself or perhaps to him. "Chicken."

Fuggle stared at her with hard, shiny eyes like a pair of boiled sweets.

***

"The thing is, sir," PC Porter said, "it was odd. That's all."

"What was?" Thornhill asked.

"The car, sir. The one in Little Russia." Porter had waylaid Thornhill on the stairs at police headquarters. He was a very large young man, and he loomed like a mountain of flesh over the Detective Chief Inspector. "Sergeant Lumb sent me out to fetch it with the truck from the garage," he went on apologetically. "There it was, little Ford Popular, terrible state, windscreen gone. Shame really, couldn't have been more than a year or two old but it's only good for scrap. Mind you, could have been worse – he was smoking, look, and the whole thing could have gone up in flames if the petrol had leaked, yes and him too, not that it—"

"But what was odd?"

"Sorry, sir. Well, for a start, the car was in first gear."

"Damn it, Porter, what's so odd about that?"

The young constable flinched as if Thornhill had hit him. "If he was coming up the hill from Lydmouth he'd be in third, maybe, and then change down to second for the bend. But not first. Not unless he'd stopped for some reason."

" "Why would he have done that?"

"Maybe he pulled over on to the layby. But then why would he have gone over the edge? So I still don't understand how it could have happened. And anyway, if he was coming up and missed the bend he wouldn't have gone over the edge there. It – it doesn't feel right. Even if he was plastered."

Porter ran out of words and stared with dumb hope at Thornhill. He had a childish faith in the Chief Inspector. Thornhill tried to ignore the knowledge that the briefing would soon be over, and therefore Jill Francis might come out of the conference room at any moment. Most of his colleagues thought Porter was stupid, and with some justification. But, as Thornhill knew, sometimes Porter's stupidity was more effective than mere cleverness could ever be; and, besides, he had a strangely profound understanding of cars and their ways.

"This layby," Thornhill said. "It's actually on the outer edge of the bend, isn't it?"

"Yes, sir. Old line of the road, maybe. There's a fence over the drop, but that's mainly gone. He went over at the downhill end. But, sir, if he'd missed the bend, he'd have gone over higher up."

"Witnesses? Anyone live around there?"

"Only the Josephs, sir, down the bottom of the valley. Sarge went to see them, said they'd heard nothing."

"What was it like where the car was?"

Porter wrinkled his broad, pink forehead. "Came down twelve or fifteen feet – slammed into a rock, that did a lot of damage, and then banged into an old cooker. Folks tip their rubbish down there, look, it's not right. Driver's door comes open, and out he comes. Head's a real mess, they say – all cut and bloody. Not nice at all."

A drunk in a car, Thornhill thought, a winter night, poor visibility, an unexpected bend with a dangerous drop beyond. What was so odd about the fact that the car was a wreck and the drunk was dead?

"I found the wallet down there," Porter was saying, his mouth forming the words very slowly as if no one had ever said them before. "Just by the cooker. Sarge wondered where that had got to. Must have been loose in the car and fell out when he did."

Thornhill glanced at the conference room door. "Any sign of theft?"

Porter shook his head. "Six quid in the wallet."

"Where is it?"

"Upstairs, sir. With the rest of his stuff. Sergeant Lumb's got it."

"I'll take a look at it," Thornhill said reluctantly. "And the clothes."

The relief on Porter's face glowed like a neon sign. Thornhill led the way upstairs. Lumb's desk was almost invisible beneath a mound of files and papers, lightly powdered with pipe ash. Porter pulled out one of the cardboard boxes on the floor beside it. Thornhill looked quickly through Wynoll's clothes – a khaki-coloured duffel coat, a college scarf, a tweed jacket, flannel trousers, an Aertex shirt, vest, pants and socks. No hat, no tie, no jersey. The shoes were black Derbys, stained with mud. One shoulder of the duffel coat was thickly encrusted with blood, still tacky to the touch.

He looked up. "Where is he?"

"Up the RAF, sir," Porter said, which meant in the mortuary of the town's RAF Hospital on the Chepstow Road.

"Possessions?"

Porter held out an old shoebox. Thornhill looked at the wallet first. No surprises – a cheque book; a letter from the aunt, postmarked Southampton and addressed to a student hostel in Bloomsbury; a membership card for the Photography Club at University College; a driving licence with an address near Ashbridge, presumably the home of the aunt; a condom, carefully disguised in an outer wrapping torn from the corner of an envelope; a book of stamps with one used, a bus ticket from Lydmouth to Ashbridge, a return train ticket to London and six pound notes.

Wynoll had kept a running total on his bank balance in his cheque book. He had had well over a hundred pounds in his current account, so lack of money hadn't been one of his problems. According to the letter, the aunt had expected her nephew to come down yesterday afternoon. The dates on the tickets confirmed it.

There was also a packet of Park Drive with two cigarettes left. Another cigarette, half-smoked but not stubbed out, had fallen inside the duffel coat, where it had caused a burn before going out. Wynoll's other possessions were car keys, a Chubb door key and a handkerchief, once white and now almost the colour of the duffel coat. And a bottle of Teacher's, still with nearly an inch of whisky in the bottom and a smudge of blood on the label.

"What about in the car? Anything there?"

"It's in the yard, sir."

"Let's have a look."

They went down to the yard at the back of police headquarters. There was a separate shed reserved for cars under investigation and equipped with an inspection pit. The Ford Popular was still on the trailer that had brought it back to Lydmouth. The front off-side of the car was like crumpled wrapping paper. One of the headlights had come adrift and was dangling by the side, attached only by wires. The windscreen and the driver's window were broken.

Thornhill pulled open the door, which was hanging drunkenly on its hinges. He looked along the row of instruments on the dashboard. He turned the handle that had wound the driver's window up and down. At the moment the glass had broken, the window had been closed. He crouched to peer at the floor.

"Put some gloves on," he said, straightening up. "I want everything out of the car."

Porter stared open-mouthed. "What?" There was a pause. "Sir."

"Everything that moves. Mats, whatever's in the glove compartment, contents of the ashtray, even the sweet wrappers. Put it all on the bench. I'll be back in ten minutes."

The briefing had finished. Thornhill found Lumb skimming through a file in reception.

"The Little Russia crash," Thornhill said. "Keep me posted, will you?"

The sergeant frowned. "Any reason, sir?"

"Just in case."

Lumb tapped the file. "We've traced Wynoll's movements yesterday. He was drinking in the Bathurst most of the evening with a young man about the same age as him. Barmaid didn't know who it was but she said they were having a bit of an argy-bargy about something at closing time. Couldn't say what about."

"Description?"

"Little chap. But she said he wasn't bad-looking, for what that's worth. Trouble is, kids all look the same these days. They left together."

When Thornhill returned to the yard, Porter was waiting by the door of the shed. Thornhill picked his way through the contents of the car. Apart from a surprising quantity of small stones and pieces of dried mud, there were half a dozen cigarette ends, more Park Drive by the look of them, along with used matches, an AA handbook and ten or twelve vividly green and purple wrappers from Brashers Mint Imperials. He put to one side a selection of less predictable items from a piece of string to a brown-paper bag containing two dried apple cores, from a travelling sewing kit to a half-used jar of Marmite.

Marmite, he thought, mints and matches. String. A sewing kit. Apple cores. His mind strained to combine them into something that made a pattern.

Matches?

When he had finished he went back outside. Porter stared expectantly at him. The constable's mouth was open as though he was hoping his superior officer might feed him with a titbit.

"Yes," Thornhill said at last. "Perhaps it is."

"Yes, sir. But what, sir?"

"As you said, Porter: perhaps it's odd."

* * *

"Chicken," Jill said aloud.

She was alone in the layby, standing under an umbrella in the rain beside her green Morris Minor. Behind her was the road, snaking up to Ashbridge and the Forest, divided from the layby by a ragged crescent of saplings, bramble and long grass. It was unexpectedly private. In front of her were the rusting remains of a barbed wire fence, draped on rotting posts. Sections of it had fallen away.

The view was beautiful. The densely wooded Little Russia valley stretched downhill, narrow and steep-sided, funnelling outwards and curving to the north in the direction of the invisible river below. The layby itself was less attractive. A rotting mattress, disgorging its horsehair bowels, lay at one end, among rusting tins, empty bottles and the remains of a sack of plaster that had left dirty-white streaks in the mud.

She walked slowly across the cracked tarmac to the largest of the gaps in the fence, a stretch of about five yards towards the end closest to the road downhill. The drop was almost vertical. The underlying sandstone was exposed. At the bottom was a jagged rock about the size of a small caravan. Beside it was a rusting gas cooker on its side, a selection of empty tins and a couple of bald tyres. It would be possible to scramble down there, but it was not something to attempt in a decent coat, a snugly-fitting skirt and two-inch heels.

Farther down the slope a roof was visible through the branches, the clay tiles streaked with lichen. A little barn, perhaps, she thought, or a shepherd's hut. It must be invisible in summer. The Forest was studded with these mysterious little buildings, usually ruinous, which must once have had necessary reasons for being where they were. Unlike her.

She stared at the rock. This was where the boy had died. Shards of glass glinted beside the rock. She wondered if she was imagining a smear of pale grey paint on one side. What had she expected to find? An explanation? The confirmation of a hunch?

There was a rustling below her, somewhere in the bushes below the rock. Jill felt suddenly guilty, as though detected in a small, shabby crime. She glanced down into the ravine and at the same time took a step backwards.

Her movement was too little, too late. Not five yards from the rock, a face appeared among the branches. There was no possibility of a silent and dignified withdrawal now.

"Hello, Richard," Jill said.

Formal as ever, he touched his hat. "Good afternoon, Miss Francis."

"When we're alone you might as well call me Jill, don't you think? I know things between us have – well, things have changed, but it's quite absurd to be so pompous."

Colour rose in his face. "Very well. What are you doing here?"

"I'm a journalist," Jill said. "Remember?"

"I can hardly forget." He touched his hat again. "I won't keep you."

Jill turned on her heel, leaving Thornhill in undisputed possession of Little Russia. She climbed into the car, lit a cigarette and started the engine.

Her hands were shaking slightly. Chicken, she thought. That's the trouble with all of us – we're all bloody chicken.

***

When he was alone in Little Russia, Thornhill methodically quartered the scene of the crash, picking his way among the rubbish, the shattered branches and the fragments of rock. It was a shocking waste of time to be doing this himself, he told himself, particularly as his reason for doing was so tenuous – in fact not really a reason at all. And what had Jill been up to? Damn it, she was editing the *Gazette* now – if they wanted local colour for their piece on the crash, why not send a minion?

Shivering because of the cold, Thornhill set off towards the

Forestry road where he had left his car. He followed a winding track that pursued an eccentric four-footed logic, for Little Russia was more frequented by deer and rabbits, badgers and foxes than by humans. He stumbled into a puddle, spattering filthy water on the skirts of his navy-blue overcoat. It began to rain, and he had not brought his umbrella.

The track passed the corner of the small stone building with its sagging roof of double Roman pantiles, patched in places with corrugated iron. There was an unglazed opening high in the gable but no other windows. The door, held in place with a rusting, hand-forged Suffolk latch, was still sound.

A unexpected colour, a vivid mauve, caught Thornhill's eye on the ground immediately outside the door. He stooped. There were two ticket stubs a few inches from the door jamb. He picked them up and felt them between finger and thumb. They couldn't have been there long, for they were still dry. A tiny oddity? He slipped them between two leaves of his notebook.

Thornhill lifted the latch, pushed open the door and went into the barn. The air smelled damp but unexpectedly fresh. The roof was still weathertight. He stood in the doorway and watched the rain drifting over the treetops towards the valley below.

He turned his back on the weather and, as he moved, his foot snagged on a soft, yielding obstruction. He looked down. There was a filthy brown blanket on the earth floor.

His immediate thought was that at some point a tramp must have passed a chilly night here. He walked about the building, automatically looking for something that would confirm or refute the theory. He found nothing. In the doorway again, he bent down to the blanket and examined it more closely. There was a cluster of darker spots on the coarse wool, fresher-looking than the ancient dirt on the fabric. He angled the blanket towards the light from the doorway. The spots were rust-red and dry to the touch. Blood? If it was, then the colour suggested it was relatively recent in origin.

Thornhill straightened up. The rain was petering away, driving north-east up the river valley below with a freshening wind behind it. Suddenly he was in a hurry to get back to Lydmouth, to the warmth and familiarity of police headquarters.

The path between the barn and the Forestry track was easier going than the path to the site of the crash. In less than ten minutes he reached the broad ride, surfaced with rubble. From there it was only a few yards to the junction of the track and the road, where he had left his car.

A brick house stood on the corner – a square modern building in an unkempt garden overshadowed by gangling conifers. As Thornhill approached, an ambulance was pulling out of its concrete driveway. It swung on to the road, where it turned left towards Lydmouth.

Thornhill unlocked his car door. He glanced up at the house. He was just in time to catch sight of a face, little more than a pale blur, before it vanished from an upper window.

***

"He's not absolutely sure," Amy Gwyn-Thomas said. "The boy doesn't come to chapel very often now. Of course they change so quickly at that age, don't they? And he's been away in the army."

"Who isn't sure?" said Jill, who had not been listening to her secretary.

"Ronald – Mr Prout." Amy blushed. "I happened to bump into him in the Gardenia, quite accidentally. The rush at lunchtime is getting worse and worse. We had to share a table."

Jill didn't believe in that sort of accident. She suspected Amy of conducting a clandestine courtship with Mr Prout, who kept a toyshop and played the organ in the Baptist Chapel.

"Whatever was Mr Prout doing in the Bathurst Arms?" Jill asked. "I hadn't put him down as a drinking man."

The blush intensified. "Of course not. He was collecting for the Mission Society. Anyway, he said, there were two young men in there, obviously rather the worse for wear if you know what I mean, at one of the tables in the saloon bar. They didn't give him anything – just waved him away; people can be so rude, can't they?

Ronald was almost certain that one of them was Little Joe. He wasn't sure, or he would have said something."

"Has he got a car?" Jill said. "Little Joe, I mean. What's his real name, by the way?"

"Mark. Mark Joseph. And I don't think he's got a car. He can't be more than nineteen or twenty. He couldn't afford it. But he might have the use of his father's. I know Mr Joseph's got one, I've seen it at chapel. It's black. Why do you ask?"

"I just wondered." Jill picked up her handbag, which was beside the desk.

"Are you going out again?"

Before Jill could answer, Amy's telephone rang in the next room. She went to answer it. As Jill was leaving her office a moment later, Amy waylaid her. There was a pink, moist spot on each of the secretary's powdered cheeks.

"Well, I never," she said. "That was Ronald – Mr Prout. He went to see his mother at the hospital after lunch. And guess who he saw being carried out of an ambulance there? Little Joe."

* * *

Acute carbon monoxide poisoning turns your cheeks cherry-pink and gives them a misleadingly healthy appearance. By that time, however, you may well be dead or comatose.

Mark Joseph was alive, but only just. The consultant thought it likely that, if the boy recovered, his neurological functions would be considerably impaired, perhaps in the long term. Translated, that meant it might be a long time before the police would be able to get any sense out of him – assuming, of course, that he survived.

Sergeant Lumb and a policewoman had been to the house in Little Russia. On his return Lumb told Thornhill that Little Joe had used strips of dustsheet to attach the hose of the vacuum cleaner to the exhaust of his father's car, which was parked in a garage beside the house. He had run the hose through the driver's window and sealed up the cracks with Sellotape and brown paper. Then he had climbed into the car, started the engine and waited to die.

"It was the sister that saved him," Lumb said. "Sylvia – she's ill, having a day or two off work. Came downstairs to make herself a drink, and she heard the engine running. Doc said he'd have been dead in another half-hour."

"Why did he do it?" Thornhill asked.

"Don't know, sir. But it was suicide – he left a note: but all he said was sorry. And he sent his love to his sister."

Thornhill considered. Then, "Not to his parents?"

"Mother's dead. He don't get on with his dad. To be fair, not many people do – they call him Uncle Joe round here. As in Stalin. He's a nasty old bugger, excuse my French, the holier-than-thou type."

"Has he been told?"

Lumb shook his head. "He's staying with friends in Scotland. No telephone. We've contacted the local boys, asked them to take a message over."

"I'll go and take a look at the house. I'd like to talk to the sister, too."

Thornhill took his own car, along with the uniformed WPC who had accompanied Lumb to Little Russia earlier in the day; it was all too likely, Thornhill thought, that Sylvia Joseph would be difficult to handle – emotional, possibly hysterical – and dealing with that sort of thing was woman's work.

The problem was, he realized when he drew up outside the Josephs' house in Little Russia, the wrong woman had already turned up to deal with it. A green Morris Minor was parked outside. He walked quickly up the concrete path, buttoning his overcoat for the air seemed much colder here. Jill Francis opened the door before he had time to ring the bell. For an instant they stared at each other, both of them conscious of the silent police-woman at Thornhill's side.

He raised his hat. "Good afternoon, Miss Francis. We've come to see Miss Joseph."

"She's downstairs now," Jill said. "In the sitting room."

"How is she?"

"Shocked. Miserable. Just sits there eating sweets and hoping it will all go away. Would you like to come through?"

"Perhaps you and I might have a word beforehand." He turned to the WPC. "Go and see Miss Joseph. I won't be long."

The young woman glanced at him, the confusion evident on her face. But she said nothing. Jill showed her into the room where Sylvia was sitting. Thornhill glimpsed a childlike figure in a dressing-gown. She seemed scarcely older than his own daughter. She was sitting in a chair, her fingers delving into a green and purple box on her lap, and she did not raise her head to look at him. Lank brown hair curtained her face. The door closed.

Jill draped her coat over her shoulders like a cape and joined him on the doorstep.

"What are you doing here?" Thornhill whispered to Jill, conscious that once again she had put him in an absurd position.

"I told you this morning – my job." She stared ahead, declining to look at him. "It's a story. A boy tried to kill himself. You'll want to see the garage, won't you? Why don't we talk there?"

It was as good an idea as any. The garage was a brick building that leaned against one side of the house, with double doors now propped open. The car was a large black Austin, at least twenty years old. The vacuum cleaner hose still ran from the end of the exhaust to the driver's window.

"You'd better not go inside," he said. "We'll need to look in here."

"I already have been inside." Her voice was flat. "Sorry. Shall I tell you why he did it? Little Joe, I mean."

He stared at her. "I think you'd better."

"In a way it's because Timothy Wynoll had seen a film up in London. *Rebel Without a Cause*. James Dean and Natalie Wood. It only opened a week or two ago. I saw it the other day when I was up in town."

"For God's sake. Jill, I haven't time for this."

"Bear with me. There's a scene in which James Dean and another boy have what they call a chickie run. Each of them has a car. They drive towards a precipice. And the first one to bail out is chicken. In the film, the other boy tries to jump out but a strap on his jacket catches on the door handle. And he goes over the edge inside his car."

"But there's nothing to—"

"Mr Prout saw Timothy Wynoll and Mark Joseph in the Bathurst Arms last night. Arguing about something. I think it ended with Wynoll challenging him to play chicken. But Wynoll didn't bail out in time."

"You've no evidence for that."

But as he spoke, Thornhill remembered the mauve tickets he had found near the barn this morning. Cinema tickets? Or was that too fanciful? Anyway, what had the tickets been doing outside the barn?

"Look at the nearside wheel," Jill said.

Thornhill stared at it. There were spots of the pinkish-brown mud on the rim, just as there were on the rims of his own car, and also something white embedded in some of the tread and smeared on the side of the tyre.

"I think it's plaster," Jill said. "Someone dumped a sack of it in the layby above Little Russia. So that car was up there, and recently."

Thornhill smiled, not at her but because, as he grasped what she was suggesting, a possible solution to a small puzzle slotted into his mind. "I wondered how he lit the cigarette."

"Who?"

"Wynoll," he said. "You see, he was smoking when he went over the edge. But he didn't have any matches or a lighter with him. And the car doesn't have a cigarette lighter, either. I thought it was odd from the start. Then Wynoll kills himself without meaning to, is that what you're suggesting?"

"Yes," Jill said. "And then Mark tries this stunt" – she glanced at the car – "because he blamed himself for Wynoll's death. It's—"

"You don't have the ticket stub, by any chance?" he interrupted.

"What?"

"From when you went to see that film." But perhaps she wouldn't have the stub, Thornhill thought, because a man had taken her, and of course the man would have paid.

"I don't know." She looked up at him. "Perhaps." She opened her handbag, took out her purse and rummaged inside it. "I'm not sure – so much rubbish accumulates – what about these? Yes, look, you can make out 'ion' on that one. The film's on at the London Pavilion."

He looked down at the palm of her hand at two mauve ticket stubs. *A man would have paid.* He felt a small and squalid relief, almost worse than the absurd jealousy that had preceded it.

The front door opened. They both turned towards the sound, pulling sharply away from each other as though jointly guilty of a nameless crime. The girl was walking stiffly towards them, an overcoat over her dressing gown. The policewoman hovered anxiously behind her.

"Sylvia," Jill said, starting forward, "you shouldn't—"

"It's my fault," the girl said in a thin, dull voice. "I can't wait."

"Miss Joseph," Thornhill said. "Your brother's alive. He's very ill but—"

"Not him," she snapped, with a flash of temper. "Tim."

He stared at her. "You'd better say what you mean by that."

Sylvia nodded at Jill. "She guessed some of it. Did she tell you? Tim was down at Christmas. We met at the Young Conservatives party in the Ruispidge Hall. I – I was a bit tiddly. And we – well, I was stupid and so was he. And I realized what had happened when I was late." She ran out of words.

"Her period," Jill said, and touched the girl's arm.

"You're pregnant?" Thornhill said to Sylvia.

She didn't speak.

"She was," Jill said. "She miscarried last night."

"Dad would have killed me if he found out," the girl whispered. "Me first, then Tim."

"So you got rid of it?" Thornhill said, thinking that the last thing he wanted was an illegal abortion on his plate as well.

"No!" she glared at him. "It wasn't like that. I wanted Tim to marry me, to make it all right. But he laughed at me. Mark was home on leave so I told him, and he said he'd talk to Tim and make him see sense. They met in the Bathurst. All they did was quarrel and get drunk and do the chickie run in Little Russia."

"Did your brother tell you?"

"Yes." Sylvia gave a brittle laugh. "When he came in last night. It was because of that James Dean film. Tim thought it was marvellous. He took me to see it when I went up to London – to tell him about – about the baby. I told him after we'd been to the cinema. I thought perhaps if we got married … " The thin, anguished voice sank to a murmur. "He said I wasn't a patch on Natalie Wood. He didn't really like me at all. He only went with me that one time because he was drunk. And all he really wanted to talk about was that stupid bloody film."

The ticket stubs, Thornhill thought. The blood on the blanket. The lighted cigarette. The wallet. Something was missing. Something that made it all add up. Then suddenly there it was – the connection: two colours glowing brightly and freshly in the forefront of his mind. Tenuous but undeniably there. *Freshly*, that was the point.

"Sylvia should be sitting down," Jill said. "She's lost a lot of blood because of the miscarriage. And a doctor should see her."

Thornhill ignored Jill. "Where were you last night?"

Sylvia's eyes widened. "Here, of course." She touched her stomach. "I was already feeling – you know – funny down there."

"Richard," Jill said. "Is this really necessary? Here?"

The policewoman took a step forward, looking to Thornhill for direction.

"But you weren't here at all," Thornhill said to Sylvia. "You were in Wynoll's car, weren't you? Waiting while he was in the pub, perhaps, maybe hoping for a reconciliation? You were with him when he drove up the hill to the layby. You lit the cigarette he was smoking when he went over the edge."

Sylvia clung to Jill's arm for support.

"You survived," he said harshly. "Timothy Wynoll didn't. You took out his wallet after the crash. What were you looking for? A letter from you? A photograph?"

The girl's expression changed, cracking like ice on a frozen pond when someone throws a stone in the middle.

"The ticket stubs for that film were in his pockets," he went on, "probably in his wallet. I found them this morning near the barn in the woods between here and the car. Still dry, so they hadn't been there long – they wouldn't have lasted long like that in this weather. You must have dropped them last night."

"You can't be sure of that," Jill said. "He might have dropped them there himself – before last night, I mean."

Thornhill shook his head, his eyes still on Sylvia. "Wynoll didn't reach Lydmouth until yesterday afternoon. The tickets in his pocket prove that. So who dropped the tickets in the woods over there? It can't have been Wynoll or your brother, Sylvia. It must have been you. How else could they have got there?"

"She – she might have paid for the tickets herself," Jill said in a voice not much more than a whisper.

"I doubt it. Why should she, when she was with a man who wasn't exactly short of money?"

Jill glared at him. But he didn't notice. The tickets were by the barn, he thought, and there had been blood on the blanket.

Another link in the chain?

"You stopped in the barn on your way back here last night," he said to Sylvia. "You were already bleeding from the miscarriage."

Sylvia let go of Jill's arm. She stared at the grubby concrete of the path, her face invisible behind the lank hair. "I hate you," she muttered. "I hate you."

Who was she talking to, Thornhill wondered – himself or Wynoll? The entire world? The unwanted baby? Or even herself? He turned to the policewoman. "Take Miss Joseph inside. Stay with her until I tell you otherwise. Don't leave her alone for any reason."

When they were alone, Jill turned on him. "What in God's name are you doing? She's a victim, can't you see that? Anyway, there's nothing to show she was there, nothing to *prove* it."

"She was there." He stared at her. "And I think she might have—"

He broke off. Sylvia had had the presence of mind to search Timothy Wynoll after he was dead. All along, there was something cold and calculating about her behaviour. Had she prevented Wynoll from braking? Or had she hit him afterwards, with a rock or even the whisky bottle with the blood on the label? He had nothing like hard proof, of course, he was far short of that. But he'd send the SOCOs into Little Russia immediately, and once they had the pathologist's report on Wynol and his head injuries—

"Tell me what you think happened," Jill said softly. "What gave you the idea she was in the car in the first place? Trust me."

He shook his head. Accepting the invitation would be like signing a blank cheque.

"Chicken," she said.

Thornhill looked at her. A blank cheque? Who cared? He would bankrupt himself if she asked him. He opened his mouth to speak, to say, "Brashers Mint Imperials are wrapped in green and purple papers."

The wrappers on the car floor hadn't been there long. Sylvia had been eating them in the house this afternoon as if her life depended on them.

But the front door opened before he had time to say anything at all. The policewoman was running down the path towards them. He knew at once what had happened from her white face and her open mouth, from the red smear on her navy-blue skirt and the door hanging open behind her. He knew that it was too late for Sylvia, and also perhaps for himself and Jill.

LITTLE OLD LADIES

Simon Brett

Brenda Winshott was an unwilling investigator of crime. But then she'd never been one to push herself forward. Given a more forceful manner, she might well have been elected Chairwoman of the Morton-cum-Budely Village Committee. She certainly had the administrative skills and people skills to discharge the job efficiently. But because she generally kept so quiet, no one considered her for the role. Instead, the members had elected as "Chair" (an appellation that Brenda Winshott silently detested) Joan Fullerton, whose administrative skills were minimal and whose people skills non-existent.

But Joan Fullerton was a woman of unassailable conviction in her own rightness. The thought had never occurred to her that she might be wrong. Throughout a long marriage, she had worn down her husband to such a point that, when he finally found peace, there was so little of his personality left that he did not so much die as simply evaporate. Her two sons had been subjected to a similar emotional bludgeoning, with the result that they had almost as little will left in them as their deceased father. Piers had repeated the errors of the previous generation by marrying Lynette, who was almost as bossy as her mother-in-law. She ran Morton-cum-Budely's only restaurant, The Garlic Press, which prided itself on its locally sourced organic menu, and where her husband acted as an ineffectual greeter. Tristram, the younger son, far too terrified by seeing what had happened to his father ever to risk taking on a wife himself, was equally ineffectual in his job as a French teacher in a nearby girls' school, Grantley House. Neither son would dare to admit, even to themselves, how much they loathed their mother.

Nor did Joan Fullerton endear herself to the other residents of Morton-cum-Budely. It was a Devon village of almost excessive prettiness, populated largely by the retired. And since men were made of frailer stuff, most of those who survived were little old ladies, punctiliously polite to everyone they met face-to-face, and equally poisonous about them as soon as their backs were turned.

So the loathing in which Joan Fullerton was held by the entire village would never have been guessed from the genteel charm with which all the locals greeted her in her perambulations up and down the High – and indeed only – Street of Morton-cum-Budely. For Brenda Winshott, naturally quiet, there was perhaps not so much difference between her public behaviour to and private opinion of Joan Fullerton, but in others the contrast was more marked. Queenie Miles, who lived in Yew Tree Cottage and had always felt that chairing the Village Committee was her birthright, never ceased from vilifying the incumbent "Chair", except in Joan Fullerton's presence, when her unctuous obsequiousness was as exaggerated as her inner hatred.

The social life of Morton-cum-Budely had been compared by one rather venturesome local to "a stationary cruise". Gainful employment did not feature in anyone's daily routine, and housework was generally done by women shipped in from adjacent, but less picturesque and well-heeled, villages. At lunchtimes some of the residents might meet in the local pub, The Old Trout; substantial cream teas were ingested at the Chintz Café; and in the early evening there was usually an exchange of gin-and-tonics in one or other of the daintily appointed cottages. At all of these encounters the same topics of conversation were recycled, rather like the air in a hotel lounge. Excitements, except for the regular *anno domini* demise of the older of the little old ladies, were rare. In recent years the only mystery in Morton-cum-Budely to make the pages of the local newspaper had been solved by the headline, "Dead Ducks: Ferrets Blamed".

That was, until the murder of Joan Fullerton on May the first.

* * *

Initially her death was assumed to have been natural and, though greeted with more relief than regret, not so different from any other in the village. It was only when the victim's home, Arbutus Cottage, was taped off as a crime scene, and policemen arrived from as far afield as Exeter, that the word "murder" came to be used – with appalled excitement – in Morton-cum-Budely.

Theories as to the reason for Joan Fullerton's killing grew more exotic as the days passed. The suggestion that she had been hit over the head by a burglar surprised in the course of his theft quickly gave way to stories of a homicidal prisoner escaped from Dartmoor. By the end of the week Joan Fullerton was said to have fallen foul of Triad gangs operating out of Plymouth Chinese restaurants, and some people spoke in hushed tones of her past as a double agent during the Cold War having finally caught up with her. In none of these conjectures did the inhabitants of Morton-cum-Budely allow their imaginations to be inhibited by complete lack of information about the circumstances of their neighbour's death.

Brenda Winshott had her own views about how and why the murder had happened, but characteristically she kept these to herself.

And would have continued to do so, had she not been visited by Detective Inspector Dromgoole.

He was a bulky man, whose bluffness of manner, Brenda could tell, masked a sharp intellect. He wore plain clothes, a shapeless sports jacket and thick cords whose nap had here and there been worn away. He arrived at her home, Honeysuckle Cottage, alone and was at pains to insist that his visit was not official.

"Just come for an informal chat really," he said, his voice softened by a Devonian burr. "Not taking witness statements or anything like that. Just trying to get a flavour of what life's like in Morton-cum-Budely."

Brenda Winshott smiled. Wrinkles radiated out from her perceptive blue eyes and deepened the lines on her powdered pink face. Sitting in her little tapestry-covered armchair, with a cup of tea on the adjacent table and her voluminous leather handbag at her side, she looked the archetypal harmless little old lady.

"And why have you come to me, Inspector?" she asked. "I'm hardly one of the movers and shakers of the village. I keep myself to myself."

"Which is exactly why I have come to you, Miss Winshott. You may keep yourself to yourself, but everyone knows you and everyone seems to like you. They all mentioned how quiet you were." He left time for a reaction, but she gave none. "I find, Miss Winshott, that quiet people are the ones you have to watch. They are frequently more observant than their neighbours. Those you call 'the movers and shakers' tend to be so busy thinking about themselves that they don't notice anything else that's going on."

Brenda Winshott nodded, accepting the accuracy of his assessment. "But you've been round Morton-cum-Budely for nearly a week, Inspector. You must have got some impression of what's going on."

"Maybe, but I think I need an insider's view."

He was rewarded with another smile. "You mean," Brenda asked, "that you can't find anyone who had a motive to kill Joan Fullerton?"

The Inspector shared the joke with her. "Hardly that. Spoilt for choice in this place. Once I get through their good manners and their mustn't-speak-ill-of-the-dead pretences, everyone seems to have hated the old bat." Again Brenda Winshott didn't comment. "Quite frankly, what I want from you is a bit more background. You know how a village like this works. I want you to sort of keep an eye open ... let me know if anything happens that you think's odd ... "

"Keep a watching brief, as it were, Inspector?"

"Yes, precisely that."

"You're not telling me the police are baffled, are you?"

"How do you mean?"

"There was a tradition in Golden Age crime fiction that in the investigation of village murders the police were always so thoroughly baffled that they ended up asking a little old lady to solve the case for them. Is that the situation you find yourself in, Inspector Dromgoole ... ?" Brenda Winshott enquired sweetly.

He coloured. "Not exactly. Mind you, any thoughts you have ... don't be shy about sharing them with me."

* * *

She rather relished having an official mandate from the police to do what she had intended to do anyway. Brenda Winshott had her own reasons for wanting to construct a watertight case that would have someone arrested for the murder of Joan Fullerton.

And maybe Inspector Dromgoole and his professional colleagues really were baffled ... He'd certainly been surprisingly ready to supply her with information, more information than the police traditionally vouchsafe to curious amateur detectives.

He had told her that Joan Fullerton had been poisoned, and expressed the opinion that poison was a murder method favoured by women. He didn't say "little old ladies", but somehow the implication was there.

The poison too had a "little old lady" quality about it. Lily of the valley. A flower whose delicate aroma belies its toxicity. And, coincidentally, a perfume much favoured by little old ladies.

What was odd, though, the Inspector confided, was that no traces of lilies of the valley had been found anywhere inside or in the grounds of Arbutus Cottage.

Inspector Dromgoole had also been generous to Brenda in filling in details of the last evening of Joan Fullerton's life. The deceased had had tea with her younger son Tristram in the cottage at Grantley House which came with his teaching job. She had then moved on to an early dinner at The Garlic Press, which, because it was run by her son and his wife, Joan Fullerton regarded as her private canteen. After the meal, she had visited Queenie Miles at Yew Tree Cottage for a nightcap, what she always insisted on referring to as an "O be joyful". On that occasion she had opted for a gin and lime juice.

Back at Arbutus Cottage, forensic examination of the premises suggested that Joan Fullerton had started to feel unwell, vomited profusely, fallen into a coma and died in the middle of the night.

The poison contained in lily of the valley, a glycoside called convallatoxin, would not automatically be fatal, but could easily have put paid to someone as old and frail as Joan Fullerton.

And indeed, had she received prompt medical attention, her death could probably have been prevented. But when she started to feel ill, she had been unable to summon help, as both her mobile phone and her two landline handsets were missing from Arbutus Cottage. The finding of those, Inspector Dromgoole confided to Brenda Winshott, together with the revelation of who had stolen them, would make identifying the murderer considerably simpler.

Brenda had decided, as soon as the Inspector left, that the best procedure in her investigation would be to retrace Joan Fullerton's movements on the evening of her death, and to pay her visits at the same times as the victim had done. So four o'clock the following day found her driving in her neat Volkswagen Golf to Grantley House.

* * *

The school did not pride itself on academic achievements. Few of its girls ever made it to proper universities. The nearest any of them came to further education was through cookery courses, wine appreciation classes, model agencies or marriage to well-heeled young men with degrees. But Grantley House did have its own stables, tennis courts and swimming pools, and no pupil was allowed to leave without having had her thighs thickened and her vowels ground to cut-glass perfection.

The quality of the teaching staff in non-sports subjects reflected the school's priorities. Which is why someone as inept as Tristram Fullerton could get a job teaching French there.

He had showed no surprise when Brenda Winshott asked if she could drop round "to express her condolences about his mother". When she arrived at his small school house, he offered her tea, just as he must have done to his mother the previous week. Brenda accepted the offer, wishing to replicate that encounter as closely as possible – though one might have thought not too closely, if Tristram turned out to be the murderer.

He was a harassed man in his forties, whose hair and confidence were thinning. Being one of the few males in a girls' school might be some men's idea of heaven, but for Tristram Fullerton it was clearly nothing but a source of stress. Teenage girls, like hyenas, have an uncanny knack of identifying weakness and, when they've found it, going in for the kill. Every pupil in the school had perfected her own impersonation of the French teacher's hesitant manner, and they paid him the ultimate insult of not treating him like a man at all.

His sitting room reflected his despair. The gloomy, downhearted furniture looked as if it had seen out many tenants. The only personal touches were a few French books and dictionaries slumping against each other on the dark shelves, and a faded fold-out calendar entitled "Les Jours de Fête de la France".

"I was very sad to hear about your mother," said Brenda Winshott, placing her capacious handbag on the grubby carpet. What she said was a lie, but in places like Morton-cum-Budely certain formalities had to be observed.

"Thank you." Tristram Fullerton stood awkwardly, teapot in hand, his eyes darting constantly downwards, as though he were afraid his flies were undone.

"And how's the teaching going?"

"Well … " A lifetime of disappointment was expressed in that single monosyllable.

"I suppose you learnt your French when the family was living in Bordeaux … ?" Brenda remembered Joan talking at great length about how her husband's job had necessitated various foreign relocations, where she had always made a point of learning the local language. This had enlarged the repertoire of tongues in which she could lash her spouse's shortcomings.

Tristram Fullerton agreed that he'd started to learn French while living in Bordeaux. "Not that I was ever very good at it. I'm still not."

His personality's default mode seemed to be apology. Having known the poor young man's mother, Brenda Winshott had no doubts as to what had caused his abject surrender to life. And she was well aware of how dangerous the suppression of his inevitable anti-maternal feelings could have been. But whether the frustration within might ever build up sufficiently to turn Tristram Fullerton into a murderer she could not be certain.

"Presumably the police have spoken to you about your mother's death?"

He was startled by the directness of her question. "Yes, yes, of course," he stuttered. "I still can't really believe that ... you know, what they say happened actually did happen."

"They seem pretty sure of their facts."

"Yes. But who on earth would want to do that to my mother?"

Brenda Winshott bit back her instinctive response: anyone who had ever met her. Instead, she enquired, "I take it the police asked you what you were doing the evening she died ... ? After she came to see you here, that is?"

"Oh, yes, yes, they did."

"And I'm sure you were able to give them a perfect alibi ... ?"

"Well ... " He looked more hangdog than ever. "Not really. I mean, I was here, marking some books. But nobody saw me here. Nobody can vouch for me."

"Ah." There was no intonation in Brenda's voice, certainly no sign of suspicion or accusation. "And did the police tell you what killed your mother?"

"Some poison. Convalley ... something or other ... "

"Convallatoxin."

"Right." He had sat down by now, and had his cup of tea raised to his lips.

"A poison found in lilies of the valley," Brenda pressed on. "*Muguets.*"

The effect of the French word was instantaneous. Tristram Fullerton's hand shook as if he had a sudden onset of Parkinson's. Tea slopped down all over his thighs. He leapt to his feet in pain and confusion.

Brenda Winshott did not appear to have noticed his reaction. She just looked curiously up at the French calendar on the wall. "*Le premier mai*," she said. "*La fête du Muguet.*"

The schoolteacher slumped back down into his chair with an air of defeat.

"The day," Brenda went on, "when the French give to those they love little bouquets of *muguets* – or lilies of the valley – to celebrate the arrival of spring. Now, your mother told me that that was a little custom that you'd picked up when you were in France, and that she'd be very out of sorts if a first of May came round and she didn't receive her bouquet of *muguets* from you. Surely you wouldn't have let your mother down this year, would you?"

"No," Tristram Fullerton replied brokenly. "I did give Mummy a bouquet of lilies of the valley this year."

"Thank you for telling me," said Brenda Winshott politely. "Strange, though, that you didn't mention that to the police ... "

***

The Garlic Press was not particularly full that evening. Indeed, it was never particularly full. The residents of Morton-cum-Budely might use the place to entertain visitors they wanted to impress, or cadge meals there from passing relatives who they reckoned could afford it, but their general view was that the restaurant was ridiculously expensive. The principle of local organic sourcing of ingredients was one to which they might pay lip-service, but not at those prices.

The other drawback of The Garlic Press was that its ambiance was very definitely affected by the barely concealed hostility between the couple who ran it.

Of this Brenda Winshott was made aware as soon as she arrived that evening. In spite of the likely emptiness of the restaurant, she had booked a table for one at 7.15 (again mirroring the movements of the murder victim). She had arrived and parked the Golf in characteristically good time, but found no one there to greet her. From the kitchen, however, came the all-too-recognizable sounds of a marital row.

"You are not going to buy a new car!" shouted a voice Brenda identified as Lynette Fullerton's. "When we finally get the old bat's money, we are going to pay off the debts on this place and then start investing in it. That's what's been holding The Garlic Press back all these years – lack of investment. Constantly having to cut down on staff, doing everything ourselves, relying on you to do things that never get done properly. Huh. Now we've actually got the prospect of some money, you're not going to get your filthy paws on any of it!"

"Look, she was *my* mother," came Piers's whining reply. "So I deserve to benefit from her will."

"Why?" demanded his wife implacably.

"Because of everything I've done! There was no point in her dying if I don't get to see any of the money!"

At this undeniably interesting stage, the conversation stopped. The arrival of a brash young man who, to impress his sluttish girl-friend, had immediately banged the bell on the desk, interrupted more tantalizing revelations from the kitchen. Piers Fullerton issued forth, ignoring the solitary little old lady, and oozed welcome over the young couple.

Brenda Winshott was finally seated at a table laid up for two and, after lengthy sycophantic joking between Piers Fullerton and the other diners, she was granted a menu. This she made a great display of studying, though she had long known what she was going to have. Exactly what Joan Fullerton had ordered the week before.

What particularly interested her was the starter. "Devon Field Mushroom with Locally Sourced Forest Salad Garnish." Brenda wasn't aware of many forests in the locality of Morton-cum-Budely, but it was not her mission to question the authenticity of the menu's claimed provenance. Her concern was for more serious crimes.

Piers Fullerton delivered her Field Mushroom with great condescension. He had mumbled something earlier about the "regular staff being absent due to illness", and every bone in his body conveyed the conviction that he was not used to such menial tasks as being a waiter. Brenda Winshott, from the conversation she had overheard earlier, reckoned that he performed that function most evenings.

The Field Mushroom was juicy and Brenda enjoyed it. But the garnish was what interested her. Lamb's lettuce, chives and wild garlic. She waited for a moment when Piers Fullerton was in the kitchen and, having checked that the noisy couple were too interested in each other to notice her, put her plan into action.

From her handbag she produced a small spray of lily of the valley and quickly substituted it for the wild garlic. Then she ate up the lamb's lettuce and chives.

When Piers Fullerton arrived to collect her plate, he looked down at what lay on it and observed rather sniffily, "One of those hidebound English people who can't stand garlic, are you? I'll have you know that the wild variety has a much more subtle flavour than the kind you've usually had."

"I'm actually very partial to wild garlic," she said calmly. "It's just that that isn't wild garlic. It's another plant that looks very similar."

"What?" demanded Piers Fullerton brusquely.

"Lily of the valley."

His pale-blue eyes seemed to wobble in their sockets. For a moment he gaped and gulped. When he finally found words, he said, "I'll go and fetch my wife."

Lynette Fullerton might well have once been a pupil at Grantley House, certainly if the breadth of her thighs and the cut-glassness of her vowels were anything to go by. Her husband hovered and havered behind her, like a fly around the tail of a large horse.

"What's the problem?" Lynette's tone implied that, whatever had gone wrong, she was not the one to blame for it.

"It's just ... " Brenda Winshott repeated meekly, "that what is supposed to be wild garlic is in fact lily of the valley."

The anger rose in Lynette Fullerton like water in a kettle coming to the boil. But it wasn't directed at the little old lady who had made the complaint. No, as usual, it was her husband who was due for a sand-blasting.

"You idiot!" she screamed. "Are you incapable of doing the simplest thing right? Because of the way you spend all our money, we can no longer afford to get our salads from the organic farm.

Which is why I have to send you out into the countryside to collect the stuff. And you can even screw that up, can't you, Piers? I've shown you enough times what the plants you're meant to be fetching look like, but you still get it wrong. Of all the incompetent, useless, lame-brained ... "

The diatribe was set fair to continue for some time. While Brenda Winshott let its tides wash over her, she observed the warring couple. Lynette Fullerton's anger was triggered only by her husband's eternal inadequacy. Lily of the valley had no particular resonance for her.

It did for Piers Fullerton, though. On his face was the greenish pallor of guilt.

***

"Now you will have an 'O be joyful', won't you, Brenda?" Queenie Miles offered winsomely.

This description of a late-night drink had been introduced by Joan Fullerton, and soon everyone in Morton-cum-Budely was using the expression. Brenda Winshott found it an irritating affectation, another example of the many things that had annoyed her about her deceased neighbour. But as ever she kept such thoughts to herself.

She loathed Queenie Miles's taste in interior décor too. Brenda would never have given houseroom to the little coloured glass animals, clowns hanging from balloons or Italian ceramic figurines of urchins with large tear-filled eyes, which covered every surface of Yew Tree Cottage. Even the profusion of fresh flowers in evidence was spoiled by the over-elaborate crystal vases in which they had been placed. But Queenie would never have suspected this repulsion from her guest's courteous demeanour.

Brenda Winshott asked for a gin and lime juice, just as Joan Fullerton had done the week before. Queenie's drink of choice was a gin and bitter lemon. She raised her glass, and made the toast "O be joyful", which Brenda echoed without evident rancour.

As she had driven in her Golf the short distance from The Garlic

Press to Yew Tree Cottage, she had had some anxiety about raising the subject of the murder, but she needn't have worried. The first sip of gin was scarcely past Queenie's lips before she said, "Terrible what happened to Joan, wasn't it?"

"Oh, appalling," Brenda agreed. "The things people do these days defy belief. Standards of behaviour in this country have never been the same since they ended National Service."

This was not necessarily her own view, but it was an article of faith amongst the little old ladies of Morton-cum-Budely. Brenda had only said it to put Queenie Miles at ease – or possibly even off her guard.

"Is it true about her having been a Russian agent?" asked Queenie.

"Oh, I don't think so, dear," Brenda replied. "I can't imagine Joan ever having the discretion to keep any kind of secret. No, I don't think we should give credence to every opinion expressed at the bar of The Old Trout."

"Maybe not ... " Her hostess was thoughtful for a moment. "Of course it means there'll have to be a new Chair of the Village Committee ... " she observed.

Brenda Winshott's benign face registered mild surprise. "I hadn't thought of that. But yes, it will."

"I wouldn't dream of putting any pressure on you, Brenda dear ... "

"No, I'm sure you wouldn't."

" ... but I was very surprised, at the last election, that Joan was selected as Chair, when I – putting false modesty aside – was obviously much the most qualified person in Morton-cum-Budely for the job."

"Mm."

"So, come the moment, I hope I can rely on you to do what's right."

"Oh, you can certainly rely on me to do that," said Brenda Winshott with quiet conviction. She looked around the cluttered surfaces of Yew Tree Cottage's sitting room. "The flowers look lovely. Very natural."

"That's the effect for which I always aim." Queenie was totally unaware of how markedly she failed in her ambitions.

"No lily of the valley, though, I notice ... When I was last here, I'm sure you had lots of lily of the valley ... "

"I think you must be mistaken, Brenda dear," came the firm reply. "I've never much liked lily of the valley."

"You know, I would have sworn that the last few times I've been here—"

"I can assure you," Queenie insisted, "that I have never had lily of the valley in my house."

"I must be mistaken. Dear oh dear, getting so absent-minded these days. *Anno domini* catching up with me, I'm afraid." Brenda let a silence hang between them. Then she said, "I suppose you've heard the rumour that it was lily of the valley that killed Joan?"

"I've heard it, yes."

"One theory somebody had," Brenda went on vaguely, "was that Joan might have drunk the water from a vase in which lily of the valley had been standing. Apparently in certain circumstances that can be fatal."

"By why on earth would she want to do that?"

"I'm not sure that she *wanted* to."

"What do you mean?"

"It's possible someone may have *made* her do it."

"Forced her to drink it down?"

"Yes." Brenda Winshott nodded charmingly. She raised her glass and looked at the light through it. "Funny, gin and lime juice isn't a very attractive drink to look at. That pale green. Looks almost like water that flowers have been left in too long, doesn't it?" There was no response from her hostess, except for a narrowing of her beady eyes. "And now, if I may before I go, Queenie dear, could I take advantage of your facilities to go and powder my nose?"

"Of course. You know the way."

"Oh yes. I know the way." And picking up her bulky handbag, the little old lady went to find the "facilities".

* * *

When she got back to Honeysuckle Cottage, Brenda Winshott poured herself another gin, and this time didn't bother about the lime juice. As she sipped, she couldn't suppress a feeling of satisfaction at her evening's work.

She had met three people who might have killed Joan Fullerton. Three people who certainly had a motive. Tristram Fullerton could have done it as revenge for the humiliations his mother had heaped on him from the cradle; his brother Piers for the inheritance that might transform The Garlic Press and perhaps get Lynette off his back; and Queenie Miles for the opportunity to take over as Chair of the Village Committee. To an outsider the last might have sounded like insufficient motive, but Brenda Winshott had lived long enough in villages like Morton-cum-Budely to know the lengths little old ladies would go to to obtain that kind of preferment.

She didn't want to leap to conclusions. She would sleep on it. Sleep always resolved dilemmas for Brenda Winshott. Then in the morning she would decide who the murderer was, and tell Inspector Dromgoole.

***

He came round to Honeysuckle Cottage. Again he was unaccompanied. Again he said he wanted to keep their discussion informal, though Brenda Winshott wondered if what he really wanted was to keep it secret. Maybe his colleagues wouldn't think much of a Major Crimes investigator consulting a little old lady.

She told him her conclusions. The Inspector looked amazed. "But my people are meant to have searched the premises," he said.

Brenda Winshott shrugged. "Well, it seems as if their search wasn't quite thorough enough."

"I'll get men round there straight away," said Inspector Dromgoole.

And indeed his men found exactly what Brenda Winshott had told him they would find. A glass vase, together with the mobile phone and two handsets which had been stolen from Joan Fullerton's home. They had all been hidden in the high metal cistern of the old-fashioned lavatory in Yew Tree Cottage.

After the discovery Inspector Dromgoole asked Brenda Winshott whether she wanted her contribution to the investigation to be publicly acknowledged.

"Oh, good heavens, no," the little old lady replied. "I like to keep myself to myself. Also, it might cause bad feeling in the village, if it were known that I had ... as it were, *shopped* one of my neighbours."

"Well, that's very generous of you." There was no doubting the relief in Inspector Dromgoole's voice.

"My pleasure," said Brenda Winshott with a teasing twinkle. "After all, it wouldn't do for the police to have been baffled, and to have turned to a little old lady to help them out ... would it?"

Inspector Dromgoole coloured and eased a finger round the inside of his collar.

* * *

Queenie Miles was arrested and tried for the murder of Joan Fullerton. When sentence was passed, she continued vehemently to protest her innocence. But then, thought Brenda Winshott, people in that position always do.

* * *

She looked around at the other members of the Morton-cum-Budely Village Committee with quiet satisfaction. With the incumbent and her natural successor both, for different reasons, out of the running, Brenda Winshott had suddenly seemed the obvious candidate for what was now once again called "Chairwoman". She'd never have pushed herself forward, but everyone liked her, and from the opening of her first committee meeting, she had demonstrated just how efficient she would be in her new role.

Her efficiency was what gave her cause for satisfaction. Her efficiency in visiting Arbutus Cottage on May the first after Joan

Fullerton had returned from her "O be joyful" with Queenie Miles. She had also been very efficient in getting Joan to drink down another gin and lime juice, even though it did taste rather odd. Waiting until her victim had shown signs of ailing and then stealing her telephone handsets had also showed great efficiency. As had planting the phones, along with a vase containing traces of lily-of-the-valley-tainted water in the cistern at Yew Tree Cottage when she went to visit Queenie Miles the following week.

Yes, a job well jobbed, as Brenda Winshott's father used to say. She looked round at her assembled committee of little old ladies, and wondered who would be the next to step out of line. And how that one would be dealt with.

As Inspector Dromgoole had observed, it's the quiet ones you need to watch.

IN PURSUIT OF THE INEDIBLE

Brian McGilloway

THE ZIGZAGGING OF his movements between the trees made it difficult to keep a grip on the forest floor. The hounds were not far behind, their low baying echoing through the damp woodland. Beneath the sounds of the dogs crashing through the undergrowth thudded the beat of horses' hooves. The Hunt Master and the Harriers would be pounding after him.

The sack he dragged snagged on brambles, forcing him to stop and untangle it. He could feel the sheen of oil through the cloth, could feel its slickness on the latex gloves he wore.

He sprinted the final distance to the edge of the precipice, then, gripping the sack in both hands, he swung it above his head then released, watching it arc into the air above the drop, turning as it did so, opening and spilling out its contents which rained on to the trees in the basin of the quarry below.

The barking grew ever closer. He turned, peeling off his gloves and flinging them into the undergrowth to the right, then sharply cut left, towards the safety of the small hide.

After a moment, the first of the hounds arrived, their snouts pressed close to the ground, the wattles of skin at their throats vibrating lightly as they moved. Some of them twisted towards where he hid. Most, though, crashed into the dense thicket off to the right, attracted by the gloves he'd thrown there.

Soon after, the Hunt Master himself appeared in view, his horse moving as quickly as the proximity of the trees would allow. He dismounted, calling the dogs, but they ignored him, continuing to fight over the retrieved gloves. Cursing, he trod to the quarry edge and looked over, as if in expectation that a fox had plunged over.

The snuffling of the dogs in the undergrowth, their low whining, must have covered the sounds of the footfalls on the forest floor, for the Master did not see the figure approaching him, arms outstretched. His screaming as he fell was enough to cause the dogs to pause in their searching, to raise their heads and sniff at the damp air.

Inspector Devlin used the siren to disperse the crowd of protesters blocking the roadway into the woods. One woman, holding aloft a placard reading "Meat is Murder", thudded on his windscreen. Like many of the others, she carried a digital video camera and was filming him. Usually they brought the cameras to record the identities of those in attendance at the hunts, and in the hope they might witness something particularly barbaric during the pursuit that they could post on YouTube.

At the head of the crowd, Devlin saw, was the anti-hunt leader, Michael Walker, a megaphone clenched in his fist. Walker had been threatening for weeks to disrupt the hunt. It appeared that he'd got his wish.

The Medical Examiner, John Mulronney, was already working on the body by the time Devlin made his way down to the quarry basin.

"Doc," he managed, puffing for breath. "After that climb, you might have a second patient."

"Give up the smokes then," Mulronney replied, just as Devlin lit up. "I've IDed your victim: Sean Cassidy."

"Butcher Cassidy? The dentist?" Devlin asked.

Mulronney smiled. "That name's a little unfair," he chided.

"I think I've earned the right to use it. I was a patient of his. Looks like he's about to fill his final cavity."

Mulronney shook his head, tried not to laugh. "Smokes out," he said quickly, nodding to where two figures lumbered through the trees towards them, the Garda Superintendent uniform on the heavier of the two recognizable even in the dim light beneath the foliage. Devlin nicked his cigarette and looked around for somewhere to hide the butt. Finding nowhere suitable, he pulled a wide leaf from the sycamore branch above his head and wrapped it around the remains of the cigarette before stuffing it in his pocket so as not to leave his trousers stinking of burnt tobacco.

"Good morning, sir," Devlin said to his boss, Harry Patterson. He nodded to the second man.

"This is Charles Hasson, the deputy Hunt Master," Patterson said before the man had the chance to speak.

Hasson approached the body of Sean Cassidy reverently. He blessed himself, sniffed back his tears, rubbed at his face with the palms of his hands before turning to face the Guards again.

"I know Mr Hasson already, sir," Devlin said. "I was a former patient of the dental practice he and Mr Cassidy ran together. I'm sorry for your loss, Mr Hasson."

Hasson glanced at Devlin and sniffed loudly. "I'm sorry; I don't recognize you."

"I moved with Mr Cassidy when he set up his own new surgery a few months back," Devlin explained. "Were you part of the hunt today, sir?" Hasson wore riding breeches and a scarlet jacket, like Cassidy.

Hasson nodded.

Patterson spoke for him. "Mr Hasson was the one called the incident in."

"I knew we should have called the whole hunt off earlier," Hasson said. "It was a disaster from the start; the hounds began rioting."

Devlin suppressed a smile. "Rioting, sir?"

"They were running everywhere, following scents all over the place."

"Why was that, sir?"

"I don't know," Hasson replied. "It was very embarrassing for Sean. His first hunt as Master and the hounds riot. It's bad form. He headed into the woods ahead of the rest of us to bring them back. Wanted to save face I suppose. We went after him and when we reached the lip of the quarry he had ... he was lying down here. Like this." His eyes filled and he stepped away from the men a pace.

"It's a terrible accident, sir," Devlin agreed."

"Accident?" Hasson snapped. "We were warned the saboteurs would try something. Michael Walker specifically threatened to harm the new Master. You saw the crowd of them out on the roadway. Looking to ruin Sean's first day."

"So being Master's a big deal?" Devlin asked.

"It carries a certain, prestige, yes," Hasson said. "As does Deputy."

"Butcher – Mr Cassidy – would be a target for protesters, then?" Hasson stared at Devlin. "Of course," he snapped.

"Bring Walker in for questioning," Patterson concluded. "And no more smoking at the scene, either."

Devlin waited long enough for Patterson's retreating figure to disappear from view, then took out the butt he'd rolled in the sycamore leaf. Opening out the leaf fully, he saw on its back flecks of flesh, congealed in oil. He rubbed the flesh between his fingers and sniffed.

"What was Oscar Wilde's comment? The unspeakable in pursuit of the inedible," Mulronney commented, packing away his instruments.

"Smell that," Devlin said, passing the leaf to Mulronney. "And tell me you don't smell something fishy."

Hasson was at the edge of the woodland when Devlin struggled up the final incline to the road way, a hessian sack held in one gloved hand.

"Have you found something?" Hasson asked, helping him up through the tree line.

"Do you know what this is?"

"It's a drag-hunt sack," Hasson said, glancing at the object. "Some of our hunts are not allowed to track animals anymore, so we fill sacks with sponges soaked in gravy and leave a trail for the dogs to follow instead. Not as much fun, obviously."

"But nothing dies, I suppose," Devlin said. "What about fish?"

"Fish?" Hasson wrinkled his nose in disgust as Devlin opened the sack.

"Smoked fish. Kippers, perhaps."

"*We* don't use it, but it would divert the hunt, yes."

"So why would someone want to do that?"

"To sabotage it?" Hasson suggested irritably.

"Have saboteurs ever done anything like this before?"

Hasson considered the question. "They've disrupted the hunts in various ways. *He's* really the man you need to ask."

Devlin followed Hasson's nod to where Michael Walker stood in the distance with a group of protesters, laughing soundlessly as he watched Devlin.

The interview room in the station was stuffy yet, despite that, Walker seemed relaxed, sitting back in his chair, playing with his now empty polystyrene teacup while a Scene of Crime Officer took final swabs from his hands and arms. He pulled the cup apart, piling the pieces of foam in front of him. His solicitor watched him perform the act without comment.

"You threatened disruption," Devlin repeated.

"We're covering old ground here, Inspector," the solicitor said.

"Which is ironic," Devlin replied. "Since the hunt today covered new ground. And lots of it. Someone laid a decoy trail for the hounds to follow. Using drag-hunt sacking and smoked kippers."

Walker glanced at Devlin and smiled.

"Red herrings," he said. His brief laid a warning hand on his arm.

"Quite literally," Devlin agreed. "It led Sean Cassidy to his death."

"My understanding was that Mr Cassidy fell over the quarry edge," the solicitor said. "Are you trying to blame my client for that?"

"I'm awaiting lab work," Devlin said. "Unless Mr Walker wants to save me the bother."

Walker smirked again and turned his attention to the pile of polystyrene.

A tap at the door broke the uneasy silence. The SOCO re-entered the room with a thin folder. He whispered something to Devlin, opening the folder and pointing to one of the sheets. Devlin nodded and thanked him.

"So, Mr Walker. It seems your hands are clean."

The solicitor sighed and gathered together his papers.

"Your wrists, however, just above the glove line, aren't so much."

"Who said I had gloves?" Walker asked.

"You have traces of talc all over your hands," Devlin said. "The type of talc inside latex gloves. On your wrists and forearms, apparently, you have traces of fish oil."

"That proves nothing," the solicitor said.

"It proves you laid a trail for the hunt to follow. You led Cassidy to that spot. That's reckless endangerment at least."

"*That's* ridiculous," the brief spluttered.

"Nor will it help that the local Magistrate is a past Hunt Master," Devlin added.

Walker raised his hands lightly. "OK. I laid a trail for the hounds to follow. So what? I didn't kill him though."

"You'll take the fall for it though," Devlin said. "The Deputy Master tells us you made threats to hurt Cassidy."

Walker shifted suddenly forward again. "Hasson said that, did he? Get me my camera. I've something to show you."

Devlin stared at Walker for a second, then nodded to the arresting officer to hand it back to him.

"I admit I did lay a trail," Walker began. "To disrupt the hunt. The dogs were almost on top of me though, so I panicked and flung the sack over the quarry, then ducked into one of the hides we use to monitor the hunts. I'd the camera with me. Anyway, Cassidy arrived and went to the edge of the quarry. He just stood there, dumbly, looking over the edge for the fox. It was like he couldn't process what had happened to his hunt. I filmed him doing it; I was going to post something on the net, you know; him, the horse, the dogs – 'which one's the stupid animal?' Walker laughed mirthlessly looking to Devlin to see if he shared his humour.

"It's not quite up there with Wilde," Devlin commented.

Walker frowned. "Anyway, he never heard the other man arrive."

Devlin leaned across and stared at the display on the camera, interested now. The only sound was Walker's own harsh breathing, rustling in the speakers. In the small screen, Cassidy stood at the quarry edge. Then, from the other side of the shot, Hasson stepped into frame. He glanced around quickly, then approaching Cassidy from behind, he gave him a single two-handed shove, pushing Cassidy out of the shot, and over the edge.

"It was no secret that he was jealous of Cassidy getting the Master's position," Walker continued. "Whoever gets it can make a mint with the connections it opens up. Cassidy stiffed Hasson over their business, then beat him to Master when they started up separate firms."

Devlin nodded.

"Why didn't you hand this in earlier?"

Walker reddened. "Hasson will be the next Master. He'd scrap the hunts completely if he knew I had this."

"That's enough to withhold evidence of murder for?"

"To me? Yeah," Walker said.

"You and the hunters aren't that different, after all," Devlin said, shaking his head. "You're both in pursuit of the inedible."

Walker stared at him blankly. "Eh?" he managed.

MOPPING UP

Col Bury

---

*I*T'S ALWAYS SURPRISING *how far brain and skull fragments fly from the back of your head when shot at close range. An odd mix akin to cheap ketchup and mushy peas splattering a whitewashed wall is never a pretty sight, but it can be perversely satisfying to see in this relentless process of mopping up.*

***

"The Hoodie Hunter? He sounds like a real pussy to me, man."

"I'm telling you, Castro, he's one mean muvver. Dunt fuck about. Takes out three at a time. According to the *Sun*, he once ... "

"The *Sun*? Rah, yeah, right, man, it must be true then." Castro drew hard on his spliff. "C'mon, shock me. He did what?"

"Well, they said he took out five in one go on the other side of town, but the cops denied they were all down to him, innit. Said it was gang shit."

"The Hoodie Hunter?" he said, disdainfully clicking his tongue on his teeth. "So he took out five hooded sweatshirts ... in one go? Sounds like an aggressive shoplifter to me, innit. Hoodie Hunter, my arse." Castro sneered under his own dark hoodie. Everything about him was dark, from his skin right through to his thoughts.

Big-un was worried. All the papers had said this "one-man crime-wave" was responsible for up to a dozen hits this year alone, and he knew the net was closing on the likes of the Bad-Bastard Bullsmead Boys. They'd done some bad shit and this appeared to qualify them for whatever this crazy muvver was doing. He stroked a hand over the tattooed "B"s on each of his knuckles, signifying membership. "But, bro, he single-handedly fucked up the Moss Range Crew on the Westside."

"Rah, rah! Yeah, yeah, yeah. Those pussies? Blam, blam, fuckin blam. Heard it all before, man," spat Castro, sucking the dregs of the spliff. He had to admit, though, their rival gang had been a bit quiet recently since their two main men had been smoked by someone. Granted, it saved him a job, but he knew it wasn't any of his crew. He'd heard the MRC had been branching out their business into Manchester city centre and had dissed a few doormen, so that was the most likely reason they'd been smoked and not this vigilante prick. He killed the weed stub in the ashtray.

"Rah, bro. I had twos up on that."

"Fuck you and your bullshit, Big-un. You sound scared, man."

"Am not scared ... just a bit ... wary, innit."

"Rah, rah. A bit? Well, if that pussy ever fancies his chances, then I'm ready." He withdrew the Browning revolver from his waistband and pointed it at an imaginary target. "I was fuckin born ready, man. Just ask Leroy Bright ... or Mad-dog McPherson ... or Lenny Jacobs ... "

Big-un knew he couldn't ask them, because they were all dead.

***

DI Jack Striker had seen a pattern emerging. It was simple, but this guy must know someone close enough to access criminal records, as each one of his victims had been career criminals and menaces to society. He'd certainly done his research, having hit the bull's-eye with each of his eight victims to date. The papers were calling him the "Hoodie Hunter", and Striker had to concede that in the four months since this all started, the streets had become safer for Joe Public. Decent folk were off the killer's radar completely and the vibes from media phone-ins, polls and news reports were, on the whole, edging toward being favourable to this accomplished assassin. After the initial bravado of the mini-riots from hooded demonstrators had waned, diminishing numbers of alcohol-fuelled youths were hanging out on street corners terrorizing their neighbourhoods.

However, this was tempered significantly by the fact that Striker, and his sidekick DC Eric Bardsley, had had to tell eight mothers that their sons had been murdered. Striker could still hear the mothers' screams now, haunting him.

This was his first case since his promotion to the force's Murder Investigation Team. Just his damn luck that it was the biggest murder case Manchester had seen since the notorious Doctor Harold Shipman. The pressure was mounting and, despite reinforcements being drafted in from outside the force, The Brass was not happy.

Alone in his office, he continued scanning the fat file of statements and photos gleaned from the eight confirmed slayings to date. He must have missed something.

The irony being, the Hoodie Hunter had done in four months what GMP had been struggling to do for four years. Striker castigated himself for fleetingly almost admiring the man's work. Then, he swiftly reverted back to Detective Inspector mode and stared down at the fanned photos of dead sons.

**

He thought of his younger brother and bubbled with controlled anger. He'd learned to channel his rage into focus years ago in Kabul: an unforgiving place. He'd been watching the news and wasn't overly impressed at being dubbed "The Hoodie Hunter" by the media. However, to the streetwise, the nickname did sum up his actions, he supposed, as he'd certainly sent shockwaves ripping through the hooded youth fraternity. And from what he'd seen of that Detective Inspector Jack Striker in the many press conferences, he did seem like a decent cop; another reason to focus.

His latest reconnaissance now complete, he highlighted the last five names on the list, knowing exactly where to find them.

**

"He's been quiet, Eric. Too quiet," said Striker to the non-PC DC.

Bardsley stirred the tea, splashing it round with the subtlety of a Sumo wrestler doing a pirouette. He rolled his eyes, his Scouse tones as bullish as ever. "Now you've gone and said it, Boss. Jinxing us with the Q-word."

"Well, nothing for ten days. You don't start what he's started and then suddenly stop. He's planning something."

"He may've just finished. Had enough. Completed his ... er ... mission."

"Nah, there's more to come. I know it. How's our list of suspects looking?

"Well, I've done four more today and, again, nothing too obstructive and all with solid alibis. I think DC Collinge has done a couple, too, with pretty much the same results. But we'll keep plugging away, Boss."

The list of fifty possible suspects was drawn up by Striker and the Chief Inspector of the Operational Policing Unit based on intell', and was just another tool in the investigation. It was almost certain the killer knew the area and had a decent IQ, which narrowed the possible perps down drastically. Nonetheless, frustratingly, without a DNA profile of this highly skilled individual, Striker wasn't holding his breath on the list coming up trumps. But every angle had to be covered, including the remote possibility that the man was not even known to the Police, which would make things a whole lot harder. Striker also knew that they all slip up in the end, more so if they become prolific, as complacency creeps in, even with the best.

Bardsley handed Striker a cuppa, a stray drop splashing on to a witness statement the Inspector was reading at his desk.

"Shit, Eric!" Striker quickly dabbed the statement with the back of his silk tie. "No wonder Margaret does the brews in your house."

"That's all she bleedin' does though."

"Why, what's up?"

Bardsley said nothing, but Striker sensed there was more and raised his eyebrows expectantly.

"Well, I know I'm not the best hubby in the world. A bit brash, always in work ... I am polite though ... I always tell her when I'm coming."

Striker half-smiled, a tad confused.

Bardsley continued, "But only problem is, I have to shout it because she's upstairs in bed and I'm on the settee."

Striker grinned, shook his head.

"If the truth be known, I've not had a shag for six months, Boss."

Striker was surprised at Bardsley's sudden openness and briefly thought of his own non-existent sex life, especially since the first murder. But at least Bardsley had a missus. Well, one that was still with him. And, more importantly, he did still live with his kids, unlike Striker.

"And with trying to catch this psycho I hardly ever see her."

"Nature of the beast, Eric ... you could go back to uniform."

Bardsley stroked his greying goatee. "Fuck that! I'd rather be celibate!"

Striker laughed, and at that moment realized that this was the first time his brain had had a conscious break from concentrating on the case. It also dawned on him just how much the whole thing was affecting them. Not only were The Brass – and himself – squirming in the incessant gaze of the media, but personally Striker had twice missed picking up the kids from school on his "arranged visits" and Suzi needed no excuse to block his access completely, such was her acrimony. He needed to call his solicitor some time soon.

"Saying that, I wouldn't mind getting stuck into some of those new probies," said Bardsley with a pervy glint in his eye.

And timed to perfection, as if God was both teasing them and refocusing them simultaneously, the porcelain face of stunning trainee detective Lauren Collinge peered round the door and both men stared agog.

"Boss ... quick ... there's an attack in progress ... it might be our man."

***

The call box door squeaked shut and he undid the top couple of buttons of his black trench coat; his funeral coat that held the memories which spurred him on. After a deep intake of the chilly night air to compose himself, he dialled the number. Three rings later and an official-sounding female answered.

"Emergency services ... which service please?"

"Police."

*A few beeps later, another female, same officious tone.
" ... Greater Manchester Police ... which town, please?"*

"Moss Range, Manchester."

"What's the nature of your call?"

*"It's about that killer on the news ... The Hoodie Hunter, I think
they call him."*

"Oh, really?" She sounded surprisingly unconvinced. Silly bitch.

"Yeah, really."

"And what about him?"

"Well, he's attacking a lad on Moss Range Park."

"Oh, right ... and your name is?"

*"That's not important, but you'd best send someone down
here ... pronto."*

*"How do I know this isn't another crank call? We get loads, you
know?"*

*"You'll know when you get here cos there'll be another dead
lad!"*

"OK, OK. So how do you know it's him?"

*"He uses a baton, right?" Silence on the other end. "Well, he's
using it right now. I saw him. It's him. Listen ... " He pushed play
on his Dictaphone and intermittent screaming could be heard in
the distance.*

*"OK ... can you still see him?" There was urgency in her voice
now.*

"No."

"Can you stay on the line until we get patrols there?"

"No." With that, he hung up.

*He was beginning to enjoy this, and adding creativity had
brought a sense of fun to proceedings. Thinking up new ways to
outwit the police, and the fuckwits, had brought a new feeling of
accomplishment to his work. And, he knew Striker and his cronies
were as far away from catching him as ever.*

***

"I'm off to drill me baby-muvver," said Castro with a smirk.

"Which one?" asked Big-un.

"Laticia, of course. Need a fix of her Babylons." His smile revealed a gold incisor.

"Don't blame you, bro." Big-un pictured the said Babylons: impressive to say the least and well worth a juggle.

"So meet me back 'ere in a coupla hours, OK? And bring some funds for tomorrow."

"Do I ever let yer down, bro?"

"Never ... so let's keep it that way, man."

Their fists met in a show of respect and Big-un left Castro's flat, then headed to meet up with the boys. They'd jack a few pissed-up students, inflict some pain, have a bit of Sniff, then go back to Castro's to discuss business, like they did most nights.

**

Ten minutes later, he was driving in the opposite direction towards the city centre, having passed half a dozen speeding police vehicles. Blue lights and sirens in full flow, plus a couple of plain cars carrying what he suspected were detectives. He could've sworn he'd seen DI Jack Striker amongst them.

If so, job done.

He pulled the black VW Golf GTI into a side street, checked his mirrors and got out. As he descended the steps of the dim, dank subway, what others would construe as fear intensified. Unlike many, he knew fear was his friend and it was just adrenalin heightening his senses, preparing him for battle. He rolled down his hat, which doubled as a balaclava.

On his approach he could hear their voices growing louder. There was laughter, too, but not for long. He saw the first one, then the second, and soon clocked that there were six in total.

Careful.

They were listening intently to a big lad in the middle who was gesticulating as he described beating his latest victim. The words "Rah, rah" and "innit" were prevalent. His instant recognition of the big lad known as "Big-un" gave him a surge of excitement. The others were dressed in usual dark sports gear with their hoods predictably up. He stopped at the subway's entrance, straining to identify his prey from twenty metres away. He withdrew a small pair of binoculars and soon sussed the one he had no interest in had a white stripe across his hood.

He saw that two were going through the pockets of a young curly-haired lad who was clearly shitting himself; probably a student.

Right.

"Oy, dickheads!"

They pivoted in unison, looking surprised.

"Want some?"

"You fucking with us, man?" shouted Big-un.

"What do you think, you bunch of low-lives?"

The student was discarded like a rag doll. They all surged forward as one, a mass of arms, legs and aggression, their profanities resounding off the subway's walls.

He turned and ran, like a fox being hounded. He took the steps three at a time and soon passed a cul-de-sac on the right ... one ... then ignored the second right turn ... two ... he could hear them closing ... three ... he turned into the third cul-de-sac, stopping at the end before turning. Breathlessly, he withdrew a baton from his left sleeve, his preferred weapon due to its silence and his dexterity with it.

And he waited ...

The noisy throng emerged at the top of the dark street.

"There he is ... the cheeky fucker!" Toward him they ran, their footsteps resounding.

He stood his ground, baton at the ready. They slowed up, still cursing, a wariness creeping into their psyches, perhaps. Big-un drew a blade, glistening under a streetlamp. "You're fucked now, gobshite!"

He backed off from the gang, slowly edging round them, baton outstretched, cutting the night air with threatening swings. Eyeballing Big-un, he subtly manoeuvred them into the opening of an adjacent alleyway just a few metres to his right. They edged forward, cursing, spitting their venom, spreading across the alley's entrance. One tried to sneak behind him, but the baton cut noisily through the air.

"Wanker! Am gonna shank you," said Levi, clicking a flick-knife open.

He knew all his targets' names, and more, much more.

He jockeyed them back a few paces with a few sharp forward steps and vicious swings of the baton, further into the alley, capitalizing on their hesitancy.

He spotted a third knife appear and took a step back.

"He's bottling it now. Ha! His arse has fell out. Fuckin slice him, bro."

Two metres away, if that, their anxious faces just visible in the darkness.

Big-un lunged forward, the others followed, yelling. He sidestepped Big-un, grabbed his arm and jerked it behind his back, before wrenching it up to his neck until it cracked. He threw in a kidney punch for good measure.

"Aaargh!" Big-un's blade clanged on the floor and he dropped like a bag of shit, clutching his broken arm. One at the back shaped to throw something and he ducked as a bottle smashed beside him on a wall. They surged forward and a 360 turn impacted the baton on to a couple of stray skulls. Spotting Big-un trying to get up, he stamped on the broken arm, producing a girlie squeal.

But the throng were getting too close.

Plan B.

He expertly swung his baton and connected on the nearest cheekbone with a thud. The youth yelped like a puppy and the others hesitated again, giving him a second to remove a brick in the wall.

"That won't fuckin stop us, you muppet."

Behind the brick was his trusty Glock 17. "This fuckin will though!" He retracted his baton in a blink and slipped it up his left sleeve. Gripping the handgun in both hands, he took aim. All swagger now gone, their fear-etched faces froze. Levi turned to run.

"It's a dead end, boys … just like your lives!"

Three shots blasted out, one for each forehead. They dropped like dominoes.

Big-un tried to clamber up the wall, but fell to his knees and glanced up.

He heard someone sobbing and looked up at the last lad standing. The one with the white stripe on his hood, his face pallid and still as the moon.

"Go, now. Speak to no one, or you won't be so lucky next time. Go sort your life out." The lad left like shit off the proverbial shovel.

He spun, pointing the Glock at Big-un.

"Pleeeease ... you're Him, aren't you ... The Hoodie Hunter?"

He scanned up the street and saw that a few lights had come on. Time to get things moving. "Yes ... I'm Him."

"Aw nooo ... can I go ... pleeease?" asked Big-un, pathetically.

"What do you think?"

Big-un began whimpering, ironically akin to many of his own victims.

***

"Sorry, Boss, nothing," said the dogman with the powerful dragon lamp, his German shepherd, Reece, straining at the leash.

"Fuck!" Striker kicked a discarded beercan, knowing he'd been suckered. He scanned the vast park to see numerous dipped flashlights dotted about, all heading his way.

Bardsley and Collinge returned with torches from a sweep of the children's play area. "All clear."

"Never mind, Boss. It's just a hoax call. At least no one's dead."

Striker bit his lip, hard. The last person he wanted to snap at was Lauren Collinge.

"Give us a fag, Eric."

"Thought you'd stopped?"

"Just give me one."

Bardsley did as he was told and Striker took an exaggerated drag, instantly feeling dizzy, albeit briefly.

As they were joined by uniform, Bardsley looked at Collinge and whispered, "Lauren, it could still be a decoy. We're all *here* now, aren't we?"

Collinge nodded and looked a little embarrassed.

"Right. No one goes off duty tonight. He's up to something." Striker's voice notched up a decibel. "I want house to house done around that phone box, the CCTV tapes from the garage on the corner ... and those bloody 999 tapes ... now!"

***

Castro's mobile finally rang and he looked at Big-un's name on the screen.

"About fuckin time, man. Thought you'd got nicked or summat. Where've you been?"

"Hi, Castro," said the deep voice.

"Who the fuck is this? Where's Big-un?"

"You'll know me soon enough. As for Big-un ... for a big-un, he's a right cry-baby, isn't he?"

"Yo, dickhead! If you touch him you're dead meat. Do you know who you're fuckin with, man?"

"It's too late for Big-un. And, yes I do know you ... *man*. That's why I'm coming up, right now."

The phone went dead. Castro was confused and felt a surge of panic. Who the fuck would have the balls to take out his number two and diss him like that?

He took out his Browning and paced the flat. A quick glance out of the window revealed nothing. Shit ... who was this muv ... ?

Then it struck him like a Tyson punch. It's that Hoodie Hunter guy!

A fear he'd never known engulfed his soul, but he fought it. "OK, Mr Hoodeee-fuckin-Hunter ... let's see who the man is. I'm not just some punk-arsed-muvver you can trample all over ... *I'm* the man."

Even as he spoke, he could see for himself the pistol shaking in his grip.

There was a bang on the door. Castro's heart flipped. He wished he'd gone easier on the weed today. He pointed the Browning and edged closer.

Another bang.

He moved to the wall away from any line of fire. He needed to check the spy-hole. He took a sharp intake and moved swiftly to take a quick look. What he saw made him jump to the wall beside the door. He registered a snapshot of a man in a balaclava, holding a handgun.

He weighed up his options. He'd have to get the boys to clear the flat of money and merchandise pronto, before Five-0 got here, but this was self-defence, right? Bizarrely, he pictured Laticia's Babylons.

Fuck it!

Castro cracked out six shots, splintering the door, each bullet piercing through. Cordite filled the air. Adrenalin pumped. He felt sickly. He heard nothing, except his own heartbeat. Cautiously, still pointing the pistol, he peeped, but saw nothing. He slowly unlocked the latch and jolted the door open.

Relief.

"Woo-yeah, man!" Castro eyed the body. No movement. Definitely smoked. Black trench coat with blood seeping out. He jumped on to the body and began to dance. "Who's the man now, Mr Hoodeee Hunter?"

As he danced, he noticed the floor was wet and got a whiff of something. He crouched and touched the carpet, then smelled his finger. He laughed maniacally, his gold incisor glowing, and resumed his celebrations.

"I was right about you, man ... the Hoodeee Hunter's only gone and pissed himself ... what a fuckin pussy!"

He watched the fuckwit dancing over the corpse and rolled down the dual-hat balaclava, then readied the Glock 17. He stepped out from the doorway into the corridor.

"You're all the same," he hissed in disgust, causing Castro to pivot like an owl on speed. He cracked a slug into the fucker's gun hand and the Browning bounced a few feet away.

Castro shrieked and clutched his hand. His eyes wide with shock. A woman's petrified face appeared in a doorway down the hall. "Get back in and you'll be safe!" he said and her door slammed. A man's muffled voice now: "It's OK, Beryl, I've called the cops." He refocused on Castro. "Pull back the balaclava," he said, gesturing with the Glock's barrel.

Shaking, Castro slowly peeled the facemask back and it revealed a duck-taped mouth. He peeled it further and Big-un's vacant eyes looked up at him.

"Now pass me my other Glock."

Castro had tears in his eyes. "Look ... fuck you man! Who the fuck do you ... ?"

"OK, I'll get it myself." He blasted Castro in the chest " ... That's from arkid ... "

Castro buckled and gasped for air, his expression a grimace with a dash of disbelief. He leaned against the corridor wall.

" ... And this one's from me." The second shot hit the top of Castro's brow and he collapsed in slow motion.

He stepped over the bodies, resisting the strong urge to spit on them, and retrieved the empty Glock. Still no DNA for Jack Striker. As he heard the sirens, he glanced down the corridor at the wall.

It's always surprising how far brain and skull fragments fly from the back of your head when shot at close range. An odd mix akin to cheap ketchup and mushy peas splattering a whitewashed wall is never a pretty sight, but it can be perversely satisfying to see in this relentless process of mopping up.

* * *

Later that night, he opened the bottle of triple-distilled Jameson Irish Whisky he'd been saving and he toasted the photo of his brother on the mantelpiece. After taking a mouthful, he started working on a new list ...

AUL YELLAH BELLY

Gerard Brennan

"*B*ELFAST CITY COUNCIL *has announced its first amnesty to hand over pit bull-type dogs. Owners of pit bull terriers and other illegal breeds can hand them in without fear of prosecution. Confirmed illegal breeds will be humanely …* "

Niall O'Hagan thumbed the standby button on the remote control. *Newsline*'s Donna Traynor disappeared to the pop and fizz of screen static.

"Lewis has to go."

Ach, shit, Niall thought. *Too late.*

Niall turned to his ma. She stood in the living-room doorway and sucked a lungful from her Mayfair Menthol. The barcode of wrinkles on her upper lip flexed.

"We agreed," she said. "Remember?"

Niall nodded. He didn't know what to say.

"I know he's your pet, love, but if he gets reported to the USPCA it'll mean a bigger fine for your da. Maybe worse. You don't want that, do you?"

Niall shook his head.

"Good. At least you've a few weeks left with him, eh? You can take him for loads of walks around the forest and spoil him a bit before he goes." Niall's ma shoved a hand into the hip pocket of her Levis. "Here, love. Go to the butchers and get him a couple of steaks. You'll have enough change to get yourself a wee chocolate bar and some sweets. Maybe even a squeaky toy for Lewis from the pound shop."

Niall heaved himself out of the sofa and took the tenner off his ma. He mumbled a thank you and she laid her hand on his shoulder.

"Dinner'll be ready soon. I've got your favourite in the oven. Crispy Pancakes and Potato Waffles. The proper ones. I know you don't like the store brands."

"OK, Ma. Be there in a minute."

"Call me Mummy, love. You know I hate it when you call me Ma."

"Sorry, Mummy."

She stepped out of the doorway to let Niall past. As he trudged up the stairs he ran his fingers along the diagonal dado rail that separated the paint and the wallpaper. The machine-cut grooves in the wood had almost disappeared under years of glossing.

Niall rested his belly on the rim of the bathroom sink, and studied his upper lip in the mirror. He had the ghost of a moustache. He rubbed his chubby cheeks. Red as ever, but not as round. Maybe his puppy fat had finally gone into remission. He might even be good-looking underneath.

He dropped his Adidas bottoms before he noticed the toilet roll situation. Down to the last two sheets. He cursed and whipped them back up. No point shouting to his ma for the kitchen roll. She'd never hear him over the sound of the knackered oven fan. He pulled open the bathroom door and walked into his da.

"Fuck's sake, Niall. Watch where you're going."

"Sorry, Da."

His da looked at him and tilted his head. "Your ma told me about the dog. Aul Yellah Belly's days are numbered."

Niall shrugged. He hated his da's nickname for Lewis but had given up protesting.

"Look, son. I'll get you a wee Staffy for your birthday. They're almost as good as a pit bull anyway."

Niall shrugged again. His da tutted. "Come with me. I've something for you."

He led him to the computer room. They called it the computer room, but really it had a bit of everything in it. Weights, stereo speakers, old books about the Troubles, rolled-up carpet remnants, the shitty pictures his da had painted in prison and, of course, the PC on its desk.

Niall watched the aul fellah pull the bottom desk drawer out. He reached in and took out a wee black tube.

"Don't tell your ma about this."

He pushed a little silver button on the side of the tube. It bucked in his hand and a thin blade flipped out. Niall blinked and took a step back.

"Son, they call this an Italian stiletto. I call it a flick-knife."

He folded the blade back into its handle and passed it to Niall. Niall held it at arm's length, half expecting it to snap open and take off his fingers.

"Your uncle brought me that home from Thailand. I want it back when you're done with it, so don't lose it. And for God's sake, don't show it off to your mates. I don't want you getting scooped for acting the big lad."

"When I'm done with it?" Niall felt like he'd missed something important.

"Yeah, when you've taken care of Aul Yellah Belly."

"What? Why do I need this? They have injections for that."

Niall's da shook his head and rubbed the SNIPER AT WORK tattoo on his forearm. "I don't care what big Gerry says. No O'Hagan is ever going to cooperate with the peelers. You'll take care of your own dog yourself." He drew his index finger across his stubble-dashed throat to illustrate.

Niall clenched his arse. He wished his da had broken this to him after he'd been to the toilet.

"You want me to use this on Lewis?" Niall tried to sound casual. He squeaked his dog's name and spoiled the act.

"Grow some balls, son. You're near sixteen."

* * *

The trees of Colin Glen Forest whispered secrets as the wind coaxed branches together and riffled through the fresh leaves. The river shushed the gossiping oak and ash on its way to the Lagan. Hyper sparrowhawks flitted between the trees, sticking their beaks where they weren't wanted and mixing it up. The midges kept out of it. They were more interested in Niall's damp suede-head. He waved them away with his baseball cap.

Lewis snarled and shook the rubber bone from side to side. His lips curled back to reveal the strong teeth gripping the squeaky toy. The thick muscles in his neck and shoulders bunched. Niall barked at his dog, the sound echoing in the clearing. The powerful black pit bull dropped the toy and backed away from his master.

"Grow some balls, Lewis. You're near dead."

The dog responded to his master's gentler tone and shuffled forward, hunched but hopeful. Niall knelt and patted his flat head. The dog's cropped ears flopped forward. His tongue lolled and he panted enthusiastically. Niall scratched the soft patch under Lewis's jaw.

"You big wimp."

Lewis licked Niall's wrist.

"This isn't fair, Lewis. I shouldn't have to do this. But I can't let you fend for yourself. You'll just follow me home, and Da'll knock me out. Can't pass you on to one of my mates either. They're fucking useless. Wee John's been through about ten goldfish this year."

Niall grabbed Lewis's head with two hands. He leaned in closer and looked his dog in his brown eyes. He earned a slobbery face for his efforts.

"Ach, thanks, you big bitch. Right in the mouth too."

Lewis used to be Uncle Peter's dog. According to his da, Peter had bought him as a pup from a Donegal breeder, the year Lennox Lewis retired from boxing for good. Peter kept him for two years. He'd wanted to train him as a fighter. But Lewis hadn't the heart for that game. It didn't matter how long Peter starved him nor how many times he poked him through chicken wire with a walking stick. Lewis refused to snap. In a last-ditch effort to build the dog's confidence, Peter had thrown him into a makeshift ring with a wee Cairn terrier. Lewis pissed all over the place and backed into a corner while the wee dog barked for Ireland.

Peter gave the dog to Niall's da after that. Niall asked if he could walk him for pocket money, thinking he'd look hard with a black pit bull on a thick chain. His da didn't really want the responsibility anyway, and said Niall could have him.

Niall slipped his sweaty baseball cap back on. The stiletto weighed his pocket down. Lewis had lived the fortnight of his dreams since the amnesty was announced. Fed well and spoiled for attention every day. But each day went by quicker than the last and Niall's guilt increased with each passing minute. He'd woken the night before, hyperventilating after a nightmare involving a ninja with a pit bull's head and a sword with a folding blade.

"OK, Lewis. Let's just do this now. Any longer and I'll bottle out."

Niall pulled the flick knife out. The *schnick-schnack* of the blade unfolding ripped through the peaceful forest soundtrack. The dog growled.

"Come here, boy."

Niall reached out for Lewis's collar. Lewis lowered his haunches and growled another warning. Niall hesitated. *Animal instincts?*

"Stop it, Lewis. This is hard enough. Come here!"

Niall reached out again and Lewis laid back his ears and barked. Niall retreated a few steps. Lewis curled back his lips and a line of drool escaped from his maw. More barking. It bounced around the woods like gunfire.

"Take it easy, Lewis."

Niall stepped back again and stumbled over a tree root. As he pinwheeled his arms for balance the knife slipped out of his grasp. He caught himself but Lewis reacted to the sudden movement by bounding forward, stopping inches shy of his master.

"Sit, Lewis. Sit!"

Lewis jumped and toppled him.

Stunned and breathless, Niall rolled about in the mulch. He wrestled to hold off the slavering, scrabbling pit bull. Thoughts of Lewis's powerful jaws around his throat chilled him. His struggling arms shook then folded. Lewis's breath warmed his face. Then his cheek went warm and wet. Lewis slurped on his master like he'd been dipped in honey. Niall chuckled.

"No way I'm going to kill you. Da must be soft in the head."

Eventually Lewis tired of slathering Niall in saliva, wandered over to a tree and raised a leg in salute. Niall dug the flick-knife out of a nearby mound of leaves and pocketed it again. He'd hand it to his da and then tell him Lewis was going back to Donegal where Niall would visit him every Christmas and every twelfth of July. His Uncle Peter would get in touch with the dog breeder there as a favour for his favourite nephew. Problem solved. Piece of piss.

Niall travelled home via the cover of the dense redbrick housing estates from the Suffolk Road to the Lenadoon estate. He was worried that a dander down the Glen Road might attract the attention of a passing PSNI patrol.

He could smell the sausages sizzling under the grill as soon as he pushed open the front door. The oven fan droned irregularly. He led Lewis through the house and out into the mossy concrete backyard. As was his ritual, Lewis sniffed the pile of cigarette butts in the far corner by the big wooden gate, then padded back towards the scent of cooking. Niall pointed at the cushioned wicker basket against the yard's wall and the dog obediently curled up in it for a nap. Niall closed the back door and turned to find his ma shadowing him. She leaned forward until their noses almost touched.

"Your da is going to freak out if he sees that dog here tonight." She whispered as if Da was in the next room, rather than stuck in the rush-hour traffic on the M1.

"Chill out. I have a plan."

"Oh, a plan? Well that's OK then." She shook her head and went back to poking the dinner with a fork.

"Don't worry. I'll talk to Da when he gets home."

"Aye, dead on." His ma clattered a lid on to the steaming pot of potatoes and drained the starchy water into the sink.

Niall left her to it. He flipped on the TV and went straight to Sky One for a *Simpsons* repeat.

Halfway through the episode, his da barged in the front door and stormed into the kitchen, blanking his son and wife, focused only on the fridge. The source of Harp lager. Niall stood up but didn't know what to do with himself. His heart beat like a dinger

and his armpits got sticky. Instinct ordered him to slip out the front
door and disappear for a few hours, but his loyalty to Lewis froze
him in place. He waited for the crack and hiss of the ringpull and
gave his da a few seconds to gulp down a mouthful. Deep breath.
He baby-stepped into the kitchen to face the music.

"Hiya, Da."

His da shot him a little head flick. Acknowledgement of his presence without an invitation to chat. Niall's hands instinctively crept
towards his tracksuit bottom pockets as his shoulders slumped. His
fingers brushed the cold, tubular knife handle and he shook himself
out of his natural silence.

"Lewis is out back, Da."

Niall flinched as his da's dark eyes widened. The big man planted
his Harp tin on the kitchen worktop and jutted his chin.

"You what?"

"Lewis." Niall swallowed hard. "He's out sleeping in his basket."

"I told you to get that done today!"

"I don't want to do it."

"You mean you *can't*." He rubbed at the SNIPER AT WORK
tattoo. "Good job nobody was relying on you when our streets
needed the Provos."

"Leave him alone, Frank." His ma twisted the tea towel in her
bony hands. "You're too hard on him."

"You too, Trish?" He turned back to Niall. "Have you finally
turned your ma against me?"

Niall struggled to breathe without sobbing. "No. I just want to
look out for my dog." He sniffed back watery snot.

"You mean you're standing up for that yellah bastard of a useless fleabag? Standing up to me? Your da!"

Niall went against every instinct in his body and inched forward.
Towards the man who'd taught him fear. "That's right. You got a
problem?" It would have been a perfect moment of defiance if he'd
dropped his voice an octave or two.

His da fired the uppercut from his hip. It moved in a blur
and stopped less than an inch from Niall's chin. It would have
popped Niall's head right off his neck if it had completed its arc.

Niall barely had time to blink. His da misinterpreted his lack of reaction.

"Fucking hell, son." He flashed his crooked, nicotine-stained teeth. "You've found your spine." He clapped a heavy bricklayer's hand on Niall's shoulder.

"Get yourself another beer, Frank," Niall's ma said. "I'll put your dinner out in a minute. Niall, go you upstairs and get out of them tracky bottoms. I've just noticed how stinking they are. What were you doing today?" She went on and on, diluting the atmosphere with chatter. Her voice sounded normal, but Niall thought her complexion paler than usual. He gave her a nervous grin and retreated to his bedroom.

* * *

After he'd pulled on a fresh pair of jeans, Niall flopped on to his bed. He lay spread-eagled atop the faded duvet his ma patted straight with military precision every morning, and waited for his heart to slow down and his mind to catch up. He'd just stood up to his da and saved his dog's life. In that moment, he felt like he could do anything. Then the mingled shouts of his parents arguing cut through his victory buzz.

Niall sat up on the bed and cocked his ear. He couldn't make out the words, but his da seemed to be making most of the noise. His scalp tightened when he heard the back door slam shut. *Lewis*. He bounced to his feet and thundered down the stairs.

He stormed past his apologizing ma and yanked open the back door. Lewis cowered in the fag butt corner. Blood trickled down his shoulder. His da gripped the chef's knife from the wooden block in the kitchen. He glanced over his shoulder at Niall and sneered.

"You should have been man enough to do this yourself."

"Da, don't."

"Or what?"

Niall went for the flick-knife in his pocket. Empty. He'd left it in his tracky bottoms, now in a heap on his bedroom floor. Before common sense could freeze him in place, he darted forward and grabbed two handfuls of his da's thick black curls. He jerked back hard and smiled when his da yelped. Then his breath whooshed out as a vicious elbow caught him in his solar plexus. He stumbled back.

His da turned to face him, rubbing his scalp. "You're going to regret that, you wee bastard."

Niall got swept up in an adrenalin wave. He sucked in as much air as his winded lungs could take and wheezed his words. "Come on then, you fucking psycho. Teach me a lesson."

Niall heard a sharp growl. He looked beyond his da to see Lewis had come out of his corner. His peeled-back lips framed his canine maw. Twin lines of drool swayed back and forth. Niall's da tutted.

"Jesus Christ. Now the mutt is going to stand up to me. Fuck this shit." Niall's da kicked out. He cracked Lewis's jaw. Lewis backed up and shook his big head.

"Go on, Lewis," Niall said. "Sic the bastard!"

Lewis loosed an aggressive bark. Niall's da backed away from the dog, into his son's reach. Niall punched him low in the back. His da wheeled on him and grabbed the front of his T-shirt with his free hand.

"You wee fucker!" He head-butted his son.

Niall felt his nose crack. Warm blood streamed over his mouth. His head lit up with pain and his legs buckled beneath him. He crumpled on to the concrete. Instinctively, he raised his hands to his face then recoiled from his own touch. He closed his watering eyes and curled into a foetal position, sure his da would kick lumps out of him.

Lewis barked louder then yelped with pain. The bastard had hurt his dog again. Somewhere in the midst of his own pain, he registered his ma's screaming protests. He felt bony but warm hands on his cheeks and risked opening his eyes. His ma gazed down on him with concern. He gripped her wrists and tugged on them. She nodded and helped him to his feet.

Then Lewis attacked.

Niall watched as his wounded dog leapt at his da. Lewis took down his target with blinding speed and accuracy, leaping higher than Niall thought possible. As the powerful jaws clamped down on his throat, Niall's da screamed then gurgled. He fell back under Lewis's weight and passed out with shock. The bloody chef's knife tumbled from his grasp. Lewis ripped at his fallen prey.

"Oh Jesus, Niall, stop him."

Niall knew it was too late, but he called his dog's name.

Lewis ignored him.

Slowly, he approached the wild animal tearing chunks out of his father. As he did, he couldn't believe how calm he felt.

Blood ran down Lewis's heaving flank, spattering the ground. Niall's da had inflicted a lot of damage before Lewis finally snapped. Careful to avoid the wounds, Niall reached out to Lewis. On contact the dog scuttled backwards, away from his kill. He hunkered low on his hind legs and rumbled a warning through his bloody teeth. Niall made soothing sounds and approached Lewis, presenting open palms.

Master and dog faced each other, both bleeding. Niall saw only fear and anger in his pet's brown eyes. Lewis had been replaced by a feral beast and Niall wouldn't risk his wrath.

"Mummy." Niall spoke in a soft tone, aware that the slightest hint of a threat would set off another murderous attack. "Get in the house."

"You first."

"No, he's watching me. Get in while you can."

"I'm not leaving you here."

"I'll be right behind you." He tried hard to keep his voice calm. "Please, get inside."

"No!"

Lewis flinched and shifted his focus to Niall's ma. His muscled haunches twitched. Niall cursed and smashed his shin into the dog's throat to buy time. Lewis huffed and wheezed.

"Run!"

Niall grabbed his ma by the arm and pulled her into the house. He heard the scrabble of Lewis's claws on the concrete but didn't look back. They charged through the house and out the front. Niall cursed himself when he realized he'd left the front and back doors open. Too late to go back. He dragged his ma up the middle of the street. Lewis's screeching barks bounced off the redbrick terraces lining their escape route. Niall felt his balls shrink. His ma's arm slipped out of his sweaty-palmed grip. She stumbled and fell. Niall looked around for help. Ahead, two small boys on chrome folding scooters watched the commotion. Further up a little girl peeked out from behind a parked car. Niall's heart thudded.

He heard Lewis growl. His dog was close. His dog, his responsibility.

Niall thought of the little kids, less than fifty yards away. Too close and too slow to be safe from an enraged pit bull. He looked down. His ma struggled to her feet, but he could see the fight was out of her. No time to think. Niall took a deep breath and turned to face his dog.

Lewis was on top of him in a streak of black fury. They collapsed on to the potholed macadam side-by-side. Niall beat at the dog's muscled side with one fist as he tried to keep him at bay with his other hand. He felt the heat of fresh blood with each punch. Lewis whined but wriggled closer and fought harder. Niall pushed his head against Lewis's neck to avoid gnashing teeth. The dog wriggled and snapped its jaws. Niall screamed. He wrapped his arms around Lewis's body, hugging him close.

Niall bit into his dog's neck. It tasted awful.

The slippery pit bull skittered backwards, bleeding hard from a fresh wound and yelping. Niall spat out a hunk of flesh and fur, then scraped at his tongue with clawed fingers. He clambered to his hands and knees and braced himself for Lewis's next attack. He could hear the kids screaming and his ma crying, but he didn't dare spare them a glance.

Niall raised one hand and inched forward slowly on his knees. Lewis backed up. The end of his lowered tail whipped softly across his hind legs. Niall stood and Lewis seemed to shrink as he lowered his head and looked up at Niall like a scolded toddler. The big brown eyes almost distracted him from the pinkish blood and slobber foam on Lewis's black muzzle.

"Shush, Lewis. Shush-shush-shush."

Lewis peeled back his lips and flopped his tongue over his lower teeth.

"Shush-shush-shush-shush-shush." He lowered a splay-fingered hand to Lewis's head.

"Niall. Stop that." His ma almost broke the spell with her gravelly whisper.

"You shush too, Mummy." He kept his voice light and Lewis tilted his head to direct Niall's hand to the sweet spot. He cupped Lewis's ear and gave it a gentle jiggle. Lewis wagged his tail and lapped at his master's wrist. Niall shuddered at the thought of how much of his da's blood Lewis had lapped up with that tongue.

Still shushing and calming, Niall hooked his fingers under Lewis's collar and led him off the street and back to the open front door. He glanced over his shoulder to see his ma following at a safe distance. She pinched an unlit, white-filtered cigarette in her shrunken slit of a mouth.

"Just wait there until I come back out, Mummy."

She drew her plastic lighter from her hip pocket and gripped it between two shaking hands. The flint sparked and God held back the breeze to allow her a wee puff.

Niall wanted to go to her. Comfort her. But he had to get Lewis's chain. He wasn't ready to let go. One last walk. His ma needed time to grieve for her husband and Niall needed to take Lewis for one last walk. Tears welled in his eyes.

He didn't know who to cry for first.

A TOUR OF THE TOWER

Christine Poulson

THE FIVE O'CLOCK tour was the last of the day.

Sadly, for Miriam it was to be the last one ever.

The grey-haired American – in his early sixties, Miriam judged, around her own age – had been the first to arrive. He was wearing a cream linen jacket: good material and very nicely cut. Miriam's working life had been spent in the menswear department of a big store and she couldn't help noticing what people were wearing. She glanced down at her chocolate-brown linen shirt and trousers: a devil to iron but worth it.

She stole another glance at the American. He was talking to a middle-aged couple (matching red anoraks) and their teenage son (hooded blue sweatshirt).There was also an older couple: a T-shirt that he really shouldn't be wearing with a paunch like that, and a pale-blue cotton sweater for her. The Australian couple in their twenties (chinos and a short skirt with high-heeled slingbacks) looked like newly-weds. There were a couple of French girls (cropped top and shift dress), who were probably from the local language school. The two young men, a tall blond (ancient Fruit of the Loom T-shirt), and a shorter, shaggy-haired youth (blue waterproof) were campers, she guessed, judging by their wrinkled clothes.

The group was a typical mix of nationalities and ages and Miriam had seen hundreds like them in her time as a cathedral guide. She was already leading them across the nave to the locker room, when two late-comers, a middle-aged woman in a cream raincoat and a stocky young man in a blue anorak, came hurrying up. That made fourteen – fortunately. She didn't like having thirteen in a group.

After rucksacks and umbrellas had been placed in lockers, Miriam asked for a volunteer to stay at the back of the group so that she could be sure that no one was left behind. The American raised his hand and she smiled her thanks. He'd probably ask the best questions, too. She led the way to a door in the corner of the locker room. From there a spiral staircase wound up through the wall of the west front.

"It's a long climb," she warned.

One by one they followed Miriam through the narrow entrance. The staircase was lit by electric lights that threw a shifting pattern of shadows on to the walls. The group toiled up the steep stone steps, hollowed by generations of feet. When they were almost at the top Miriam made her usual comment to the people behind her.

"It's just when you think you can't go any further that you get there!"

She had timed it just right. They emerged on to the narrow gallery as the choir came in for evensong. There were exclamations and gasps of surprise when people realized how high they were. To Miriam's mind this was the best view of the cathedral. There was a lump in her throat as she watched the white and crimson robes moving in stately procession down the nave.

When she had heard about the new regulation, she had gone to see the Dean, but he had explained to her that his hands were tied: " … new rules … insurance company … no one over sixty."

"It's not fair, I know," he said, smiling at her, "when one feels as fit as one ever did." And that was kind of him, because she knew for a fact that he was a good three years younger than she was *and* he was in good shape. He might be a Very Reverend, but he was also a keen sportsman who coached a cricket team and ran half-marathons to raise money for charity.

His cropped hair and natural tonsure gave him a monastic look. He had asked her to call him Jim, but she really couldn't bring herself to be so familiar, and after that she tried to avoid calling him anything.

The Dean was right. It really *wasn't* fair and Miriam was as fit as she had ever been. Even after this climb, she was scarcely out of breath, unlike the woman in the red anorak, who was leaning on the parapet and breathing heavily. The stocky young man in the blue anorak was suffering too: beads of sweat were standing out on his forehead.

When everyone had had time to recover, she led them up the next flight of stairs to the space over the clerestory. Her voice seemed to run on independently of her, weaving in the history of the cathedral with little jokes and anecdotes.

"Pardon me," said the American, "but this render on the walls, what would that be?" He had an "aw-shucks" kind of voice that made her think of James Stewart.

"That's pumice stone covered with lime wash," she told him, thinking she'd been right about his asking the best questions.

"You really know your stuff," he said admiringly.

She did. It was scarcely an exaggeration to say that she knew every inch of the building. At nights when she couldn't sleep, she explored the place in her imagination, roaming the vast dark spaces of the nave and the glorious soaring transept, wandering through the tranquil cloister and the chapter house, where the treasures of the cathedral were displayed. There were some wonderful things in there – early printed books, embroidered altercloths and vestments, silver plate and, most precious all, St Edmund's silver-gilt chalice. It had escaped being melted down during the Reformation, when the bishop had buried it in the garden of the palace.

The cathedral was the only thing that had kept her going after Bill had died so soon after they had retired here from London. But perhaps she shouldn't have let it become her whole life. Maybe she should take up bowls again. She and Bill used to play at competition level ...

Someone coughed. She came to herself and realized that everyone was looking at her.

"This way," she said brightly and led the way across a gangplank to the room at the base of the tower that housed the working of the medieval clock. This was the first place on the tour where one could get a view of the close and the surrounding landscape. Pewter-grey clouds were massing over the water meadows. Miriam pointed out the bishop's palace through the rain-flecked window. She noticed for the thousandth time that the crevices of the windowsill were clogged with the desiccated corpses of dozens of butterflies. She had been meaning for ages to bring up a little battery-operated vacuum cleaner and now she never would.

I'm looking at things for the last time, she thought, and that's almost like looking for the first time. She was struck all over again by how strange it was to be up here, like seeing behind the scenes at the theatre.

An open wooden staircase like a piece of scaffolding wound up around the inside of the tower. They climbed it and emerged into the bell chamber. Miriam had timed this to coincide with the chiming of the hour at six o'clock. They ranged themselves on wooden benches or leaned against the wall and waited. The sound, when it came, was stupendous. It swelled to fill the whole space and got into your head. It was impossible to speak, scarcely even to think.

When the reverberations had faded away, it was time for the final climb up to the walkway that ran around the base of the spire. Today, the view was literally breathtaking. When you tried to speak, the wind whipped the words out of your mouth. The Australian girl didn't want to go out, and in those heels, no wonder. The metal rails were chest-high, but it felt as if the wind was about to lift you off your feet.

All that was left now was to retrace their steps. She kept up her flow of patter – it wouldn't do to short-change the visitors – but when the door at the foot of the spiral staircase thudded shut behind her, it had such a final sound that she felt like crying.

She got a grip on herself. Her last task was to count heads before the group dispersed. She counted thirteen. She frowned – must have missed one – and asked everyone to stand still so that she could count again. She did count again – and again – but it still came to thirteen.

Someone was missing.

"Did you count them in the clock room on the way down?" asked the Dean.

Miriam blushed to the roots of her hair. She had clean forgotten. That had been the rule ever since a visitor had got stranded on the walkway around the foot of the spire. The guide hadn't realized that he was still out there and had bolted the door. The poor chap had been up there for hours.

The American had been adamant that no one had been left behind. No, he hadn't actually counted them, but he had been the last to leave every room and each time he had checked that it really was empty. Miriam had felt a momentary doubt, but she clung to the knowledge that there had been three dark young men on the way up and only two when they reached the bottom. The trouble was that they were all dark and stocky and they had all been wearing something blue. No one else thought that anyone was missing.

It was just her luck that the dean should have been hanging around to witness her discomfiture. Not that he was censorious, far from it, but that only made her feel worse.

"I'll go back," she said.

"You most certainly won't," said the Dean. "I've been in my office all day. I could do with the exercise. I'll be there and back before you know it."

Miriam could only submit. She took a seat at the end of a pew. The other guides were drifting into the nave one by one. Miriam glimpsed one of the posher ones, a woman who was a leading light in the local Pony Club. She was pleasant enough, but Miriam never felt comfortable with her. She was whispering something to one of the others. From the corner of her eye Miriam saw them glance at her and look away. She wished the earth would open up and swallow her.

It seemed to take hours, but couldn't have been more than fifteen minutes before the Dean emerged from the locker room. As he walked briskly towards her, the skirts of his cassock flicking out behind him, he smiled and gave her a thumbs-up.

"All clear. There's no one up there," he said. "And there's nothing left in the lockers either."

Miriam felt a surge of relief. She got to her feet and the smiling Dean took charge of her. Chatting at her side, his hand under her elbow, he steered her towards the cathedral café. She was surprised to see that the little gathering of guides had swelled to a crowd. The door was opening, there were balloons, and someone was holding a bottle of champagne. The Dean released her and held up his arms like a conductor readying an orchestra. He brought them down and there was a loud chorus of "For She's a Jolly Good Fellow."

"Happy birthday, dear Miriam," said the Dean, and he leaned forward to kiss her on either cheek.

Perhaps it was the excitement or the champagne or both, but Miriam couldn't sleep. It was almost two o'clock when she gave up and pushed back the single sheet that was all she'd been able to tolerate. She put on her dressing-gown, padded into the sitting room, and switched on the light. Rain was spattering the window and buffeting the geraniums in their pots on the little balcony.

The top-floor flat wasn't in the close, but it was near enough for a view of the cathedral. On sunny days, the massive structure looked as vast and improbable as Mont Blanc. Tonight it was like a black ocean liner rising up in the dark. The floodlights were switched off at midnight and only a red warning light on the very summit of the spire remained.

If Miriam craned her neck, she could see part of the top floor of the dean's house. The windows were dark tonight. In the months after Bill's death, when Miriam had found it hard to sleep, she had often seen a light there in the early hours. It was comforting to think of the Dean working late on a sermon or reading some weighty theological tome and to know that she wasn't the only one awake.

Miriam thought about that last tour. She was certain that fourteen had gone up the tower and only thirteen had come down. Of course, *feeling* certain and *being* certain aren't the same thing. That's what Bill would have said. How infuriating he could be and how she missed him. If he were here now, he would be complaining about being woken up. "Stop fussing, woman." She could hear him saying it. And yet when push came to shove, he would have been on her side, and in the end, wasn't that what marriage was about?

The cathedral clock struck two. In her mind's eye Miriam saw the clogs turning and meshing together, the ropes growing taut, the pealing of the bell vibrating through the empty cathedral and floating out into the night air.

And that was when she knew how the disappearing trick had been pulled off.

She had already started to dial the Dean's number, when she asked herself what she thought she was doing. She couldn't ring him at this time of night and he had already been up the tower once. And suppose she did instigate another search and there was no one there after all, how would she feel?

She went back to the window. If only there was some real evidence, lights in the cathedral maybe ... But she could see only the spire from here. She bit her lip, considering. Well, why not, she wasn't going to get any sleep, that was for sure. She went into the bedroom and got dressed.

She was about to leave when her eye fell on her bowling bag, open on the chest of drawers. Buoyed up by champagne after the party, she had decided to polish her woods, thinking that maybe she could find a new partner and begin again. She picked up the nearest wood, and cupped the familiar, almost spherical object in her hand. It wouldn't make much of a weapon, and if it came to self-defence, she couldn't see herself putting up much of a show. Still, there was something reassuring about its smooth weight in her palm. She slipped it into the pocket of her cagoule. It just fitted.

Miriam was no stranger to the close at night. After Bill had died, insomnia had often driven her out to stroll there alone, but she had never been there when the rain was pelting down and the wind was blowing so hard that her umbrella was turned inside out. Two of the spokes were actually broken and she dumped it in the bin next to the kiosk that was occupied by the constable of the close. There was no one there at the moment – he must be on his tour of the close – but that would be her first port of call if she did see anything suspicious.

She pulled up her hood and pushed her hands into her pockets to reassure herself that the wood was in one and her mobile phone was in the other. She set off along one of the paths that dissected the grassy space around the cathedral. She didn't need a torch. Her feet knew the path and took her confidently forward. She reached the paved area outside the west front. Her eyes had adjusted to the dark now and the cathedral was no longer one black undifferentiated mass. She could distinguish window arches and the shadowy forms of saints in their niches. Out of the inky darkness of the porch a figure stepped forward. Her heart jolted and her hand shot to her mouth. The beam of a torch light dazzled her.

"Jeez, you nearly scared the pants off me," said a laconic American voice. "That hood. Thought for a moment you were some kind of monastic ghost."

"*I* scared the pants off *you*! What are you doing here?"

"Same as you, I guess. Couldn't sleep. Look, you'd better come in out of the rain."

She stepped into the porch. The American held the torch so that it illuminated both their faces. The strong light exaggerated his features, giving him deeply shadowed eyes and flared nostrils.

"I don't think we introduced ourselves. I'm Tom, Tom Leverens." He thrust out a hand. His clasp was firm and his hand felt dry and warm in hers.

"I'm Miriam. And I think you'd better switch the torch off. If there is something going on … "

"Yeah, yeah, OK." There was a click and his face vanished. "If I'd had my wits about me, I'd have actually counted heads, but – well, my mind was elsewhere. I've been planning this trip for years – it would have been our fortieth wedding anniversary – me and Louise. After she passed away last year, I wasn't going to bother, but the kids thought I needed a break. Tell the truth, I thought one of them might come with me, but Jeannie's expecting her second and Martha got offered this internship … "

The homely litany was reassuring. He was a solid presence in the dark beside her. She could smell an aftershave or cologne with an aroma of lime.

"Hey, you don't want to hear all that. Thing is, I know when someone might have slipped away."

"Me, too."

"The clock striking, right?"

She nodded, forgetting that he couldn't see her. "No one would have heard him going back down the stairs. There'd be plenty of time to hide in the roof space above the clerestory."

"But why?" he said. "For a bet? To steal something? All the valuable stuff must be in the chapter house. That chalice ... "

"St Edmund's chalice. That's what I'm afraid of. All the security is aimed at keeping people out of the building, but once you're in there ... "

"I've already been round the building looking for lights, but what say we do another circuit?"

As they stepped out of the porch, Tom took her arm and tucked it in his. It was a long time since a man had done that, but it felt natural. They fell into step with Miriam leading the way. The rain had slackened, but the sky was still overcast. They kept close to the cathedral, moving out to skirt flying buttresses, staring up at the windows, straining their eyes against the darkness. It wasn't until they were rounding the east end that something occurred to Miriam. She pulled Tom in against the wall.

"You said you'd already done a circuit," she whispered. "Did you see the constable?"

"Didn't see a soul."

"He wasn't in his kiosk when I passed it, so where is he?"

"Maybe he's there now."

They looked across the close towards the kiosk. But an avenue of mature beeches blocked the view. They saw a light glinting through the leaves, nothing more.

"We'd better see," Tom said.

They set off across the broad expanse of lawn. The wind pushed Miriam's hair back from her face and made her eyes water. From time to time, she glanced back and they had almost reached the shelter of the beeches, when she thought she saw something moving on the tower.

"What's that?"

Tom's arm stiffened in hers and he said, "What – I can't see—"

Something was dangling from one of the windows of the clock room like a spider letting itself down from a web.

"We'd better call the police." Miriam pulled her mobile phone out of her pocket.

"I don't think so." Tom's hand closed round her wrist and he didn't sound like James Stewart any more. "I'd hate to hurt you, Miriam, so I think we'll just stand here and let my confederate make his escape."

The night exploded into dazzling whiteness. The cathedral sprang out of the darkness. The floodlights had been switched on.

Tom released Miriam. He turned on his heels. The next moment she heard the thudding of his feet on the paved path between the beeches.

A figure in tracksuit bottoms and a sweater emerged from the porch door. Was it another member of the gang? No, it was the Dean. He was looking up at the tower. In the stark light she saw a young man with a rucksack on his back hanging about ten feet from the ground. The rope on which he was descending had snagged on a gargoyle. In an effort to free it, he was bouncing himself off the wall with his feet.

The Dean was sprinting towards him. Without pausing to think, Miriam set off too.

The gargoyle gave way. The young man fell heavily to the ground. Miriam prayed that he had twisted an ankle, but the next moment he was on his feet. The Dean was closing in on him. The young man slipped off his rucksack. For a moment Miriam thought he was going to drop it and run. Instead he gripped it by both straps and swung it at the Dean. The Dean swerved and the rucksack hit him only a glancing blow, but it was enough to send him spinning out of control. He fell awkwardly on his side. The young man was off, sprinting towards the west front.

In the distance there was the wail of a siren. Over by the constable's lodge flashing lights appeared and there was the sound of a car screeching to a halt. The dean was getting to his feet, but he wasn't going to be in time. Once the youth had reached the other side of the close and the bridge into the water meadows, he could lose himself in the darkness. Even if Miriam could intercept him, what then? He was young and fit and desperate and she was sixty.

She pulled the wood out of her pocket, drew back her arm, and bent forward in one fluid movement. The wood seemed to flow out of her hand and float across the shaven grass. Time slowed down. The wood reached the path at the precise point where its curved trajectory met that of the fleeing youth. The sole of his right foot made contact with the wood as if the two of them had always been destined to meet. His arms flailed, he wobbled, he teetered. For a moment it seemed that he was going to regain his balance. Then he was down with a crash that must have knocked the wind out of him.

"Ouch," said the Dean.

"Sorry," said Miriam, "but it's a nasty graze and it should be disinfected."

She put the top back on the bottle of TCP. The Dean rolled down his sleeve. They were in the kitchen of his house and there was a bottle of brandy on the table between them.

"I should be the one worrying about you," the Dean said. "You must have had an awful shock when that scoundrel turned on you."

"He'll get his just deserts."

Tom Leverens and the driver who was waiting for him had been stopped as they tried to leave the market square.

"You're sure you're all right? Delayed shock can be a nasty thing." He took one of her hands in both of his and squeezed it.

"Something I've been meaning to ask you," she said. "What were you doing in the close at that time of night? How did you know there was something wrong?"

"I didn't, but I know *you*, Miriam, and you were certain you'd left someone up the tower. When I went up to bed I saw that there was a light on in your flat and I guessed that you were still worrying about it."

"In my flat?"

"You can just see it from my bedroom window." Could it be? Was the Dean blushing? "I tried to ring you, but there wasn't any answer. I couldn't raise the constable of the close either. I went out and found the poor fellow trussed up by the wall of the bishop's palace. That was when I called the police."

"Thank goodness you were working late!"

"Actually I wasn't working. I was reading a detective story." Now the Dean was definitely blushing.

He wasn't looking at her, but he was still holding her hand.

Hunting for the first-aid kit, Miriam had noticed tins of soup for one in the cupboard. For the first time it occurred to her that someone might be a busy and important person, but still come home to an empty house.

She cleared her throat.

"Tell me, Jim," she said, "Have you ever thought of taking up bowls?"

DEAD MEN'S SOCKS

David Hewson

1

PERONI BENT DOWN to take a good look at the two bodies in front of him and said quite cheerily, "You don't see that every day."

"Actually," Silvio Di Capua replied, "I do. This is a morgue. Dead people find their way here all the time."

The cop was early fifties, a big and ugly man with a scarred face and a complex manner, genial yet sly. He frowned at the corpses, both fully clothed, lying on gurneys next to the silver autopsy table. One was grey-haired, around Peroni's age, short with a black – clearly dyed – goatee, tubby torso stretching against a dark suit that looked a size too small for him. The other was a taller, wiry kid of twenty-two or so with a stubbly bruised face and some wounds Peroni didn't want to look at too closely. Dark-skinned, impoverished somehow and that wasn't just the cheap blue polyester blouson and matching trousers. Rome was like everywhere else. It had its rich. It had its poor. Peroni felt he was looking at both here. Equal at last.

"What I meant was you don't see *that* ... " He pointed at the feet of the first body. "And that ... " Then the second.

Di Capua grunted then put down his pathologist's clipboard and, with the back of a hand cloaked in a throwaway surgical glove, wiped his brow.

Peroni was staring at him, a look of theatrically outraged disbelief on his battered features. Di Capua, immediately aware of his error, swore then walked over to the equipment cabinet, tore off the present gloves, pulled on a new pair.

It was nine o'clock on a scorching July morning. Peroni and Di Capua had just come on shift. The day was starting as it usually began. Sifting through the pieces the night team had swept up from the busy city beyond the grimy windows of the *centro storico* Questura. Today was a little different in some ways. The head of the forensic department, Teresa Lupo, had absented herself for an academic conference in Venice leaving the Rome lab in Di Capua's care. Leo Falcone, Peroni's inspector, was on holiday in Sardinia. Nic Costa, his immediate boss, was taking part in some insanely pointless security drill at Fiumicino airport. Their absence left Peroni at a loose end, with no one to rein in his inquisitive and quietly rebellious nature.

"Don't try to distract me with minutiae," the pathologist said.

"I like minutiae," Peroni replied. "Little things." He looked down at the kid in the cheap blue blood-stained clothes and thought: little people too. "Who are they?"

Di Capua glanced at his clipboard and indicated the older man. "Giorgio Spallone. Aged fifty-one. An eminent psychiatrist with a nice villa in Parioli, fished out from the river this morning. Probable suicide. His wife said he'd been depressed for a while."

"Do psychiatrists do that?" Peroni asked straightaway. "Wouldn't they just climb on the couch and talk to themselves instead?"

Di Capua stared at him and said nothing.

"Where?" Peroni continued.

"Found him beached on Tiber Island."

"That's a very public place to kill yourself," Peroni replied. "Bang in the centre of Rome. I've never known a suicide there in thirty years."

"He probably went in elsewhere," Di Capua said with a shrug of his spotless white jacket. "Rivers flow. Remember?"

"Time of death?" Peroni asked. "He's dried out nicely now. Shame it's shrunk his suit. That won't do for the funeral."

"I don't know. I just walked through the door. Like you."

The cop glanced at the second corpse. "And this one?"

Di Capua picked up his notes.

"Ion Dinicu. Twenty-two years old. Some small-time Roma crook the garbage disposal people came across in Testaccio."

"Small-time Roma crook," Peroni repeated. "It sounds so ... judgemental."

"He lived in that dump of a camp on the way to Ciampino. Along with a couple of thousand other gypsies. We got him straightaway from the fingerprints ... "

"Oh yes," Peroni said, smiling. "We printed them all, didn't we? Man, woman and child, guilty of nothing except being Roma."

"I'm not getting into an argument about politics," Di Capua told him.

"Fingerprinting innocent people, taking their mugshots ... that's politics?" Peroni wondered.

"Don't you have work to do?"

"I knew his name already," Peroni went on, ignoring the question. "Got here before you. Looked at the records downstairs. The kid never went inside. Couple of fines for lifting bags from tourists on the buses. Got repatriated to Romania when we were bussing people there. Came back, of course. They never take the hint, do they?"

"Maybe he should have done," the pathologist suggested.

The cop went to the other end of the body and leaned over Dinicu's bloodied, bruised features.

"What killed him?" he asked. "And when?"

Di Capua sighed.

"You've worked here a million years, Peroni. You know what a man looks like when he's been beaten up. When did it happen? I apologize. The battery died on my crystal ball. Come back later when I've got a new one."

"Some big tough guy who liked to use his fists," the cop said. He pointed at the corpse of Spallone. "The other guy's got a messy head too."

Di Capua folded his arms.

"Not unusual with river deaths. Could have hit the stonework falling in. Got washed around by the swell. When we've done the autopsy then I'll tell you."

Peroni leaned over the dead psychiatrist and said, "Nah. If you hit stonework you get grazed. The Roma kid could have gone that way. He's cut. Spallone here ... " He looked more closely. A bell was ringing but too faintly. "He's bruised. Swollen. No blood."

"Blunt force trauma," Di Capua said.

"That tells me a lot."

The pathologist folded his arms and looked a little cross.

"Why should I tell you anything? You're not dealing with either of these guys. Not as far as I know. Inspector Vieri's been round seeing Spallone's widow. He sent some wet-behind-the-ear agente to wake up the little hood's camp at seven. No one talking, of course. If it wasn't for the prints and photos we couldn't even ID him. Agente said even his own father wouldn't help. Chances are it's a gang rivalry thing and some other Romanian hood will wind up dead a couple of days down the line ... "

"Dead quack gets an inspector and the full team. Dead immigrant gets a visit from an infant. The Roma mourn their dead, Silvio. Just like we do. Also you're forgetting the deal."

"The deal?"

"You don't do cop work and we don't dissect your corpses."

Di Capua was starting to get mad.

"Yeah, well ... One drowned doctor. One beat-up street kid. And you hanging round here as if you care. Don't you have work to do?"

"There's always work if you look for it," Peroni answered. "Right now I'm ... " He searched for the right word. "Foraging."

"Then why don't you go forage somewhere else?"

"What next?" the big man answered, ignoring him again. "Slice and dice. Weigh the organs. Check the spleen and things. Peek inside at every last little bit of them, working or not, until you get something to write down on your report ... what? Tomorrow? The day after?"

Di Capua opened his arms wide.

"That's the way it goes. Custom and practice. One mistake and we all could hang. As you know. Now ... "

"Just a favour," Peroni said quickly, coming close, putting a huge arm round the skinny, balding pathologist.

"Why should I ... ?"

"The socks," Peroni interrupted. "Those ... " He pointed at the two sets of feet in front of them. Shoes off already. Ankles splayed. Very dead.

"What about them?" he asked.

Peroni laughed, took away his arms, clapped his big pale hands. Then he retrieved a pair of scissors from the kidney bowl on the silver autopsy table and carefully cut up through the front of all four trouser legs. Spallone's expensive dark blue barathea didn't give in easily. The Roma kid's garish polyester was so flimsy he could slice it apart just by lifting the lower blade.

"Are you kidding me?" he asked when he finished.

Both men were wearing long socks pulled up close to the knee. Odd socks. The one on each right leg light-blue and unpatterned. The other pale-grey and ribbed so subtly the markings were scarcely noticeable.

The fabric of the blue socks seemed as cheap and thin and as artificial as the kid's shiny jacket and trousers. The toes were close to going on both. The grey ones were newer, wool maybe. Expensive.

"I never knew a young guy who wore long socks like that," Peroni murmured. "Curious ... "

"Gianni ... "

"But not as strange as the fact two dead men, found the same morning in different parts of Rome, seem to have dipped into the same sock drawer before they went out for the night."

"You don't know that!" Di Capua protested.

Peroni retrieved his phone from his pocket and took a picture of the dead legs. Then he reached forward and very lightly tweaked Spallone's dead big toe.

Di Capua shrieked.

"That was the favour," the big man added. "I don't leave till I get it."

The pathologist grumbled. But he still went and got a pair of tweezers and, very carefully, pulled each sock from each dead limb, depositing them in four separate plastic envelopes.

Then the two men peered at the plastic bags. One set, the grey ones, had a brand, a pricey one from Milan. The others looked the kind people picked up three pairs to the euro from a street stall. No name. Nothing to identify them.

"I can check on the fabric to see if they're the same too," Di Capua said, serious now. "Give me till the end of the afternoon."

"Thanks," Peroni said, and slapped the pathologist hard on his white-jacketed shoulder. "That would be good."

2

Inspector Vieri's team worked on the floor below, in an office next to Falcone's unit. Peroni's customary home was empty now. Costa had taken everyone except him to Fiumicino for the drill there. Peroni knew why he'd been left behind. He always found it difficult to keep a straight face when the management decided to lead everyone in the merry dance known as role play.

Vieri had arrived the previous month sporting the finely tailored suit and standoffish manners of a young officer eyeing some rapid progress up the ranks. He had all the traits that mattered when it came to catching the eye of promotion boards: a couple of degrees from fancy universities, a spell at business school, periods in some of the more fashionable specialist units involving terrorism, organized crime and financial misdemeanours. The man was all of thirty-three and had never, Peroni suspected, punched or been punched once in his entire life. To make matters worse he hailed from Milan and spoke in a gruff, cold northern voice that matched his angular pasty face. He never set foot in the Questura without shoes so polished they looked like mirrors. No one ever saw a hair out of place on his bouffant, gleaming black-haired head. The general opinion in the Questura bar round the corner was he'd make commissario before he turned forty, maybe even thirty-five. After that the direction of his golden future was anyone's guess. Just to rub salt in the wound the man's wife was a beautiful redhead who worked as a producer for the state TV company RAI. All things considered, as far as the average grizzled Roman cop was concerned Vieri might as well have worn a sign saying "Shoot me" on his back.

This morning's suit was dark-blue barathea, not unlike the shrunken jacket and trousers clinging to the corpse of Spallone upstairs. Peroni, who had barely met the man, strode over smiling, introduced himself and asked if he could help.

Vieri gave him a taciturn stare. He'd brought a handful of officers from Milan with him when he arrived in Rome, turned them into his personal confidantes, people he spoke to before any of the locals whenever possible. An unwise decision for such a clever man.

"Don't you have work in your own unit?" Vieri asked. He didn't look in the least grateful for the offer of free manpower. Just suspicious.

"Sure," Peroni replied pleasantly. "But sometimes a little local knowledge can help an officer who's new around here. I hope you don't mind my saying. Rome's a village really, sir. The peasants tend to stick with their own and … "

Vieri wasn't listening. He was staring at his phone, a model that was decidedly fancier than anything handed out as stock issue to the average Questura officer. Another innovation from Milan.

"The socks," Peroni added.

The young inspector scowled and waved him down. He was reading his email. It seemed to Peroni he was the kind of man who thought every message, whatever its contents, was of overriding importance, if only because it was addressed to him.

Vieri barked out a couple of orders to two men across the room. Local guys. Peroni knew them both. One of them nodded. The other briefly stared at Peroni with hooded eyes.

"The socks," Peroni repeated. "If you'd care to come upstairs to the morgue I can show you. Better to see than try to explain sometimes." He scratched his ear. "I keep trying to work out how many possible solutions there might … "

"I don't approve of police officers interfering with the work of the forensic department," Vieri said rather pompously, not once taking his eyes off the phone.

Peroni felt his hackles rising and wondered whether he cared if this man noticed or not.

"It's cooperation, not interference, sir … " he began.

To Peroni's surprise Vieri's hard stare managed to silence him.

"I know it was once fashionable for police officers to watch and sigh and groan as pathologists go about their business," the inspector declared. "Truthfully it's a waste of time. Theirs and ours. When forensic have something useful to tell us, they will do so and I will listen. In the meantime ... "

Peroni watched him bark out yet more orders. Hunts for CCTV images. Mobile phone records. Car details. A call to the media to see if anyone had seen a man answering Spallone's description near the river the previous night. Nothing about the Roma kid.

"You don't think it was suicide?" he asked when Vieri was finished.

"I don't know, agente," the man replied curtly. "I have no preconceptions. His widow assures us he was a troubled man. He absented himself from home at regular intervals." Vieri shrugged. "I have no reason to disbelieve her. Spallone was a widely respected man. He sat on the board of several public bodies. He was a patron of the opera. Known in political circles. We will investigate and report in due course." For the briefest of moments his stony, ascetic face displayed something approaching doubt. "I imagine she's right. They were a wealthy couple, well-connected. Hard to see anything else."

Peroni stood there, wondering whether to point out that Vieri had contradicted himself already. Instead he said, "I would really appreciate two minutes of your time to see these socks."

"You didn't listen to a word I said, did you?" Vieri snapped.

"On the contrary. I hung on every one."

The young inspector turned away from him. He was listening to someone else speaking on the phone.

"The Roma kid ... " Peroni began, not moving a centimetre, speaking a little more loudly to regain Vieri's attention.

"If the father can't even stir himself to come and identify the body there's very little I intend to do at the moment. They can stew until they want to talk, or sort it out between themselves and then we'll pick up the pieces."

Peroni blinked, struggling to believe what he was hearing, though, with a moment's reflection, he knew the man's callous words should not have come as such a shock. This was the modern force, not the one he'd joined thirty years before. Priorities, procedures, resource management ... and the keeping sweet of bereaved relatives of men who sat on public boards and patronized the opera. All these mean, inhuman practices had come to swamp the previous shambling chaos through which officers sifted hopefully, trying to sort good from bad, the crucial from the inconsequential, with little to help them other than their own innate intelligence and knowledge of their fellow men and women.

"You'll never get a thing out of the Roma if you send kids to talk to them," he said with undisguised brusqueness. "It doesn't work like that."

Vieri's eyebrows – which were, the old cop now noticed, manicured and shaped – rose as if in a challenge.

"You think you could do better?" the man from Milan asked.

"I know it," Peroni replied straight away. "You want me to go there?"

"You don't work for me," Vieri said, looking him up and down. "Frankly I prefer younger officers. My problem, not yours ... "

With that he turned and started talking to his men again. About phone records and databases, video and intelligence. Peroni guessed this team could try to work two cases – no, one and a quarter at best – for the rest of the day and never set foot outside the building, never do a thing without having a phone to their ear, their fingers on a keyboard, their minds tuned for a call from the morgue and the delivery report that said: it's fine, go home, there's nothing you can do.

One of the men Vieri had brought with him from Milan was watching Peroni with a look that spoke volumes. It said: get out of here.

"You know," Peroni said, touching the guy's arm and nodding at the sunny day beyond the window, "it's really not scary out there. You won't even get sunburn, I promise. You should try it some time."

Then he marched out of the room, along the corridor, back into his own empty office, looked at the vacant chairs there, the silent phones, the desks, the computers, papers strewn everywhere.

Years before Peroni had been an inspector himself. As arrogant as Vieri. Maybe more so. Maybe with better reasons. He was good at that job, a leader, a man who let people run with their own imagination at times, and always – or usually – managed to reel them in before they went too far. Then his job and his private life collided and when he woke up from that crash everything he held dear was gone: family, career, a good few friends. He was lucky to keep any kind of position in the police after that, even one as a lowly agente, maybe the oldest, lowliest officer there was by now. Lucky too that, for some reason he could never understand, love came back into his life in the shape of Teresa Lupo, the morgue boss now in Venice. And friendship in the form of Costa and Falcone.

But they weren't here. He was and he could do what he damned well liked.

Afterwards Peroni would try to convince himself it was a considered, reasoned decision, one weighed and balanced, pros and cons, before he made up his mind. But this was, he knew, a lie, a conscious act of self-deception. The proof already lay in his pocket. On the way out he'd subtly lifted a very full notepad from the desk of one of Vieri's taciturn Milanese minions.

There was one sentence in it about Ion Dinicu and three pages about the eminent psychiatrist Giorgio Spallone and his business-woman wife Eva. They lived in a fancy street in Parioli. It seemed a good place to start, but only after he'd checked a couple of things on the computer first.

3

The villa was, like everything in the couple's quiet, rich, suburban cul-de-sac, daintily perfect. A three-storey detached home from the early twentieth century, soft orange stone with colourful tiled ribbon decorations over the green shuttered windows. A small orchard of low orange and lemon trees ran between the ornate iron gate and baroque front door with its stained glass and plaster curlicues and gargoyles. In the finely raked gravel drive stood a subtle grey Maserati saloon and next to it a lurid red Ferrari.

He glanced through the window of the low sports car. There were magazines on the passenger seat, titles about women's fashion, a few coarse gossip mags and, somewhat oddly, a glossy about men's health, with a cover of a muscular bodybuilder type straining at a piece of exercise equipment. There was nothing on the seats or the dash of the Maserati. The car looked clean and tidy. And, like the Ferrari, not much used except as some icon placed behind the iron gates, one advertising the wealth of those to whom these vehicles – so unsuited for the busy, narrow roads of Rome – belonged.

Showy jewellery for the drive, and it wasn't hard to work out which was his and which hers.

Parioli, he thought. The place was such a byword for bourgeois snobbery that the term *pariolini* to describe its residents had become, for some, an insult in itself. It was a little unfair. But only a little.

He walked up to the door, rang the bell and showed his ID when a maid in a white uniform answered. She was foreign, of course. Filipino he guessed. The name "Maria" was embroidered on the uniform. She'd been crying recently and didn't look into his face after she read the ID.

"I know we've been here already. How upsetting this is, Maria," he said. "But I do need to check a couple of small details with Signora Spallone. Please ... "

She wasn't there, the maid said, still staring at the ground.

"Where is she?"

"Down at the gym."

Peroni was thinking about this when the woman sensed his puzzlement and added quickly, "It's Signora Spallone's job. She and the signore own it. She wanted to break the news to the people there. They all knew him."

"Of course," he said, nodding. "This is such a very small thing. I just need to check some clothing in their bedroom. Giorgio's. One quick look. The boss won't let me off shift until it's done. Can I ... ?"

She opened the door and he walked in. The place was beautiful, spotless and palatial, walls covered in paintings, old and new, corridors dotted with what looked like imperial-era statues.

"Their bedroom?" he asked.

"They sleep apart," she said quietly and led the way upstairs.

The first bedroom they came across was huge, the size of many working-class apartments. It had its own separate lounge and a bathroom with two sinks, one toothbrush by the nearest.

He opened a wardrobe and saw line upon line of elegant dresses there.

The husband's room was as far away as it was possible to get. Right at the back of the house. He could hear the drone of traffic from the busy main road. It was small and functional and hadn't been decorated in years.

"When did Giorgio move in here?" he asked.

She looked at the bed, all perfectly made for a man who'd never sleep in it again. Then she brushed some stray cotton fibres off the sheets and said, "Two months." Nothing more.

Peroni opened the wardrobes. Plenty of expensive suits and shirts, drawers with underwear and socks. All wool or cotton. Nothing cheap or artificial.

"He was a careful dresser," he said.

She nodded.

"The signore took pride in his appearance. He was a gentleman."

"A depressed gentleman?"

Her chin was almost on her chest.

"I am the maid, sir. You ask those questions of the lady."

Peroni got the address of the gym, a back street near the Campo dei Fiori in the city centre, not far from the Questura. An awkward place to get to from Parioli, twenty-five minutes if the traffic was light. Then she showed him to the door. He couldn't help noticing a pile of unopened letters on a sideboard next to it. A few looked like bills. Several bore the names of banks.

He stood on the threshold for a moment, gazing at the Maserati and the Ferrari.

"Those are not cars for Rome," Peroni said. "Too big, too expensive. Too easily scratched by some stupid little kid who hates anyone who's got the money to buy them. Why anyone ... "

"They hardly use them," the woman said. "Only when they

leave the city. Every morning I wash them down. But when those big ugly things last went anywhere … "

She shrugged.

"How do they get around then?"

"I call a driver," she said as if he was being dim.

4

Peroni didn't approve of exercise. So gyms didn't impress him much. The one the Spallones owned was called the "Palestra Cassius" and occupied the first floor of a vast palazzo in the Via dei Pellegrino, the old pilgrims' street from the city to the bridge to the Vatican. The name intrigued him until he saw plastered behind reception a black and white picture of the man most people knew as Muhammad Ali, not Cassius Clay. There was a debt to history being paid here, but it wasn't a Roman one.

The place smelled of aromatic oils and sweat. There was a blank-looking girl with a ponytail behind a computer, rows and rows of unused exercise machines, and close to the small windows at the back a boxing ring. A sign leading off to the right said "Sauna".

"Exercise I can do without," Peroni told the kid behind the desk when he walked in. "But sitting around sweating doing nothing … that I can manage. Is it good?"

She gave him a leaflet. It boasted of the biggest, most traditional Finnish sauna in Rome. She had her name embroidered on her T-shirt: Letizia. Someone, Spallone's wife he guessed, liked to tag the things they owned.

"I could break into a good sweat looking at the prices," he said.

"We've got great introductory discounts," she piped up. The girl looked around at the lines of empty machines. "And discounts after that if you ask nicely."

"I always ask nicely. How many people work here? Trainers, fitness people and the like?"

"Ten, fifteen guys. Plus me. We're good."

"I'm sure you are," Peroni said, showing her the police ID. "But I'd really like to see Signora Spallone now if you don't mind."

The woman was in her office with ten or so of her men. Every one of them was big and fit, under thirty he guessed. Names embroidered on their shirts. Mostly foreign from the way they spoke and muttered as he showed his ID. More than half of them blonde, Nordic. Like Eva Spallone herself, he now saw.

She ushered them out and gave him a hard stare, the one civilians used when they thought the police were paying them too much attention.

"You're not Italian," he said.

"Is there something wrong with that?"

"Not at all. It's just that I always try to place people. It's a game."

Eva Spallone looked no more than thirty-five. She had short blonde hair, the face of an angel, bright blue eyes, and the curvy, almost carved kind of figure Peroni normally saw in the magazines, not real life. She didn't look as if she'd been crying recently.

"Finnish," he said.

"You guess well."

"Not really." He pointed to the books and trinkets behind her desk. "You've got that blue and white flag there. The sauna makes a thing about being Finnish and not many do that. Two and two tend to make four. Usually anyway."

On the desk stood a picture of her with a man he took to be the living Giorgio Spallone. She was in a wedding dress, he in a suit. The Colosseum was in the background. So many weddings used that location for pictures after the ceremony. From the look of her he guessed this couldn't have been more than four or five years before.

"I went to your house," he said. "There was a detail to be cleared up. We thought you'd be at home."

Her eyes misted over then. Very quickly it seemed to him.

"This was Giorgio's business too. It was how we first met."

A tissue came out of a very expensive rose-coloured leather handbag so small it couldn't have contained much else. She wiped her pert nose then rubbed her bright blue eyes with the back of her hands.

"In a sauna?" Peroni asked.

"He loved the silence, the tranquillity. When his mind was troubled it was the place he went. On his own."

She didn't want to answer that question.

"So you two started the business?"

"It was a wedding gift." Another dab of the eye. "He was the kindest man. Everyone here loved him. I had to tell them myself. Lately he'd been so ... melancholy."

Peroni found he couldn't take his eyes off the wedding photo.

"What detail?" she asked.

"Was your husband a fastidious man?" Peroni asked.

Eva Spallone blinked.

"Fastidious?"

"Was he careful about what he wore? How good his clothes looked? How neat they were?"

"Very much so," she said.

"Thanks." Peroni got up.

"You came all the way for that?"

"I don't need to take up any more of your time, signora. Will you be here long? Just in case my boss thinks of anything else."

"I'm having lunch with a friend. Round the corner. So many people to tell. And you won't let me do anything with poor Giorgio. No funeral arrangements. It's OK. I understand."

He asked himself: was that what most widows did the day their husband was found floating in the Tiber? Have lunch with someone to tell them how awkward things were?

He wondered. Most people reacted by staying close to the home they shared. A few found that too full of memories. Too painful.

"Here," she said and gave him a business card for the gym with her mobile number on it.

On the way out he stopped by the ring. Two of the hulks were sparring, landing not-so-gentle blows with puffy brown leather gloves.

Peroni watched them, thought about the gloves and said quietly to himself, "Boxing."

The rest of the hulks stood around watching, commenting in a variety of accents, none of them native Italian. None of them looked to be in mourning. Next to the ring was a glass door marked as the sauna entrance. Peroni wandered over and took a look. He'd no idea what a sauna was like really so he opened the door and found himself gasping for breath almost instantly. It was like peering into a hot, damp fog. All billowing steam, so thick he couldn't see his hand in front of his face.

"You wanna try?" asked a hulk, taking him by surprise when he walked up behind.

"Isn't there someone in there already?"

The hulk laughed.

"Who knows? You share a sauna, man. That's what it's about. Togetherness." He squinted at the fog. "But no. I don't think there's anyone there. Thursdays are quiet."

"Spallone used to come here alone, I thought," Peroni told him.

"Yeah, well … " The hulk shrugged. He looked and sounded east European, Russian maybe. Peroni couldn't quite make out the name stitched on his shirt. "That's more business than choice I guess. Sauna's a sociable thing." A big elbow nudged Peroni in the ribs. "A place for men to talk. Get things off your chest."

"Maybe I'll try next week," Peroni told him and walked out of the building, back into the bright day. It was just after noon now. Lunchtime. He wondered what Teresa was doing in Venice, how the play acting was going at Fiumicino, what kind of culinary delicacy the ever-picky Falcone had chosen for his solitary meal in Sardinia. All this speculation made Peroni hungry so he bought a panino stuffed with rich, salty porchetta from the market and ate it from his big left fist as he drove out to Ciampino and the Roma camp.

5

He didn't need any directions for this place. Every cop knew where the Roma lived, dotted around the city in shifting encampments, bulldozed from time to time by the authorities only to reappear a few weeks later, a kilometre or so down the road. Several hundred, even a thousand men, women and children lived in these places, crammed together in hovels built out of scrap wood and corrugated iron, huddled around makeshift braziers in winter, sweating out in the open in the scorching summer. For years now the Italian government had been trying to push them back into Romania and Hungary. It was like trying to sweep away the tide with a broom.

Peroni pulled through the camp gates and found his car immediately surrounded by scruffy urchin kids, hands out begging for money. He pushed through them and found himself confronted by a tall, surly-looking man with a beard. Grubby clothes, dark, smart eyes. Security around here.

"Police," Peroni said, showing his ID. "I need to see Ion Dinicu's father."

"Not here," the man said immediately.

Peroni sighed, looked around. There were eyes glittering in the dark mouths of the makeshift homes, all watching him. He'd dealt with these people many times in the past. It was never easy. They liked living apart from everyone else. They didn't want the police to solve their problems, offer them protection. In their own eyes they were a separate nation, detached from a world which failed to understand them. That didn't mean they were without rules or principles or beliefs. Faith even.

"If Ion isn't identified ... claimed by someone ... " Peroni told the man, " ... then it's up to us to deal with his funeral. If that's what you want, fine. But bear this in mind. We'll pass the work on to a charity in all probability. A Catholic one since we're in Rome. If anyone wants an invitation ... "

The bearded man stood there, silent.

"If Ion's father speaks to me now, just for a few minutes, I will make sure a request goes through for an Orthodox service. Romanian Orthodox if you like. It can be done. It won't be unless I ask for it."

He waited.

Orthodox and Catholic. It was like football. Same game, different teams. Bitter rivals.

Two minutes later he was in a corrugated shack at the end of the camp, seated at a low plastic table with an elderly bent man who smelled of cheap dark tobacco and wood smoke.

"What do you want?" Ion Dinicu's father asked.

"To find out who killed your son."

"Why?"

Peroni shrugged and said, "It's what I do. Don't you want to know? Don't you want some kind of ... " He hesitated. The word sounded odd, wrong, in these circumstances. " ... justice?"

Dinicu's father had the same kind of eyes as the man on the gate. Dark and intense. Blazing now.

"Find me the man who killed my Ion and I'll show you justice," he said. "He was a good boy."

Peroni sighed.

"He was a pickpocket. A petty thief. Petty. But a thief all the same."

"That was then!" the old man cried. "Not now."

"Now he's dead. I want to know why."

The Romanian was silent for a while then he murmured, "Everyone hates us here."

"Why did Ion come back then? After we deported him?"

"Everyone hates us there too. At least here there's money. Work."

"Tourists on the bus. Women with purses in the park."

"No!"

"Then what?" Peroni wanted to know.

"When he came back he was a chauffeur. People wanted to go somewhere, they called. He was good. Cheaper than those taxi guys. Reliable. He had his own car."

This was interesting.

"Where's the car?"

"Gone. He went out on a job yesterday. Next thing you send round some kid in a uniform to tell me he's dead. What am I supposed to say?"

Peroni folded his arms, stared out of the opening of the shack, watched the kids playing with their grubby toys, the women sitting round, darning clothes, hanging up washing.

He couldn't shake from his head what he'd seen in the morgue that morning. How many possible explanations were there?

"This is going to seem an odd question," Peroni said. "What kind of socks did your son wear?"

The man blinked and looked at him sideways.

"Is this a joke?"

"Not at all. What kind? Short? Long? Medium?"

Ion Dinicu's father rolled up the legs of his cheap black trousers. His socks ran all the way to the knee.

"These socks," he said.

The cop nodded.

"I mean," the man went on, "*these* socks. We shared. Socks. Shirts. Was cheaper. Easier that way."

"Right," Peroni murmured and found his mind wandering back to the city.

"What happens to my son? You won't let the Catholics have him? Don't do that to him. He don't deserve it."

Peroni said, "Give me some way I can get in touch with you. When his body's released I'll make sure they know he needs an Orthodox service. If you want to come in to the Questura ... "

The father was shaking his head briskly.

"Then give me some way ... "

The man reached into his pocket and handed him a card. It read, "Deluxe Ciampino Limousine Service" and had two mobile phone numbers printed beneath a colour photo of the front of an elderly but very shiny Mercedes, a young man standing beside it, smiling.

"The second phone number's mine. First was Ion's," he said.

Peroni said thanks then walked back to the car.

6

By the time he was back in the city, looking for somewhere to park near the Campo dei Fiori, most of the smell of tobacco and wood smoke had left him. Peroni squeezed the battered unmarked police Fiat into a diagonal space that left the front wheels up on the pavement of the Via dei Pellegrino and would, to his regret, force pedestrians into the cobbled street. He hated doing this, but there was work to be done.

He got out and called the Questura. Prinzivalli was the duty sovrintendente running the uniform officers out on patrol. This was good news. He was an old-time cop, a colleague going back three decades.

Peroni said, "If I asked for five strong men outside an address near the Campo dei Fiori in twenty minutes would you want to know why? Time's a little short, see."

There was a pause on the line. Trust was an odd thing. Delicate, easily broken.

"I've got officers round there all the time," Prinzivalli said. "I'd still need to give them some idea what exactly they're looking for."

Peroni told him, then passed on Eva Spallone's mobile number and some more instructions.

"You know the new guy from Milan? The inspector? Vieri?" he said when he was finished.

"Mr Cheery we call him," Prinzivalli replied.

"He's the one. Well, Mr Cheery's busy right now. It's best he doesn't know. Not straightaway."

There was that pause again, then Prinzivalli said, "Vieri hates being interrupted when he's busy. I've learned that already."

"Me too," Peroni said, then finished with a few more details and cut the call.

He read the notes he'd made on the computer that morning. Detailed notes. There was a stationery shop on the way to the gym. He went in there, bought the things he needed, then walked down the narrow street to the Palestra Cassius.

7

It was now close to four o'clock. Peroni smiled for the girl on reception and said, "It's me again, Letizia."

She was chewing a nougat from the bowl on the counter, looking bored in the way only teenagers knew.

Eva Spallone wasn't there. Must have been a long lunch. Prinzivalli could deal with her then.

There seemed to be one customer in the place, a fat guy sweating and grunting on an exercise bike. The hulks were still crowded round the boxing ring. Peroni walked over. Two of the biggest blondes were in boxing shorts, bare-chested, tanned pecs and biceps gleaming with oil, sparring lazily off and on the ropes. They looked bored too.

Peroni clapped his hands and brought the fun to a close. Ten sets of eyes turned on him. He waved his ID card high, chose his most authoritative of voices and ordered them all into Eva Spallone's office. That instant.

They obeyed straightaway, shambling over to the far side of the gym in a long line. Peroni watched them. Bodybuilding did something bad to the way people walked, he decided. It was like health stores. They always seemed to be full of sick, sniffy people.

The ten hulks filled the small office. The smell of sweat and oils and liniment was a little overpowering. None of them spoke, which he found interesting.

"This is a simple, routine check," Peroni announced, forcing his way to the desk. "I want ... "

He began coughing. Kept on coughing. The hulks stared at him. They looked worried they might catch something.

"Sorry ... sorry," Peroni said, gasping. "Got a really bad throat today. Hurts like hell. Tell you what ... "

He pulled out the dark grey paper he'd bought in the stationery shop and the blue pen then scrawled a single word in large capital letters.

"Any of you guys ever been ... " He coughed and roughed up his voice even more. "Here?"

Then he walked down the line showing them the paper. Eight of them shook their heads. A thuggish-looking guy with the name Vladimir embroidered on his T-shirt glared back at Peroni and said, "Was years ago. In Russia."

"Must have been fun," Peroni replied.

Only one, halfway down the line, didn't answer at all. He was the biggest of them all, one of the boxers, a good deal taller than Peroni, muscle-bound with a flattened nose, dim close-set eyes and a stripe of Mohican-cut blonde hair. His chest gleamed with sweat and oil, his muscles looked as if they'd been sculpted somehow.

There was a name embroidered on his bright red satin shorts. Eva Spallone did take great care to tag her possessions.

Peroni looked down at it and said, "Sven?"

"What was the question again?" the man asked.

Peroni held up the paper. The close-set eyes glanced at it nervously then darted round the room.

"The rest of you leave," Peroni ordered and he didn't take his attention off the man in front of him for a moment as they filed out of the office.

"Swedish?" Peroni asked when they were gone.

"Finnish."

"Like Eva Spallone. Isn't that nice?"

The hulk just stood there. Big, stupid Sven, with his beady blue eyes and blonde cockatoo stripe.

Peroni looked at him and said, "You know when my daughter was four years old the doctors thought there was something wrong." He indicated his eyes. "Here. With her sight. We went through all these tests. Pretty nurse in the clinic." He grinned. "I never said no when it came to running her there."

"What?" Sven asked.

"Bear with me," Peroni went on. "One of the things they thought was maybe to do with the way she saw colours. That perhaps she was colourblind." He sighed. "Scary when you think there's something wrong with your kid. There wasn't. She just needed better glasses. But that nurse was so pretty, so careful, I kept going back and talking to her. I thought I knew everything then, of course. Colourblindness. Red and green. People couldn't see traffic lights and things. I was a smartass. She put me straight. Sure they can't see red or green. But they can see something, which light is on for one thing. So they can drive if they want. No problem usually. And also ... "

He reached into his pocket and found his own notepad where it sat, next to the one he'd stolen from Vieri's guy that morning.

"It's not just red and green. That may be the most common kind there is but you find lots of others. Like one called ... " He glanced at the note. "Tritanopia. You heard of that, Sven?"

The Finn stood there stiff as a gleaming rock, saying nothing.

"I looked it up. They call it blue-yellow colourblindness but it's not that simple. Specially with the blues. Anyone who's got this thing really struggles with those. Can't see the difference between blue and black easily for one thing."

"What're you talking about?" Sven asked.

Peroni's eyes narrowed, "I'm talking about you. How did it go? Let me guess. Eva's been monkeying around with you for a little while. She says, 'Oh Sven, oh darling Sven. If only it was the two of us. You and me running the gym. Then we'd be together and make lots of money too. But Giorgio won't ever divorce me ... '"

Beads of sweat were beginning to build on the Finn's broad, tanned forehead.

"So all you've got to do is wait one night until he's in the sauna on his own. Walk in there, boxing gloves on, beat him about the head until he's out stone cold. You got those gloves on, remember. No serious marks. No cuts. Dump him in the river. Eva says how sad, how depressed he was. Suicide. Stupid cops nod and then you're done."

Sven cleared his throat and stared down at his own broad chest.

"I guess Eva thinks a sauna's a clever place," Peroni went on. "All that evidence – sweat and blood and everything – gets washed away down the drain. Not sure about that frankly but it doesn't matter. You see Giorgio Spallone's a nice guy. Really. His maid in Parioli calls him cars from some poor Roma kid called Ion. He likes Ion. Feels sorry for him. Sneaks him into the gym for a sauna last night as a favour. And there's the Roma kid, hidden in all that steam, when you go wading in with the boxing gloves, punching Giorgio in the head."

Peroni reached down and lifted Sven's vast fists. He undid the lace ties of the boxing gloves at the wrist and gently tugged them off his enormous hands. There were cut marks on the knuckles. He touched them. Sven flinched. Then he looked more closely at the hulk's face. There was a graze near the right cheekbone.

"Middle-aged psychiatrist's a piece of cake for a thug like you. A Roma kid like Ion doesn't go down so easily. I guess the gloves came off there. But he was a little guy. You punched him out in the end."

"This is stupid ... " Sven murmured.

"It was," Peroni agreed. "See, when it's done you now have two bodies in all that steam. Both naked. One, Ion, dead, I guess. Giorgio out for the count. You got to dress them – Eva won't do that for you. You got to get them out of there."

He cocked his head and looked up at the Finn.

"Ion's car, I guess. You got his keys, beat where it was out of him. Put the two of them in there. Giorgio goes in the river somewhere near the Ponte Sublicio in Trastevere. Then you drive over and dump Ion with the trash near the nightclubs in Testaccio, the sort of place a Roma kid might find himself in trouble."

"Stupid," Sven said again.

"Here," Peroni told him, "is the problem. Tritanopia. You got to put their clothes on and it's hot, you're scared, you're all alone. And you don't see what everyone else can. Those two guys are wearing different coloured socks. They'd know it. I'd know it. But not you."

He pulled out his phone and showed the hulk the photo from that morning: four dead legs, two sets of odd, long socks.

Peroni put the phone away and picked up the paper sheet he'd written on.

"See this? The paper's just about the same colour as Giorgio's socks. The pen the colour of Ion's. You can't read what I wrote there, Sven. Because it all looks the same to you. Here. Let me help."

He took out a red pen and scribbled over the letters he'd written earlier in blue.

"How's that?"

Sven could see the word now. He stared at it with his tiny, frightened eyes.

"P. R. I. G. I. O. N. E." Peroni spelled it out.

"Prison. Jail. Incarceration. That's the place you're headed. One murder's bad enough. But two."

He sighed, put away the paper, reached up and lifted the Finn's chin so he could look into his face.

"Two is so much worse. My advice is this. Tell the truth. Think about cooperation. Tell everyone how Eva put you up to it and led you by your beat-up nose. We'll find out anyway. You don't think you were the first one she made goo-goo eyes at, do you? We'll talk to all the other guys. But if you help us now you're talking years off the sentence. Otherwise ... "

He stood back and looked up and down at the shining, sweating man in front of him, quaking in his tight red satin shorts.

"Otherwise it's just more fisting time in jail, and really I do not recommend ... "

The Finn pushed him out of the way and raced across the gym towards the stairs.

They run oddly too, Peroni thought. Arms pumping, legs going up and down like mechanical dolls.

He walked over to the receptionist, watched by the line of wide-eyed, open-mouthed hulks who'd stayed behind and the fat customer now stationary on his exercise bike. There he picked up a couple of fistfuls of nougats from the bowl and stuffed them into his pockets before calling Vieri.

"There's good news and there's bad," he said when he got through to the inspector still in his office in the Questura. "The Spallone case and the Roma kid are done. Bad is ... " – he popped a nougat in his mouth – " ... you're going to have to unplug yourself from your Blackberry and take a walk outside."

8

When he got down the stairs he found Sven cuffed, hands behind his back, face pressed against a blue police wagon blocking the narrow street. Prinzivalli was there, seven men with him. Peroni handed out nougats from his jacket pockets.

"I only asked for five," he said. "You didn't need to come."

Prinzivalli watched the hulk make one last effort to struggle then give up. The Finn looked shocked and a little teary-eyed.

"It's on my way home. End of shift." He popped Peroni's nougat into his mouth. "I thought perhaps this was something I didn't want to miss."

"It's just an arrest," Peroni answered.

Eva Spallone was being marched down the street in the custody of two women officers leading her firmly but politely by the arm.

"Wife?" Prinzivalli guessed.

"The ice queen of the north," Peroni murmured.

Moments later a Lancia saloon drew up behind the van. Vieri got out, face like thunder, with three of his minions from Milan.

Peroni looked at the men holding Sven, nodded for them to let go a little. The hulk looked up, saw the Spallone woman and started to squawk in broken Italian, "Was her idea! *Her idea!* I tell you … "

"Tell him," Peroni cut in, indicating the approaching Vieri.

"Her idea!" he yelled again, at Vieri this time. "Not mine!"

By now the Spallone woman was close enough to hear.

"Shut up, you moron!" she screamed at him. "Shut the … "

She glanced at Peroni, looked as if she felt stupid for a moment. Then the abuse started again, this time in an incomprehensible stream of gibberish, a language so strange Peroni couldn't begin to guess a single word.

He took out his phone and hit the record button. When she was done he stopped the phone, walked out in front of the van and said to the officers there, local and Vieri's crew from Milan, "Listen to me. I want these two taken into separate custody. No chance they get to talk to one another. No shared lawyers." He held up the phone. "I want a Finnish translator. Call Di Capua and … "

Vieri broke stride and leapt in front of him, then roared, "*I* am the inspector here!"

Peroni put a hand on his shoulder and said, "Of course." Then he turned to the men again and said, "The *inspector* wants these two in custody. No contact. Finnish translator. Forensic are going to seal off the sauna in this place. The Roma kid was killed there, Spallone got beat up. Whatever this woman thinks there's got to be some trace left. Check bank records and the financials for this gym of hers. This place was bleeding old man Spallone dry. Talk to the maid. She's got the Roma kid's number and called him when Giorgio needed a ride. There's your link. And the car." He pulled out the business card Ion Dinicu's father had given him. "This is an old Mercedes. Dinicu used it as an illegal cab. Spallone was his customer. My guess is Sven here ferried them away in it after he hit them, then dumped the thing. Find this ... " – he squinted at the picture and read out the licence plate – " ... and we're in court come Friday. My guess is start looking around Testaccio." He glanced at the Finn. "Sven here's not the brightest button in the box."

The Finn squeaked.

"And you," Peroni added, glaring at the hulk in the red satin boxer shorts, "remember. Tell the truth. One word. Fisting."

They all stared at him in awed silence. Peroni eyed a minion from Milan. The man had his notepad in his hand. He hadn't written a word.

"I'll repeat the licence plate once more," he said. "After that ... " He touched Vieri on the shoulder again. "The inspector gets cross."

They all scribbled it down that time. Peroni looked at Vieri and asked, "Anything else?"

The man's hair didn't look as perfect as it had that morning. He was lost for words.

"I'm off shift in thirty minutes," Peroni added, glancing at his watch. "Take off the fact I never got a lunch break, in truth I'm done now." He eyed Prinzivalli. "Beer? The usual place?"

The uniform man stripped off his uniform jacket, turned it so the lining was on the outside, and said, "The usual place."

"Come ... with ... me ... " Vieri ordered, gripping Peroni by the arm.

9

They walked round the corner, back towards the Campo, and Peroni filled him in on the details along the way.

To the man's credit, Vieri listened, furious as he was.

When the explanation was done, Vieri shook his head and said, "I could have your job."

"No, no." They stopped by the place Peroni had bought his porchetta panino that morning. "I've done much worse than this and I never got kicked out then. Besides I've only got a few years left. What's the point?"

He looked Vieri in the face.

"Anyway what are you going to say? Fire this man because he tracked down a couple of double murderers on evidence I wouldn't even walk upstairs to look at? Not when he pleaded with me? I was too busy on my Blackberry, see. Too tied up watching CCTV and waiting for the mobile phone records to land in my inbox." He scratched his head. "Is that how you get on the up escalator in Milan? If so, let me offer some advice. Don't try it here. Won't work."

Vieri stiffened.

"We would have found all this," he insisted. "When forensic reported, when we got round to the detail ... "

Peroni felt a little red light rise at the back of his head.

"You didn't need the detail. Two dead men, odd socks, same pairs. How many questions does that raise? How many possibilities? They didn't get up that way. All you have to do is work out how they got naked. Then ask yourself why whoever dressed them didn't spot the socks were wrong. Really. That's it."

The man from Milan was silent, a little down in the mouth.

"You use your eyes," Peroni added. "Watch what people do with theirs. You know the only person who's looked me straight in the face all day? That poor Roma kid's father. He didn't have anything to hide. He wasn't choking on some stupid obsession with systems and procedures and idiotic theoretical ... "

"OK, OK," Vieri interrupted. "Point taken."

"And yes," Peroni added. "You would have got there in the end. But this case maybe hangs on our golden boy Sven getting scared enough to cough it all up and put Eva beside him in the dock. Get his confession and before long she'll realize she can't wriggle out of it. You won't have to prove a damned thing. You could have spent months trying to do that, and I'd bet a politician's pension somewhere along the way Sven would have gone missing, by himself maybe or courtesy of some other hulk Eva was keeping sweet between the sheets."

Vieri nodded. He seemed to agree.

"It's Toni, isn't it?" Peroni asked. "I'm Gianni."

Vieri glanced behind him to make sure no one was watching. Then he took Peroni's hand.

"The trouble is, Toni, all that northern crap doesn't really cut it here. Not sure it does anywhere frankly. Walk around staring at your Blackberry and your computers all day and you're as blind as that stupid Finn, to a few things, maybe ones that matter. At least he's got the excuse he was born that way."

"The paperwork ... " Vieri began.

" ... is your problem. This is your case. You get the credit. Tell them you sent me out to see Dinicu's father on a hunch. It all fell into place from there. You've got someone itching to confess to two murders and cut a sentencing deal. No one's going to ask a lot of questions."

The inspector nodded.

"And if none of this had worked out? All your hunches came up empty?"

Peroni grinned.

"Then you'd never have been any the wiser. Here."

He gave him the minion's notepad, the phone with the recorded exchange in Finnish between Eva Spallone and Sven, and the keys to the unmarked police Fiat.

"I stole the notebook from your guy. A translator might find something useful on the phone. And me and Prinzivalli ... it may be more than one beer. You get someone to deal with the car."

"Fine," Vieri said and started to turn on his heels.

"Hey," Peroni called. The man stopped and looked at him. "You should come for a pizza with me and my friends. Falcone, Costa, Teresa. Well ... " He shrugged. "She's more than a friend. You'll like them."

Inspector Vieri laughed. It made him look human.

"Oh," Peroni added.

He reached into his pocket, took out a nougat, held out it for the man from Milan.

"Welcome to Rome."

ACKNOWLEDGEMENTS

MEET ME AT THE CREMATORIUM by Peter James © 2010. First appeared in *The Sounds of Crime*, an audio anthology edited by Maxim Jakubowski.

WRONG 'EM BOYO by Nick Quantrill © 2010. First appeared in BYKERBOOKS.

WHERE ARE ALL THE NAUGHTY PEOPLE? by Reginald Hill © 2010. First appeared in *Original Sins*, edited by Martin Edwards.

A BULLET FOR BAUSER by Jay Stringer © 2010. First appeared in *Crime Factory*.

WHOLE LIFE by Liza Cody © 2010. First appeared in *Ellery Queen Mystery Magazine*.

A FAIR DEAL by L. C. Tyler © 2010. First appeared in the *Sunday Express*.

DEATH IN THE TIME MACHINE by Barbara Nadel © 2010. First appeared in *Ellery Queen Mystery Magazine*.

SHOOTING FISH by Adrian Magson © 2010. First appeared in *Plots with Guns*.

THE MINISTRY OF WHISKY by Val McDermid © 2010. First appeared in *Ellery Queen Mystery Magazine*.

THE ART OF NEGOTIATION by Chris Ewan © 2010. First appeared in *Original Sins*, edited by Martin Edwards.

JUNGLE BOOGIE by Kate Horsley © 2010. First appeared in *Pulp Ink*, edited by Nigel Bird & Chris Rhatigan.

ROTTERDAM by Nicholas Royle © 2010. First appeared in *Black Wings*, edited by S. T. Joshi.

SMALL PRINT by Ian Ayris © 2010. First appeared in *A Twist of Noir*.

EAST OF SUEZ, WEST OF CHARING CROSS ROAD by John Lawton © 2010. First appeared in *Agents of Treachery*, edited by Otto Pensler.

SISTERHOOD by Nigel Bird © 2010. First appeared in *A Twist of Noir*.

RULES OF ENGAGEMENT by Zoe Sharp © 2010. First appeared in *Original Sins*, edited by Martin Edwards.

LOVELY REQUIEM, MR MOZART by Robert Barnard © 2010. First appeared in *Ellery Queen Mystery Magazine*.

BEASTLY PLEASURES by Ann Cleeves © 2010. First appeared in *Original Sins*, edited by Martin Edwards.

THE WALLS by Mark Billingham © 2010. First appeared in *The Sounds of Crime*, an audio anthology edited by Maxim Jakubowski.

MOON LANDING by Paul Johnston © 2012. First appearance in print.

PARSON PENNYWICK IN ARCADIA by Amy Myers © 2010. First appeared in *Ellery Queen Mystery Magazine*.

THE LONG DROP by Tony Black © 2010. First appeared in *Out of the Gutter*.

TERATOMA by Keith McCarthy © 2012. First appearance in print.

CLUTTER by Martin Edwards © 2010. First appeared in *Original Sins*, edited by Martin Edwards.

COLT by Ken Bruen © 2010. First appeared in *Ellery Queen Mystery Magazine*.

OPEN AND SHUT CASE by Marilyn Todd © 2010. First appeared in *Ellery Queen Mystery Magazine*.

QUEEN OF THE HILL by Stuart Neville © 2010. First appeared in *Requiems for the Departed*, edited by Gerard Brennan and Mike Stone.

GHOSTED by Peter Lovesey © 2010. First appeared in *Original Sins*, edited by Martin Edwards.

TEXAS IN THE FALL by R. J. Ellory © 2010. First appeared in France in a Sonatine Editions sampler.

THE FEATHER by Kate Ellis © 2010. First appeared in *Original Sins*, edited by Martin Edwards.

THE DECEIVERS by Christopher Fowler © 2010. First appeared in *The Sounds of Crime*, an audio anthology edited by Maxim Jakubowski.

LOVE AND DEATH by Michael Z. Lewin © 2010. First appeared in *Alfred Hitchcock Mystery Magazine*.

BLOOD ISLAND by Barry Maitland © 2010. First appeared in the *Newcastle Herald* & the *Canberra Times*.

FEST FATALE by Alison Bruce © 2010. First appeared as a chapbook.

THE GIFT by Phil Lovesey © 2010. First appeared in *Ellery Queen Mystery Magazine*.

THE SKIN WE'RE IN by Matt Hilton © 2010. First appeared in *More Tonto Short Stories*.

LITTLE RUSSIA by Andrew Taylor © 2010. First appeared in *Original Sins*, edited by Martin Edwards.

LITTLE OLD LADIES by Simon Brett © 2010. First appeared in *Ellery Queen Mystery Magazine*.

IN PURSUIT OF THE INEDIBLE by Brian McGilloway © 2010. First appeared in a Radio 4 reading.

MOPPING UP by Col Bury © 2010. First appeared in *Even More Tonto Short Stories*.

AUL YELLAH BELLY by Gerard Brennan © 2010. First appeared in *Crime Factory*.

A TOUR OF THE TOWER by Christine Poulson © 2010. First appeared in *Ellery Queen Mystery Magazine*.

DEAD MEN'S SOCKS by David Hewson © 2010. First appeared as an e-read Amazon book.